Praise for *Fortunes of France*

"Modern-day Dumas finally crosses the channel" *Observer*

"An enjoyable read, distinguished by its author's
erudition and wit" *Sunday Times*

"Swashbuckling historical fiction… For all its philosophical
depth [*The Brethren*] is a hugely entertaining romp…
The comparisons with Dumas seem both natural and deserved
and the next 12 instalments [are] a thrilling prospect" *Guardian*

"Historical fiction at its very best… This fast paced and
heady brew is colourfully leavened with love and sex and
a great deal of humour and wit. The second instalment
cannot be published too soon" *We Love This Book*

"A highly anticipated tome that's been described as *Game of
Thrones* meets *The Three Musketeers*"
Mariella Frostrup on BBC Radio 4's *Open Book*

"A vivid novel by France's modern Dumas… [there is]
plenty of evidence in the rich characterisation and vivid
historical detail that a reader's long-term commitment
will be amply rewarded" *Sunday Times*

"A sprawling, earthy tale of peril, love, lust,
death, dazzling philosophical debate and political
intrigue… an engrossing saga" *Gransnet*

"A master of the historical novel" *Guardian*

"So rich in colourful characters

Born in 1908, ROBERT MERLE was originally an English teacher before serving as an interpreter with the British army during the Second World War, which led to his capture by the German army at Dunkirk. He published his hugely popular *Fortunes of France* series over four decades, from 1977 to 2003, the final instalment appearing just a year before his death in 2004. *League of Spies* is the fourth book in the series, after *The Brethren, City of Wisdom and Blood* and *Heretic Dawn*.

League of Spies

ROBERT MERLE

PUSHKIN PRESS

Pushkin Press

71–75 Shelton Street

London WC2H 9JQ

Original text © 2018 Estate of Robert Merle

English translation © 2018 T. Jefferson Kline

League of Spies was first published in French as *Le Prince que voilà* in 1982

First published by Pushkin Press in 2018

1 3 5 7 9 8 6 4 2

ISBN 13: 978-1-78227-392-9

Designed and typeset by Tetragon, London

Printed in Great Britain by the CPI Group, UK

www.pushkinpress.com

LEAGUE
OF SPIES

1

I T WAS ONLY by the slimmest of chances that my good valet, Miroul, and I had finally made good our escape from the horrendous St Bartholomew's day massacre, aided throughout by our massive Swiss Guard from Berne and our master-at-arms, Giacomi, and found refuge with the Baron de Quéribus in Saint-Cloud. As this gentleman had a rich estate in Carcassonne, he decided to head south, thereby providing a well-armed escort for the three of us as far as Périgord, warning us that the roads and towns of France were now quite dangerous for anyone reputed to be a Huguenot. And since Dame Gertrude du Luc, who'd managed to save the life of my beloved Samson by preventing him from returning to Paris, was desirous of accompanying us, I invited her and her chambermaid Zara to join us, knowing full well that her interest in meeting my father was motivated by her burning and tenacious desire to marry my brother.

We arrived at Mespech during the grape harvest, but after the initial delight of our reunion with my father and Uncle de Sauveterre, for the first time in my life I was unable to enjoy seeing the beautiful bunches of grapes trampled in the vats by the bare feet of our women, for the red juice which flowed from them suddenly brought back the horror of the oceans of blood we'd seen covering the streets of Paris on 24th August and the days following.

At the end of the first week, however, remembering all my peregrinations on the highways of France and my incredible adventures in the capital, I began to feel some impatience with the quiet rusticity and slow pace of life in my father's chateau. In any case, I'd already decided not to spend the winter with my family, but to move to Bordeaux to set up my medical practice there. But my readers know as well as I do that Fortune holds in great derision the will and projects of men, and plays at undoing them just as the waves of the ocean undo the sandcastles that children so painstakingly construct on the beach. I thought I'd stay but two months in Mespech. I stayed two years.

And though my primary object in these pages is to provide a portrait of my good sovereign, Henri III, as he really was, and not as he was so shamefully smeared by Guise's people and others in league against him during his lifetime, who spewed out their hateful venom through thousands of libellous verses and lampoons, as well as execrable accusations made from the pulpit, this memoir is also intended to chronicle the life of my family. So I don't want to rush through those two years of family joys and domestic sorrows shared by my beloved Samson, by my older brother François, by my little sister Catherine, by the Brethren (my father and Uncle de Sauveterre), by Dame Gertrude du Luc and by my Angelina. To the best of my memory the most contentious affair that clouded my return to Mespech in 1572 was the marriage of Samson to Gertrude, a union that should have seemed very advantageous to our Huguenot economy, since the lady wanted to offer him as dowry the flourishing apothecary shop of the Béqueret family in Montfort-l'Amaury.

"You shouldn't let Samson do this!" snarled Uncle de Sauveterre to my father as we were riding, along with François, to visit Cabusse at le Breuil. "The lady's a papist and has been on a pilgrimage to Rome!"

"Can I prevent my youngest son from such a marriage," replied Jean de Siorac, "when I allowed myself to marry Isabelle de Caumont?"

"And you know what a bad decision that was! She's such a devout Catholic!" croaked Sauveterre, who resembled more than ever an old crow, with his bent back and his increasingly thin neck.

"The mistake," replied my father, whose bright eyes went sombre at the memory of it, "was to try to convert her publicly and by force, since the lady had so much tenacity and pride... But she was a good wife to me," he continued, glancing at François and me, "and I loved her dearly."

At this Sauveterre had no more to say. Although he was too good a man not to have tried valiantly to offer her his affection during her short life, he'd had more success in grieving her when she was dead than in cherishing her while she was alive. For Sauveterre, so biblically convinced as he was of the necessity of fecundity, believed that every woman was but a fertile womb by which God's people grew and multiplied. But the fact that this fecundity required sowing one's seed in such hostile ground left him quite devoid of sexual appetite and any feelings of tenderness.

"Have you thought about the fact," he continued gravely, "that if this lady marries Samson, your grandchildren will suck the superstition and idolatry of the papists with every drop of their nurse's milk?"

"Well, I'm not convinced that such milk counts for much," answered Jean de Siorac. "Charles IX had a Huguenot nursemaid and you saw how much that mattered during the St Bartholomew's day massacre! Moreover, my brother, since the persecution has broken out again, it may be a good time to disguise our faith. I'm more worried about Samson's excess of zeal than about his lack of spine. Dame Gertrude will serve as a mask over his innocent face. Not to mention the fact that no one will want a Huguenot apothecary in a papist town! At the death of the first patient they'll all be crying 'Poison!'"

"I see that you've decided to support this business," growled Sauveterre.

"Well, would you prefer to see Samson continue to live in sin? Or live emasculated like a monk in his cell?" replied my father, who must immediately have regretted this last phrase, since, as he glanced at Sauveterre, he saw his brother wince at the idea that chastity could be equated with impotence.

"At least, Baron de Mespech," came Sauveterre's icy reply, "see that these ladies depart as soon as possible. I'm tired of their cackling, their affectations and the way of life they're imposing on us. Ever since their arrival, our expenses for meat, wine and candles have been exorbitant! Especially in candles! Why do Dame du Luc and her chambermaid require ten candles to be lit the minute the sun goes down, when one is enough for me in the library?"

"Ah, that's because you don't primp yourself enough!" smiled my father.

"But that's the point!" growled Sauveterre. "What need have they, since the Lord gave them one face, which they hasten to counterfeit with another in its place?"

"Good *écuyer*," soothed my father, "would you have blamed any of our soldiers of the Norman legion for burnishing his arms before a battle?"

"What battle are you talking about?" sputtered Sauveterre.

"The one they wage, day in, day out, against our defenceless hearts!"

"Defenceless!" gasped Sauveterre reproachfully. "A whole month! It's been a whole month since this plague of locusts fell upon our wheat!"

"Since there are only two of them, they haven't ruined much of the crop," smiled Jean de Siorac. "And how can I chase them away? They can't go off alone in their coach. You must realize they're waiting for Quéribus to escort them back to Paris. The baron is enjoying himself at Puymartin's estate…"

"Worse than just enjoying himself," muttered Sauveterre.

"Yes, Puymartin is so taken with him that he insists on his staying every time Quéribus talks about returning to Paris."

"Well, let Puymartin know how we feel."

"Not on your life! I'd never dare offend a faithful friend over such a trivial matter—especially a man who's stood by us through thick and thin!"

I noticed that my brother François suddenly opened his eyes and pricked up his ears, given that his dearest project, should Diane's mother ever marry Puymartin, was to marry her daughter, and thereby acquire half a share of the Fontenac estate, and, as the eldest male heir, the title that accrued to that domain. In this way, he'd bear the title of baron even before my father died. Happy François, who had only to open his beak for all the crumbs to fall into it! This was especially galling to me, since my older brother, who loved me so little, owed this good fortune to me for having killed in loyal combat the brigand baron whose sweet, very Christian daughter was going to marry him, papist though she was—a marriage that would doubtless set Sauveterre croaking again! But since the fertile lands of Fontenac so conveniently bordered our own, and since that well-defended chateau could only reinforce the security of Mespech, his strict Huguenot visage could not conceal his secret acquiescence.

Sensing this, and judging that, papist for papist, Gertrude du Luc was every bit as advantageous a match as Diane, my father couldn't keep from adding:

"Dame Gertrude comes from noble lineage. She's wealthy—and saved Samson's life by preventing him from heading back into the slaughterhouse of Paris in search of his brother. And as for me, I'm not sorry to see her blonde head brightening our old walls. I like her well enough!"

"And her chambermaid even better," added Sauveterre drily.

11

At this my father decided to hold his tongue and pretended not to have heard, which was his wont when he desired no further debate on a subject. "Ah, beautiful Zara!" I thought. "How far will you go in your devotion to your mistress?" And this thought so amused me that I shot a look at François and gave him a knowing smile. But François did not return it, his long, regular features remaining thoroughly inscrutable, which was his way of suggesting—hypocrite that he was—that he was content to draw a veil over the foibles of his father, who did not inebriate himself with wine, but rather with women, our good Franchou not being enough for him, if I understood Uncle de Sauveterre correctly.

I said "Uncle" de Sauveterre, and perhaps my reader will recall that my father and Sauveterre were not brothers by birth but had become so attached to one another during their years in the Norman legion that they had decided to "brother" each other before the magistrate in Rouen (as was the custom then) and join their estates together legally. So, although there was but one Baron de Mespech, the estate belonged to both of them, Sauveterre, though only an *écuyer*, having the same authority as the baron to decide all matters pertaining to the management of the property—but not, thank God, in matters regarding Sauveterre's "nephews".

That afternoon, the Brethren had gone to le Breuil, at Cabusse's request, to examine a sheep that seemed to be suffering from a disease called "toad foot" (in which case it would have to be isolated and treated, lest the malady spread to the whole herd, which would be disastrous). Scarcely had they returned to Mespech when Zara knocked on my door, and told me that her mistress required my presence in her room. She managed to use a hundred words for this message when one would have sufficed, accompanying her speech with devastating expressions and inviting looks, smiles and childish lisps, tilts of her head and undulations of her body, all of which, despite my sense that they were the habitual weapons of this arch-coquette, nevertheless had some effect on me, even though I knew that Zara couldn't help expressing herself in this way.

She was dressed, as usual, as if she were of noble birth, in a silk gown with diamond earrings, pearl necklace and ruby rings—Dame Gertrude was unable to refuse her chambermaid anything; she was so crazy about her that Quéribus had joked with a wink that he'd never known a maid spend so much time in her lady's private chamber. Seeing me frown at this, he'd laughed uproariously and added, "Better these inconsequential games among wenches than for Samson to be cuckolded by some Don Juan as soon as they were married!"

"Monsieur," I scolded, "remember, I beg you, that you promised you wouldn't be—or at least would no longer be—that Don once their vows were done!"

"I keep my promises!" cried Quéribus, throwing his arm around my shoulder and hugging me to him. "And all the more so since I'm so afraid of your terrible sword now that Giacomi has taught you his 'Jarnac's thrust'!"

"You're making fun of me!" I objected. "Though *certainly* I have made some progress with it—"

"Though *assuredly* I've made some progress," corrected Quéribus, pinching my shoulder painfully to emphasize his emendation of 'certainly', since the term was a dead giveaway that I was a Huguenot, as the Baronne des Tourelles had already warned me.

"…I'm but a novice fencer when compared to you," I conceded. And although this was no longer entirely accurate, it made Quéribus blush with pleasure, since he adored flattery.

Zara, for her part, didn't covet words so much as appreciative looks at her inviting back, as she rolled her ample hips like a sloop in a swell when preceding me down the hallway to her mistress's room. From a quick glance back at me, I could see that she was estimating my degree of interest out of the corner of her golden eyes, which were partly hidden by the shawl, through which she looked invitingly at me like a mare from beneath her mane.

Gertrude du Luc was seated in a large, tapestried armchair in front of a bright, crackling fire of pine logs, the only fire allowed this early in the season, by special courtesy of the Baron de Mespech, since it was already quite chilly for an October morning. When I entered, she did not rise and throw her arms around me, pulling her body close to mine in an "innocent" hug, as she usually did given her great appetite for men's bodies. How quiet, reserved, well behaved and angelic she'd become under the watchful eyes of the Brethren! We were, moreover, not alone: Little Sissy, her little fingers clasping a handful of candles, was busily placing them in two candelabra that stood on either side of a mirror set on the dressing table.

Gertrude remained quietly seated and languorously extended her hand for me to kiss. Little Sissy's eyes darkened ominously as I did so, which did not escape the notice of the blonde Norman.

"My girl," she said, somewhat haughtily, "when you've finished placing the candles, go fetch me some more logs for my fire."

"Madame, I cannot!" said Little Sissy in a most abrupt manner. "I cannot do that. I will not go!"

"And why not, you impertinent girl?" gasped Gertrude, open-mouthed to hear herself addressed in such a tone.

"Because I'm pregnant, and cannot carry such weight," said the little serpent. "But," she added in a hiss, "the more important reason is that I don't want to!"

"Zara!" cried Gertrude, quite undone. "Did you hear that? Did you ever see such a little earthworm put on such airs! By my conscience! I could die! Zara! Give this silly goose a good smack!"

At this, Zara, who was certainly not pleased by such a mission, approached the miscreant rather lazily, but the latter, who was barefoot, easily slipped away from her and, in the blink of an eye, ducked behind the table, saying:

"More logs! And ten candles a day! You're going to ruin us at this rate!"

"Quiet there, you little rascal!" I hushed, fearing that she'd continue to chatter on if I didn't. And taking her by the collar, like a little kitten, I relieved her of her candles and handed them to Zara, who received them very unhappily, as if fearing some contagion.

"Come, Madame Sharp Tongue," I continued, pushing Little Sissy before me towards the door. "If you need a taste of the whip to mend your manners, we'll give it to you!"

"Oh, no! Not the whip!" cried Gertrude, who, her anger now abated, was so good and full of pity that she would have wept to see a cat toying with a mouse.

"Monsieur," said Little Sissy as soon as the door had closed behind us, "are you going to whip this poor wench who cannot keep from caressing you the minute you so much as brush her with your finger?" And immediately she pulled me to her and, cooing softly, pressed her body so tightly against mine that there'd have been no way to strike her except in a laughing, loving parody of cruelty.

"Ah, you daughter of a Gypsy!" I gasped. "There you go again with your impertinence! What honey bee stung you to make you dare confront that noblewoman?"

"My jealousy," she answered straightaway, lowering her head like a little goat. "Oh, my Pierre! I hate these two great whores, who hide their old age and wrinkles beneath all that powder and grease and who look at men as if they were going to swallow them whole!"

"Old age!" I laughed.

"It's true! Dame du Luc is old enough to be my mother!"

"Enough!" I said. "She's going to marry Samson and not me. And they'll be leaving soon enough."

"And thank God for that!"

"Peace, my little warbler!" I soothed, softened by the firm flesh that she was pressing into me, and the sweet nothings she was whispering in my ear. "Be off with you, little viper, and ask Miroul to bring some firewood."

"Madame my sister," I announced as I re-entered her room, "I beg your pardon for this nasty business. I would have punished the miscreant if you hadn't pardoned her."

"Nay, Monsieur," she said, her eyes shining. "I believe I heard that the wench is pregnant? Is this your fruit?"

"'Tis grafted from my stalk, yes."

"Well, then!" smirked Gertrude. "Surely you're not going to spoil a crupper that's so serviceable…"

"'Tis true, Madame."

"And since the wench knows it all too well, am I to suffer further insolence from her?"

"No, Gertrude," I promised. "Miroul will serve you in her place."

"What? A manservant!" exclaimed Zara, who pretended not to like men. "A man in here! By my conscience!"

"You'll not die of it, Zara," said Dame du Luc. "Miroul is very respectful of you."

"Well, it's to his credit!" answered Zara, who, having placed the candles on the table without having set them in the candelabra, was rubbing her hands with ointment.

There was a knock on the door, and since Zara was so engrossed in her ointments I went to open it, and Miroul came in with

"each eye a different hue,
the right one brown,
the left one blue!"

as my poor little Hélix used to love to chant. He went to pile some firewood in the corner of the chimney to warm it, since the recent rains had dampened it. Then, with a deep bow to Dame Gertrude and a slightly less profound gesture of reverence to Zara—so subtly derisive that I was the only one to notice it—he was heading towards the door when Zara cooed:

"Sweet Miroul, might I ask you a favour?"

"Madame, I'd be delighted to oblige," replied Miroul, bowing, his chestnut eye twinkling brightly.

"I need you," replied Zara, very happy to see herself called "Madame", "to place the candles on the candelabra."

"Madame," smiled Miroul, "with pleasure! Better these large hands than your delicate fingers!"

I burst out laughing, and Gertrude smiled wryly, while Zara couldn't help looking wounded, since she immediately understood the extent to which this malicious compliment was meant to put her in her place. For our household domestics have their points of honour, just as their masters do: valets bring firewood; chambermaids set candles. And no doubt Miroul understood that Zara believed she could get away with such behaviour simply because her mistress clothed her in such finery.

Miroul took his leave as soon as he had set and lit the candles, which were not only the subject of Sauveterre's bitter remonstrations but the object of the scorn of the entire household (excepting my father)—from the chambermaids to the scullery maids, who were free to express their disapproval of this wasteful practice openly, since Dame Gertrude didn't understand a word of the local dialect.

As soon as Miroul had left the room, Dame du Luc said, "Zara, close the door, if you please." And this done, still sitting, Gertrude held out her hand and bade me sit on a little stool at her feet, so that my back was to the fire and my face close up to her dress, which was beautifully brocaded and awash with perfume.

"My brother," she asked, "where are we in our great affair?"

"Uncle de Sauveterre is very recalcitrant and my father has but half consented." Which was only half true, since my father had given his full consent to their marriage.

"What?" she gasped, her green eyes full of alarm. "Not given his full consent?"

"Neither my father nor I," I replied.

"What? You! Ah, what treason! You, my brother, whom I so dearly love!" And saying this, she leant forward and placed her hands on my shoulders, in such a way as to expose to their greatest advantage her bodily charms for my enjoyment—and subjugation. "Aha!" I thought. "Now I see the why and the wherefore of this stool that's so artfully placed as to prevent my retreating without backing into the fire if the enemy presses my front line." However, knowing that my greatest weakness presently was my eyes, and that the attack was aimed directly at them, I closed them halfway, and, behind this defence, fortified my resolution, saying in a firm voice:

"Madame my sister, I cherish you as well, and hold you in great friendship. But, as you yourself have confessed, there is a certain licence given to widows such as you, one that the world may close its eyes to but a husband could not forgive."

"But did I not," she answered, lowering her eyes, "already give you my oath about any further goings-on with Quéribus?"

"It's not about Quéribus," I countered, "but about certain immoral adventures to which, as a widow, you became all too accustomed."

"What, you heretic Huguenot! You dare call my pious pilgrimages 'immoral'?"

"The goal may have been pious," I replied stiffly, "but not the paths that led to it. And those paths, as everyone knows, abound in dangers for a woman's virtue."

"Oh, my brother!" she countered, and brought her face up close to mine so that the firelight illuminating her blonde hair appeared to create a halo—an adornment I doubted she could lay claim to. "Oh, my brother!" she cooed, feigning a charming confusion. "What unjust suspicions! I who thought only of my indulgences on my travels!"

"I think you've put the remedy too close to temptation—or the other way around," I said with a smile. "And these indulgences will be unnecessary once you've committed to a life without sin in your marriage to Samson."

"True enough," she sighed, withdrawing her hands from my shoulders and leaning back against the chair's cushions with a great sigh. She remained silent for a few minutes with Zara standing by her side—but certainly not in the role of her guardian angel, her beautiful compassionate eyes moving back and forth between her mistress and me, and, no doubt, at this point hardly loving me more than my valet.

"So I must promise to give up my pilgrimages!" said Gertrude with yet another sigh.

"You must."

"Ah, cruel man!" she sniffed. "How you harry me!"

"For the love of you know very well whom!"

"But," she said, temporizing, "would I marry him if I didn't love him?"

"Well, Gertrude," I said, rising to my feet with sudden impatience, "I see you all too clearly there! You want to have it all: Samson and your pretty little adventures! But it cannot be!"

"Ah, Monsieur!" Zara burst out angrily. "Don't you see how you're mortifying my mistress terribly with all your high and mighty airs! What brutes men are, putting knives to our throats like that! Fie! What wickedness! And what's it to you how things go in your brother's marriage? Is it really any of your business?"

To which I answered not a word, pretending not to have heard, and no more looking at Zara than if she'd been a log beside the road. My attitude clearly saddened her, since ordinarily she could count on looks that showered her as if with flowers, not to mention words that I lavished on her unsparingly and that she drank up like grass the morning dew.

"Easy there, Zara!" scolded Gertrude. "Calm down, my little sparrow! Monsieur de Siorac is very concerned about the innocence of my pretty Samson and would never want him to suffer from my feminine weakness, which he's trying, as a good brother, to help me to overcome. And that's all there is to it. And he's doing the right thing, even if it goes against some of my natural proclivities. Oh, Pierre!" she continued with a sigh. "Widowhood wasn't such a bad condition, you know. I was free to spend my money as I wished, free to open my wings and travel year in, year out to Chartres, to Toulouse, to Rome, to Compostela—anywhere I wanted! But I understand that if I want my Samson, I'm going to have to put an end to my wandering ways."

"So you're truly resolved in this?" I said more gently.

"Completely."

"Ah, Madame!" said Zara, the tears in her eyes telling me just how much she felt she had to lose as Gertrude's partner in the comforts and delights of these travels.

"My sister," I said to Dame du Luc, putting knee to floor and taking her hand to kiss it, "I beg you not to resent me too much for my zeal. But you know how innocent and naive Samson is, yet how implacable. At your first lapse, he would cut you off from him like a rotten limb, even if it meant mutilating his heart forever."

Hearing this, Gertrude, whose own heart was as tender as her morals were weak, began to weep uncontrollably, a sight that overwhelmed me with pity—and Zara as well—who knelt beside me at her knees as together we comforted her with kisses, caresses and soothing, sweet words until she finally calmed down.

"Oh, my Pierre," she confessed when she'd regained her composure enough to speak, "if you didn't already love Angelina and I didn't love Samson, it's you I should have married, for you're so direct and honest with me that I can't help feeling some solace in obeying you even in the teeth of my resistance."

"Oh, Madame!" warned Zara, who saw this confession as a betrayal of her sex.

"Zara! Zara!" scolded Dame Gertrude. "For heaven's sake! Don't be so querulous! And make your peace with Monsieur de Siorac! I don't want to hear you calling him 'mean' or 'stupid brute' any more as you've been so bold as to do."

"Madame," said Zara with one of those little pouts that, once they'd left her pretty lips, began to agitate her whole person and move in a kind of undulation throughout her body, right down to her toes, "if Monsieur de Siorac requires me to ask his forgiveness—"

"Stop right there, my pretty!" I exclaimed. "Your beauty is ample warrant that all your impertinence shall be forgiven—plus a few kisses on your pretty cheek and your alluring neck" (which I applied as I named each spot, before finishing off with a languorous kiss on her mouth).

"Good my brother," interrupted Gertrude, suddenly rising, whether because she didn't fancy having her chambermaid thus praised and petted, or because she judged any compliments that were not addressed to her to be a waste of chivalry, "I believe I heard you say that Samson and you converted to the reformed religion at the age of ten."

"And I have very good reasons for remembering it, for my father got quite angry at me on that occasion for not wholeheartedly embracing the new faith."

"Ah!" crowed Gertrude, raising an eyebrow. "And why was that?"

"I loved Mary. And at that age I thought that any religion that didn't have a woman to adore would never wholly win my heart."

"Listen to that, Madame," laughed Zara. "When he was in his swaddling clothes, Monsieur de Siorac was already entranced by the fairer sex."

"Well, he can be pretty intransigent about morality when it comes to anyone but himself!" added Gertrude. "But never mind," she continued, as soon as her arrow was aloft, "so you were baptized in the true religion then, my brother."

"If you insist on calling it that," I conceded, with a very cold nod of the head.

"And Samson as well, then, who's born of a different mother but is the same age as you."

"Samson as well."

"Pierre," she coaxed, stepping up very close to me, her green eyes sparkling, "may I ask you to request of the priest of Marcuays that he provide a written attestation that Samson was baptized as a Catholic and that he hears Mass?"

"That he hears Mass?" I said, flabbergasted.

"He'll hear Mass next Sunday with me in the chapel at Mespech, since your father has asked your priest to come here to say Mass for Zara, *maestro* Giacomi and me."

"Well, Gertrude, it's quite amazing what you've managed to obtain from my father!"

"Well, to tell the truth," confessed Gertrude, lowering her eyes, "Zara had a hand in it."

"Oh, Madame!" protested Zara.

I couldn't help laughing.

"In any case," I continued, "Pincers, our priest, won't celebrate your marriage if Samson hasn't renounced loudly and clearly the new religion. He's too much under the thumb of the bishop of Sarlat."

"Don't worry, my good priest from Normandy won't be so difficult. He'll be satisfied by the written attestation I mentioned, if you'll be so good as to get it in Marcuays."

I'd already resolved to do that very thing, and had decided it wouldn't be a bad idea to ask Pincers for a similar attestation for myself, which would be very useful should the very Catholic Monsieur de Montcalm ever agree to let me marry my Angelina.

But presently I found this room to possess great charm, since I'd never seen it illuminated in this way, both by the crackling fire and by the profusion of candles; nor had the dark walls of Mespech ever been so brightened as they were by the golden locks of Gertrude, and the beauty and the accoutrements of such fine ladies—who, no doubt, recalled to my father, as they did to me, my late mother. I found I wasn't in such a rush to accomplish the task Dame Gertrude had set before me, and began presenting some objections to the lady's plan in order to prolong as much as possible this sweet scene, and they obligingly began begging and caressing me to help me put off my resolve to visit Pincers.

Carrying their message as well as one from my father, I went to see Pincers, the local priest, the next day at nightfall, accompanied by some protection whom I hoped not to employ unless absolutely necessary: my good Miroul, my master-at-arms Giacomi and Fröhlich, my faithful Swiss Guard from Berne, who'd never left me since the St Bartholomew's day massacre, feeling no dishonour at quitting the service of Henri de Navarre, who was to all intents and purposes a prisoner in the Louvre, to offer his services as bodyguard to a young Périgordian whose resources lay more in his wisdom than in his wallet.

Having attached our horses to the hitching posts in the place de Marcuays, I banged loudly on the priest's door, and his serving girl, after requesting me to identify myself through a small peephole, finally unlocked and opened up.

"How are you, Jacotte?" I asked with a tap on her derrière.

"Well enough, my noble Monsieur," laughed the fluttering, sprightly wench, so much more amply endowed in bosom than any other woman in Marcuays, her face so smooth and her body so firm that you had to doubt that she was even close to the canonical age required of women who are in the service of priests—and seemed even less appropriate for the job given her complexion. In the village, ever since the silly business in which our priest had earned the nickname "Pincers" (which I recounted earlier), people quite simply referred to her as the "priestette", though never to her face. Although ordinarily quite a fearless wench, she blanched a bit when she saw my escort.

"But who's this?!" she stammered, pointing at Giacomi, standing as tall and thin as a sword.

"This is *maestro* Giacomi," I replied, "assistant to the Great Silvie, the fencing master of the Duc d'Anjou."

"And this mountain of a man?" she queried, pointing to Fröhlich, who, at that very instant, was having to bend over to cross her threshold and to squeeze his shoulders together to avoid damage to the door frame.

"He's one of the king's archers, who's now working for me," I replied, careful not to refer to his Huguenot leanings.

At this she fell silent and just stood there staring at us (including Miroul, whom she knew already), taking in the fact that all four of us were armed to the teeth.

"Monsieur," she stammered, now clearly terrified, "what business have you with my master?"

"My good woman," I replied as casually yet as coldly as I could, "that's between him and me."

"Well, Monsieur!" cried Jacotte. "Are you going to take your revenge on him for bearing witness against you in your duel with Fontenac? Don't you realize he only did so with a knife at this throat?"

"Or maybe it was his knife that was all polished up for evil business," I mused, not wanting to relieve her fears. "But enough, Jacotte. I'm not here to argue with you. Go straightaway and fetch your master and bring him here. Miroul, follow her wherever she goes. I don't want the wench running off before we've finished our business here."

At this Jacotte shook more violently than a poplar leaf in a high wind and was too nervous to object to Miroul's advances as she led him to the oratory of the priest.

"Ah, good master," Miroul laughed later, "I could have turned her into a Huguenot right then and there, she was so afraid I'd dispatch her once the priest was dead."

Her double-dealing master didn't look so confident when he arrived in the room—or rather was hauled before us—where the three of us awaited him in front of his fireplace, each with his right hand on his sword hilt. To tell the truth, Fröhlich's attention was distracted by a terrine of pâté de foie gras and a flagon of wine that awaited our host, his table already set for his evening meal—our priest being as much of a glutton as our giant Swiss Guard, and, according to la Maligou, who'd been groped by him, an insatiable lecher and drinker. You could have easily guessed these habits from his crimson complexion, his huge nose, which practically obscured his fleshy lips, the glint in his tiny eyes and his low forehead. As I looked at him, I mused that Pincers had just enough brain to serve his appetites, but not an atom of room for any knowledge or manners, for he was not a godly man, however much he pretended to be one.

No sooner had he entered the room than Giacomi closed the door behind him, and leant up against it in a way that would have made Pincers turn pale if his bright-red complexion had allowed it, but caused his eyes to roll uncontrollably in their sockets like a scared rodent's and his lips to tremble like jelly:

"Well, venerable doctor!" he lisped and stammered in French, giving me a deep bow. "I am exceedingly honoured—"

"But I am *not* honoured in the least, priest!" I broke in rudely. "I would have been released had it not been for your testimony."

"Ah, Monsieur!" snivelled Pincers in Provençal. "The Sieur de Malvézie forced that testimony out of me with his dagger on my Adam's apple!"

"Yes, but once his dagger was removed, you repeated it to the bishop, you miscreant!"

"Blessed Virgin!" whined Pincers. "How could I refuse my bishop when he was demanding it of me?"

"Comrades!" I cried in French. "Did you hear that? What an odious trap was set for me!" And, at this, my three companions shook their heads gravely, including Fröhlich, who'd not understood a word of the Provençal, his eyes glued to the pâté de foie gras on the table.

"Priest!" I commanded immediately. "Sit down on this stool, and you, Jacotte, bring his writing desk, and make haste, woman, make haste!… Shadow her, Miroul!"

Which he did, except that this shadow had hands that surely would have slowed her errand had not Miroul feared my anger. As for Pincers, he was quite unhappy that anyone but him was allowed to fondle his housekeeper, but dared not breathe a word of reproach.

"Priest," I asked, when all was ready, "do you know how to write?"

"Certainly," replied Pincers, regaining his composure.

"In Latin?"

"Alas, no," he confessed. "I can say my Mass in Latin and my prayers, but I'm not used to writing it."

"Then I'll dictate it to you."

But this turned out to be impossible since his spelling was so full of mistakes. So, in the end, I wrote attestations for Samson and myself in Latin and he copied them, submissive and sweating from his effort, though not without resisting a bit when it came to the passage about the Mass.

"Monsieur," he said in French (perhaps so as not be understood by Jacotte), "that's false: you don't hear Mass; nor does your brother."

"We'll hear it on Sunday when you come to say Mass at Mespech!"

"But only once!" countered Pincers, as though terrified of anger-ing me.

"Well, the document doesn't say that we hear Mass regularly."

"Ah, now that's true!" conceded Pincers, who only half understood the Latin he'd copied.

"Jacotte," I said in Provençal, when her master had finished his note, "you will testify, if called to do so, that the priest of Marcuays wrote all of this without threats or harsh words of any kind; nor was he paid to do it, but did it of his own free will."

"Yes, Monsieur," agreed Jacotte.

"And here, my good girl," I said, reaching in my purse, "are two sols to recompense you for any inconvenience we may have caused you."

"I thank you, Monsieur. It was no bother at all," smiled Jacotte, as she threw an unrancorous look at Miroul over her shoulder. Miroul was still standing directly behind her, his two hands on her hips, which were as large as her big strong shoulders, though her stomach was far from large since, unlike her master, she didn't drink like a shoe with a hole in it, but worked from dawn to dusk and sometimes all night, according to some—although she seemed quite happy to be so vari-ously occupied.

"Priest," I soothed, as I slipped the two attestations in my doublet, "since you have written this, which is God's truth, you have thereby righted the wrongs that you were constrained to do against me."

"Monsieur," replied Pincers, so greatly relieved that his voice was now more assured, "I would be most happy if you were to forgive me, and your father as well, for these unfortunate testimonies."

At this, and not wishing to over-reassure him, I rose and, turning away, held my boots up to the fire that was crackling in the hearth, and realized that the fellow was less careful about his firewood than we were at Mespech, since his flock provided him with his wood, his wine cellar and his venison, and filled his larder with liver pâté. Indeed, there wasn't a lamb in this flock, any more than in the parish at Taniès, who, in addition to his annual tithes, didn't make sacrifices every month, good years and bad, to lavish provender on his pastor. So, in exchange for a few paternosters, the hypocrite lived like a rat in a wheel of cheese, his back to a warm fire, his stomach filled with delicious meals and his bed with Jacotte. The more I thought about this, the more it pained me to ingratiate myself with him, since he was nothing but the eyes and ears of the bishop of Sarlat, whom he visited each week, riding either on some labourer's cart or on his mule. But I didn't want him to go and undo verbally the Latin attestations I'd got him to sign.

"Priest," I said, "I've heard tell that the beautiful statue of the Blessed Virgin in the church at Marcuays has had all her paint rubbed away by the hands of the faithful, who need to touch her while praying."

"'Tis true, alas!" confirmed Pincers with a huge sigh, his face suddenly illuminated. "But the parish has no funds with which to regild her."

"Here," I offered, placing an écu on the table, "perhaps this will help return her shine. This gift," I added in French, holding up my palm to silence his gush of thanks, "should remain a secret in both Marcuays and Taniès, but not from you-know-who in Sarlat, where I hope he will see me in a better light, as one whose life was preserved by the Duc d'Anjou and the king in the travails he had to endure."

"Monsieur," Pincers confirmed, bowing deeply, "I can assure you that it shall be as you wish; and, as for me, I will spare no effort to make it so."

As we stepped from his little nest, a cold breeze slapped us in the face, and the sudden chill seemed to be a harbinger of snow rather than rain.

"Well, Monsieur," said my lively and wiry valet as he pulled his mount up next to mine, leaving Giacomi and Fröhlich in the rearguard, our horses' shoes ringing strangely on the rocky road, "is it not a damnable offence to give money to gild a papist idol?"

"Well, this cost me only one écu," I pointed out, "whereas it cost the Brethren 500 écus to win the bishop's approval for their purchase of Mespech, since Fontenac was so opposed to our Huguenot presence."

"But an idol, Monsieur!"

"Well, Miroul," I joked, "to gild her arouses no guilt, as long as one doesn't worship her."

"But to so adorn her makes others adore her!" rejoined Miroul, without missing a beat, for, valet though he was, he loved puns and plays on words as much as any Italian courtier.

"No matter, Miroul," I replied. "What do we care if the villagers kiss her hands and feet? Should my sweet brother be prevented from marrying his Gertrude, should I be forbidden to marry Angelina simply because a few colours are splashed on a piece of wood? It seems to me this kind of talk is all too easy for you, Miroul!"

"What do you mean, Monsieur?"

"Well, my Miroul, you're lucky enough to be in love with a Huguenot, whom you can marry without all of these ruses and abuses!"

At which, had the night not been dark as pitch, I would have seen Miroul turn scarlet, so thoroughly was he bewitched by his chaste Florine, yet so attached to me that he'd promised not to marry her before I'd led my Angelina to the altar. This was a promise I'd never have dreamt of exacting from my good Miroul, since my own marriage prospects were so precarious. Monsieur de Montcalm was so tyrannized by his confessor that he couldn't accept a heretic for a son-in-law, even though I'd saved his life and those of his wife and daughter in a fight against the outlaws of Barbentane, who were holding them captive. But luckily Angelina and Madame de Montcalm were on my side, and, in their letters to me, encouraged me to continue to hope, since this confessor was old and infirm, and they hoped to replace him soon with Father Anselm, who was Montcalm's secretary and fond of me since we'd fought together against the outlaws, as I've recounted elsewhere.

Lest the reader judge me for having worked so hard to obtain attestations that Samson and I had been baptized in the "true faith", but not sought the same document for my brother François, I should explain that this would have served no purpose, since Diane was lodged in the Château de Fontenac, and their marriage must necessarily be celebrated in Marcuays, under the watchful eye of the bishop of Sarlat, who was very little inclined to give away the advantage the papists had secured on St Bartholomew's eve. For I have to say that the massacre perpetrated in Paris and in cities throughout the kingdom had struck such terror into the hearts of the survivors that a large number of them—excepting those who were to fight so valiantly against the king at La Rochelle—either tried to accommodate themselves with the papists or simply converted straightaway to the Roman Church, among them Rosier, our good pastor in Paris, who preferred to live a Catholic than die a Huguenot. The Brethren, on the other hand, who'd never taken up arms against their king, felt they had little to fear from him, and found ways to make peace with the local clergy, going so far as to grant them, *gratis pro Deo,** a property that we possessed in Sarlat so that a monastery of Capuchin monks could be built to allow them to enlarge their community.

At the same time, my friend Quéribus, who enjoyed the favour of the Duc d'Anjou, not only spread the word throughout the Sarlat region that I, too, benefited from the duc's good graces—which wasn't exactly false since the duc had given me 200 écus from his treasury—but that the duc had personally assured my safety during the night

---

* "Free, for the love of God."

of 23rd August, a happy lie that I repeated as often as I could, since nothing protects a man better than princely protection, even if it's merely a rumour.

However, even if these prudent steps—and I include those of the Brethren with my own—had arranged things in the Sarlat region so well that we felt quite assured of our safety, it was nevertheless quite improbable that our bishop would consent to the marriage of Diane de Fontenac with a heretic, unless François agreed to convert—which he doubtless would have done with my father's consent, had not Sauveterre imposed his unshakeable rigour on us all.

All of which is not to say that every bishop in the kingdom, even after the St Bartholomew's day massacre, was as implacable as ours. Some, for whom their families and alliances came first, even went so far as to declare that it could be profitable for the Church if papist women were allowed to marry Huguenots on condition that their children be raised in the religion of their mother, thereby allowing the Huguenot faith to die out with no hope of perpetuating itself. They argued that this form of extirpation of the heresy could be accomplished without struggle or injury, but ultimately by the sweet intervention of women.

No, not all the prelates in the kingdom were as haughty and fierce as our bishop of Sarlat! His opposition had forced Gertrude to resort to her flexible Norman priest to celebrate her marriage, on the sole condition that she produce the Latin attestation we'd sweated out of Pincers, which, rushing upstairs to her warm, brightly lit room, I presented to the lady, who slipped it between her breasts, where it was assuredly more happily ensconced than in my doublet, which was frozen from the cold winds and covered with snowflakes.

"Well, my brother! How good, brave and caring you are!" cried Gertrude, who was so happy she didn't even know what she was saying, and threw her arms around me in a fond embrace.

"Miroul," I said to my good valet, who was watching this with a twinkle in his brown eye, "go and tell my father that it's snowing, and ask him to have a fire lit in the fireplaces at either end of the great hall. It's getting cold enough to crack a stone out there!"

"At your service!" called Miroul over his shoulder, happy enough to rush off to the kitchen where Florine, the blonde Huguenot wench he'd saved from the St Bartholomew's day massacre, was helping la Maligou prepare the evening meal. It was hard to believe that la Maligou was the mother of my slender little viper Little Sissy, for she was a corpulent woman in every aspect—stomach, breasts and buttocks—and was now wailing like an abandoned heifer since she'd been fighting a bout of diarrhoea for three days.

There was a knock at Gertrude's door, and Zara, consenting to interrupt her application of more unguents to her hands, went to open it. Baron de Quéribus stepped into the room, entirely covered with snowflakes since he'd galloped all the way from Puymartin to Mespech in order to dine with us. He was dog-tired, but splendidly clad and remarkably handsome, with blond hair, blue eyes, dark eyebrows, chiselled features and such youthfulness in his sunny smile that you couldn't help liking him despite his swagger. For, as one of the favourites of Anjou's entourage, he seemed always to put on such airs, with his svelte figure, his feet planted proudly, his hand on his hip.

"By my conscience!" he burst out. "It's snowing so hard you can't tell the road from the fields! And the cold pierces right through you! Madame, I throw myself at your knees!" But he was careful to kiss only her hand and not to take her in his arms, hoping to convince me that he remembered our agreement. On me, however, he lavished a great hug.

"Madame," observed Zara, who, though she professed not to like men, couldn't do without their adulation, "the baron likes Monsieur de Siorac better than us! What's more, they resemble each other like peas in a pod. It's as though, when the baron looks at Monsieur de Siorac, he thinks he's looking in a mirror! So that's why he loves him better than us!"

"Oh, Zara, what are you saying?" cried Quéribus, and, wheeling around on his heels, he seized her waist and held her to him. "Do you think I could ever forget you, beautiful Zara, and that I don't love you and your mistress more than anyone alive? God alive! I'm like to die," he continued, his voice rising in pitch, as he swore like Charles IX on a tennis court, but careful nevertheless to ensure that the Brethren could not hear him, given his respect for them.

"Baron, if you love me," cooed Gertrude, "you will not delay your departure another minute, since I have some business in Normandy that cannot wait!"

"Ha!" laughed Quéribus, glancing at me conspiratorially. "If this business is so dear to you, I promise not to crawl like a tortoise! However, I cannot start back until the fifteenth of November."

"The fifteenth of November!" cried Gertrude, which Zara immediately echoed:

"The fifteenth of November!"

"Oh, Monsieur," pouted Gertrude, "that's such a long time! What a bore and a pain to have to wait till then!"

"Madame," Quéribus replied with a bow, "though I'd love to accommodate you, I cannot do so any earlier. My cousin Puymartin is inviting the nobility of the Sarlat region to a great soirée in my honour on the tenth of November, where I expect to enjoy myself deliriously. I don't think I'll be recovered from my fatigue until the fifteenth."

"What?" gasped Gertrude, her eyes lighting up and suddenly all ears. "A soirée? A great celebration! The tenth? Will there be dancing? Will I be invited?"

"But of course, Madame!" laughed Quéribus. "Along with your betrothed and his brother here, and François, and Catherine, and the Brethren of Mespech."

"And what about me?" asked Zara coyly.

"That goes without saying!" roared Quéribus, somewhat derisively, it seemed to me. "How could I deprive such a noble lady of the company of her lady-in-waiting?" he continued with a somewhat mocking smile, for secretly he did not believe the lady to be so noble, since Gertrude was a member of *la noblesse de robe* and he the more ancient and knighted *la noblesse d'épée.*[*]

"Well then!" cried Gertrude, running to embrace her chambermaid. "Did you hear, Zara? A soirée! The tenth! With all the nobles in Sarlat. In Puymartin's chateau!"

Of course, there was no possibility (as Quéribus would have pointed out) that Zara hadn't heard, especially since Gertrude reminded her of the event several more times, and so delighted was she to be invited to such a celebration that she forgot all about her haste to go to marry my brother in Normandy.

The object of this forgetting made his entrance at that very moment, waving a flagon containing a liquor of a particularly unappetizing greenish colour, on which his blue eyes were so happily fixated that he appeared not to notice any of those present, not even Gertrude, whom he now approached without even seeing her—like filings drawn to a magnet.

"Well, my pretty Samson," she cried, running to his side like a hen to her chick, "look at you! You're not wearing your collar, your doublet's all unbuttoned and your sleeves are rolled up! Your socks are falling down and your hair looks like a distaff that's got all tangled up!"

"My love," he replied softly, his innocent face looking like that of a saint in a stained-glass window, "I've spent the last five hours concocting this medicine"—at this, he brandished the flagon—"out of

---

[*] "The nobles of the gown" (the judicial and administrative class of nobility); "the nobles of the sword" (the feudal, knightly class of nobility).

twelve different elements, some extracted, some sublimated or ground to powder; carefully combined according to my own prescription, they will cure the stomach disorders that la Maligou is suffering from."

At this, Quéribus, ever the gallant, could hardly suppress his laughter, and turned away, attempting to stifle his mirth.

"Monsieur!" scolded Gertrude. "I won't have you making light of this. Have you no appreciation for the evangelical charity of this angel of God, who's laboured for five long hours in order to relieve the ailments of this simple servant?"

And turning to Samson, she added with supreme illogic and with the same choleric tone:

"Samson, aren't you ashamed to have locked your door to me for a whole afternoon in order to concoct this horrible potion? Zara, take that flagon and put it on the table."

"Oh, but I cannot, Madame! My hands are covered with ointment," protested Zara—an astonishing response from a chambermaid, to pretend that she had such delicate hands she couldn't touch anything from dawn to dusk.

"Good heavens, Zara! Well, at least run over to Samson's chambers and fetch his collar!" said Gertrude, who, even when angry, tolerated a stunning degree of laxity from her lady-in-waiting, as she insisted on calling her chambermaid.

Zara obeyed with obvious reluctance, little pleased with the prospect of leaving the warmth of Gertrude's room to venture into the cold of the rest of the chateau. As for me, seeing the lady very hesitant to approach Samson as long as he was holding the flagon of greenish fluid, I suggested he place it on the table, which he did, seemingly still under the spell of the labour that had consumed the better part of his day.

"Come here, my pretty sorcerer," beckoned Gertrude, taking Samson by the wrist and making him sit on a stool before her lit mirror. After which she undertook to clean his stained fingers with spirits of wine.

I took Quéribus's arm and we left our beauty to her cleaning, having no doubt she'd need no help at it, especially since Zara reappeared with Samson's lace collar and was preparing to put it on once she'd buttoned his doublet.

We descended a little winding staircase, which felt absolutely glacial, as though the wind had found a way to pass right through the stone walls of its construction. But soon we stepped out into the warmth of the great hall, with its enormous fireplaces at each end. The various members of the household were already seated, each of them in their places at the lower end of the table, their hats under their arses, their hands washed and their lips sealed, while Sauveterre and Siorac walked up and down the room, not side by side, but in opposite directions. Each time they met in the middle they'd exchange a few rapid words and then continue, Sauveterre, as was his wont, careful to avoid stepping on the joints of the stone flooring, which forced him every few steps to shorten or lengthen his stride—not an easy task given that he limped from the wound he'd received twenty-seven years before at Ceresole.

"Zounds!" he complained (this being the only swear word that he permitted himself). "What extravagance! Two fires in the same room!"

"But isn't that why two fireplaces were built?" asked my father as he passed him. "Each one warms half the room."

"But two fires!" grumbled Sauveterre. "When we might have made do with one!"

"Yes, we might have," replied Siorac over his shoulder as he continued, "but these ladies, whose bodices are so exposed, could not have." That this response was calculated to set his brother off, I'm quite certain.

"The plague take their ruinous bosoms!" muttered Sauveterre, continuing all the way to the far end of the room, his eyes fixed on the joints of the stones. "Can't they put some wool over them to save on firewood?"

"What a pity that would be," said my father to himself as he reached the end of the hall.

But Sauveterre's hearing was too sharp.

"At this rate," he said, "our supply of firewood will scarcely last out the year!"

"Come now, my brother," objected Siorac, "we've got enough wood stacked out there for two winters!"

"But not such a cold winter as this one will be," warned my uncle. "Just ask Faujanet!"

"Faujanet," said my father, stopping short, his eyebrows raised, and turning to face the lower end of the table, "what do you know about the coming winter?"

Faujanet, who was of dark complexion and had a limp like Sauveterre's (which is doubtless why they had such affection for each other), rose from his seat. But before he said a word, he pulled his hat off the seat of his stool and held it in front of him with both hands, signalling that he was speaking to the baron with his hat respectfully doffed.

"Monsieur, I was out this morning, working on the pathway to les Beunes and I came across a burrow. 'Well,' I thought, 'must be a rabbit.' So I started digging, and dug and dug. But couldn't reach 'im! 'Twas a marmot! And he'd dug down at least a good half a toise! Proof that winter's come early this year and is going to be a cold one. The snow's here to stay for a while."

This prediction—which seemed to all of us quite certain, no one doubting the wisdom of the hibernating marmot seeking warmth as deep as possible—led all of our people to put on long faces. Noticing this, my father immediately made a joke of it to ease their worries.

"*Cand avetz fred,*" he said in Provençal, "*cal tener lo tiol estrech.*"* Which of course made them all laugh uproariously and, as they did so, look

---

* "When winter's cold and clothed in white, you've got to keep your arse squeezed tight!"

adoringly at their master, grateful that he knew the proverbs that had nourished their childhoods.

"With your permission, Monsieur," said Faujanet, whose turn it was to quote a proverb, given that he'd discovered the marmot burrow, "*annada de neu, fe de jintilóme, annada d'abonde!*"* Well, this created another wave of laughter from the table, not because there was anything comic in this comforting maxim, but because our cooper had said, speaking in his own name, "*fe de jintilóme*", and had said it as he addressed a baron. Nor were they sorry to take Faujanet down a peg or two since they could see he'd spend the winter all puffed up with pride for having made the prediction based on the marmot burrow, especially if it turned out to be true.

The laughter ceased and the whole table rose to honour her, as the door opened to admit Gertrude du Luc, preceded by Zara and Samson, this last decked out in his lace collar and all buttoned up, his beautiful copper-coloured curls all brushed out, and carrying the two candelabra (which were dissipating with each flicker of their light the finances of the Brethren). Zara even deigned to open the door for him, which evidently her smooth hands could do without injury.

To tell the truth, our people didn't have to be forced to be silent at her arrival, since the golden locks of the Norman lady and all her splendid accoutrements recalled to the eldest of them my late mother in all her finery, and some of them—out of earshot of Sauveterre of course—opined that, however great the additional expenses were for meat, firewood and candles, one had to admit that the chateau seemed much gayer since the "ladies" had come to stay. Barberine, papist that she remained under her Huguenot crust, added that Dame Gertrude was "as beautiful and good as the Blessed Virgin", and that it was a

---

* "Year of snow, by my faith as a gentleman, year of plenty!"

pity that the "Monsieur" (meaning François) couldn't just go and marry her equal in Sarlat since Mespech could no more do without a baronne than a blind man without his cane.

Since the only light in the great hall had been from the fireplaces, the arrival of Samson bearing the two "wasteful" candelabra suddenly illuminated Quéribus and me, who'd kept to the shadows to avoid disturbing the oscillating and disputatious stroll of the Brethren. Seeing us now, my father smiled graciously at us from across the room and, after placing a mustachioed kiss on the hands of the two ladies, hastened over to us and gave each of us a warm embrace. He was fond of Quéribus, despite the Parisian's mannered and bejewelled affectations, and was happy to accept the invitation to the soirée on the 10th on behalf of both Brethren. Meanwhile, Sauveterre was making a stiff and deep bow to the ladies from far across the room, as though he felt there to be some peril to his soul were he to approach these ornately painted vessels of iniquity. We took our places at table, and, as we were sitting down, Samson suddenly slapped his forehead, murmuring "I'm crazy!" and sent Miroul off to retrieve the greenish flagon he'd left in Gertrude's room—no doubt forgotten given the attentions he'd received from Zara and her mistress.

My valet was back in the blink of an eye, though he'd had no candle to light his way through the dark hallways, his variegated eyes able to see as well at night as during the day, like those of a cat, which he resembled as well in his remarkable agility. Neither of these traits would have described la Maligou, who, when she emerged from the kitchen with the soup tureen, walked with tiny steps and trembled at each like a bowlful of jelly, so swollen was the excess of flesh on her bones. As soon as she placed the soup on the table, Samson offered her the greenish concoction, explaining the why and how of its use. La Maligou listened with great reverence, and bestowed many benedictions on Samson for his good medicine, which, however, ended up having no curative effect. Her uncontrollable stomach troubles continued for days afterwards, getting worse and worse, and only seemed to improve when she swallowed a concoction of walnut leaves and blackberry brambles that Barberine was accustomed to giving her cows when they suffered from the same malady. So great was the respect our people had for Samson's vials and flagons, however, that none of them made light of his failure. Barberine later explained that his remedy was too beautiful and too complex to cure a simple servant.

As my father was seated at the head of the table, he had Sauveterre on his right and Dame Gertrude du Luc on his left.

"My brother," ventured Siorac in French, "did you hear that Puymartin has invited us to a grand soirée at his chateau on the tenth?"

"Humph!" growled Sauveterre, for whom "soirée" meant dancing, and dancing meant perdition, but who also knew that he could not refuse to appear, since Puymartin would be closely allied with us, should the marriage of François and Diane be celebrated.

"Did you hear what I said, François?" asked Siorac with a knowing air.

"I heard, Father," replied my elder brother, opening his mouth to speak for the first and last time during the entire meal. In particular, he refused to speak to—or even look at—Dame du Luc, who, in his estimation, was not of noble enough birth to merit his attention, and even less Zara, who possessed no claim to nobility whatsoever. My brother's eventual claim to the two baronies he would inherit apparently gave him the right to swagger like a peacock. But whom would he have talked to? Was I not his younger brother and Samson a bastard? The one a lowly doctor, the other an apothecary! Of course, there was Quéribus, but this gentleman had eyes and ears only for the Brethren and the ladies. The Parisian was so infatuated with his own nobility it didn't occur to him to worry about their rank—it was enough that they were present, their sparkle embellishing his world.

"My brother," Siorac whispered in Provençal, since Dame Gertrude was momentarily in deep conversation with Quéribus, "you seem quite upset and out of sorts about this matter of the soirée."

"Well, not just about that," grumbled Sauveterre, casting a disapproving eye on the two candelabra and the two fires. "I won't hide from you, my brother, that I don't like the way things are going here. Everywhere I look I see needless expense and dissipation. *Non ego mendosos ausim defendere mores.**

"In that case," replied my father, quoting Romans 12:15 in Provençal, "rejoice with those who rejoice! Our two papists will be leaving on the fifteenth with our friend here."

At which, Quéribus, who spoke some Provençal (since his own estate was near Carcassonne), threw a look at my father, another at me, smiled, and immediately continued his conversation with Gertrude.

"I find this news infinitely comforting!" sighed Sauveterre. "*Nulla fere causa est in qua non femina litem moverit.*† So, just between you and me, the end is finally in sight for this never-ending month. You know that our quarrel has never really been so much about the cost of candles and wood, but rather about the '*odor di femina*'‡ that has impregnated our walls."

"What?" exclaimed my father. "You mean you couldn't detect it before, with Catherine and her chambermaids here?"

"Yes, of course," conceded Sauveterre, "but *she* never managed to subjugate you completely."

"Well!" replied Siorac with some gravity. "You've hit on a point of great consequence, and one that has always amazed me: it may be possible not to love women, but it's not possible to love them without loving them excessively!" These words so perfectly captured Jean de

---

* "You won't find me defending immorality" (Ovid).

† "There are almost no cases where a woman hasn't been the cause of a quarrel."

‡ "Odour of woman."

Siorac's nature (and mine) that to this day I still remember them, along with my father's face when he pronounced them and Sauveterre's as he took them in, for he would have preferred a response in which nature had not won out over virtue. On the other hand, at that moment he was so happy, in his jealous affection, to have learnt of the imminent flight of our pretty birds, that he didn't press the argument with Siorac. Alas, poor Sauveterre was very nearly disappointed in this, as you shall soon learn.

My little sister Catherine, whose *odor di femina*, to use my uncle's phrase, didn't seem to bother her uncle's nostrils, wasn't so little as I liked to imagine, but had become a woman from head to toe, svelte yet well rounded, her eyes like asters, her face ruddy with health and devoid of any interest in make-up or trinkets—other than the gold necklace I'd given her to compensate her for the ring I'd offered to Little Sissy. She overheard the Brethren's exchange with that quiet, shy demeanour that we teach our girls from their infancy. But since I knew her well, I was all too aware that she was not the least bit sorry to see our ladies depart— though she liked to babble with them in their room, try on their finery and play with the colours that they used in their make-up—because she was convinced that her father, whom she adored, gave them the attention that should have been bestowed on her. Indeed, ever since my mother's death, Catherine saw herself as mistress of Mespech, at least until she married, though this event did not seem imminent. Having reviewed with Barberine all the possible matches for her in the Sarlat region, she'd not discovered a single one worth sinking her claws into.

For she possessed a set of sharp claws, and a pretty good mouth as well, treating her brothers tersely and haughtily, using the formal *vous* with us, scolding us, teasing us, tolerating neither kisses nor hugs, calling us stiffly "Monsieur my brother", and at the least provocation turning on us a cold shoulder with an irritated swish of her skirts. When I say "her brothers" I do not mean François, whom she never graced with the slightest look, so much did she despise him, but rather Samson and me, whom she loved, though you'd have never guessed it, with a great and jealous love—yet another reason for demonstrating little affection for Gertrude and even less for my Little Sissy, whom she'd grown up with, being a mere three days older than her maid.

When dinner was over, and while Alazaïs, Miroul and Florine were arranging our chairs in front of the fire—the library being too cold on this frigid, snowy night to permit us to withdraw there with the ladies—Catherine pulled me aside at the other end of the table, put her arm in mine and said:

"My brother, I've heard from Samson that after he leaves Mespech with Gertrude du Luc, your thought is to set yourself up as a doctor in Bordeaux."

"That is, indeed, my plan," I confirmed, somewhat annoyed that Samson had informed her of our intentions, since Catherine tended to twist what she'd heard according to her fancy.

"How does it happen, then," she demanded, withdrawing her arm from mine, shaking her blonde curls in annoyance and, doubtless, feigning an anger that she didn't actually feel, "that Samson knew of this before I did?"

"My sister," I replied testily, annoyed that she was already accusing me of sins I hadn't committed, "have we ever signed a contract that stipulates we'll tell each other everything?"

"Never! And yet brotherly love should have dictated that you do so," she replied with a little pout.

My stonily silent reaction to this taught her that this approach wasn't going to work, so instead she took the road of reconciliation, extending her hand and a smile, and offering her cheek, saying:

"'Tis of no consequence, Pierre, I pardon you. Give me a kiss."

Which I did, overcoming my own anger and embracing her sweetly, but, like a cat, prepared to retreat at a moment's notice, whiskers bristling and inquisitive, put on guard as I was by her scolding of me, and wary of the sharp claws concealed within her velvet paws. It also worried me that I could see Little Sissy on my left, who seemed to be hanging about, all ears, apparently engaged, though she was normally so lazy, in vigorously polishing the long table behind us.

"Pierre," she continued after returning my kiss, "I know that you're going to take up your medical practice in Bordeaux, and, until you marry Angelina, you'll have no one to manage your household and your servants, Florine and Miroul. Why don't you take me with you? I think I could manage things quite well!"

Even if I'd known how to answer this question (which frankly astounded me), I wouldn't have had time to get a word in, for suddenly Little Sissy had rushed between us, her black Gypsy eyes aflame with fury.

"Madame," she proclaimed, her hands jauntily set on her hips, "if there's a woman in this house whom Pierre should take with him to Bordeaux, it's assuredly me! I'm his wench and I can give him things a sister could never pretend to!"

"What?" cried Catherine, startled and wholly beside herself. "You little bird! How dare you interrupt this conversation? And presume to confront me! Get yourself to the kitchen, slattern! Be gone, you toad! You viper! You slinking lizard!"

"Madame," Little Sissy replied, giving her a sarcastic bow, "a serpent I may be, but I've got a handsome gentleman in my bed, and have conceived his child!"

"Scorpion!" screamed my sister. "Do you think your ugly sins give you any advantage over me?" And so saying, she stepped up to Little Sissy and viciously slapped her twice.

"Well, Madame! Now you're beating a pregnant woman! That's treachery!" screamed Little Sissy, who would have returned her blows if I hadn't stepped between them and held her arm, offering Catherine my back to block further assault, something she seemed eager to commit, trying to push me out of the way.

Seeing me caught between these two Furies, my father rose and came to the rescue, ordering Catherine to withdraw to her room and Little Sissy to the scullery. Which they did, grinding their teeth, their eyes shooting daggers at each other.

"Pierre! What on earth," my father queried, once they'd left the hall with a furious flouncing of their skirts, "was the reason for this caterwauling?"

As I quietly explained what had happened, my father walked back and forth before me with his impatient step, incapable as ever of remaining at rest, but, despite his greying hair, alert and always at the ready: carriage straight, hands on hips, strong of leg. To honour our lady visitors he was decked out in a velvet doublet of a handsome pale green—a tribute to my mother, for green had been her colour. In all, the Baron de Mespech cut a handsome and alluring figure.

"Well, Pierre!" he laughed, glancing at me from the corner of his eye. "It doesn't seem, as Quéribus would say, that there'll ever be a lack of wenches around you, but rather an overabundance of 'em, since you're so excessively generous and soft: a combination to which even your sister is sensitive, who is never without the gold necklace you gave her—even at night. As for Little Sissy, though I don't like a pregnant woman to be struck in my house, I sense that she deserved these slaps, since she's insufferably cheeky with everyone here. Casual love," he continued, taking my arm and pulling me close to him, "always seems easily won, but there are always dangers there, because we too often forget that our good chambermaids are women every bit as much as the gallant ladies—they are always trying to slip a halter around our necks as soon as they get their hands on us."

He sighed—a sigh that led me to believe that Franchou was giving him a hard time because Zara had been hunting on her territory.

"As for Catherine," he continued, "she's so much like your late mother: very affectionate with those she loves, but haughty by nature and deprecating towards everyone else, suffering neither reins nor bridle, always riding hell for leather and impossibly indomitable. So, my son," he laughed, "which will it be, Catherine or Little Sissy, whom you'll take to Bordeaux?"

"I'd never thought about it till now," I confessed, "but now I'll have to consider it. I understand that Catherine is not very happy in the countryside, since she can't find a suitor here, so of course she'd love to live in a big city, hoping for a miracle there. But I'd never dream," I added after mulling it over a bit, "of depriving you of her radiant smile."

"Which isn't very radiant when you and Samson are gone," he lamented. "Catherine yearns for younger stallions than we've got within our old walls. If you think she'd do, Pierre, take her with you without a second thought for me."

"Ah, but do I want her? I just don't know," I mused. "No doubt I love her, with a great and fraternal love, and yet…"

"And yet?" continued my father with a laugh. "Don't finish that sentence until you've thought about it some more. There'll be plenty of time to make up your mind before Samson leaves on the fifteenth."

The next morning, the snow continued to fall in flakes so thick that, from the window of the fencing room, I could hardly distinguish the church tower in Marcuays on the other side of the meadow, as if a white tapestry had fallen from the sky, partially obscuring the horizon and so muffling all the normal sounds that, though I heard our cocks crow, I couldn't hear the cocks from the neighbouring farms answer them. Worse still, even the noises from Samson's fencing lesson with Giacomi seemed muted to my numbed, lazy ears.

Miroul and big Fröhlich, seated beside me, were rendered speechless by the sight of Giacomi, with an almost imperceptible movement of his wrist, parrying my brother's blade and touching his own to my brother's chest as quickly and effortlessly as a bird flits through the air.

"Well, now, Samson!" cried Giacomi, with that wonderful Italian lisp that gave his speech such grace. "Were you backing away? Pure heresy. It's the blade's business to deflect the blade. Not the torso's job to sound the retreat!"

"I'll remember," promised Samson, who, of the three of us, was the most docile, and, as a consequence, hardly the best swordsman, being slow to understand and late in learning.

Giacomi seemed almost preternaturally quick by comparison, his flesh so thinly spread on his bones, long arms and legs, and his movements so economical and well executed that it was a marvel to watch him achieve so much with so little effort! And how I loved to watch his oval, tanned face, all of whose features seemed joyously to pull upwards: the corners of his eyelids and his lips, even his turned-up nose. He was a person of great quality, the mirror of courtesy, a man of good and rare mettle, who, though a papist, had risked his life to help me navigate a safe route out of Paris during the St Bartholomew's day massacre.

"Giacomi," I said, pulling him over to the window embrasure once his assault was ended, "I'm ashamed to watch you exercise your art with such insignificant folk as ourselves, you who were Silvie's assistant in the Louvre and the teacher of such great and important noblemen. And as much as I would love to keep you here, and my father as well, I wouldn't wish to shackle your fortunes for anything—"

"What are you saying?" interrupted Giacomi, raising his eyebrows.

"That if you'd prefer to leave on the fifteenth with Quéribus and his escort—"

"What, my brother!" he cried, feigning anger. "Have I displeased you? Are you annoyed with me? Have I been banished to the borderlands of your affection?"

47

From this speech, couched in such gaily humorous terms, I knew that Giacomi would be staying with me. I laughed from the comfort I felt, but with my heart beating and my throat all knotted up, I gushed:

"Ah, Giacomi! You know that my heart is forever attached to yours by hooks of steel—ever since St Bartholomew's eve!"

"My brother," answered Giacomi, "let's not get too emotional about what each of us owes the other, and start crying like fountains over our blessings. Friendship is like a viol whose strings mustn't be tightened all the way to tears!"

These very poetic Italian thoughts were spoken with a gracious gesture of his left hand, and, as he walked away, he said over his shoulder:

"But what about you, Pierre?" And glancing at the snow, he added, "Do you plan to stay the winter at Mespech?"

"Absolutely not! After the departure of our ladies, I plan to set up my medical practice in Bordeaux, which is a beautiful, large city that prospers from its maritime trade."

"Well then," smiled Giacomi, "if you want me to accompany you, Pierre, I'll follow, along with the arms and baggage. I have no doubt I can find as many fencing students there as you will patients."

I looked over at Fröhlich and saw that he was looking very sullen, since he had little love for the farm work he'd been doing at Mespech, but didn't dare ask me to take him with me to Bordeaux, knowing full well that I already had Miroul in my service and was doubtless not rich enough to support two valets.

But I didn't have time to comfort my good Swiss Guard: Escorgol stuck his enormous nose and even larger stomach through the door and announced breathlessly that a horseman, followed by a page, was outside requesting entry to Mespech and claiming to be my friend.

Our Escorgol had the peculiarity of possessing a very large nose but a weak sense of smell, and tiny ears but the finest sense of hearing in the whole region. He could, it was said, hear a child walking barefoot along the grassy road to Mespech fifty toises away. Which is why we employed him as our porter. He also had very keen vision, though it was hard to see his eyes through all the folds of his eyelids.

"Did he tell you his name, Escorgol?"

"He flatly refused, Monsieur, arguing that he would reveal his name only to you."

"Did you recognize his voice?"

"No, and even less his accent, which is definitely not from here."

"And his face?"

"I couldn't see it. The fellow is covered up to his eyebrows by a great cloak, which itself is covered with snow."

"'Sblood!" I cried. "Let's solve this mystery!" And off I ran, with Escorgol, Miroul, Giacomi and Fröhlich at my heels, leaving Samson frozen in place, magnetized suddenly by a more attractive metal, for Gertrude had just entered the room from the opposite door.

After crossing the two drawbridges of the little island in our moat, I ran to open the peephole in the main gate and spied a large fellow on horseback, whose cloak was so closely drawn over his face that you could hardly see his eyes. Indeed, the brown mantle covering him was completely blanketed with snow, and his horse was only black on his underside, but our visitor seemed less bothered by it that his pretty little page, who was blowing on his fingers to try to warm them.

"Who are you, my snowy companion?" I shouted through the peephole.

"Is that really Pierre de Siorac who's speaking to me through the iron grid there?" said the fellow, whose voice had a familiar ring to it.

"'Tis really I."

"Well, if that's really the case, then I curse the treacherous peephole that's preventing me from seeing your handsome face!"

"And who are you to speak thus?"

"A man who loves you. But tell me—relieve me of my doubts: is this really the venerable Dr Pierre de Siorac, younger son of the Baron de Mespech, who's speaking to me?"

"Didn't you hear me? 'Tis I!"

"And you don't recognize me, Pierre de Siorac?"

"Not all cloaked up like that, no."

"Nor my voice?"

"Not yet."

"Well!" laughed the fellow. "It is the voice of blood."

"The voice of blood?"

"Or rather, if you prefer, the murmur of milk: I was your nurse, Pierre."

"My nurse, a man?"

"Am I a man?" mused the fellow sardonically. "Sometimes I wonder. But never mind. I was not your wet nurse Pierre, as Barberine was, but the nursemaid to your mind."

"To my mind?"

"Indeed! I nourished you in Montpellier at the teats of logic and philosophy that hang from that cow Aristotle."

"What?" I cried, unable to believe my ears and throwing open the door in my joy. "Fogacer! Is it really you?"

"*Ipse, mi fili,*"* he said, lowering his cape. And smiling, his head now slowly covering with snow, he looked at me with those dark eyes, and arched his diabolical eyebrow.

---

* "Myself, my son."

2

M Y FATHER WAS delighted to meet Fogacer, having heard so much about him, though I'd omitted certain particulars about his habits, which no doubt would have been difficult for him to swallow given how foreign they were to his own temperament and since they were so vilified by our religion. And Fogacer, for his part, accustomed as he was to the persecution of persons of his stripe, had learnt so well how to disguise his voice, gestures and behaviour that the Baron de Mespech was a thousand leagues from suspecting anything, even when Fogacer requested that his young page not be bedded down in Miroul's room, but in his own, since the poor lad suffered from suffocation fits in the night that only his master could calm by massaging his epigastrium.

Fogacer made this request without batting an eyelid, and my father was entirely persuaded by the reason, since, as you will remember, he'd studied medicine in Montpellier himself before choosing a career as a soldier. As for Sauveterre, convinced as he was that all evil in this world derived from womankind, he had no particular sensitivity about such "devilishness and other detestable enormities", as Calvin labelled them—both he and the Pope condemning the practitioners of this vice to the scaffold, doubtless the only subject on which they'd found reconciliation.

I chose for their lodgings the room at the top of the north tower, since it was the most isolated of all of our living spaces and would afford them the privacy they'd need.

"*Mi fili*," said Fogacer when we were able to sit down alone together, "please allow me to stretch out on the cot here. I've been on horseback for three solid days, and almost haven't dismounted since Périgueux—and though I prefer the present discomfort to the flames that were intended for my derrière in that town, the inflammation is nevertheless quite painful!"

"Does that mean, Fogacer, that you were threatened with being burnt at the stake in Périgueux? Who or what got you into such a mess?"

"My virtue," replied Fogacer, arching his eyebrows.

"Your virtue," I observed, seating myself on a stool beside his cot, while his valet—or, as Fogacer termed him, his page—squatted on the floor nearby, and never took his eyes off his master, as though he feared that the man might evaporate into thin air if he turned his back for a quarter of a second, "your virtue, Fogacer, was already under some debate back in Montpellier, if I remember correctly."

"And yet," replied Fogacer with that slow, sinuous smile of his, "wouldn't it be cowardly to cease to be what I am, just because who I am doesn't please those who construct gallows, build pyres and christen my virtue a crime, in the name of obscure precepts that have come to us all dusty from the dark night of belief?"

"Crime or virtue, my friend, what did you do in Périgueux that got you condemned to be burnt alive?"

"I loved," lamented Fogacer gravely and, this time, without a trace of a smile, "in the only way I know how, and the only object that I deem lovable. But though my love was noble and, in my heart, pure, it was suddenly labelled 'abominable and diabolical' by the powers that be, who are governed by certain narrow-minded, weak, hypocritical and zealous persons. And so suddenly I found myself in desperate flight, galloping furiously over hill and dale, fearing for my life—and fearing for *his* especially," placing his hand on the blond curls of his page, who immediately took it and covered it with kisses of infinite gratitude.

"This little fellow," Fogacer continued, taking his hand from the boy's, and with more feeling than I'd ever witnessed in him, "was in the employ of an acrobat in Paris, who was teaching him his tricks and had him working long hours under perilous conditions for a pittance. What's more, he would beat him mercilessly and shower him frequently with a thousand insults. But it happened that our impresario, having been caught in some villainy in Paris, had to flee the capital with his band and travel from town to town, earning his bread by his antics and acrobatics. So what could I do but follow them across France, wholly captivated as I was by the charms of my pretty Silvio, and caring for the injured and sick in the troupe without receiving a sol for my services?"

"Oh, Fogacer! To think that you were one of the doctors of the Duc d'Anjou! Fallen so low and prey to these vagabonds!"

"*Trahit sua quemque voluptas!*"* mused Fogacer with a wistful sigh. "But allow me to continue. When we reached Périgueux, I decided to take this little angel—who's as angelic in his heart as he is in his bodily beauty—and flee our tyrannical impresario. But the villain, who'd turned a blind eye to my passion as long as it served his interests, 'realized' at my departure that his Christian conscience was outraged by our love and ran to denounce us to the bishop of Périgueux"—and here Fogacer lowered his voice—"as a monster and an atheist, since he'd also observed that I only rarely and without interest heard Mass. At this, the bishop sent a cleric to my inn to conduct an inquiry, but I bribed him to let us go. Which we did that same day, smelling fire and brimstone all around us, and knowing that the damned can expect no justice in this kingdom."

"The damned, Fogacer?"

"The Huguenots, the Jews, the atheists and the sodomites. And since I belong to the last two categories, I was in great danger of being

---

* "We are all governed by our own particular pleasures."

burnt twice! Ah, what a cruel world, my Pierre. So many try to please God by zealously killing their fellow men."

He laughed at this, but with the face of one who's decided to laugh to avoid crying.

"Did you know I was here in Mespech?" I asked after a moment of silence.

"Not before arriving in Sarlat, where, to my intense relief, I heard that you'd escaped safe and sound from the St Bartholomew's day massacre. May I have your permission, Pierre," he said, sitting up on his cot, "to remain at Mespech long enough for this clerical vigilance to calm down? My idea is to go from here to Bordeaux, and from there to La Rochelle, where, from what I've heard, my master has decided to massacre the Huguenots who have occupied that city."

"My dear damned friend," I said with a smile, "does it make any sense to help Anjou slaughter other damned people?"

"Not in the least, *mi fili*," replied Fogacer. "The point is not to help him in this effort, but to try to cure his ills. The only blood I'll draw when I'm there will be his, and since it's blue, I'll be protected from persecution."

I laughed at this, of course, and assured Fogacer that he could stay at Mespech as long as he liked, my father being indebted to him for having saved my life in Montpellier when the judges tried to send me to the scaffold for the "murder" I'd committed as well as for my amorous activities on a tomb with a diabolical petticoat.

The snow continued to fall so hard and unremittingly over the next several days that it threatened to close the road from Sarlat, cutting us off from the seat of the seneschalty there—something the elders of our villages hadn't seen in Périgord for sixty-seven years. In consequence, the Brethren consulted with their neighbours and decided to send all of their labourers to clear the roads of snow at least as far as Marcuays. This was a Sisyphean task for the poor folk, who suffered in the bitter cold, shovelling the snow to the sides of the road, knowing they'd only have to start all over again the next morning—an exhausting task, one that they performed for their lords and that they accepted very begrudgingly since they earned no salary for doing it. Mespech was the only chateau to serve them some hot soup at noon, the only meal they had throughout their interminable day.

I wanted to help with this effort on Mespech's roads, along with Samson (but not François, who considered this labour beneath him). As soon as my resolution was known, there wasn't a healthy man in Mespech who didn't want to accompany me—including Giacomi, Fogacer and even Quéribus, who, dainty fellow though he was, felt it a point of honour to shovel as much as I did. Lord! What a rough, tough and exhausting day it was, and how painful for the palms of our hands (except for those of Giacomi, who'd thought to bring gloves, not wishing to blister his fencing hands). And how sweet our return to Mespech at nightfall, where we enjoyed hot punch before dinner! And with what comfort and joy Quéribus, Samson and I found ourselves in Gertrude's room afterwards around a warm fire under the comforting glow of the candles, as we watched the ladies prepare their gowns and accoutrements for the grand soirée on the 10th at Puymartin's. The rustle of their satin gowns! And the brilliance of the pearls and gems! The inebriating effect of their perfumes! Their soft babbling and the graceful gestures of our nymphs as they went about their pleasant work! I felt so happy to have been born in a chateau and not in a farmhouse, where, at this hour, I'd still be sweating over my labour.

My little sister was there, showing more affection for Gertrude than ever before, since the lady had given her a very pretty dress for the occasion that needed only to have the waist taken in and the length shortened in order to fit her perfectly—an operation that wasn't as simple as one might have thought, judging by the intense discussion it provoked among the women. Just as animated was their exchange over which set of pearls to choose to set off Catherine's soft white bosom, which was discreetly displayed by the lacy collar of her gown.

"Monsieur," commanded Gertrude, after Quéribus had greeted her with great restraint (no doubt because of the presence of Catherine), "you must choose, I beg you, since you know the latest fashions of the court: I think that rubies would be best since they match the pink of her gown. Catherine is more inclined to wear the pearls."

"Well, that depends," replied Quéribus, taking his role as arbiter very seriously, more seriously than many judges in parliament did theirs. "If the pink dress were worn by you, my beautiful Gertrude, then rubies would be required, since the two colours have a natural affinity to one another. But since it will be worn by Catherine, who's only sixteen and unmarried, I would vote for pearls, as their milky whiteness are more suited to her modest virginity."

And at this, with a smile, he made a deep bow to Catherine, who batted her eyelashes at him and blushed excessively.

"Monsieur," said Gertrude, for whom Quéribus as a familiar of the Duc d'Anjou could not err in these matters, the duc being considered *urbi et orbi*[*] as the arbiter of elegance, "as you have spoken wisely and gallantly, we will follow your advice."

And indeed, Catherine was to shine so brightly at the soirée on 10th November that she even outshone Gertrude du Luc and her lady-in-waiting, with such inimitable éclat that there wasn't a single gentleman in all of Périgord who didn't request a dance with her. Even the Baron de Quéribus, who had known all the beauties of the court, was so dazzled by this bright star that he requested no less than three dances with her, and would have asked for a fourth had not my father dispatched me to ask him to desist, in order to keep tongues from

---

[*] "In the city and in the world."

wagging. Quéribus consented to this request, quite crestfallen, and with what seemed to me to be very bad grace.

Even though the roads from Mespech to Marcuays, and from Marcuays to Puymartin, had been shovelled by our labourers on the day of the ball, the snow had continued to fall so thick during the evening that our horses and Dame Gertrude's carriage had a devil of a time getting back home. Our delay caused terrible throes for poor Sauveterre, who waited up for us in his library, accompanied by Fogacer, who'd also declined the invitation to attend, having, as he said, no taste for such festivities.

"My nephew," Sauveterre told me the next morning, looking more and more like a bent old crow in his black clothes, "you have a friend in Fogacer, whom you should take as a model. He's a paragon of virtue. Still young and though a papist, I congratulate him for having preferred the company of an old fogey like myself and his little page to that of those Delilahs."

"Delilahs, my uncle? But everyone who is anyone in Sarlat was there last night!"

"The men running after the women!" answered Sauveterre bitterly. "I have to tell you, my nephew: it's women and women alone that men go to seek out at these sorts of gatherings. And anyone who isn't out to satisfy his lubricious instincts has no interest in such events."

"Alas!" I agreed, affecting humility. "I well know that in this respect my virtue is a thousand leagues from equalling Fogacer's…"

"You're right, my nephew, and for me, such austerity in a man of so few years provides me great comfort, papist though he may be. Did you know that he's teaching his little valet to read, so that his intelligence will be opened through good books? Is it not a marvel in this world we live in, that a venerable doctor of medicine should take such pains to raise a simple servant in the light of righteous ideas?"

To that which required no response, I gave none, secretly admiring Sauveterre's holy simplicity and the perfect control Fogacer exercised on himself, as if the perpetual persecution that hung over his life like the sword of Damocles forced him to be like a captain always on the alert, clad in his coat of armour, his sword at the ready, his bulwarks already constructed. "Ah," I mused, "what a pity to be forced by the inhumanity of our customs to advance through life wearing a mask, constrained by the zealotry of others to so hide the truth that our good Sauveterre can't see what's going on right under his nose."

But we had other concerns when the snow simply refused to stop falling after 10th November and accumulated in drifts so high that, other than the roads in our vicinity that we'd laboured to clear, the highways were rendered impassable, so that you couldn't take a step, whether on foot or on horseback, without feeling the futility of it. Quéribus was forced to put off his departure *sine die*, and though ever since he'd heard Fogacer report that the Duc d'Anjou was laying siege to La Rochelle he seemed to be burning with impatience to join the fray—a plan I had no reason to doubt given the man's bravery—he didn't seem as disappointed about delaying his leaving as I would have imagined. Indeed, fortune dictated that (with the snow persisting) he had to take up his winter quarters at Puymartin, and thus galloped every day from Puymartin to Marcuays and from Marcuays to Mespech to spend the day in our company. This arrangement surprised my father, who thought that it would have been more fitting and courteous to spend more time with his host.

My father and Sauveterre, seeing all of us ensconced at Mespech through these frigid, wintry months, turned two very different faces to the situation: the former happy to have Samson and me with him for several months longer; the latter, though he loved us dearly, found the pleasure of our company spoilt by the *odor di femina* that Gertrude and Zara continued to spread throughout our walls—his displeasure multiplied by the extravagant spending on firewood and candles that their presence required. My uncle even went so far in his miserliness to complain bitterly about the amount of meat these two "gluttons" consumed. To which my father replied that Giacomi, Fogacer and Silvio consumed triple what the ladies did.

"But," growled Sauveterre, "at least they're earning their keep by helping out with the livestock."

"My dear *écuyer*," laughed my father, "would you really like to see Dame du Luc grooming our stallion?"

"Women belong in the house," snapped Sauveterre, and seeing my father shrug his shoulders at this, he added: "It's one thing for Dame du Luc—she's of noble birth. But what does this creature Zara do with her ten fingers every day?"

"She rubs ointment on them."

"Zounds! Her laziness is a scandal! Why can't she help with the housework?"

"You forget, my brother, that she's not in our employ, but in the service of her mistress."

"And yours as well on occasion," observed Sauveterre drily; and, turning away in his irritation, he limped to the other end of the library, bending over, with his hands behind his back. My father watched him retreat with a mixture of irritation and affection, having listened to him cough and spit out his daily screed of displeasure these many years without ever losing patience with him.

"And I'll say again," continued Sauveterre, heading back towards my father and not mincing his words, "that I don't like what's going on here. Your Dame du Luc has turned her room into Circe's palace, where she charms and traps our younger sons and Quéribus."

"Hardly!" laughed my father. "Why, I've seen them enter her room often enough, but never seen them emerge as pigs!"

Hearing this, I looked up from a treatise by Vesalius, which I'd been reading—or at least trying to read—in the enclosure of the nearby window, smiled and added:

"Gertrude's power isn't as strong as all that!"

"But she's corrupting our little Catherine," objected Sauveterre, "who's now enchanted with her—and with Quéribus as well. He never seems to enter her palace of delights but she follows him there."

"Well, that is, indeed, more serious!" frowned my father. "We'll need to keep an eye on this—and perhaps a hand as well. Pierre, what do you think of Quéribus's daily visits to Mespech?"

"That the filings know very well why the magnet attracts them," I replied, rising and walking over to them. "But, my dear father, as sweet as Quéribus is, with all his courtly mannerisms, to Dame Gertrude, he's so grave and respectful with Catherine that the strictest censor would have nothing to object to."

"What about Catherine?"

"Colder than a rock frozen in a winter snowstorm."

"A rock!" snorted Sauveterre, raising his hands heavenwards. "What kind of rock is that that burns with such an inner fire? Don't you see the flame that lights up her eyes every time she looks at him?"

"My brother," soothed my father, to whom this outburst seemed unnecessarily quarrelsome, "if God had not put that fire into men and women, what reason would they ever have for coming together, given how different they are? But Pierre, is it true that you've never noticed any secret notes being passed between Catherine and Quéribus? Or surprised them in a private conversation in some corner?"

"Never. These two fires are aflame, to be sure, but separately, as though each were afraid of the other."

"Well, we know how to measure *that* form of separation!" growled Sauveterre, limping furiously back and forth in the library. "Zounds! Another papist!"

"Yes, along with Gertrude," agreed my father with more forgiveness than condemnation. "And Diane. And Angelina. Should we punish our daughter because our sons are marrying papists?"

My father said no more, but, as far as I could tell, he'd said enough to persuade me that he would not reject Quéribus if he should approach him, especially as the baron was a match that was well above any that she might have found in Périgord. He was not only of high birth, but exceedingly well-to-do—and rich, too, in his alliances, especially in his connections with the Duc d'Anjou, whom many believed would soon ascend to the throne, since Charles IX had no heirs and was gravely ill.

One of the hardships during these long months of snowy weather was that the roads were so hard to travel on that very little news could reach us from outside Périgueux. I felt particularly desolate to have no word from my Angelina, who was in my thoughts from dawn to dusk. Though I was plunged into the intricacies of Vesalius's magnum opus each day, her beautiful doe's eyes seemed to be beseeching me from between the lines of this austere treatise, hope and despair alternating in my poor divided heart. 'Tis true that man is able to separate his heart from his more urgent appetites, my little viper Little Sissy completely satisfying the latter needs. But did she really satisfy them? In truth, I don't know, for despite all the pleasures and relief that a woman's body can offer us, there is none that can truly fulfil the soul if love doesn't accompany it. Assuredly, Little Sissy made those long, dark days at Mespech more bearable for me in the bloom of my youth, but she was far from evoking in me the depth of friendship I'd had with little Hélix, or even for Alizon back in Paris, whom I remembered with such gratitude and affection for the help and shelter she provided for us on that bloody morning of St Bartholomew's day.

I'd only caught sight of Angelina for a few seconds in Paris as I ran alongside her coach, trying to raise the curtains they'd hung over the windows to shelter her from my view, but what a look she'd given me! What volumes I read in it! I read, reread and read again the letter she'd sent me after my return to Mespech, before we were snowed in for the winter, isolated from the rest of the world. But it had given me hope that soon Father Anselm (who was Quéribus's cousin) would become Monsieur de Montcalm's confessor, and he was likely to be less rigid than his predecessor about his daughter's marriage to a Huguenot. Ah, what a beautiful thought, that Angelina might be mine after so many years of waiting. And by what magic that, out of all the women I'd encountered in different parts of the kingdom— many, such as the ladies-in-waiting of Catherine de' Medici, among the most magnificent and stunning women in France—Angelina alone had, in a single glance, captured this heart that now yearned only for her? What charms, what potions, what enchanting brew concocted by Love had transformed her hand into one whose mere touch took my breath away?

The snow finally consented to melt in early April, but given the sheer size of the drifts that had been accumulating since November, the melt flooded the valleys of Périgueux and left our roads so wet and muddy that, for a while, they remained impassable. But luckily our region is so hilly that there was a rapid run-off from the steep roads, which flowed into the dales and swelled the river of les Beunes so much that Coulondre Iron-arm's mill was transformed into an island, and could only be reached by boat. And, just as in Genesis—when, after the Deluge, God promises that the land will be dry and fruitful again—the sun eventually came out and dried out our fields. Now Quéribus, looking like death warmed up, gave the order to saddle up, as he'd promised six months before, and swore to me that if he weren't killed in the siege of La Rochelle, he wouldn't fail to write to me and that he'd return to Mespech, having left here such friends—he specifically used the plural—that his heart was sore pained to leave them. He then embraced me and called me his "brother"—which he'd never done before—and kissed my cheeks with a warmth he clearly would have loved to bestow on a sweeter cheek than mine.

The ladies shed a few tears at this parting, which in Zara's case were doubtless purely ceremonial, since she was so anxious to return to Paris—but not so Gertrude, who'd become very attached to my father, and even to Uncle de Sauveterre, being entirely ignorant of the troubles she'd inflicted on him, both by her excessive consumption of his goods and by the perfumes she'd spread throughout his chateau. I couldn't help noticing that when she looked at Samson, her eyes lit up like those of an eagle carrying off a lamb in its talons, although these talons would be tenderly applied to the milky flesh of my gentle brother and would never harm a single copper-coloured hair on his beautiful head.

"Well, Samson," said my father as he gave him an embrace that I thought would never end. "Ah, my son! When will I see you again?"

He said no more, but as the coach and horses faded from sight he withdrew with Sauveterre, François and me into the library, sat down in the large armchair in front of the fire, put his right hand over his face and quietly wept. We were silenced and stunned—as much by his melancholy as by the quiet that had suddenly descended on the house after all the laughter and merriment that Quéribus and the ladies had brought, and then suddenly taken from us.

There was a knock at the door, which I opened to welcome my younger—though no longer little—sister into the room. Catherine was dressed in an azure gown, with a ribbon of the same colour in her golden hair, and she entered with that assured and lofty demeanour that reminded me of my mother, her head held high as usual—but it looked to me as though she'd been crying.

"My father," she announced, after making him a deep curtsey, "I found this note in my sewing basket, and though it's addressed to me, as I am still but a girl under the protection of her father, it seemed to me that you should read it."

"Let's see it, then," agreed the Baron de Mespech, not without some gravity. And, having unfolded the note, he read it, his face inscrutable; then he handed it to Sauveterre, who, having read it in his turn, frowned deeply and gave it to François, who, glancing at it with disdain, handed it to me at a sign from my father. This is what I read:

Madame,

Although I've said goodbye to you, I beg you to allow me with this note to kiss the hands of the woman I honour and love more than anyone in the world. I shall by my acts and words proclaim this love and am ready to witness it before God and man.

The days will seem like years as long as you are absent from me. Ever since this blessed snow had the misfortune to melt and the ground to harden, I swear that not a night have I passed dry-eyed.

I kiss your hands a hundred thousand times more.

Quéribus

"Catherine," said my father at last, "have you read this note?"

"Would I have brought it to you if I hadn't read it?" replied Catherine with a somewhat impertinent respect.

"I understand perfectly. But what do you think about what it says?"

"My father," answered Catherine, "I shall think of it what you tell me is suitable for me to think of it." And saying this, she made an even deeper curtsey to my father, who was clearly astounded that one so haughty could bow so low and put so much mute rebelliousness in her pretended submission; this strange mixture so embarrassed him that he doubtless would have preferred to confront five or six desperadoes, sword in hand, than to engage in this peaceful conversation. He so loved his daughter, calling her "my sweet, my soul, the apple of my eye", that the enemy had rushed into the breach before he'd even drawn his sword.

"Very well," he concluded, choosing to break ranks rather than continue the battle, "you may retire, Catherine"—which she did with a majestic rustle of her skirts, a flame in her eyes and her head held high, leaving me amazed that someone so young had known how to put so much defiance into a gesture of respect, and communicate such implacable resoluteness in the language of obedience.

"Well then!" breathed my father, when the door had closed behind her. "What do you think of all this, my brother?"

"That we must end all commerce with this scoundrel immediately!" cried Sauveterre, his eyes aflame.

"And why would that be?" frowned my father.

"Because he has broken the laws of hospitality in sending a secret note to the daughter of his host that's false and mendacious!"

"Mendacious?" asked my father, raising an eyebrow. "I find it rather touching. In what way does it seem mendacious to you?"

"My brother," snarled Sauveterre indignantly, "was there any sign that Quéribus has been crying every night since the snow melted? Who would believe such a thing other than a virginal little girl?"

"My uncle," I broke in quickly. "Quéribus is not a liar! 'Not a night have I passed dry-eyed' is simply a figure of speech. That's simply how they talk at court ever since Ronsard."

"What?" stormed Sauveterre, now beside himself with fury. "Ronsard! Have you read Ronsard, my nephew? This sworn enemy of our faith?"

"I've read his love sonnets," I replied, somewhat ashamed to admit such a thing in this library where there were no frivolous poems, except perhaps those of the Greek poet Anacreon.

"This is hardly the point," said my father. "My brother, for Quéribus, the courtier no doubt hides the man. The man is of good mettle.

Nothing required him to go to a great deal of trouble and take such a risk in order to hide Pierre after the St Bartholomew's day massacre and then bring him home safely to us. And as for his note, I don't find it so damnable to assure one's lady of one's respect and say that one is 'ready to witness one's love before God and man'. I think we should let this run its course."

"Run its course!" trumpeted Sauveterre.

"Certainly! Let's wait for the baron to declare his love openly, especially since Catherine is so infatuated with him, given the way she brandished his note in front of our noses."

"She was defying you!" said Sauveterre bitterly.

"Forget the defiance! I'm not going to cross swords with my daughter, as I so regret doing with my late wife, whose haughty and rebellious temperament she's obviously inherited. A gentle hand is the only thing that will work with this tough lass. What's more, I don't want to hurt her if I can avoid it."

During the week that followed, and though the baron affected a calm demeanour, I felt that he was suffering so terribly from Samson's flight from the paternal nest, having no idea when he'd return, that I decided to delay somewhat my own departure so as not to add so soon to the distress of the man whom I believed to be the best father there ever was. Assuredly, he would never have said what Montaigne had said, that he'd "lost three of four children in infancy, not without regret, but without great anger". For, great warrior that he was—having, as everyone knows, distinguished himself at Ceresole and at Calais—he showed those he loved a degree of tenderness and affection that was truly maternal, always placing our well-being above his own. Indeed, during these melancholy days after Samson's departure, I heard him say more than once that he was delighted that his pretty bastard was going to marry Gertrude in Normandy and that he would receive the apothecary shop in Montfort as dowry from her. He was also heard to say, begging my reader's pardon for these rustic words from a man of the countryside, "There's no greater happiness for a man than to spend his nights enjoying amorous 'encunters' with a good woman and his days in work that he's chosen."

I had another reason for wanting to linger. Spring was disclosing its beauties in the myriad flowers that were budding as Mespech entered the verdant months that I so yearned to enjoy here after the rigours of the long winter. As soon as the thaw had rendered the roads passable again, I wrote to Angelina to assure her that I would always keep her image in my heart as fresh as the day I first laid eyes on her. But a lover's heart is so crazy and unreasonable that, of course, no sooner had my letter departed than I began to be impatient for a reply even though it was manifestly impossible to expect one before the middle of the summer.

Fogacer, his little page in tow, had left Mespech in the company of Quéribus, no less impatient than the baron to see the Duc d'Anjou, especially after the business in Périgueux, hoping that the duc would quickly reassure him of his protection.

His was the first letter I received, towards the end of August. After a thousand compliments and thanks to the lords of Mespech for their hospitality, he informed me that, since the duc had been elected king of Poland, he had raised the siege of La Rochelle, not wishing to alienate the Protestant minority in his future kingdom. In this wise, he made a treaty with the French Huguenots that they never would have dared hope for after St Bartholomew's day. This news delighted the Brethren, though they were very sceptical about the duration of this precarious peace, since the French papists were so fanatical about the eradication of our people.

Fogacer added that Quéribus intended to follow the duc to his new kingdom, though with a heavy heart (for reasons which he thought I would understand), and that he himself would do the same, not so much because Dr Miron needed him, but rather because where his shield went, he could not but follow. It seems he preferred this frosty Polish exile to the flames I already knew about. Nevertheless, he was convinced that this separation wouldn't last long, having observed while at the Louvre how sickly Charles IX was becoming. I had a little trouble understanding this last sentence, and had to go in search of a dictionary, since Fogacer had written it in Greek, fearing that his letter would be read in transit.

Although Catherine had little taste for study, she insisted on standing behind me and leaning over my shoulder as I was working at this, and when I'd translated the Greek, she said, "What does this mean? What difference does it make to Fogacer that the king should be coughing and feeble?"

"Well, if the king renders up his soul to God, then the Duc d'Anjou will come back to France with his entire retinue."

"Well, in that case," she replied with a sly smile, "I'm very happy for Fogacer!"

I smiled at this, but made no reply, since, for all the months that Fogacer had spent at Mespech, Catherine had never once taken notice of him.

My knowing smile didn't fail to induce Catherine to open up a bit more, and, putting her hand on my neck (she who was so sparing in her caresses), she asked if I would read her Fogacer's letter, which I did immediately—it was something she couldn't have done herself without a lot of effort, since she knew her letters scarcely better than my Alizon in Paris.

"Dear my brother," she cooed sotto voce when I'd finished, "why was the baron's heart so heavy to have to leave France for Poland?"

"But, Madame my sister, you know all too well why!"

"Me?" she replied raising her eyebrows with an air of childlike candour that struck me as half-natural, half-feigned.

"Didn't the baron tell you in the letter you found in your sewing basket that 'the days will seem like years as long as you are absent from me'?"

"But do you think I should believe him?" Catherine asked with a kind of anxious urgency, as though all her most secret thoughts of love were about to be realized. "Didn't the baron write love notes like this to all the gallant ladies of the court in Paris? Can I really trust him? What a pity the baron must hide himself away in this villainous city of Warsaw! Who forced him to go there? Don't you think he'll forget me when he gets there?"

Hearing this, I stood up, turned to face her and burst out laughing.

"What?" she cried, frowning, her hackles raised. "You dare laugh at me?"

"It's just that I don't know which of your questions to answer first!"

"Well then, answer them all, you heartless creature!" she cried, stamping her foot. "All of them! I shan't be satisfied until you do!"

"Hear me, then," I answered, suddenly quite serious. "Here's your answer, Catherine, my dear, sweet sister, as best I can respond. I believe Quéribus loves you deeply and that he will not fail to ask your father for your hand in marriage before he leaves for Warsaw."

"You really believe that?"

"Assuredly so."

"Oh, my brother!" she cried; and, forgetting her usual haughty airs, she threw her arms around my neck, pulled me close as though I were the object of her affections, and gave me a hearty kiss, saying, "Oh, Pierre! Oh, my brother! You're the most lovable of men!"

"Now, now, my sweet!" I laughed. "You're exaggerating! The most lovable of men is the one who has written that his eyes have not been dry since the snow melted."

My father received a beautiful letter from this same man a month later that was so full of spelling mistakes that he was as appalled by the anarchy in the arrangement of the letters as he was moved by the sincerity of Quéribus's expressions of his great love for my sister. But there are plenty of clerics in this kingdom, not to mention educated gentlemen, who admit that they're uncertain of their writing, and this "malady" has even invaded the printers, as is evident by the fact that the same word may take on, like a coquette wearing different clothes, a plethora of different spellings in the same book.

So my father, assuredly one of the most learned men in the whole of the Sarlat region, didn't hold this foible against Quéribus, but wrote him a long letter in response in which he acquiesced in principle to his overtures, but in very prudent terms, not wishing to commit his daughter's hand entirely to a lord who might be away in Poland for God only knew how long.

As for me, as the summer was drawing to a close and the August weather, as often happens in Périgord, dissolved into storms that brought lightning and cold rain, I began to pack my bags for Bordeaux, feeling that Giacomi, Miroul and his Florine were growing impatient to live in a big city—Giacomi because he was from Naples, Florine because she missed Paris and Miroul because he simply loved strolling through the streets of a big city. So I sat down with my father and we decided on 1st September as the date of my departure from Mespech. Alas! Once again it was not to be.

We were all sitting around the table at nightfall on 31st August, each in his accustomed place—Cabusse, our stonemason Jonas and Coulondre Iron-arm had all joined us, accompanied by their wives, for this Sunday dinner—when our porter, Escorgol, rushed in, breathlessly asking to raise the portcullis to let Jacotte, the priest of Marcuays's chambermaid, inside our walls. It appeared that she was breathless from running and screaming at the top of her lungs, begging to be given protection and banging with both fists on the gate. The Brethren agreed, so Escorgol hurried off, and soon returned with the poor girl, who was trembling, out of breath and dripping with water.

She threw herself at my father's feet and begged him with hands joined in supplication, and in a voice broken by sobs, to hurry to the defence of our priest and the town of Marcuays, which, without the succour of Monsieur the baron and Monsieur the *écuyer* of Mespech, would be completely destroyed, and all its inhabitants killed by a band of vicious brigands who were sacking the place. She herself had been able to flee out the back through her garden, and cut across the meadows, but fell into a ditch that had been flooded by the recent rains—which explained why she was soaked through like a crouton in soup.

"La Maligou," ordered my father as he rose to his feet, "give this poor wench some hot milk with a shot of spirits of wine. And you, Barberine, fetch her one of your dresses for dry clothing. Jacotte, undress in front of the fire, right away! Miroul, stoke up the fire!"

"What, Monsieur?" pleaded Jacotte. "Naked! In front of all these men! Ah, no, Monsieur, that's a sin!"

"There's no sin where necessity is the preacher," replied my father. "Would you rather catch your death of cold from your bath in the icy water? Then do what I told you, Jacotte, and while you're doing it, answer me."

"All right, Monsieur," conceded the "priestette", who, having sacrificed her Christian modesty under orders, wasn't so unhappy about playing Eve to this assembly, since she was reputed to have the most abundant and firm bosom of any wench in the whole region.

"Cabusse, take Jonas and Coulondre and fetch our cuirasses, helmets and arms," continued my father, who'd picked them for this mission because their wives were getting jealous. And, certainly, that's how the other unmarried lads understood it, for they were secretly laughing and elbowing each other, greatly enjoying this order, which deprived their Herculean companions of the spectacle and allowed them to get their fill of the charms before them, forgetting for a moment their fear of the combat that awaited them outside.

Their emotions seemed entirely foreign to Sauveterre—or, if they weren't, he repressed them by prayer and simply turned away, not daring to countermand his brother's orders, doubtless understanding that this was the only fire in the chateau and that the girl was indeed chilled to the bone and trembling so violently it was heartbreaking to watch.

But for these two eyes that were averted, many others opened so wide you'd have thought they'd pop out of their sockets at this unexpected and unheard-of display of the priest's chambermaid, who was standing as naked as the day she was born. It was a thing they'd never believed possible even in their wildest dreams: an event that surpassed in consequence even the battle they were about to wage against the ruffians in Marcuays—and one they couldn't wait to brag about to anyone who hadn't seen it.

However, their anticipatory laughter was suddenly followed by a silence, in which you could have heard a chicken feather turning in the wind, when Jacotte removed the last of her soaked clothes and appeared in all her robust flesh: large of foot, with finely muscled legs, rounded croup and incredibly generous but firm breasts.

Taking advantage of Sauveterre's lack of interest in this spectacle, Miroul threw a large log on the fire, which flamed up suddenly, illuminating this statue of flesh and blood in all its feminine beauty. And, no doubt encouraged by the additional warmth of these flames, poor Jacotte (but could one really call her "poor" given the riches with which she'd been endowed?) turned this way and that to warm herself even more, and not one among her audience had eyes enough to take in this invigorating sight. My father noticed that even François, who had feigned indifference, was secretly eyeing this idol through half-closed lids, and called out in the language of the province, "Well now! The duchesse or the working girl—it comes down to the same thing when you see them as nature made them!"

"Well, I've never seen a duchesse in my life," laughed Barberine, who was arranging some clothes for Jacotte in front of the fire, "but no one's ever seen teats like that around here! Heavens! Even mine when I was nursing these little gentlemen were never so large and beautiful!"

"Oh, yes they were!" I shouted. "I know because I drank from them for three years!"

"Four!" corrected Barberine. "And I even suckled you occasionally, glutton that you were, when I was nursing Catherine!"

"Ah, how well I remember!" I agreed. "Round they were and soft to the touch!" At which she laughed wholeheartedly.

At this, poor Petremol, our saddle-maker, who'd lost his wife and children to the plague six years previously, spoke up in his scratchy bass voice: "Excuse me, Jacotte, and you too, Barberine, but Sarrazine's boobies, when she was nursing the kids at the table here in Mespech on Sunday, were smaller, maybe, than yours, but they were marvellously golden brown. And I loved watching her—no offence, Sarrazine!"

But Sarrazine, who well understood that Petremol was suffering terribly from loneliness, looked at him with compassion in those beautiful, gazelle-like eyes of hers, smiled and—realizing (as all the women present did) that the pleasure of this nourishment was simply for the mother and babe, as God certainly intended it to be—said simply, with a voice I would have said was as sweet as the Blessed Virgin's if I weren't a Huguenot, "Thank you, Petremol."

"For pity's sake," growled Sauveterre in French (which none of our servants understood), "are we going to stand around admiring these teats while they're pillaging Marcuays?"

Certain it is that he couldn't have expatiated very long on Jacotte's mammaries, since he was so obstinately turning his back on her.

"Wait, my brother," said the Baron de Mespech. "We need to arm ourselves for battle! We can't go charging into the fray with our doublets on!"

Cabusse was soon back, followed by Coulondre and Jonas, all three burdened by a plethora of armour and arms, which they carefully laid out on the table, and from which each of us quietly selected the weapons we'd need, attaching each other's breastplates from behind, our eyes now turned inward, focusing on the threat of injury or death that awaited both us and the villagers (though outwardly our eyes were still fixed on Jacotte, who was now drinking some warm milk that la Maligou had brought her). It was a prospect that filled us with courage and valour, for we knew all too well what these ruffians would do to the sweet girls in the town if we didn't arrive in time to dispatch them.

"So, Jacotte," said my father, "time is of the essence. Tell us what you know of these marauders: their number, their weapons and, especially, whether they have firearms—pistols or arquebuses."

"Excuse me, Monsieur, but I can't tell you how many there are since I didn't dare look out of the window, which I closed as soon as I heard them attacking and because I rushed away to tell my poor priest."

"But you must have seen them, Jacotte," said Siorac. "You must have *some* idea how many there are!"

"Perhaps she doesn't know her numbers," observed Sauveterre.

"Excuse, me, Monsieur *écuyer*," Jacotte corrected, "I know my numbers up to twenty, and may the Blessed Virgin strike me dead if I'm lying."

"God is the only one who can strike you dead!" cried Sauveterre wrathfully. "And not Mary, who is not God!"

"Excuse me, Monsieur *écuyer*," replied Jacotte with dignity, "that's not what my priest taught me."

"Now now, my brother," broke in Siorac in French, "this is not the time to argue about theology! Now, my girl," he said, turning to Jacotte, the fingers of his two hands extended, "were there ten of them? Or fifteen?"—keeping his right hand open and extending his left twice. "Or twenty?"—holding out all ten fingers twice.

"Well, I'm going to say, Monsieur, it was maybe ten, maybe fifteen."

"Maybe twenty?" said Sauveterre disdainfully.

"Maybe twenty," said Jacotte unaware of his malice.

"Well, now you know, my brother," snarled Sauveterre. "And what about their weapons, Jacotte?"

"By my faith," replied the girl, walking over to the table, "there were some like this"—pointing to the swords—"and some like this"—pointing to the pikes.

"And some like this?" said my father, pointing to a pistol.

"Maybe."

"And some like this?" he continued, pointing to an arquebus.

"Maybe."

"'Sblood! And what about these?" he asked, pointing to the armour.

"Oh no! I didn't see any armour on them!"

"Well, that's a good thing!" said my father between clenched teeth.

"Zounds!" hissed Sauveterre. "If there are twenty of 'em, carrying firearms, with or without armour, there are too many of them for us. My brother, I think we should send a messenger to Puymartin, asking for help, and that we wait till dawn tomorrow to attack, since we'll be more numerous and will be able to see more clearly."

"Ah, Monsieur *écuyer*," moaned Jacotte, tears in her eyes, "these brigands are like starving wolves! If you wait any longer, you won't find anything left of Marcuays but burnt-out houses, dead men and women raped and gutted."

"What do you think, my brother?" said Siorac in French.

"That reason rarely wins out over one's heart," replied Sauveterre, clearly shaken by Jacotte's words. "And so it is with me. Let's send Miroul post-haste to Puymartin, and though the battle be uneven, by

God's grace, Mespech can't allow her village to be burnt right under our noses!"

"Well then, let's pray Puymartin arrives in time!" agreed Siorac. "La Maligou, Barberine, tie a white strip of cloth on the arms of our men so they won't kill each other, though thankfully there's enough moonlight to see tonight. Miroul, tell Puymartin to do the same. My brother," he said in French, "I want you to guard the chateau in our absence with Faujanet, Coulondre Iron-arm, Escorgol and François."

"Oh no!" cried Sauveterre in French, beside himself with rage that my father wanted to leave him behind with a bandy-legged man, a one-armed man, an obese man and a coward. "I'm going to fight, and that's all there is to it!"

"But your leg, my brother!"

"It'll carry me!" said his fellow lord, angrier than I'd ever seen him. "What else do you want to say?"

"But I can't leave the defence of the chateau to François, who's so young!"

"Oh, yes you can! François is very good at firing our little cannon, and we won't be too far away to hear them if he does."

"François, can you do this?" asked my father coldly, terribly disappointed that François hadn't adamantly insisted on joining the fight in Marcuays—as, assuredly, I would have done in his place.

"Monsieur my father," François replied, with his long face fixed in that inscrutable look he wore most of the time, "I will do whatever you command. With you in Marcuays if you command it, here if you prefer. And I assure you I'll keep a good watch out while you're gone."

His reply was not dictated by cowardice, as Sauveterre no doubt believed, being a soldier of the old school and having served under a soldier king. No, my older brother was more calculating. Having no warmth, no heart and no stomach, he was less inclined to save the poor women of the village than to safeguard the seat and chateau of his future barony—which he would have done bravely if the fortunes of war had required it.

We saddled our horses, and when Escorgol raised the portcullis, I rode up next to my father, who had Jacotte behind him, holding on to his hips. By the light of the moon I could see worry written large on his face. And, certainly, there was plenty to worry about. If there were twenty of these rascals, we were not half as many as we should have been for such a fight: the Brethren, the two Siorac cousins (one already bearing a scar from our battle at la Lendrevie), Cabusse, Jonas, Petremol, Fröhlich, Giacomi and me. Ten in all, given that we couldn't rely on Miroul, since we'd sent him off to Puymartin and couldn't count on his arriving at the battle in time—especially since Puymartin was probably off at a soirée in some chateau in the area.

We dismounted behind a deserted farm called la Fumélie, which lay just outside the town walls—proof that our enemies were not protecting themselves, since they should have posted a guard at this house, which commanded the road coming from Mespech.

We left Petremol with our horses, since my father had never seen him fight and wasn't sure how he'd do, and the nine of us (with Jacotte behind) quietly approached the village wall with its strong oak gate strengthened by a lookout turret, in which was posted an old, one-legged drunk named Villemont—who was no doubt asleep when the marauders arrived, and who probably lay dead on the other side of the wall.

"Jacotte," whispered my father as we rode up, "go and knock on the door and tell them you're the priest's servant coming back late from the fields. As soon as these villains unlock the gate, get away as fast as you can and hide in the cemetery."

"Monsieur," replied the "priestette", "I'll pray to the Blessed Virgin to save my priest and protect you and"—she hesitated for a moment—"the *écuyer*."

"Amen!" whispered my father. "My friends," he continued quietly as the eight men gathered around him, "unsheathe your swords—but no noise!—and keep your sword points low in order not to wound each other. Not a sound from any of you! Walk like cats, one paw after the other! Silence before any claws come out! Don't fire your pistols unless it's absolutely necessary, because any shot will alert our enemies within. The rascals are probably out pillaging before they start drinking. No mercy! The *écuyer*, my son Pierre, Giacomi and I will attack the parish house where most them are probably grouped. The rest of you will remain here as reinforcements with Cabusse in charge. May God keep you, my children!"

Brave and strong wench that she was, the priestette played her little role without batting an eyelid, demanded entry with a strong voice and even made a little joke as though she believed Villemont was still at his station, instead of lying dead in the mud—which is how we found him a second later, his throat cut from ear to ear, having traversed from his wine-induced slumber into eternal sleep without ever knowing the difference.

One cut throat deserved another, and, without a cry being raised, the murderer was dispatched in a trice by Fröhlich's knife, the knave falling like a sack of grain onto the body of Villemont. Our Swiss Guard then threw his entire weight against the chain, broke it and pushed the gate open wide. We were in! My father and I were the first to rush into the parish house through the door they'd left open, and found four miscreants engaged in torturing Pincers, who was hanging by his wrists from a beam—they were trying, no doubt, to get him to tell them where he kept his gold. We ran them through with our swords, though not before one of them had taken a wild shot at my father, who buried his knife in the brigand's throat.

"Damn!" cursed my father. "I don't like that one bit! The noise and commotion are going to bring the cockroaches out of their nest!"

He headed for the stairs leading up to the loft, but I was quicker than he, wishing to protect him from any shots coming from above; as I did, I tripped over the body of one of the rascals, who was half drunk, half dead from fear, and whom I grabbed by the throat. "Villain!" I hissed, squeezing his throat like a vice, my knee on his chest. "How many are up there? Your life, if you answer!"

"Just one. The captain."

I levelled a blow of my iron glove at his ear and a kick in his side that sent him down the stairs—a blow that saved his life, as I found out later. But when I glanced out of the window, to my horror I could see by the moonlight that our men had been surrounded on the square by about a dozen brigands, who were shouting, "Kill 'em! Kill 'em!" Pulling my pistol from my belt, I dispatched one of them and Sauveterre, on my right, another.

"My brother," called Siorac, "go and get the captain with Pierre! I'm taking Giacomi to help our men outside!"

Since the door at the top of the stairs was closed, I burst it open with a kick and rushed into the room, and was surprised to see a tall fellow preparing to leap out of the window to help his men below; but when he saw me enter, he turned to face me with a sword in one hand, which didn't worry me much, and a loaded pistol in the other, which worried me a lot, since mine was now discharged—as was Sauveterre's. I stopped dead in my tracks and my uncle as well, amazed not only that the wastrel didn't fire, though he continued to point his gun at me, but also because he was naked and, over on his right, lying on Pincer's bed was one of the village girls, whom the villain had been busy raping—if rape it was, for he was an unusually handsome man, broad-shouldered, barrel-chested, long-legged and with a proud air about him: a fierce brigand, destined for the scaffold but scorning his fate. "Monsieur," he yelled to Sauveterre in a mocking tone while keeping his eye on me, "if I don't shoot, will you spare my life?"

"If you shoot," said Sauveterre, imitating the rascal's mocking tone, "I'll kill you in a trice!"

"I don't doubt it," came the fellow's retort. "May Heaven keep me from believing I'm the equal of a gentleman with a sword in his hand. And yet, even if you kill me, your son will also be dead and will be eaten by the same worms that eat me!"

"Villain!" cried Sauveterre, trembling with rage. "Am I going to stoop to bargain with the likes of you?"

"I'm afraid you don't have a choice, Monsieur! 'Tis as true as that my name's Big Jacquet! My pistol is faster than your sword."

"So you think, you rascal!" cried Sauveterre, lunging at him with all his might, but falling short of his mark, since his treacherous bad leg didn't allow him a full thrust. Seeing this, the fellow whirled and fired his pistol at my uncle, who fell from the shock of the bullet—as did the shooter, a second later, pierced by my blade.

I leapt to my uncle's side.

"It's nothing," Sauveterre assured me in no uncertain terms. "I'll be on horseback in a week! Pierre, throw this scoundrel out of the window so his men can see him and lose heart."

But the villain was so big and heavy, and my armour so cumbersome, that I had to call the wench to come and help. Which she did, though she hadn't had time to get dressed, and the two of us easily managed to do as Sauveterre had ordered.

"This was a handsome fellow!" she mused when he'd fallen to the courtyard below. "What a pity!"

"Zounds! It would have been a good deal more of a pity, my girl, if he'd killed you after having deflowered you!"

"That's what I thought too," she answered. "The bird who sings so pretty in the morning will be plucked that evening. But now I've been dishonoured without even having had the pleasure of being so! Monsieur, if you tell anyone about this I won't find a husband in all of Périgord."

"Now now, don't worry, I won't tell a soul."

"Not that you deserve it, you hussy!" hissed Sauveterre, who'd pulled himself into a sitting position against the wall and was reloading his pistol, though very pale and breathing heavily. "Get yourself dressed, get out of here and pray to God for forgiveness for your sin. Pierre, don't show yourself at the window!"

At this moment we heard a cry below: "Big Jacquet's dead!" So Sauveterre handed me his pistol and I stole a look out of the window and opened fire, dropping the fellow in this tracks.

This done, I reloaded my own pistol as quickly as possible, though it turned out to be unnecessary. When the band of brigands saw their leader down, they fell back in confusion and ran helter-skelter towards their horses with our fellows in close pursuit, cutting them down from behind. But when a sudden cloud covered the moon, my father immediately ordered them to fall back, since he didn't want us to shoot one of our own by mistake in the darkness.

"Pierre," gasped Sauveterre, his face resolute but his voice seeming to weaken, "cut down the priest from his beam. As dissolute and untrustworthy as he is, he doesn't deserve being treated as a common thief, or even as an evil devil."

As I reached the floor below, my father was just coming in; he bounded up to me, crying, "Thank God, Pierre, you're safe!"

"Amen!" I cried. "And you, my father?"

"Not a hair out of place!" he laughed, giving me a bear hug and rubbing his scratchy moustache on my cheek. "And Sauveterre?"

"He's wounded by a pistol shot, but says he'll be on his horse again in a week."

"Ah, let me see!" said my father, suddenly growing sombre.

I was going to follow him when I heard a voice from above, crying, "Hey! Monsieur! Help me! I'm dying up here! My arms are breaking!"

As Giacomi came rushing in at that moment, I asked him to hold Pincers's feet up to relieve the weight on his arms. That done, a couple of slashes with my sword cut the ropes, and down he came, like a puppet, onto Giacomi's shoulders, moaning that his wrists were broken. I untied them and, though the flesh around them was discoloured and swollen, there was no bleeding. I felt the bones and detected no breaks, so I was pretty sure that the worst he'd suffered were badly stretched tendons and some torn muscles, which would bother him at least until the new year.

Jacotte arrived from the cemetery at that moment, and, seeing her priest in such a predicament, fluttered about like a terrified mother hen and began turning every which way, babbling like a mill in white water. I told her to calm down and rub her priest's arms with spirits of wine, then to lay him on his bed and give him some opium, which I knew she had, to help him sleep—since Pincers, to earn a bit of extra money, served as a kind of apothecary for the locals, but was so miserly that he never gave out enough of anything to kill anyone.

As I was finishing my instructions for Jacotte, I saw my father coming down the stairs with a heavy step; approaching me with lowered eyes and a very grave expression, he said in French, "It's not a light wound at all. The bullet pierced the lung through and through. It was madness not to give safe passage to that villain! His life was nothing compared to Sauveterre's and yours!"

"But," I stammered, my mouth suddenly parched and a knot in my throat, "Ambroise Paré claims that one can recover from a bullet wound to the lung."

"Assuredly so, but the prognosis is not good for a man of that age and who has so little appetite for life. Pierre, go and find a cart and an ox in the village so we can bring your uncle back to Mespech. He'd certainly never make it on horseback."

82

I found some people in the village still gripped by fear and trembling, and who were already singing the praises of Mespech, for none doubted that, had we not arrived, the marauders, their pilfering and pillaging done, would have put the entire population to the knife, wenches and priest included. They were so relieved to have but two to mourn—if mourn them they did: the watchman Villemont and a fellow named Fontanet, who'd died with a pike in his hands attempting to protect, tooth and nail, his worldly goods—for which he was roundly blamed by the villagers, since, having no skill in swordplay as gentlemen did, he'd merely tried to show off by aping the bravery of the nobility.

Scarcely had the villagers provided me with cart and ox, amid a great deal of excited chatter, before I heard the sound of a pistol shot, and then a second, which I knew must be coming from the la Fumélie farm, where the fleeing brigands were doubtless trying to make off with our horses, and Petremol was shooting at them from the window of the farmhouse.

"My friends!" I cried. "Hurry! We need to get to la Fumélie. They're trying to steal our horses!"

Already I was running full tilt towards the village gate, followed by our little band, when all of a sudden I heard my father's voice roar from behind us, filling the village square with its thunder: "Pierre! I order and command you to remain here! Cabusse, Fröhlich, Jonas and my Siorac cousins, run to la Fumélie and carefully make your presence known to Petremol! Do not take any risks! This business has cost us too dearly as it is! Better to lose our mounts than the horsemen!"

Although I was very ashamed and chagrined to be thus dressed down before our servants, I fully understood that he'd only done so out of fear of losing me in this skirmish, sharing the soldier's superstition that misfortune never comes alone. And, indeed, he was very nearly right, for in the dust-up at la Fumélie, Fröhlich was hit by a bullet that tore open his helmet and came within half an inch of piercing his skull, but merely ripped off half of his left ear. Luckily, I was able to sew it back together when we returned to Mespech an hour later. All he got from this nearly fatal wound was some immediate pain and a handsome scar that later he was able to show off to the ladies.

Alas, Sauveterre's wound was far from benign. At every breath he took, some blood bubbled up out of the hole in his chest. And even when I'd succeeded in suturing the wound, which was extremely painful for him, he didn't regain any strength and his fever remained constant and acute, his pulse irregular, his heartbeat weaker and weaker, and his breathing more and more difficult. For three days, neither my father nor I left his bedside, urging him to remain as still as possible, to refrain from speaking, to take shallow breaths and to drink milk and hot broth—which he agreed to do only to please us, for he had no hope or faith of recovering.

Since we told him that he *must* remain silent, he looked at my father and me, when we took turns at his bedside with such a sweet air of deep affection that neither of us could manage to hold back our tears. It seemed that the implacable rigour that he'd shown throughout his life had completely dissolved at the approach of death, laying bare his sensitive and infinitely benign soul, which had been so hidden by pride and by his Huguenot austerity.

On the morning of the fourth day, his fever fell, and, given that he'd been able to sleep thanks to the opium we'd prescribed the night before, my father said to him: "My brother, you're getting better."

"No, no, I'm dying," Sauveterre assured him—with such absolute conviction that I saw that my father dared not contradict him, especially when, as the day wore on, his breathing became more and more laboured, painful and halting, and from time to time he stopped breathing altogether, so that we thought we'd lost him. There was no longer any point in asking him not to speak: he did not have enough breath to do so, and just lay there, his mouth open like that of a fish out of water.

And yet, towards evening, he regained some strength and asked my father to call Catherine and François to his bedside. But all he said to them was: "Always remember that you were raised in the reformed religion." Then he made a gesture for them to leave, clearly having much less love for them than he did for Samson and me, Catherine being a girl and François being... well, François.

He began gasping for breath at about six o'clock, but towards seven the gasps subsided; he turned to my father, looked at him for a long time, gave a faint smile and finally said, in a voice so weak it was barely audible, "Jean, you have been, these last thirty-seven years, my only earthly joy."

My father gave him his hand and I saw Sauveterre squeeze it with all his might, which gave me a moment of mad hope for his recovery despite all of the indubitable signs that should have dashed it. And then I understood better what I was seeing: he was holding fast to the hand of this man who, all his life, had sustained their immutable friendship, in order to gain the courage to wage his last earthly battle, which all of us must someday lose, and follow the dark, treacherous passageway to death. But then, at about nine o'clock, he managed to speak again, in a barely perceptible voice:

"My presence here..."

And then took a deep breath. My father leant close and nodded, to show him that he was listening.

"My presence here," continued my uncle in fits and starts, "was only a long and arduous separation from eternal happiness."

My father and I looked at each other in silence, both of us realizing that Sauveterre hereby summed up the rigour of a life that had only been a long approach to what was to follow. I saw that my father wanted to speak, but couldn't, his voice strangled by the knot in his throat; large tears were running down his cheeks.

But, by then, any words would have been useless. Sauveterre, his tanned face now pale and wrinkled, had already lost the words and thoughts of his native tongue; his look was now troubled and fixed, his breathing so laboured that my heart ached sorely in my despair of easing his pain.

"Pierre," my father said, as the clock struck ten, "go—take some dinner and drink a pitcher of wine."

I was rising to obey him, my shoulders heavy with grief, when all of a sudden Sauveterre gave a violent start. A sea of blood gushed from his mouth; his hands clenched, and then he fell back into such immobility that we knew even before listening to his heart that this stillness was to be as eternal as the felicities that he'd promised himself.

3

J EAN DE SAUVETERRE's death at the age of sixty-two left an
open and painful wound for Jean de Siorac, who was five years
younger than his brother and now sole proprietor of Mespech, as the
brothers had arranged back in 1545 when they merged their worldly
goods in the presence of the notary of Sarlat.

There was, however, one gift that they weren't able to provide
each other, and that was to leave this earth together after thirty-seven
years of a relationship forged under the duress of war and battle;
they had fought together in the Norman legion, and had never been
separated since, despite the incredible perils of the persecutions
against the Huguenots, standing side by side like two rocks fused
together and never broken or divided by the series of floods that
battered them.

Alas, death had achieved what the malice of men had failed to do
to the Brethren, as they were known throughout the region, now cut
in two, bleeding from a wound that no surgeon in this world could
dress or heal. And from my father down to the least of our servants,
who loved Sauveterre with deep respect, and were never put off by his
implacable virtue, the walls of Mespech now resounded with tears and
lamentations—or, worse still, fell into a mournful silence as though
now suddenly deserted.

As for my father, it seemed to me that at Sauveterre's death he
was widowed for the second time, so unhinged was he by the loss of

his partner, much like an ox who'd lost its teammate, with whom he'd daily shared the management of their estate, read the same books, followed the same religion, decided everything with one mind—not without arguing ceaselessly, as we've seen, for these two, united in the same faith and the same unshakeable friendship, were so opposite in temperament that it was a miracle they'd come to love each other so much.

My father's moustache turned completely white in the single night after Sauveterre's death. He seemed wholly lost in anxiety and mourning, his eyes fixed on the ground, lips sealed, conversation rare, gestures slowed and hesitant, as if he were constantly searching—by his side, at table, on horseback, in the library, in the stable or in the fields—for this grumbling and fractious brother. No doubt Jean de Siorac had come to love his brother's very remonstrations because they were *his*—and, I often thought, because they reminded him of the most severe Huguenot maxims and, in some sense, excused him from having to obey them, Sauveterre's inflexible virtue compensating, as it were, for my father's profligacy.

My father's despair and distress were so great that I decided, yet again, that I must put off my departure from Mespech, knowing that Jean de Siorac would derive no comfort from my older brother, François, whose manner remained icily cold even in the face of my father's affliction and sadness.

As for my little sister, Catherine, although she adored my father, she was completely focused, ever since receiving Quéribus's letter, on Charles IX's imminent demise, which would bring Anjou back from Poland, and, along with him, his brilliant retinue. Lost in the clouds of her great love, she danced over the flowery paths of her future, imagining that she was already living in Paris, a baronne and a guest at the Louvre, scarcely aware of her surroundings at Mespech, whose melancholy she hardly noticed in her new-found happiness.

And so I stayed on at Mespech, at first just for a few days, and then, when my father seemed unable to emerge from his grief, a few weeks more, and, as his pain seemed to grow rather than lessen (which caused me some disquiet about his health), an entire second winter. How interminable those long, cold months seemed, in a Mespech now devoid of the company of Samson, Quéribus, Gertrude and Zara. All that beauty and gaiety was now flown from our walls; Catherine was wrapped inaccessibly in her dreams, and my Little Sissy was first ravaged by a cough that tormented her chest and caused her to lose a lot of weight, and then made bitter after a miscarriage in March robbed her of my child.

At first I tried to help my father with his stewardship of Mespech, but, realizing eventually that my efforts brought more pain than relief to Jean de Siorac, I tried another approach altogether and attempted to revive his former great love for medicine. On the pretext of needing to brush up on my own knowledge, which was getting rusty from lack of practice, I involved him in my reading and in various dissections—of the animals we slaughtered for our food as well as of some of the poor devils that died along our roads during that hard winter. And after three months of this continuous and daily study, I saw my father begin to regain his former liveliness. His posture improved, along with a renewed vigour, as he gradually emerged from the excessively morose devotion into which Sauveterre's death had plunged him—this excess driven, I suspected, by the sins that his natural tendencies had led him to, and would, no doubt, again, since to renounce his natural appetites would mean renouncing his appetite for life itself.

Talking about this casually in front of the fire in the library, after a ride over our domain, I dared tell him without hesitation that his decision to close the door between his room and the one next door, as he'd done ever since the death of his brother, seemed to me completely nonsensical, depriving Mespech of the sons and daughters he might still have—a fecundity that was often recommended in the Bible, as he knew all too well, having read, meditated on and quoted to Sauveterre the passage in Genesis 29 in which we see Jacob repeatedly impregnate Rachel, Leah and her servants.

My father made no response to this reference, but instead rose and walked back and forth in the library with a more vigorous step than I'd seen for a long time, his hands on his hips, a sight that gave me such joy and the hope that he would now recover the posture that I'd always admired.

"It's true," he confessed, "that I quoted this text to my brother Jean, as well as others I found in the Good Book. But don't you think it was sacrilegious to cover my sins with such high authority? And when I was fooling around with the poor wench who gave me Samson, was it not just plain adultery, your mother being still alive and my wife before God?"

"Perhaps," I conceded, "but the tree must be judged from its fruits: that sin was assuredly forgiven in heaven since it gave you Samson, this beautiful angel whom everyone in the world admires, and whom even my uncle, who made so many reproachful sermons when he was conceived, holds in higher esteem than any of your legitimate children."

"You said 'holds'," my father exclaimed in surprise. "You speak of Sauveterre as if he were still alive! And so he is, in my heart," he continued, as if in a dream. "In my thoughts I'm still arguing with him constantly and about everything. But it's quite true, as you say, Pierre, that your uncle was not angry—quite the contrary!—at seeing the increasing number of children by which Mespech grew and fortified itself. He abhorred my sins, but glorified their results."

I gave no answer to this, but watched him drift silently into his thoughts and didn't want to disturb them further. I know all too well, being my father's son, how powerful the world of our imagination can be: our thoughts are like fillies that need space to gallop, head held high and mane flowing in the wind, and shouldn't be bridled in their youth. The bit can be applied later, if bit be needed.

As soon as Little Sissy had been confined to bed, I stopped going to her at night—not because I feared contagion from her illness, but because the poor wench was so feverish and restless that I got no rest sleeping by her side. Moreover, I got my father to agree to have a fire burning in her room at night since I believed the heat would allow her to sweat out the rest of her sickness. I wasn't certain the remedy would cure her, but the result was that I was chased from her room, except for brief visits, by the excessive heat there, and had to sleep in a little chamber adjoining Franchou's.

Every night I'd hear the wench turning over and over in her bed like a crêpe on a pan, at times sobbing, at other times sighing like a bellows in a forge, finding herself so alone ever since the Baron de Mespech had refused to spend his nights with her, more dissuaded by the remonstrance of a dead man than he had been by the same man while he was alive. And yet, Franchou being so appealing, so fresh and benign, I had no doubt that my father, given the disposition I'd just observed in him, would satisfy her again soon—which augured much better for his health and happiness, the doctor in me outweighing the moralist, and may my readers forgive me if they're of a different opinion.

My Angelina had written me two letters, which I reread so often in the silence and reclusion of my little room that my eyes were like to devour the very paper they were written on if they could. Not that they brought me the news I'd so hoped for. Monsieur de Montcalm's confessor, who was near his last breath, used this breath to continue to deter his penitent from the certain damnation that awaited him if he were to give his daughter to a heretic. The Latin note that I'd obtained from Pincers attesting that I'd been baptized in the Roman

Church—which was true—and that I heard Mass—which was only true on three or four occasions—was unable to shake the zeal of this moribund priest, who, before he would agree to our marriage, demanded that I kneel on the floor of the Barbentane chapel, holding a candle, and make a full confession of the sins and heresies of the Huguenot faith. Angelina knew full well that, because of my attachment to my father's religion, I could never be pushed to such extremities. Her only recourse was to pray to God to call to His side this priest, who had certainly earned his rest, given how well he'd served Him—which she reported to me with such naive innocence that it left me half-moved and half-joyful.

At the end of June, now fully two years since the St Bartholomew's day massacre, the news reached us of Charles IX's death in the Louvre on 30th May. I learnt later from Pierre de L'Étoile that the king was tormented by remorse for having spilt so much blood in the massacre of our people in Paris on the night of 23rd August 1572—a remorse that showed he had more heart than Catherine de' Medici, who'd planned and carried out the entire massacre without batting an eyelid, and then imposed tortuous lies on her son without ever a breath of repentance.

"My brother," whispered Catherine as she tiptoed into my little bedroom, candle in hand, as I was about to retire for the night, "I've heard the king is dead. Is this true?"

"It is. My father heard it directly from the seneschal of Sarlat."

"May God rest his soul!" said Catherine, making the sign of the cross. But this done, she couldn't keep her face from radiating with joy. "And so," she continued, "the Duc d'Anjou will return to France from Warsaw?"

"'Tis certain," I smiled, "that he'd much prefer to reign in France than in Poland if he can."

"If he can?" she breathed, her blue eyes widening with fear at the word "if".

"Well, it's not yet certain, my Catherine, that his good Polish subjects, who worked so hard to find themselves a king, will let him leave now that they have him."

"What?" gasped Catherine, pulling herself up in anger. "His subjects would dare make him their prisoner?... Oh, you wicked brother!" she cried. "You were kidding!"

"Not at all!" I replied. "All you have to do is ask your father: he'll confirm it. But, my sister," I continued, "don't get so upset! The Duc d'Anjou is a great captain, and he'll surely figure out some trick to get away, along with his retinue."

This "retinue" nicely cancelled out the "if", and so pleased my sister that she put her hand on my shoulder and said, "You know, Pierre, you bear an uncanny resemblance to Baron de Quéribus!"

"Yes, so I've heard. But I'm not half as good-looking," I added with a laugh. "He and I have already agreed that I'm the sketch and he's the finished drawing."

"Yes, I see that," she agreed, and I laughed again, though she didn't really notice since she was so wrapped up in her own thoughts. "And you're not so well appointed," she continued with great seriousness, "since you have but one doublet that's in the Parisian style, and you got that one from him."

"Well, that's because I'm not as rich as he is," I said, laughing again, absolutely delighted with the turn this conversation was taking.

"'Tis true," she frowned.

"Nor am I a baron."

"Assuredly not," she agreed. "You're not and never will be. And yet," she added after a moment of reflection, "I'll still always love you, Pierre, no matter how poor you may be—and a doctor as well."

"Madame," I replied, bowing, "I am infinitely grateful for your generous regard."

At which she suddenly emerged from her dreamy state and stamped her foot:

"Oh, Pierre! You're making fun of me again!"

"Not in the least!" I answered. "And I swear I will love you every bit as much when you have become a baronne."

"Will I really be a baronne?" she cooed, her eyes alight. "It's not so much the title that dazzles me," she explained with a return to her usual haughtiness, "Mespech being what it is and my mother descended from such noble blood. But the baron is so amiable! My brother, may I give you a goodnight kiss?"

"Do you have to ask?" I smiled.

But instead of a kiss, she put her arms around my neck and nestled her head against my shoulder, her blonde tresses all unbraided for the night, and just stayed that way for a moment, all dreamy and thoughtful, her eyelids half closed. "All right," she said with a sigh, "it's off to bed. Pierre, these wicked Poles won't kill our king if they catch up with him on the road to France, will they?"

"Are you serious? Lay a hand on the person of the king?!"

"Or on his retinue?"

"Not on them either. Now, Catherine, go to bed and sleep well! The baron will be here by mid-August, I'll wager it on my doctor's bonnet! And who could he ever marry but you, the most beautiful daughter of any baron in France?"

At this she smiled a candid and confident smile, pursing her lips in contentment—still such a child and yet already fully a woman, an arithmetic puzzle of the first order!

And so for Catherine, a long period of waiting set in that ran exactly parallel to mine, each of us with our sights set on our respective lovers. And isn't it amazing what sway the future holds over the present, whether we await it with intense ardour or tremble in apprehension at what it will bring? And isn't it a strange form of madness to stop living fully the few days of our brief life because of the hope or the fear of what's coming?

My poor Little Sissy could no longer dream of the eternal happiness and glory—and easy life—that bearing my heir would have provided her at Mespech. She struggled hard against death, who wanted to steal her away, and when she had finally triumphed over the fever and was able to rise from her bed, she was so pale and faltering, the flesh having fallen away from her bones and all colour so absent from her face, that she looked like a ghost. She appeared so frightening that la Maligou actually screamed on seeing her emerge from her cavern in her white nightgown that first morning, and cried in a terrified stammer, her eyes wide in fright, "Ah, poor soul, why do you come here to torment me? I never did you any harm when you were alive!"

Little Sissy was alive, but now a mere shadow of her former self: raw-boned, eating little (and little enjoying what she did eat), haggard, slow in her movements, distant towards others, speaking only when spoken to—and then answering in such tenuous, almost benign tones that you would have said her sickness had wiped out her ability to secrete her customary venom. She wished me to return immediately to her bedroom to take up our former relations, but I couldn't. I told myself she was too weakened to be able to tolerate such activity, but the truth is that my appetite had been replaced by mere compassion, and I also thought that if Heaven granted my wishes regarding Monsieur de Montcalm's confessor, it would be better not to risk fathering a son or daughter with Little Sissy, whom Angelina would obviously resent.

In the middle of August, we received a long letter from Dame Gertrude du Luc accompanied by two notes addressed to my father, one from Samson, the other from Zara, both of these written in such a horrible hand that you would have thought a cat had arbitrarily made scratch marks on them. My father laboured a good hour attempting to decipher them, but, in the end, was happy with what he'd read—though for very different reasons. Gertrude, who wrote a longer letter and beautifully formed characters, brought us happy news of her marriage to Samson, their move to Montfort-l'Amaury and the prosperity of the apothecary's shop—despite the absence in the town of a doctor who could prescribe remedies that would need to be purchased there. For this reason, Samson had written to our friend and colleague the venerable doctor Merdanson, who had been my co-conspirator in the exhumation and dissection of two bodies buried in the cemetery of Saint-Denis, near Montpellier. (The reader may also remember that I'd had a disastrous encounter there with the beautiful sorceress Mangane.) This Merdanson, who was a jolly, strapping fellow, had a strange sort of mania: from his lips there flew a continuous scatological stream—the solid sort outweighing the liquid kind—such that I'd once told him, before we became friends, that his anatomy must have been scrambled at birth since he seemed to confuse his mouth with his anus.

This is not at all to say that he wasn't a good man, quite the contrary—and he was an excellent doctor: well informed and devoted to his patients day and night—so I wholly approved of Samson's wish to join forces with him if he could get him to come to Montfort, since it was against the rules (not to mention quite dangerous) for an apothecary to distribute medicines without a doctor's prescription.

We were just sitting down to our evening meal on 29th August when Escorgol, preceded by his enormous paunch, arrived all out of breath to announce that there was a large escort outside the gates asking that the Baron de Quéribus be allowed entry.

"What! The baron?" cried Catherine, half rising from her seat, but down she fell in a dead faint, which brought la Maligou, Barberine and Franchou running to her side, each believing that her distress was a "woman's matter", but since none of them knew what to do, they scratched around her like hens in dust.

"Enough of your chatter!" yelled my father, suspecting that this loss of consciousness was a malady that a healthy and vigorous girl was in no danger of dying from. "Loosen her bodice and give her some spirits of wine. If that doesn't help, put her to bed for two days."

These last words and the spirits did wonders. Catherine quickly regained consciousness and her colour, and, as Barberine was attempting to loosen her bodice, she told her maid in no uncertain terms to desist and leave her as she was—though this wasn't exactly what she intended, since she then asked permission from my father to withdraw to her room to prepare herself and asked Franchou to follow her to give her a hand.

When my father gave his consent, Catherine stood up without any help whatsoever, turned with a great whoosh of skirts, ran to the stairs and disappeared. I exchanged a quick smile with my father, knowing full well that the "preparation" was not a matter of catching her breath, but of arranging her hair and changing her clothes.

"But, Escorgol," my father said, turning to his porter, "you know the Baron de Quéribus well—you've seen him a thousand times! And how did one with hearing as sharp as yours not recognize his voice?"

"Well, of course I thought it was him. But it's dark outside and he has a large escort. I didn't want to raise the portcullis until I received permission to do so!"

"My son," said the Baron de Mespech to me, "will you go and see?"

Well, I did better than "go and see"—I rushed out of the hall and was at the gate in the blink of an eye! And, leaning out of the little window of the tower, I called:

"Quéribus, is it really you, my friend?"

"'Tis I, Pierre, and no doubt about it! I nearly killed my horses getting here! And how is…" He was going to say Catherine, but stopped himself; then, after hesitating, he said, "…the Baron de Mespech?"

"In excellent health, as is his daughter!"

"Ah, my brother!" was all he could say in answer.

"The Devil take this portcullis and this door!" I cried. "I can't raise the one and unlock the other without Escorgol, who's dragging his arse back here like a snail on its stomach. By the belly of St Anthony, Escorgol!" I shouted. "Get over here!"

"Ah, Monsieur!" panted the poor porter, completely winded, having never run this fast before, and carrying such a load of flesh that it was a wonder he didn't trip over it on his way. "Ah, Monsieur! Be patient! Where's the fire?"

"The fire?" I replied, but in French so he wouldn't be insulted. "I'm going to light one in your drawers to catapult you here faster!"

Quéribus broke into gales of laughter and, after a great grinding of metal, unlockings and unboltings, we exchanged a hearty embrace and much back-slapping.

I told Escorgol to stable their horses and, with Quéribus, set off at a run towards the great hall, where, after a deep bow to my father, he couldn't help betraying his confusion at not seeing the object of his affections. He was able to mask this confusion, however, when, enquiring after Monsieur de Sauveterre, he learnt of my uncle's death. My father asked the baron to take a seat on his right, ordered that a silver plate be brought for his supper, and proceeded to recount our bitter combat with the brigands at Marcuays, and the mortal wound his brother had received there. Quéribus listened to this tale courteously while swallowing his food without even looking at it, his attention divided between my father's narrative and the door by which he believed Catherine would enter the hall. But Catherine didn't appear during the entire meal, whether because her toilette took so long or because she wanted to whet the baron's appetite to see her—an appetite she must have been aware of, since her own desires were growing more intense every minute she delayed (the Creator must have provided the gentle sex with this calculating ability as a compensation for their lesser physical strength).

As soon as Quéribus had eaten his fill, my father led him off to the library, leaving the hall to the baron's retinue, who, now that they had unsaddled and brushed down their horses, must have had some pretty dry throats and sharp teeth after their forced march. La Maligou and Barberine bustled about these men, very enticed by such handsome and vigorous fellows, who must have excited the jealousy of some of the men at Mespech. But, thankfully—for them and also for our economy—they were due to depart the next day and be lodged with Puymartin, Quéribus's cousin, who would have been offended if the baron had not accepted his hospitality.

My poor Quéribus sat down in the library at my father's right, in the straight-backed chair that Sauveterre had occupied for so many years, trying to put a good face on his despair at seeing Catherine's absence prolonged ever longer, wondering, no doubt, if his place in her heart had been taken by some gentleman from Sarlat during his long, wintry exile. Indeed, my father had made no firm promises to the gentleman, as you will recall, since he had no idea how long Quéribus would remain in Poland. Meanwhile, my father was deriving great amusement from the baron's suffering, since he knew that it was to be relieved at any moment, and not at all sorry that this handsome courtier had fallen under the spell of a damsel of such rustic origins. Indeed, he pressed his guest to continue the narrative of the king's adventurous escape from Warsaw, but Quéribus, at the limit of his anxiety and impatience, demurred, pleading fatigue from his long ride.

"Monsieur," laughed my father, "you astonish me! I understand your backside is tired, but not your tongue! And here"—he interrupted himself—"is Franchou with a pitcher of hot wine to comfort you!"

But Quéribus, whose eyes had lit up when the library door opened only to go dark again when Franchou appeared, allowed the chambermaid to fill his goblet without a murmur of thanks or a sip of the contents, unaware, I'll warrant, of what he was holding in his right hand.

Meanwhile, Franchou had stepped over to the Baron de Mespech and slipped a note into his hand, which he unfolded and read to himself, a smile playing along his lips. The good wench was, meanwhile, watching her master avidly, hardly able to contain her delight.

"My dear Quéribus," ventured my father, half in jest and half choked with emotion, "my daughter requests, in this note, the honour of coming in to greet you. Would this meet your fancy? Or are you so exhausted from your travels that you'd prefer to retire?"

"Oh, not at all! Not at all!" stammered Quéribus, who was unable to say more, for all the colour drained from his face and he looked like he too might faint away, and would certainly have fallen had he not been seated. Seeing this, I seized the goblet that was now at such risk in his trembling fingers, applied it to his mouth and had him down it in one swig. The brew did marvels. And you might have thought that, instead of a modest local wine from our grapes, Quéribus had imbibed a magic potion, so sudden was his return to his usual liveliness and vigour. He sat upright in his seat, squared his shoulders, raised his head and, eyes afire, glanced over at the door through which Franchou had just disappeared. On the other side of the door, she was now joyfully preparing to tell Catherine how pitiable the baron had looked a minute earlier, before introducing her young mistress into the library.

Back in her chambers, there is no doubt that Catherine had gone through some very anxious moments deciding whether she should reappear before the baron in the gown she'd worn at Puymartin's ball on 10th November, when she'd won the heart of this gentleman—or whether she should appear in her fresh and natural grace, wearing a simpler and more common dress. Would the former not be too obvious an attempt to court him? And mightn't it risk comparisons with all the stylishly clad ladies of the court?

Finally she had the sense to choose the latter, and appeared in the library clothed in a pink cotton dress without lace collar, but with a very virginal neckline set off by a few modest pearls, and without any make-up, her beautiful face washed with clear water, her golden hair combed and tied with a pink ribbon. To add to her stature, she was wearing tall heels, which were hidden by the low hemline of her dress. There was, in short, so little in her clothing to distract from her native beauty that the baron could not but admire her young body and her beautiful face, graced with those large, blue, shining eyes—artfully illuminated by Franchou, who preceded her carrying a candelabrum with four candles, the only excess that Catherine permitted herself.

She stepped forward and made a deep bow to my father and another to the baron, who leapt to his feet with the speed of an arrow leaving a crossbow, his eyes wide with the excitement he felt at seeing her. He stammered that she should take his chair, as she would be more comfortable there, and that a stool would suffice for him. He then sat down, but so abruptly that he grimaced in pain, his backside still very tender from so many days on horseback, furiously traversing hill and dale at a gallop in the excitement of seeing her again after his wintry exile in Poland. And here she was, finally! He'd envisioned her day after day as he rode towards her, since our mental images can never be fully satisfied once love gets hold of us.

But of words, once Quéribus had been able to balance himself gingerly on the stool, not a one! And by my faith, I thought that this silence was going to last a century, so absorbed was he in his contemplation of the object of his affections; and so happy was the object herself to be contemplated that she remained silent as well, her complexion rosy with excitement, her bosom heaving with emotion and her eyelashes fluttering modestly, secretly stealing looks at the baron to make sure that he was as lovable as her dreams had painted him.

"My dear Quéribus," my father said, breaking in, thinking that this mutual bewitching had lasted long enough, "now that I see you're restored by the glass of claret, I wonder if I could hear the story of the king's escape from Poland?"

"Ah, Monsieur," cried Quéribus, rising, "I'm mortally ashamed not to have told it already! My fatigue must have gone to my brain for me to have so thoroughly failed in the courtesy due my host! I beg you, Monsieur, to accept my humble apology!"

This said, he made another deep bow to my father, but this bow could not be accomplished without another grimace, so he decided to remain standing throughout the recital of his adventures, marching back and forth in the library, a position that allowed him more secret glances at Catherine, who, for her part, followed his movements back and forth, all eyes and ears.

"'Tis said," prompted my father, "that these Poles did not want to allow their king to leave since they'd taken so much trouble to elect him."

"Well, it's also said," laughed Quéribus, "that they believe the kingdom of Poland to be every bit the equal of France and that they felt that their king should name a viceroy to serve in Paris so that he could remain king in Warsaw."

"A pretty good bargain that was!" said my father, laughing in turn. "Not that the kingdom of Poland isn't a large and noble country, but France is much richer, and the sun shines here more often. And what city in the world is more glorious than Paris?"

"Assuredly so," said Quéribus, "but the palatines were quite resolved to keep their king, so we had to find a clever ruse to escape them."

"Who are these palatines, Monsieur?" asked Catherine.

"The most important nobles, governors of their provinces, Madame," replied Quéribus, making a deep bow to her, "who, when they meet in their assemblies, have more power than the king himself in this strange country. But, to continue: on the eighteenth of June, a very hot night, the king—having promised to remain in his country of Poland—gave a huge Pantagruelian banquet in his palace with lots of good French wine for all the palatines. These gentlemen, being great womanizers and drinkers, drank themselves silly and fell under the table by midnight. Seeing this, the king withdrew to his chambers and pretended to go to bed, while Count Tęczyński, who could scarcely stay on his feet, drew the curtains over him."

"What was the name of this count?" asked my father.

"Tęczyński. He was the marshal of the palace, a man with a copious beard and proud of his gigantic proportions. In short, after he'd staggered out of the room, the king arose, put on his valet's clothes and headed for the postern, followed by Du Halde, Villequier, Du Guast, Soubré, Quélus, Pibrac, Miron, Fogacer and me."

"Ah!" I exclaimed. "Fogacer!"

"And me," added Quéribus, with a meaningful glance at Catherine.

"Ah, Monsieur, please continue!" begged Catherine. "I'm all atremble for these fugitives!"

"So you should be, Madame!" he replied with another bow. "For scarcely had we passed through the palace gates when a cook recognized the king and ran to tell Tęczyński, who managed to rouse himself from his stupor, sound the alarm, leap into his saddle, drunk as he was, and set off after us with a group of fierce Tartars! Ah, my friends, what a ride that was! A few leagues from the Austrian border, as dawn was breaking, we saw them behind us, galloping at full speed to catch us. Heavens! If they'd succeeded, they would have taken the king prisoner, of course, but the rest of us would have lost our heads!"

"Your heads, Monsieur?" gasped Catherine, her hands on her heart.

"They would have rolled!"

"God forbid, my dear Quéribus," said my father in a half-serious, half-amused tone, "that such a handsome head should fall under a Polish sword!"

"Well, it came within a hair's breadth!" came Quéribus's fiery response. "Just as we reached Plès, the first Austrian village, the king's mare fell under him, dead as a doornail, and Tęczyński and his Tartars were right behind him. There was no help to be got from the villagers, who, at the sight of the band of Tartars, had boarded themselves up in their houses."

"Ah, Monsieur!" panted Catherine. "So what did this terrible Tęc... what's-his-name end up doing?"

"Tęczyński. Without a word, he looked at the king—who had stood and was bravely looking back at him—signalled a halt to his Tartars, walked his little white horse alone towards the king, dismounted... and fell flat on his face in the dust of the street. We were, in fact, amazed that the fellow had lasted so many hours in his stupefied condition on his steed. Finally, he managed to get to his feet, and staggered forward. The king cried, 'My friend, do you approach as friend or foe?'

"'Well, sire!' replied the giant in French as he staggered uncertainly towards the king (no doubt very moved that his monarch had called him 'my friend'). 'I come as the very humble servant of His Majesty.'

"'Well then,' shouted Soubré, 'order your Tartars to withdraw!'

"At this, Tęczyński, who was holding a hunting whip in his hand, turned and gave it a furious crack, with such force that he almost lost his balance; then he shouted an incomprehensible order in Polish, whereupon the Tartar cavalry turned their mounts and rode away in a trice, leaving the little white horse alone in the town square, who now began to follow his master step by step as Tęczyński walked towards the king. This man was at least two heads taller than anyone in the king's retinue—though I myself am not a little man," added Quéribus proudly. "His beard was sticky from all the wine he'd spilt on it, and white from the dust of the road; his doublet was torn and unbuttoned over his hairy chest; his breeches were falling down and his arms were decorated with enormous jewels—but he was armed, thank God, with only a knife, which reassured us, since we had swords and pistols, all of us except the king.

"'Well, sire!' cried Tęczyński, throwing himself at the feet of His Majesty, and speaking French with his jarring accent, but with enviable eloquence for one as inebriated as he was. 'I beg you not to leave Poland, but to return to your poor subjects who, if you return to your capital, will wake up tomorrow orphans and stripped of their beloved monarch.'

"'This I cannot do,' replied Henri. (I'm among the few people who can call him by his name and with whom he uses the familiar *tu* on occasion.) 'I must go and reclaim the kingdom that God has given me through legitimate succession. However, my friend, I am not abandoning the throne to which I was elected. And I am only leaving for a while and will return here when I have been crowned king of France.'

"'Oh, sire!' cried Tęczyński, in the depths of despair, since he didn't believe a word of what he'd just heard, yet couldn't accuse his king of dishonesty. Then, falling silent and crying hot tears, beating his chest, tearing at his beard and hair, and encircling the king's legs with his whip, he fell to his knees and kissed the king's feet, sobbing, 'Sire! Sire! Come back now to your poor orphaned people!'

"We all put our hands to our swords at the sight of the king tied up this way by the giant, but Henri, with his usual grace and pleasant manner—and, as far as I could tell, quite moved by the loving protestations of the palace marshal—signalled to us to remain calm, and said:

"'Monsieur, are you a faithful subject of your king?'

"'Oh, sire!' cried Tęczyński, staggering to his feet, the huge gold earring in his left ear trembling with the effort. 'Could you ever doubt it?' And at this, he staggered back three steps, drew his knife, cut a gash in his right hand and drank his own blood—which, in his people's bizarre customs, meant, I suppose, that he was swearing eternal allegiance to His Majesty.

"'Monsieur,' said the king, who hadn't blinked an eye when the giant drew his knife, 'since you are a good, loyal and devoted subject, I order you to return to Warsaw and tell the palatines what I have decided.'

"'Sire, I will do your bidding,' replied Tęczyński, tears flowing down his cheeks into his beard; and suddenly, unsteady as he was, he thrust his knife back into its sheath in a single movement and without even looking; then he ripped from his hairy, muscular forearm a gold bracelet, dropped to one knee and held it out as a present for the king. Henri accepted it with a thousand thanks, weighing it in his hand as though surprised by its heaviness, and embarrassed that, dressed as he was in a valet's clothes, he had nothing of value to give to the count other than a tiny gold pin of such little consequence that it would have been an insult to offer it, given that he was the king of two great Christian countries. And finally, at his request, Soubré handed him a diamond that was very beautiful and certainly of a size to represent a suitable response to Tęczyński's offering, clearly worth at least 1,200 écus.

"The count was so happy that, holding it up in the dawn sunlight, he turned it over and over in his thick fingers, and then, having no safe place to put it in his doublet, which was torn to shreds, he stuffed it in his mouth, bowed to the king, leapt on his little white horse with surprising agility and galloped off like a shot.

"'My God, I hope he doesn't swallow it!' gulped Pibrac.

"'If he does,' smiled the king, who loved to jest, 'that stone will be the purest thing he's ever drunk!'"

We all burst out laughing at this, and Catherine harder than any of us, her periwinkle-blue eyes gazing at Quéribus as if he were the most handsome, valiant and witty person in all humankind. My father's admiration was perhaps less extreme, but I could see he was delighted by the swagger with which Quéribus had recounted his little epic. As for me, knowing our guest much better than either my sister or my father, I couldn't help but be moved by the ardent admiration he displayed for my beloved sister, knowing as I did that his rough-and-tumble exterior hid a very generous heart.

"So at what point," asked my father, "did you ask the king permission to leave his service?"

"In Venice, where His Majesty was received with great pomp and where he allowed himself some rest and relaxation after the Polish winter. As for me, after having begged permission to depart, just as Tęczyński had done—though," he said with a knowing look at Catherine, "I hope I don't resemble him in any other wise—I quickly crossed the Alps with my little escort, and, finding myself in the sweet climes of Provence, I went to pay my respects to my cousin Montcalm in Barbentane."

"Barbentane!" I cried, leaping up so abruptly from my stool that I knocked it over with a great clatter.

"Well, I certainly could not have passed through Provence," he said with a sly smile, "without going to greet Montcalm and embrace my three other cousins: mother and daughters!"

"Three?" I asked in disbelief.

"Madame de Montcalm, Angelina and Larissa!"

"Larissa? But who's Larissa?"

"Angelina's twin sister. But let's not talk about Larissa. It's a sad and most painful story, one that I shall recount another time. I have here," he said, rising and stepping towards me, "two letters. One addressed to your father and the other to you."

"Ah, you scoundrel!" I hissed. "Why didn't you say so sooner?"

I tore the letter from his hands and opened it by the light of the candelabrum Franchou had just placed on the table nearby. My father did the same, though with a much greater display of outward calm than

I could manage, my hands all atremble like poplar leaves in the evening breeze and my heart pounding so hard I thought it would burst from my chest. I dared hope that finally Angelina's prayers had been answered and that heaven had opened its gates to the prelate who'd promised a life in hell to Monsieur de Montcalm if he married his daughter to me.

"Monsieur de Montcalm," announced Jean de Siorac at last, to a room so silent you could have heard a pin drop, "has written me a very civil letter, in which he assures me that he would be infinitely happy to see his daughter Angelina married to my son, Pierre, at the same time that my daughter Catherine is joined in wedlock to the Baron de Quéribus, provided that each of my children, being Huguenots, agree to a condition that his confessor, Father Anselm, has imposed on them. And this condition being what it is, I shall have to give it some thought and sleep on it. I shall tell you tomorrow what I have decided. Monsieur," he concluded, "I bid you goodnight and a welcome and deep sleep after your long journey. Pierre, please show the baron to his room. Catherine, take my arm, please! And Franchou, what are you doing, standing there crying like a cow who's lost her calf instead of lighting our way?"

"Ah, Monsieur, my good master!" replied Franchou in Provençal. "I couldn't help hearing what you said, and I'll go on crying the entire time you're away marrying off your son and daughter in Provence."

"Well, you silly goose," he laughed, "then you heard something I haven't said yet! Far from it!"

At this "far from it", I gave Catherine's arm a little pinch to reassure her that the words were pure facade, given how happy my father must be with this double marriage, yet how reluctant he'd be to rush into anything without due consideration. There was no doubt he took as much care managing the affairs of his barony as he had in the military exploits that had won him that title. As for the condition that had been imposed, I learnt of it the next morning after a long sleepless night—sleepless not because of my anxiety about the decision but because of the intoxicating delights that I felt were soon to be mine, having loved my Angelina for so many years without being able to marry her, or even approach her as long as her father's confessor held sway over him. Since my father hadn't immediately refused, and since I knew Anselm was very fond of me, I believed that his conditions wouldn't be too severe. And finally, towards dawn, just as I had finally fallen asleep, exhausted from the turbulence of my emotions and visions of Angelina, I was awakened by Miroul, who'd come to tell me that my father was awaiting my presence in his room.

I hurried to dress, knowing that he needed to head off to Marcuays to look at a pair of oxen that had been highly recommended to him by his drover.

"Ah, there you are, Pierre!" said my father, as Franchou was fluttering around him, trying to dress him. "Out you go, Franchou!"

"But Monsieur, you can't go out undressed!"

"Leave us! Pierre, give me a hug! Well, in two words, here are the conditions! Leave me alone, dammit, Franchou!"

"Monsieur, just a second: I have to button up your doublet! Your workers can't see you in your undershirt!"

"So, Pierre, the conditions… A plague on this fly who's buzzing around me! What are you doing to my collar?!"

"I'm fastening it. Surely you're not thinking of going to Marcuays without your lace collar?"

"Pierre, you'll have to promise Father Anselm to hear Mass every time you're lodged with a Catholic lord."

"Is that all?" I answered. "That's not so much to worry about!"

"It's not much and it's a lot. You're choking me, you silly witch. Take your fingers off of my throat!"

"Monsieur, your lace collar is hanging like a cow's udder! I have to fasten it!"

"My father, I don't understand. Where's the 'lot' in this 'not so much'?"

"Well, suppose you end up at the Louvre, commissioned by the king to help Miron and Fogacer in their medical duties? You'll have to hear Mass every day, since you'll be in the king's service. You silly goose, are you not yet done?"

"But Monsieur, your breeches are hanging loose and your aiguillette is unfastened!"

"My father," I interjected, my voice barely clearing the knot in my throat, "is there really any possibility of such a commission? Could I fulfil it? Has it been decided?"

"Yes, it's done! Franchou, by the belly of St Anthony! Take your fingers out of there!"

"Monsieur, I will not let you go through the streets of our villages with your flies hanging open! By my faith! They'd have a good laugh at your expense!"

"The king's physician!" I answered dreamily. "Is that not marvellous? What could be better?"

"Of course—but Pierre, hear Mass?"

"I'll listen to it with a Huguenot ear."

"Which is to say you'll be sitting with your arse on two stools: one buttock in Geneva and the other in Rome, and that's a pretty wide spread! Franchou, my little hen, have you still not finished?"

"Indeed so, Master! Now you're set!"

"Amen! Pierre, look before you leap! A Mass every day?!"

"But, my father, in Paris! At the Louvre! The king's physician!"

To which my father answered nothing further. Hadn't he, too, loyally served, good Huguenot that he was, our Catholic king, Henri II—who was, after all, the one who began this persecution? But off he went, humming to himself a ribald tune in the sunshine of this beautiful summer day, with his sprightly step, his back as straight as a board and, as Franchou would say, "like a rooster after a hen in heat and as gay as an Easter hallelujah". And may she be pardoned for mixing the sacred and the profane as she did, for she was merely using a saying that the wenches of Périgord often repeat without any malice whatsoever...

I rushed up to Quéribus's room and, hearing no answer when I knocked, entered. He was lying asleep, naked as the day he was born, on his cot, no doubt dreaming the same dreams I would have been immersed in, though with a different object, had Miroul not awakened me.

I hesitated a bit before awakening him from such pleasure, but then, realizing that when he opened his eyes he, at least, would be able to see his great love in the flesh, I reached out to touch his shoulder. But as I did so, I was struck by our uncanny resemblance to each other: though I know his eyes are of a different shade of blue from mine, we have the same dark eyelashes and delicately chiselled noses, as well as similarly shaped mouths. Yet my features are less striking, I must admit, though I'm certainly not lacking in self-esteem—and again I sensed that he was the finished portrait for which I'd been only the sketch.

Mirrors are indeed treacherous friends, who always manage to reveal the ugly along with the beautiful aspects of one's face, as well as the wrinkles that age makes around one's eyes—though, thank God, at twenty-three I didn't yet bear her claw marks. But Quéribus was a more benign mirror, whose beauty and strength comforted me greatly, as long as I was able to forget that he was better looking than I, which I usually succeeded in doing when I loved him, and even more so when I loved him less. For though my friendship for him never cooled entirely, it couldn't help fluctuating somewhat, according to which of his two faces I beheld: the man or the gallant.

"Baron," I said shaking him, "what are you doing lazing about in bed when I know someone who's already up, fresh as a daisy, and happily enjoying her bread, milk, ham and other meats in the great hall?"

"What say you?" groaned Quéribus, blinking himself awake and sitting up. "My beauty is awake? 'Sblood! I must fly to her side!"

"Well, don't fly there with nothing on, you'll offend her modesty! And, for heaven's sake, don't swear within these Huguenot walls! And third, Monsieur my brother, hear this while you're getting dressed: my father has accepted the condition that Father Anselm stipulated for me, and so there's no reason he would refuse to do so for Catherine."

"Well, my brother! My good brother!" cried Quéribus, rushing to embrace me. "What a good angel of God you are to bring me such news!"

"By the belly of St Anthony," I joked, "if I'm an angel, then that divine cohort is better hung than they're reputed to be! But, my brother, I need you to answer a question that has immense consequences for me: is it true that I've been commissioned as the king's physician? And by whom?"

"By the king, of course!" laughed Quéribus, his hand over his mouth in the manner of the favourites of the court.

"Yes, but of his own accord?"

"His, mine, Fogacer's."

"Aha! So Fogacer's behind this!"

"And me!" corrected Quéribus, visibly a bit stung. "Do you think I go mute when it's time to sing your praises to His Majesty? Who, by the way, remembers you very well and considers you a good man, along with your father, whose loyal and devoted service to François I and Henri II has not gone unnoticed. And as soon as he learnt of my desire to ally myself with your family by marrying your sister, and of your desire to ally yours with Montcalm's by marrying my cousin, he conceived the project of bringing all of us together at court—you, me, your father and Montcalm (to whom he'd like to assign some duties at the Louvre). He wants to gather round him a group of steadfast and loyal friends who owe him everything, knowing how much his power is threatened on all sides by the factions which are destroying his kingdom."

"But, my brother, I'm a Huguenot, and my father as well!"

"The king has no fear of Huguenots as long as they love him and agree to serve him loyally. He's less the enemy of Henri de Navarre than of Guise, of the Spanish king and of the priests loyal to Guise."

"Well I certainly can't answer for Montcalm," I replied after a moment's reflection, "but I doubt my father would agree to leave Mespech, being so invested in the management of his lands, and especially since he's made so many innovations that he's become a model for the entire region."

"I've already explained all this to the king, and he certainly doesn't wish to put pressure on your father. But he thinks that the Baron de Mespech, if he believed the king were in danger, would, like Cincinnatus, quit his plough to take up the sword."

"Well," I exclaimed in my delight, "I shall certainly repeat these words to my father, who will be very honoured to have been spoken of so highly by such an august personage."

Quéribus's escort was so numerous and well appointed that my father decided to ask only Giacomi, Cabusse, Fröhlich and Miroul to accompany us—these last two being our valets, Giacomi our master-at-arms and Cabusse our devoted friend ever since the rewards he'd received from the siege of Calais had provided him the means to purchase the farm at le Breuil, although he'd never lost his taste for adventure.

Four men was but a small escort for the Baron de Mespech to provide—if he'd dared, Quéribus might have bemoaned the fact that his company wasn't more magnificent, but he'd already had a hard time convincing my father to provide Catherine with an appropriate trousseau for her wedding, as well as outfitting our little company for our voyage, and so he didn't insist on an increase in our number, preferring to focus on questions of quality rather than quantity. He spared no expense—in terms of labour or lucre—for our sartorial needs, inviting the master tailor of Sarlat to Mespech to take our measurements and to provide each of us with a doublet and hose *à la mode de Paris*, whose design left this poor artisan dumbfounded. Miroul and Fröhlich were each fitted for liveries.

"Liveries!" exclaimed my father in the privacy of the library. "What do I need with liveries for my servants? Isn't their work just as good without them? By my faith, this fop is going to ruin us with such unnecessary excesses! What would my poor Sauveterre have said of such silly vanities? The hose look like women's girdles, the way they hug your thighs!"

"But that's the style in Paris now, my father!"

"And who decides this style?"

"The king, I suppose."

"The king should spend more of his time worrying about his kingdom and the various factions that are pulling it apart. My old clothes fit me well enough! I don't like leaving them in my chest to dress up in such finery! Zounds! I can't bear these expenses and this ridiculous style!"

"But Father! There's nothing we can do! This is the style in the capital!"

"Well then," he exclaimed raising his two hands heavenwards, "I wish I could give *la mode* a great kick in the arse so she'd gallop back into Paris!"

Of course, I laughed at this little witticism—though, along with its humour, this outburst also contained some tenderness, as though my father had wished to play Sauveterre's role to bring him back to life for a moment. And looking back on it now, I am quite certain that I wasn't wrong in this conjecture, for more than once I surprised my father in this affectionate and almost magical doubling of the shadow of his brother, as though he were imitating Ulysses, who had one of the shades in Hades drink blood to get him to speak his thoughts.

Meanwhile, when the tailor returned with the doublet and hose—which were of a light green (my late mother's colour, which the Baron de Mespech wore throughout his life)—my father, having abandoned Sauveterre to re-embody Siorac, didn't disdain putting them on and prancing around in front of his mirror, and only with great difficulty hid his guilty pleasure at wearing "these silly vanities" from Quéribus and me.

It took nearly a month to finish our preparations, which I watched impatiently from day to day, gnawing at my fingernails till there was nothing left—my Angelina now so close and yet so far, and my Miroul undoubtedly happier than I, since, having heard about the voyage, he'd got permission to wed his Florine in the Huguenot faith at Mespech. Seeing this, my little sister, Catherine, who couldn't have Franchou for her chambermaid since she was still breastfeeding her new baby, and who refused to take Little Sissy, whose insolence was so intolerable to her that she referred to the wench as "scorpion" and "snake" to her face, asked my father to give her Florine, half to oblige herself, half to oblige the girl. I agreed to this, but only for the duration of the trip, since I wanted to engage this sweet and gentle wench in the service of my Angelina, Miroul having asked to remain in my service, despite all the gold he'd taken from the bearded monster he'd killed during the St Bartholomew's eve horrors, as I've already recounted. (On my father's advice, he'd given the gold to an honest moneylender in Bordeaux to invest for him.)

The day finally arrived when we were ready to depart from Mespech. Catherine was mounted on a white palfrey, and so Quéribus's energetic steed was forced, despite its own sense of protocol, into service beside it, frothing at the bit, its legs all atremble at having to maintain such a slow pace. From time to time he'd give it full rein and my own Pompée, who'd never consented to let anyone pass her—stallion, gelding or mare—burst, whinnying, into a gallop in pursuit of the insolent mount that dared run ahead, so off they both went at full speed until they encountered too steep or too rocky a patch of road to keep running, and would slow to a walk, happy and snorting from their exertions, with Quéribus and me now side by side.

"My brother," I confided, seeing that we were some distance from the main body of the escort, "help me understand this mystery! I spent more than a month at Barbentane, recovering from the wound in my arm those bandits inflicted on me when Father Anselm and I were delivering the Montcalms from their clutches, but during that time I never laid eyes on—or heard either her mother or father speak of—Larissa."

"Well," sighed Quéribus, his demeanour suddenly sad and serious, "there's a good reason for that! And it's only fair that you should know about it, especially since the comte bade me inform you of it, since you'll be joining the family. Poor Larissa was the cause of terrible suffering and despair, though initially there was every appearance that she would bring them as much joy as your Angelina."

"Do they look alike?"

"Two peas in a pod. Their height, hair, eyes, traits, voice, step and manner—everything is so uncannily alike that you wouldn't be able to tell them apart if nature hadn't decided to place a distinctive mark on Larissa's face: a small mole on her chin, an 'imperfection' she's always been ashamed of and tried to hide under her make-up."

"Well, at least there's a way to tell them apart!"

"Well… no! For Angelina, who is the most benign and accommodating daughter of any mother in France, has often allowed Larissa to persuade her to wear a mark in the same spot, a doubling that, when they were children, often spared Larissa the whip that she deserved, and gave it to Angelina though she didn't deserve it in the least."

"Oh, what a nasty business!"

"Well, not really. Larissa isn't as malicious as you might think. She's quite charming, though has always had a wild and fantastical side, ever since she was a child. But, alas! it pains me terribly to tell you the rest." And he fell silent for a few minutes, his head lowered, his eyes fixed on his stallion's mane. "Isn't it a pity," he mused, "that such a noble family, so rich, so virtuous and so well known for its honour and good works, is so prey to the workings of the Devil?"

"The Devil?" I replied, unable to believe my ears.

"Who else?" replied Quéribus, looking more serious than I'd ever seen my normally brave and light-hearted friend, now visibly uneasy about what he was about to tell me. "Listen to the infinitely deplorable tale I witnessed when I was a young lad visiting my cousins at Barbentane. Larissa was going on thirteen when Madame de Montcalm took an interest in a poor young fellow from one of their villages, cleaned him up and made him her page. And when I say 'page', I do *not* mean her minion, for the lady's virtue is irreproachable and, as everyone in the area knows, she treated him almost as the son she'd never had, intending to have him serve as her little valet, as is often the custom among Parisian women anxious to make their mark in society. As for me," Quéribus continued, a little stiffly, "I know what I know, and if I were the husband of one of those women, I wouldn't suffer such an extravagant and daily commerce with these common pages, these little brown-skinned Africans, or even these dwarves whom our gallant ladies of the court are so fond of. To my mind, that's placing temptation too close to appetite. And it's no surprise, given such imprudent customs, when, one fine morning, your wife bears you a little dark-skinned baby, or a little short-legged one—and how can one avoid confessing to such progeny without completely dishonouring the family? But, 'sblood! That's all beside the point! Madame de Montcalm is not of such coarse cloth, and, in a word, the danger didn't come from her, but from Larissa."

"What! Larissa? But she was thirteen years old!"

"Barely! But she hid her guilty commerce so successfully that no one would have ever known of it had her chambermaid, who was in on the secret, not become afraid someone would discover it, and decided to tell Monsieur de Montcalm. Unable to govern his fury, her father burst into her room in the middle of the night and, finding the little rascal in her bed, drew his sword."

"Merciful God—did he kill him?"

"He didn't have time. The terrified page leapt from the bed and jumped out of the window, but fell awkwardly and broke his neck. Seeing this, Larissa, who was making cries that sounded more bestial than human, guessed who'd betrayed her, seized a small dagger from under her pillow and plunged it into the breast of her chambermaid, and would have then killed herself had her father not seized her wrist. After which, she threw herself on the ground and rolled about with atrocious contortions, foaming at the mouth and for the next several hours continuing her terrible screams, wild-eyed, her face distorted, her skin as red as the flames of hell, and hitting and biting anyone who dared approach her."

"Good God! Two deaths and a madwoman for a little pleasure!"

"Not two. Against all expectations, the chambermaid survived, but the doctors, having examined Larissa and found her physically healthy in all respects, opined that this so-called malaise of the patient could not be explained or cured by any known remedy and that consequently it must be the work of the Devil."

"Ah, what a marvellous diagnosis!" I cried indignantly. "Are we supposed to believe that all human maladies have been inventoried and remedies found?"

"Well, I certainly don't know about that," replied Quéribus, "but Larissa's subsequent behaviour certainly seems to lend credence to the doctors' judgement, for at times she would lie pathetically in a corner of her room, weeping silently and shaking her head; at other times she would take up her unbearable wailing and roll around, foaming at the mouth, striking and scratching the floor; at still other times she would undo her braids, strip naked and run through the chateau, seizing every man she encountered, no matter what his age or condition, hugging and squeezing him, her face enflamed, crying a thousand obscenities."

"And did my poor Angelina observe any of this wild behaviour?"

"No. She was sent away from the chateau. And as for Larissa, the Montcalms decided to consult a Capuchin friar in Montpellier, Father Marcellin, very learned in demonology, who, having observed the poor wench, declared he'd discovered unmistakable evidence of satanic possession: first, her flushed face, wild eyes and hideous countenance; second, her great torments and the pains in her stomach, bowels and sexual organs; third, an extreme twisting of her torso and hips when she fell to the floor; fourth, a continuous and frenetic desire for sexual contact; and fifth, a tendency to employ obscene, lubricious and outrageous language any time her will was thwarted. Father Marcellin concluded that Larissa was prey to five different demons that had got hold of her, but he was confident that he could rid her of them by virtue of his practice of exorcism."

"And did he?"

"Not at all! He tried on at least three occasions and failed each time. So Monsieur de Montcalm paid him handsomely and sent him away."

"But," I gasped in surprise, "did he have to grease his palm if he repeatedly failed to cure her?"

"Absolutely! Otherwise, Father Marcellin would have denounced her to the bishop as a witch, which would have put her in great danger

of being burnt at the stake, whatever her claim to nobility. Which is also why Monsieur de Montcalm, despite his great love for her, had her locked up in a convent, where the poor girl remained for years, and would have spent the rest of her days if Samarcas had not managed to have her withdrawn from it."

"And who's this Samarcas?"

"A Jesuit. Venerated by the Montcalms because he managed to bring Larissa back to Barbentane, exorcize and purify her and restore to her the possession of her soul."

"And when did this Samarcas complete his miracle?" I asked, at least as astonished by the cure as I had been by the sickness, since I do not believe in demonic possession, maintaining, as Monsieur de Montaigne does, that these "witches" are simply poor madwomen, possessed by no other devil than their tortured imaginations. However, I didn't share my scepticism with Quéribus, since it so goes against the grain of popular opinion in our times and would be considered sacrilege to both the Huguenot and Catholic Churches.

"Two months after the St Bartholomew's day massacre," replied Quéribus. "So it's been nearly two years since Larissa has been released from her convent. And since I saw her on my return from Venice, I can testify that today she is as healthy as Angelina. The two sisters now share such a close and constant bond that you almost never see the one without the other, almost as though they're reflections in a mirror, one of the other."

I couldn't help feeling some discomfort at hearing this—not, of course, that I wished Larissa had remained confined in her nunnery, but I couldn't help thinking that this poor girl's past must have left some traces in her and that these might end up being dangerous for her twin sister, who was so naive and childishly affectionate.

*

The Montcalms lavished a wonderfully warm welcome on my father, on Catherine and even more on me, not only because I was going to be the son that fortune had denied them (their two male children having died in infancy), but also to undo the very unpleasant impression they'd given me when they'd rebuffed me in Paris, in their attempt to marry their daughter to that big oaf, La Condomine.

Our little company arrived at Barbentane at dinner time, and Madame de Montcalm, splendidly attired in an azure gown and wearing her finest jewellery, whispered in my ear, after I'd kissed her hand in the Spanish manner, "Patience, Monsieur! You'll see your Angelina presently. She's finishing her toilette."

"Well, Madame," I gushed, quite moved by hearing her say "*your* Angelina", "patience I have aplenty, having learnt it over these long years—but I swear I bear no grudge to anyone, and entirely respect the scruples imposed by your conscience that caused the delay."

"Pierre," she replied, barely able to hold back her tears (which would have ruined the kohl around her eyes), "you're going to be a good son to us, I'm sure. Give me a kiss!"

She tendered her cheek, and I placed a discreet peck upon it, careful not to disturb the ceruse make-up that covered it, or to get too much on my lips, unsure of the digestibility of this white powder, which, I'm told, contains large amounts of lead and is thought to be poisonous by our apothecaries. From the smooth cheek of Madame de Montcalm I passed to the rough cheek of the comte, who gave me a big hug and several slaps on the shoulder and back, but wordlessly, a tear in the corner of his eye and his throat in a knot—being, I believe, excessively happy to have finally found a way to thank me for having saved his life that didn't compromise the rigour of his Catholic beliefs.

Father Anselm, patiently awaiting his turn, then stepped up and embraced me warmly, planting a kiss on each cheek in the peasant manner, and, as was his wont, commenting on my health in a wry and jocular tone that made an immediately favourable impression on my father. I was very happy to be reunited with this man, whose straightforwardness, open expression, large neck, muscular frame, hair cropped like a field after harvest, square jaw, white teeth and sonorous voice produced an instant sense of complete well-being. His laughter shook his plentiful belly so soundly that one couldn't help joining in his mirth.

To Montcalm's left stood another prelate, whom my host introduced as the Jesuit Father Samarcas, whose costume surprised me no end, since he wore neither surplice nor cassock, but a black velvet doublet with a large ruff collar and a sword at his side. I judged that he knew how to use this blade, since he resembled Captain Cossolat of Montpellier: large-shouldered, not an ounce of fat on his very muscular body, and with something very quick and supple in his every movement that suggested he was well endowed in athletic prowess. And indeed, no sooner had he learnt that Giacomi was our master-at-arms than he proposed that they face each other the next morning, and subsequently proved himself very adept in the art of fencing. What's more—or perhaps what was worse, if you will—when he believed he'd sufficiently gained Giacomi's good graces, he told him in confidence that he'd heard in Paris (which he knew well, along with Rome, Madrid, Lisbon and London) that the Italian was the sole possessor of Jarnac's secret thrust, and, being an adept of the Jesuits' own secret thrust, he suggested that they exchange their respective insights. Giacomi immediately rejected this suggestion, though with his usual courtesy, and, the next day, explained his reason for doing so.

"No doubt you are aware, Pierre, that Jesuits are bound to obey their order *perinde ac cadaver*.* To reveal Jarnac's thrust to a Jesuit would be to reveal it to everyone in that society."

---

* "Like a cadaver."

"Even if he were to swear never to reveal it?"

"The Jesuit general would relieve him of this oath. A few signs of the cross, a few Latin words, *e il gioco è fatto.*"*

"My brother," I smiled, "you know the papal orders better than I do, but wouldn't you be tempted to learn this famous Jesuit thrust?"

"Of course! But not at the price that Samarcas is exacting! My conscience (and the oath I pledged my master that no one will ever learn it from me) has created an obligation never to reveal Jarnac's thrust, which cuts my opponent's hamstring but spares his life."

"And yet you taught it to me."

"To you alone, my brother," replied Giacomi, throwing his long arm over my shoulder, "on condition that you never divulge it and because I have complete confidence in you. But Samarcas! Do we even know what nation this mysterious fellow hails from? This religious dagger-bearer! This monk without a monastery! This tonsured fellow who gambols from country to country and speaks in a jargon of French mixed with Spanish, Italian and English!"

"God," I smiled, "gave the gift of languages to the Apostles."

"A nice Apostle he is! Who's he serving in all these missions to faraway places? The Pope? Felipe II? Guise? He's just come back from London. What did he do there? Do you think he tried to convert Queen Elizabeth to Catholicism? And what are the origins, causes and powers of the control he exercises over Larissa, which is so great that she looks at him with a veneration so fearful and grovelling that you'd think he were God himself!"

"Well, it's because he exorcized her," I replied, wishing to hide from Giacomi my disbelief in demonic possession and exorcism.

"But exorcism is a public and solemn rite," countered Giacomi gravely, "and, against all rules, Samarcas's was private and secret,

---

* "And the game's up."

conducted in a locked room, where he remained alone with her for three days and three nights, and from which Larissa emerged quiet, subdued and angelic, according to what I've heard. That stinks of magic!"

"Oh, Giacomi," I laughed, "if the exorcist is suspected of black magic, where will the Inquisition ever end?"

"But do you know," Giacomi continued, "that I've never seen anyone so inflamed as Monsieur de Montcalm was when he swore never to marry his Larissa out of the fear Samarcas instilled in him that, if he did, the Devil would take possession of her once again on the day of her wedding? But there's worse still! Monsieur de Montcalm has abandoned his paternal prerogatives and given Samarcas the governance and education of his daughter, to the point that, when the monk leaves Barbentane on his secret missions, he takes her with him!"

"What! She goes with him? And Madame de Montcalm has consented to this?"

"Indeed! She's terrified by the thought Samarcas has planted in her that the Devil will re-enter Larissa during his absence."

"But Giacomi," I replied, feeling stunned, "how did you discover all this?"

"From Montcalm's master-at-arms."

"Aha! The Florentine?"

This Florentine had been in Montcalm's service for ten years, and kept his eyes open, his ears pricked and his mouth closed. Even since our arrival he'd not left Giacomi's side, so happy was he to be speaking Italian again.

But I'm getting ahead of myself. Samarcas was hardly in my thoughts on this first night at Barbentane, where, sitting at dinner with my amiable hosts, I thoroughly neglected my plate, my eyes fixed on the door through which my beloved would appear—just as Quéribus's had been at Mespech. The stool on my right was vacant, but it was not the only one, for the place on Samarcas's left was also unoccupied, which should have alerted me to what was about to happen and thus prevent me from appearing so utterly at sea when the door suddenly opened and I saw not one, but two women enter the hall, so uncannily alike in every way that there was no sign on earth that would have allowed me to distinguish which was Angelina and which Larissa. The resemblance was even more pronounced since each had a small, dark stain to the left of her mouth (a feature that Quéribus had explained at Mespech), Larissa having transmuted her mole into a beauty spot and Angelina having counterfeited the same out of the goodness of her heart at her twin's request.

I rose from my seat, my heart fit to burst from my chest. Although my astonishment initially provoked some laughter, this merriment quickly died away, to be replaced by a growing sense of dismay: not one of us, not even their parents, could have distinguished between the two sisters as they stood on the threshold, not moving a muscle, hand in hand, each the reflection of the other, while I continued to stand dumbstruck at my place, trying desperately to guess which was my pure and stainless beloved, and which the miserable madwoman who'd allowed herself to be seduced at thirteen by a little valet, then stabbed her chambermaid and abandoned herself to delirious howling. A deathly silence gradually took possession of the hall, which only added to the malaise that reigned there, but what really shook my own nerves to the core was that both of these beauties were looking directly at me with expressions of passionate love—though assuredly one of the two was seeing me for the first time, and was as much of a stranger to me as I was to her.

Meanwhile, I could not help noticing that, despite their smiles, there was a strange tension between the two, and that one of them was squeezing the hand of the other, holding it fast while the other

125

tried in vain to undo her grip. And I imagined that the former must be Larissa, since it seemed unimaginable that Angelina would not want to hurry to my side and take her place on my right. And so I began to smile tenderly and confidently only at the captive, rather than at her sister; seeing this, the captor stopped smiling at me, bit her lip and cast down her eyes sadly, yet maintained her vice-like hold on her sister's hand. I also surmised that, though Angelina was strong enough to free herself, she was prevented from doing so by her goodness and pity for her twin.

This indecent constraint obviously signified some odious meaning. Surely Monsieur de Montcalm could not help but see it; yet he could not stop it, since he would have been too ashamed—and perhaps too horrified by the idea of a sudden return of Larissa's demon—to dare open his mouth.

From what Giacomi told me later, all he could do was look pleadingly at the Jesuit, who'd watched the entire scene with indifference and pretended not to meet Montcalm's glances, so that Madame de Montcalm finally leant over to him and whispered a few words in his ear. At this, Samarcas turned on his stool and, giving Larissa a single brief look, said in the most negligent tone imaginable,

"Larissa, come over here this instant and sit down beside me."

At this, trembling from head to toe, Larissa dropped Angelina's hand, stepped forward, eyes lowered and looking quite contrite, and sat down as he'd commanded, while her liberated twin hurried to me like a goose to her gander.

When I'd drunk my fill of her beauty and voice, on which my eyes and ears feasted with incredible delicacy, scarcely able to believe she was at last in my presence, and indeed so deliciously present to me after these two years of separation—and especially after seeing her in Paris without being able to speak to her—I couldn't help sneaking a glance at Samarcas and his strange pupil. The latter sat quiet and subdued, her eyes lowered, her bosom heaving, while the Jesuit, his large, hairy hand pinning Larissa's to the table and holding her imprisoned there like a cat with a mouse under its claws, whispered in her ear in a quiet but grave voice, like a muted drum, a long incantation, which the poor girl listened to, mechanically nodding her head and blinking constantly without ever daring to look in my direction. Samarcas's voice emerged in a low humming sound that was incomprehensible to the rest of us at table but held her as if crushed under the weight of all her sins. But his intense focus on her allowed me to study him at my leisure out of the corner of my eye.

Samarcas's face was of a yellow-brown, sepia colour, with a long, curved nose, hollow cheeks and flesh drawn so tight over his cheek-bones that you could see the muscles of his big, square jaw working when he chewed on his meat. His lips were thin and pinched; his eyebrows were bushy and very dark, and met over the bridge of his nose, emphasizing the squareness of his forehead above them. His hair was still quite black, though some white was beginning to appear around his temples. His jet-black eyes were deeply set in their sockets and gleamed maliciously out from them, animated by rapid, search-ing, probing, ferreting movements. Indeed, though he appeared to be completely focused on Larissa, his mobile glance met mine at one point and, realizing that I was watching him, he threw me such terrible look that my blood nearly froze in my veins; but he immediately gave me such a charming, amiable and suave smile that I was dumbfounded, unable to decide what to conclude from this first skirmish: was this a declaration of war or a peace offering? Before leaving the field, however, I was able to observe that he wore moustache and beard, immaculately trimmed—as were the nails of his hairy hands. He was dressed in the latest style, with a carefully ironed ruff, and his hair suggested that its curls owed more to art than to nature.

*

My sister Catherine's marriage contract had been drawn up at Mespech in a trice, Quéribus being so accommodating. It took a good week, however, for mine to be worked out at Barbentane between my father and the comte—Madame de Montcalm having been deployed to ensure that Angelina and I were never alone together, and the gorgon who was dispatched to watch us considerably hampering our liberty to exchange the kisses and innocent caresses that even the most careful parents normally allow engaged couples. Moreover, as soon as Samarcas left, Larissa attached herself to her sister like her shadow, and always sat quietly nearby, her eyes lowered but, I imagined, her ears devouring our every word, just as her eyes would have devoured me had she dared break the tablets of the law that was imposed on her.

This gorgon was a kind of intendant in the service of the comtesse—there being twice as many servants at Barbentane as there were at Mespech, even though Montcalm was only half as rich as my father, as became obvious during the discussion of the marriage contract. Moreover, I couldn't tell whether Monsieur de Montcalm was the one who had imposed such rigid conditions on our courtship, or whether his wife invented them out of her own bitter chastity, but whenever my face approached Angelina's beautiful visage, as inevitably drawn to her as a horse is by the tender green grass of spring, the gorgon began to cough and repeat in the most unpleasant tones:

"Be kind enough, Monsieur, to keep your distance!"

Angelina would sigh at this and Larissa, an octave lower, would utter a deep groan, her eyes always lowered, but seeming to share her twin's every pleasure in the moment and drink in my compliments and sweet nothings as if they were addressed to her.

As for me, I was so annoyed by the tyranny of this old hag—who, though her hair didn't harbour snakes like the original gorgon, secreted poison from her heart that made her the enemy of all life and tenderness—that I dared ask my beloved, while the monster, a heavy drinker, was away for a moment to search for some wine, if she would meet me at nightfall in the same turret of the east tower where she'd pledged her faith to me back in 1567. If at first she hesitated to agree to this illicit assignation, the memory of this earlier moment was so dear to her that she ended up by agreeing to meet me. My request, though delivered in a whisper, was, sadly, loud enough for Larissa to overhear, though Angelina trusted her implicitly, since neither sister had ever betrayed the other: they maintained such a friendship—or, rather, an incredibly unshakeable and intimate love for each other—that neither feared sharing her thoughts and plans with the other.

Towards sunset, I took my leave of Angelina, Larissa and the gorgon, and withdrew to my room, where I remained for a while, musing and waiting for darkness to fall, at which point I hurried to my post in the turret, a small shelter in the chateau wall, pierced by loopholes from which one could fire on any assailants attempting to scale the east wall, which rose some fifteen toises above the moat. Although the night was chilly, with a north wind blowing constantly on the ramparts, the turret itself was sheltered from the wind, and its stones still warm from the day's sun, and I rubbed my hand along their rough surface, enjoying their texture. I felt as secure in this little enclosure as a silkworm in its cocoon, protected as I was from the breeze, and my heart full with the excitement of our meeting, my limbs shaking with a crazy pleasure at the idea of finally holding Angelina in my arms.

I heard her heels on the stones of the ramparts, and suddenly, the night being fairly clear, I saw her in the doorway of the turret, turning sideways to get her dress through the opening; as I reached out to greet her, to my great surprise she didn't take my arms, but threw her own about my neck, pulling me close and kissing me passionately. Although I returned her kisses, I couldn't help thinking that it was very unlike Angelina, given her natural modesty, to throw herself at me so quickly and with such tumult as I would only wish to share with her when we had exchanged rings. And this thought ultimately carrying the day against the agitation of my senses, I pulled her hands from my neck and held them at arms' length, pushing her away and searching her face in an attempt to get a better look at her in the semi-darkness. "Angelina, what is this?" I asked.

I don't know whether she would have answered—I couldn't see her eyes because her lids were closed—but, in any case, she didn't have time to respond. A deep, sonorous voice behind her intoned: "You're mistaken, Monsieur de Siorac. It's not Angelina who's here. It's Larissa."

I looked up and guessed (rather than recognized him in the darkness, through which all I could make out was his lace collar) that this dark silhouette must be Samarcas, with his large shoulders practically touching both sides of the turret that enclosed us.

"What?" I gasped, dropping her hands. "Larissa? Is that you? What trickery and dastardly pretence! Have you no shame?"

"Monsieur de Siorac," replied Samarcas, whose deep voice resonated strangely around the cylindrical turret, "I beg you to remember your Christian charity—Larissa, despite her age, is only a child. In her thinking and behaviour, she's still the age she was when she was locked in that convent"—and, at the mention of this memory, I could see her begin to tremble from head to foot—"torn from Barbentane, from her loving and amiable parents, and above all, from her twin sister, without whom her being was ripped from its better half."

"But, Monsieur," I answered, more touched by his words than I would have wished, "was Larissa trying to fool me and usurp the role her sister was supposed to have had?"

"I'm afraid that she doesn't really know if she *is* her sister or not, she wants so much to be her!" replied Samarcas urgently. "Which is why she's trying so desperately to hide under her make-up the mole that alone distinguishes her from Angelina. Monsieur," he continued, with a tone of such quiet authority that I could not but obey, "your hand!"

Then, seizing her with his left hand, he imprisoned Larissa's head in the crook of his arm, and, guiding my index finger between her chin and mouth, he made me touch the mole.

"Can you feel it?" he asked. "By this little projection, which cannot be felt under Angelina's make-up—which she paints on her face out of love for her twin—you will always be able to recognize Larissa—if you wish to." (These last words were said in the most menacing tone imaginable.)

"But I'm not Larissa," Larissa cried suddenly, raising her head and stamping her foot. "I'm Angelina! Larissa is all malice and wickedness and in the sway of the Devil!"

"Quiet, you!" snarled Samarcas, and, seizing her wrists from behind, he pulled her forcefully to him. "And that's enough of your mischief! I won't suffer it! Do I have to whip you? Or do you want to be sent back to the convent?"

"Oh no! Oh no! Oh no!" begged Larissa, and suddenly, as if the air had gone out of her, she wilted and seemed to give in entirely to Samarcas. Seeing this, the Jesuit freed her hands, and Larissa, turning round to face him, encircled his waist with her hands and put her head on his shoulder, remaining quietly in this filial posture, as docile as a baby.

"From now on," soothed Samarcas with a sweetness that astonished me, and placing his hand on the head of his pupil, "remember that you are Larissa, that you must keep this body free of evil, and that if you sin, you will be pardoned as long as your confession is true and sincere."

"Amen," whispered Larissa in a tiny, almost inaudible voice.

"Monsieur de Siorac," the Jesuit continued in his sonorous voice, which seemed to fill my head, so thoroughly did it resonate in the little turret, "you can now understand and measure by what's happened here just how much your arrival in Barbentane has created terrible confusion in this poor head. Since there is no reason that this trouble should spread to other members of this noble family, which has already suffered so much, may I ask that you not mention what's happened here to anyone? And may I also entreat you"—and here I heard the same menacing tone infuse this request, which was an entreaty in name only—"to swear on your honour that you will prevent any future repetition of such a mistake, now that you have the means to prevent it?"

"Monsieur," I replied firmly and coldly, "this 'mistake', as you put it, was not mine, and it is not for me to engage my honour in preventing its recurrence, since my honour was never in question in this matter—nor, for that matter, in any other."

At this, he bowed slightly and as stiffly as my tone seemed to warrant, and, taking Larissa by the hand, drew her after him out of the turret and onto the catwalk, and then disappeared.

"'Sblood!" I thought, nearly unhinged. "He all but challenged me to a duel! Good God! A duel! Here! And with a Jesuit! This Samarcas must feel very secure in his famous Jesuit sword thrust! By living in the world, he's certainly adopted worldly ways! His tone is unctuous, but ultimately he challenges, prances and defies men like the most jealous and furious of husbands!"

Gradually my anger subsided and, as I began to reflect on what had just transpired, I resolved not to obey the first of Samarcas's injunctions, but instead that, while I would hide Larissa's mischief from her parents and my father, I would tell Giacomi all about it, since he seemed to feel some interest and compassion for this poor girl, and Angelina as well, who should not remain in the dark regarding the awful encounter between her twin and me—also, quite simply, because I felt some obligation on my part to reveal to her what had happened.

I thought I must be dreaming when I suddenly heard the sound of her heels on the stone pathway, and when, by the light of the risen moon, I saw her profile enter sideways through the narrow door of the turret, and felt her take my outstretched hands, but without approaching further, appearing somewhat ashamed to be meeting with me in secret at this hour and in such an enclosed place. Seeing this, and observing that she was out of breath from the emotion of the moment, I renounced—at least for the moment—the pleasure of exchanging a kiss with her and kept my distance (as the gorgon would have us do), and recounted what had happened with Larissa, a story that I believe she listened to attentively, but, due to the darkness, I couldn't really see her face or her expression, except for the wonderful luminosity of her large black eyes. When I'd finished, she remained silent for a while, sighed deeply and, in a voice that didn't betray a trace of anger or bitterness, said,

"Ah, the poor girl! She would like to be me: that's the entire story! She's wanted this since we were in swaddling clothes, suffering so much from her unfortunate mole, which caused her to feel so terribly worthless, sure that she was inferior to me and so undeserving that she would have destroyed everything if we'd let her. So that's why the Devil, seeing that she was divided against herself, could get inside her!"

This view of the Devil left me aghast, though of course I understood that Angelina was just repeating what she'd heard, not wishing to contradict a theory that was so generally accepted by those around her that it had become "the truth". On the other hand, I didn't want to endorse it, so I decided that humour would be the best way out:

"The Devil's a busy fellow! Was it the Devil who pushed her to let that little page into her bed?"

"Assuredly so!" Angelina replied with tranquil certainty. "Who else? My mother, as my cousin must have told you, was very fond of this fellow, who was pretty enough to eat, lively and amiable, played the viol beautifully and wrote verse as well. I loved him as a girl loves at that age, madly, but never permitted him any intimacies, and ultimately it was I who infected Larissa with this ill-fated passion."

"But how did it happen, if Larissa wanted so much to resemble you, that she was unable to maintain her modesty and self-esteem in this affair?"

"Because," she answered in the most matter-of-fact way, "the Devil had already got possession of her."

"Well," I thought, feeling unable to shake this unbreakable certainty, "I'll never get to the bottom of this 'truth'—all I seem to be able to do is scratch the surface!"

"But," I added, "if I'm to judge by what happened tonight in this turret, can we believe that the Devil has completely left her?"

"But that's precisely the point!" corrected Angelina in a voice tinged with worry and sadness. "Father Samarcas, who's venerated here as if he were a great saint, believes that the Devil, having left Larissa, is still residing on the outskirts of her soul, and at the first occasion will insinuate himself back into her if he doesn't watch over her. Which is why, in his great saintliness and marvellous devotion to this soul whom he has saved, he doesn't want her out of his sight, day or night."

"What, at night as well?"

"Oh, especially at night. He sleeps in a little cabinet adjoining her room, both bolted from within and protected by heavy oak shutters over the windows. Father Samarcas considers Larissa to be under siege by an evil spirit during the night, and that he is the garrison who defends her."

This gave me much food for thought, and might have given me much to question if I hadn't been convinced that Angelina was too rigidly set in these beliefs to be able to listen to my doubts. It's a strange error that many fall prey to, to imagine that the wench that we're madly in love with would be the least disposed, in marrying us, to marry our opinions and philosophies as well. Far from it—and even further in this case, since Angelina was a papist and I am of the reformed religion, which, as everyone knows, is little inclined to accept the immense power that the direction of their souls gives priests over Catholic families.

Ever since my arrival here, it had become obvious to my stupefied eyes (and to those of my father, who was quite scandalized by it) that Father Anselm and the Jesuit Samarcas, amiably sharing their immense power (despite the little love they bore for each other), governed every aspect of life at Barbentane: the one because he was the comte's confessor, the other because Larissa was his pupil. To view the situation with open eyes, it was not Monsieur de Montcalm but Father Anselm who gave me Angelina in marriage, along with the condition that he had imposed and that, good Huguenot though I was, I could not fail to obey. Likewise, it wasn't the comte but the Jesuit Samarcas who had decided that Larissa would never marry, since the demon that was lurking on the "outskirts of her soul" might then reinvade the city.

Angelina stood silently in the shadows of the turret while I was thus lost in thought, but at length I took her very gently in my arms and gave her a few kisses, but very respectfully, and without hugging her to me, especially since I was still feeling sad about Larissa's punishment, sensing that she'd destroyed the charm of the moment—and Samarcas even more so. The events of the evening had sadly taught me the great extent to which I was a stranger both to this family that I was going to enter and, worse still, to the sweet woman whom I loved.

I shared these feelings with Giacomi that next morning in the fencing room, while we were catching our breath on a small bench set in the recess of a window, our legs extended in front of us, his well beyond mine.

"In order for Angelina to see Samarcas as you do," lisped Giacomi, "you just need to be patient. That's what's usually required in human affections. Should I be sorry for you?" he smiled. "You who love and are loved?"

"Ah, Giacomi," I joked, "are you in love with someone who doesn't love you?"

But to this he made no answer; instead, eyes lowered, his face suddenly very serious, he began tracing indecipherable signs on the floor with the point of his sword. At length he said, "If I were you, I wouldn't resent Larissa. The poor girl calls for infinite compassion. And isn't it a pity that, the Devil having renounced her soul, it has been taken over by this other, whom everyone here treats like one of the great saints!"

"Monsieur," came a voice from the other end of the hall, "would you do me the favour of crossing swords with me in a friendly bout?"

Absorbed as I had been by what Giacomi was saying, and by my vain attempt to decipher the arabesques he'd been tracing on the floor, I hadn't heard the door open, but, raising my head, I saw Samarcas standing at the threshold, sword in hand, a smile on his lips belying the fire in his eyes.

4

THE DOUBLE MARRIAGE of the Baron de Quéribus to my sister Catherine and myself to Angelina de Montcalm was celebrated on 16th November 1574 in the chapel of the Château de Barbentane, after I'd solemnly sworn on my salvation "to hear Mass wherever and whenever I find myself in a Catholic household and to allow my lady and wife to raise the fruits of our union in the faith of her ancestors". My father had also been required to adhere to this condition when he had married Isabelle de Caumont, the difference being that at that time he hadn't yet pledged his faith to the Huguenot religion, so that I was raised in the Catholic faith until the age of ten. And thus, as I swore on my faith to abide by the condition imposed by Father Anselm, I again found myself, now twenty-five years old, neither fish nor fowl—or, as the Baron de Mespech put it so delicately, with my arse between two stools. This situation troubled me less than it had my father, since I have no love for religious zeal of any kind, having seen with my own eyes both the massacre of the Catholics in the "Michelade" in Nîmes and the slaughter of our people in Paris on 23rd and 24th August 1572. Which is not to say that I'd become, like Fogacer, a complete sceptic, but I believed that the sincerity of one's worship was of much greater importance than the form, since the Roman Church is so troubled with errors, inventions and superstitions.

My father, who had such a strong sense of his manorial duties back in Mespech, wished to depart Barbentane virtually the day after the wedding, but Monsieur de Montcalm would hear nothing of it, arguing that Mespech had begun its winter season by now, and that all the work of the harvest, grape-pressing and gathering of nuts and firewood would be finished, and hence the presence of the master in his household was no longer so necessary. And although my father disagreed with the comte, feeling that the master's presence was useful even in winter, when there was still much to be done, he also realized that both Catherine and I would doubtless be settling in Paris, and that there might be many months, perhaps even years, between our visits, given how perilous travel was during that unsettled era in the kingdom. And so he agreed to my sister's repeated requests—and to mine as well—that he give in to his affection for us and delay his return to Périgord, at least for as long as Monsieur de Montcalm would need to settle his affairs before leaving for the capital.

I was delighted with this decision, since the unbelievable joy I felt at being united with Angelina at long last would have been tempered by the sting of my father's sudden departure, and by the sadness that engulfed me whenever I thought of how Jean de Siorac was going to find himself very alone in Mespech, deprived of Sauveterre—and now also of Samson, Catherine and me—in his old age, despite his sprightliness, suffering bitterly from the emptiness created by our absence. It made me even sadder to imagine myself alone in Mespech without the children I hadn't yet had. Is it not a pity, when you think about it, that, as the ribbon of our life unremittingly unravels, and the advancing years inevitably sap our strength, we should also have to be diminished by the flight from the nest of the progeny of our flesh and blood?

I was somewhat relieved when, the day after our double marriage, Samarcas, who wasn't coping well with the evident interest Giacomi was showing Larissa, suddenly decided to depart for Reims, carrying off his pupil in his terrible talons—thereby causing much grief to the Italian, but, by the same token, ending the malaise that my own ambiguous relationship to Larissa was causing me. And how could it not have been thus, since neither my heart nor my body could remain indifferent to one who so thoroughly resembled my beloved in looks, though not in the matter of corruption, which was so troubling to me? For at the very same time that I was endeavouring to knock down, one by one, Angelina's bastions of modesty, Larissa's fortress was so invitingly weak and undone that it would have required no effort to overcome it. All of her senses were awakened, begging for attention, where my dear wife's were still dormant. And so, when I met her in a corridor, her large eyes fixed on mine, and her hand brushing against mine, I recognized her by the way my senses began to tremble at her silent appeal.

Samarcas led me to believe that he was travelling to Reims to visit the famous Jesuit seminary there, but from a few hints dropped by Larissa I gathered that they were only stopping in Reims before going on to London.

"So what the devil," Giacomi asked when we were alone in the fencing room, "is this demon going to do in a country which has so few Catholics? *Chi lo sa?*"*

"You seem to know the answer!" I laughed. "Your tone tells me in no uncertain terms that you think he's up to some dastardly business, evil as he is!"

"Indeed, that's exactly what I think! He's a man for whom the darkest ends justify the most savage deeds. Did you notice that if I hadn't been totally on my guard, he would have skewered me like a roasting pigeon during our last scrimmage?"

"Good God! Did he touch you?"

"Not on your life! I parried his thrust! But with a shameless parry—not with my blade but with my arms! Blessed Virgin, I'm still embarrassed! And I was so furious at that moment that I engaged his

---

* "Who can tell?"

blade with mine and made it fly from his hands. Ah Pierre, if his eye had been a pistol, he would have dispatched me! But that was only for an instant, for he quickly regained his calm, picked up his sword, resheathed it and said in that sonorous bass voice he's so proud of, '*Maestro*, is that the famous "Jarnac's thrust"?'"

"'Heavens no, *padre*—if I'd used that, you'd have been crippled for life!'

"'But with this one, you had me at your mercy! And with those two tricks,' he joked, but with a black flame lighting his eye under those dark eyebrows, 'you could go a long way! *Maestro*,' he continued with a suave but menacing smile, 'if I were the Grand Inquisitor of Spain, I'd torture your tricks right out of you!'

"'But *padre*, I'm a good Catholic!'

"'Who could claim to be so,' he said, eyes blazing, 'who frequents Huguenots?'

"'Anyone who hears Mass.'

"'With half an ear! But *maestro*,' he continued tapping his hand on his scabbard, 'thank you so much for showing me that you can't be persuaded by arms!'

"'Persuaded?' I said, surprised. 'What's this evangelical language?'

"'I wouldn't put it any other way,' he hissed. 'You've understood me well enough.'

"And at that he made a deep bow and left—and, Pierre, believe me, this man is more beholden to the Devil than to God, I'd swear it on my life! And it makes me choke with rage that he should hold sway over Larissa!"

"Ah," I thought, observing his furious wrath, "my Giacomi, love surely changes a man!"

"And do you know what I've learnt form Angelina?" I said. "This man requested and obtained from Monsieur de Montcalm 1,000 écus for the 'education and welfare' of his pupil."

"Surely you don't think I'm surprised!" snarled Giacomi. "The snake couldn't help but be an extortioner! *Samarcas è un uomo che scorticare un pedocchio per avere la pelle.*"*

I laughed at this, of course, not wishing to believe Samarcas to be as evil and zealous on questions of religion as Giacomi portrayed him, but—alas!—I could certainly think of Huguenots in Nîmes and Montpellier, and even Huguenot ministers like Monsieur de Gasc, who were easily his equal in this respect. On the other hand, in my attempt to maintain an even-handed position, I well understood that the Montcalms, though they pushed their veneration of Samarcas beyond reasonable limits, were not wrong to feel some gratitude towards him. Whatever methods he'd used to cure Larissa, and whatever the nature of the strange control he exercised over her (though in this regard I had a theory which I'm not yet ready to share), I had to admit that he had succeeded where others had failed and had managed to wrest Larissa from the clutches of the prison-like convent where she was wasting away, and the poor girl clearly owed to him, and him alone, the reflowering of her life.

Angelina shed some tears at her sister's departure, which I drank from her fresh cheeks, doing everything I could to calm her. And, while I'm on the subject, I will repeat that I disagree with what Michel de Montaigne told me when I visited him in his tower: that I should be very careful not to caress my future wife, for fear that such extravagances of amorous licence should unhinge her reason. On the contrary! I believe a man should teach his life's companion the delicious enhancements that make love-making so intense and so pleasurable! Is it reasonable to set to work on her quickly and precipitously like a dog, leaving her no possibility of feeling anything? Isn't it better to awaken her senses little by little? And should we forgo the immense pleasure of

---

* "Samarcas is a man who would flail a louse to get his pelt!"

exploring the provinces of her body with touch and tongue, and the enjoyment of seeing in her visage and hearing in her voice the signs of the pleasure we've afforded her?

If man must enter life alone and exit it alone, I pray that at least he be not alone in the moment of his conjunction with his life's partner, so that from this conjunction a new life will come, convinced as I am that there's no solitude worse than that of pleasure received without pleasure given. The soldier who rapes girls and women in the sacking of a city doesn't hold in his arms a being, but rather a thing, so that possession and destruction, for this desperate villain, amount to the same thing. That's not pleasure. It is—I'll say it again—a sad and bestial solitude. But the body isn't as important as are caring, tenderness, generosity and human consideration, when the first duty of a husband is to bring his wife, by delaying if necessary his own, the pleasure that it would be basely selfish to deny her. And when you consider that the Creator bestowed this pleasure on her in compensation for the pain of pregnancy and childbirth, then we should be doubly grateful for our own pleasure, since He's spared us the suffering she must endure.

We'd been at Barbentane for two months already, Monsieur de Montcalm being in no hurry to prepare his own departure, when my father sent Fröhlich (now serving as his valet) to ask me to join him in his rooms. As I arrived, I was happy to see a lively little chambermaid name Jeannotte just leaving, whom my father had been eyeing lately, but was surprised to see him looking more surly than I would have expected given the amiable company we'd been keeping.

"Father," I asked as pleasantly as I could, "what's wrong? Why so grumpy? Did Jeannotte displease you?"

"Not at all!" he replied. "Thank goodness the wench is amiable enough. But alas I have other worries. Here, read this letter from François that I just received." He handed me the missive and threw himself scornfully onto his armchair, crossing his legs impatiently and watching me closely as I read the note from my brother:

Dear Father,

I have only good news to share with you about Mespech. Everyone—including our animals and servants—is well, and I'm managing the chateau according to your wishes.

I regret, however, that I must inform you that, finally, I have converted to the Holy Roman and Apostolic Church, finding no other way to marry Diane, divide up her estate with Puymartin or inherit the title of Baron de Fontenac, which will be mine with the first male child she provides me.

The bishop of Sarlat wanted to make much of my conversion, and celebrated it in the cathedral. I suspected that these circumstances would be sad and painful for you, and so I preferred to convert in your absence and beg you not to resent me for it. I desire nothing more than your affection and assure you that I will, till the end of time, be,

With all my heart, your humble, obedient and devoted servant,

François de Siorac

"Well," sighed my father, "what do you think?"

Of course, I was in an awkward position, not at all liking the stiff tone of this very correct letter, but not wishing to criticize my older brother (though, in truth, I didn't like him) and feeling, almost in spite of myself, some sympathy for his reasons. "What do I think?" I temporized.

"Yes, tell me!"

"That I don't know what I myself would have done, if I'd been in François's predicament, given that the bishop of Sarlat is not as accommodating as Father Anselm."

"I just want you to say, Pierre," said the Baron de Mespech, "that you would have consulted me *before* you acted!"

"Assuredly so! But François is François: he wouldn't have dared confront you."

"In short, he's a coward!" cried my father as he stood up abruptly and, frowning, began pacing back and forth in the room. "And what's worse," he continued furiously, "a Catholic coward!"

"Well, not entirely a coward," I observed. "If, someday, someone tries to take something from him, he'll fight tooth and nail!"

"Don't defend him!" cried my father, suddenly drunk with rage. "That little hypocrite knew full well even before my departure that he was going to change sides, and said nothing to me! And now he tells me in this note that he 'desires nothing more than my affection'! And this 'with all his heart'! But—'sblood!—would he have dared to switch camps while Sauveterre was alive, and still in Mespech? Oh, Pierre, I'm devastated to think that our Huguenot faith will have lasted but the length of my brief life, the second Baron de Mespech returning to the Catholic faith like a dog to his vomit, along with all my grandchildren—all of them! The sons and daughters of François—and Samson! And Catherine! And you as well!—will be raised and nursed on papist idolatries from the minute they're in swaddling clothes!"

I fell silent for a few moments and walked to the window to look out on the daylight dropping in the west over the stony hills of Provence—more luminous than our Périgord but less verdant—having no idea how to answer my father, understanding his immense grief at seeing his religion abandoned successively by his descendants, even including me, alas, who loved him so well.

"Ah, Father," I urged, after much reflection, "forgive François: his conversion isn't, sadly enough, an isolated thing, but one among innumerable others after the twenty-fourth of August last. That's the second harvest of the St Bartholomew's day massacre: after so much grain cut down and crushed underfoot, now the priests are gleaning what's left. Everyone lives in peril of death. You yourself, in order to appease the bishop of Sarlat, agreed to make a gift of land to the Capuchin monks, and invited Pincers to Mespech to say a Mass for our papist guests. I myself gave an écu to Pincers to have an idol regilded, and from now on, against my soul and body, I will be hearing Mass every day we remain here, being forced to become a Janus with two faces, one Catholic and the other Huguenot, like the Sephardim of Montpellier, who pay lip service to papism but remain faithful to their Jewish roots and traditions."

"But the difference is that you go to Mass!" groaned my father.

"I *hear* it," I smiled, "but as the saying goes, listening with only one ear to the fields and with the other to the city—secretly a stranger to this Roman cult."

"*You* do perhaps, Pierre, but will your children?" asked Jean de Siorac with a sudden wave of tenderness that clouded his eyes with tears; and, stepping over to me, he threw his arms around me and embraced me tightly. "But your children! Your grandchildren!"

"I shall make very sure that they hear from my lips the unspeakable persecutions that we suffered at the hands of the priests. And who knows whether some of our family won't, when things become less dangerous for us, return to the purity of our faith?"

"And yet, Pierre," mused the Baron de Mespech, looking askance at me, "it seems to me that, of my four children, you are perhaps the least zealous of the lot on the question of religion. How does that happen?"

"It is because I hold zeal in great disdain, having seen the terrifying effects of it in Nîmes and in Paris. But, Father," I continued, not wishing to get into a debate with him, "I beg you to allow me to withdraw. I promised Angelina to help her choose between two dresses for the evening meal, and she's waiting for me in her room."

"Well then, don't delay any longer!" laughed my father. "The choice of which jewellery she will wear is very important to a woman in her wish to please us and please herself. If the gentle sex didn't take so much care in their adornments, where would we find such beauty in our daily lives?"

The day finally came when it was time to take our leave of this excellent man and set out for Paris, leaving him to return to Périgord and live in a kind of double solitude at Mespech: that of a father abandoned by his children, and the equally bitter solitude of one who must watch his children turn their backs on the religion that not only had been the founding principle of their lives together, but was to have been the glue that bound a Huguenot line that joined their material prosperity to the truth of their purified beliefs.

Oh, such tears were shed at this parting, both by my sister Catherine, as enamoured as she was of her Quéribus (with whom she seemed to be floating on a cloud of mad happiness), and by my Angelina, whose natural compassion told her how painful this separation was for the Baron de Mespech. But I have to add, without any shame whatsoever, that I too wept to be separated from this man, whom I cherished as much for his good and pure mettle as for certain weaknesses that we shared and that had drawn us even closer.

I was to remember the raw bitterness of this parting several years later when, hearing Mass with the king in the chapel at the Hôtel de Bourbon (opposite the Louvre), I observed two lords who had entered the chapel in the king's retinue, but who appeared to be listening to the Catholic service with a sad and bitter expression, as if what they were hearing made them sick to their stomachs. And Fogacer, being seated next to me, and his sharp eyes noticing the direction I was looking in, smiled at me with a knowing look, but said not a word. A few moments later, as we were standing in the Salle des Caryatides, waiting to be summoned by the king, leaning against one of those giant statues sculpted by Jean Goujon, my friend asked me whether, as a great petticoat-chaser, I wouldn't be overwhelmed by the giant stature of these wenches were they to suddenly come alive, and I replied, laughing, "Not at all!" And, as I added in English, "You can't have too much of a good thing!" I suddenly remembered the two grave faces of the gentlemen we'd seen at Mass, and asked Fogacer who they were and why I hadn't seen them at court before. He told me their names (which I won't repeat here) and added, sotto voce, "They're like you, *mi fili*, lip-service Catholics but Huguenots at heart, who've just arrived here and whom the king has asked to 'trim their sails' if they want to serve him."

"Trim their sails? What does that mean?"

"It's a nautical term that His Majesty learnt recently and likes to use. It means reduce the size of your sails when the wind gets too blustery."

"Ah, certainly, God knows that's how things are!"

"And, *assuredly*, God knows that's how things are!" smiled Fogacer. "*Mi fili*, what's the point of hearing Mass if you betray it by this 'certainly'?" To which he added, "'Certainly! Certainly!' says the Huguenot, for he's a man full of certitudes."

"And the papist?"

"The papists are full of zeal. And, as I see it, very few of them today would allow themselves to be burnt at the stake for their faith."

"Would the king die for his faith?"

"My dear chevalier," replied Fogacer (using the title the king had conferred on me but a week previously, along with a small estate in Montfort-l'Amaury called "the Rugged Oak"), "don't say 'the king'— say, simply, 'Henri'. That way, if someone overhears you, they won't know whether you're referring to the Duc de Guise, Henri de Navarre or 'Henri the One-third', who's mocked by this sobriquet because the other two are making such inroads into his kingdom."

"What an ugly and thoroughly demeaning expression," I whispered, "which you'd be wise not to repeat!"

"Well, it's because I've got a sharp tongue myself," smiled Fogacer, arching his diabolical eyebrow, "though my heart is faithful to Henri."

"But, venerable Dr Know-it-all, you haven't answered my question about Henri's religious convictions."

"That's because it's a debatable point. Henri loves monks, the monastery and the cowl. He goes on pilgrimages. He goes on retreats. He walks in processions."

"I know all that. He even puts on the hair shirt of the penitent and girds himself with a belt ringed with skulls."

"He whips himself as well. But do you know why?" Fogacer continued, his eyes ablaze. "It's because he's trying to assuage his conscience, and, every time he does this, he immediately goes back to the trough of his usual delights."

"Curb that evil tongue of yours! Answer me! Do you think Henri would die for his faith?"

"He'd probably more likely die for the faith of others, given that the Church is pushing Guise to hem him in both geographically and personally."

"I'm astonished to hear you say so," I laughed. "In the ten years that I've served him, I've heard Henri defend his zeal for serving the Church and for extirpating heresy at least ten times."

"He's *trimming his sails*!" replied Fogacer with that sinuous smile of his. "It's a manoeuvre that serves Henri very well in tempestuous times. And, as you yourself said, the Devil knows that we're in for some stormy weather!"

"I never mentioned the Devil! I said 'God knows'!"

"And you really believe it's God who's breathing such fire and brimstone on our poor kingdom?"

*

I hope the reader will pardon this intrusive leap forward from 1574, the date of my marriage and my move to Paris, to 1584, a fateful year for the kingdom and for my good master "Henri the One-third". The truth is that the ten intervening years were, for me, as calm and peaceful as a freshwater river winding through a prairie, and I feared boring my reader with tales of my domestic happiness. Not that there weren't troubles and difficulties during those years, notably caused by the king's brother, but in the main they seemed quite tranquil by comparison with the torrents of agitation and angry white-water rapids that engulfed us all in 1584.

It was on 6th May of that year that the first dark clouds appeared in the sky of France, announcing the storms that were to tear the kingdom apart and shake the throne. And I remember it was my handsome brother-in-law Quéribus who first brought me the news, one afternoon when he and my sister Catherine were visiting us in our lodgings on the rue du Champ-Fleuri, situated just a couple of steps from the Louvre. They were both waiting for us as I returned from the Louvre with Angelina, who was carrying our one-year-old, Olivier, her fifth child. Quéribus was magnificently decked out as usual, in a salmon-coloured doublet, grey stockings and a large lace ruff, his curly hair carefully arranged in ringlets under his pearl-studded cap, a diamond earring in his left ear, and wearing rings over his gloves on both hands. For our gallant, this was a somewhat modest ensemble compared to the sumptuous outfits he wore to court balls; he had at least a hundred costumes in his wardrobe that were as elegant as this one—enough so that he could wear a different suit every day, not wishing to be shamed by other glittery competitors in the presence of his king. Did I forget to mention the brown velvet cape he'd thrown over his shoulders, without which no gallant at the court would have dared show himself, even in the hottest weather?

I knew Quéribus was in my lodgings even before closing the door and spying him there, since the odour of his perfume outdid in strength the combined applications of Catherine and Angelina.

And, indeed, scarcely had I set foot in the dining hall before I saw him rushing towards me, arms outstretched, his face more heavily made up than those of most of the ladies of the court, his eyes darkened with mascara and his face so covered in ceruse that he avoided giving me the customary pecks on both cheeks, but threw his arm over my shoulders and lamented, "Ah, Pierre! Things are going from bad to worse in the kingdom. The king's brother is dying!"

"What! Are you sure?"

"'Tis certain! I heard it from Marc Miron. As sickly as he already was, all dried out, bony, exhausted, Alençon's now coughing his lungs out."

"Well, by heaven, I won't go mourning him!"

"Nor shall I!" agreed Quéribus.

"But stay!" cried Angelina in her usual concerned and caring way. "Will there be no one in the kingdom to shed a tear over this, our brother, who's dying?"

"This 'brother'," corrected Quéribus, "was an execrable brother to our king. He raised armies against him. He created problems and fomented conflicts of all kinds. He's a traitor to his blood! Unfaithful to his brother and sovereign."

"It's true," conceded Catherine, "that Alençon is excessively ugly: small-boned, dark as a prune, his legs all bent, his face all swollen and pockmarked from smallpox. There was never a more despicable little runt in the whole of the Valois family!"

"And his soul is worse than his face," added Quéribus, "being both cruel and cowardly."

"Cruel?" said Angelina.

"Ah, there's no doubt about it!" I confirmed. "In Issoire, Alençon had seventy-seven peasants murdered after they'd surrendered."

"Well, as for that," laughed the baron, "the Huguenots are like the Hydra of Lerna! Cut off one head and seven grow back!"

"Monsieur!" scolded Catherine, frowning haughtily. "If you make fun of my Huguenot relatives, you'll find the door of my chambers closed to you tonight!"

"Madame my wife," soothed Quéribus, kneeling before her, taking her hands in his and kissing them tenderly, "to such a punishment I'd prefer the wheel and rack! Forgive my little joke, I pray you!... The fact remains," he added as he stood up, "that Alençon has been a calamity for this kingdom. He never contributed a thing to the welfare of France. And the worst part is that, having ill-served the king while alive, his death will be even worse for His Majesty."

"But how can that be?" asked Angelina. "Can he really do any damage when he's dead?"

"Alas, he can!" Quéribus explained. "His death raises the thorny question of succession, since, after ten years of marriage, Henri still has no heir. Alençon would have succeeded him, just as Henri succeeded Charles IX and Charles his brother François II."

"But the Blessed Virgin may yet grant him a child," ventured Angelina. "My sweet sister Catherine was childless for seven years before she brought fruit."

"Assuredly, the Lord was gracious to me," agreed Catherine, who, in her Huguenot heart (though she was, like me, constrained to hear Mass), could not bring herself to name the Virgin Mary as the author of this divine gift.

"Which is why," Quéribus observed, "the king has spent the last two days wearing out his royal shoes in pilgrimages from Notre-Dame de Paris to Notre-Dame de Chartres, and has got nothing more out of it than severely blistered feet, which the Chevalier de Siorac has been treating."

"Which chevalier," I laughed, "has been treating his own as well, and had to resole his shoes when he got back, though I've heard that His Majesty simply tossed his away, since he wasn't raised with a Huguenot sense of economy."

As I was saying this, our hungry little Olivier raised an ear-splitting cry, and Angelina immediately unlaced her bodice and gave him her breast, because I'd convinced her that no foreign breast would equal hers for milk, though I promised to find a wet nurse if her milk ever dried up. Which never happened.

We all four fell silent while this sweet spectacle continued, amazed and moved as we were by the beauty and generosity of the mother, as well as by the insatiable appetite of the little urchin.

When the babe had drunk his fill, Angelina silently signalled to me to take the child, and walk him back and forth so that the little devil would do his burp, while she relaced her bodice, looking all the while at me as if she were afraid I'd drop the nursling on the floor. At length I gave him back to her, and, as the little fellow was falling asleep in her arms, Florine came to take him from her and place him in his little cradle, which she rocked with her foot, while continuing her knitting.

"But I don't understand why this question of succession is so vexing," Catherine said. "If Heaven were not to grant Henri a son, I've heard my father say that the Bourbons would succeed the house of Valois, and that Henri de Navarre would be the legitimate heir to the throne."

"Alas, my beloved," said Quéribus, as he pulled a stool over to sit at her feet, "Navarre converted to the Roman Church after the St Bartholomew's day massacre, with a knife at his throat. But once he escaped from the Louvre, which was nothing more than a gilded prison, he reconverted to the reformed religion, and so is thought to be not only a heretic but a relapsed one, and is in great danger of being excommunicated. Do you think we'll see a heretic on the throne of France? Maybe there are some among the nobles who would accept this, but the people? Never. And the clergy would execrate him. Which is why Guise, who covets the throne but would never admit it, is promoting this idiot, the Cardinal de Bourbon, who's a Bourbon of the cadet branch, and the uncle of Navarre."

"The cadet branch!" smiled Angelina.

"And a cardinal!" said Catherine.

"And old!" laughed Quéribus.

"And," I added, laughing in turn, "having so little brain that he wouldn't know how to boil an egg, being the most brainless dotard in creation!"

"And," concluded Quéribus, laughing still harder, "being thirty years older than the present king, whom he hopes to succeed, his head is so unsteady on his shoulders the weight of the crown would probably break his neck! Not to mention holding the sceptre with his frail arms. He's got the strength of a hen—but not her brains! 'Sblood! I know why Guise is pushing this thick purple cushion onto the throne: it's so it'll be more comfortable when he himself sits on it."

And the four of us laughed our fill at the immense perils, troubles, wars and devastation that this problem of succession was creating for the kingdom.

Our laughter had scarcely died down when my good Miroul (who, ever since his marriage to Florine ten years ago, had awakened every morning in such happiness that he himself was astonished at it) came to tell us that Samson, Gertrude and Zara had just arrived. I'll leave you to imagine the noise and confusion this announcement provoked, as these ladies burst into the room with their silks and brocades and swept around embracing each of us in turn. Since Montfort-l'Amaury was a day's carriage ride from Paris, I didn't get to see Samson more than five or six times a year, so that our reunions were always accompanied by lengthy hugs and kisses and much rejoicing. Although we'd all passed the age of thirty, Gertrude was still quite beautiful, and Zara indestructibly seductive, but there was no danger in showering her with kisses, since Angelina was not the jealous type and Zara had no taste for men. When Giacomi joined us for dinner later, I could see that our pleasant mirth only served to sadden him, since Larissa would not be among our guests, as he would have hoped. So I rose from the table, took his arm and led him into the fencing gallery, which was situated in the loft, hoping to distract him from the disappointment of not having seen Larissa for three long months.

"Ah," he moaned, "what a pity to know the poor girl is in the hands of that miscreant, who, however religious he claims to be, is little better than a dagger-wielding brigand!"

"My brother," I reflected, "if he lives by the dagger, sooner or later he'll die by it. You must give as good as you get!"

"But Larissa!" cried Giacomi with a long face. "Since she's inevitably mixed up in his affairs, she'll end in the same way—or worse! What if she landed in jail? She'd fall back into her madness and would be burnt for being possessed by the Devil!"

I found nothing to say to this, having no doubt that Samarcas was involved in some very nasty business that frequently required suspicious trips to London, so Giacomi's fears seemed to me all too well founded.

Our discussion was interrupted by Miroul, who announced that there was a fellow at the door in a large black coat, who'd asked him to tell me he had a matter of consequence to share with me concerning my family, but who refused to give his name. I stuck a pistol in my belt, giving one also to Giacomi, and the two of us unsheathed our swords and went downstairs. This nocturnal visit seemed so suspicious that I asked Miroul to put a lantern in the upstairs window to determine whether others might be waiting nearby.

"Monsieur," I said, opening the peephole but not putting my eye to it, fearing a pistol shot. "Who are you and what do you want?"

"Are you the Chevalier de Siorac?"

"The same!"

"In that case, I have business with you and I beg you to let me in."

"Monsieur," I countered, "it's dark out, and you refuse to tell me your name. I must be careful. Are you armed?"

"I have a pistol and a sword, just as you do… And as Giacomi does, and the Baron de Quéribus, and his escort of five men who are dining in your kitchens—and not counting your valet, Miroul, who's armed with a lantern and an arquebus upstairs and who'd kill me in an instant on your signal."

"Monsieur, how is it you know so much about my household?"

"And outside your household as well, Monsieur. It's my business to know other people's business, which is how I make my living. People pay handsomely for the information I have."

"Monsieur, are you alone?"

"No. I have an escort waiting for me at the corner of the rue du Champ-Fleuri and the rue de l'Autruche. I beg you, open your door! The wet pavement's seeping through my soles and the gutter stinks to high heaven!"

"Monsieur," I countered, "I must require you to open your coat and show your hands before you come in. Don't be disturbed by the pistol I'm carrying. I'm not in the habit of dispatching men I don't know."

"Your obedient servant!" the fellow replied, holding his hands up to the peephole.

At this, I bade Giacomi to unbolt the door, while I stepped to one side, holding my pistol in my left hand and my sword in my right; the *maestro* opened the door just wide enough for the fellow to squeeze through, and then closed and bolted it immediately after the man had entered.

I brought our guest into the little cabinet with locked windows where I occasionally retired to read or compose letters, so as not to be disturbed by the play and chatter of my children.

"Monsieur," said the stranger, seating himself on a stool, "since I'm not required to tell you my real name, you can call me Mosca."

"Mosca means 'fly' in Italian," explained Giacomi.

"But also in Latin, *maestro*," said Mosca with a slight bow.

He then fell silent, studying each of us in turn by the light of the candelabra, while I returned his look with great curiosity. He looked more like a fox than a fly, with slits for eyes, a shifty and searching look, a long thin nose, an untended, bristly moustache and huge ears. It's as though his entire face had been pulled forward by his eagerness to see, hear and surprise others, and there was something about his walk that betrayed an aptitude for flight at the least sign of danger, oddly balanced by a sort of impudence, which must have stood in for courage on occasion. There was, moreover, a great deal of intelligence in his mobile and cunning expression. He was of medium height and slight of build, though not without some reserves of strength and agility, which led me to believe that this fly must have known how to sting with his sword and dagger. He was dressed all in grey, and could have been mistaken for a notary had it not been for his weapons.

"Monsieur," Mosca began with one of his usual little bows, "might I ask whether you've seen Larissa de Montcalm in Paris recently?"

Needless to say, at the mention of her name Giacomi gave an involuntary start.

"I saw her in Paris towards the end of January, I think—that is to say, about three months ago."

Mosca smiled at this, revealing a set of sharp little yellow teeth, and said, "She was here again three days ago."

"Where?" cried Giacomi.

"*Maestro*," replied Mosca, "I don't give out information *de gratis*. I sell it for hard cash."

I could tell Giacomi was on the verge of throwing his entire purse at this fellow, so I put my hand on his arm and whispered, "*Lasciatemi parlare*,"* trusting to my Huguenot sense of economy when it came to bargaining.

"Monsieur Mosca," I proposed, "since I don't know your name, I'd like at least to know your condition, since it's clear that the value of your news must in some way be connected to it."

"Monsieur," replied Mosca, after hesitating a bit, "I am called 'the fly' because I am the eyes and ears of my employer."

"And who might that be?"

"The same man whom you serve," said Mosca with his slight bow.

"And you also sell your news to him?"

"Assuredly."

"And you've already sold him the news we're bargaining about?"

"Yes."

"In that case, since my master is very fond of me, he'll give me this news *de gratis*."

"Not on your life! This news touches on state secrets, and our master is very tight-lipped about such things. Not even his mother would reveal this."

I had to think about this for a moment, but I couldn't doubt that Mosca was telling the truth, since the king was of necessity very distrustful and secretive, surrounded as he was by so many traitors, even in his throne room.

"Monsieur Mosca," I ventured, "would you sell your news to the king's enemies?"

---

* "Let me do the talking."

"Well, to do that I'd have to confess that I'd spied on them, which would be a rather dangerous enterprise for me."

"I would have thought," I smiled, "that you wouldn't wish to sell them these secrets, out of affection for our master."

"Monsieur," said Mosca, "I won't mince words. I am fond of the person you've mentioned, but I'm more fond of myself, of my neck— which I'd like to preserve—and of my purse."

"I'm beginning to enjoy your company, Monsieur!" I confessed. "You're not a hypocrite… So how much are you expecting to add to your purse tonight?"

"Ah, now that depends; if all you want to know is Larissa's whereabouts, it's twenty-five écus. If you want to know about Samarcas, it's a hundred."

"One hundred écus!"

"That's because Samarcas is involved in the secrets I've mentioned."

"Monsieur Mosca," I replied, "let's start with the whereabouts. Then we'll see about the Jesuit. Well? What's the matter? You're not talking?"

"You'll first have to untie my tongue."

And for this untying, we had to empty my purse and Giacomi's. After which, handing my purse to Miroul, I asked my valet in Provençal to go and fill it immediately from the cache he knew about, in case I wanted to know more about Samarcas.

"My thanks to you, Monsieur—and to you as well, *maestro*," Mosca said, stroking his bristly moustache with his right hand. "And thanks as well for this money, and for not resorting to force and torture to get my secrets out of me."

"Monsieur," I assured him, "I would never lay a hand on one of the king's spies."

"You have my sincere thanks for that! And I'm also going to tell you more than I'd planned to. Dame Larissa and Samarcas set sail from Dover at daybreak on the twenty-eighth of April, and disembarked in

Calais that afternoon, lodging at the Golden Ram. On the twenty-ninth, they rented a carriage to bring them to the capital, and the ostler who rented to him, being a fly from my swarm, gave them a coachman, who came and told me where they're lodging in Paris—an address that surprised me, since normally they are lodged with Monsieur de Montcalm."

And, since Mosca fell silent, Giacomi cried, "So where are they, Maître Fly?"

"Alas, *maestro*, you wouldn't be welcome there, any more than our chevalier here would. The place is inviolable. It's the abbey of Saint-Germain-des-Prés. The king himself wouldn't even dare ask such admission for members of his provostry, given how thoroughly he's drawn and quartered by every priest in Paris on Sundays."

"So how," I asked, beginning to regret the waste of my money, "can we know whether Larissa's really there?"

"Monsieur," replied Mosca archly, "I don't sell merchandise that isn't guaranteed: my information rings as true and valuable as your coins. You won't see hide nor hair of Larissa outside the walls, but if you were to post your valet near the gate of the abbey, you'll see Samarcas emerging tomorrow, sword at his side and looking very much the gentleman. But for heaven's sake, don't have him followed. I already have a fly on his tail and your man would spoil everything."

"You're having him followed? But why?"

"I beg you, Monsieur, to remember our bargain."

"Well, Monsieur, 100 écus is a lot of money!"

"It's not so much when it's a matter of state secrets."

"I know nothing about that, but have every interest in knowing!"

"You have, Monsieur, the *greatest* interest in knowing this, since unfortunately, it's linked to a lady in your family."

I saw Giacomi pale at this, and struggle to remain silent, as I had asked. And as for me, my heart was beating wildly at the thought of the peril that Larissa was in, caught in the middle of the web that the Jesuit was spinning.

"Miroul," I conceded, "count out 100 more écus for Monsieur Mosca."

Which Miroul did, but not without obvious reluctance and resentment, being deeply devoted to my interests. I wasn't much happier at the sight of these gold coins passing from my purse to Mosca's, but it was now evident that this fellow, far from being a common spy, flew far above the swarm, and was indeed their chief and guide, and that he conducted his dishonest dealings with a certain honesty—his information being both accurate and of immense consequence, not only for my family, but for the beloved sovereign whom I served. From what he'd said, Henri now appeared to be in extreme peril, and I placed no limit on the price of helping him escape from the treason and attacks that beset him on all sides.

When my poor coins had tintinnabulated sadly into Mosca's purse, he pulled the strings closed, as though he wanted to strangle it, stuffed it in a secret pocket in the side of his doublet and again stroked his fox-red moustache—with such pleasure that my stomach almost heaved at the sight.

"Monsieur," he said, seeing my discomfort, "I understand it's painful for you to part from your money, good Huguenot that you are—though you 'go under duress', as those at court who 'trim their sails' say."

"That I 'go under duress'," I repeated. "What do you mean?"

"That's the term they use for going to Mass."

"Ha," I laughed, "I had no idea! That's very clever!"

"Monsieur," replied Mosca with a slight bow, "I'm delighted to give you a good laugh. And now, listen to my story, which now belongs to you since you've paid for it. In January of this calamitous year, Queen Elizabeth of England dismissed the Spanish ambassador, whom she suspected of being the origin of all the plots that Felipe II and the

Jesuits had hatched against her. In February, she arrested a Welsh Catholic by the name of Parry, who'd tried to kill her in an ambush. This Parry was a hothead, but he'd been carefully guided by the Jesuits from the seminary in Reims."

"Reims!" I exclaimed, glancing at Giacomi.

"Yes, Reims! And from that city and from Treves emanated a whole series of attempts on the life Prince William of Orange, who is the strongest ally of the reformed Church in the Low Countries. If he were killed, the Spaniard would find it easier to impose his will on that unfortunate country. And, likewise, if Elizabeth were dispatched, it would be easier for Felipe to place Mary Stuart on the throne and conquer England."

"Conquer England!" I gasped in disbelief.

"No less, Monsieur."

"But I don't see what interest the Jesuits would have in all this," mused Giacomi.

"The Jesuits have no interest in secular matters, but they possess infinite zeal regarding spiritual ones, and in their zeal they are sincere, devoted and valiant. Their aim is to re-Catholicize England and the Low Countries. And, sadly, to reach these ends, all foul means are acceptable: war, inquisition and murder."

"Well," I said, looking Mosca in the eye, "you make me shudder, Monsieur! Queen Elizabeth, William of Orange, no doubt the Lutheran princes of Germany and… who knows? The king of Navarre! Do their dastardly plans stop with these sovereigns?"

"Not at all!" replied Mosca, lowering his eyes meaningfully.

"What?" I cried beside myself. "Our master? But he's a Catholic!"

"Not zealous enough, in the opinion of the zealots, to stamp out all the heretics, since the power of the Huguenots in his kingdom counterbalances the power of Guise."

"Will they kill him?"

"No, all they want to do is cloister him, since he loves monks so much. But you know as well as I do on what a thin thread the life of a prisoner of state hangs when he gets in the way of those in power. And, under the circumstances, those in power will be named Guise."

"Does the king know about this?"

"About this and a lot more," replied Mosca.

"Well!" I thought, now wholly terrified by what I'd heard. "I'm not surprised by my poor sovereign's distrustful and melancholy looks lately. How can one keep calm and maintain one's appetite for life when one feels the sword of Damocles hanging over one's head?"

"But," asked Giacomi, whose worries focused less on the king than on Larissa, "what's Samarcas's role in all of this?"

"Samarcas, *maestro*, has just left the seminary in Reims, like the worm from the apple, and this fruit has been expressly cultivated to nourish those worms, whose principal and ultimate goal is to make the spiritual reconquest of England."

"By assassination?"

"Among other dastardly methods. But I beg you to observe, Monsieur: Samarcas makes frequent visits to London, and when he comes to Paris, he visits Mendoza, who's presently the ambassador of Spain to France, the same ambassador whom Elizabeth kicked out of England for having plotted against her. Which is why Samarcas is poking his nose around Paris, and why I've got a fly on his tail, given my master's manifest interest in preventing the assassination of Elizabeth."

"God preserve her!" I exclaimed, believing as I did that this great queen was our prime and principal bulwark against further oppression by the Roman Church.

"God," observed Mosca, "and Walsingham…"

"Walsingham?" I asked, hearing for the first time this name, which would soon become so familiar to me.

"He's the English minister tasked with the security of the queen and, Lord knows, he keeps a good and sharp watch over her! Monsieur," Mosca continued, rising, "I'm pressed for time and I know my escort risks catching cold waiting for me out there; I beg you to hear now the strangest news of all: Samarcas is being followed not only by my fly, but also by another, and that one's employed by the English ambassador in Paris."

"Well," I said, "that entirely explains the little role Samarcas is playing!"

"I think so too."

And, making me a deep bow, and another to Giacomi, this fox-like Mosca took his leave, leaving my purse diminished but my mind enriched with a wealth of secrets that more than made up for it.

"Monsieur," said Miroul, his brown eye maliciously glowing, while his blue eye remained cold, "would you like me to tell you the real name of this Mosca?"

"What? Miroul! You know who he is?"

"Certainly, Monsieur, but I don't know if I'll say it, since I learnt it when 'frittering away my time on the streets of Paris' when you send me out with messages for your friends."

"Miroul, what are you saying?"

"It's just that you're always scolding me for 'frittering away my time', with my nose in the air and my eyes wide open in the streets of the capital; always accusing me of wasting my time with your frowns and scowls!"

"Come then, Miroul, speak! Speak! You'd try the patience of a papist saint the way you're always thwarting your master's will!"

"Alas, Monsieur!" he countered, his eyes shining. "There you go again, finding fault with me. I only loiter in order to serve you, constantly enriching myself with thousands of details that I see and hear on the streets! Would I know what I know if I hadn't stopped in front of the Grand Châtelet last Monday?"

"Oh, you obstinate valet!" I cried. "Are you going to tell me or not?"

"Monsieur," Miroul replied, pretending to be angry, "if you insist on thinking me wicked then I'll lose my tongue and shut up!"

"Dammit, my man! I beg you! Enough with these complaints! *Diga me!*"*

"If I'm 'your' man," he replied, "then I can't be so wicked as all that! And you 'beg' me, but your prayer is an order. But, Monsieur, are you going to keep criticizing me for 'frittering away' my time in Paris, seeing how my 'frittering' teaches me so much?"

"Ah, Miroul!" cried Giacomi, who was growing red from impatience. "You have assuredly one of the best and most good-natured masters in Christendom! How many others would suffer such insufferable impertinence without taking the rod to you!"

"*Maestro,*" replied Miroul, seriously and almost haughtily, "we are not on such terms, my master and I! He knows very well that I'd give anything (except Florine) to save his life, and that I serve him with love and respect, especially given that my savings in Bordeaux would allow me to set myself up if I wanted."

Having said this, he suddenly looked as if he were going to shed a tear—seeing which, I felt very chagrined that I should have made him unhappy, and with a knot in my throat took him in my arms and kissed his cheek. At this his brown eye lit up and a tear trickled down his cheek, so that, crying and laughing, like a ray of sun through the rain, he said, "Ah Monsieur! Did you really have to dress me down last Monday for half an hour's lateness? What's the point of living in Paris if you can't stroll about as you want?"

---

* "Tell me!"

"Miroul," I said soothingly, embracing him contritely, "should I beg your pardon?"

"Ah, Monsieur, not on your life! That would be beneath you! But as for our man, here's the news: last Monday, at about eight in the morning, as I was delivering a message for you, I saw three pickpockets being escorted from the Grand Châtelet, whom they were taking to hang at Montfaucon. Alas, for these poor fellows the week was beginning very badly." (He laughed heartily at his little joke.) "And the one leading them, surrounded by the guards, pikes in their fists, was, as I learnt afterwards, the lieutenant of the provostry, Nicolas Poulain."

"What! Mosca?"

"*Ipse.** Unfortunately, badly lit as he was tonight, I only recognized him when he was leaving, otherwise I would have been able to whisper it to you in time to save you a handsome sum of money!"

"What? What are you saying?"

"Could he have extorted money from you if you'd known he was an officer of the king? One who, to be sure, is not so highly placed that you'd have seen him at court and been able to recognize him when he arrived here. Thus, it would seem, Monsieur," added Miroul (who could not resist—*in cauda venenum*†—teaching me a lesson), "that it's sometimes more profitable to stroll through the streets of Paris than to do so though the courtyards of the Louvre."

I smiled at this barb, but didn't react, not knowing, after so many years spent side by side, which of us was the master—for the more I scolded him, the more he chided me, never missing an opportunity to get his revenge for any wounds I'd inflicted. And isn't it always thus between master and servant whenever real affection exists between them? Even the king is, so to speak, "commanded" by those who obey

---

* "The same."

† "The venom's in the tail."

him: by imparting to him only the news that they themselves want to hear, they end up governing to a great degree his reactions to it.

My poor Giacomi was disconsolate to learn that his Larissa was so near, yet so inaccessible, imprisoned behind the walls of the abbey—where Samarcas had sequestered her doubtless because he'd discerned the progress that the *maestro* had made in the affections of his pupil, and, for this reason, no longer wanted to stay at the Montcalms' lodgings, where the *maestro* was always welcome and from where he himself had so often to be absent, attending more to his business than to his prayers. As for me, it hadn't escaped my notice that, for the last ten years, Giacomi had room only for Larissa in his heart—notwithstanding the humble petticoats he chased upon occasion, not wishing to live in total abstinence; but he refused any and all offers of marriage in the hope of one day taking Larissa as his wife. He seemed entirely unconcerned by the former disorders of the poor woman, since they'd been caused by "the devils that had managed to inhabit her".

And I couldn't help thinking too that, if Samarcas were to disappear, the Montcalms wouldn't have turned up their noses at this offer, since Giacomi was clearly a man of quality: he was in great favour with the king, who, in gratitude for his lessons, had ennobled him with the title of *écuyer* and enriched him with a little estate called la Surie—which Giacomi had also taken as his own name in order to "Frenchify" it. What's more, since the royal fencing master, Monsieur Silvie, was getting old, Giacomi now had as his students some of the great lords of the kingdom, and had put their largesse to good use, buying a very beautiful house in the grand'rue Saint-Honoré, with gable and loggia, and though he lived modestly, people thought him more well-to-do than he was.

As for the relationship between Larissa and Giacomi, though they'd been unable over these last ten years to exchange more than ten words, their blushes at seeing each other and pallor at parting from each other—not to mention, during every interview, the heaving chests, the oppressed hearts, the stuttering tongues and trembling hands, the sudden perspiration and weakness in the legs, and, above all (though they were virtually never alone), the mute eloquence of their shining and joyful eyes, drunk with yearning and blurry with tears—had allowed them silently to pledge their mutual and eternal fidelity to each other better than the whispered orisons of ten papist priests could have done.

And thinking about this, in my great friendship for my brother Giacomi, and my brotherly love (less great, but perhaps more ambiguous) for my pretty sister Larissa (the ambiguity one more reason to want to join them together), I frequently imagined confronting Samarcas and, suddenly crossing swords with this progeny of the shadows, my "Jarnac's thrust" pitted against his Jesuit's feint, finally dispatching him. But this dream was like so many others: it never transpired. The outcome was quite different, as we shall see.

I took Giacomi into my fencing room, but fearing that if he unsheathed his sword for a lesson with me, in his present despair, he might put it through his own heart, I took him by the arm and walked him up and down, allowing him to let out all his anger and fury. His eyes were now shooting flames, now flowing with tears, and, from time to time, he gnashed his teeth, clenched his fists, stamped his foot or moaned, his head on my shoulder—all this accompanied by a flood of words that I could remember only half of, since the rest were in a Genoese dialect that I couldn't follow at the speed he was talking.

When he was finally exhausted from all this grief and anger, I made him sit down on a chest of arms and said:

"My brother, as we take stock of everything Nicolas Poulain told us, what do we conclude? If the peril Larissa faces—of being locked up in an English jail as an accomplice to an assassination plot—is all too clear, we obviously can't solve the situation by informing the Montcalms: they venerate Samarcas too much to believe our word against his. Moreover, to warn the Montcalms would be to warn Samarcas himself, who is, moreover, caught in the nets of both English and French spies. And it's certainly not in the interests of our king, or of Queen Elizabeth, that he be forewarned."

"So what can we do in such a predicament?"

"Verify that Samarcas is indeed lodged at the abbey, but do so without following him and without being seen, as Maître Fly recommended. In this way, we'll know how much trust to place in Poulain and his stories."

I asked Gertrude du Luc to lend me her travel coach, and the next day, before dawn, Giacomi and I—dressed in black, our faces disguised by masks, with Miroul in the driving seat, his hat pulled well down over his eyes—posted ourselves on the little square opposite the great doors of the abbey of Saint-Germain-des-Prés. At this hour there were very few people other than a few ruffians in rags, who, seeing us stationed there, came limping out of their hovels like woodlice from a hole, and tried to steal our horses.

Seeing this, we leapt out, swords unsheathed, and, with Miroul's help, gave them such blows on their backs and backsides with the flats of our blades that they fled, never to return. After which we remained on guard, this area of Saint-Germain being, as everyone knows, of evil repute, in which there huddled many ramshackle dwellings, many falling into ruin, where there swarmed a collection of beggars, thieves, whores and pickpockets. It's a miracle that in the middle of such a cesspool rose this beautiful, rich abbey (which was surrounded by abandoned fields so thickly covered with nettles and thistles that even an ass wouldn't have found provender there), with walls so high that no ladder would have been tall enough to scale them, erected to protect its monks and treasures from the lowlifes who teemed at its feet.

As the dawn was chilly for 7th May, we climbed back into the coach, thinking we could keep better watch from there without being seen, Miroul standing guard for us outside, to prevent the population of very destructive "rabbits" who surrounded us, and who disdained the grass pushing up between the paving stones, from satisfying their more murderous appetites.

After a few moments, as the first glimmer of the sun was showing on the horizon, I saw a beggar in dirty rags slip along the walls, and squat down a few yards from the gate, remaining so immobile there you would have thought he was one of the stones of the abbey. This blending in didn't seem to me to be the least bit accidental: I surmised that this caiman had arrived not from the hovels of the surrounding neighbourhood, but from Paris, and that he must be one of the spies Poulain had directed to follow Samarcas. There was, moreover, no reason for a beggar to be here, since there was no one to beg from— except us, and he showed no interest whatsoever in asking us for alms.

Scarcely had he taken up his position, however, before another fellow appeared, dressed entirely in black, like a cleric, except that he had a dagger, a sword and a doublet that was definitely not cut in the French tradition. After an indifferent look at Poulain's man, and another, somewhat more interested, in our direction, this fellow went and leant against the wall at a fair distance from the abbey gates and began cutting his nails with a pair of small scissors. This, I deduced, must be Walsingham's man, but he didn't appear to play the game with as much grace or skill as Mosca's man, since he didn't blend in as well with his surroundings.

I judged from the presence of these two spies, one nearly invisible and the other less discreet, that Poulain had told us the truth, and that the stage was set for the emergence of the dramatis personae we four—the two spies, Giacomi and myself—were expecting. Giacomi, from what I could see, was clenching the hilt of his sword with his long, thin hand. At this, seeing his emotion and afraid that it might interfere with his judgement, I told him to allow me to take the lead in this action, and not to move a muscle until I'd given the word.

Scarcely had I said this before the gate of the abbey opened (which was as much of an operation as opening the one at the Louvre) and two huge guards emerged, swords at their sides, looking more like soldiers than monks; after taking a look around, they went back inside. A minute later they reappeared, followed this time by Samarcas, who, seeing Walsingham's man, headed directly towards him as if shot out of a crossbow, and, when he was about a yard away, unleashed a torrent of insults and drew his sword. The Englishman drew his weapon and laid into his opponent, but the clash of swords didn't seem to press the soldiers into action: they just stood, hands on hips, and watched from a distance, quite assured of the fight's outcome.

"Blessed Virgin," cried Giacomi, "are we going to stand here and let this man be assassinated? Samarcas will kill him! I can see it coming!"

"Ah, Giacomi," I hissed, "don't go getting yourself killed! If you show yourself, even masked, Samarcas will recognize your sword and will sound the alarm. We'd have an entire monastery of monks on our backs in no time—and, worse, the Jesuit will know that his presence in Paris has been discovered, along with his plots against the king."

"Well, I'll obey you, but, by heaven, to sit here and do nothing! Samarcas has so much skill and so little heart."

"But the Englishman doesn't seem so bad either!"

"He parries well. But now you're going to see the famous Jesuit feint! Watch closely, you're about to see it! I can tell by the sounds of their swords. The Englishman is valiant and skilled but he's only got a second more to live!"

"Miroul," I called, "show yourself, hat down over your eyes, and give a good crack of your whip, as loud as you can!"

Miroul quickly stepped forward, and it seemed to me that the sound of the whip troubled our swashbuckler enough to stop him from killing his opponent, missing his heart but hitting his lung. However, seeing Miroul, the soldiers at the gate unsheathed their swords and headed towards the coach. I decided it was time to show ourselves, and, with Giacomi at my side, our swords drawn, I shouted in English, to make them believe we were compatriots of the wounded man,

"Come here, damn you! We shall kill you!"

At this, Samarcas evidently decided that the whole affair was too public, as some passers-by were now watching the proceedings, so he called back his troops and they withdrew into the abbey, closing the gate.

I ordered Miroul to drive the coach between the gate and the wounded man to create a shield that might be the target of their arquebuses, and ran to the wounded man, who, seeing me coming, made a weak effort to grab his knife, believing no doubt that I wanted to finish him off. But, before he did, I shouted,

"Do not move! We're friends. We shall take care of you!"

He was reassured at this and allowed Giacomi and Miroul to seize him by the shoulders and feet and lift him, bloody as he was, into poor Gertrude's coach. As I started to climb into the vehicle, the beggar dressed all in grey who'd been squatting next to the wall and hadn't moved a muscle throughout, extended his hand from his rags and, throwing me a quick look, murmured:

"A sol, just one sol, for God's sake!"

His prayer was, unlike his look, quite humble, so I very conspicuously took a couple of coins from my purse, walked over to him and placed them in his hand.

"Monsieur," he whispered, "do not take the wounded man to his embassy and do not show yourselves there either! A number of Spanish flies are flitting about there!"

I was struck by the poetic turn of this sentence in the mouth of a spy, not yet aware that such metaphors were in daily usage in the jargon of their work. I also found it strange that I should have such a thought in the midst of this commotion—a moment when I had to have my wits about me if we were going to survive.

Once we'd brought the coach into my stables, unhitched the horses and placed the wounded man on a bed, I had him undressed and, examining his wound, discovered that it wasn't as serious as the one that had sent Sauveterre to his grave—that one being the result of a gunshot and this one of a sword that hadn't entirely passed through the lung, though it had penetrated at least two inches into the organ. But the Englishman was young, of robust complexion, strong and healthy in every part of his body, and thus very desirous of living, and not a bit impatient, as was my uncle Sauveterre, of achieving eternal happiness. Seeing this, I tried to reassure him and said in his language: "My master, Ambroise Paré, whom perhaps you've heard of, claims that a wound to the lung will heal as long as the patient remains in repose, and avoids speaking, coughing and any sudden movement."

To this, with a very obedient air, the Englishman, whose name was Mundane, blinked twice, and I could see from this exemplary docility that he was one of those patients who aid the physician rather than encouraging the sickness.

From this I predicted that he'd be on his feet in a month if his wound did not become infected. Meanwhile, as I was getting ready to retire after having washed and bandaged the gash and given him some opium to assuage the pain, he said to me in English, in a thin and breathless voice,

"Sir, will you be so kind as to tell my embassy of my predicament?"

I nodded in affirmation, though I had no idea how to go about this, given the urgent advice of the other spy. Musing on this dilemma, I went downstairs and out into the courtyard, and thence to my stables, where I saw Miroul busily cleaning the blood from the interior.

"Ah Miroul! Excellent work! And how thoughtful of you not to leave this job to the indiscretion of a chambermaid. But, unfortunately, cleaning it won't be enough. We can't take the risk of this carriage being recognized by those people, so I'd like you to paint it pink—especially since that's Dame du Luc's favourite colour."

"Monsieur," replied Miroul, stepping from the coach with a most unhappy expression on his face, "don't count on it! I am not a painter, nor do I aspire to be one, since I'm well above such manual trades. Moreover, I hate that colour!"

"Well, Miroul, no one's forcing you! If you don't want to do it, don't do it! We'll just ask some painter from around here, but he won't do it any better than you and will likely go off chattering about the work."

And I walked off, pretending to heave a sigh of resignation, all the while knowing that the minute I was out of sight, he'd set to it and do it with great care.

As I returned to our room after these early-morning events, I found Angelina just finishing her nursing of our little babe and eager to see me, since she hadn't found me there when she'd awoken earlier. But she didn't want to converse or cuddle with me until she had had a chance to wash her face, brush her beautiful blonde tresses and perfume her neck, which I loved to kiss, since her skin was so soft there. This I did as soon as she'd ceased being, as she put it, "too horrible to look at", and, taking her sweet body in my arms, I teased her a bit about her foibles while her beautiful doe eyes looked at me full of mute questions about where I'd been since dawn. I understood very well what she was thinking, but I didn't want to tell her the naked truth in order to spare her excessive worry about Larissa. Finally, I said,

"Angelina my love, I can't tell you where I was this morning, since I must keep it secret out of loyalty to my king, but I'm glad I was there, because I was able to help a young Englishman who'd been wounded in a villainous attack; I've brought the young man here to our blue room in order to bind and heal his wound. We need to tell our servants not to disturb him because he's taken some opium to help him sleep off his pain."

At this point, Gertrude and Zara burst into our room to say good morning, still dressed in their flowing nightgowns, which revealed their beautiful shoulders and more, and gave us each a hug (never an unpleasant event with two such beautiful women, though I would never press such intimacies beyond a casual embrace). They exploded into joyful cries to see us so happily ensconced, and leapt into bed with us, distributing sweet caresses to Angelina and me, both of them so avid to receive the compliments I showered on them throughout the day. When it comes to women, it's my belief that it's best to go at it not with a teaspoon but with a trowel, like a mason, given how insecure these creatures are about the duration of their beauty. But I must add that I felt no constraint or hypocrisy in doing so, given how sensitive I am to the graces of the feminine body, and how unable I am to see a pretty girl without feeling a sharp desire to caress her—and, since I can't go at it straightaway with my fingers and lips, I must do the best I can with words, so that whatever compliments I pay to my lovers are really part of my pleasure in making love to them.

It's true that, with Gertrude and Zara, I could have gone a little further than words alone, though exactly how far I'd never tested, having decided not to go beyond the point of no return, but instead to substitute verbal caresses for physical ones in order to avoid offending Samson or my Angelina. Perhaps the excitement of such delicacies derives from the fact that, however innocent they appear, they aren't completely so, allowing us to enjoy the secret dreams or regrets that they may provoke.

When I'd done with such sweetness in the warmth and delicious disorder of their soft and flowing nightgowns, which are free of all the stays and rigid hoops that our current style imposes on them, and had caressed them and been caressed by them to my heart's content (though my heart isn't so easily satisfied), I took on a grave expression, and explained to them how I'd found a badly wounded English gentleman in the street, and brought him to our house. I urged them to help care for him since, other than Florine, I didn't want our chambermaids to see him, since we mustn't be compromised by others hearing of his presence here.

They were suddenly all aflutter at the idea that there was a veritable Englishman in our house. When I ventured to add that he was not only English but very good-looking, despite his red hair, Gertrude exclaimed:

"Ah, my brother, how can you speak of him with such disparagement? Didn't I hear you just last month praising Lady Stafford to the skies precisely because of her red hair?"

"That's different: hers is Venetian red; he's a carrot-top!"

And, as I opened the door, she sniffed, "You're leaving? Have I so pricked you by pointing out your meanness?"

"Not at all! No one in the kingdom is more charming than you, my sister!"

"What about me?" pouted Zara.

But I didn't bother to reply, since Gertrude's allusion to Lady Stafford had just given me a way out of our predicament, and I needed to visit Madame de Joyeuse post-haste.

I had Miroul take her a note, and he was, of course, delighted to have to abandon his painting for a leisurely stroll through Paris—so leisurely that he didn't return till an hour after the midday meal, having taken two hours where one would have sufficed. I derived a double pleasure from this: the first from the relief that Madame de Joyeuse agreed to receive me, and the second that Florine set about Miroul with ten times the fury for his "loitering" than I would have dared apply, and so saved me from having to do it!

No sooner was I admitted to Madame de Joyeuse's apartments than Aglaé de Mérol appeared and welcomed me to the house, just as she had done when I was a medical student in Montpellier and Monsieur de Joyeuse was the governor of the city.

At that time, Aglaé had despaired of ever marrying, since her father was so rich that he would only allow her to marry a man of very considerable means, and the three or four suitors that possessed such wealth were entirely unacceptable to her. Heavens! Eighteen years had flown by, like sand in the wind, since I'd kissed her pretty dimpled cheek for the first time. In the meantime, her father had died; she'd followed Madame de Joyeuse to Paris, and met the Marquis de Miroudot, a handsome gentleman ten years her junior, who was from an ancient and good family but poor as Job, having only his debts to live on—and whom, being finally mistress of her own destiny, she married.

This turned out to be both a good and not such a good thing. For though Philippe de Miroudot, who was a very refined gentleman of great wit and cultured tastes, became her most delicious friend—spending hours in her boudoir, dressing her, coiffing her and helping her put on her make-up—his nature led him to no greater intimacy than this, oriented as he was in another direction. So Aglaé had a devil of a time to get him to give her a child, since her young husband went at it so half-heartedly, despite his great affection for her, his enjoyment of her company and his love of her clothes. She valued all of these feelings very highly, but they were not enough to satisfy her, and, after her feelings for her husband took a more maternal turn, she found what she needed from one of those young pages who are, as Quéribus had explained to me, all the rage among the noblewomen of the court.

"Monsieur de Siorac," said Aglaé, to whom I offered a discreet kiss, following the custom we'd established eighteen years earlier, "I'm delighted to see you here! Indeed, I'm always complaining that I never get to see you as much as I'd like! Of course, it's true that, given your looks, an old woman has no attraction for you, especially now that I'm over thirty and Madame de Joyeuse—"

"Stop right there!" I broke in, giving her another kiss on her dimple. "Don't tell me the maréchale's age—and, as for yours, it's the same as my Angelina's, and you know how I love her! And I swear that in your case, as in hers, the years have passed without making any inroads into your imperishable beauty!"

"Well, Monsieur," she answered wryly, "I must be very old indeed to require as much hyperbole as you used to shower Madame de Joyeuse with in Montpellier."

"But that was entirely different! They were employed as was dictated by my role as her official lover!"

"Well, Monsieur! I'd advise you to keep quiet about that!" said Aglaé, placing her finger on my lips and pretending to be shocked. "Don't breathe a word in this house about your former role, nor about the 'school of sighs'! No surprise that you bring it up first thing! But within a year of your departure, Madame de Joyeuse fell into the most zealous devotion! You simply wouldn't believe it! Other than eating and drinking to sustain them, we are to consider our bodies as having no value! Our life here is like that in a convent: we hear Mass every morning, take Communion every Sunday, spending at least two hours a day in the chapel; we go on retreats, and run after poor people to give them alms. In a word, we are now enflamed only by the love of God!"

"We?"

"She, I meant to say."

"Thank Heaven!" I cried. "But do I dare appear before her? Won't she revile me for reminding her of her past?"

"Not if you adopt, Monsieur, an air of modest contrition, scarcely brushing her hand with your kiss, lowering your assassin's eyes in humility, restraining your body and maintaining a funereal expression."

"Funereal, Madame? When Madame de Joyeuse has so many reasons to be proud of her sons, the king showering favours on both of them? Anne is now a duc, a peer and an admiral! The Comte du Bouchage is master of the king's wardrobe, and a bishop awaiting his cardinal's biretta!"

"Showering is the word! It's been a veritable storm of favours, and we have become great as a result—greater even than Épernon. But our greatness has not made us happy."

The most sanctimonious Tartuffe never put on a more priestly face than I did as I entered Madame de Joyeuse's salon. My eyes lowered, my spine reverential and my voice a mere whisper, I presented her my respects, which she accepted with a benign air and one visibly innocent of any excesses she may have once shared with me back when I was a student of medicine in Montpellier, a memory that had, no doubt, been completely effaced.

"Monsieur," she intoned, "you've abandoned me! It's true that I have mostly withdrawn from the world and its vanities"—a description that conveniently omitted the dozen superbly attired great lords and ladies who regularly paid court to the mother of Henri's favourite—"but don't I remember that your family is descended from the Caumonts of Périgord, my little cousin? And, in such wise, are you not under the obligation of assiduously paying me your respects?"

"Madame," I conceded, "I would be devastated to have failed in such an obligation, but you must remember that you and your family have risen so high, and now shine so brilliantly at the head of our kingdom, that I would have been afraid to approach you too often, for fear of being blinded by your splendour."

"Oh," she objected, her golden-brown eyes full of melancholy (the only feature of her face that reminded me of our past), "you cannot be serious, my cousin! That's exactly where the shoe pinches the most! We've risen too quickly and too high! I'm terrified of such heights and of the fall that must inevitably follow! You know, of course, that the king married my son" (he'd actually married off two of her sons, but she was referring to Anne, whose ambiguous sobriquet—"the king's favourite"—caused some nasty smiles at court) "to a princess of the house of Lorraine, thereby making him his brother-in-law. But I found myself so stupefied by such a rapid elevation, and the incredible benefits that accompanied it, that I had to remain closeted in my chapel for two whole days and nights, pretending to be ill and praying God to slow the course of this immense fortune, stricken with the apprehension—that I still feel—of our inevitable decline."

"Madame!" I exclaimed in surprise. "May Heaven be deaf to your fears! Why should you fear for the future? There's not a soul who doesn't believe that Anne is solidly ensconced in the king's favour!"

"But the king is mortal, my cousin!" she whispered. "And if he dies, what will become of us? Are you aware of the history of the chateau the king bequeathed to my son as a wedding gift? François I ripped it from the hands of his treasurer, Ponchet, to give it to Madame d'Étampes. When the king died, Henri II gave it to Diane de Poitiers, from whom it was confiscated at Henri's death, and now it's in the hands of my son! Do I not have good reason to be afraid?"

I tried to console her, but couldn't help being secretly amused that Madame de Joyeuse had spoken with such pleasant naivety of this domain in Limours, whose strange destiny had somehow caused it, as my friend L'Étoile said, "to fall prey to a succession of mistresses and sweethearts of our kings".

"But Madame," I reassured her, "your son, Anne, is married to one of the princesses of the house of Lorraine! Who'd dare confiscate this land from the sister of the king?"

"Well, my cousin," sobbed Madame de Joyeuse, "that's precisely why I'm so afraid! If the king were to die, how would my son continue to maintain the princess in a manner befitting her rank? She'd be the ruin of us! I shared my fears with His Majesty, who replied, 'But Madame, I'm neither old nor infirm. Don't go worrying about my death more than I do myself! In any case, I shall know how to guarantee your son's safety because of the great friendship I feel for him, and because, after all, he's my brother, having married my sister!'"

"Madame," I said soothingly, "given such assurances from the king himself, can you not put your worries to rest?"

"Alas, my cousin!" she moaned, tears welling up in her amber eyes. "Nothing seems to help! I'm consumed by my anxieties!"

Alas for me as well! We weren't yet done with this subject, which dragged on for another quarter of an hour, Madame de Joyeuse, her plump hand posed on my wrist, continuing her moans and lamentations, trying to impress on me the terrible future portended by the power, glory and riches of her son. "Oh heaven!" I mused. "The poor lady is consumed with fear! And isn't it interesting how this paragon of piety, who spends her life in prayer trying to fortify herself against the infernal fires, is in fact much more worried about her treasures on earth? One of these fears should have calmed the other, instead of combining to make her so miserable!"

Luckily, instead of taking my leave of this tedious teller, I managed to continue my audience long enough to catch sight of the red hair of Lady Stafford, whom I knew to be most assiduous in her attentions to her friend, visiting virtually every day, in part out of friendship—and in part, I suspected, in order to pick up the latest court gossip to pass on to her husband.

When, finally, there came a pause in this flood of fears and recriminations, I seized the opportunity to come up for air, and exclaimed, as if surprised, "Isn't that Lady Stafford I see over by the window? Might I ask you, Madame, to introduce us? I understand she speaks beautiful English, and I'd love to practise mine, which is much in need of improvement!"

Madame de Joyeuse shot me a sharp look, as if she immediately suspected that I had some frivolous designs on the wife of the English ambassador, but seeing only pure innocence in my eyes, and recalling that I was now married and reputed to be very much in love with my wife and faithful to her, she took me by the hand, led me over to the lady and said,

"My Lady, may I introduce my cousin, the Chevalier de Siorac, who is of good, noble stock, and who has had the strange notion of studying medicine—doubtless the only nobleman in France to do so—and the good fortune to become one of the king's physicians."

To which Lady Stafford, after giving me a penetrating look with her hazel eyes, and judging me to be worthy of her attention, extended her hand with a gracious but cold smile. I had no doubt that she had every reason to be wary when meeting people in this country, since she was surrounded by so many sworn enemies of her queen.

I kissed her fingertips in the Spanish manner, and immediately began speaking English to her, spouting a stream of banalities, hoping that we'd soon be rid of the dowager with whom Lady Stafford had been conversing, as well as of Madame de Joyeuse. And, as soon as we were alone, I told her, sotto voce, that I was a Huguenot who went *under duress* to Mass; thus having to some extent gained her confidence—since the English Church, despite its continued adherence to many of the errors of the papist practice, had no worse enemy than the Pope—I told her about Mundane, his wound and the circumstances in which he'd received it. She listened with great attention to my story, looking me directly in the eyes the whole time, which prevented me from looking at her lips and appreciating her English beauty.

"My Lady," I continued, "Mr Mundane must not be moved from his present bed. Therefore, I will keep him in my house until he's well, if God wills that his wounds should heal."

Lady Stafford remained silent for quite a while, looking me over with those fine, sagacious eyes of hers. I must say that it was a rare pleasure to be studied by one so beautiful, and when she finally spoke I was even more delighted, for I'd never heard such a sweet feminine voice speaking English with so ravishing an accent—indeed, I believe the English language is one of the most melodious in the world, so fluid, supple and elegant you'd think you were listening to the music of the spheres! She assured me that her husband would be most obliged to me for the care I was providing Mr Mundane, but she found it quite inexplicable that I would put myself at such risk and peril unless it was in service of my king, who clearly had an interest in the stability of the English crown.

I told her that, indeed, I served my king ardently, which naturally inclined me to be a friend to his friends, but I added that I also had a personal interest in the matter, since Mundane's assailant held my wife's sister in his power and control, and that I couldn't help fearing for her safety, seeing that she was so implicated in his plots against the English—despite her complete innocence in these affairs, given that she was somewhat deranged.

"And what is the lady's name?"

"Larissa de Montcalm."

"I shall not forget it," she assured me, extending her hand to signal that our interview was concluded, and throwing me such an enchanting smile that, to this day, I can remember the emotion it produced.

Satisfied that I had now accomplished to my satisfaction—and to Lady Stafford's—the mission that had brought me here, I was heading towards Madame de Joyeuse to ask her permission to leave, when suddenly the double doors of the salon were thrown open with a great racket by the swarthy valets who guarded them. Through them, arm in arm and with great panache, marched Anne de Joyeuse and his younger brother, Henri, Comte du Bouchage, master of the king's wardrobe. They were followed by a swarm of the gentlemen of their households, though only the first few gained entrance before the doors were closed again on the rest, who were thus forced to wait in the antechamber.

The two brothers, who obviously enjoyed each other's affection, were quite tall, of elegant bearing, possessed of the same long face, aquiline nose and azure-blue eyes, and could have been mistaken for identical twins except that Anne's beard was blond and his brother's red. The other difference was that Henri's demeanour was as austere and melancholy as his brother's was joyful.

Indeed, the Comte du Bouchage's expression accurately mirrored his character, for he was every bit as devout as his mother, having been, from earliest childhood, indoctrinated in churchly beliefs and behaviour. Against these the delights and vanities of the court had no force whatsoever and could not prevent him, when his wife died, from cloistering himself with the Capuchin monks, exchanging his pearly doublet for a cassock and rope belt.

Anne, whose bearing was much less serious than his brother's, seemed wholly intoxicated by the magnificent favours the king lavished on him. Unlike the Duc d'Épernon, Anne's talents were vastly inferior to his fortunes, but he believed his gifts were superior to others', and, watching him burst into his mother's salon with such a self-satisfied air, I discerned in his eyes, voice and gestures, and in his way of throwing himself into an armchair, that this naive belief in his own strengths led him to behave as though he were the king himself, though he was only a pale reflection of his monarch. He was like the foam carried on the crest of a wave: frothy but of little consistency.

There was no denying, however, that he was good-looking, well built, youthful, gay and gracious, and infinitely amiable to all those who crowded around his armchair to pay court to him.

When it was my turn to greet him, he said, "Ah! Monsieur de Siorac, I'm very happy to see you! How well I remember the little soldiers that you gave me in Montpellier when I was just a child, and which you employed to portray the glorious campaign at Calais, where we retook that good city from those nasty Englishmen!"

Of course, this was a very handsome thing to say to me, though it was the tenth time that Anne had mentioned it, forgetting with each repetition that he'd already said it. But what a heedless and inappropriate thing to say of the valiant English people in front of Lady Stafford, whom, in my view, he should have greeted when he first entered her salon, rather than waiting till she came forward.

I was in the midst of these reflections when the doors of the salon burst open yet again, despite the valets' efforts to prevent this, and the Baron de Quéribus, after paying his respects to his hostess and to the Duc de Joyeuse, pulled me aside into an alcove and whispered urgently:

"I've just come from your lodgings, Pierre, where Angelina told me you'd be here: the king demands your presence in his chambers immediately."

"What! In his chambers?"

"He's taken to his bed."

"Already! Is he sick?"

"He is, or is pretending to be—I know not which. I found him extremely agitated, looking very sad and eaten up by anxiety."

5

PEOPLE TALKED SO MUCH about the health of my good master, and both Guise's people and the Catholic League spread so many false rumours about it, that others came to believe that Henri wasn't fit to reign. I have to say, however—speaking not only from my own observations of Henri but also from those of Miron, Fogacer and His Majesty's other physicians—that, while it's true that the king was beset by many ills that greatly pained him, some of which even humiliated him, none of them seemed to us to be life-threatening. Indeed, all of us believed that he would have lived to the ripe old age at which many men in this kingdom die, had not the knife of his assassin monk severed his life's thread in his thirty-eighth year.

Since my duty to my readers is to make my account reliable, recounting the facts as they were, however shameful, I have to report that Henri suffered from various abscesses, sores and fistulas, one under his left eye, another under his right arm and others in his groin and on his testicles—these last doubtless the cause of his sterility. These were cold humours; they never grew enflamed or enlarged, produced acute fevers or suppurated, but certainly caused the patient much discomfort and worry.

The king also suffered terribly from haemorrhoids, which sometimes became so enlarged that they made sitting uncomfortable, which is why, despite his excellent horsemanship, he preferred his carriage. Of course, this preference caused rumours that he'd gone soft, but the truth was that it was due instead to this particular condition, which is so difficult to treat. This was also the reason he didn't like jousting or hunting. And though he went hunting more often than his critics claimed, the gentleness of his nature gave him little taste for it, since he had no appetite for killing animals, as his brother Charles IX had, but was more like Montaigne, who professed no pleasure "in hearing the screams of a hare caught in the dogs' teeth".

Unlike his brother Charles, or Guise or Navarre, he had little interest in tennis, since he doubtless found it beneath him to appear on a tennis court in shirtsleeves, with a racquet in his hand. On the other hand, he delighted in the noble art of fencing, and, thanks to the lessons Sylvie had given him, and thanks as well to constant practice, he was an excellent swordsman, and few gentlemen in the kingdom were his equal in this regard. Anyone who'd seen him with a sword, as I did more than once, would never have dared claim that he was soft, weak or sickly, for he went at it furiously, without stopping, breathing hard and sweating but rarely exhausted.

And as for me, I can testify better than anyone to his robust nature, having, as I mentioned earlier, already accompanied him on his pilgrimage from Notre-Dame de Paris to Notre-Dame de Chartres, a very long trek that he covered on foot in two days—after which, after resting a day and a night, he undertook the return journey in two days as well. From this he suffered no other discomfort than blisters on his feet and some stomach pain, after having eaten too much on the road.

This is strange behaviour for a man purported to be so near death, wearing out his shoes on the gravelly roads and then eating too much at the inn! For although he took no spirits, Henri ate like an ogre— sometimes two whole capons in a single sitting; he was never one, as the saying goes, to turn his back on a feast—or on his enemy in battle.

It's true that, with such an appetite, he'd developed a bit of a paunch by the age of thirty, but, in conversation one day with Monsieur de

Thou, the president of parliament, who was quite old but in very good health, Henri asked him the secret of his marvellous youthfulness. De Thou answered that he'd always maintained an even disposition, lived a well-ordered life, dining, sleeping and waking at the same hour every day, always eating the same foods and never to excess. This so impressed Henri that, from that day forward, he never took more than two meals a day, and never again ate more than one capon for his dinner. Naturally, he was the better for it.

I will dare to say, after all this, that the veritable malady from which Henri suffered was not rooted in his body but in his soul, which the harshest and most continuous persecution had bruised and mutilated. For being of an infinitely magnanimous nature, he pushed this rare virtue to the point of pardoning the many priests who dragged him through the mire every Sunday in their sermons. But since Henri III aspired only to keep the peace among his subjects, and didn't believe that one could vanquish heresy by the knife, he met only the most pitiless execration from both Huguenots and Catholics. I can only pray that, in future centuries, the crying injustice that comes from such partisan approaches to religion, and that so overwhelmed my poor master during his lifetime, may at last come to an end. Our children and grandchildren will hopefully look back with horror on the excesses perpetrated by this religious zeal and on the way in which such zeal blinded people to the most manifest truths.

Henri was such a hard worker that he would spend hours with his advisors and in his study, and yet the minute he sought some recreation, people would accuse him of sloth. If he studied Latin, the rumour-mongers would say he was "declining". Though he was very pious, both by nature and by practice, his detractors nevertheless accused him of being a secret enemy of the Church, a fomenter of heretics, an instrument of the Devil—and who knows what else? Too valiant to howl with the wolves, he displayed a marvellous constancy in his service to the state, but he was accused of being a coward. His determination regarding the great principles of government, and notably the question of succession, remained unshakeable to the end, and yet he was accused of weakness and vacillation. And lastly—as I've already said and can never repeat enough—he was, by nature and by reflection, good-natured and forgiving, but people called him cruel.

This entrenched hatred that was relentlessly spewed out about him; the thousands of insults and calumnies that were spread about him on all sides; the betrayals that were perpetrated by the nobility, his ministers, his officers, his servants, his favourites and even (with the exception of the queen) his family—his brother Alençon, his sister Margot and his mother Catherine (the latter two of whom passed over to Guise's side); and, beginning in 1584, the flurry of threats, which became increasingly grievous and seditious and weighed on his freedom and his life, all rained down bitterly on this sensitive soul, to the point where it became totally enervated, and Henri went from tears to fury, and from fury to melancholy, and from melancholy to despair.

At one point, I saw his face bathed in tears after hearing the report of an insult the Duchesse de Montpensier had directed at him. I also saw him, when Anne de Joyeuse made an unforgivable comment, become so angry that he beat and kicked his favourite practically unconscious. I once saw him tremble helplessly at each burst of lightning from a violent storm in his belief that Heaven had taken up the complaints of his subjects and was about strike him dead. I watched him, in the coldest winter months, shiver in the gloom of wind and rain, fall into despair, and experience the discomforts of life as so many insufferable stings. At such moments, totally withdrawn, his mouth twisted in bitter resentment, his wild eyes darting about in defiance and suspicion, he saw evil everywhere. Gradually the gentlemen in his retinue learnt to refrain from any humour or impudent remarks, as poor Monsieur X learnt, who, hearing the king's manservant, Du

Halde, say to His Majesty that it sufficed for him to appear somewhere for the plague to disappear from that place, exclaimed, "One plague chases out another!" So outraged was the king that he threw himself on X and beat him like a new-cut stalk of barley, and might have killed the man had Épernon not grabbed his fists.

According to what I'd heard from Quéribus in Madame de Joyeuse's salon, Henri had fallen into one of those dark moods, and so it was not without a great deal of apprehension that I requested permission to enter his apartments from his butler, Monsieur de Merle, who, understanding the reason for my visit, immediately bade me enter and whispered in my ear to be very careful not to aggravate His Majesty, who seemed exceedingly overwrought.

The king was stretched out on his bed, lying almost as rigidly as if he'd been the recumbent effigy on his own tomb, wearing the mask he wore in his sleep to preserve him from the unhealthy night air, which he believed ruined his complexion (despite the fact that his face was quite ruddy and resisted both sun and wind quite well). He was flanked on both sides by chambermaids, who were kneeling next to him, rubbing his hands with a yellowish unguent that smelt like musk. Du Halde stood nearby, watching this application and directing their work. The king's fool, Chicot, was seated on a stool, looking very upset, being very devoted to his master and unhappy to see him in such anguish. Chicot, unlike most members of his profession, was neither small nor deformed, but a strapping Gascon gentleman, whose bravery with a sword was to be demonstrated by the manner of his death.

"Who goes there?" came the muffled voice of the king from beneath his mask.

"Sire, 'tis the Chevalier of Bloodletting," replied Chicot, who loved giving pseudonyms to all the personages of the court, calling Guise "the Magnificent", the Cardinal de Guise (the duc's brother) "the Great Whoremonger", the Cardinal de Bourbon "the Great Halfwit", and the king himself "His Double Majesty", alluding to the crown of Poland (which, however, he'd recently lost).

"Chicot, give your stool to the chevalier and keep quiet!" said the king from beneath his mask.

"As for my stool, I gladly cede it," replied Chicot rising, "but, Henri, must I be quiet when the Magnificent speaks so loudly to you? What is a fool who doesn't make a sound? If you no longer wish me to serve you, Henri, tell your treasurer to pay me my wages, for I cannot bear to ask alms from this son of a whore. I'll find work elsewhere. Already the Guise brothers are paying court to me to get me to work for them! To the scaffold with all of them! But if you'd like me to keep working for you, Henri, my sweet, I'll remain, despite better offers from your enemies, and despite the wretched odours wafting from your privy this morning!"

"Chicot!" laughed the king. "Stay, I beg you, but quietly! I need to talk to Monsieur de Siorac."

"But, Henri," insisted Chicot, delighted to have succeeded in making his master laugh, "what can the Chevalier of Bloodletting tell you that I haven't already told you? He hears Mass half-arsedly. I hear Mass whole-arsedly. And didn't you know that to be king of France today it's enough to be Catholic? Which is why the Great Halfwit is aspiring to succeed you."

The king laughed again, pulled off his mask and, raising himself on one elbow, commanded, "Du Halde! Send these women away and put on my gloves!"

At this, the chambermaids, without waiting for the manservant's orders, backed towards the exit with three bows, and disappeared as Du Halde closed the door behind them.

"Slide the bolt, Du Halde—and you, Chicot, keep quiet!"

"If Your Double Majesty so commands," replied Chicot, "I'll obey twice. And if I disobey twice, I'll give myself a double whipping. As the Magnificent says, 'Let everyone whip himself in whatever *guise* he chooses!'"

"Ah Chicot," laughed the king, "if I didn't love you so much, I'd hate you!"

"And vice versa," replied Chicot.

"Siorac," began the king with a wan smile, "are you surprised that so many gentlemen in this kingdom disregard my commandments? Even my fool won't listen to me!"

"Ah, but there's a difference," corrected Chicot, "which is that I disobey you out of love."

"What, Chicot!" smiled the king. "What impertinence! Are you going to claim that my cousin the Duc de Guise is not crazy about me? He tells me so every day!"

"And, assuredly, 'tis true!" agreed Chicot. "Why, to save you he'd give the last drop of your blood!"

"Now, Chicot!" warned the king, who did not appreciate this last witticism. "You're going to exhaust my patience!"

"That's not possible. How can the king lose his patience when he has none?"

At this, the king laughed outright, proving that he loved a good joke even when he was the target.

"Sire," said Du Halde, "if Your Majesty keeps shaking and moving about, I'll never get his gloves on!"

"Go on, Du Halde, go on!" replied the king, for he always wore these gloves to bed, and kept them on all night to preserve the ointments that had been rubbed on his hands. I never ceased to be amazed at this precaution, since I would find it such a discomfort that I wouldn't be able to tolerate it. It's true that my own hands, which had no other merit than being washed daily, were not as beautiful as the king's.

"My little Henri," announced Chicot, who knew infallibly when it was time to keep silent, "you've listened to me long enough. I won't open my mouth again until you've finished your business with Monsieur de Siorac, unless you ask for my advice."

Henri smiled at this, and I realized how much he relied on his fool's wisdom when I saw him ask Du Halde to withdraw, but kept Chicot as a witness to our conversation.

"Monsieur de Siorac," he began, "I heard from Mosca what happened this morning at the gates of Saint-Germain. But since Mosca cannot appear in the Louvre without losing the trust of those he's spying on for me, I had to learn of the event through an emissary, who gave only the briefest account of the thing, so I'd like you to give me a fuller one."

I immediately satisfied the king, and told him the particulars of this adventure, being careful to give as elegant a description as I could, knowing how much Henri loved beautiful language, having studied elocution with the scholar Pibrac, whose eloquence was renowned *urbi et orbi*.

"Monsieur de Siorac," he observed when I'd finished, "that was well done and well presented! It was very humane of you to help Mundane under the circumstances and to warn Lord Stafford by such indirect means. The safety and well-being of Elizabeth are very dear to us, since if she and her kingdom were to fall into the hands of foreigners, our people would be infinitely more vulnerable. As you know, the Prince of Orange, Queen Elizabeth and I, though we are of different sects—the prince being of the reformed religion, the queen an Anglican and I Catholic—share the same enemies, who hide their evil designs under the cloak of religion."

"Well, that cloak has many holes in it," Chicot couldn't help interjecting, "to let the assassin's daggers through."

"Well said," rejoined the king with a brief, raucous laugh. "Monsieur de Siorac," he continued after a moment's reflection, "I would like to make a request of you."

"A request, sire? No, sire, you command me!"

"Not in this case. I want to make sure that you freely and willingly accept my commission, knowing that it has nothing to do with your service as my physician, and that it will undoubtedly place you in great danger."

"All the more reason, sire!"

"Henri," interjected Chicot, "the Chevalier of Bloodletting is ready to bleed for you! *Talis pater qualis filius.*"*

"You're right, my son," agreed the king. "And I remember well how loyally the Baron de Mespech served my grandfather at Ceresole, and my father at Calais."

"Henricus," observed Chicot, "luckily I'm not your son and wouldn't wish to be. You've fathered nothing but ingrates!"

"All but one!" corrected the king.

I wondered, of course, hearing these enigmatic words, which of the two arch-favourites was the ingrate and which the faithful friend, the latter seeming, the more I thought about it, to be Épernon rather than Anne de Joyeuse, a guess that the rest of the conversation confirmed in the most dramatic fashion.

"Monsieur de Siorac," continued the king, "the intermediary between Mosca and me is not in the least to my liking. He's of limited intelligence and has way too big an appetite."

"But Mosca himself…" I smiled.

"Mosca," said Chicot, "takes money from all hands, both those of the king and those of his enemies."

"But Mosca can betray in only one direction," corrected the king, "since he knows nothing of my plans, and everything of theirs. While his intermediary could betray Mosca—in which case I would be betrayed."

---

* "Like father, like son."

"That's remarkably well reasoned for a king!" observed Chicot.

"Sire, if I understand you correctly, you would like me to serve as intermediary between Mosca and Your Highness, since you have entire confidence in my fidelity, which is to my infinite honour."

"But also because," explained the king, "being my physician, your access to me is so natural and necessary that it won't excite anyone's curiosity."

"But sire," I confessed, "how great is the peril that I risk in this role?"

"Immense," he replied, fixing his large, jet-black eyes on mine. "If Mosca is taken by those he betrays, he'll give them your name, and these zealots, as you know, breathe fire, brimstone and murder."

"Well, sire! I've encountered many other dangers!"

At this he dropped his eyes an instant, sensing that I hadn't mentioned the St Bartholomew's day massacre by name because he'd taken part in it. I also knew that, ever since the siege of La Rochelle, he'd become convinced that "knives resolve nothing" against the reformers, and was struggling with all his might against Guise, who wanted to force him to undertake a new crusade. Which was also why I was so dedicated to this monarch, who dared protect my people—who were still my people even though I now went to hear Mass. But it's also true that I just plain liked Henri for himself, both for his thoughtfulness and for his heart—the most affable and generous there ever was. I am persuaded that Henri perfectly sensed my feelings about him, since his judgements about people (except when passion interfered) were usually very penetrating and sure.

"Monsieur de Siorac," the king continued, looking up at me again, "you had occasion to meet, some twelve years ago, my cousin, the king of Navarre"—a discreet allusion to the assassination of Coligny.

"Yes, sire. We rode side by side one night from the Louvre to the rue de Béthisy"—where Coligny lived, though I was as loath as the king was to mention him by name in this conversation—"and we talked as we rode."

"And do you believe he'd remember you?"

"I believe so, yes, sire, if it's not too presumptuous. The king of Navarre praised me highly for having studied medicine despite being of noble birth, a circumstance that seems to have impressed him greatly."

"That's him all right!" he smiled. "The king of Navarre practises the religion of usefulness."

"That's all the religion he's got!" observed Chicot.

"Quiet, fool!" snapped the king. "Let no one be a judge of conscience, not even you, Chicot, wise and crazy though you may be. Monsieur de Siorac," he continued, "since my brother is dying and my queen has given me no child, I want no other successor than Henri de Navarre. Moreover, I hold him in high esteem. He is of high birth and a naturally good disposition. My inclination has always been to love him and I believe he loves me. He is sometimes quick to anger and can be prickly, but at heart he is a good man. I am sure my temperament would please him and that we could get along well. I think that in a week or so I'll dispatch Épernon to ask him if he would agree to be my successor, on condition that he consent to convert to the Catholic religion; on this occasion, I would like you to accompany Épernon to Guyenne, since he suffers constantly from throat pain and his own physician is himself sick and bedridden."

"Sire, I shall do *everything* you command me," I replied, emphasizing the word "everything", since I understood that my medical attentions to Épernon were not all there was to my mission, and that he preferred to leave to my imagination the part that he didn't yet wish to reveal.

"My little Henrikins," said Chicot, "your decision drives me, a devout henchman of the Magnificent, to despair! What? You prefer this relapsed heretic Navarre to his uncle the Great Halfwit, who must be a good Catholic since he's a cardinal, and so senile that he shits himself! What a wicked choice you're making! You're going to have all the Guisards nipping at your heels, along with the priests, the preachers and the Duchesse de Montpensier, who limps with her right foot but is as nimble with her left thigh as her brother the Whoremonger! Ah, Henrikins! To hell with the most sacred rules of succession! Believe me, we should be choosing the younger branch over the older branch. And the shit-covered uncle over the valiant nephew! Heavens, once the Great Halfwit is king and trades his cross for a sceptre, then you'll have the Magnificent as constable. A celestial choice, Henricus! The most fervent desire of the Lord God, the Pope, the Spanish king, the people of Paris and the most vociferous priests in the capital! How many strident enemies you've made! Aren't you hated enough already?"

"I'm hated enough to suit me," declared Henri III, who, having listened carefully to his fool, responded with a seriousness that frankly surprised me. "But, Chicot, never forget this! The rules of succession govern the king and he cannot violate them to suit himself without shaking the kingdom to its foundations. Navarre happens to be my legitimate successor according to those rules. And I shouldn't choose just any so-and-so in order to thwart him. I made no vows at my coronation to exclude a prince from succeeding me on the basis of his religion. And this is not a decision I can make on my private authority. The state orders it. And so, convinced as I am that the good of the state orders it on this occasion, I am at ease with my conscience in naming Navarre as my successor."

At this Chicot, forgetting his role as fool, fell silent, as did I, both of us struck beyond all words by this beautiful and strong expostulation, by which the king's fidelity to the principles of the kingdom appeared with such strength. He considered them to be above him as he was above his people.

"Monsieur de Siorac," continued the king, handing me a piece of paper folded in four, "it is important, as you travel to Guyenne, to be properly outfitted so as to make a good impression on the Duc d'Épernon. When you present this paper to my treasurer, he will provide you with 300 écus."

"Sire, I offer you a thousand thanks for this marvellous munificence."

"Oh, don't thank him!" growled Chicot. "His generous nature is his greatest defect. If we hadn't given so much money to all the ingrates, we'd have more to arm ourselves against the Magnificent."

"May God," continued the king, pretending not to have heard his fool, "keep you safe, Monsieur de Siorac, and stalwart in my service! You have greatly obliged me by your acceptance of this mission, and it cannot but redouble the friendship I bear you. I would give you my hand, Monsieur chevalier, if it hadn't been gloved for the night. Chicot, my mask, if you please."

"Sire," said Chicot as he arranged as best he could the mask over Henri's face, "may I sleep on the floor beside your bed tonight?"

"Alas no, Chicot. Your feet stink. Call Du Halde. This mask isn't set the way I like it. Monsieur chevalier, I shall sleep soundly, confident in your obedience and certain of your fidelity."

"Ah, Chevalier of Bloodletting," said Chicot after we'd left the king and he'd informed Du Halde that His Majesty was asking for him, "of all the brave and good people on this earth, Henri is the most generous and affectionate with his servants. I am enraged at the evil that they want to inflict on this lamb! And that they use us to get at him! Oh, if only I could find in this kingdom a sack large enough, I'd stuff it with the Magnificent, the Whoremonger and Madame Limp and drown them in the Seine!" He said all of this with a tear in his eye, partly out of pity for the king and partly out of fury at his mortal enemies.

"Ah, where shall we find a sack large enough?"

"Patience!" replied Chicot as he gave me a huge hug, which I returned with all my heart—though I did notice, as I embraced him, that the king was absolutely right about his feet. Nevertheless, as witty, incisive and rambunctious as he was, and sharp though his claws may have been, beneath that irreverent exterior beat an immense heart. After this moment we'd spent together, I loved him till his death, which was heroic, as I've said.

My poor Angelina was pained and sad when she learnt that I'd have to leave her, and though I assured her that this would be an affair of but two months, she refused to believe me, knowing full well that when great men travel in this kingdom, followed by all their servants and effects, they're received in every town with banquets and feasting, and thus increasingly delayed by all these delights. And though she was aggrieved by this separation, and perhaps jealous of all the Circes that I might encounter in my journey, she had too much dignity and nobility to cover me with tears or to betray any of her suspicions. And yet, as I watched the pensive way that she looked at me, her beautiful doe eyes filled with such candour and trust, it seemed to me that they sometimes misted over in melancholy, which her dignity and her scrupulous concerns for me prevented her from expressing.

And bursting with love at this new appreciation for her exquisite kindness, I pulled her to me passionately and kissed and hugged her, murmuring those many tender expressions we'd exchanged over the years, and assuring her of my undying commitment to her. I told her again that what her beauty had set in motion, those many years ago, her admirable goodness had completed, and that I would love her till the end of time—or, at least, as long as I remained in the world of the living.

Leaving her side to begin outfitting myself for my mission, as the king, in his generosity, had commanded me to do, I could think only of expressing my feelings for Angelina in some way that would feel adequate, for my boundless love seemed to surpass any earthly measure of recompense. As I wandered about the streets purchasing the necessary items for my trip, I couldn't help seeing her everywhere and desiring to please her with every beautiful object I saw in the shop windows, wishing I could offer her the very universe.

In the midst of these dreamy fantasies, I was staring at some very expensive necklaces in the window of a jeweller's shop, when a lady wearing a black mask got out of a coach behind me, followed by her chambermaid, also masked. She stepped unabashedly to my side, and pretended to examine the display in the window that I'd imagined being able to offer Angelina.

I suspected that this mysterious lady was some well-dressed debauchee in search of a young gentleman to fleece, but my suspicions vanished as soon as she spoke: her low, musical voice was as sweet as honey and her French remarkably refined, though marked by an accent that seemed familiar.

"Monsieur," she ventured, "I'm going to guess that, of all the rings displayed here, the one you like best is the luminous Hungarian opal, set with little diamonds."

"Madame," I stammered, astonished by such on opening, "you're very perceptive! That's the very one! But I'm afraid my pockets aren't deep enough to afford it."

"Ah, what a pity!" she sighed. "Or, rather, what a half-pity, for I know a noble lady who'd be very pleased to offer it to your wife, to thank her for the expense and bother of taking into her home a gentleman in need of medical attention."

"Madame," I replied, suddenly suspicious, "I know not which gentleman you could be referring to! Nor who this noble lady might be! Nor who you might be, for that matter!"

"I serve the woman I've mentioned," said my mysterious friend, "and she's good enough to lend me some of her jewels from time to time, which are much like these you see on my hand. And as you have such a good eye for jewellery, perhaps you will recognize the owner of these stones…" And so saying, she slowly removed her glove from her left hand; when it was bare, she raised it to her mask as if she were intending to adjust it, and allowed me to admire the set of rings that had adorned the fingers of Lady Stafford when I'd kissed them in Madame de Joyeuse's salon.

I now saw that this was no attempt to trick me, and I was struck by the subtlety of my English friend's feminine intuition, for, though I'd not said a word, Lady Stafford, seeing my admiration of her jewellery, had subsequently had the idea of using it to express her gratitude for what I'd done.

"The gentleman is well on his way to recovery. He'll be able to ride a horse in a week or so."

"Then he'll be able to accompany you on your trip to Guyenne," said my mysterious friend, leaving me dumbfounded that she knew of this voyage and the unexpected request of the king.

"And these are your mistress's wishes?" I asked when I'd recovered my voice.

"Yes, Monsieur."

"Assuredly," I conceded, "her wishes are important, but I cannot accept without first having discussed it with my master, to see if he agrees, so I won't be able to answer you before tomorrow morning."

"Well then, Monsieur, let's agree to meet here again tomorrow at the same time, so you can inform me of his decision."

"Agreed," I consented, "as long as you'll share with me the identity of your mistress, which is more persuasive than your rings."

At this, my masked friend, whom I imagined to be one of Lady Stafford's ladies-in-waiting, gave a saucy laugh and departed with a great swish of her generous skirts.

I was able to speak to the king the next morning while appearing to take his pulse, and apprised him of my previous day's encounter. He gave his consent to her request, on condition that no one should know that the fellow was English, since His Majesty was convinced that in the Duc d'Épernon's retinue there would be some of Guise's spies. On the other hand, he understood that Queen Elizabeth wanted to use the offices of this gentleman to consult with Navarre on ways to foil the assassination plots of their common enemies, and this was what ultimately convinced him to sanction the project.

As I did every day, I accompanied the king to Mass in the chapel of the Hôtel de Bourbon, and, when I returned to my lodgings, I found Giacomi in despair after having received a report from Mosca indicating that, after losing any trace of Samarcas for the past several days, he'd discovered the Jesuit had embarked from Calais two days previously with his pupil. I comforted my Italian brother as best I could, and decided to obey the sudden inspiration of my feelings by asking him to accompany me to Guyenne, since I'd also be bringing Miroul and Mr Mundane with me. He hesitated at first, until I suggested that he tell the Montcalms that he'd be away for six months, pointing out that they'd doubtless communicate this information to Samarcas, who then might stay with them during his next visit, believing the *maestro* to be conveniently separated from his pupil.

From the change that came over his face at my suggestion, I could tell that I'd given him some hope with this dazzling possibility, however fragile, given that I wasn't certain that we'd be returning before six months had elapsed, or that Samarcas would be returning to Paris during that period. It's well known, however, that the lover who lives in perpetual fear of losing the object of his affections thrives on speculations about his mistress, some sombre, others radiant, and all of them unreasonable. At least what I'd told him was neither impossible nor nonsensical, since, when he was in Paris, Samarcas wouldn't stay with the Montcalms if there were any chance of seeing Giacomi there.

In the examination I performed on Mr Mundane after my midday meal, I found him well on the way to recovery and had no doubt he'd be able to saddle up by the date the king had set for the departure of the Duc d'Épernon, so I immediately informed him of what the sovereign he served was expecting of him. He answered that he was aware that when his mission in Paris had been completed he would be sent to Guyenne to support the king of Navarre, and that he'd be delighted to join me in this voyage, especially since he spoke French with an accent and would need my help to avoid the suspicions of the Guisards, who held the queen of England and all of her loyal subjects in particular execration.

"Mr Mundane," I replied, "I've already considered this problem, and I thought we might resolve it by proposing that you play the same role as Miroul in my service, and that you wear my livery. No one will pay any heed to the speech of a valet, whereas that of a gentleman would doubtless draw unwanted attention. I hope, Mr Mundane, that my proposal in no way offends your dignity."

"Why, Monsieur, I find your idea outrageous!" exclaimed Mundane, who loved to say the opposite of what he thought, a joke that was habitual with him and that he accompanied with a huge guffaw, his face becoming brick red in colour, just like his beard and hair. "But I'll have to put my security ahead of my dignity! One punctured lung is enough for me! I wouldn't like a second…"

"Mr Mundane," I cautioned, placing my hand on his shoulder, "in your condition I would avoid laughing, coughing, speaking and any excessive movement. I'm afraid you've been overtired by Zara."

"Not at all! She's the one doing all the talking, not me! I can't get a word in edgewise! She loves talking about herself, a subject she's excessively fond of! But though I listen only with one ear, I use both my eyes to look at her."

"Ah, but your eyes could cause you undue agitation all by themselves!"

"Not at this stage of my recovery, venerable doctor," he replied with a grateful wink, in self-mockery. "I'm being reborn and reliving my infancy in Zara's arms."

"What? In her arms?" I laughed. "Already?"

"Thank God, she's very affectionate," replied Mundane, his face inscrutable but for the sparkle in his eyes.

I left my happy Englishman to his thoughts, very comforted to see with what sharp teeth he was taking a bite out of life after having nearly lost it, and hurried to my rendezvous in front of Corane's jewellery shop, which was then situated on the Pont au Change, and still is to this day. This time, however, I had myself shadowed by Miroul and Giacomi, who, in addition to their swords, carried pistols in their leggings; I, in the Italian manner, concealed a long dagger behind my back, hidden by my cloak, which, if necessary, could be drawn more quickly than a sword up close to an assailant. Not that I feared an ambush from the ladies I'd talked to, but rather from any Guisards who might have followed them.

I felt a sting of disappointment when I arrived at the jewellery shop only to discover that the opal from Hungary set with little diamonds that I had admired the day before was no longer displayed in Corane's window, an absence I found quite aggravating, even though I knew I couldn't afford the jewel. The 300 écus the king had advanced me for the trip would scarcely suffice to cover my expenses, and of these 300 écus, the king's treasurer had taken a cut of fifty, and so the 250 remaining would scarcely pay for meals for the four of us—Giacomi, Miroul, Mundane and myself—not to mention the cost of oats and hay for our four mounts, plus a packhorse.

I was at this point in my unhappy deliberations when suddenly the masked lady of the day before appeared at my side and, pretending to admire the jewels in the window, said, "Monsieur, if you'll consent to follow me to the rue de la Vieille Pelleterie, you'll find my mistress waiting in a coach there. She'd like to have a word with you. However, I should warn you, Monsieur, that there are two men over there who have been watching you."

"What do they look like?" I asked, since there was such a crush of people on the Pont au Change.

"One is tall and thin, and the other quite slender."

"They're with me," I smiled. "Lead the way to the coach, Madame! I'll navigate in the wake of your skirts."

I recognized the coach I'd seen the day before waiting in the middle of the rue de la Vieille Pelleterie. Instead of climbing in herself, my mysterious guide motioned for me to step inside. The coachman leapt from his seat, pulled open the curtains, lowered the steps and silently signalled for me enter. Which I did warily, my left hand reaching for the dagger in my cape. At first glance, however, I determined that the only weapon in the coach was the beauty of the women who were awaiting me. Inside I found not one but three sets of petticoats, but I was unable to identify any of my fellow passengers, for the coachman immediately lowered the curtains, leaving us in a perfumed penumbra in which I could scarcely make out the lady I was seated next to, clearly the most richly attired of the three. However, as my eyes grew accustomed to this obscurity, I decided that I was comfortably enough lodged here to patiently accept whatever awaited me. Finally, my neighbour removed her mask, threw me an enchanting smile and, placing her gloved left hand on my right arm, asked in her sweetly musical voice whether my master had agreed to her proposal regarding Mr Mundane. Even in this gloom I was able to recognize—both from the timbre of her voice and from the colour of her Venetian-red hair—that I was in the presence of a lady of high birth and great beauty. We were sitting so close that our faces were practically touching, and I told her in a voice much less calm than I would have liked where things stood with the king, and noticed that she was pressing my arm with increasing fervour as I explained the situation. When I'd finished my report, she exhibited a degree of joy and gaiety that surprised me, given the haughty and cold demeanour she'd displayed in our first conversation:

"Monsieur chevalier, I hope that your pockets are sufficiently deep, for I have much to give you on behalf of Lord Stafford. First, a letter for Mr Mundane. Second, this purse containing 200 écus, which should cover all of Mr Mundane's expenses during your trip to Guyenne. And third, a ring that I would like to offer to Madame de Siorac, to express my gratitude for the trouble she's gone to in receiving Mr Mundane in her household."

One can easily imagine my difficulty in adequately expressing my thanks, which included a vain effort to dissuade her from such an extravagant gift (since I could easily guess which ring she had chosen, without even having opened the case), and how thrilled Angelina would be, given her love of jewellery. Lady Stafford would not, of course, be dissuaded, because she was of a generous yet obstinate disposition, and argued that the compensation was twofold: firstly to thank us for our care of the wounded man and secondly to take care of his travel expenses. But, she added, this reasoning was irrelevant given that she was only obeying her husband's orders, and she expected the same obedience from me. She said this in French, with a charming accent and an imperious little pout that would have routed my most steadfast legions even if she, Lady Stafford, hadn't added, this time in English, "Chevalier, we have argued enough. I shall kiss you if you do not accept it."

"Well, Madame!" I replied. "You're too condescending…"

But I never finished my sentence. She closed my mouth with a kiss that was, though suave enough, exceedingly brief, as though to let me know that nothing would follow it—although I never would have flattered myself by thinking otherwise, knowing full well how much this noble lady treasured her birth and her virtue, the first fortifying the second, as sometimes happens. After which, having accepted this light kiss and the heavy purse, nothing remained but to shower her with professions of gratitude and praise and assurances of my infinite respect. Which I did profusely as was my wont. I had no doubt that she was very happy with me—and with herself, for having served her husband and her queen so well.

This mission of the Duc d'Épernon to Henri de Navarre was no paltry affair, and no expense was spared: Épernon was escorted by a train of some 500 gentlemen, each of whom had received a gift from the king equal to mine, on condition that each be splendidly attired and accompanied by at least five servants. I would have been very ashamed in the midst of such grandiose company, given that I was accompanied by only two valets bearing my livery, and a master-at-arms, had Quéribus, who had taken the trouble, as one would have expected, to surround himself with a large number of servants (including a fool, a masseur and an astrologist), not instantly invited me to join his party—as much because he would enjoy my company as because he didn't want to have to blush at his brother-in-law's very Huguenot economy.

So, if you add to the 500 gentlemen their retinues, not to mention the Duc d'Épernon's guards (and the wenches who followed them, since the duc did not want any defilement along the way), as well as the valets, cooks, baggage carts and mules, you can imagine the interminable ribbon of humanity, moving at a heavy, snail-like pace, under a leaden sun, to the din of thousands of hooves beating the dusty road.

On my advice, Quéribus had requested and obtained from the Duc d'Épernon a position in the avant-garde, whose responsibility it was to prepare the accommodation at each of the staging post, a difficult task to be sure, but one that allowed us to escape from the unbelievable din, halts, falls, disputes, turbulence and, worst of all, clouds of dust that pitilessly whitened the ruddiest of faces and most colourful clothing of the travellers.

Moreover, since we were the first to arrive at each staging post, we could take our time to obtain all our provisions before meat became first dear, then scarce, and then disappeared altogether, to the despair of every town or city we passed through and left as empty as if we'd been enemy troops intent on their devastation! The labourers in their fields who watched our superb procession open-mouthed would have been wise to mix some terror in with their admiration, for we passed through their farmlands like a cloud of locusts, leaving nothing behind us.

Moving as slowly as we did, it took ten days to reach the Loire valley, where we stopped in Loches, a large town, which the Duc d'Épernon admired for its formidable defences, the strength of its walls, towers and square dungeon, which is one of the highest I've ever seen.

At the rate we were moving, it took us a month to reach Pamiers, where the king of Navarre had sent word to Épernon that he'd meet us. However, desirous of honouring Henri III's ambassador, the king of Navarre, in a remarkable display of condescension, advanced to meet him at Saverdun. There was much discomfort and embarrassment among the troops on both sides, since Épernon's train was so numerous and magnificent, and Navarre's so poorly attired, as if the rich north were meeting the poor south, and Catholic splendour were confronting Huguenot parsimony.

Henri de Navarre, having signalled to his retinue to halt, advanced alone on his white horse, as if to place himself in the hands of the king's representative and display before this assembly the trust he placed in him. Seeing this, Épernon signalled to his people to stop, rode out to meet Henri on his beautiful Andalusian mount, and doffed his plumed hat, whereupon Henri immediately did the same. They exchanged princely pleasantries for a few minutes in the manner of noblemen who wish not only to express their friendship for each other, but to put it on display before the world.

Their conversation ended, Navarre turned his mount and rejoined his men, who led the way to Pamiers, arriving there well before we did, being as unencumbered as we were heavy-laden. (Quéribus and I had not had to make our usual avant-garde preparations, since we were Navarre's guests here.)

I imagine that Navarre was forced to reflect on the relative impoverishment of his escort, for, instead of awaiting us on horseback, he dismounted and welcomed us on foot, surrounded by no more than a dozen gentlemen and guards with little display or fanfare. In his welcome to the Duc d'Épernon, he behaved less like the king of Navarre and more as though he were merely the first citizen of his city, with his open and healthy demeanour.

Épernon, who was, like his host, a Gascon, well understood the subtlety of Henri de Navarre, who, unable to match his guest's splendour, wished to outdo him in simplicity; so, bending to the finesse of Navarre, he dismounted, threw his bridle to his servant, removed his plumed hat (though the noon sun was hot enough to boil an egg) and stepped forward, bareheaded, to pay homage to the presumptive king. The latter, charmed that he'd understood so well, stepped forward, embraced him heartily and, taking him familiarly by the arm, led him into the city, where, happily for the duc, who always went bareheaded, the houses offered some shade, while the joyful crowds loudly acclaimed the king of Navarre, and through him, the king of France.

Henri did not seem to have changed much over the twelve long years that had elapsed since that fateful night when we'd ridden side by side from the Louvre to the lodgings of Coligny, though he seemed smaller, perhaps because Épernon was walking beside him now. But he still had the same long nose in his angular face, the same sparkle in his eyes and the same open and jocular expression. And though he'd gone to some expense to dress appropriately for this occasion, his unpolished and brusque manners were more those of a soldier than those of a prince. And yet one could easily see that he wasn't a man who would allow himself to be slighted: he had about him that air of self-confidence that comes from a long habit of leadership and an aptitude for action.

Pushing my way to the front, I bumped into a mountain of a man who was positioned right behind the king, and who was wearing the red and yellow livery of his guards; feeling the push from behind, he turned his head only slightly and growled:

"*Herrgott!* Watch where you're going, *Mensch!*"

Recognizing this voice, I seized the arm of this colossus with both hands, trying to whirl him around to see his face, but this had no other effect than to get him to raise his arms and me along with them. But as he did, he glanced backwards and, catching sight of me, made a great shout that would have been audible on the other side of town if the crowd hadn't suddenly broken forth in clamorous cheers that would have penetrated the ears of the deaf.

"*Ach!* My noble master!" he trumpeted as he slowly lowered his arm to restore me to firm ground. "You—here?!"

"Fröhlich!" I exclaimed. "My good Swiss! What are you doing in Pamiers? Did you leave my father's service?"

"*Nein! Nein! Nein!*" he crescendoed, tears bathing his large, round face. "Me? Leave the baron? *Schelme! Schelme!*"

"And yet you're here!" I said in surprise. "You're neither a dream nor a phantom, but a man, made of flesh and bone! Good Lord! It's really you, Fröhlich! And wearing Navarre's livery, which you last wore twelve years ago! Here! In Pamiers! Which means you *must* have left my father's service!"

"*Schelme! Schelme!*" he repeated. "I'd never leave the baron! You think I'd leave your father, a man so valiant and generous there's never been his like in the kingdom?! *Nein! Nein!* I'm his man, now and forever."

"But, Fröhlich," I laughed, "how can you serve the king of Navarre in Pamiers and my father in Périgord?"

"But," cried my giant, his huge, rubicund face breaking into a smile as he realized why I thought he'd abandoned my father, "it's because Monsieur your father is here—serving, as I do, the king of Navarre!"

"What? My father's here?! Ah, my good Fröhlich, take me to his lodgings straightaway!"

"My noble master," Fröhlich replied, "wait a bit till I've restored some order to this crowd, who are pressing up around the king like to suffocate him! *Herrgott!* Is this any way to behave? I'll be with you as soon as the princes are safely behind closed doors. Wait for me!"

Having said this, he grabbed his staff with both hands and, holding it horizontally in front of him, ran to push away a group of labourers who were surging forward and blocking Henri's access to the city hall. "Ah!" I thought. "Now I understand why the king assigned me to serve as Épernon's physician on this trip to Guyenne! He knew I'd get to see my father!" Besides the joy he'd offered me, he must also have considered that I'd learn many things that were hidden from Épernon and that would be most useful to know.

I retraced my steps to find Giacomi, Miroul and Mundane, which wasn't easy in the press and confusion of the horses in these narrow streets, the noise of acclamation still ringing, as though the throats of these fellows were made of the same bronze as their church bells, which were also clanging to burst your eardrums, as if to prove their conversion to the new religion. I couldn't help enjoying the sight of all the pretty wenches leaning from their windows, preferring this view of the festivities to risking their hides in the midst of all these hungry men. From one balcony to another, you could hear them trading jokes about the new arrivals that would have made a papist saint blush. Anyone who assumed that these people had suddenly become solemn when they joined Calvin's ranks would have been sadly mistaken, for, from every side, we were welcomed with cries of happiness, garlands of flowers and shouts of "Long live the king!" This demonstration of the reconciliation between the kings of France and Navarre had clearly renewed their hope of a return to peace in our kingdom.

This long and tiring journey from the north of the kingdom to its extreme southern point, where the towering Pyrenees formed a rampart against Felipe II of Spain and his morose, murderous zeal, was finally at an end, and we could all now bask in the friendship of this good city—and I more than anyone, since I was to be reunited with my father. When at length I was able to meet up with Giacomi and Miroul, they too were overjoyed at the prospect of seeing Jean de Siorac and at being reunited with their gigantic companion, Fröhlich, who'd fought tooth and nail with us on our odyssey through the terror of that bloody St Bartholomew's eve in Paris.

There are so many joys in our brief life, but perhaps none greater than to be reunited after so many years with one's father, to see him still hale and hearty, still of good cheer, and to watch him coming and going in his lodgings with his customary stance, hands on hips, straight as a board, his hoary head still held proudly, blue eyes still asparkle and still enjoying life's sensual and intellectual pleasures—and as disdainful of appearances and glory as ever.

"Well, Pierre," said he, after enquiring about Catherine, Samson and me, "I'm so unhappy being around that pompous ass of a brother of yours! He's become so stuck-up and self-important now that he's got an heir and can call himself Baron de Fontenac. Certainly, he manages that estate and mine diligently enough. But, by the belly of St Anthony, I so miss my brother, Sauveterre, and my poor Franchou, who died in childbirth! It feels like pissing vinegar to have him constantly at my side with his long, Lenten face! And now that he's switched sides and become a papist, he's become more Catholic than the Pope! He goes to Mass every day, worships the saints, mumbles his Ave Marias and, would you believe, goes on pilgrimages! Dammit! My blood boils at these hypocritical mummeries! I've left him in charge of Mespech for these two months, happy to be following Navarre from town to town, with no care whatsoever for the modest lodgings I'm in, and managing with but one valet and a single chambermaid—who is, by the way, a devil of a good wench."

"Ah," I thought, looking at this little darling, "is she a devil of a good girl, or a good she-devil?" My father's sixty-seven years certainly didn't seem to weigh heavily on him, and I'd have been very worried if he ever stopped behaving this way. As for me, I'm convinced impotence is the daughter of abstinence and not the other way around!

After we had ravenously demolished our dinner, Giacomi, sensing that my father wanted to converse with me alone, told me that he wanted to see the town of Pamiers, and took with him Mundane and Miroul, leaving us to ourselves. My father took advantage of this tête-à-tête to ask me why Henri III had asked me to accompany Épernon on this journey, and I explained that, in truth, there were three likely reasons, a sure one and two conjectures.

"Well, tell me the one you're certain of," laughed Jean de Siorac.

"Since the duc seems to complain constantly of a sore throat, the king wanted me to try to cure it as his personal physician was confined to his bed."

"And the duc, indeed, continues to complain of this affliction?"

"Assuredly."

"So what do you prescribe?"

"Gargling with boiled salt water each morning, at noon and at six. Between times, I recommend honey."

"And water. Tell him to drink lots of water."

"I shan't fail to do so. And the second reason—"

"Which is conjectural," he interrupted with a laugh, as though the word itself tickled him.

"…is that the king wanted to please me, knowing that you'd be here."

"Yes, he knew it. Duplessis-Mornay saw me with Navarre, and he's been in Paris since April."

"The third reason," I continued, "is that the king wanted to test you, using me to trick you."

"Careful now! Careful!" laughed my father. "My son, are you spying on my king to serve yours?"

"I serve the one in serving the other, since I believe their fortunes are now linked."

"Well said! And they are. They are in principle and someday will be so in reality. Against Guise, the Pope and Felipe II, the king has no other ally than Navarre."

"And Elizabeth."

"Ah! Elizabeth!" smiled Jean de Siorac. "So that's the reason that you brought along this Englishman, whose servant's appearance belies what I suspect is his true condition."

"Indeed! He's supposed to contact Navarre on behalf of his sovereign. Is this something you could arrange?"

"I'll think about it. Venerable doctor," he continued with a smile, "are you the king's physician or his spy?"

"Both."

"Be careful!" warned my father, shaking his head. "If there's a profit in the first, there's danger in the second."

"The king warned me of this. Father, do you think Épernon's mission will be successful?"

"That's up to Navarre to decide."

"But what do *you* think?"

"My son," queried Jean de Siorac with a twinkle in his eye, "are you sounding me out?"

"Yes, Monsieur."

At this my father burst out laughing, so hard he couldn't stop, and his chambermaid, Mariette, raised her head in surprise—she had not understood a traitorous word we'd exchanged, since she spoke only *langue d'oc*, but, delighted to see her master so joyful, she began to laugh along with him. Seeing this, Jean de Siorac got up, walked over to her stool, which was set before the window, and began caressing her shoulders, arms and breasts; then he mused, "The human body is symmetrical, which is why we need two hands to caress it."

"My father," I persisted, "you haven't answered me."

"That's because I believe you're capable of answering yourself."

"How so?"

"You're only two years younger than Navarre. Try to imagine yourself in his place in 1572, a rustic child of the mountains of Béarn, a little kinglet who's scarcely out of swaddling clothes, speaking *langue d'oc* better than French. Imagine that you arrive open-mouthed at the Louvre, and are greeted with hostility by the foppish court favourites, despised by those in power and by the people because you're a Huguenot. What's more, you've got short legs, a long torso and a nose that's said to be 'bigger than your kingdom'. You're not very handsome, or clean, or perfumed, and you smell of garlic, dirty feet and sweat. And then you become an immediate cuckold by marrying the Princesse Margot, who's known to have lost her virginity as Guise's whore, and become the laughing stock of the entire court. You're hooted at and spat on and lampooned. You're hated by Catherine de' Medici, since Nostradamus prophesied that 'the Béarnais will inherit everything'. On St Bartholomew's morning you see all of your gentlemen massacred before your eyes in the courtyard of the Louvre; Charles IX practically holds a dagger to your throat and declares, 'Mass or death! You decide!' So you go to Mass and take Communion amid the jeers of the court, while Catherine bursts out laughing as she looks at the foreign ambassadors. There follow four years of captivity—four years, Pierre!—within the walls of the Louvre where, as 'the little kinglet of a prisoner', you must cool your heels, your life perpetually threatened. Your chambers are searched every day. You have but one valet to serve you. When the court travels, you're forced to ride in the carriage of Catherine, the queen mother, who keeps her round raptor's eyes on you all the time. When the court goes hunting, you're followed by two gentlemen, who never leave your side, even when you piss. When you fuck, it's with women chosen by Catherine, who report everything to their mistress, even your sighs. Heavens! How many indignities you've had to swallow! Finally, you escape, and become king in your kingdom, the titular head of a powerful party, now ready to confront your former jailers. My son, if you were Navarre, would you go back to this sinister Louvre, where this same Catherine is waiting, along with the same ministers, the same Guise and the same populace beating on the walls of the chateau—the same St Bartholomew's mob, who hold Navarre in more strident execration than Beelzebub?"

"Not on your life."

"Well, there's your answer. You provided it yourself."

"But, Father, the predicament is no longer the same. Henri III is not Charles IX. He loves Navarre, and though he's still 'trimming his sails' when necessary, he never strays from his will."

"But you're forgetting, my son, that Henri III has no support from any side that will back him, no matter what he chooses, and that he's presently in as much danger in the Louvre as Navarre would be if he were mad enough to return."

"My father," I mused, after reflecting a moment, "will you permit me to repeat to Épernon the contents of this discussion?"

"Absolutely not!" replied my father with a smile that belied his refusal. "Let Épernon plead his case with Navarre! There are doubtless other considerations than those we've discussed. And they're of such enormous consequence for peace in the kingdom that Navarre may very well temporize."

I examined Épernon's throat that very evening before he went to bed, and found it still very raw and somewhat swollen, but devoid of any white spots or blotches, from which I concluded that, if he continued to gargle with water and consume honey, he'd be well on his way to being cured—as long as he took care to avoid the cold when in a sweat.

When I'd finished my examination, Épernon, who lacked any of the exquisite civility of our good master and sovereign, demanded in the brusque and imperious tone he used with everyone, "What says Mespech of my mission?"

"What I'd also say, Monseigneur."

"And what do you say?"

"That to house Navarre right away in the Louvre would only discourage him."

"But it could be arranged to have him lodged elsewhere! For example in the Château de Saint-Germain-en-Laye, with a strong garrison of troops."

He said nothing more, but the vivacity of his response convinced me that Épernon sensed the enormous difficulties of his mission and that he greatly feared failing at it.

I never heard one iota of what was said between Épernon and Navarre that day in Pamiers, nor at Encausse on 29th June, where they met again. On the other hand, I gleaned a few echoes of the long discussions they'd had at Pau from the 3rd to the 11th July from my father, who, though he'd not attended those meetings, was present when Navarre conferred with his principal advisors: Marmet, a minister of the reformed religion, Du Ferrier, his chancellor, and Monsieur de Roquelaure, who, though Catholic, had faithfully attached himself to the person of Navarre and to his fortunes, whatever they might be.

To tell the truth, my father never opened his mouth in this discussion. Navarre never once asked for his advice, and my own view is that if he invited Siorac to attend it was so that the king could learn the terms of the discussion from another source than the Duc d'Épernon. At least, that's the way my father understood it, otherwise he wouldn't have shared a word of it with me. The strangest thing of all was that Navarre never once, in all those days, gave any sign that he remembered me, neither addressing a word to me nor looking at me directly, he who was so familiar with everyone down to the last slip of a page or saddle boy, despite the fact that he'd specifically asked Fröhlich at Pamiers how my fortunes were advancing at Henri's court.

What gave this secret council such weight was that, at the very time it was meeting, all the participants knew that Henri's brother, whose health had been deteriorating since May, had died on 11th June—news that we received on 8th July from a messenger sent from Paris by the king. Thus, it had become imperative, Henri now having no successor, that he urgently come to an understanding with Navarre, if he didn't want the Cardinal de Bourbon (Guise's brother) to make his hair curl by pushing his advantage.

Later on I had access to the letters that His Majesty sent to Navarre, admonishing, begging, exhorting him to join him in Paris and go to Mass with him so that he could recognize the Béarnais as his legitimate successor to the crown of France, and thereby receive all the rights, honours and advantages that would accrue to him in that role. It is never formally stated in these letters, but it is nevertheless strongly suggested that Navarre would be named lieutenant general as soon as his conversion was consummated, a position that would make him second only to the king of France, without his having to renounce the throne of Navarre.

On the seventh day of the discussions between Épernon and Navarre at Pau, Navarre, departing from his usual habit, withdrew into his cabinet after the repast, with Roquelaure, Marmet, Du Ferrier and the Baron de Mespech, whose presence he requested with a nod of the head as he passed him. Dismissing all his valets and guards, he closed the door and, without saying a word, began pacing up and down, hands behind his back, lost in thought. According to the participants in the room, his demeanour wasn't much different from that he'd adopted during the entire round of discussions: silent, occasionally shaking his head, posing a question or two, but never revealing his own position—until this moment with his counsellors, when he would no longer have to disguise the worries and confusion that had plagued him. My father reported the discussion as follows:

"'Well, sire,' said Roquelaure, who is a tall, portly gentleman, whose scarlet complexion suggested that he is little apt at dissimulation, 'whence this new sadness? Haven't you every reason to be happy? The king of France not only recognizes your rights to succession but is ready to receive you at court and establish you as the first and firmest support of the throne.'

"'Yes, but on one condition,' countered Marmet."

"Father," I said, interrupting him, "what does this Marmet look like?"

"I'm not surprised that you haven't noticed him," my father laughed. "He looks like a shadow. It's as though he has no body, being so tall and skinny and all dressed in black, his eyes deep in their sockets, lips thin as blades of dead grass. But he's surer in his faith than the firmest of rocks and has escaped from countless gibbets. My son, if you'll promise not to interrupt me, I'll continue:

218

"'On one condition, however,' warned Marmet.

"'Well, I know what you're going to say!' said Navarre over his shoulder, not without some bitterness, since this condition was a thorn in his conscience. And he continued to pace back and forth on his short but energetic legs. The country of Béarn is all hills and valleys, as everyone knows, and its inhabitants have a mountaineer's stride—lengthy and indefatigable. I think of Navarre as one of our local barns set on a hill: not very well proportioned, but built to withstand all weathers."

"And what about the chancellor, Du Ferrier?"

"You're interrupting again! You've seen wise old Du Ferrier—with the Ten Commandments etched on his noble brow. His sagacious eyes were moving back and forth between Navarre and Roquelaure, and from Roquelaure to Marmet, and, having too much on his mind to trust himself to express it, he simply held his tongue. But you can guess, my son, that this silence wasn't just anybody's silence—*Nein! Nein! Nein!* as my good Fröhlich would say. Du Ferrier's silence had a kind of strength and majesty to it: Moses standing on Mount Sinai waiting for illumination from Heaven. And yet he's a very political man. He's only recently converted to the Huguenot faith and is a lot less zealous than Marmet.

"But all this silence—Navarre's, Du Ferrier's and Marmet's (this last had said but five words, but they were fearsome words)—this triple silence was becoming increasingly intolerable to Roquelaure, who, being a man of action and plain speaking, suddenly burst forth in a torrent of feelings.

"'Well, sire!' he cried. 'Here you are inwardly debating whether to embrace this good fortune and accept the king's offer, or whether to refuse it in order to please your minister here and others of his stripe, who advise you according to their own passions and concerns, with no respect for your service and the public good!'

"At this brutal attack, Mamet didn't blink an eye, for indeed, how could such a rock be the least bit affected by a cataract falling from the greatest heights?

"'I am not,' he hissed in a voice that was barely audible, 'indifferent to the public good. Whether or not the king of Navarre agrees to hear Mass or not is a matter of conscience. Fourteen years ago, he was forced into it, a knife at his throat. Today, they're begging him to do it. But who is begging him? The victor of Jarnac and Moncontour and one of the architects of the St Bartholomew's day massacre! Assuredly, the king's predicament has changed him, but what circumstances can fashion, circumstances can also undo. Navarre might well be Henri III's right hand at the court, just as Coligny was—alas!—for Charles IX. But the court's favour is fickle. In Béarn and in Guyenne the reformers are the lance and shield of our king, but if he agrees to hear Mass, he will be disarmed. If he returns to the court he will fall into the hands of his enemies. He will be doubly stripped bare.'

"At this, Navarre, as he continued to pace back and forth with his mountaineer's step, glanced meaningfully at Marmet, who'd just let him know, in his gentle and veiled way, that if he chose to hear Mass, he'd lose the support of the Huguenot party from which he drew his strength.

"'But stay,' cried Roquelaure passionately, 'if he doesn't resign himself to hear Mass, isn't he renouncing the throne of France? On the other hand, as soon as the court learns that the king of Navarre has converted, everyone in France will run to him to offer him their support, their means, their riches...'

"'Must he lose his soul to win the approval of men?' asked Marmet.

"'But he doesn't have to hear Mass in his heart!' Roquelaure replied with naive impudence. 'Can't he be a Catholic only on the outside?'

"At this a silence fell over the room so heavy, so cold and so prolonged that poor Roquelaure, who was himself a Catholic, but of the most worldly variety, was quite abashed, scarcely able to understand how the Huguenots felt about this question, which he'd raised with such unexpected light-heartedness. However, anchoring himself firmly on his two powerful legs and appearing, like Antaeus, to gain strength from his very contact with the earth, he added, his black eyes shooting thunder and lightning, 'If we rebuff and refuse the king of France, there's every danger that he'll make peace with Guise and the Huguenots will pay the price for this alliance. And so I ask everyone here: wouldn't it be better to hear 500 Masses than to revive the civil war and face its accompanying horrors?'

"To speak of massacres to Huguenots, who had so often suffered from them, was a language they understood all too well, and Roquelaure's argument, even though it stuck in their craws, had a visible effect on everyone present: but Marmet made no response, because he'd already said his piece; Du Ferrier held his peace because he had too much to say, and the king remained silent because he couldn't open his mouth without announcing his decision—and he wasn't ready to decide yet.

"'Well, my father,' said the king to Du Ferrier, 'what do you think?'

"'That we must,' replied Du Ferrier in a very measured tone, 'try to imagine the effects of an immediate recantation of your faith. I believe they would be deplorable, both for the Catholics, who wouldn't believe you to be sincere, and for the Huguenots. And what would the advantages be? In my view, very dubious ones, the court in Paris being what it is. I don't think the hour has yet come for such a considerable concession, one that would confuse everything and solve nothing. The king of Navarre has already changed his religion too often. So I think it's better that he remain what he is than put himself in danger of being reputed to be changeable and unserious, without any certainty of being able to take advantage of the conversion. So what should we do? Remain faithful to the law, to try to prevent the Catholics from attacking the Huguenots and the Huguenots from undertaking any action against the Catholics. Our entire kingdom is hungry for such a time. The two factions who seem today so incompatible will discover themselves reunited through clemency.'"

"Well, father," I cried, "those are noble words indeed, and recall what Étienne de La Boétie once said to us while visiting Mespech, and what Montaigne says in his *Essais*."

"And before him, Michel de L'Hospital," added Jean de Siorac, "since the great minds of our times are friends of tolerance. But to continue: at the silence that followed Du Ferrier's declaration—which didn't absolutely rule out Henri's abjuration but saw it rather as inopportune—you could sense that Roquelaure had lost the argument, though the king, without agreeing with either one, leant over to Du Ferrier and whispered a few words in his ear. After which, making a stiff bow to our assembly, and a friendly smile, he unlocked the door and left the room."

The next day, which was 11th July, my father received a visit from the king of Navarre, who was accompanied only by Roquelaure, and stayed for a breakfast that was served by Mundane, who'd been hastily awakened. Afterwards, my father withdrew, while Navarre and Roquelaure remained with the Englishman, and so I've never learnt what was said on this occasion. I strongly suspect, however, that Elizabeth had no interest in seeing Navarre weakened in any way, since Guise was threatening to throw France into the Spanish camp, which would isolate England on its island—a suspicion that was fuelled by rumours that Felipe II was amassing an immense armada to invade England and restore Catholicism there.

On that same day, our party heard news of a disastrous event of enormous consequence for world peace, and, although I only received word of it a month later, I will report it here. My heart is as heavy now, years later, as I write these lines, as it was when I learnt this news: the Prince of Orange, known as William the Silent—because he spoke so little but always so very thoughtfully—was assassinated by a man named Balthasar Gérard, who, having just handed him a letter, pulled a pistol from beneath his coat and, while the Dutch head of state was reading it, shot him through the heart. Put to torture, Gérard confessed that he had been exhorted to act by a Jesuit in Rome, who'd assured him that this would be a deed of infinite merit and that a choir of angels would carry his soul straight to Paradise, where he would take his place at the right hand of Jesus Christ and the Blessed Virgin. Travelling from Rome to Paris, he'd been strengthened in his resolve by the Spanish ambassador, Mendoza, and in Flanders by the Duke of Parma, who promised him immense riches if he succeeded in his mission. Worse still, a Jesuit from Treves covered his body with new parchment that had been blessed, to assure his invulnerability after his deed.

Thus fortified with a promise of impunity, heaps of gold and a trip to Paradise, this poor fool, believing he was serving God in this business, in which many other interests than his own were being served, dispatched one of the most magnanimous princes on the continent, and the most solid bulwark of our Huguenot faith. As soon as he received the news of this "triumph", the Duke of Parma set in motion the enormous machine that was to capture the port of Antwerp, reduce Flanders to ruins and menace the English.

We were in Lyons when the news reached me, and I informed Mundane of it immediately, and remember vividly that, when he heard it, he fell onto a stool, head in hands, and cried hot and bitter tears. I was astonished at this sudden display of emotion, since he was normally so calm, slow to act and inscrutable, even when he was making a joke, which was always accompanied by a little chuckle rather than a burst of laughter.

"Ah, Mr Mundane," I enquired, "did you know William the Silent personally, and were you so fond of him?"

"No, no!" he replied in English, forgetting his French in his distress, "I've never set eyes on him."

"So why are you taking this so grievously?"

"Oh, my queen!" gasped Mundane, still in English, overcome with sobbing. "My queen! My poor queen!"

"What has this got to do with your queen?" I asked, amazed.

"She is next on the list," he replied, taking his head from his hands and looking at me in great distress.

Understanding the extremity of his fears for Elizabeth, since Felipe II and the Jesuits had so easily succeeded in their assassination of the Prince of Orange, I did my best to comfort him, reminding him that, as England was an island, any miscreant would easily be apprehended as he arrived in port, and that Walsingham was said to have a hundred eyes, half of which were constantly on the lookout for any enemies of the queen. At the name of Walsingham, who was the minister whom Mundane must be working for, my companion seemed somewhat heartened and dried his tears, leaving me wholly impressed with the great love he bore his sovereign. I could only wish to God that someday in France my countrymen would display such devotion to their king! And that our swords might forever protect him against the throng of knives that surrounded him!

It was in Lyons that Épernon joined Henri III, who'd come there to remove Monseigneur Mandelot from his post as governor of the city (since he'd got wind that he was a Guisard) and transfer the office to the Comte du Bouchage, Joyeuse's brother. For the same reasons, he removed La Mante from his role as captain of the citadel and gave it to Montcassin, whom he trusted because he was the cousin of Épernon—a trust that was, alas!, misplaced, since Montcassin later betrayed him with Guise. Things had become very ticklish for the king at this juncture, since Guise's followers were infesting the country like worms rotten wood, making it difficult for him to find supporters who had not already joined these worms.

As Épernon approached Lyons, a very stupid accident nearly cost him his life. A good number of gentlemen from the king's retinue had come out from the city to meet him, which they did on a very narrow road that bordered a ravine. These last, after greeting their ally, turned their horses round to return to the city, preceding the king's favourite, but, unfortunately, as they did so one fellow caught his sword in the duc's bridle and the terrified horse reared and rolled into the precipice with its rider.

We thought both rider and mount had been killed, as indeed the horse had been, but no—Épernon had merely fainted away, and suffered a dislocated shoulder, but no break. I had it back in place within an hour, and, when we got to Lyons, I bandaged the cuts he'd received. I went immediately to reassure the king, who was extremely uneasy, since rumours had reached him of Épernon's demise; he was very relieved to hear that the wounds were of little consequence.

"Épernon, my little man!" laughed Chicot. "If you'd seen the great joy on all the faces of the workers and inhabitants of Lyons, you'd have been impressed by how much they love you!"

"I don't give a fig about being loved," replied Épernon without so much as a smile at this joke. "I serve the king."

"And faithfully," added the king.

"Nay nay, my little friend!" countered Chicot. "Was it to serve the king that you stripped Monsieur de La Châtre of the captaincy of Loches, or was it to acquire the post yourself?"

"To serve the king, of course!" responded Épernon without missing a beat. "La Châtre is a Guisard, no matter how much he tried to ingratiate himself with me. He was intending to betray us."

And in this the king's favourite was not mistaken, for La Châtre did indeed go over to Guise's side after that, handing him the city of

Bourges as a gauge of his fidelity. I'm writing this in my chronicle in order to be completely fair to Épernon. And, as for his reputation of forever grasping for money, I'd like to add that, although the king bestowed innumerable heaps of gold on him, they did not all end up in his purse, but were often spent in the service of his master—as were, for example, the monies he used to recruit and pay the famous "Forty-five Guardsmen" with whom he surrounded the king day and night to protect him from assassination.

On the evening of Épernon's terrible accident, I saw Henri III at his bedtime in his alcove, on the pretext of taking his pulse, and told him in detail what I'd learnt from my father regarding the secret council of the king of Navarre.

"It's just as I thought," he mused when I'd finished, with a distracted and dreamy look. "He and I were bound to end up as allies someday. Separated, we'd be destroyed, one after the other. Together, we will destroy them!"

Mundane was very anxious to return to Paris, to deliver a note to Lord Stafford that Navarre had written to his queen, and I too was anxious to return, having sorely missed Angelina and my beautiful children these past three months. Therefore, I asked leave of my king, not wishing to remain in Lyons with him and Épernon while they attended a festival that was being held there in their honour—the king loved such amusements, especially theatrical productions, ballet and poetry.

Henri granted my request quite reluctantly, especially since, as he said, he feared for my safety—since I'd be travelling through the countryside, where, ever since the troubles had begun, there were thousands of brigands, who attacked travellers and left them only their bodies and souls. I explained to His Majesty that there were four of us, all well armed with pistols and all four able swordsmen—not to mention that Miroul could throw a knife better than any mother's son in France. But the king, who was like a father to all of his servants (though he was my age), would hear nothing of it, and insisted on providing me with a sergeant and three guards as reinforcements, and on adding 100 écus for their expenses (which was reduced to sixty-five by his treasurer). The astonishing thing about this transaction was that the royal treasurers, who amassed such great fortunes, often ended up lending money to His Majesty (with interest), even though the monies were his own!

This sergeant was named Delpech, and he was from the Sarlat region, which immediately endeared him to me—no surprise, especially since he was, in the Périgordian manner, amiable and very helpful, with no other vices than a penchant for the bottle. I would have preferred to do without him and his three men, since, dressed as they were in the king's livery, they identified us as allies of His Majesty, which naturally provoked many hostile looks from all the Guisards along our way. My unease was also provoked by the feeling, once or twice, that we were being followed on the road from Lyons to Paris, a feeling that was confirmed when, at one point, we suddenly turned our horses to confront our followers, only to see them turn round and scurry away. This led me to consider the fact that brigands always set up their ambushes ahead of you—in some woods or behind a bridge—but never attack from behind, since, coming from the rear, they couldn't hope to catch you, gentlemen's horses being always stronger and faster than theirs. So our followers must have been of another species than highwaymen, and must have had other reasons to be spying on us than a taste for our money, rings or horses. I became so alarmed that I discussed with Giacomi whether we shouldn't leave the main road, where our followers could always catch up with us at an inn, and throw them off the trail by taking a longer route to Paris. But Giacomi disagreed, arguing that the main road was so full of carts and horsemen that it would be difficult for these rascals to attack us without others coming to our rescue, not to mention the fact that a group as well armed as ours would be able to inflict heavy losses on our attackers given that they didn't appear to outnumber us.

At this, Mr Mundane, who'd been listening to our conversation, vehemently intervened and begged me to continue on the shortest possible road, since the message he had to transmit could tolerate no delay. At first I resisted his request, but poor Mundane renewed it with such desperation that you would have believed the life of his queen depended on it. So, in the end, I accepted Giacomi's and Mundane's advice, very much against my own better judgement, and abandoned my plan.

In the end, this turned out to be a grave error, as the irreparable damage that followed proved only too well. I still feel terrible pain and regret to this day, and have, ever since, been convinced that the natural leader of a band—though he should certainly consult his companions when in danger—should nevertheless make his own decisions, no matter how unpopular, if he is sure of them, since he alone is responsible for the success of the enterprise and the welfare of all. I failed to accept this responsibility that day for the first time in my life—and I pray to God that it will be the last.

We found lodgings at the Black Horse, situated at the north end of Mâcon, at a crossroads called "the dead horse", which inspired Miroul to comment that the horse must have died of the plague since, on the inn's sign, it was entirely black—apparently also the colour of the heart of the landlord, who scorched us properly, extorting five écus for a room that was worth two at the most. He justified this fleecing by pointing out that traffic on the main road was so heavy that he didn't lack for customers—a claim that was quickly verified, for, less than an hour after us, four fellows arrived, who asked for lodgings and were placed at the lower end of our table, where they threw themselves at their food like pigs after slops. They were all scruffy-looking, bearded and unwashed, and took their meal with their hats drawn over their eyes, making only grunts instead of words, their leader ending the ceremony by cleaning his teeth with his knife. I called him "their leader", for he appeared to have some authority over the other three, though he was the smallest of the lot, as thin as a weasel, with a snout like a fox.

The sight of these swine splattering themselves with grease in their avid gluttony was, frankly, revolting—Miroul observing that you could tell from the stains on their doublets everything they'd eaten in the last week—and so I turned away to watch the chambermaid at work. She was a lively and frisky girl, whom our innkeeper from hell called Marianne, and who'd made some advances and caressed our hands as she'd served us our wine—most obviously to Giacomi, but more subtly to me. But seeing no encouragement from either of us—Giacomi being so constantly melancholic and myself consumed with thoughts of my Angelina—she'd turned her artillery on Miroul. My gentle valet, though he loved his Florine dearly, was not a man to resist a petticoat, and weakened at her first onslaught. The minx therefore redoubled her assaults and pressed her bosom up against his face as she served him his wine. At this rate I doubted Miroul would ever find the resolve necessary to block her advances in the night that was fast approaching. Seeing the affair as good as concluded, and believing, with Montaigne, that "one should always give one's valet leave for some imprudences"—especially when that valet serves you as well as Miroul did me—I decided to feign complete blindness to the progress of the couple, and instead engaged Giacomi in a discussion of Larissa, trying to fan the dying embers of his hope.

Meanwhile, I couldn't help watching the comings and goings of the wench, since there's a kind of invincible attraction in the body of a woman who's bustling about. I noticed that she was engaged in a rather lengthy conversation with the fox-faced weasel, which suddenly excited feelings of antagonism towards the girl, and these increased when I saw her, as she returned to our end of the table, give a harsh slap to Miroul's hand as he started to caress her backside. After that she paid no more attention to him than if he'd been a mouldy biscuit, suddenly redirecting her fire onto Mr Mundane, who'd never taken his eyes off of her the entire time, and so she was able to breach his walls and occupy his stronghold in a trice. "Well!" I thought. "So many of the fair sex are like the moon, whose face takes on so many different expressions in one month! But in this case it's not one a day but one a minute!"

After dinner, our skinflint of an innkeeper came to warn us to keep our windows closed and locked, since they looked out on the road, and the area was teeming with miscreants who wouldn't hesitate to lay siege to any opening, climbing up to it by ladder or along the eaves. He also advised us to hobble our horses in the stable and have our valets keep a close watch over them, so that no one would steal them, for as well shuttered and locked as the barn door was, one must keep an eye open for thieves who'd pass through the eye of a needle to steal other people's goods.

Giacomi and I would certainly have wanted to keep the windows open in our room, since the August night was stifling, but we preferred our safety to any breeze that might blow our way, and kept them tightly shut. I repeated the innkeeper's instructions to Mundane, who was to share a room with Miroul, fearing that the Englishman might not have understood his particular dialect.

No sooner had I closed my door, however, than someone knocked; opening it, I saw Miroul standing there, entirely clothed, pistol and sword prominently displayed in his belt (and two other knives doubtless hidden in his boots).

"Monsieur," he explained, "I thought it would be a good idea to sleep in the stables so as not to have to go down there two or three times to make sure no one's trying to get at our horses."

He said this with a mix of pride and chagrin, and, as I raised my candle to get a better look at his face, I found him looking somewhat crestfallen, which gave me to believe that, having been suddenly deprived of Marianne's attentions, he had decided to vacate the room in order to allow Mundane to enjoy the fruits of his victory, and to make his bed in the straw of the stables—to "chew on the cud of his disappointment", as they say in Périgord. For never did a dream replace a wench, as everyone knows, and a chambermaid in an inn is worth more than a thousand dreams of a princess in her palace…

"Go on, my Miroul," I agreed reluctantly, feeling sorry for him for now having such a dry mouth after previously drooling so much. "You're right, we can never take too many precautions when the roads are so full of danger and the inn is invaded by these swine we saw wallowing in their slop, and whose necks have grown fat for the rope!"

This said, and having softened his pain as much as I could through my praise of his work and worth, I embraced him and sent him away happy in his virtue and in himself—small consolations, perhaps, when he'd expected to bite into such sweet, forbidden fruit.

I didn't fall asleep as quickly as I'd hoped, having such a sore backside from all our riding, as well as suffering pangs of regret for the decision I'd made to take the main road, given the presence of these scoundrels who'd followed us. I believe there's no greater vice than impatience—which, in this case, had caused us to leave the king's procession, thereby exposing us to the dangers of travelling without their protection, and, subsequently, to choose not to take the longer route. All of these thoughts so disturbed me that my heart was beating like a drum, so I got up and went to verify that our windows were securely fastened, and then went to knock on Mundane's door. He had not yet gone to sleep, as you can easily imagine, and opened the door so I could take a look at his windows, which were sealed as tight as a tomb. I wished him goodnight, and urged him to bolt his door and to sleep with his sword unsheathed at his side.

"Well, good chevalier!" he laughed, his eyes shining, his red hair and beard aglow in the lamplight. "If you'd had a wife as cold and thin as your good blade, would you have had so many beautiful children?"

And, though my heart wasn't into it, I laughed at his little joke and then repeated my warning that, if he were to receive a nocturnal visitor, he should be very careful to lock the door behind her when she left. He heartily assured me that, like Ulysses, he'd know how to ward off all Circes, Calypsos and sirens, and that, in any case, he had no use for the gentler sex and preferred the company of dogs and horses. That was Mundane in a nutshell: enjoying his disguise and laughing at me from behind his mask.

I left his room and went to knock on the door of Sergeant Delpech, whom I saw already snoring on his bed (since he'd drunk copiously beforehand), with his three guards spread out on the floor beside him. Seeing their leader disabled so quickly, I checked on the window bolts and then sent two of his guards down to the stables to help Miroul keep watch there. As for the remaining soldier, I advised him to bolt the door behind me.

Having taken these precautions, I felt a bit more light-hearted, though I took great care to make sure my pistol was loaded, its wick at the ready beside the candle, and my sword unsheathed. As soon as I blew out the flame, I fell into a deep sleep, though in my dreams I kept realizing that I'd lost something—I didn't know what it was, but was sure it was a thing of great consequence. Moreover, I had the impression that I hadn't slept at all when, suddenly, a loud noise and uproar, followed by a piercing cry, awakened me. I leapt to my feet, grabbed my sword and pistol and ran to bang on Mundane's door, but there was no answer and it was locked from the inside. Giacomi joined me, candle in hand, and behind him Delpech's guard, both of them, like me, naked as the day they were born. Following them, the innkeeper ran up, armed with an axe, but begged us not to break down his door—which of course we did, after promising him two écus for the damage, whereupon we quickly split the oak.

We didn't need Giacomi's candle to determine that poor Mundane was dead, as the moon was shining brightly through the open window and bathed his bloody body in her light. He'd been stabbed who knows how many times before he'd been able to defend himself, his sword still sheathed by his side. As for his rings, there was not a trace, though I didn't believe for a second that robbery was the motive for this murder, or that Mundane had opened his windows to his killers. And, observing on the bed a woman's bodice and skirt, I sent the innkeeper and the guard away, the latter observing that this couldn't have been the work of soldiers, who would have slit the man's throat to keep him from crying out and sounding the alarm.

This alarm having now been sounded, the entire inn was quickly roused and very shaken by the cries and the axe blows, and all the guests, wrested from their sleep, came running up in their nightgowns, candles in hand, to see what had happened. I decided to play the part of a bravo, and emerged from the room entirely naked but with pistol and sword in hand, scowling like the Devil, and shouted:

"Good people, I'm an officer of the king, as you saw this afternoon from the livery of my guards. So in the name of the king I order you to return to your rooms and to go back to bed without further ado!"

And since there were still some among them bold enough to attempt to push into the room to see what had happened, I pointed my sword at them and thundered:

"By God, I'll make a ghost of the next man who dares to take a step forward!"

That was enough to disperse these rabbits, who scurried back to their rooms, allowing Miroul, who was at the back of the crowd, to come to my aid, sword in hand and so relieved to see me alive and unscathed that he scarcely batted an eye when he spied Mundane lying dead in his bloody bed.

"Ah, Monsieur!" he cried, unable to say anything but this—"Ah, Monsieur!"—three or four times in a row.

"Miroul," I said, cutting him off, "hurry back to the stable and wake up those louts, if they're still sleeping, and keep a sharp watch! And tell me," I added, having no doubt as to who were the authors of this murder, "did those pigs we saw last night already ride away?"

"Yes, an hour ago!"

"Shouldn't you have told me?"

"But, Monsieur, they departed less than two hours after we'd finished our meal, and did so quietly and peaceably, like good subjects of the king, with neither swagger nor threats, but were quite civil with us."

"Ah, Miroul," I sighed, "why didn't you come to warn me? From now on, if any of the hotel's guests attempts to saddle up before dawn, come and tell me!"

At this reproach, Miroul left, very crestfallen, bitterly unhappy to have failed me and feeling badly stung for being blamed, sensitive as he was about his honour, despite being a valet.

His departure left me alone with Giacomi, so I took the candle from his hands and, kneeling down beside the bed, looked underneath it.

There, in one corner, cowered Marianne, naked, mute and apparently half-dead with terror. I ordered her to come out of hiding; once she'd emerged, she looked as though she would faint when she saw Mundane lying there—a weakness that struck me as oddly discordant with the resolution in her face. Seeing this, I told her in the coldest possible tone to get dressed. Which she did, much more calmly than I would have expected from a wench who'd just witnessed such violence, but, observing this, I forced myself to put aside the feelings that such women normally inspire, and to see her as someone with whom I must cross swords, rather than as the frisky brunette she was, thin and supple and yet sweetly rounded in the right places, with black eyes and a pretty face.

"Marianne," I warned with as much severity as I could muster, "if I handed you over to the provost of Mâcon, it is certain that he'd first put you on the rack and then hang you for having been an accomplice to this murder, since you were found under the bed of the assassinated man."

"Accomplice, Monsieur?" she protested, losing all the colour in her face but not a whit of her wits. "Assuredly, I am not! If I were, why would I have stayed here and not run off with those miscreants?"

"Who found it remarkably expedient to abandon you once they'd done their business."

"No, no!" she cried. "I swear on my salvation! Oh, Blessed Virgin, hear my plea! And let the Devil devour me in one gulp if I'm lying! I never saw these rascals before last night's meal, and I was an idiot to have taken that good-for-nothing's five écus to lie with the Goddam"— by which she meant Englishman—"and open the window once he'd fallen asleep. That fox-faced villain told me he just wanted to play a joke on the fellow and make him believe he was my husband, which is why he pulled his hat down over his eyes at supper."

"And you believed him, you silly wench?"

"Why should I question him when my hands were full of his money? Though I confess I was surprised that he told me to flee the room as soon as I'd opened the window—which I didn't do but hid under the bed to enjoy the joke they were going to play on him! Oh heaven! I thought their swords were going to go straight through the bed and pierce me right through! And remember, Monsieur, that my bodice and skirt were still on the bed! I was mortally afraid they'd look under the bed and kill me too! But they never thought of it, thank God! They were too busy pulling his rings off."

"So they didn't take them right away?"

"No. They only removed them when they heard you banging on the door."

"Giacomi," I said in Italian, "it's clear that these *spadaccini** were looking for the letter."

"Monsieur," broke in Marianne, who seemed to be regaining her colour and self-assurance, "I speak Italian—my mother was from Florence. And I know what happened to the letter. While I was getting undressed, I watched the Goddam in the mirror as he was hiding it."

"And where is it?"

"I'll tell you," she said, regaining her confidence, "if you'll promise not to deliver me to the provost."

"'Sblood!" I cried in anger. "This is a cold wench! They kill a gentleman right under her nose and here she is bargaining like a Florentine."

"That's because I *am* a Florentine," said Marianne without batting an eye.

"You minx!" I snapped. "If I hand you over to be tortured you'll loosen your tongue."

"But you won't be the only one to hear what I say," said Marianne, who was clearly smarter than I'd imagined.

"Giacomi," I said in Latin, "what do you think of this wench? Don't you think she's too sly to be honest? Do you believe her story?"

"If she were stupid I'd believe it," replied Giacomi in the language of Cicero. "But, on the other hand, if the letter is a state secret, as you believe, should we allow the provost of Mâcon to get his hands on it? I think we have to make a deal with her."

"All right, but not before trying to frighten her!" And suddenly grabbing Marianne by her long hair, I pointed my sword at her breast. "That's enough!" I cried at the top of my lungs. "No bargains. Talk if you want to live!"

---

* "Swordsmen."

"Monsieur," replied Marianne with a sudden smile, "you must be kidding! Would you really kill a woman, you who are so repulsed by the idea of letting her hang?"

"Pierre," interjected Giacomi in Latin, "the wench had you figured out in the blink of eye, and as for understanding her, she's got more depth than either of us can gauge. I really don't know what to think, except that, if she were conniving with these murderers, she would have told them where the letter was, since she saw Mundane hide it."

I was so struck by the justness of this observation, which seemed to clear the girl of any complicity with the assassins, that once again I was weak enough to ignore my own feelings, which inclined me in the opposite direction, and resolved to let her go if she provided us with the letter. In this I was miserably wrong, as events proved all too well.

"Wench," I said, "it's a bargain: the letter for your freedom."

"Monsieur chevalier," said Marianne, looking me in the eye, "do I have your word as a gentleman?"

"You have. But how do you know I'm a knight?" I asked.

"I heard the sergeant of the guards address you that way," she answered.

And though the thing was possible, I didn't believe her, but decided to let it go, since I was so anxious to have the letter, which touched on the interests of three kingdoms, for although it was addressed by Navarre to Queen Elizabeth alone, I had no doubt that it also involved my master.

"The Goddam put his letter under that chest over there," said Marianne with a very reluctant air, as though she were as unhappy about giving me the letter as I was about setting her free.

The chest was so large and heavy, being adorned with many iron clasps and bars, that I was unable to lift it by myself, and had to ask Giacomi to help, quite amazed that Mundane could have succeeded in this exploit all by himself.

"I will keep my promise, Marianne," I said once I had the letter. "You're free to go."

"Thank God and thank you, Monsieur chevalier," replied Marianne, making me a deep curtsey that seemed to contradict her expression, which seemed neither tender nor forgiving.

"I believe it's the Devil she should be thanking," observed Giacomi, who, approaching Mundane's body, added in a very melancholic voice, "Isn't it a pity that the life of such a good man should be so little mourned, while this accursed letter has occupied all our attention?"

"Sad but true, my brother," I agreed. "I too feel the injustice of our neglect. And yet you can't mourn a companion who's fallen in combat as long as the combat continues, and it's my belief that we're still in great peril, as long as we have this in our hands."

Giacomi made no reply—I guessed that he was silently praying for the soul of the poor Englishman—so I took my leave to return to my room to get dressed and secure the letter in my doublet, since the missive felt like it was burning my very hands, so deadly was its effect. When I returned to Mundane's room I found Sergeant Delpech, who'd been awakened by his men and appeared to have recovered from his drunkenness, but who was very distressed and ashamed to have slept like a dormouse through such an uproar. I sent him off to search for the innkeeper, and, Giacomi having gone off as well to get dressed, I was able to examine Mundane's body at my leisure. I noticed that the entrances to the wounds were entirely in his chest, but that there was no evidence of their exit through his back. Thus I concluded that he had been stabbed with a dagger and not run through with swords, as Marianne had fallaciously recounted, claiming that they'd even pierced the bedding and threatened her own life.

"Innkeeper," I asked of this skinflint as he came in, "what do you know about this Marianne who's in your employ, as regards her lodgings, her family or her village?"

"Nothing at all, my noble Monsieur," the fellow replied. "I hired her yesterday afternoon about an hour after my chambermaid unaccountably quit her post, and this strange wench arrived to offer to take her place without any discussion of wages, which is surprising, since I don't pay well because of the very marginal profits of my inn. But, Monsieur," he added, "I must, in all reverence, ask you as a matter of simple justice to pay for the bed, which is bloodstained beyond repair, as well as for the missing sheet."

"What?" I asked, amazed. "What's this about a missing sheet? Do you think these miserable pigs ran off with your sheet? Of course, it would be a handsome heist for these scoundrels who're now enjoying the spoils taken from this gentleman!"

"But Monsieur," countered our host, "you can see that there's only one sheet here! Where's the other one?"

"How should I know? It must have slipped onto the floor!"

At this, getting down on all fours and looking under the bed, the innkeeper cried out, and produced a sheet that had been rolled tightly into a ball, and which was quite bloodstained. When we unrolled it, out fell a dagger.

"Oh my God!" I cried almost beside myself. "Where is this devil of a wench?! Innkeeper, show me her room immediately!"

But, as we were hurrying towards her room, we bumped into Miroul, who was beside himself and breathless. "Monsieur," he cried, "Marianne has just fled on your Andalusian mare!"

"What? On *my* horse!"

"Ah, Monsieur, she's a devil! She came down to ask me to saddle your horse for you. This done, and as I had to let go of the bridle to open the stable door, she offered to hold it. Then, while I was busy taking down the bars, she jumped on your horse as if she were a man, spurred it out onto the road and disappeared."

6

THAT SHE HAD COMMITTED the murder, and that she alone had committed it, without help or complicity from any of the swinish fellows I'd suspected, now appeared incontrovertible and turned our search wholly in her direction. Marianne had taken advantage of the nocturnal departure of the good-for-nothings (who doubtless had other sins to confess) to shift all of the blame onto them by placing the ladder under Mundane's window. Then, once the deed was done, she'd opened the window, thrown the Englishman's rings outside to make us believe the swine had stolen them, wiped the bloodstains from her body on the sheet, wrapped the dagger in the same sheet and hidden it and herself under the bed, pretending to be in terrible shock at the murder she herself had perpetrated with such cold resolution, having stabbed poor Mundane at least a dozen times.

We calculated that she'd arrived in Mâcon well before we had, and that she must have visited all of the inns, discovered they were full with the exception of the Black Horse, and deduced that that's where we'd stay. She'd then bought off the chambermaid, convincing her to quit her job, and taken her place, guessing that Mundane, though likely to be suspicious of any traveller, would not suspect a serving girl, since throughout the kingdom these girls are chosen for their youth and beauty in order that they might charm the clientele into handing over a few coins in exchange for their company for the night. As for her behaviour during the previous night's meal, her rejections of Giacomi, Miroul and me, and her whispered conversation with the fox-faced weasel were all coquetry designed to whet Mundane's appetite, gain access to his room and, having exhausted him with her caresses, dispatch him while he was asleep.

She made only two mistakes: the first (which the guard had justly observed) was that, unlike Judith sacrificing Holofernes, she didn't begin by cutting his throat, so that Mundane was able to cry out loudly enough for me to sound the alarm; the second was that, never having laid her hands on the trunk, she believed she could lift it, as Mundane had done, to steal the letter he'd slipped underneath. And in this her whole plan failed, for she killed Mundane for nothing, and, finding herself in great peril of the gibbet or of being drawn and quartered, she managed to get herself out of her predicament by pulling more wool over my eyes than is found at a sheep-shearing in May, and then, to seal the bargain, by stealing my horse, which was the only steed in the stable that could have caught her had she chosen any other.

It's not impossible that she was the chief of the little band who'd been on our tails ever since we left Lyons, but she must have decided that, given our number and arms, the chances of beating us in combat were not good, and so decided to use a ruse where strength wouldn't have succeeded. As for me, other than the loss of my Andalusian mare (who had cost me 500 écus, being very robust and fleet of foot), I now realized that I was blacklisted by some powerful enemies of the king, this Marianne clearly being a Guisard, as zealous as she was bloodthirsty in her execution of the designs of her master.

With fury in my heart, I purchased another horse, and this time taking the longer route to Paris along a series of smaller roads, we arrived in the capital without further difficulties, and I hurried to deliver Navarre's letter to Lady Stafford, whom I found in the salon of Madame de Joyeuse. She offered me copious thanks, but expressed much less grief at the news of Mundane's death than I would have wished. But I've noticed that the English are much more attentive than we are to differences of birth, rank and degree, having, as they do, two words for the nobility: the *gentry*, who are the lower, and the *nobility*, who are the higher. As Mundane belonged to the first category and Lady Stafford to the second, she doubtless thought herself too highly placed to weep over his death, and contented herself with a very reserved encomium for the deceased, saying that, without doubt, he was a gentleman entirely devoted to his queen, but nevertheless too "rash". No doubt this last term was meant to communicate her displeasure that any English gentleman would be capable of consorting with a chambermaid in a hotel—especially a French one!

I was a little disappointed that neither the Duc de Joyeuse nor the Comte du Bouchage visited the maréchale that day, but gathered from what I overheard in my hostess's salon that they were being very hard on the heretics, and that this judgement smelt too distinctly of Guise for gentlemen who owed the great fortunes of their houses to the king. The Marquis de Miroudot, who was very sharp and guessed my astonishment despite my efforts to hide it, took me by the arm and said, sotto voce:

"How unjust people are to me to call me ungrateful! It's the wind that's changing, not me!"

Miroudot belonged to the type of people whom the Guisards had come to hate almost as much as the Huguenots, calling them "politicals"—a term that designated Catholics who did not want to break with the reformers, whether because of secret connections to them, because they were suspicious of the zeal of the Pope, the clergy and the Spanish king and didn't want to appear sympathetic to the tyranny of the Inquisition, or because they were faithful to the king and could clearly see that the civil war that Guise sought to launch would profit only himself, and that religion was only the mantle with which he covered his ambition.

These "despicable" politicals were, truth be told, very good and honest folk, like Miroudot, like L'Étoile, like Roquelaure, but they had so many subtle nuances in their opinions and such prudence and zeal in their hearts that they were unable to join together to resist the Guisards' oppression, and struggled against them only through their numbers and their inertia.

As soon as I'd learnt that the king had returned from Lyons with Épernon, I went to visit him and met a crowd of courtiers in his antechambers, who were besieging him with requests for favours and handouts of various kinds, since they hadn't had access to him for two months. Most of these were royalists, but some were Guisards who ate at two troughs and were devouring the riches of this kingdom with their eyes already fixed on the next regime, or at least hoping for a change.

"Well, *mi fili*!" Fogacer greeted me as he emerged from the crowd and gave me a welcoming embrace with his spidery arms, his eyes ablaze under those diabolical eyebrows of his. "So you're back from your mission, smelling like sulphur and embers, just like the days when you were chasing diabolical petticoats around cemeteries! But this is much worse," he whispered in my ear. "All they can talk about in there are the infernal spells and other evils you use to serve the tortuous designs of the king."

"Well, as for my magic," I laughed, having no idea about what he might have heard about my own setbacks, "I was able to prescribe a boiled saline solution for him to gargle for his sore throat."

"But tongues are wagging, *mi fili*," whispered Fogacer.

"And what are they saying?"

"That you were the member of Épernon's retinue whom the king charged with offering Navarre 200,000 écus if he'd declare war on the Catholics of this kingdom."

"But Navarre never spoke to me, or even saw me!"

"That's precisely why you're suspected, since there was no way Henri could have forgotten you after your meeting on St Bartholomew's eve. So it's bruited that you worked this deal through your father, the Baron de Mespech."

"That's a pure and simple fabrication!"

"*Mi fili*," he said, arching his black eyebrows, "a fabrication is never pure and rarely simple."

With a laugh he turned away to join the venerable Dr Miron, who was looking for him. Of course, I was much alarmed at the rumours that were circulating about me in Paris and that clearly called for my assassination, since, in these troubled times, there was no lie too enormous for the uninformed populace to swallow it. I wanted to hear Quéribus's thoughts on this, and went looking for him among the press of people, finally spying him in conversation with a Guisard sympathizer, who, the minute he caught sight of me approaching, quickly took his leave of the baron, casting a terrified look over his shoulder and fleeing as though he'd just seen the Devil himself.

"'Sblood!" exclaimed Quéribus, nearly suffocating me in his embrace. "You've become a decidedly unsavoury character in Paris! Those 200,000 écus are a distinct stain on your reputation!"

"But who would believe such an absurd story?"

"No one at court, except perhaps for the idiot I was just talking to, who fled in terror at the sight of you. Few people at court are ignorant of the fact that if the king gave Épernon 200,000 écus when he left, it was to cover the expenses of his mission. But you can be assured that the zealots of Paris will believe the other version as if it were gospel."

"But who invents these lies?"

"What! You mean you don't know? It's the Madame Limp herself, the Duchesse de Montpensier! She has a natural talent for inventing stories that are designed to harm the king and serve her brother. She then sends her inventions, accompanied by significant monetary contributions, to all the Guisard prelates in the capital, who immediately sprinkle their sermons with them on Sundays as if they were the word of God."

"But who'd ever believe the king would give such a sum to Navarre to attack his own army?"

"The Parisians, my friend! There's no nonsense that can't be fed to Parisians if you repeat it often enough. And here's another: that the king spent 400,000 écus in Lyons purchasing miniature greyhounds."

"What are they?"

"Tiny dogs that the ladies like to put on their laps. Notice the immensity of the sum! At 500 écus per puppy, the king would have purchased 800 of 'em! Heavens! What would he have done with them all?"

"So that's what's being repeated in the pulpits?"

"No, it's reported in the sacristy, whispered in the confessional, alluded to in the sermons and trumpeted in the processional! The seminarians teach it as gospel to their aspiring priests! And the professors at the Sorbonne gloss it for their students! You know, Pierre, there are nearly 500 streets in Paris and there's no street so small that it doesn't house at least ten men of the cloth, whether monks or priests, so you can imagine what an immense net is thrown over the people of our city by Guise's 5,000 zealots!"

"So, it's Quéribus the Quarreller!" snorted Chicot, pushing his way between Quéribus and me, his long nose perennially dripping. "And you, Bloodletter! I couldn't help overhearing!"—for indeed he had excellent hearing. "You're plotting against the Magnificent! You know that's a capital crime in this kingdom! Don't you go to church? Aren't you familiar with the Gospel according to Madame Limp? The Book of the Great Whoremonger? The Epistle of the Pig? The Psalms of the Magnificent, who never tires of singing his own praises?* You will

---

* In order: the Duchesse de Montpensier, the Cardinal de Guise, the Duc de Mayenne and the Duc de Guise.

note that these four evangelists are all from the house of Lorraine—four paragons of all the virtues known and unknown. The four columns and caryatids of our Holy Mother the Church!"

"Chicot, you're becoming bitter," growled Quéribus, who, though he was an anti-Guisard, didn't like to hear princes maligned, even if they were from Lorraine and therefore foreigners.

"It's Paris that's growing bitter," replied Chicot. "Paris suffers from two great evils: 100,000 horses and 5,000 priests. The first shit piles of manure, the others piles of Guisardist sermons."

Our laughter attracted the attention of other courtiers, who loved hearing Chicot's bons mots, which would then be bandied about from one end of the Louvre to the other. Chicot took each of us by the arm, the drip from his nose falling happily on his own doublet, and dragged us over to a table laden with food, where, after observing that none of us had yet breakfasted, we three set to—but our repast was to be short-lived.

"Bloodletter," said Chicot in my ear in a suddenly serious tone, "the king is very unhappy that Épernon failed in his mission, since, if Navarre had been converted, Henri could have counted on him to fortify his throne. He's also worried about your safety, having got wind of the business in Mâcon."

"What! Already?"

"Henri has his spies," said Chicot. "Did you think you were the only one? Moreover, he wants to see you as soon as he's finished spilling his guts to Father Auger."

"Chicot," I answered, "you whose madness is so full of wisdom—"

"Nicely begun!" interrupted the fool.

"Given that the Jesuits are occupied in London, Treves, Reims and Rome with such 'worthy' endeavours, explain to me why he has chosen one of them to be his confessor."

"There's an answer to that," replied Chicot, "which is that Auger is, first and foremost, a royalist, and always has been."

"There's another answer to that," added Quéribus, "which is that the Jesuits never put all their eggs in one basket."

"True enough," agreed Chicot, "but in this case they've got nine eggs in Guise's basket and but one in Henri's."

"Excuse me!" said a tall, well-built courtier as he elbowed his way to our table. "I'm sorry to dislodge you, but I need a bite to eat!" I recognized this intruder as Alphonse d'Ornano.

"Corsican," smiled Chicot, "the table is yours, given that you're the best Corsican alive and so devoted to your king!"

"That's true enough!" cried d'Ornano, seating himself with alacrity. "I'd give my life for the king."

"But not your stomach," laughed Chicot.

At this moment, the door to the king's chambers opened, and Du Halde trumpeted at the top of his voice, "Monsieur de Siorac, the king's physician!"

With Chicot at my heels, I pushed my way through the press of gentlemen, trying to look as meek as possible, but inwardly delighted to take precedence over all these peacocks. Surprisingly, however, Du Halde stopped the fool as he tried to cross the threshold. "I said 'the king's physician'," growled Du Halde, stiff as a German reiter.

"And so I am!" Chicot replied. "I heal his soul!"

"Let him pass, Du Halde!" cried the king from within.

"Du Halde," hissed Chicot, "from now on, it's going to be '*Du Halt*'!"

The king was standing with his left hand on the mantel of the fireplace, dressed in a pale-green doublet with yellow slashes embroidered in gold and covered with innumerable rows of pearls and gems. Under his beautiful white ruff he wore a double necklace of gold-studded amber that, as I noticed when I got closer, gave off a sweet odour. On his right hand he wore two rings, and on his left three. On each ear hung at least two pendants, one of diamonds, the other of pearls.

Under the little bonnet topped, in the latest style, by two sprays of diamonds, his hair was arranged in fluffy rings.

Henri, who could sometimes be open and amusing with his intimates, as he had been the last time I'd seen him, was in a much more sombre mood on this morning, which meant that I shouldn't expect him to laugh, smile or even extend his hand for my reverential kiss. He appeared to be as immobile as the marble behind him and stiff as a statue, and fixed me with those deep, black, Italian eyes, without blinking.

He was decorated like an idol, with as many gems, pearls and jewels as Queen Elizabeth, whom I'd seen in London in 1586 when I was accompanying Pomponne de Bellièvre on a state visit. He was tall and elegant in stature, despite the increasing portliness that was threatening him, but his handsome face was now overshadowed by worry and melancholy. He was not without an air of real wisdom, as though he'd worked at creating an image of a monarch who was able to impose his authority by his virtue alone. When he opened his mouth to speak, his flowery speech added a sovereign grace to his thoughts, which were always the finest, most considered and most equitable of any of the voices around him. His generosity was legendary, for he showered all those who served him with innumerable gifts, a largesse which derived not only from his natural complexion, but from his belief that he was a "father to his subjects", although he had no children of his own—a liberal and forgiving attitude that prevailed for as long as his subjects were faithful to him.

If he had a fault (which I'm reluctant to name, so great was my love for him), it was that this image that he'd so carefully cultivated—his splendid appearance, the studied etiquette of his entourage, the crafted eloquence of his public speeches, his marvellous intelligence about affairs of state, which was demonstrated on so many occasions, and his boundless generosity with his officers and servants... in short, it was that this beautiful, noble and wise image was just that: merely an image, almost as inflexible as his beautiful hand resting on the mantel—you might have said it was marble on marble.

For the entire time that I served him, that is, right up until his death, Henri seemed to me to suffer from a deep reluctance to act, to move or to strike when necessary, as indeed these times demanded of him. It's not that he was weak-willed, or that his soul was irresolute. But since he read Machiavelli every day, he'd convinced himself that it was better to feign blindness, to dissimulate and to temporize with a smile and without batting an eye—tactics that followed altogether too closely his own inclination to suffer stoically the many intrusions, injuries, dispossessions and even humiliations that were showered on him. And although these humiliations irritated him at times, he never abandoned in his heart of hearts the firm intention of someday turning them to his advantage. But his very patience gave his emboldened enemies, and sometimes even his own people, the impression that he was soft and cowardly—though he was neither, as events would eventually prove.

This infinitely logical prince had the folly of believing in reason in a century that was dominated by zealotry. He wanted to use argument, rather than beheadings, to sway those who conspired to ruin him. Heads did eventually roll, but it was as a last resort, and in the despair of not knowing what else to do, or how to do it.

I well remember, on the subject of the preachers and doctors of the Sorbonne who were insulting and bombarding him with calumnies, that, a mere three years after the meeting that I've been describing here, the king, being furious with their lies, called them together with his parliament at the Louvre, where he delivered a bitter and forceful reprimand that lasted a full two hours, lambasting their insolent and unbridled licence in preaching against him.

The knaves trembled with fear as they listened, the most fearful of all being Boucher, the priest of Saint-Prévost, whom His Majesty called "wicked and impudent" for having included calumnies and obvious lies in a sermon against him—which even included the assertion that he'd had an Orléans theologian named Burlat drowned in a sack in the river, whereas this same Burlat was not only still living, but daily consorting with other priests in the taverns in that town.

"Boucher!" cried the king. "And all the rest of you priests and doctors of the same cloth, you can't deny that you're doubly damned!

"First, for having publicly conspired against your legitimate king, and propagated calumnies and lies, which are forbidden by the Holy Bible.

"Second, for having administered the Blessed Sacrament after having spoken such lies and calumnies without having either reconciled yourselves with me or confessed your sins, despite telling your congregants that such reconciliation and confession are necessary before presenting oneself before God!

"And as for you, Messieurs masters of arts at the Sorbonne, I've heard on good authority that on the sixteenth of this month, after a good dinner, you secretly passed a resolution authorizing my subjects to remove from power any prince who should be found wanting in any way. I've been told to take no notice of this resolution since it was taken after a meal. And yet, Messieurs of the Sorbonne, and you, Messieurs preachers, I'd like to remind you that the reigning Pope, Sixtus V, recently sent to the galleys a good dozen Cordeliers for having spoken irreverently of him in their sermons. And, finally, I'd like to remind you that there is not one of you—I say, not one!—who is more worthy than one of those Cordeliers. However, I'm willing to forget and pardon everything as long as you agree not to return to such calumnies and lies, else I will instruct my parliament to wreak immediate and exemplary justice on you."

This was doubtless a strong and beautiful speech, but its very reasonableness flew too high for the base group of souls who were listening, and who, when they failed to see in it any threat of a well-deserved rope around their fat necks, discovered in this impunity a redoubling of their audacity and of the hatred they bore their monarch.

De Thou once told me that the king's laziness and slowness to make decisions and act on them were due to the fact that he was a man more devoted to quiet meditation than to leadership, preferring the study of the habits, customs and laws of the kingdom in order to right the wrongs he discerned, and that Henri was never happier than when he could, during the more peaceful years of his reign, devote himself entirely to the writing of the immense body of laws that were later called, in legitimate homage to this work of immense consequence, the Code of Henri III.

I don't know that I can contribute very much grist to this mill, since I witnessed this king, so beloved of his private study though he was, make so many decisions that seemed excellent at the moment—such as to send Épernon on a mission to Navarre—but that ended in failure. It wasn't so much that the king's meditations led to the wrong course of action, but rather that the action, once engaged, seemed somehow divorced from all the planning that went into it, since our times were so unsettled and unpredictable. Indeed, if one were to compare the actions of the Duc de Guise during this same period, from 1584 to 1588, one would observe that he seemed no less paralysed, hesitant or inconsistent than the king. Which is to say that he had to confront as many predicaments as Henri did. Despite receiving heaps of Spanish gold and enjoying the support of the people, Guise lacked Henri's legitimacy as sovereign. Also, having adopted religion as his armour and shield, this armour ended up weighing him down, forcing him to march crab-like towards the throne.

My poor master, for his part, found himself nearly crushed by the enormous weight of his conscience, which was unable to condone his particular pleasures, which were roundly despised and condemned by both the Huguenot and Catholic Churches, the clergy, the ministers and the people. Indeed, it was to purge himself of this unbearable burden that Henri so often went on retreats to monasteries, locking himself in a tiny cell to pray and mortify his flesh, or else walked barefoot through the mud and muck of the Parisian streets in interminable processions in his hair shirt, chanting, praying and flagellating himself. Indeed, however much spittle (in the form of calumnies, lies and slander) fell on this poor soul from the sacred pulpits, whatever the affronts to and incursions into his power that Guise subjected him to, his inner spirit was already much darker than any of their attacks could make it. So, however much the king in him might have sought revenge, the sinner in him was resigned to drinking down, without flinching, the gall and vinegar of these humiliations.

I do not claim that all of these ideas occurred to me between the moment when Du Halde unlocked the door and the moment when I knelt before the king and he offered me his beautiful hand to kiss, which I took as delicately as I could in my rough paw, knowing how much care he took to keep his hands soft and smooth. But all of these aspects of Henri now invade my thoughts as I recollect this conversation in particular, not because it differed so much in content from all the others, but because I was struck by the king's bearing, for he seemed in his absolute immobility to be posing for his own statue. Alas! the vile enemies who so besmirched him while he was alive still bedevil him after his death, since, in their engravings of him, they represent him standing, holding a miniature greyhound in a basket (a fancy he had on one particular day) or playing *bilboquet* with a cup and ball, something he once enjoyed for an hour or so. It is through such puerile and grotesque images that they have detracted from the dignity of a prince who struggled valiantly for fifteen years to maintain the unity of his kingdom and the legitimacy of the succession of the monarchy.

Boquet, who made the little ball that is named after him, spent years in a miserable workshop making these toys until the day that he was recognized by one of the king's servants for having been the man who led Henri through the Polish forests when he was fleeing from Warsaw twelve years previously—a service that had never been required of him, nor rewarded. And when the king learnt of his whereabouts, he immediately went to his shop, followed by the entire court, bought all of Boquet's balls—ordering more—and was immediately imitated by all the courtiers and then by pages, horsemen, lackeys, university students, artisans, bourgeois, thieves and even farmhands from the villages around Paris. As for the king, having enjoyed launching the game that was all the rage throughout his kingdom and that enriched the modest little inventor, he gave his ball to Chicot, who made little use of it, preferring to string words together than to catch a little ball on a string. And yet that's how the fidelity, gratitude and graciousness of the king were eternally ridiculed by the hatred of the Guisards, despite the fact that Henri's enrichment of Boquet hadn't cost the royal treasury a penny!

"Siorac," said the king, when I'd risen after kissing his hand, "I heard about your difficulties in Mâcon from a lieutenant in my guards who took the shorter route here while you were taking the longer, slower one. However, since his report was quite succinct, I'd like to hear a more complete version from you."

I satisfied His Majesty as best I could, remembering how much he liked to hear everything in the greatest detail and enjoyed a well-told, lively and colourful account that would appeal both to the intellect and to the imagination.

This account given, the king appeared lost in thought for a few moments, but then explained:

"On the one hand, it would have been better to assign Mundane to Quéribus's retinue. You were too carefully watched by Guise's spies, firstly because you're my physician (and they know I use Marc Miron

253

on my missions), secondly because you're a Huguenot 'trimming your sails' at court, and thirdly because you're the son of a famous father who's in the service of Navarre. On the other hand, Quéribus wouldn't have conducted the inquest in Mâcon as well as you did, or so quickly, *my child*, discovered the letter."

By this "my child"—the king being the same age as myself—Henri was expressing both his gratitude and his affection. With him everything was conveyed in such nuances: he knew the art of expressing a great deal in few words.

"Tell me about this Marianne."

"She was lively and trim, with a dark complexion, black eyes, hair black as a crow's wing and a delicious mouth."

"Which doubtless you would have kissed if you'd had the opportunity…" the king replied, without smiling.

"No, sire. I wouldn't have trusted her, since we had a letter to deliver. In such circumstances a rat must be clever to escape a clever cat."

"Bloodletter," Chicot interrupted, "since the wench was so enticing, you should say rather that 'a rat must be clever to escape a beautiful cat'."

"Chicot," said the king, "do you know a wench of this description?"

"Indeed I do," replied the fool. "She's of good birth and serves two thighs."

"Two thighs?" Henri said quizzically.

"One too short, the other too light."

"Well, Siorac!" warned the king. "You and your friends are going to have to be on your guard. Madame Limp's nest of vipers are extremely bloodthirsty. They've already accused you of taking 200,000 écus, and the knife will follow. You must leave Paris, my child—get away today, within the hour. Go to your estate, the Rugged Oak, fortify it and don't leave until I call you back here. My treasurer will give you 2,000 écus, which should be enough for you to arm yourselves and fortify the place. And while you're gone, my fool here, who's got the nastiest tongue in the court, will spread the rumour that you've had a falling out with the king and that he's exiled you to your estate."

"Ah, sire!" I moaned. "Leaving you is already an unhappy and painful enough task! Must you add this nasty rumour of my disgrace?"

"Bah! It's nothing but wind! But a wind that will protect you better than two squadrons of arquebusiers! In fact, who knows whether, instead of seeking to kill you, some Marianne might not come and tend to you in your solitude, hoping to win your sword to Guise's cause?"

"By heaven, I'd sink it two inches in her heart!"

"What an original form of fornication!" mused the fool. "But one which has the weakness of not allowing any repeat performances."

The king did not smile at this witticism, as he was in one of those melancholic moods that no one in the world, not even Chicot, seemed to be able to lighten, explain or cure.

I was no less sober as I left my good master, in that I had no idea when I'd see him again, and was sorely distressed by the idea that I could render him no service until all the dust of the 200,000 écus had settled. I could look forward to who knew how many long, morose months spent waiting at the Rugged Oak, with no other pleasure than fortifying its walls, for the expense of which the royal treasurer very disobligingly paid out but 1,500 of the 2,000 écus promised by the king. He pretended to be surprised that I was not overjoyed to see them pour into my wallet, but, in truth, I was so overcome with grief, and my cheeks so tear-stained, that I doubtless gave credence to the rumour that Chicot must have already spread by the time I reached the Louvre gates in the rue de l'Autruche, since Fogacer, Quéribus, Giacomi and Miroul had already heard it, and Captain Rambouillet, the portly guard who sat at the gate, held out his hand and said, "Farewell, my friend! The king is too fond of you to allow this exile to last very long."

His words comforted me more than I could say (even though I knew that my disgrace was counterfeit), and so I leant over, teardrops as big as peas bathing his shoulder, and gave a kiss to each of his large red cheeks, which looked like nothing so much as hams that had yet to be cooked.

"My Pierre," Quéribus urged, "let's go into the chapel in the Hôtel de Bourbon. It would be good if we were seen hearing Mass on your last Sunday in Paris, and we can talk there without fearing the knife or any other disturbance at this early hour."

As soon as he saw us, the paunchy verger of the chapel headed over to us, no doubt expecting a handout, given our rich attire, for seating us in a "good and worthy place", but Quéribus informed him that we wished to sit at the back, "in all humility" and in order to pursue our devotions in tranquillity. Of course, the verger understood immediately, since so many affairs, even amorous ones, were negotiated in the shadows of this chapel located so conveniently close to the Louvre—affairs to which, once his palm was appropriately greased, he happily turned a blind eye. Accordingly, he placed us behind a large pillar and departed, very happy with us, given the generosity of our contribution, praying that the Lord might keep us forever in his holy protection.

"Amen!" confirmed Fogacer.

"Monsieur," cautioned Miroul, "perhaps I should step out onto the porch of the chapel to keep an eye on our surroundings?"

"Go ahead, Miroul!" I replied sadly. "Stroll about as much as you'd like, my son. God knows how many months it'll be before we see the streets of Paris again! But don't go far. We have to leave today for the countryside."

He took his leave and, with Quéribus on my right, Giacomi on my left and Fogacer behind us, flanked by the page he called Silvio (after the youngster he'd saved in Périgueux some ten years before, but who'd died of appendicitis, leaving him disconsolate), all three pressed me with questions about my disgrace, but I was careful not to mention

Mundane, or Marianne, or the theft of my horse, instead saying only that the king wanted to get me out of Paris because of the rumours about the 200,000 écus that I had supposedly given to Navarre.

"Ah, my brother!" whispered Giacomi in my ear. "Although I'm devastated that you've been exiled from Paris, this exile happens to fit perfectly with my own affairs, if you're willing to take me with you to the Rugged Oak!"

"What, my brother?" I scolded, quite put out by his request. "My exile is a comfort to you? My disgrace is merely a good thing for you!"

"Ah, Pierre!" returned Giacomi, blushing in shame. "I expressed myself very badly! But I need to tell you that Samarcas, thinking that we were still in Guyenne, has returned to Paris and is lodged with the Montcalms, where I saw Larissa this very day. She swore her love for me and begged me to free her from the clutches of this devil. But Samarcas arrived at that moment without being aware of my presence, and announced he was leaving within twenty-four hours, since he'd heard of our return. So, if he discovers that you've been exiled to the Rugged Oak, he may delay his departure, which would allow me, after ostensibly having left with you, to return to Paris."

"Well, one man's misfortune is another's happiness," I replied with a weak smile. "I am happy for you, Giacomi, and want you to be happy as well. I'll leave today, if Quéribus would be willing to lend me his coach."

"His coach, his escort and himself!" replied Quéribus.

"And me!" Fogacer chimed in.

"But, Fogacer, what about the king's medical needs?"

"*Mi fili*, even though lies may sometimes be inoffensive, among friends they may be too obscure to be understood. I would love to be able to pretend that I am coming with you for your security. But with the baron? With Giacomi? Where could you find more able swordsmen? And no one's better at throwing a knife than Miroul... who's just coming in with his cheeks all swollen with some bit of news he's about to spit out for you. *Mi fili*, the truth is neither pure nor simple, as I've already said. I must flee as far as possible from my street, my lodgings and my neighbourhood, since people are beginning to suspect that I don't like petticoats as much as I should."

"What about Henri?" I asked.

"Henri believes I'm at the bedside of my old mother, who's been dead these twenty years. Another lie. But what can I do? The consequences of my fellow men's foolishness are that I must constantly prevaricate and disappear. The wandering Jew? That's me!"

"Monsieur," broke in Miroul, his blue eye lighting up the shadows, "may I have a word alone with you?"

I rose and went to join him behind a pillar.

"Monsieur," he repeated, "isn't it amazing just how much one can learn when strolling about the streets if one keeps one's eyes and ears wide open!"

"Miroul," I snapped, "this prologue is way too long! Get to the point!"

"Ah, but this point needs some glossing!"

"Gloss away, I pray you."

"Monsieur, when I think about how severely you've scolded me these past ten months for having strolled about for an hour or so, when in fact I learnt the name of the lieutenant of the provostry."

"Are my errors and repentance a necessary part of your gloss?"

"Not at all—my gloss is all about the power of coincidence."

"Well, explain yourself!"

"A lady leaves her lodgings and goes to post herself at the gates of the Louvre to bring you a warning. At this very moment, in order to go for a stroll I emerge from the chapel. From which it emerges," he said, very happy with his play on words, "that if I hadn't been strolling along, I wouldn't have met the lady."

"Well, I suppose I must be convinced of the power of the coincidence."

"What's wrong, Monsieur? You're not yourself! You're not scolding me! You're sad and patient!"

"That's what exile does to you."

"Monsieur, don't you want to know who the lady is?"

"Do I know her?"

"Very well, once upon a time. As a friend now."

"Her name?"

"In her work, she's a seamstress and bonnet-maker."

"My Alizon, my little fly from hell!"

"Well, now, Monsieur, you're reviving!"

"Miroul, run and fetch her!"

"Monsieur," replied Miroul, "observe that I'm leaving without further teasing, your chagrin makes me so sad."

And, seeing him depart like an arrow shot from a crossbow and very relieved that he'd ceased his glossing, I made a sign to the verger; slipping him a few coins, I told him that I needed to speak to a lady about our common devotions, and that we'd need a private place to meet.

"Behind this curtain," he offered, "you'll be able to discuss the elevation of your souls. My good Monsieur, I'll add my own prayers to yours."

Even when we'd pulled the curtain in front of us and she'd removed her mask, I could scarcely recognize my Alizon, so splendidly was she decked out—in a pale-green petticoat embroidered with gold threads, and a beautifully brocaded bodice of the same colour.

"Alizon!" I exclaimed as she threw her arms around my neck and showered me with kisses, despite the distance between us enforced by her hooped petticoat. "Alizon! My pretty fly! How you're done up! You look like a lady in all this finery!"

"Ah, Monsieur, you're teasing me! I'm still the same bonnet-maker, though now I'm a mistress of my trade. But you can't imagine what a perilous time I've had tracking you down, since you've now such a bad reputation on account of those 200,000 écus—"

"Lies, Alizon! Fabrications! A damnable character assassination!"

"Well, Monsieur! I'm so happy to hear it from your lips! Now, give me a kiss, my Pierre! I haven't seen you for three months!"

"But these fancy clothes, Alizon!"

"I have just finished them for one of my clients who's the same size as me, and I was cheeky enough to wear them so no one would recognize me, since I wanted to speak to you in person."

"But what if you'd met the lady on your way here?"

"Monsieur, she'd not resent me, since I only put it on in order to save the life of her brother."

"What! Catherine! My sister Catherine! Good heavens! How I'd like to see her expression if she knew you were here! Ah, my little fly from hell!" I laughed, taking her in my arms and covering her face with kisses. "What a pretty trick this is!"

"Monsieur!" hushed Miroul, raising the curtain enough to stick his head in. "May it please you to quiet down! You're disturbing the Mass. And the verger is casting dirty looks in this direction!"

"So go and grease his palm, Miroul! Alizon has just cured my melancholy!"

"Ah, that makes me very happy, Monsieur! It grieved me to see you so patient with me!"

"My Pierre," whispered Alizon when the curtain was lowered again, "you're a strange one! I run to denounce an ambush that's been laid for you and you're laughing!"

"If you knew Catherine as I do, you'd be laughing too! The lady is so incredibly haughty that if she saw you in her clothes she'd throw herself in the mud in mortification! Alizon, if she refuses this dress, I'll pay for it: it's yours."

"Monsieur, I thank you! But we're wasting time! They're waiting to shoot you from the first floor of the needle shop opposite your lodgings."

"But the shop has been closed for a month."

"Which is why they could rent it."

"Little fly, this news is worth its weight in gold! How did you find out about it?"

"From two women who were whispering this morning behind a curtain, and when I heard your name, I pricked up my ears."

"And what were you doing on the other side of this curtain?"

"I was delivering some bonnets."

"And who are these ladies?"

"Monsieur!" sniffed Alizon archly, pulling herself up. "I couldn't tell you their names, since they're my clients!"

I would have laughed outright had she not covered my mouth with kisses.

"I beg you, Monsieur, don't laugh! You're disturbing the Holy Mass!"

Which would have made me laugh even harder, if I'd been able, but it also caused me a few bittersweet regrets, since I'd sworn to be faithful to my Angelina.

"Alizon," I began, pulling myself away, "I'm certain that I know those two ladies. One is quite tall, though small, and the other is smaller, though fairly tall. And the latter is, like you, a lively brunette, except her eyes aren't as sweet as yours. And her name is—"

"Mademoiselle de La Vasselière," Alizon blurted out, almost in spite of herself.

"Alizon," I said, closing her mouth with my hand, "you must be careful not to bandy your clients' names about so! You'll lose business! I'm going to look into this matter, but know that I'm in your debt every bit as much as on that St Bartholomew's dawn, when you sewed me a white armband to help me get away."

"Ah, Monsieur, it was nothing!" she said, blushing, not because of the memory of the danger but because of how close we were back then.

"Nothing?" I replied. "Nothing less than my life. Alizon, I know how proud you are, but I beg you, take this ring." And taking a topaz ring from my little finger I placed it on her ring finger, over her glove.

"My dear Pierre," she said, "I am of too low an estate to wear so precious a ring, but I will keep it among my treasures out of love for you."

As she was saying these words, the curtain was suddenly raised and she had just enough warning to whirl around and put on her mask, before the verger announced in his sonorous bass voice:

"Good gentleman, the priest has pronounced the *ite missa est.** Perhaps it would be best if the lady disappeared before the faithful begin to leave?"

"Indeed! I appreciate the thought!"

Alizon was outside in the blink of an eye, and, returning to my place behind the pillar, I found myself between Quéribus and Fogacer, our eyes respectfully lowered and our hands joined in prayer, for the entire time it took the few faithful that were there to exit the chapel and, as they did, to glance or to glare at me according to the great or little love that they bore me. As I peeked at them out of the corner of my eye, I could gauge just how much my disgrace had grown, spread and been discussed. What an edifying image we offered, Fogacer, Quéribus and I, to these gentlemen as we continued our devotions despite the fact that the first was an atheist, the second so lukewarm a Catholic that one got chills around him, and the third a Huguenot! But that's how it is in this century, when zeal is measured in grimaces.

"*Mi fili,*" counselled Fogacer sotto voce, "wipe your cheek! It's smeared with rouge! Are you not ashamed to let yourself be kissed by a person of the opposite sex in Our Lord's temple?"

"This temple," observed Quéribus, "has often been put to far worse use! Why, Princesse Margot once offered her body to the Baron de Vitteaux in here in order to persuade him to kill Du Guast."

---

* "Go, the dismissal is made" (the concluding words of the Catholic Mass).

"Excuse me, but you're mistaken, Monsieur," corrected Fogacer. "That fornication did not take place on these holy stones but on the floor of the Grands-Augustins chapel."

"'Tis true," I agreed, "but it was here that Catherine de' Medici piously took Communion the day she had Coligny assassinated."

I didn't want to inform Quéribus or Fogacer of the ambush that had been planned, since I wasn't sure whether the king wanted them to share the secret of this business, whereas Giacomi and Miroul had necessarily been involved ever since the business in Mâcon. And so I let the baron take his leave to prepare his coach and the escort that he'd promised to have ready by noon.

Fogacer having assured me that he'd be ready and waiting with his Silvio, I remained alone with the *maestro* and Miroul, and, in a hushed voice, since the verger was hanging about with his ears pricked, I told them what was up.

"Monsieur," said Miroul, "you remember good Thomassine's needle shop in Montpellier, which had two entries, as everyone knows these little houses often do, since they do other kinds of business than just selling needles? Wouldn't it be the same for this one, since it's unthinkable that the assassin, once he'd shot his arquebus, would walk quietly out into the street where you lay bleeding! No, no, it can't be. I'll wager that his horse is waiting for him in an alley behind the shop so that he can leap on it as soon as he's shot you, the way Maurevert did after the murder of Coligny."

"You're talking sense, young man," said Giacomi. "Let's go and find the horse in the alley that runs parallel to the rue du Champ-Fleuri and from there go up and get the man."

I fell silent, admiring the fact that Giacomi could easily have refused to be involved in such a perilous adventure, one that had such potentially grave consequences for him both in the present and in what might follow. I winced with remorse at how I'd just rebuked

263

him for having said that my exile came at just the right time for his own affairs, so I whispered to him, pressing his arm:

"My brother, I owe you an apology for the brusque way I just treated you. I beg you to forgive me."

"It's nothing," he replied. "I spoke without thinking, and your remark did not wound me. My brother, let's surprise this rascal in his lair! Once we find the trap, victory is ours! I can't wait to see the look on this fellow's face!"

And so, proceeding from the tethered horse to look for its rider, and finding every door in the needle shop open, so anxious was the fellow to flee once his shot had been fired, we came upon him from behind as he sat on a stool looking out of the front window, from where he could shoot me as I opened the door to my lodgings.

"All right," I said quietly, putting the point of my sword in his neck, "put down your arm, my friend, and show us your face!"

Which he did, turning suddenly and seeing our three swords surrounding him.

"What's this?" he stuttered. "What business do you have with me who have none with you?"

"Ah, but you do!" I said, looking at him at my leisure, frowning deeply, letting him sweat a bit in apprehension of the rope. He did not have as evil a face as I might have expected: though it was pudgy and ugly, with his upper lip deeply scarred and one ear missing, his were eyes neither menacing nor stupid.

"I am," I announced, "the Chevalier de Siorac."

"Good gentleman," he replied, "I recognized you already. They pointed you out to me as you left the Louvre this morning. But isn't this treachery to sneak up behind me while I was waiting for you to appear in the street before me?"

"You're the traitor," observed Miroul as he placed the point of his knife on the man's throat.

"Good gentleman," he said, without batting an eye, "if you're going to kill me, get it over with. Don't hand me over to the provost, who'll torture me before hanging me, all of which is horrible, slow and painful."

His response made me look at him with less severity, remembering what Espoumel had told me in his jail cell in Montpellier.

"There will be no torture," I assured him, "if you answer my questions. First, your name."

"Nicolas Mérigot," said the man, "but they call me 'the Guard'."

"Where did you get that nickname?"

"I was in the French Guards, but was thrown out for having robbed my sergeant."

"And your present employment?"

"Hooligan and vagabond," said Miroul.

"Not only," said Mérigot. "I'm a Paris boatman—side to side only."

"What?"

"I'm not allowed to go upstream or downstream, just ferry. There are 500 of us, all outlaws."

"What? All of you?" said Giacomi.

"It's the tradition."

"What a pity," mused Miroul, "that to take a boat across the river you have to put yourself in the hands of men who profess neither faith nor law!"

"What are you saying?" cried Mérigot, outraged. "No faith? We're all good Catholics and hold the Blessed Virgin in particular veneration."

"I thought," I put in, "that it was the butchers of the slaughterhouses who venerated the Virgin."

"Well, they have their Virgin and we have ours, whom we carry in all our processions."

"Listen to this miserable idolater!" said Miroul in Provençal.

But Giacomi was smiling, since he prayed to the Virgin every morning and evening and was nearly in love with her.

"Mérigot," I pressed, "who paid you to do this murder?"

"A fellow who came and found me yesterday on the hay wharves. He bought me a bottle, we got talking and he offered me thirty écus."

"Thirty deniers!" corrected Miroul.

"Monsieur," objected Mérigot, looking at him with his watery eyes, "I would never have done this for so little."

"But why you," I asked, "rather than somebody else?"

"Because I'm an excellent shot, having been a member of the French Guards. Still, at first I refused to do it."

"And why was that?"

"I'm a thief. I don't deal in blood."

"So what changed your mind? The horse?"

"They only lent it to me. Once I was outside Paris and I'd reached Saint-Cloud, I was supposed to attach it to a ring behind the village church, where this fellow was to pay me my écus."

"Or the prick of a stiletto to guarantee your silence."

"Ho! Ho!" said Mérigot, his eyes opening wide. "Not a bit of it! The fellow told me he was the major-domo of a great house, and, what's more, that his master would be able to get me out of jail, if I were caught. I decided he must belong to Guise since he told me they had to kill you because you were for Navarre, that agent of the Devil."

"Well," I laughed, "that's interesting! So that's what convinced you to 'deal in blood'?" With my left hand, I opened my doublet to show him the medal of Mary that my mother had given to me on her deathbed, and that I still wear around my neck, and explained, "They misled you, Mérigot. I'm as good a Catholic as you are. The fellow is a cousin of mine with whom I'm involved in a lawsuit over an inheritance that he wants to win by killing me."

Mérigot was clearly quite surprised by this and visibly took every word as gospel, being the sort of hulking fellow who's not got enough brains to cook an egg.

"This man you're talking about, what does he look like? Isn't he kind of—"

"Small," said Mérigot, "with a thin face, black eyes and a scar under his lower lip."

"That's him all right!" I exclaimed. "That's definitely my cousin! But I'd already recognized his horse! Mérigot, don't you think it's a shame that these crafty scoundrels coerce you honest outlaws of the Seine to commit murders under the pretext and mantle of religion?"

"It's pure treason!" cried Mérigot, squeezing his hands into fists that were made for rowing against the fiercest winds on the river.

"Miroul," I prompted, "fetch me a pen and paper from our lodgings."

"Good gentleman," pleaded Mérigot, "what are you going to do with me?"

"First of all, we're going to write down your deposition, so that you won't be tortured. After that, we'll see."

When Miroul returned, I said to Giacomi in Provençal, which he'd learnt from Miroul during our stay in Mespech, "So, what shall we do with this fellow?"

"If he were a member of the Magnificent's household," said Miroul before Giacomi could answer, "it would be a pleasure to kill him to get reparation for the blood they intended to spill. But since the rascal is simply a river rat…"

"I think we ought to deliver him to the provost," said Giacomi. "The law is the law. Without Alizon, Pierre would be dead now."

"I disagree," countered Miroul. "If the Magnificent plucks him out of the provost's hands, as he's done for other men who were to be hanged, then this fellow will be indebted to him forever, and he'll be all the more dangerous, given that he's the biggest idiot in creation. No, Monsieur, free him or kill him. That's my judgement."

"I'm going to think about it," I replied in French. "But I'll begin by writing his deposition."

I, Nicolas Mérigot, boatman on the Seine, unmarried, and frequenting the community of the hay wharves, do testify and swear as true on my death and salvation the following facts:

There followed the report of his being hired to wait for me and assassinate me, and the description of the fellow who hired him. There was no reference to my supposedly being this fellow's cousin. I closed the deposition as follows:

Following the above confession, the Chevalier de Siorac, recognizing that I had been led into this enterprise through lies and misrepresentations, was good enough to pardon me for this attempt on his life, and, given that luckily no blood had been spilt, and that he, being a good Catholic, didn't wish my blood to be spilt either, set me free, recommending that I tell the truth of this affair to all the other boatmen of the hay wharves, and gave me five écus to entertain them in his name and in the name of our natural and sovereign king, Henri III, praying God and the Blessed Virgin to keep him safe, in their holy favour.

Hearing this, the boatman threw himself at my feet and kissed my hands, asking a thousand pardons and assuring me that I would never regret my goodness and mercy as long as he lived. This said, he began trembling from head to foot of his enormous body like a poplar leaf in the wind—he who, only a few minutes before, had faced down Miroul's knife without batting an eye in his raw courage.

"Mérigot, I am now heading back to my estate outside Paris," I explained, "but on my return I will have Miroul, my secretary, send for you"—and hearing this title, Miroul flushed with pleasure—"so that you can tell me about your life. However, if I discover that my evil cousin has come back to the hay wharves to hire you…"

"I'll throw him head over heels into the Seine!" Mérigot burst out, clenching his huge fists.

"But don't let him drown," I cautioned. "Sign here, Mérigot, if you know how to write."

"Know my name, at least," muttered Mérigot, who was sweating profusely, the goose feather appearing heavier in his big hands than an oar made of ash.

After having extinguished the fuse of the arquebus (whose odour would have terrified our neighbours had we been out in the street), Miroul seized it, while Giacomi took hold of the bridle of the horse that was tethered in front of the needle shop, and my two companions, now in possession of our booty from this great battle, sent our prisoner off without weapons or rings, but very happy to have saved his neck from the noose and his guts from the points of our swords.

Once back in my lodgings, I embraced my Angelina and hugged my children, then left Giacomi to ask my good wife about her twin sister and the hopes that she'd reawakened in him, and went downstairs with Miroul so that we could shut ourselves in the little study—where I'd received Mosca—in order to continue my correspondence.

"Miroul," I announced as I sat down opposite him at the table, "I need you to write a letter that I'm going to dictate."

"Well, Monsieur," he cautioned, "my spelling is going to ruin it! It's not as good as yours!"

"Yes, but yours is better than the queen mother's. So write, Miroul, without further stalling. And first of all the address:

"TO MADAME DE LA VASSELIÈRE
HÔTEL DE MONTPENSIER
PARIS."

"Indeed! Is this the one I think it is?"

"Or whose name you likely heard when you were listening at the curtain in the chapel."

"*Nosse velint omnes, mercedem solvere nemo*,"* observed Miroul, who loved to produce such quotations when he was in a jam. "So it is with me, with your permission, Monsieur."

"Permission granted. Write, Miroul.

"Madame,

Although you managed to run through my valet in Mâcon, I made you a bargain and, as promised, granted you your freedom, which you immediately used to steal my horse, valued at 500 écus, from under the nose of my other valet—"

"'From under the nose of my secretary'," corrected Miroul.

"If you wish.

"And today, redoubling your outrageous behaviour, you tried to have me assassinated by a fellow who, luckily for me, was too focused on the street in front of him and not enough on the stairs behind him. Which means we have him. My men wanted to kill him—"

"Monsieur, what would you think of: 'My secretary, in his wrath, wanted to dispatch him'?"

"If you insist.

"But I did not grant him this wish, having no stomach for spilling the blood of a Christian; also, I elected not to hand him over to the provost, to whom he certainly would have given the name of his

---

* "Everyone wants to know, but no one wants to pay the price for the information" (Juvenal).

employer, who happens to be the major-domo in your household. And so I sent him back to his boats. However, Madame, I have decided to keep his horse as compensation for the horse that was stolen from me in Mâcon—"

"One bad turn deserves another!" laughed Miroul.

"'And I am also keeping his arquebus out of love for you.' Next line.

"I must say, Madame, that I would have found it thorny indeed to be assassinated by you on the very day I was being sent into exile. Is it not enviable to manage to be shamed from both sides at once? I would have been twice slain: first by your bullet, then by ridicule."

"Ah Monsieur, that's profound!"

"Next line.

"Since my talents are no longer required, I am heading off to rot in my country estate, where, I assure you, I will not eat any of the mushroom dishes that you might send my way."

"Monsieur, what's all this about mushrooms?"

"That's how Annet de Commarques poisoned my cousin Geoffroy de Caumont."

"But does she know that?"

"Geoffroy de Caumont also happens to have been her cousin."

"Heavens! Are you a blood relative of this Fury from hell?"

"'Tis more than likely. Next line: 'So that if I ever have the pleasure of meeting your unforgettable beauty—'"

"Unforgettable more for the knife than the beauty!" interjected Miroul.

"…may it be, I beg you, on an occasion when it will no longer be a question of daggers and arquebus, but rather one of admiration, with which I have the honour of being, dear Madame, in spite of everything, your humble and respectful servant.

"And then sign for me."

"What, Monsieur, sign for you?"

"Sign 'S'. Nothing more. 'S' followed by a full stop. Then add this postscript: 'My mother's maiden name was Caumont-Castelnau. Might we be cousins?'"

"Monsieur," asked Miroul, as he traced an "S" that was pot-bellied at both ends, "what do you call a letter in which one caresses a person who has just tried to bite you?"

"A *captatio benevolentiae.*"*

"And just why do you wish to obtain the benevolence of this murderess?"

"So that she'll stop wanting to kill me."

"Is that what she wants?"

"She may end up loving me if she thinks I've been shamed by the king."

"She may just *pretend* to love you," corrected Miroul, "if she doesn't believe your story of being out of favour."

"Ah, now you're the profound one, Miroul!" I smiled. "What else can I do? There are always two players in a game like this and it's always dangerous. But I'd rather try to get her sword on my side than to fear it will suddenly emerge from the shadows behind me. I won't always have an Alizon to warn me!"

"Or a Miroul," said Miroul with pique.

"Or a Miroul," I agreed with a grin, "who's both a sort of a mentor

---

* "Winning of goodwill."

to me and much, much more besides. Miroul, may I ask you to make a copy of Mérigot's deposition with your beautiful hand, as well as a copy of this letter to La Vasselière?"

"Monsieur, what you say about my 'beautiful hand' is a straight-out, shameless *captatio benevolentiae*, since you know very well that it's eleven o'clock, an hour when any self-respecting man should be dining. I'm starving!"

"Just one more effort, I beg you, Monsieur secretary! Moreover, I will work opposite you, since I must compose a letter to the king."

"What? In your own hand?"

"But I'm writing to the king and so it must be in my own hand!"

"Ah, well then!" said Miroul, half in jest, half in earnest. "I'm infinitely honoured. But honour does not nourish a man!"

He must have made twenty more such bitter comments, which was his way of expressing his affection through teasing, and yet he made two beautiful copies without missing a line or a word, and that were quite legible, while I provided a brief report to Henri of all that had just transpired, adding that I'd had my letter to Marianne written and signed by Miroul, in order to keep these she-devils from forging my writing and my signature, since I'd heard that Madame Limp kept a stable of secretaries working on forgeries and copies of seals, and that they were working on a copy of the king's own seal.

"Did you know, Miroul, that they burn the right hand of anyone who tries to copy the king's seal?"

"With Madame Limp," Miroul answered, "that won't be necessary. She's already burning internally. And the same for the queen mother. They also claim that she has already copied it more than once."

"Ah, but that's different. Henri refuses to allow anyone to treat his mother or his sister with disrespect, no matter how treasonous they are."

I enclosed the three missives under a single seal and, after a brief repast, asked Miroul to carry them without delay to the Louvre.

"Monsieur, let's be clear," he said stiffly. "Am I your secretary? Or your messenger?"

"Right you are, Miroul," I conceded. "Now that you're my secretary, I'll have to find a little valet to replace you in these menial tasks."

"What?" scowled Miroul, his blue eye darkening. "A little valet? Here? I wouldn't tolerate it! Monsieur I would quit your service immediately if I ever saw a little tyro in here who would inflict his ignorance on us! Monsieur, you're not unaware of the fact that I am a man of means and can set myself up if and when I want to!"

"So, no little valet, Miroul?"

"Monsieur," he replied solemnly and in French, "I would never tolerate it for a second, I swear it!"

"I'll take this letter to the Louvre myself, and place it in Chicot's hands so that he can give it to the king."

"Monsieur, you must be joking," said Miroul, mustering all the dignity he was capable of. "I shall go myself. Is it not natural that a secretary should carry the letters he's just written? Could we entrust such a mission to the first good-for-nothing to come along? Would they even let him in the gates of the Louvre? And would he know how to find Chicot in such a labyrinth?"

I spent five months at the Rugged Oak, using the king's money to raise my walls above ladder height, build a tower that would allow a view of the surrounding area and dig a tunnel that led from inside the walls to a glen in the forest of Montfort-l'Amaury, which would enable us to send a man for help if our walls were assailed by our enemies. I even purchased a small culverin that I had hoisted to the top of the tower, though I doubted it could do much damage to any besiegers, other than to strike terror into them with its explosive noise. It was also a way of sounding the alarm, as I discovered the first time we fired it, for it could be heard as far away as Méré and

Galluis, and a group of the townsmen rushed to our walls to find out what was happening.

Two days after he escorted me here, Giacomi slipped away to Paris, where he was able to see Larissa at the Montcalms' lodgings and hear her renew her promise to try to escape the clutches of the Jesuit as soon as she was able—a proposal that aroused in me some scepticism, since I believed that Samarcas exercised more of a moral than a physical control over her, holding sway over her soul rather than her body.

Five months after having left Paris, I received a letter from Madame de La Vaselière that I found quite perplexing.

Dear Cousin,

I find it strange that you wrote to me—legitimately, I believe—of our common parentage and interests at the very moment that you accused me of having run through your valet in Mâcon, stolen your horse and attempted to assassinate you.

My cousin, this is madness! You must have been hoodwinked by some wench who had the impudence to resemble me and, perhaps, usurp my name.

As for me, I protest that my weapons are entirely feminine: I thrust with a pout, shoot with a smile and steal a horse with a glance—and, with the same glance, though a more severe one, I assassinate. However, I also know how to heal such wounds, and, strange to say, with the same arms that have caused such damage.

My cousin, if you're not afraid of my artillery, come and see me, when you return from exile, at the Montpensiers' mansion, where, in the delightful prospect of seeing you, I shall be your humble and devoted servant,

Jeanne de La Vaselière

I dared not show this letter to my Angelina, who would have feared for my life night and day if she'd known the truth of the matter. Moreover, she had enough worries and troubles with six beautiful children to nourish and care for, all hale and hearty, having been left as little as possible in the care of servants—who were certainly not lacking in our household, but who were always closely supervised by Angelina, since our nurses and chambermaids often entertained gross and dangerous ancient superstitions that one had to guard against, to protect the children's eyesight, hearing and general health, if not their very lives. Indeed, the parents who rely on the false experience and claims of knowledge of such women are exposing their children to all sorts of remedies and secrets that have been handed down since time immemorial but do not stand up in the light of reason: for example, the custom of pouring a spoonful of alcoholic spirits in the nursling's milk so that he will go to sleep straightaway at night and not bother his parents with his crying—a remedy that serves the parents' happy repose rather than the welfare of the infant, who, rather than being fortified by such treatment, will likely be less vigorous and healthy later in life.

I named my oldest daughter Elizabeth, because I admired the bravery and energy of the English queen; the next child was also a girl, whom we named Françoise after my maternal grandmother, whom I loved dearly, though I hadn't known her well; our third child, my oldest son, was named Philippe, since I would have wanted to bear this name myself; my second son we called Pierre, because he resembled me from the day he was born. My third son I named Olivier, since Olivier was, of all the knights of Charlemagne, the one I admired the most; my fourth son bore the name Frédéric, at Angelina's request, simply because she liked the sound of this name and believed it portended a great destiny for him.

Dame Gertrude du Luc, for her part, had ten sons by my brother Samson, but lost two to smallpox in early childhood and was all the more devastated since she was approaching that period of life when Nature normally prevents women from bearing any more children. And, in truth, to see her in such full bloom, her face so fresh, full of colour and unwrinkled, one might doubt that Nature was so wise, or fair, to set so early a term on feminine fecundity since she extended men's fertility to a much more advanced age—indeed, in some cases very advanced, if we are to believe the Bible.

I hadn't seen Samson for quite some time, and when I saw him buried in his apothecary's shop among all his vials, I found him quite thickened around the middle, his complexion very splotchy, his eyes dulled, his posterior grown heavy and his pretty face lacking the beauty it once possessed, presently all pale and swollen. And though Gertrude was always pestering him to get more exercise outside his shop, claiming he preferred sleeping with his vials to sleeping with her (a reproach quite difficult to believe given how many children he'd fathered, and the urgent appetite of the lady), I also understood that her friendly admonitions would never suffice to conquer the passion his alchemy inspired in him. So I decided to counter his pharmaceutical passion with a stronger one and, taking him aside, begged him to help in defending our stronghold against a likely attack. I suggested that, together, we patrol the woods around Montfort, take up fencing and shooting practice, and practise scaling walls, in order to help our band of Giacomi, Quéribus and Miroul ensure our common safety.

Samson was much aggrieved to hear of the peril I faced and threw himself into my Herculean travails like the beautiful angel of God that he was, so much so that his pharmacy would have been left entirely deserted had it not been for his assistant, who, to tell the truth, was quite capable of replacing him. And without Gertrude's vigilance, the conjugal bed would have gone unoccupied, given the fatigue that my brother faced after running uphill and down dale all day long. But the cure worked miracles, for, besides keeping me good, brotherly company in the absence of Giacomi (since Larissa and Samarcas had not yet departed Paris), we rediscovered the great fraternal love that we'd shared in our infancy and youth but that had later suffered due to our very different interests and ranks, his religious zeal, his excessive naivety, his inflexible nature and, ultimately, the distance between Paris and Montfort. It was a pleasure to see him regain his vigour from our exercises and rediscover the virile symmetry of his body, as well as the former marvellous youthfulness of his face, with its freckles and those azure eyes, which were so luminous and candid that no one could gaze on them without loving him.

In her carriage filled with her eight children, Zara and herself, Gertrude came to visit us at our manor almost every afternoon, weather permitting, and this February was so mild that we could all frolic about on the grassy courtyard of my stronghold, where there was enough space for their children and mine to run and play, and for the mothers to chat about their incessant work—a conversation to which Florine and Zara could contribute their own experiences, though the latter had never wanted to marry.

"Zara," said Gertrude, "please bring Alexandre over here, since I see he's just gone in his pants."

"Oh no, Madame!" exclaimed Zara throwing up her hands. "He is quite beshitten and I'm not going to touch him or even go near him, he smells so awful! It's enough to make you sick!"

"You just have to get used to it when you're a mother," replied Gertrude, making a sign to one of her nursemaids to bring her the howling bundle.

"Which is why I'll never be a mother, Madame, seeing how disgusting this business is: the terrible brutality of men, the ugliness of pregnancy, the pain of childbirth and then the infant himself, who would doubtless be very sweet, with all his smiles and looks and fresh little body, if he didn't shit and piss himself all the time! Ah," she continued, putting her hand over her mouth, "I nearly gag at the very thought of it, so abhorrent do I find it."

"But Zara," countered Angelina, who, as the wife of a physician, wanted to inject some reason into the discussion, "we must all pay our debt to nature! You yourself do so!"

"But I do not pay my debt where others can see it! And I do it as quickly as I can! And, even so, I am ashamed that these horrors and smells could emanate from my body! Heavens! I have to wash and perfume myself immediately, so disgusting do I find that business. It's all well and good for men, who are naturally such coarse beings! But couldn't things have been arranged differently for our sex, which is by nature so tender and delicate?"

She had hardly finished this outburst when the porter came to announce that the priest of Montfort was at the gate and requesting permission to enter. Hearing this, and desiring to honour him, I went myself to open the gate, having established a friendship with him that wasn't conducted without feelings on both sides that were better left unsaid. I believed him to be a good man, not at all as zealous as one might have feared, who never attacked the king in his sermons, only providing sketchy lamentations and jeremiads about us heretics (without sabre-rattling or veiled calls for slaughter)—a degree of moderation that would have had him labelled as a "political subversive" by the Guisards in Paris.

And yet his big long nose, which was always sniffing out the affairs of his parishioners (including myself), was nettled that neither Angelina, I, our children, Miroul nor any of our servants confessed to anyone but Father Anselm. In this arrangement he smelt, with those enormous nostrils of his, an odour that, prudent man that he was, he wouldn't have called sulphurous, but that nevertheless provoked in him a vague presentiment of evil.

"Well, Monsieur Siorac!" exclaimed Father Ameline, raising his two hands heavenwards. "What a charming and bucolic tableau this is! And how happy I am to see these fourteen lovely Siorac children, frolicking about like little angels!"

These angels were, at this moment, making enough noise to raise the dead, screaming at the top of their lungs, pummelling each other, some with their hands, others with their feet, like a bunch of devils incarnate, crying, laughing, their noses running and some even having soiled or wet themselves.

"The so-called reformed Church," continued Father Ameline, squinting at me out of the corner of his eye, "expects its ministers to marry. But I've always thought that the Holy Roman and Apostolic Church displayed a truly divine wisdom in denying its priests the bother and hindrance of a large family, given the enormous expenses that are entailed, the chains by which it restricts a man's life and, though I make no reference to present company," he added with a sly smile, "since the ladies present are assuredly exceptions to this, the bilious moods of a spouse.

"It is true," he continued, "that the Lord intended in some wise to correct the domestic tyranny of women by recalling them to His side almost always after the fourth or fifth birth—proof, my ladies," he added, bowing in their direction, "that the Most High considered each of you too sweet and willing to bend to the wills of your husbands here to subject you to the common law."

To this, Angelina and Gertrude smiled but made no answer, having learnt from both my father and me that it was the ignorance, uncleanliness and superstition of the midwives that led to death in childbirth, much more than the will of the Lord.

Meanwhile, having decided that he'd paid enough attention to our beautiful children and the vessels of iniquity that had raised them (without, however, having broken after the fourth birth), and wishing to pursue our conversation as far as possible from the din of our little angels and the chatter of our women, Ameline begged me to show him the tower we'd just built, "no doubt at great expense of time and money!"—a hint, I'll wager, that if I could spend so liberally on my estate, I should also be able to help with the repairs to the roof of his sacristy.

"Monsieur de Siorac," he began, "have you heard of certain stirrings among some of the great men of this kingdom, who are reputed to have allied themselves, perhaps with the Pope's blessing, with King Felipe of Spain in order to take up arms, if necessary, against Henri de Navarre's accession to the throne?"

"I have heard of a league," I replied, "but never of any alliance with a foreign prince. And if it turns out that this news is true, I thoroughly deplore it. Only the king of this kingdom has the power to establish treaties with foreign sovereigns. That would be pure treason on the part of a subject!"

"But the king," countered Ameline, who clearly felt very uneasy about the application of the word "treason" to Guise, "is so weak, so hesitant! And isn't it true as well that he has been secretly supporting the king of Navarre?"

"Father Ameline," I said, looking him straight in the eye, "if, perchance, you are referring to the infamous rumour about these 200,000 écus—"

"Absolutely not!" he cried raising both hands. "Not at all! You've been cleared of that frightful scandal, and, from what I hear, there is no more talk of it whatsoever in Paris, nor at the Louvre, neither among the nobility nor in the sacred pulpits. It seems that people even feel sorry for you for having been so wickedly slandered."

At this moment, my secretary, Miroul, entered the tower room, opened his mouth to speak, but closed it abruptly on seeing Father Ameline; then he opened it again and said in Provençal:

"Monsieur, your brother-in-law has just arrived and wishes to speak with you immediately in the blue room concerning a matter of great consequence."

"What's this?" said Ameline, poking his nose into the matter.

"He's speaking *langue d'oc*, Father. My secretary and I are in the habit of practising the four other languages we speak: Provençal, Italian, English and Latin!"

"Indeed! Latin!" exclaimed the priest. "It's often so little understood, even by the great dignitaries of our Church! Why, the Cardinal de Vendôme has a lackey who knows it better than he does, and once, when the cardinal was hosting a canon, who spoke to him in that language, said angrily,

"'What on earth is this silly jargon you're babbling?'

"'But Monseigneur,' exclaimed the canon, 'that's Latin!'

"'Knave!' shouted the prelate, turning to his lackey. 'Couldn't you have warned me?'"

Of course, I laughed at this little joke, which I was hearing for the third time, and before escorting him to the gate of our manor (where he insisted on blessing every member of my household), I greased his palm with a few écus to help with the sacristy roof, which he slipped into a pocket of his large cassock, which was so thoroughly outfitted with secret pockets that my coins disappeared before you could say "Amen"!

From the gate, I recrossed the grassy courtyard where the fourteen little Sioracs were cavorting so noisily, and suddenly caught sight of my little sister Catherine in conversation with Angelina and Gertrude (but, as usual, turning her back on Zara). She gave a little cry when she saw me, and was good enough to throw herself into my arms—forgetting for a moment that she was a baronne—and showered me with kisses that, if not passionate (since she was always reserved even in her enthusiasms), were at least tender, reminding me of those she'd given me when we were growing up at Mespech and I would carry her up two flights of stairs to bed in the evening. I hadn't seen her for five months, and hugged her to me, whispering, "Catherine! My sister! My little sister!"

"Little!" she sniffed, pushing me away. "Where do you get the idea that I'm little? Quite the contrary! I'm as tall as you are! And maybe taller!"

Which, given the height of her heels and the crown of pearl-studded hair that graced her head, was indeed true. And as I stepped back to take a good look at her, splendidly decked out in a petticoat of pale green, brocaded with golden threads, which, though I was seeing it for the first time on her, I well remembered from my brief conversation in the church with Alizon, I simply couldn't keep from bursting out laughing. I left her standing there, furious with me, her blue eyes blazing, and, still laughing uncontrollably, headed upstairs to the blue room, were Quéribus awaited me.

The baron, dressed, as usual, like a court dandy, was much more effusive in his embrace than his sister, with whom, however much we loved each other, spats and sulks were more numerous than rainy days in the Île-de-France.

"Well, my Pierre!" he exclaimed, our salutations duly made. "Hurry and pack your bags! The king requires your presence in Paris."

"What?" I said in amazement. "In Paris? At the Louvre? At his side?" But, suddenly realizing that Quéribus knew nothing about Marianne, about the murder in Mâcon, or about the attempt on my life, I decided to perpetuate the fable of my exile, and added, "What? My disgrace is over? But how? Tell me what you know! How did it happen?"

"Nothing easier!" replied Quéribus. "When he awoke yesterday, the king said, 'Siorac did so marvellously at curing the sore throat of Monsieur d'Épernon, I don't doubt that he'll cure mine as well.

What is he doing so far away on his estate? My Quarreller! Go and fetch him!' You know, of course," continued Quéribus, with a hint of swagger, "that ever since my interrupted duel with you, the king loves to call me 'Quéribus the Quarreller', or, better still, 'my Quarreller'?!"

Of course, I knew this as well as he did, never having forgotten the duel in which I would have lost my life had not Henri intervened. But since I also knew what response Quéribus expected from me (our respective roles having solidified over these past twelve years), I dutifully replied:

"That's because the king has such great affection for you."

"Yes, I believe so as well," gushed Quéribus, preening his wasp-like figure.

But, thinking that my recall to Paris must have some connection to the "stirrings among some of the great men of this kingdom" that the priest had referred to, I asked:

"So how are things with the king?"

"Delicate, indeed. The princes of Lorraine and other nobles have formed a Holy League for the financial support and defence of the Catholic Church and the eradication of heresy."

"That's nothing new."

"What is new is that they've signed a document at the Château de Joinville excluding Navarre from the throne of France as a heretic, and recognizing the Cardinal de Bourbon as the legitimate successor of Henri. And what's worse is that this document was also signed by representatives of Felipe II."

"But that's treason and open rebellion!"

"Open, no," replied Quéribus with a smile. "You know Guise: he moves like a cat, always ready to flee. It's a secret document—all very cloak-and-dagger. It's not open defiance of the king, it's pressure on him."

"So how has the king responded?"

"Since it is not an open challenge, he's being careful not to respond to it."

"And that's all?" I asked in disbelief.

"What else can he do?" replied Quéribus. "He's 'trimming his sails'."

"But," I observed, greatly troubled, "by continuing to trim his sails, Henri runs the risk of having his enemies come aboard and throw him into the deep."

I left Quéribus there and, wishing to prepare our household for an early departure the next day, went to tell Angelina to ready our baggage, news that she received with visible joy, having languished far from Paris for these past six months. Gertrude, on the other hand, was very put out not to be able to follow her, and the beautiful Zara even more so. Samson was too steeped in his pharmaceutical vials to be able to leave them.

I found Fogacer in my library, rereading the treatise of Ambroise Paré in his favourite armchair, with Silvio on a stool at his feet, leaning his back against his master's knees, lost in his dreams, his eyes vacant except when Fogacer spoke.

"Well now, venerable Dr Fogacer," I asked, "isn't this the tenth time you've read this treatise? What's your conclusion about it?"

"It is marvellous for everything having to do with anatomy and surgery. But adding nothing, I mean absolutely nothing, alas, to our knowledge of common diseases, containing only the superstitions and fallacies of the Greek, Arab and Jewish traditions. 'Shoemaker, don't try to pronounce on anything above the shoe!'"

"What?" asked Silvio, shaking his black curls as though he were awakening from a deep sleep. "What does a shoemaker have to do with it?"

"He's very famous in the history of art," smiled Fogacer. "Listen, Silvio. When the painter Apelles publicly exhibited a painting of a man, the neighbouring shoemaker criticized the way he'd painted the sandals. But after Apelles corrected this error, the next day the shoemaker commented on his portrayal of the legs. To this, Apelles replied as I did."

"So you believe," observed Silvio, "that the surgeon should write only about surgery?"

"And about anatomy," I added, "since he shouldn't cut into what he knows nothing about."

"*Mi fili*," said Fogacer, placing the book on a low table before him, and resting his left hand on Silvio's curly black mane, "you didn't come here to talk to me about Ambroise Paré, but about your imminent departure for Paris."

"How do you know about that?" I asked in surprise.

"I received a letter this morning," Fogacer answered with his diabolically raised eyebrow, "from the Marquis de Miroudot, who informs me, among other things, of the signing of the Treaty of Joinville between the Guise brothers and Felipe II."

"So you know the marquis?" I asked, moving from one surprise to the next.

"It would be a calumny to say I knew him intimately," laughed Fogacer. "But you know all too well that in our brotherhood any distinction of rank or wealth is abolished by the force of our common interests."

"So you're friends," I smiled. "But what connection do you find between the Treaty of Joinville and my departure for Paris?"

"It's obvious," replied Fogacer. "*Mi fili*, I'm not as credulous as the baron, so I never believed the story about your disgrace, given how much money you were able to spend on fortifying your domain—an amount so lavish that it could only have come from the king. Would the king so handsomely support a man he'd just sent into exile? Answer, Silvio."

"No, Monsieur."

"You heard him, my chevalier. Moreover, when I observed from the library window your handsome minion, Quéribus, prancing and pawing the ground, it was only too obvious that he could be here only for one reason: to bring you orders from the king, who always needs the support of his advisors when he's in a desperate predicament."

"Desperate, Fogacer?" I asked, my heart suddenly beating frightfully.

"Completely. First, the queen mother (and therefore all the ministers that she's had appointed and who belong to her) are betraying the king, and have secretly joined Guise's party."

"What, Catherine has been won by Guise?!"

"Both the strength and the weakness of Guise," replied Fogacer with his slow, sardonic smile, "is that he makes promises to everyone, hatches too many plots and burns too many bridges! And so he's promised the throne to this crazy old Cardinal de Bourbon once Navarre has been dispatched. To Felipe II, he promises nothing less than France herself, once Navarre has been killed. And as for Catherine, he offers to present the sceptre to her grandson, the Marquis de Pont-à-Mousson, once the cardinal dies. The child is the son of Catherine's daughter Claude and the Duc de Lorraine."

"What?" I gasped. "Pont-à-Mousson would accede to the throne through a woman? What about Salic law?"

"It is not a law," replied Fogacer. "It's just a tradition that Catherine can ignore since she's Italian."

"I can't believe my ears! Is Catherine really such a bad mother to our poor king?"

"Not at all! But she's already figured out that Guise's victory over Henri is inevitable, and she believes that by joining the Guisard faction, she can ultimately soften the fate of her son and at least save his life."

"Do you believe that is true, Fogacer?"

"No. But I'm convinced that she's right in believing that the king has been ensnared in Guise's nets and is very unlikely to untangle himself."

"Fogacer!" I moaned, feeling stunned and my heart beating like a mad thing. "Heavens, what are you saying? The king has lost! But he hasn't even begun to fight Guise!"

"He can't possibly win! I've heard from Miroudot—and don't ask, *mi fili*, where he got this information—that Felipe II has promised Guise 600,000 écus a year to gather arms and men enough to defeat the king! And since the king has now exhausted his liberalities, how can he expect to get anything more from the parliament or the Estates-General? If it comes to war, the Spaniard will win."

"But what about Navarre? And Queen Elizabeth?"

"*Mi fili*, you've hit the nail on the head. The king cannot ally himself with Navarre unless Navarre converts, and Navarre can't convert without losing his army. As for Elizabeth, what can she do for Henri when she herself is in perpetual danger of assassination by a Jesuit or of invasion by Spain? And, what's more, since the population of Paris is mostly made up of Guisards, the king can't even guarantee the support of his capital! Silvio," Fogacer continued, less to ask his page's opinion than to check to see whether he was still listening carefully to the conversation, wishing to instruct him in everything and sharpen his judgement, "what do you think the king's chances are in this predicament?"

"Slim," replied Silvio as he rose as nimbly as a cat and stood, hands on hips, looking at Fogacer with his big brown eyes, "but…"

"But what?" said Fogacer, looking at Silvio with what one might describe as a mother's pride rather than a devil's glee.

"But the king is our natural and legitimate sovereign. Is that not a great source of strength?"

"Indeed it is!" gushed Fogacer in his glee, leaving me stunned at this burst of genuine enthusiasm from one whose attitude had always seemed so callous and dismissive. "*Mi fili*," he said, as if to hold me witness to the prowess of his student, "did you hear that?"

"I heard it," I smiled, "and would only like to add that the king is distrustful, secretive and very capable, and has more cleverness in his little finger than there is in the head of the Magnificent, in the bloated face of the Great Whoremonger, in the paunch of the Pig or in the thighs of Madame Limp!"

"By Jupiter! Well said, my friend!" laughed Fogacer. "One could only surmise from hearing you, *mi fili*, that you were a great admirer of the Holy League and the Guisards! But I am not! I cannot trust anything that calls itself 'holy': the *Holy* Church, the *Holy* Council, the *Holy* League or, emanating from all of these 'holies' like a worm from fruit, the *Holy* Inquisition! 'Sblood! The *Holy* Inquisition in Paris! Say goodbye to the joy of living. I've already been 'inquisitioned' enough in my life! In Paris, trouble and setbacks stick to me like crabs on the skin of a monk! *Mi fili*, I wonder if I would be abusing your liberal hospitality by staying here a bit longer. All I need is for Miroudot to find me and my page lodgings in a neighbourhood where I won't be recognized, since my former neighbours want to see me hanged, drawn and quartered and then burnt!"

"Burnt?"

"Don't they burn the buggers and the atheists?"

"But won't the king protect you?"

"Alas! The king can no longer do so since he himself has been accused of being a bugger. Of course, you understand, *mi fili*, that my sexuality wouldn't bother any of my good neighbours if I weren't also reputed to be 'political'. We don't even need the Spaniard in Paris! The Inquisition has already arrived! Do you realize that they've secretly inventoried all the houses of the 'politicals' to massacre the lot as soon as Guise arrives in the capital?"

"But how do you know that, Fogacer?"

"Well!" said Fogacer arching his diabolical eyebrows. "I have a better sense of smell than a Jew: I can smell massacres coming from the distant horizon!"

At this, Silvio suddenly buried his face in his hands and began sobbing uncontrollably.

"Fogacer," I said, "you may remain here with Silvio as long as you like. My people will treat you as the master of the house. But how shall I explain your extended absence to the king?"

Fogacer hesitated before answering, doubtless wanting to take Silvio in his arms to comfort him, but not presuming to do so in my presence. "Tell him," he said, turning slightly away from me to hide his tears, but still forcing his lips into that sinuous smile of his, "tell him that Heaven has inconveniently prolonged my mother's illness despite my best remedies."

"What's this?" broke in Angelina as she swept into the library with a great rustle of her petticoats. "Silvio in tears? Fogacer as well? My Pierre, have you been scolding our two great friends here?"

"Not at all!" I replied with a smile. "And I'm am greatly distressed that they'll be unable to return to Paris with us tomorrow. It seems they'll have to wait here until they find new lodgings, since their former dwelling is no longer available."

"Why don't they come and stay with us in the rue du Champ-Fleuri?" she cried. And saying this, she took each of them by the arm and, pulling them to her, smiled sweetly since she loved them dearly, and especially Fogacer, who'd been so fond of her for so long that his affection would have troubled me had it been anyone else. But I knew very well that the love they shared was not even like that of a father for his daughter or a sister for her brother, but rather an entirely spiritual tenderness. Everyone who knew Fogacer believed him to be sceptical, derisive and diabolical, but not Angelina, who was blind to all of his vices and did not believe his atheism, his negativity or his sexual orientation—and what she saw must have been real in some way, for Fogacer responded to her view of him with perpetual and immutable adoration.

"Oh, my friend!" stammered Fogacer, his voice suddenly reaching such a clarity and pitch that it sounded infantile. "I never would have dared ask you for such a boon, no matter how much I wished it, for fear of inconveniencing you, but if this is what you want, I could not ask for better! You are so good, beneficent and forgiving that if I were more religious I'd compare you to the Blessed Virgin!"

"Silly fellow!" replied Angelina, standing up on tiptoe to give him a kiss on the cheek, for Fogacer was a good head taller than she, though he behaved as if he were one of her children. "That's blasphemy!"

"My friend, you dare scold me?" replied Fogacer, secretly delighted to be so chided.

"You're blaspheming, silly fellow that you are!" Angelina insisted imperiously. "It's a sin to compare me to the Mother of God; I'm simply the mother of six little devils—seven, if I count you!" she said, smiling sweetly at Fogacer. "No, eight!" she added, fearing in her generous nature that little Silvio might feel left out of the clutch of chicks she gathered into the warm down of her feathers. "To work, my friends," she trumpeted loudly and joyfully. "To your rooms and pack your bags and look lively! I'll come by later to check in on you," she added, giving each one a squeeze on the arm and, as she let go, a little pat on the neck.

"What about me, Madame?" I asked when they'd left. "Will I have nothing from you?"

"Monsieur," she replied, her beautiful doe's eyes shining tenderly, "you'll have everything, but in good time, which is not the present moment, or even the next—or even the one after that! I've got a thousand chores to do that you can help with. Unless…"

"Unless?"

"Unless you could ask our servants to have my bath filled with hot water at eight o'clock, since all this packing will leave me as filthy as

Queen Margot, who, if I remember correctly, once boasted of not having washed her hands for a week."

At this, she gave a joyful laugh, turned on her heels and, her petticoats swirling in time with her fine figure, ran off to do her chores.

Of Queen Margot, whom I'd seen with these very eyes on the day of her marriage to the king of Navarre, I'd scarcely heard a word since her brother had banished her from the court, given that her whole family had rejected her on account of her strange behaviour. And as for Navarre, although he had welcomed her to his chateau in Nérac, he'd caressed his "wife" with sweet words and polite smiles, but had never once touched her with his hands, mouth or member, not wishing to allow her to claim she was pregnant by him when it was a thousand times more likely that she would be carrying someone else's baby, since the lady was so profligate.

On the morning of our departure, as I went to give the signal to mount, my foot practically in my stirrup, a horseman rode up to deliver a letter, and, recognizing both the address and the beautiful handwriting of my father, I dropped my bridle and hurriedly opened the missive.

My dear son,

I am sending a copy of this letter to your estate at the Rugged Oak and another copy to your lodgings in the rue du Champ-Fleuri, so concerned am I to ensure that it reaches you, since the news I am sending you is of the greatest consequence, not so much for you as for the king, to whom you must communicate it immediately, or, if you are still at the Rugged Oak, within a day. The king of Navarre has just escaped an attempt to poison him perpetrated by one of his secretaries, named Ferraud, whom his wife had placed in his service. This Ferraud confessed under torture that he had acted on express advice and orders from his mistress, who was distressed that her husband would not consent to approach her.

In any case, it is said here that Navarre's coldness towards and negligence of the queen dates from August 1583 (following rumours that she'd had an abortion while at the court of her brother, the king, during the fifteen months she was separated from her husband). It is possible that the assassination attempt was prompted not so much by the queen's anger and bitterness towards Navarre as by her desire to rejoin Guise, since it is known that she was infatuated with him before her marriage—and so the attempt may well be at Guise's instigation.

The king of Navarre would like to know what his cousin and beloved sovereign, the king of France, would like him to do with the queen, as he does not wish to offend His Majesty by treating her inhumanely, nor to keep her against her will, given her rank and dignity.

Since it is also possible that this assassination attempt was part of a more general plan aimed at various Christian princes—as we already saw in the murder of William of Orange—the king of Navarre entreats his cousin and beloved sovereign to take measures to protect his own life, and prays Heaven to keep him safe.

My son, I am in good health and hardy, and wish the same for you and for Madame your wife and for your children.

Jean

We arrived in Paris at nightfall, and though still dusty from the road and wearing my boots, I hurried to the Louvre, where Alphonse d'Ornano, who was posted at the gate, required that I hand over my sword and dagger, since the Duc d'Épernon, who'd been promoted to colonel general of the French infantry, had decided that no armed man would be allowed to enter the Louvre, a measure I found wholly appropriate given the uncertainty of the times. I ran from the gate and up the great staircase that led to the king's chambers, where I expected to find him given the lateness of the hour, and met Du Halde in the royal antechamber, and informed him that the king had urgently required my presence. Du Halde agreed to ask His Majesty if indeed he wished to see me, and, in my impatience to convey the news of the attempt on Navarre's life, I hurried in after him. No sooner had I passed the threshold, however, than I was suddenly overwhelmed by a pair of strong arms and thrown to the floor, while I don't know how many menacing daggers pricked me in front and from behind, and a giant bearded fellow stepped up and shouted in stentorian tones and with a rough Gascon accent:

"How now, Monsieur? Is this any way to enter the king's chambers? Who are you and where do you think you are?"

"Monsieur," I countered, white with rage, "who are you yourself? And what kind of reception is this to throw an unarmed man to the ground and surround him with daggers?"

"I am Laugnac de Montpezat," he replied, "captain of the Forty-five Guardsmen, five of whom you see here, who are going to search you, however much you claim you're not armed."

"This is too much, Monsieur!" I cried, but in vain, for two of these *spadaccini*, who stank of garlic and sweat, held my legs, two others my arms, while the fifth went through my doublet and my leggings inch by inch with his vigilant fingers.

"Monsieur," I said indignantly, "I am the Chevalier de Siorac, the king's physician!"

"That's as may be," Laugnac replied with utmost arrogance, "but I don't know you and have never laid eyes on you in the six months I've been here."

"I was away on my estate."

"In exile then, were you?" sneered Laugnac, raising an eyebrow.

"Indeed, in exile. But the king has called me back to him."

"Have you got letters to prove it?"

"No. The Baron de Quéribus ordered me back here."

"Who," broke in one of the five, "hasn't been seen in three days."

"No, because he was at my estate in Montfort-l'Amaury."

"The fact remains, Monsieur," Laugnac insisted, "that none of us knows you."

"Messieurs," I observed, "six months ago, not one of you was here, since you were recruited in Gascony by the Duc d'Épernon."

Visibly, this did not please them at all, and I could see in their Gascon eyes, as they glared at me from all sides, that they would very happily have dispatched me right then and there if they'd dared.

Luckily for me, the door to the king's chambers opened and Chicot appeared, his nose running as usual; seeing me pointedly surrounded by these Gascons' knives, he burst out laughing:

"Rapier," he observed to Laugnac, "if you kill Henri's physicians you'll very likely lose your 1,200 écus in wages *and* your meals at court, which would be an extreme punishment for someone like you, who eats as much as four."

Just then, Du Halde appeared and, seeing me in this predicament, instead of laughing, frowned mightily and said in a tone dripping with scorn:

"Messieurs, I find you excessively hasty and your actions precipitous. This gentleman is expected by His Majesty."

Whereupon the five released me, looking very sheepish and abashed, yet still snarling and their fur still bristling, like dogs that have been deprived of their quarry.

7

THE KING HAD NOT gone to bed, but was, instead, in his chapel, engrossed in a piece of work that struck me as passing strange, though I'd heard tell of it already from Quéribus. But there were so many fables concerning Henri that I never would have believed this one had I not seen it with my very eyes: His Majesty was cutting out miniature images from one of the prayer books that were written by hand before the use of the printing press became widespread; and since such miniatures were drawn by the most gifted artists, the king, after cutting them out, directed his page to glue them onto the woodwork of his chapel, at places he would indicate only after a great deal of hesitation and consideration. The page was standing there waiting, his brush in hand, while the king meditated on his choice, and I stood there as well on the threshold of the chapel—or rather the oratory, which was furnished with a tiny but very ornate altar, a single kneeler, covered in red velvet, and a bookstand, on which the illuminated manuscript had been placed, from which, as far as I could tell, the king had cut about one quarter of the miniatures.

Now, I won't deny that the effect of these paintings on the walls of the chapel was a very pleasant one, since the miniatures were not distributed randomly, but according to their subjects and colours. Nor did it bother me that this activity was an affront to logic or even to art. No—what surprised me was that its very principle was one that only a child would have conceived of: the destruction of an infinitely precious book of hours in order to decorate an oratory, when he could have had a much more complete and harmonious decoration painted for him by a great artist. Nor should we forget that each of the miniatures was meant to illustrate a particular prayer, and so his display would no doubt have seemed almost sacrilegious to a papist, since it separated the images from the orisons.

The king was facing away from me, entirely absorbed by his work, and hadn't heard me come in. I didn't feel I could budge until he had seen me and offered his hand in greeting, so I stood quietly in his presence for several minutes, feeling quite ill at ease lest he feel I had surprised him at this bizarre pastime. I was astonished that he could focus so completely on this childishness while his entire kingdom was in such turmoil, his own capital a hive of Guisard sedition, his finances in such a shambles and his life in such imminent danger.

"Sire," said Du Halde finally, who, as he stood behind me, sensed my embarrassing predicament, "Monsieur de Siorac is here."

"Ah, Siorac!" said the king as casually as if we were continuing a conversation begun the night before; and, transferring his scissors from his right hand to his left, he distractedly offered me his hand, which I kissed on bended knee.

This done, the king returned to his work as though he'd forgotten the reason he'd asked me to return post-haste from my estate. So, as I stood there silently awaiting his pleasure, I observed that his face seemed horribly altered, his skin a pasty olive colour, his eyes circled with deep, dark rings—nor could I help noticing that that the fingers that held the scissors were shaking so hard that he had trouble cutting a straight line. He had to struggle so hard with this task that his forehead was bathed in drops of perspiration despite the frosty February temperatures in the room.

"Well, Siorac!" he said with a sigh as he handed the cut-out miniature to his page and pointed to the place where he wanted it to be glued. "How fare you?"

"Sire," I replied, "I received a letter this morning from my father, who writes on behalf of Navarre that there is news of great consequence concerning his wife."

"Ah!" sighed the king with an expression of great disdain and bitterness. "Margot! Margot again! What is it now? Read it, Siorac!"

I read the letter, though Henri seemed scarcely to listen, continuing all the while his scissor work, his eyes lowered, his lips pursed and a frown furrowing his brow, with so great an attention to his task that one might have thought the fortunes of his throne depended on it.

When I'd finished, he remained silent until he'd managed, despite the trembling of his fingers, to detach the image he'd been extracting from the book of hours; then he looked around, his head cocked to one side, to decide where he'd like it pasted in the strange mosaic that papered his oratory, pointed with his index finger (whose long nail was painted bright red), indicating where the page was to hang it, and handed it to him.

"If Margot hadn't failed," he remarked in the most casual tone, despite the trembling of his lower lip, "I'm sure Guise would have been very happy."

"Sire," broke in Chicot—who, until that moment, had been standing behind Du Halde and who, I now noticed, looked pale and crestfallen, entirely devoid of the happy, joking expression it usually displayed—and forgetting his role as fool, "do you believe Guise had her do it?"

"I don't know," answered the king. "Margot has as little respect for the life of a man as she does for that of a chicken. She's a thoroughly unforgiving woman and seems entirely embittered towards Navarre, whom she cannot forgive for his disdain of her body these last two years… Siorac, reread the letter, I beg you."

I obeyed, and when I reached the sentence where it was written, "The king of Navarre would like to know what his cousin and beloved sovereign, the king of France, would like him to do with the queen, as he does not wish to offend His Majesty by treating her inhumanely, nor to keep her against her will, given her rank and dignity," Henri interrupted me.

"Navarre," he said, shaking his head and putting down his scissors on the book of hours, "always writes exactly what he should. He is sensitive to the fact that it would offend me if Margot were treated inhumanely, no matter what she has done. I would like," he continued after a moment's reflection, "to have her placed under guard in some city where Navarre might see her from time to time to father some children… But," he added suddenly, "Navarre will never do this. And how could I blame him, since I'm quite aware of the lady's infidelities? So I'm not sure I'm right to ask this of him."

I was astonished to hear Henri debate such private family matters in my presence, but, on the other hand, it's true that a king belongs so thoroughly to his kingdom that he has no private concerns, not even his heart or his life, or his most personal setbacks, all of which influence our own. However, I consider that had Henri been in his usual frame of mind, he would never have repeated in the same distracted tones, as if speaking to himself, this next sentence, which I would have preferred not to hear:

"Other than Marie de Clèves, I've never loved any woman but Margot, and I would have wanted to keep her virtuous, except perhaps with me. Had she been so, I might be a different man today."

Having said these words that, on the one hand were not very clear but, on the other, were all too clear, the king took up his iconoclastic labours again, until finally Du Halde, who had established a rare degree of familiarity with the king, authorized by his unlimited devotion, presumed to speak:

"Sire, you called Monsieur de Siorac here to speak of a matter that would brook no delay."

"Well, Siorac," said the king suddenly, in such a clear, resolute voice that one would have thought Du Halde had awoken him from a long sleep. He put down his scissors and continued, "Siorac, my son, the rumours about you have quieted, perhaps because of your letter to La Vasselière. Or perhaps because of your feigned exile. But I believe that your life is no longer in danger and that you can remain in Paris and begin serving me again, but secretly. I'm going to spread the rumour that you returned in order to treat Épernon's raging sore throat, which has made his life miserable since January, and that you're going to oversee his diet and the necessary medications. But in reality, my son, your job is to contact Mosca and find out what Guise is doing to cause the Parisians to turn against me. You will offer this fellow as much money as Guise has given him to do their work."

"But, sire," I replied, "didn't you tell Quéribus that you yourself were suffering from a terrible sore throat?"

"No, no! He must have misunderstood. The only pain I feel is here," he mused, touching his heart, "since I'm so devastated to see those I love betray me, especially those who are most guilty of ingratitude."

At this, Chicot and I looked at each other in silence (Du Halde having left the chapel to enquire about a disturbance that we could hear in the antechamber) and wondered whether "those most guilty of ingratitude" referred to the queen mother, or Margot, or the Duc de Joyeuse—who, owing everything to the king, was now leaning towards Guise, according to what Quéribus had told us at the Rugged Oak—or perhaps all three of them together.

"Sire," announced Du Halde, "it is Monsieur the Cardinal de Bourbon, whom you sent for."

"Have him come in, Du Halde," replied the king with a smile, which lit up not only his own face but ours as well, by a kind of after-effect. Chicot recovered his role as fool quickly enough to add:

"Henri, do you know what I found in your antechamber, left there intentionally by some wag? Two pencil drawings, one of which represents the Great Halfwit—"

"Quiet, Chicot!" hushed the king, his smile broadening.

"...in his doublet, sword by his side, but wearing his cardinal's mitre, and underneath the drawing, this legend: '*Ah Corydon, Corydon, quae te dementia coepit?*'"*

"Hush, Chicot!" hissed the king, laughing. "The presumptuous presumptive to the throne will be here any minute!"

"And the other," continued Chicot, "representing the Great Whoremonger in his red robe and his cardinal's mitre, but with a large unsheathed sword in his hand and, underneath, this legend: '*Domine, mitte gladium in vaginam, Ecclesia nescit sanguinem.*'"†

At this, the king burst out laughing and suddenly seemed to have regained his former vigour and been so cured of his sombre and ruminant mood that his face appeared rejuvenated and restored to health.

"Page," he cried, "close the door to my chapel, so that the presumptive heir doesn't see my childish activities! It would doubtless be the subject of an infinite number of calumnies he'd spread to his Guisard friends! And yet, when you think about it, if some grown men suck or bite their thumbs to ease their minds and calm their souls, why shouldn't I, for the same purpose, cut out pictures? What's more, I've done no harm except to this unhappy manuscript, which, in any guise, will be nothing but dust in a thousand years."

"That's well said," exclaimed Chicot, pretending to have misheard. "All Guises will end up as dust, and much sooner than a thousand years from now!"

---

* "Ah Corydon, Corydon, what madness has seized you?"

† "Lord, bury your sword in a vagina, the Church does not like to shed blood."

At this the king broke out laughing again, and even the grave and austere Du Halde allowed a trace of a smile to curl his lips at all this indecent craziness, since he could see that it had enticed Henri out of his melancholy. At length, he opened the door and introduced the Cardinal de Bourbon, who appeared not in a doublet as in the drawing, but in a red robe, his mitre on his head; beneath this mitre was a curious mixture of vanity, stupidity, weakness and violence that excited in one an immediate urge to abuse and make light of him. The king, bringing himself up to his full height, stepped confidently towards his guest with a smile on his face, his handsome Italian eyes sparkling with mirth, and, without offering his hand or allowing the cardinal to kneel, gave him a welcoming embrace and showered him with caresses, compliments and cajolery, which were so exaggerated and so excessive that one might have thought that this man, who was twice Henri's age, was his son and heir.

"My cousin," gushed the king, who, taking his arm, began walking the cardinal up and down his chambers at a much faster pace than the fat old prelate would have preferred to take, "will you answer truthfully the question I shall put to you?"

"Sire," replied the old man, "providing I know the right answer to your question, I shall give it to you straight out."

"Well then!" laughed the king. "I've got you, my cousin!"

"What do you mean 'got me'?" stammered the cardinal, his stupid eyes widening.

"My cousin," Henri continued, feigning some gravity, "God has not yet given me an heir, and it would appear that He's not going to do so. Alas, we live in an uncertain world and the Lord could call me to His side at any minute! If that were to happen, the crown would fall directly to the Bourbon line. So tell me, Cousin, would you not like, even though you are descended from the cadet branch of the family, to take precedence over your nephew, the king of Navarre, and have the kingdom of France fall to you rather than to him?"

"Sire! Sire!" stammered the cardinal, his terrified, wide chicken's eyes rolling around in their orbits. "Who could ever contemplate your passing? I assure you, it's not something *I've* ever thought of," he continued lowering his eyes hypocritically. "I pray to God with all my heart that He spare us this calamity, and since I'm twice as old as you, I'm afraid the aches and pains of this old body will have ceased long before the Lord takes Your Majesty from us! What an idea, that you should disappear before me! No, sire, most assuredly I don't think about it at all," he continued, his lying, stupid eyes looking wildly around, as if to find a mouse hole to hide in. "No, no," he added, his voice pushing up into a falsetto, "I never think about it, since it's so beyond the realm of reason or appearance, and against the order of nature that ensures that old men go to the grave before the young ones."

"My cousin," insisted the king, his face deadly serious, but his eyes twinkling in amusement at the protestations of the cardinal, "haven't you noticed that, every day, Nature's orders are inverted and reversed, as the young precede the old on the road to the Styx? So, as you promised to do, tell me freely, my cousin: if that happened in my case, wouldn't you stand in opposition to the king of Navarre as regards the succession to the throne?"

"Ah, sire!" moaned the cardinal, struggling timidly to free his arm from the king's grasp and slow the pace with which His Majesty was moving him back and forth in the room. "Ah, sire, you're too insistent!"

"But ultimately, Monsieur cardinal," rejoined the king, "won't you tell me the whole truth, since your sacred position naturally inclines you to honesty?"

"Assuredly so," answered the cardinal, all out of breath from the promenade he'd been subjected to. "Well then, sire, since you command me so insistently: although the misfortune of losing you has never entered my mind, being so far from the natural course of things and from any reasonable discourse"—a phrase he must have used in his sermons, since it flowed so quickly and easily from his mouth—"nevertheless, if such a great misfortune were to befall us, and for which I could never shed enough tears, then, sire, then, indeed, the kingdom should be delivered into my hands, for I am a good Catholic, and should not be governed by Navarre, who is a Huguenot, and I should be quite resolved never to cede it to him."

At this, the king stopped his mad pacing from one end of the room to the other, led the cardinal to the door, removed his arm from the prelate's and, with a smile, said:

"My good friend, Paris might well offer you the crown, but the parliament would take it away from you."

Having said this, he turned to Du Halde and told him in mocking tones:

"Du Halde, show the cardinal out with all the honours that you owe to his person, to his estate and to his ambitions."

After which, without presenting him his hand, he made him a slight bow and turned his back on him.

As soon as the other had left, Henri threw himself down in his armchair and, hiding his mouth with his hand as women often do, burst out laughing; he was immediately joined in his mirth by Du Halde, Chicot and me, but not by the page, who stared at us with his big blue eyes but said not a word.

"Henri," laughed Chicot, "you certainly pulled the worms out of the Great Halfwit's nose!"

"Worms—or vipers!" said the king.

"Monsieur Chicot," began the page, leaving me astonished that he should presume to open his mouth in the presence of His Majesty.

"Monsieur Chicot!" Chicot repeated, pretending to be indignant. "You good-for-nothing! How dare you 'Monsieur' me? If you must know, it's just 'Chicot', fool to His Double Majesty, but when we're not in the presence of the king you may call me 'sire', since I'm the king of fools!"

"Chicot," began the page, blushing, "I shall remember."

"You may speak now, my child," said the king with his customary gentleness.

"Sire," said the page, who wasn't sure whether he should address the king of France or the king of fools, "why would the parliament take the crown away from the cardinal?"

"Because," answered the king with great gravity, as though he were addressing his great council, "the cardinal belongs to the cadet branch of the Bourbons, whereas Navarre embodies the older branch."

"Nevertheless, Henri," observed Chicot, "would the parliament dare take the sceptre away from the cardinal if Guise were in a position to hold a knife to their throats? I don't believe the members are of the stuff heroes are made of!"

"Assuredly," agreed Henri. "But if that happened, the rules of succession would be manifestly violated, and if they were, the legitimacy of the king would be open to question at any time and the state would find itself shaken to its foundations."

"Force," replied Chicot, "is a great strength."

"Not at all!" said the king heatedly. "It's a very weak form of strength, since it can only perpetuate itself by the use of more force: civil wars, usurpations that will invite other usurpations... Chicot, hear me well, for this is my gospel: the legitimacy assured by the laws of succession is the only peaceful foundation of power. If I did not hold on to the reins of government, we would soon see a swarm of presumptuous pretenders: the Cardinal de Bourbon, the Marquis de Pont-à-Mousson, the Comte de Soissons, and who knows how many others?"

"What, sire—the comte as well?" gasped Du Halde.

"He is thinking about it. And why not? He's a Bourbon, a good Catholic. And after everything I've heard, he's trying to bolster his right to the throne by marrying the sister of the king of Navarre—from which I conclude he must have a strong stomach. The lady is as ugly as the seven deadly sins!"

As I returned to my lodgings, I ruminated over this conversation that I have reported in detail, since Henri appears therein fully revealed and exposed in the curious diversity of his contrasting behaviour. However, childish though it might appear, his cutting out his miniatures should not, in my opinion, blind us to or diminish the clear understanding he had of the affairs of state, nor his remarkable cleverness in manipulating those around him when he thought it useful.

But nothing seemed to succeed, that year, in my good master's hands. This dialogue with the cardinal was hardly useful, since the man was so abysmally vain and idiotic that *nothing* could have discouraged him from the stupid ambition Guise had insufflated in him. Nothing, and I mean *nothing*: not his ecclesiastical responsibilities, nor his age, nor his infirmities, nor the laws of the kingdom, nor the parliament, nor even the open opposition of the king. Proof indeed that great evils are perpetrated as often by idiots as by the wicked. Indeed, in reality they are most often a result of the conjunction of the two, as I have ascertained, even though I have occupied such a humble place in the affairs of the kingdom.

The next morning, I asked Miroul to seek out Nicolas Poulain and ask him to come to see me at nightfall in my lodgings. And, of course, you can easily imagine that my Miroul objected at first, saying that he wasn't my message boy or my little valet, but my secretary, and that this errand was, consequently, beneath his station. And, knowing that Miroul would invariably begin by refusing whatever I asked of him (after which he always agreed to do it), I told him in the most succinct terms:

"This is not an errand, it is a mission of great consequence. If you don't wish to do it, I'll do it myself. The thing must be done post-haste."

At which, I turned away, but watched him out of the corner of my eye as I walked away, and saw that he threw his cape over his shoulder, put on his hat and checked to be sure his knives were properly stowed in his boots.

It was not at nightfall, but in the dark of night that Mosca knocked on my door, well escorted and wearing a greatcoat. And when I spied him through the peephole, he seemed very loath to uncover his nose, which, as soon as he showed the tip of it, was so fox-like that I would have recognized it among a thousand noses.

"Come in, come in, Maître Fly," I said, "I'm very glad to see you!"

He certainly couldn't have said the same of me, and, pointing his aforementioned muzzle straight ahead—his long nose sniffing in advance my future words, his oblique gaze observing my face and Miroul's, his unruly moustache bristling with suspicion—he sat down warily on the stool that Miroul offered him, not at all happy that Giacomi appeared, armed, and closed the door of the little cabinet behind him. As this room had, overlooking the ground floor, a small window that was protected by iron bars and reinforced by a solid oak shutter, Mosca found himself wholly isolated from his escort and, in a sense, caught in a trap, one against three, however smiling and accommodating we appeared.

"Monsieur Mosca," I began, "I'm very happy that you've hurried to shed some light on the situation, even though it is the middle of the night. But knowing that your time is no less valuable than mine, I'm going to come straight to the point, without further ado."

As I spoke, I saw my fox tense up in all the muscles, nerves and tendons of his frail but large frame, and observed that his eyes were rolling in their sockets like little cornered animals, so I decided to press my advantage.

"Mosca," I began with a harsh and rapid delivery, "someone is creating problems for the king in his capital. You are part of this problem—the king knows it, and orders you to come clean. It's your choice, Monsieur Mosca. Open mouth: life and money. Closed mouth: torture."

A lieutenant of the provostry who takes poor devils to be hanged at Montfaucon for the theft of a few pennies on an almost daily basis is very accustomed to seeing the cord squeeze the necks of others, yet cannot imagine it around his own, especially since he knows from experience the horrible grimace that they make on the gibbet, tongue hanging out and feet dancing very uncomfortably in the air.

My Mosca, upon hearing my brutal options, almost fainted, and seemed suddenly unable to catch his breath. When he regained his composure, he threw me an incredibly false look, closed one pious eyelid and said:

"Monsieur chevalier, it's not the promise of life and a few coins that will open my lips, but my conscience, which, for the last three months, has been nagging me over this wicked and damnable enter-prise on which I have unwillingly embarked, so astonished am I by all the blood that has to be spilt and the pillaging and murder that are supposed to take place here in Paris. In addition to all the horror and great carnage that are planned, it would mean the ruination and dissipation of the state, so that I would profit very little from the great riches that have been promised me if I were to lose my soul into the bargain and had to take the road to hell."

"I detest this wily rascal," broke in Giacomi in Italian, adding, "*El mangia santi e caga diaboli.*"*

"Mosca," I asked, in the same curt and cutting tone, "how much did they promise you?"

"Twenty thousand écus."

"The king will give you an equal amount."

---

* "He eats saints and shits out devils."

"Ah, Monsieur chevalier," replied Mosca, "it's not the gold that motivates me, but my duty as a natural-born Frenchman, citizen of the first city in France, where my king was crowned and where I pledged my obedience at the time when I served as the lieutenant of the provostry of the Île-de-France. So much so that if some revolt were planned against the state, given the wages and profits that His Majesty bestows on me, I would be bound to warn him of it. Given these considerations, together with those that I've mentioned, and that I hold very dear to my heart—"

"Repeat those words, I beg you, Mosca—I didn't quite hear them."

"Which ones, Monsieur chevalier?" said Mosca, screwing up his eyes.

"The last ones."

"I hold very dear to my heart."

"Ah, that's very good. Go on, I beg you."

"...I decided to warn the king. But in considering how I'd go about it, I found myself very perplexed and troubled, given the difficulties attendant on it (not to mention the fear of being discovered by the conspirators), so that I remained perplexed and, as it were, sitting on my arse on the ground between two saddles."

"What do you mean?" I asked.

"Monsieur," he explained, suddenly opening his eyes wide and looking straight at me, "I couldn't come to you because you had left on your feigned exile."

At this blow, I remained silent, Giacomi, Miroul and I exchanging astonished glances.

"Mosca," I said after a moment, "what do you mean, my 'feigned' exile? What are you talking about? Who considers it thus?"

"I do, Monsieur chevalier, and the Holy League. The League believes you to be the most faithful and immutable servant of the king, so much so that your house is marked as one of the first to be attacked and pillaged, and its occupants massacred."

"Bah!" I said, more shaken than I wanted to appear. "We shall see what we shall see! Monsieur Mosca, let's get back to our subject. Since I was away, why didn't you warn Chancellor de Villequier, since you know him?"

"But that's just it! I do know him," replied Mosca. "Villequier would immediately have warned the queen mother, and she, to cover herself, would have warned the king. After which, the queen mother and Villequier would have persuaded the king that I was paid by the Huguenots and that my entire report was nothing but lies and falsehoods. So I would have risked being tortured by the king or killed by the League, if Villequier had secretly denounced me to them."

"My poor Mosca," I smiled, "from what I can see, it's not easy to betray either side! Luckily for you, I am here! Standing right here before you! And all ears! So you can now completely absolve your conscience and comfort your heart. Speak, my good Mosca! Speak without further delay!"

"But, Monsieur chevalier," countered Mosca, "here's your valet with a writing desk…"

"You aren't seeing clearly, Monsieur," objected Miroul archly. "The man you see sitting at this table is the *secretary* of Monsieur de Siorac."

"Monsieur chevalier," snarled Mosca, "if it's a deposition you want, your swords will never make me sign it! There's no way a lieutenant of the provostry will incriminate himself!"

"Calm down, Monsieur Mosca," I smiled, "we're just taking notes. Your real name will not be mentioned."

"If that's the way it is," he replied, looking much more confident, "and if it's to be done correctly—with a few changes to the supposed names—then don't call me 'Mosca', the fly, but 'Leo', the lion."

"'Leo'," I conceded, "since you're a lion, roar me a beautiful story and I'll be happy."

"Monsieur chevalier, it is more worthy of a moan than a roar, given how troubled the times are and how much blood will be spilt (perhaps including mine). But, to be brief, it's like this: on the second of January, Maître Leclerc, a prosecutor at the court of the parliament, and Georges Michelet, a staff sergeant at the Grand Châtelet, good people whom I've known for twenty years, came to fetch me in my lodgings and suggested that there would be a good occasion to improve my lot, and, if I was willing, earn a good pile of money."

"What wisdom they displayed," interjected Giacomi in Italian, "to talk knavery to a knave."

"And," Mosca continued, "to win the favour of some great lords, who could see to my advancement professionally, as long as I went along with the plans they were about to execute—which, moreover, would contribute to the conservation of the Holy Roman and Apostolic faith."

"Who would not want to cooperate in such a noble cause?" observed Giacomi.

"Which is why I swore to join their League, which they call the Holy League. So, on the third of this month, I went to see Maître Leclerc in his lodgings, where I met with several others of the same party, the Seigneur de Maineville having been sent to us by the Duc de Guise to explain the enterprise. This gentleman explained that the Catholic religion would be lost if we didn't put things in order, and that there were more than 10,000 Huguenots hidden in the Faubourg Saint-Germain, who, when the moment came, would launch a St Bartholomew's slaughter of the Catholics in order to preserve the throne for the king of Navarre."

"And you believed him, Mosca?" I said, raising my eyebrows.

"Monsieur," he replied, "I'm a lieutenant in the provostry of the Île-de-France, so I know very well that the only people 'hiding' in the hovels and shacks of the Faubourg Saint-Germain are plague-carriers, thieves, pickpockets, bandits and whores."

"But you didn't contradict him?" I observed.

"Monsieur chevalier, who am I to dare to contradict the Duc de Guise when the most powerful people in the land don't dare naysay him? What's more, the Seigneur de Maineville, since he was the one speaking and not me, also told us that the king, who goes to monasteries and apes the penitents, dared in his treachery to offer 200,000 écus to Navarre so that he would secretly wage war on the Catholics."

"And you believed him?"

"Monsieur chevalier," replied Mosca with a kind of rampant haughtiness, "what I believe or don't believe is a matter of conscience."

"And of heart," added Giacomi.

"And did you believe," I asked, looking him straight in the eye, "that I was the instrument of this transaction?"

"The Holy League was the first to claim it, but then later denied it; thus I don't have to believe it any more."

"And so," I concluded, "the moment the League calls itself 'holy', fables become truth and truth becomes a fable."

"Monsieur chevalier," returned Mosca, "from the moment you are a member of a party you must either believe everything or leave."

"So you believed everything?"

"Monsieur chevalier, I beg you, let's leave what I believe and what I don't believe out of this and get to the crux of the matter. So, the Seigneur de Maineville told us on this occasion that we needed to counter all of the efforts of the 'politicals', the king's parliament and the king himself in support of the Huguenots and against the Catholic religion; and, in this pursuit, all members of the Holy League having sworn to die rather than tolerate such enterprises, we should secretly arm our supporters in Paris in order to make ourselves the superior force. He also told us that the Holy League was not supported only by the priests, but also by the faculty at the Sorbonne, by the Lorraine princes, by the Pope himself and by the king of Spain."

"Which constitutes treason for consorting with foreign powers and open rebellion," I observed with a frown. "This is starting off well, and at the end of this road lies the Inquisition."

"Monsieur chevalier, I would like you to remember that you promised me my life and 20,000 écus."

"A promise made, a promise kept. And what was your role in this subterranean business?"

"To purchase arms. The provost Hardi, who's very old, depends entirely on me as his lieutenant, and since the king forbade the sale of arms to anyone without proper identity, in my capacity as lieutenant of the provostry I can purchase them on the pretext of fortifying our strongholds, and pretend that I've received this commission from the king."

"That's a damnable fraud! And so you purchased some, Mosca?"

"Since the second of January, to the tune of 6,000 écus."

"'Sblood! Six thousand écus! And how many of these 6,000 found their way into your purse?"

"Very few, alas!"

"And where have these arms been taken?"

"To the lodgings of Leclerc, Campan, Crusset and Guise."

"And who provided the money to buy them? Did you ask?"

"I didn't fail to ask Maître Jean Leclerc, who told me that the donors were all honourable men who wished to remain anonymous for the moment, so that they wouldn't be found out prematurely."

"Ah, that's very prudent of them! And besides this cache of arms by which the blood of natural-born Frenchmen will be spilt, as you've said, Mosca, what are the other enterprises of the Holy League?"

"They've been 'working on' the labourers and inhabitants of Paris."

"'Working on'? What does this jargon mean?"

"Trying to win them to our cause. And it has succeeded."

"And who are the 'workers'?" I replied, winking at Miroul so that he'd write down the names.

"There are a lot of them," Mosca replied, noticing, of course, my wink to Miroul; not wishing to be pressed harder on this matter, he equivocated, saying, "Each one 'worked' in his particular corporation or on those over whom he held some power, based on his status or neighbourhood."

"Monsieur Mosca," I counselled, "20,000 écus is a lot of money, so you're going to have to give me a more precise account."

"Monsieur," sighed Mosca with a mournful look that accentuated his foxy muzzle, "I will accede to your demands, provided that your secretary writes 'Leo' throughout and not 'Mosca'."

"*Res effecta, Leo*,"* said Miroul, who, ever since he'd become my secretary, showed off his Latin at every opportunity. And to this he added, "*Promissio boni viri fit obligatio*."†

"All right," conceded Mosca, with another dramatic sigh. "Here are the names, though it pains me greatly to pronounce them, since I like each of them so much and wouldn't have wished to betray them if my fidelity to my king hadn't made it my duty to do so."

"Now there," exclaimed Giacomi wryly, "are some truly honest feelings!"

"The names, Mosca!" I cried, cutting short his theatrical grimaces.

In the end, he produced them, and I couldn't help reflecting somewhat on them and the great mass of information we'd received; but I needed to put on a serene and confident front, though I was devoured by anxiety, since Paris was now manifestly lost to the king, given that the city was being "worked on" by so many violent Leaguers, not to mention the abusive sermons by its priests. Of course, I couldn't reveal these feelings to Poulain, whom I trusted as much as I would a viper, so I asked him about the intended use of all of these arms, as well as about the purpose of their "working" on the people of Paris,

---

* "The thing is done, Lion."
† "The promise of an honest man is the equivalent of a legal obligation."

and the secret meetings at which the blood of the French people was discussed.

"But," said Mosca, "nothing less than the taking of Paris by the Holy League! And then the capture of the king in his Louvre, after the massacre of his advisors, officers, favourites, principal members of parliament, 'politicals' and any nobles who dare offer him their support. The plans have already been drawn up! The powder is ready! The only thing we're waiting for is the spark, which will come from two sides: the army Guise is assembling, and the Spanish."

"Well, for the latter," I mused with a smile and as if in jest, "all they have to do is cross the Pyrenees!"

"Oh, no, Monsieur!" corrected Mosca, as though annoyed by my tone. "That won't be necessary! The League has already decided to take Boulogne very soon and to deliver the port to Felipe II so his army can come ashore there."

I noticed that Mosca was biting his lip for having too quickly divulged this information, but, stunned by his revelation of this plot to take Boulogne, and of the immense consequences should it succeed, I pressed him with so many bribes and menaces that in the end he revealed the entire plan.

"It was in the Jesuits' house over the last two days that this assault was devised. They know that the provost Vétus, whom they have successfully 'worked on', is accustomed to spend three months at a time in Boulogne, and so they decided that, on his next visit, he will take fifty soldiers that he will be given under the guise of an escort, seize one of the gates of the city and, this done, open it to the Duc d'Aumale, a cousin of Guise's, who will have amassed the necessary forces in the surrounding area."

I was so terrified for the king in this enterprise that I slept very little after Mosca left us, after promising to return to see me whenever I should contact him, so that I could ascertain how great a threat this invasion of Boulogne would be—not just to France, but also to Queen Elizabeth, who was our natural ally against these papist and Guisard manoeuvres, and who would be equally threatened by this attack, which had been planned, as I now realized, by the Jesuits, who'd been introduced to the League and who burned with a passionate zeal to reconquer England.

I was able to see the king as soon as he'd risen, and when I entered his chambers under the pretext of taking his pulse, I handed him my notes from the previous day's conversation and whispered in his ear that they contained most urgent and consequential information. He promised to read them as soon as he'd been to his chapel to say his prayers and conferred with the English ambassador, who'd asked for the earliest possible meeting—but he asked, with his usual courtesy, that I wait in his antechamber for him to call me.

Meanwhile, scarcely had I left the king's chambers when I was seized by the arm, but this time in a most amicable fashion, by Laugnac de Montpezat, who offered me sincere apologies for having stopped and searched me with five of his guardsmen on my previous visit, saying that he hadn't had the honour of making my acquaintance, since he was just arriving as I was leaving with the Duc d'Épernon to go to Guyenne, and then, on my return, I had left for my long retreat to my estate at Montfort. He used the word "retreat" rather than "exile", with a subtle smile, as though he wanted to get more information out of me, knowing that in such situations words are better than silence. But I took cover behind my Périgordian amiability, which was every bit as serviceable as the pleasing Gascon manners he had on display, so that we were immediately all honey and smiles. And yet, looking him straight in the eye, I realized that I didn't like what I saw—not that Laugnac wasn't tall and handsome, with skin, beard and eyes that had a Saracen look to them, but there was something forced in his expression that I didn't completely trust.

While we were thus engaged, Lord Stafford appeared on his way to see the king; we all bowed to him, but received only a curt nod of the head in reply.

"'Tis bruited about," said Laugnac, throwing an affectionate arm over my shoulder, "that Lord Stafford has come to offer His Majesty the Order of the Garter, which Queen Elizabeth wishes to confer on him, but only with his consent. Do you think it's true?"

"Well, Laugnac! What opinion could I have about it? You know much more about it than I do!"

"And yet," smiled Laugnac, "I saw you talking to Lady Stafford in the salon of the Maréchale de Joyeuse!"

"Laugnac," I replied, smiling back at him, "who wouldn't enjoy a conversation with such a noble and beautiful lady, whose virtue could not but contribute to her beauty?"

At this, he took his leave with another exchange of smiles, leaving me feeling very uncomfortable with his inquisition and quite suspicious of his new-found favour. To tell the truth, having served my beloved king for more than ten years, I didn't quite trust these courtiers who, in ten months, had won Henri's friendship, since I couldn't help feeling that if they'd risen like the foam on a wave, they might well have the same airy consistency and that their devotion might prove to be no more than a bubble that, being half air and half water, bursts in the first unfavourable breeze.

The king, who'd received the English ambassador in the privacy of his rooms—an arrangement that set Guisard tongues wagging and conjecturing, since they had no ear to listen in on the proceedings as they would have had at a public audience—had me fetched at about ten o'clock, and, as soon as I arrived, came straight to the point:

"Siorac, if what you have written is true, it is of the greatest possible consequence. But is it true? What are we to believe of the report of this Mosca, this Leo or this Poulain?"

"Sire, he's the most venal rascal in all creation. If it happened that someone wanted to buy his mother, he'd sell her."

"So the entire thing might be a fabrication."

"It might be. And yet, sire, I believe we must proceed as though the opposite were true. For two reasons: first, because Mosca incriminated himself regarding the purchase of arms; second, because we cannot afford to ignore the possibility of this attack on Boulogne taking place at some point."

"That's very reasonable talk," admitted the king. "In any case, we must prepare for it in advance, and warn Monsieur de Bernay, who commands our troops in Boulogne. But how can I do this without leaking word of what we're up to and chasing our rats away prematurely? We can't use ordinary channels; instead we must use secrecy and stealth."

"Sire, command me and I'm away! That way only you and I will know about it."

"Ah, Siorac!" smiled Henri. "I love your eagerness to serve me and I love you for it! But I absolutely do not want to place you in such great peril! They'd assassinate you."

"In that case I won't go without a disguise. I'll pass myself off as a merchant."

"A merchant!" replied the king, who found this idea hilarious. "What would you sell in Boulogne?"

"Bonnets, sire."

"Bonnets?" laughed the king. "Men's?"

"No, sire, ladies'. I've heard tell that Madame de Bernay is a young and beautiful woman and I'll wager that, living as she does in Boulogne, she'll be delighted to acquire the latest Paris fashions."

I was well advanced on my bonnet idea, but encountered serious resistance from Alizon, who initially refused to accompany me for such a long trip, though she had complete confidence in her colleague—none other than Baragran, whom she'd known from the time they worked for the cheapskate Recroche, and whom she'd hired after the master's death, despite that fact that they'd quarrelled for ten years while in the skinflint's service. She'd then married a master bonnet-maker, who had died two years earlier. The subject of her quarrels with Baragran was that she thought he bent too easily to Recroche's every demand. But, as soon as she became the mistress of her atelier, what she had taken for servility in poor Baragran turned into obedience, fidelity and honesty, and he never cheated her out of a penny. She loved him dearly for these qualities, and might have married him, I'll wager, had she not considered herself to be above him in rank and thought she could pass for a lady, or at least a bourgeoise, in her manners and dress.

I overcame her refusal to accompany me by assuring her that she would make many sales of bonnets and other items of fashion to the noble ladies of Boulogne. But what really convinced her was that she would travel in a coach (having no appetite to subject her tender thighs to a saddle), and especially that she would pass for my wife and lodge in the inns with me, and that I would take her late husband's name as an alias. Hearing all this, my "little fly from hell" threw her arms around me and began showering me with kisses, but I told her that I'd sworn fidelity to my Angelina and that my spousal role was for public but not private consumption. But whether the very idea of our appearance as a couple was enough for her, or whether, knowing me for so long and having enticing memories of our earlier connection, she thought I would not be so valiant as to resist so many opportunities to renew it, my answer did not seem to dampen her spirits one bit. She happily set about planning our clothes for the coming voyage, arguing that they must be of the very finest quality, since the better a merchant looks, the more he sells.

It took two days to obtain these clothes, but as soon as we had put them on, Alizon observed that my every movement betrayed a certain air of aristocratic ease and high birth, something I'd got from being at court; that my left hand was too often reaching for the hilt of my absent sword; that I needed to display less nonchalance and more pomp; that I didn't walk, sit down or blow my nose like a merchant; that I shouldn't look so self-assured but act more like an ordinary fellow who had some means; and that I shouldn't prance and twirl around but go flat-footed, with my feet more splayed than straight. She said I must also remove the gold earring from my right ear, which made me look too much like a courtier, a sailor or a soldier, flatten down my curly hair, refrain from the use of any perfumes, and remove my physician's ring and my two other jewelled rings, wearing instead a silver timepiece on a cord around my neck, consulting it gravely from time to time to indicate that my time was precious. I should also avoid the high-pitched laughter of a courtier, speak slowly and roll my *r*s, and trudge soberly along in the old style rather than walk with a sprightly step as they do in Paris. As she continued with these prescriptions, she became more and more prey to hilarity, and warned me through her laughter that if I didn't alter my look and demeanour, my colleagues in Boulogne would see right through my disguise and discover the truth.

In short, I must follow her instructions in everything and also learn some of the slang of the bonnet-maker's trade before testing my new skin.

"My friend," I interrupted, half-amused, half-annoyed by the portrait she'd drawn of me (and of the court), "do you really think I'm so ridiculous?"

"Absolutely not!" she replied, planting a kiss on the corner of my mouth. "You are, my Pierre, what you are and I like you just as you are. But ten years in the court have changed you, for, just as my bonnets are moulded on the block, men cannot help but be moulded by their surroundings. And if you weren't such a precious and gracious gentleman, would I love you like I do? And, at least in your case, the man is still visible beneath the veneer of the courtier."

I spent two days learning from my little fly from hell the manners, tone and language proper to my new profession, lessons which she found exceedingly funny—and, no doubt, comforting, since she now found herself in a position of superiority, as she worked to teach me how to abase myself. During this time I also made arrangements to rent a carriage, and cajoled Quéribus into lending me his escort, which he gave up reluctantly since he enjoyed being surrounded at all times, even when he went to the Louvre, which was only a short distance from his lodgings. His escort were no happier, since they had to abandon their brilliant, gold-laced livery and clothe themselves in grey, black or brown like common people, whom our lackeys infinitely despise. However, when I explained to them that they were in fact acting in the service of the king, who would recompense them for acceding to his demands, they agreed much more light-heartedly to wear these humble clothes that gave them the feeling that they had been degraded.

Our voyage was made without encumbrance or incident, and, once in Boulogne, we found lodgings in a nice enough inn called the Golden Vessel, from where I sent one of my men the next morning to the governor's mansion to inform Madame de Bernay that we would consider it a great honour to show her, before any of the other ladies of the town, the Paris finery that we'd brought at great peril, and that she had only to name the day and the hour and we would be there immediately.

The words "Paris finery" were, I'll wager, a kind of shibboleth, for, less than two hours later, Madame de Bernay sent a great hulk of a lackey to inform us that she would receive us at ten o'clock sharp. We arrived at this rendezvous in our carriage, which was filled with our marvels, and which we left in the courtyard of the governor's mansion under the watchful eye of two other giants. Alizon reminded me in a whisper that a merchant would deeply offend any lady of her station if he presumed to look at her as a woman he might desire, and that in Madame de Bernay's presence I should be very careful to stifle the looks I was accustomed to give women—especially since she was generally admired for her youth and charms.

Indeed, her charms were very much in evidence, for she received us in her negligee while at her toilette, with one chambermaid holding her mirror, a second doing her make-up and a third brushing her hair. Her casual attire set Alizon on edge, though it was evident that Madame de Bernay paid no more attention to a master bonnet-maker than she did to the stool on which she was resting her bare feet. Her attitude allowed me the leisure, while Alizon was greeting her and displaying her wares, to take a good look at her, and even a cursory glance convinced me that the lady was even more comely than her reputation, having a trim and well-proportioned body and one of those angelic faces that might not correspond to her nature, but that are most pleasant to look at. Her eyes were of the most beautiful blue and her features finely chiselled, and her blonde hair formed a halo round her pretty head.

Whether because Madame de Bernay was seduced by the finery that was presented to her so artfully by Alizon, wished to prevent the other noblewomen of Boulogne from getting their hands on them, or else simply loved spending her husband's money, she would have bought the lot, I'll wager, had her husband not appeared. As he kissed her hands, he asked her about the bill, and, finding it too high, stopped the flow of coins and told me to follow him into his cabinet so that he could pay me what he now owed.

I was delighted by the opening that this provided me, and once the door was closed behind us, and the money safely in my purse, I said,

"Monseigneur, our business is not yet done. I have a letter to give you from the king."

"From the king?" he repeated, and, taking the letter in his large fingers, he looked carefully at the seal and then again with his magnifying glass. "Well, that's the king's seal all right," he confirmed. "But who are you, Monsieur?" he continued, giving me a curious look. "This letter did not arrive by the usual channels."

"That's because the news it contains is not ordinary news," I replied, responding to his observation rather than to his question.

Monsieur de Bernay understood immediately, being one of those apparently dull men who sometimes surprise us with their sharpness. And after one last inquisitive look, he broke the seal and read the letter; then he sighed and read it again, while I watched him with as much curiosity as he had when he observed me.

I must admit that the governor of Boulogne had much less cause to be proud of his appearance than did his wife, being fat-arsed and paunchy, with a chubby and soft face and so many wrinkles that you could scarcely see the slits of his eyes as he read the letter. And as he read, haltingly and with difficulty, those eyes betrayed his regret—being as greedy for his comfort and repose as he was—at having to choose between the king and the Holy League. Clearly, he would have preferred his present indetermination, which allowed him to avoid the wrath of either party and not put his position as governor in jeopardy should Guise come out on top.

When he'd finished his second reading, he said not a word, but sighed deeply and, turning away, stood before his window, tapping the panes, deep in thought. Finally, turning round and walking back to me, his eyes still hidden within the ramparts of the folds of his eyelids, he said:

"Monsieur, after what you told me when you handed me this letter, it would appear that you are familiar with its contents."

"I am, Monseigneur."

"Where are you lodging?"

"At the Golden Vessel."

"At two o'clock this afternoon, I shall send you Captain Le Pierre, whom I'd like you to inform of this matter so that he can take care of it."

I could not hide my doubts and displeasure at this suggestion, and replied:

"Monseigneur, I would have little authority in such a conversation. Wouldn't it be better to have that meeting here and in your presence rather than at my inn, where your captain's visit to a master bonnet-maker could not fail to arouse suspicion?"

"I could not have the meeting here, Monsieur," objected Monsieur de Bernay. "I will be away for the next few days in order to visit a property I have ten leagues from here, but Captain Le Pierre has been given command of the city and of the port in my absence, and I'm certain that, as he is a brave and good soldier, he will know how to handle the matter."

I was unable to disguise my astonishment that the governor of one of the king's good cities should decide to absent himself at the very moment that he learnt that there was a plan afoot to take the city from him.

"Captain Le Pierre will come to visit you with his wife on the pretext of buying her some of the finery that you're selling, which will give his visit a credible appearance."

"Monseigneur," I said after a moment of silence, "if you cannot attend this meeting, perhaps I could ask you to return the letter from the king so that I may show it to him and thereby justify my mission here."

"Your request is entirely understandable and I would be happy to acquiesce," replied the governor, thrusting the letter into my hands as though it were burning his fingers, happy to pass this inflammatory object on to this Captain Le Pierre so that he could hurry off to his estate ten leagues from Boulogne and wash his hands of the entire matter. He could thus argue later that he'd never received my visit, nor read the letter, having already left.

When he came to see me at our lodgings, Captain Le Pierre produced quite a different reaction in me: he carried his spare body very erect, and his bony face and black eyes communicated a firmness that was entirely lacking in the governor. Moreover, he had an honest look, quick gestures and directness of speech, all of which I found reassuring. I received him in one of the two rooms I'd taken at the inn—why I'd taken a second room the reader may easily guess; the reason I'd given Alizon was that it was so that she could receive her customers and store her merchandise in the one she slept in, and in the other I could receive the various fellows I needed to talk to.

"'Sblood!" cried Le Pierre, full of anger and bitterness after having perused His Majesty's letter. "Who would have thought that the provost Vétus would have betrayed the trust of the king and become Guise's instrument in delivering a port of such extraordinary importance as Boulogne to His Majesty's enemies! And who could fail to see that this betrayal profits no one but the Spanish king! Good God, this is outrageous! It's out-and-out treason!"

As much as Monsieur de Bernay had disappointed me, Le Pierre delighted me with his response—and all the more so since he declared that as a citizen and native of Boulogne he'd prefer to die than allow his city to be put under yoke of a foreign power, be it Lorraine or Spain. As I wanted to sound him out a bit further, I asked him what he thought of the pretext of religion as the cover for the League's seditious activities.

"Bah!" he spat. "That's nonsense! The king is as Catholic as you and me! And there's no reason to worry about Navarre, since the king is neither dead nor dying. These foreigners" (meaning the house of Lorraine) "simply want the throne! That's all there is to it! The rest is the nonsense you hear from the priests who execrate the heretics from morning to night! If the king wants to declare war on the heretics, I'll sign on! If he wants to keep the peace, I'll keep it! We have a number of these shit-and-piss-stained Leaguers in Boulogne too! But—by God!—as long as I'm here, they're not going to drag the people of this town into tumult and sedition! I'll put a stop to that!" he declared, making a fist of his right hand, which was neither small nor irresolute.

"Well then, Captain!" I exclaimed. "I'm very happy to hear this, and all the more so since Monsieur de Bernay seemed so hesitant I couldn't help but wonder which party he's in!"

"Monsieur de Bernay," laughed Le Pierre derisively, "is in Monsieur de Bernay's party. That's all there is to it! But he's honest enough. Guise offered him 20,000 écus to abandon Boulogne, but he refused. Of course, it's true that he's rich enough already, though less so since he married that noble lady—who, as anyone will tell you, looks angelic enough, but Lord! what a big spender! Thank the Lord that Madame Le Pierre has more sense in her little finger than that lady has in both her hands, which are more like sieves! But to come back to Monsieur de Bernay, after he refused Guise's offer, he began to be so afraid of the duc's vengeance that he shits his breeches every time he hears his name! That's all there is to it! So he left town to do as the snail does—pull his head and horns into his shell until the storm blows over—without realizing that he's going to get harvested anyway!" (At this Le Pierre had a good laugh.) "But—'sblood!—there's a better way to handle things! I'm going to wade in up to my elbows, set my sails and my traps and make sure that I foil the ambush of this traitor so thoroughly that they'll talk about it for a long time in Boulogne and throughout the region! As for Monsieur de Bernay, he's better off where he is than back here, where things are going to get very rough! If you're afraid of leaves, don't go wandering into the woods!"

I was very happy to discover Le Pierre's resolve and that his heart was in the right place, and, no longer doubting the outcome of the enterprise, since a trap foiled is a victory won, I prepared to saddle up and leave the next morning so that I could hurry to reassure the king. But Alizon, who was having great success selling her wares to the young ladies of the town, begged me to stay another week in the hope that she could unload the rest of her merchandise.

In addition, Le Pierre yearned so much to shine under the watch of a *missus dominicus*,[*] who would report back to the king. Ignorant of my little fly from hell's prayers to remain in Boulogne, he joined to them his own, assuring me that he'd sent a scout to determine the strength of the Duc d'Aumale's forces and another who was to warn him of the approach of Vétus, who was expected any day now in Boulogne and said to be bringing three months of pay for the soldiers in the garrison there. He urged me to stay so that I could observe the downfall of these treasonous Frenchmen.

He convinced me to remain—to Alizon's great delight, who was happy to be making so much money, and, like as not, to be passing herself off as my wife, playing this role to the hilt every night at dinner at the Golden Vessel. At night, too, claiming that she'd been terrified by a mouse, she would abandon her room and climb into bed with me, which troubled my sleep since I could feel her so close to me and since, the nights in Boulogne being so cold, she would cuddle up close to me to stay warm.

Each day of this week seemed to melt into a night both sweet and uncomfortable (since I was pulled in such different directions by my contrary desires). On the morning of the ninth day, Captain Le Pierre came to wake me, bringing me a helmet and a cuirass, and requested me to join him on the ramparts of the town, since Vétus was now only two leagues away.

I hurried to stand guard with him and watched the provost arrive, along with a heavy escort. As they approached, a sergeant posted in the entrance tower signalled for them to enter by the east gate, where

---

[*] "Envoy of the master."

a beautiful ambush was awaiting them. Scarcely had the traitor and his fifty men crossed the threshold—already shouting "We're taking the town, the town is taken!"—before, without having raised the drawbridge in front of them, Le Pierre ordered the portcullis behind them dropped, and a good hundred arquebusiers rushed up from their hiding places on all sides, their wicks lit. At this point, Captain Le Pierre shouted to the rascals to throw down their weapons or be cut to pieces.

They obeyed and were pulled from their horses and led directly to jail, confused, crestfallen and roundly mocked by the townspeople as they walked through the streets. After which, the portcullis was raised to give the appearance of a town that had already been taken and then abandoned, and that was therefore available to whoever wanted to take it. We didn't have long to wait. Le Pierre's scout rode up at breakneck speed and spread the word that the Duc d'Aumale was approaching with 200 cavalrymen and 300 foot soldiers.

"Well!" said Le Pierre happily. "Two hundred horsemen is not so many! I placed sixty in the little wood that you see over there on the right, and behind them are a solid hundred arquebusiers. As for cannon, we've placed our heaviest pieces on the east wall, so we'll tear them up pretty badly, but I don't have enough cavalry to chase them down and capture that scoundrel Aumale, which I'd love to do, so I could hand him over to His Majesty!"

In the end, we almost did, for Aumale's foot soldiers, believing they were going to sack the city, rape its girls and women and make a fortune pillaging it, started running joyously towards the gate, emitting a deafening victory cry, but were suddenly pitilessly cut down, not only by the arquebusiers hidden in the little wood, but also by those within the walls and by the cannon. After which, Le Pierre's cavalry, emerging from the cover of the trees, galloped straight for Aumale and surrounded him, but were too few to prevent his cavalry from freeing him and ignominiously abandoning the field, their foot soldiers flee-ing in panic and disappearing as quickly as they'd rushed the town.

Ah, dear reader, you can easily imagine what joy, what acclama-tion and what a quantity of wine was shared after such a victory! And what endless stories were recounted by the soldiers! But even though so much ammunition was fired precipitously, it caused few casualties among Aumale's troops, killing or wounding a mere twenty of these poor fellows, who were, alas, only Frenchmen like us, who had been misled by Guise and the so-called Holy League, and who had been enlisted in the service of the king of Spain without their ever realizing it.

But though the engagement was brief and not very bloody, the battle plans that Captain Le Pierre had drawn up seemed to me so judicious and his resolution so unshakeable that I swore to him that I would make a report to the king so advantageous that it would earn him His Majesty's eternal gratitude. And celebrating that evening with him in his lodgings in the amiable company of his wife, Henriette, and my supposed wife, he made a toast to me, and then another to Alizon, and then to me again, emptying his glass and eating the crust at the bottom. In response, I drank a toast to him, he one to Alizon and I one to Henriette, and then he toasted the king, and I the good city of Boulogne. He followed this with a sarcastic toast to the provost Vétus, and I, matching his silliness, one to the Duc d'Aumale, and then he to Guise and I to the Jesuits who had plotted this nasty coup and happily failed to bring it to fruition, so that at midnight we separated, very happy with each other, and very shaky on our legs—at least, he and I were, for the ladies had preferred talk to drink, so that Alizon had to help me stagger to the Golden Vessel and climb the stairs to our room, where, once we'd arrived, I fell, nearly unconscious, on the bed and she had to undress me.

I woke the next morning as fresh as a young maid, but when I remembered the previous evening's excesses I felt very ashamed to have become drunk for the first and, my God hear my solemn oath, last time in my life. But, observing about her a somewhat malicious air of triumph, I asked Alizon what had produced it and learnt that in my drunken state I'd spent the entire night taking my pleasure with her and she hers with me.

My shame in hearing this account was so great that I sat there voiceless and stupid. I think that if I'd been a genuine papist, I would have rushed to a confessional to wash myself of this damnable sin, since I do not countenance adultery, despite the fact that, in these times, people tend to turn a blind eye to men's sins and reserve their condemnation for women. But, since I'd remained a Huguenot in my heart, I felt that I needed to find some way to atone for this sin, which was not so much an affront to my God as one to Angelina, whose beautiful doe's eyes and loving look were imprinted on my conscience with such force that I nearly wept.

My poor Alizon immediately sensed the extent of my pain, and wished to console me, so sweet and affectionate as she was; however, she didn't dare take me in her arms or even approach me, but told me that I shouldn't punish myself so severely since, she claimed, it was all her fault, as she hadn't remained in her room but had claimed there was a mouse there in order to enter my bed, and, once in my arms, had such a great desire for me that it was too great a temptation to simply play at being husband and wife without ending up making love. She also assured me that everything that I'd done was done to serve the king and that, consequently, I should be less hard on myself, and that I should realize that the wine I'd drunk had stripped me of any will or knowledge of what I was doing.

"Ah, Alizon," I replied, "you are so kind and benevolent to want to comfort me. But anyone can see that I willingly blindfolded myself in order not to see where this voyage with you would eventually lead us, under the guise of serving my king. With all our disguises! And the roles of husband and wife, and the drunkenness! I was fooling myself the whole time! Hiding from myself the desire I'd had from the very beginning!"

"Ah, Pierre," cried Alizon, in utter joy, "I knew it! You wanted this too! Even though you pretended to be so strict and virtuous, Huguenot that you are!"

And suddenly she burst out laughing.

"But listen, my Pierre!" she continued, throwing herself in my arms, cooing as I held her to me. "Don't you owe me some of your life for having saved you—not once but twice? And don't you feel some friendly obligation to accommodate my affection for you—at least as long as we must play this charade on this voyage that you have arranged? Can't I at least be your wife on the outskirts and margins of your life? I swear that our roles here will end the minute we reach the gates of Paris!"

This was well said, and heartfelt, and clever, since some confessors wouldn't have gainsaid it, arguing that sinning one time or ten is all the same. Once the wine bottle is opened, the sinner might as well drink it. Another sophism, I fear, by which I hoped to soothe my suffering conscience—which, by the way, seemed to trouble me less once I'd assured it that I would close the "parenthesis" of my relationship with Alizon as soon as I reached the gates of Paris and that my fidelity to my wife would return once I'd done so.

Some time after the events I've just described, I alluded to them in the company of my immutable friend Pierre de L'Étoile, who, his curiosity piqued, asked to hear my account. In response, he made a comment that gave me pause, since his recollection of the events suggested that the years that had passed since these events had somewhat clouded my memory: it was his belief that this battle had occurred several months after the dates at which I'd situated it. We checked in his journal to see if he'd given an account of the events in Boulogne. We found no entry at the dates I'd recollected, but instead discovered the battle against the League had occurred on 20th March 1587. His account of this incident concerned not only the events at Boulogne but the sad fate that later befell Captain Le Pierre, who had so loyally defended his king.

I have copied this page, my heart stricken by the cowardly assassination of this unfortunate man:

At this time, the Duc d'Aumale ordered the assassination of Captain Le Pierre, a very brave soldier, for having prevented the taking of Boulogne, an operation the Duc d'Aumale and the League had planned. The king was very upset by this but dissimulated his role in the matter and pretended to believe what Aumale and the League told him, namely, that it was merely a quarrel they had, even though His Majesty had been informed of the contrary. His Majesty also ordered the Duc d'Épernon, who was most unhappy about this situation and ready to start a fight with Aumale, not to pursue the matter, but to wait for the moment when they could teach all of these Leaguers a lesson.

Dear reader, if this outcome strikes you as unjust, I ask you to accommodate, as best your heart can, this awful truth: this story is not a fable in which the wicked are punished and the good recompensed. Regarding Boulogne, it's quite the opposite, for the outcome there displayed the extremes of iniquity: the provost Vétus, traitor to his king, whom Captain Le Pierre had imprisoned in Boulogne, was freed four and a half months later as part of an exchange of prisoners that the king and the Duc de Guise arranged, following the Treaty of Nemours, by which the king pretended to be reconciled with his powerful vassal and, at least in appearance, gave him everything he asked. Upon his release from prison, Vétus had the extreme impudence to return to Paris. I learnt of this, and asked Nicolas Poulain what had become of him; Poulain, stroking his bushy moustache with his right hand, said with a sly smile:

"He was welcomed and treated very well by the members of the Holy League, who ordered me to introduce him to the best houses."

"They asked *you*, Mosca, the very man who had denounced him to the king?!"

"Yes, precisely! Which I found quite amusing," smiled Mosca, revealing his yellow teeth. "Together we visited the best houses of the League, where Vétus was welcomed, well considered and well feted, so that it took us a week to do all of these glorious visits."

I was more inclined to weep at this than to laugh at it as Mosca (or Leo, or Poulain) did—this man of two or three faces, who had neither faith nor soul, thinking only of money and his advancement, and who was quite comfortable having a foot in both camps, assured—as he thought himself to be—that he would be well treated by the future victor, whoever that might be. What honest man, however, would not have been devastated, seeing the terrible fate that met Le Pierre and the glory of the provost Vétus, to realize that in these troubled times everything ended up perverted or subverted, the king's loyal subject brought low and the disloyal one raised in stature?

On my return to Paris, I shed my skin of bonnet merchant at Alizon's place and, putting on my regular clothes and strapping on my sword, I felt myself once again become a gentleman, both inside and out. As Alizon watched me undress and then dress, she observed, with more bitterness than humour, a tear in her eye:

"You've already put on your fine airs again! You haven't even left my house and you're already the courtier, dreaming only of forgetting all my lessons and, worse, all the pleasant times we had on this journey!"

As she said this, a tear flowed down her cheek, and, moved by this, I took her in my arms, held her to me and kissed her pretty face, assuring her that I would always be her friend and that I would visit her from time to time, always conscious that she had twice saved my life, and was as fond of her as she was of me.

"Oh, no!" she cried. "That's just not true! And never was! But it's sweet of you to say so, and sweeter for me to hear it. But," she asked between sobs, "will we never return to Boulogne?"

I didn't know what to say in answer, nor what to do, other than to shower her face with kisses, and couldn't help feeling that she'd been an irreplaceable piece of my life.

When I returned to our lodgings, I learnt from Miroul that Angelina had gone out to visit my sister Catherine. Miroul himself seemed to greet me icily, clearly upset that I hadn't taken him along on the journey to Boulogne, since I'd thought that the Guisard spies might have recognized him, however well disguised he might be, by his varicoloured eyes. I ran to embrace my beautiful children, and then asked my chambermaids where I might find Fogacer. They informed me that he was with Silvio and Giacomi in my cabinet on the ground floor. I went back down and was delighted to find them deep in discussion. After I embraced each one in turn, Fogacer asked with his sinuous smile whether I was happy with my trip and if I had brought back good news for the king. I had to content myself with a simple "yes" but couldn't elaborate, since I didn't know whether His Majesty had confided in him.

"Well, *mi fili*!" he gushed. "This will give our Henri new confidence and faith, since, ever since you left, the Louvre has been inundated with messengers arriving from all parts of the kingdom bringing news of cities falling to the League without a fight, because they've been either bought or outwitted, or defeated by other shameful means. Our poor king has been watching his kingdom crumble before his very eyes! Guise lit the fuse by seizing Châlon-sur-Marne, which he's made a gathering place for his army. After this, he took Toul and Verdun. His brother Mayenne has captured Dijon, Mâcon and Auxonne. Monsieur de La Châtre, to avenge himself on Épernon, who removed him from the captaincy of Loches, has handed Bourges over to the League.

Guise's relatives and accomplices, Elbeuf, Aumale and Mercœur, have created an uprising in Normandy, Picardy and Brittany. D'Entragues has taken Orléans."

"Is that all?" I asked, terrified.

"The south, thank God, has held out. The League's efforts failed in Marseilles and the Leaguers were arrested and hanged. Toulouse and Bordeaux stand firm under the king's officers. In the east, Guise didn't dare attack Metz, where Épernon has stationed his troops. Troyes was taken, but has now been retaken."

"So all is not lost!" I cried, beginning to regain some hope.

"Well now, *mi fili*," replied Fogacer, arching his diabolical eyebrows, "I see you have lost nothing of your cheerful disposition!"

"I cannot believe," I said, "that God would permit the victory of these miscreants!"

"*Deus non est, neque diabolus*,"* corrected Fogacer, his dark eyes sparkling.

"Ah, my venerable doctor!" cried Giacomi, in terror for his friend. "I beg you by the Blessed Virgin not to speak in this way!"

"And what did you say, Monsieur?" asked Silvio, who invariably addressed Fogacer with utmost respect and politeness, despite, or perhaps because of, the familiarity of their connection.

"Nothing that bears repeating," replied Fogacer, who doubtless did not wish to share his atheist views with Silvio for fear of persuading him and putting him in as much danger of being burnt alive as he himself was. "Which is why," he added with a smile, "I said it in Latin, the language of these filthy pedants who go croaking around the Sorbonne."

"Fogacer," I observed, not without some asperity, which I tempered with a smile, "your Latin croaking would not have pleased Angelina, who has made you swear never to say *ipsissima verba*† in this house!"

---

* "God does not exist; neither does the Devil."

† "These very words."

"Oh, my Pierre!" cried Fogacer, who blushed in a most naive and disarming way, a reaction that suddenly seemed to spread over his entire face, which caused it to lose the sharpness of its features, its devilish smile and the ironic twist of his mouth, and to resemble instead the face of a child. "I beg you, don't repeat it to her! She'd scold me, or, worse still, refuse to speak to me for an entire day!"

I promised, laughing; and, begging their pardon for remaining so briefly among them, I prepared to leave, and saw my Miroul emerge from the little cabinet, sword by his side, cap on his head, requesting permission to accompany me.

I hurried to Quéribus's lodgings, where my Angelina gave a cry of happiness at seeing me and covered my face with a barrage of kisses that I returned with passion, feeling myself to be both the happiest of men and the most traitorous Judas Iscariot who'd ever crawled on the face of the earth. I realize that this kind of feeling is hardly in fashion in Paris or at the court. But, however courtly Alizon chides me with being, I am only a courtier in appearance, remaining in my heart both a provincial and a Huguenot.

However, I had to pull myself away, and thanking Quéribus warmly for the escort he had provided me, made haste to see the king and bring him the happy news of the League's failure to take Boulogne. But Quéribus, observing that I couldn't possibly appear before the king as sweaty and dirty as I was, since His Majesty had such a delicate sense of smell, had a bath prepared for me, where his three chambermaids scrubbed me, dried me and combed my hair. This done, Quéribus brought me one of his most sumptuous doublets and some colourfully waxed shoes, and told me that if I refused to wear them he would never speak to me again, explaining that the clothes were matched with the news I was bringing to the king.

"Hey, my brother! How do you know that it's good news?"

"By your resplendent face!"

I laughed at this, but said not a word more of it, handing him my purse and asking him to give five écus to each member of his escort with the message that they were to tell no one of their adventures, where they had been or what they had seen.

"Not even me, my brother?" laughed Quéribus.

"Not even you," I said, embracing him, "unless the king unseals my lips!"

I found the king had aged, his face ashen and swollen, his eyes sunken, his back bent, and his right hand inserted in his doublet and supporting his belly, which led me to believe that the burning in his stomach had returned, and that once again he was unwisely eating too much. This last was confirmed by the sight of a bright-red comfit box hanging from his belt, containing hard candies and prunes that he nibbled on alternately, believing that since the first blocked him up, the second would prevent constipation.

Although the weather had been quite clement, he'd had a huge fire lit in his hearth, and, still feeling chilled, was wearing a black velvet hat that he'd brought back from Warsaw, which came down to his ears and would have made him resemble Louis XI had his face not been so painted with red and white—make-up that looked very out of place with his unshaven beard (a spectacle so unusual that my eyes bulged at it), and even more so with his two pendants, one of pearls and the other of diamonds, which hung from his ears and were so heavy that they elongated his lobes. As for his *habitus corporis*,[*] I would have been a thousand times happier to see him, as I usually did, standing erect in front of the fireplace, his beautiful hand on the mantel and his face of marble, than to see him feverishly pacing back and forth in the room, now rubbing his belly, now pressing his two hands to his

---

[*] "Bodily posture."

temples (indicating that his headaches had also begun to recur), rings around his large, black, haggard eyes, which constantly shifted about as though suspicious of his surroundings, and his bitter lips mumbling so softly that it was impossible to catch a word of what he said.

At first he didn't see me, so enveloped was he in his bitter thoughts, but when Du Halde drew his attention to me, he paused and extended his hand, which, after having kissed it, I held in mine, intending to take his pulse, but he angrily withdrew it and said curtly:

"I am not ill."

"Except, sire, for your head and stomach."

"And how do you propose to cure me, Monsieur," he snarled, "when Marc Miron cannot?"

"Sire," I replied, "I have no other cure for worry than to give some opium to the patient so that he may sleep, and to ask him to open the windows, take a walk outside in the fresh air, eat less and throw away the prunes that Your Majesty has been devouring to excess."

"That's doctors for you!" came the king's retort along with a dismissive shrug. "They take away our little pleasures and want us to be grateful! Well, you wicked physician, now that the League is taking everything else, you want to take away my comfit box as well?"

"Sire," I laughed, "one gift deserves another! Give me your comfit box and I'll give you back Boulogne!"

"What!" he cried. "Boulogne! My comfit box is yours!"

"Yes, indeed, sire! The League failed miserably in its attempt to take the city! The city and the port are still in your hands!"

"Ah, my good doctor!" cried the king, his eyes shining; and, pulling himself up to his full height, he cried, "You have secured peace in Picardy!"

"Sire," I replied, "you give me too much credit! All I did was to warn them in time of the attack. Captain Le Pierre was the one who defeated them."

"Siorac, my son!" replied Henri, extending his hand. "What a beautiful blow you have struck against Guise! Chicot! Du Halde! Did you hear?" he said, spinning around with surprising alacrity, and in his joy extending his two hands, which the pair rushed to kiss. "Siorac, my son," he added, his eyes shining, "are you laughing? You have every reason to laugh. My gay doctor, what gay news you bring!" he cried, and, suddenly casting off his velvet hat with childlike petulance, he said, "Siorac, come over here and sit next to me! Here on this stool! On my right! Tell me everything and in the tiniest detail! Give me an earful of good news! My ears haven't been accustomed to such good news for a long time!"

I immediately obeyed as best as I could, and, to tell the truth, this "best" wasn't too bad (may the reader excuse my vanity!), for I'd been working on my story since the night before and had been thinking about it during the entire return voyage (Alizon becoming impatient with my silence), knowing all too well how much the king liked lively stories—especially in these times, when his throne rested on such shaky foundations that the wildest financier wouldn't have bet a sol on it.

"My good Siorac!" exclaimed the king when I'd finished. "That was well thought out, well done and, what's more, well recounted! I'm very proud of you! Just because Pibrac is dead and Ronsard dying doesn't mean that the art of fine speech has to be replaced by the gibberish of the priests of the League!"

"But, sire," interjected Du Halde, whose long face suggested a degree of austerity that one seldom found in the papist courtiers, "it isn't such an enormous gain not to lose a city!"

"Ah, killjoy!" replied Henri. "We shouldn't discount good things when they come, even if they are so rare! More to the point, the failures of the League in Boulogne and in Marseilles—did you know that the Leaguers failed to take Marseilles, Siorac?—put a dent in its reputation for invincibility and, at least for the moment, will put a stop to the betrayals. But Chicot, have you gone mute?"

"Sire, I have nothing to say!"

"What, not a single joke? Has the League also stolen the wit of my fool?"

"Henri," replied Chicot after a moment's thought, his nose perennially dripping, "the traitors you're referring to are turning my stomach! I'd like to vomit them up with my bile. Or shit them out with my shit."

"Well," the king replied, "what does it matter that I'm surrounded by ingrates, as long as I don't catch the infection? But my gratitude is as fresh as a daisy—and thick-skinned. Hey, Du Halde!" he continued, laughing. "Now that I think about it, call the barber right away and ask him to give me a shave! Siorac, my son, you have served me well and loyally. I won't forget it."

"I and Captain Le Pierre, sire!"

"Indeed, and I won't forget him either!"

"Alas, sire!" observed Du Halde. "For every Siorac or Le Pierre, how many Montcassins are there!" (Montcassin had been sent by the king to Metz with an armed force and a good deal of money, but made a detour to Châlons-sur-Marne and gave the troops and the money to the Duc de Guise, thereby shortening his trip.)

"Montcassin," growled the king with a look of infinite disdain, "is nothing but a little mouse compared to the fat rat who's nibbling away at my kingdom, city after city. Ah, Du Halde! Du Halde! It's obvious that if I keep letting these people have their way, they'll end up as my masters and not my companions. It's time to put my house in order!"

"Well then, sire, gather every one of your supporters among the nobility and we'll mount all together and ride against this traitor Guise!"

"Fire and brimstone, Siorac!" gasped the king with a weak smile. "Am I going to stick a firebrand down the throat of Guise?"

"Absolutely, sire!"

"And risk the entire kingdom on a throw of the dice in one battle? And start a civil war?" asked Henri, contemplating the void before him with a grave air. "A war that would profit only the financiers, the horse-dealers and the weapon-makers, and fill the kingdom with foreign fighters, division, eternal discord and endless murder and brigandage, while our poor labourers have hardly caught their breath after our past troubles?"

"But Henri," observed Chicot, "if we don't set a cat on the trail of this rat, it's going to keep gnawing away, and soon enough gnaw all of Paris!"

"It's already happening! I can hear his teeth! And I can see all the holes he's making! But that's not a reason to go waging war far from Paris, since I may not find any refuge here on my return."

"Ah, sire, are things really so far gone?"

"And worse still! Mosca's reports are rosy compared to the reality of the situation!"

"So what should we do, Henri," asked Chicot, "when they've got you by the throat?"

"Like Machiavelli," answered the king, "we should 'trim our sails'. Let the line out little by little, then reel it in, let it out again and pull it in."

"Until it breaks," finished Chicot, who'd sat down next to the fireplace and was sharpening a small knife on the hearth stones.

"What are you doing, Chicot?" asked the king.

"It's for Guise."

At this the king sighed and, lowering his beautiful Florentine eyes, murmured:

"I hope it never comes to that."

"Well, sire," I dared to observe, Guise's insolence weighing so heavy on my heart, "is this prince of Lorraine so blustery and stormy that the king of France has to 'trim his sails'? What will the nobility think?"

"Siorac," said the king, fixing me with his large black eyes, "have you read Machiavelli?"

"No, sire."

"Then think about this: it is often wise, and certainly the best sort of valour, to pretend to be soft and timid in the world's eyes, if this pretence is useful in attaining your goals. Du Halde," he added, "while it's fresh in my memory, please write to my treasurer and have him give 2,000 écus to Siorac, and the same amount to Le Pierre."

"Sire," I ventured, not without some apprehension that I'd be rebuked, "Your Majesty will forgive me, I hope, if I ask for more and less."

"More *and* less?" asked the king, pondering this conundrum. "Chicot do you understand this enigma?"

"Not in the least, Henri, unless the Bloodletter is sweet on one of the queen mother's ladies-in-waiting."

"Which ladies," observed the king, "given their morality, are hardly worth 2,000 écus apiece! Moreover, I have no sway over the gilded whores of the queen mother—who, though she's surrounded me with her ministers, has not yet encircled me with her petticoated spies."

"This has nothing to do with the flesh, sire," I explained, "but with your comfit box, which you more or less offered to grant me as a kind of reward for Boulogne."

"Then its yours, Siorac!" exclaimed the king, detaching it from his belt as if it were the most worthless bauble.

"Well, sire!" cried Du Halde reproachfully. "You give everything away! But you shouldn't so casually abandon this comfit box! 'Twas the queen mother who gave it to you!"

"The queen mother is now a member of the League," returned the king bitterly. "So who knows whether she won't take it back someday and give it to Guise!"

"Ah sire! You mustn't make light of this!"

"Rather than see it end up in Guise's greedy hands," the king answered, "I prefer to see it in the loyal hands of my good Siorac! On the one condition that he not display it at court as long as my mother does me the honour of living here."

Ah heaven! I was walking on air as I left the king, the bejewelled box stashed carefully in the deepest pocket of my doublet, and I almost forgot in my childish pleasure the misfortunes of the kingdom. Well! No doubt my uncle, Sauveterre, would have accused me of being woefully untutored in the art of bargaining, since I'd traded a comfit box worth, at most, 600 écus for 2,000 newly minted coins. And, certainly, he would also have let me understand in his Huguenot way that there was more than a hint of worldly idolatry in the immense value I attached to owning something that had belonged to the king. But, from another standpoint, when a monarch steers as best he can the ship of state through the hazards that confront him, how can a Frenchman, if he loves his nation, not cherish his sovereign wholeheartedly or be half-heartedly loyal to him—especially when this king is so likeable and so touching, as much in his generosity as in his distress?

What's more, this box was one day to save my life, as I shall later recount, and not by shielding me from an assassin's bullet, but in a much more unusual and bizarre way. Far from wearing it or showing it off to anyone, I showed it only to my Angelina when I returned to our lodgings, where I locked it away in a secret drawer in a little cherrywood cabinet that I kept in my room. This room adjoined hers, and, hearing her come in shortly after I did, I went to find her, took her in my arms and, pressing her to me in a most delicious embrace, gave her a thousand kisses on her neck and face and whispered a thousand compliments on her goodness, her beauty and her grace, assuring her of the great and indestructible love that I felt for her, feeling some remorse for what I'd done in Boulogne. Despite the strangeness of the hour, Angelina consented, not without the initial restraint and reserve that are so much part of her natural complexion, to allow me to lock the door and lead her to her bed.

Our first tumult over, we fell into tender conversation, in which each of us opened our heart to the other, I raised on my elbow, contemplating her beautiful doe's eyes, my hand on her breast, whose form and texture I never tired of. It occurred to me to ask her why, since she was so open and affectionate with Fogacer, she displayed, if not coldness, then at least a sort of distance with Giacomi.

"In truth," she confessed, not without a trace of shame, "I love them equally, each for his own qualities. But Fogacer, who puts on such airs with men, constantly looks at me with such a childish expression and without a trace of the desire that I don't like seeing in any eyes but your own, Monsieur my husband, and find so offensive in other men. It's not the same with Giacomi, though he is infinitely respectful. Because he is so in love with my twin sister, our resemblance could not but create some confusion, and put an occasional light in his eyes when he looks at me that I cannot accommodate."

I remained silent at hearing this, remembering my own confusion at Barbentane when I encountered Larissa unexpectedly in an upper hallway, and ended up being very relieved to see her depart, albeit in Samarcas's clutches.

"Do you believe," asked Angelina, observing my silence, "that there's any reasonable hope that we may free her from the claws of this Jesuit?"

"I do. It's clear that Samarcas is known to the English spies, and that he is aware of it, but that he's chosen, in his crazy, intrepid fanaticism, to continue his intrigues in London. At some point, he's bound to be caught in their net!"

Angelina looked at me wide-eyed, since she'd never heard me speak of Samarcas's enterprises, and I'd carefully hidden from her Mundane's connection to Walsingham and the Jesuit's hand in Mundane's murder.

344

And despite her usual discretion on these matters, she couldn't help asking:

"But if Samarcas were to be thrown in an English jail, isn't it possible that Larissa would be as well, since she'd be suspected of conniving in his machinations?"

"If that were to happen, my love," I soothed, "I'd be the first to learn of it and would have every hope of freeing her and bringing her back here."

So, with this small and fragile hope, Angelina had to be contented, and Giacomi as well, with whom not a day passed without our discussing it.

At the end of May, the king asked me to attend to Épernon, who, given the awful state of his health, was afraid of either dying a natural death that was predicted on all sides, given how emaciated he looked, or assassination by the League, who had vowed to kill him, since they believed he was the last mainstay of the throne. He had retired to his chateau in Saint-Germain-en-Laye with 400 guards, either to recover from his illness or to die peacefully there.

I hastened to his side, and found him terribly thin and weak, suffering from painful cankers in his throat, and attended by two great asses of doctors who had, for the last two months, been bleeding him, starving him, purging him and immobilizing him. I sent word to the king that very evening that if such a "cure" were continued, they'd reduce him to a skeleton in no time.

"As for me," I added, "I will try to restore his health and vigour by other means, on condition that these shitty quacks be removed forthwith."

Which the duc did, on advice from the king, and it was a good thing too, since their purgations had so uselessly tortured his empty bowels. I put an immediate end to their regime, and began feeding him a liquid diet that he was able to force down. Recalling how much my father hated the practice of bleeding, which some charlatan had introduced into France from Italy on the illusory pretext that the more dirty water one withdraws from a well the clearer it will get, I had it stopped. And taking the opposite tack from his previous cures, I counselled the duc to get up out of his chair and begin walking and exercising his body. Which, with the strength that he was regaining from the nourishment I provided, he did all the more willingly, since he'd always been of a very lively and robust complexion and could barely tolerate the repose that had been forced on him by the two quacks. As for his throat, I contented myself, as I had done during the voyage to Guyenne, with a prescription of gargling with boiled salt water every morning, noon and evening after each meal. But then, observing that this remedy soothed the duc without really healing his throat, and, on the other hand, seeing that he was regaining some of his former strength every day, I attempted to cauterize the cankers with a red-hot iron. Which I did very lightly, several times, and, as I believe, with some success—for, from that day forward, the duc began to recover, and by the beginning of July was fully healed.

During these two months, I saw the duc almost daily, and, as assiduous as I was in my cure, as much to save the life of my patient as because I judged his life to be very important in his service to the king, I never managed to like him as a person, finding him to be very haughty in nature. This trait naturally displeased me, even though I could see that it was linked to an admirable firmness of soul that was so much a part of his temperament that, even with his king and sovereign, Épernon displayed an air of inflexibility.

Quéribus told me in this regard that when he first arrived at court, Épernon went to meet the king with his doublet unbuttoned, and the king, annoyed by this failure of etiquette, scolded him. At the king's rebuke, bowing, but without a word of reply, Épernon turned on his heels, walked away and began packing his bags, preparing to leave the court that very day. When the king learnt of this, he sent for the duc to entreat his reconciliation.

As for his physical appearance, he struck me as exceptionally strong and tough, and, given the rapidity of his recovery as soon as the other doctors were prevented from interfering with him, I believed that he was made of hardened mortar and would last for a century.

He wanted to offer me a good sum of money as a reward for my cure, but I refused, saying that I was acting on orders from the king and was salaried by His Majesty. When the duc heard this, he sensed that there was some nobility in my refusal, and he told me with a smile (since he could be very charming when he wished) that the Chevalier de Siorac was henceforth his friend and, as such, could not refuse the gift of a diamond and a beautiful horse that he had in his stables. I consented to this, very happy that, in the end, he was treating me as a gentleman (if not really as a friend, since friendship, as far as I could tell, was a feeling entirely unknown to him).

Having no use for it, and being very happy with the steeds I already had, I ended up selling the horse, and giving the diamond to Angelina, after a jeweller had mounted it in a gold ring (and informed me that its value was easily 1,000 écus). I wryly surmised that the duc wouldn't have given half this sum to a doctor who couldn't convince him that he was of noble birth.

Judging that the king's forces, roughly 25,000 good soldiers, were not inferior to those that Guise had marshalled in the east of the kingdom, thanks to the gold Felipe II had provided, Épernon decided that he must immediately have it out with the rebel duc, a decision I'd heard him announce to the king every time His Majesty came to visit him in the chateau at Saint-Germain-en-Laye to ask about his health. But His Majesty, who had a deeper understanding of the situation, argued that he could never wage war on Guise as long as this latter hid his activities under the mantle of religion, which guaranteed him the support of the clergy and the people, whose support we most needed to win away from the League. And this was the reason that the king ended up, on the intercession of the Guisard queen mother, signing with Guise the Treaty of Nemours, which ended up being so disastrous and ignominious, by which the king of France recognized as practically legitimate the rebellion that had been raised against him, and forfeited to the duc dominion over the cities he'd seized from the king.

"The worst thing in all of that," said Pierre de L'Étoile on the morning he informed me of this news (being marvellously informed about everything), "is that the king is on foot and the duc on horseback."

"No," I corrected, "the *worst* thing is that they forced him to annul all the edicts guaranteeing peace between the two parties, and instead to sign an injunction compelling all Huguenots to leave the country within six months or else have all their worldly goods confiscated! A nice bonfire lit atop a barrel of gunpowder."

"And you're no doubt thinking," said Pierre de L'Étoile, "about all your father will suffer from such an injunction."

"Oh, no! Mespech is now in the claws of my older brother, who, having become a turncoat, is now a devout Catholic—but who cannot see that His Majesty has avoided a civil war with Guise only to start one with the Huguenots. It's Scylla after Charybdis!"

"And yet, when you think about it," said Pierre de L'Étoile with a wry smile, "this civil war against the Huguenots will be waged by His Majesty without any zeal whatsoever!"

"Well!" I responded. "I think so as well. But isn't it the height of Machiavellianism to pretend to ally oneself with one's mortal enemy in order to give the appearance of waging war against one's natural ally?"

8

T HAT SAME DAY, as I was returning to my lodgings, I found a letter that a messenger had just brought, and that immediately plunged me into an abyss of surprise and apprehension:

Monsieur my cousin,

It pains me greatly that you haven't yet replied to the invitation I made you to visit me in my Hôtel de Montpensier, where I would have been delighted to introduce you to Madame my cousin, who is most eager to meet you, having heard such diverse opinions of you that she desires to make your acquaintance and thereby form an opinion of you that comes only from knowing you. Believing, Monsieur my cousin, that you would not knowingly neglect the wishes of this high lady—as, alas, you have done mine—I pray to God to keep you in His holy protection, or at least as long as this noble lady commands me to remain, Monsieur my cousin, your humble and devoted servant,

Jeanne de La Vasselière

I could hardly believe my eyes at the extreme impudence of this Marianne, who was ordering me in a combination of threats and politeness to submit to the inquisition of the Duchesse de Montpensier, whom everyone knew to be the frenetic servant of her brother, and whose gold inspired the most strident of the priests of the League to rage against the king day and night in their sermons. From her belt dangled a pair of gold scissors, by which she meant to tonsure Henri before locking him away in a monastery, giving him his third and final crown, the first being the Polish one and the second the French. She spawned a constant stream of perverse and wicked invective that the League then bruited about in Paris and that the king, had he not been so excessively mild-mannered, should have punished by exiling her forever.

Since I couldn't share this letter with my Angelina, who was so good and naive that she could never see evil in anything or anyone—and, in addition, having decided, in order to preserve her peace of mind, never to reveal the perilous enterprises into which the service of the king led me—I decided to show the note to Miroul. He immediately bade me not to put myself at the mercy of the ferocious Guise in her mansion, which was no doubt the garrison for many armed and hostile men, and added:

"Monsieur, it's my belief that you should not go there under any circumstances! When you grab a wolf by his ears, you're pretty sure to get bitten! Especially since you're known as the king's loyal servant and your lodgings are already marked for the massacre!"

"But Miroul," I protested, "he who plays the sheep will be devoured by the wolf!"

"And he who doesn't run away is eaten all the sooner! Monsieur, wait for him to show his teeth if he must bite! Don't throw yourself headlong between his jaws!"

What he said made sense, but finding his peasant's prudence a bit too passive under the circumstances, I decided to seek the opinion of Quéribus, who, taking a position in direct opposition to Miroul's, laughed:

"Monsieur my brother, go ahead! The danger you face is no greater inside the Hôtel de Montpensier than outside it! And, once inside, you'll be able to cast your piercing blue eyes on this monster, one of whose thighs is too short and the other too light, as Chicot has said—a quip that would have had him assassinated ten times over had it not been dishonourable to dispatch a fool! Madame Limp suspects, as does everyone else, that you're secretly working for the king. She wants you to visit her in her mansion so she can pick your brain. But I think you're way too clever not to give her enough rope to hang herself. You are not unaware that the king sets great store by your opinions—which is why I'm not jealous that he uses you more than me, since I'm more agile with a blade than with my brain."

"Quéribus, I cannot imagine that you'd ever be jealous of me!" I cried, throwing an arm over his shoulder. "I who am but a sketch for your exquisite portrait!"

"Well, 'tis true," gloated Quéribus as he preened his wasp-like figure, "that, as for my earthly appearance, I am still, though well past thirty years old, enough of a beauty to turn many a head, and that, every day I spend at court presents a thousand opportunities to sin were I not so fond of Madame your sister."

His words brought a knowing smile to my face, since, though I agreed that he had as many occasions to sin as he claimed, I doubted that he didn't take advantage of some of them. He found my smile as flattering as my usual compliments, so that I left him very happy with me, as I was with him, since his advice suited my present inclinations much more than Miroul's.

I sent Miroul off to the Hôtel de Montpensier with a little note in which I threw myself at the feet of Mademoiselle de La Vasselière, and, less than an hour later, he returned, looking very mournful and not a little worried. He told me he'd met directly with this prodigious wench, and that if it wasn't the Marianne we'd met in Mâcon, it was an exact portrait of our assassin. He related that she'd read my missive with a wry smile and had said in a derisive tone, "I'm charmed by

your master's obedience and request his immediate presence here…
unless he's afraid of being devoured by the ogresses who reign herein!"

Hearing these words, I strapped on my sword without further
ado, all the while Miroul begging me not to be crazy enough to go
wandering off into this she-wolf's lair, exposing my life to these Furies
from hell who, only a month previously, had hired Mérigot to shoot
me. But since I'd already made up my mind, I refused to listen to a
single word, so he decided that the best he could do was to fasten a
small Italian dagger to my back, under my cape, explaining that it
might come in useful, as they would surely confiscate my sword at the
entrance to the Hôtel de Montpensier.

And, of course, he was right, for without this little Italian stiletto
I would have felt very vulnerable and exposed when an enormous
blackguard of a lackey ushered me into a small salon, where I was to
wait. But no sooner had I got my bearings than the door flew open
and Marianne appeared, offering me her hand to kiss, with a haughtiness I could barely credit; she then stood glowering at me and ordered
me to be seated without the faintest trace of a smile and in the most
cutting tone. She herself remained standing and began pacing back
and forth in front of me without another word, darting looks at me
from time to time as if they were arrows from a crossbow. She was a
lively brunette with few charms to recommend her, other than her
constant movement. La Vasselière was not without some resemblance
to Alizon, but she was a full head taller and her black eyes expressed
only variations of disgust as opposed to my sweet seamstress's inevitably
benevolent looks. She was robed in white satin, with gold embroidery
and strings of pearls, finery as splendid as that of any of the ladies
of the court. Her white-laced collar was adorned with a multitude of
little diamonds and other precious stones.

"My cousin," she said, coming to a halt in the middle of the room,
"may I ask you to satisfy my curiosity?"

"Madame," I replied, with a smile that hardly masked the impatience I felt, "I would be happy to satisfy it if only I knew who was asking the question: Mademoiselle de La Vasselière, or Marianne?"

"Monsieur chevalier," she countered without the slightest sign that I'd shaken her haughtiness, "this Marianne whom you presume to name is my dearest and closest friend. But she who is speaking to you here, with all the weight that her relationship derives from him, is the cousin of the Duc de Guise."

"Madame!" I exclaimed, leaping to my feet and making her a deep bow. "Although I am a faithful and devoted servant of my king, I am not ignorant of the respect I owe to a great lord who is second only to the king of France."

This said, I sat down again, knowing full well that this phrase had only partially satisfied her, and not wishing to go any further in the contentment that I'd just provided her.

"Some people think," she said with a less-than-generous look in her jet-black eyes, "that it is the Duc d'Épernon who is second to the king in this kingdom. And it may be surmised that you share this belief, since you cured him of the cankers in his throat."

"Madame," I answered stiffly, "I care for, cure and do whatever is necessary to heal those the king orders me to attend to. If he ever ordered me to offer medical attention to the Duc de Guise I would not leave the latter's bedside until I'd cured whatever malady beset him."

"Well, that's good!" replied La Vasselière curtly.

After which, finally understanding that I could not be shaken from this position, she seated herself in an armchair, arranged her skirts about her with care and, suddenly staring at me intently, snapped:

"Who was this Mundane fellow? Where did he come from? What was he doing among your servants? What happened to the letter he was carrying? To whom was it addressed?"

"Madame," I replied with exquisite calm, "I shall answer this hailstorm of questions if you would only be so good as to answer a single one of mine. Why did Marianne kill him?"

"She didn't intend to," she answered with surprising animation, "but when she tried to lift the heavy chest to take the letter, she was surprised by the Englishman, who'd pretended to be asleep, and when he grabbed and unsheathed his sword, she had no recourse but to draw her dagger, throw herself at him and stab him."

"So many times!"

"Yes, because he had his hands around her neck and was choking her!"

"I thank you, Madame," I breathed after a moment of silence, "for this report, which certainly reveals Marianne to be more humane than I'd thought."

"I'll tell her so," replied La Vasselière with a grain of irony. "She'll be charmed to learn of your feelings."

After this, I urged her to repeat her own questions, having asked mine only to allow me time to calculate my answers.

"As for Mundane," I said, temporizing, "I'm unable to satisfy your curiosity at this time. I know neither who he was nor where he came from. All I know is that the king ordered me to include him in my retinue and to provide him protection and any help he required. Which is why, when he asked me at Pamiers to arrange a meeting with the king of Navarre, I got my father to help with this."

"Who is, if I'm not mistaken, a Huguenot," she observed. "And you, Monsieur?"

"As for me," I improvised, "as you know very well, Madame, I go to Mass and to confession."

"With your words or with your heart?"

"Well, now, Madame," I replied stiffly; and, rising to my feet, I exclaimed, "This inquisition is intolerable! I will answer to my confessor on this matter, not to you!"

"Sit down, my cousin," she soothed, smiling for the first time. "If you find this question offensive, I withdraw it, and will content myself with the information you've provided that Mundane met Navarre thanks to your father. Which, of course, we already knew."

And which, of course, I suspected, otherwise how would Guise's people have known about the letter and the importance attached to it? Which also explained the counterfeit frankness with which she praised my "honesty".

"And to whom," she asked, "was this letter addressed?"

"There was no address on the letter," I said, looking her directly in her blue eyes.

"So to whom did you deliver it?"

"To the king, judging that it must be of very great portent if someone had been ready to kill the messenger in order to obtain it, and then attempted to kill a second man once the letter had been delivered."

To which, without batting an eyelid, Mademoiselle de La Vasselière replied with utter calm:

"Unfortunately, you happened to witness a murder which could have inculpated my closest friend, and me as well, since you couldn't help learning my name, living at court as you do."

"Madame," I answered with a feigned look of surprise, "you astonish me! Can you imagine that the king would have accused a cousin of the Duc de Guise of any wrongdoing?"

"I realized as much afterwards, which is why there was no further attempt on your life. Especially since, dear cousin, in the letter you addressed to me, you showed yourself to be more open to our position than I would have thought, by liberating your prisoner and refusing to incriminate the major-domo of this house, who, since he is not a nobleman, could have been hanged. In truth, I don't give a fig about his life. But I do worry about the stain his death would have caused to our family."

"Well, Madame," I cried, attempting to convey a sudden bout of honesty, "had I known sooner of your good offices towards me, I could have been spared my voluntary exile!"

"Voluntary, Monsieur!" gasped La Vasselière. "You mean you weren't sent into exile for the disgrace you caused to the throne?!"

"Well, not as entirely as I pretended," I said, again counterfeiting some confusion. "I was also seeking to protect myself from you. I had to leave Épernon's bedside, so it's true that the king was quite unhappy with me since he would have wanted me to continue my cure of the duc."

"Monsieur my cousin," said La Vasselière, rising, "I am truly charmed that you have been so forthcoming with me as to share the truth about your exile, since we knew of course that it was feigned and that the king's treasurer had provided you with 2,000 écus on the eve of your departure from Paris."

"Well!" I thought. "My Guisard friends have ears everywhere! I was right to let slip this bit of truth. As Henri has often said, the best and most Machiavellian lie is the one that's closest to the truth!"

"Madame," I observed, looking her directly in the eye, "I am also delighted that you've become so much more amicable!"

"Amicable?" she queried, raising an eyebrow. "I will only be so, in fact, if you have the good fortune to please Madame de Montpensier, who will receive you shortly, if you'll please await her here."

And at this, she made a small curtsey, and left me astonished at the frigid haughtiness of this wench, who, to serve Guise, hadn't hesitated to prostitute herself to an English gentleman in an inn, stab him to death with her own hands, and then steal my horse.

"Shortly" certainly did not describe the length of time I had to wait. For more than an hour, I had ample opportunity to meditate on the peril in which I found myself, given that I was in the hands of these maenads who took no more account of the life of a man than of that of their cat, or of a mouse for that matter. They called you "my cousin", but they could, just as easily, throw you into a sack at night and drop you in the Seine from one of their windows overlooking that river. Thus it is that religious zeal has come to override every moral consideration in this strange century!

I was left to kick my heels for a long time, stewing in the most absolute disquiet—and you can imagine, dear reader, how much worse it would have been had I learnt the fate that the Guise faction had reserved for poor Captain Le Pierre. Eventually, the same great hulk of a lackey reappeared to lead me to his mistress, but instead of taking me to a princely salon in which I would confront the elegantly attired sister of the Duc de Guise, surrounded by her ladies-in-waiting, I was taken to a small chamber in which the only furniture was a great gilded bed, whose curtains of white brocade had been drawn, hiding from my sight the person who occupied its interior, but whose voice I could hear as she loudly scolded her chambermaid, who was attempting to put in order a room strewn from one end to the other with various clothes, shoes and other feminine accoutrements.

"Yes, I am sure," whined this voice bitterly, "that it was you, Frédérique, and none other, who mislaid the draft of the letter that Henri sent to Felipe, which I had in my hands only yesterday."

"Madame," replied Frédérique, whom I took to be from Lorraine given how tall, robust, blonde and blue-eyed she was, with broad shoulders and a large bosom that looked more muscular than inviting, "that cannot be. I never touch your papers! I've got enough to do just sorting out this mess, in which a bitch wouldn't be able to find her pups! If I don't straighten this room it'll look more like a pigsty than a princess's chamber!"

"That's enough, you silly wench!" said the voice, reaching an ever-higher pitch and nastiness. "You've got too sharp a tongue, it seems to me! But you'll be talking out of the other side of your mouth if I have to have you whipped in front of the entire household for your impertinence! So I'm a boar's sow and live in a sty?"

"Madame," Frédérique replied without batting an eyelid or pausing in her work, "you are assuredly the most beautiful princess in the universe, but may the Devil throttle me if you're not also the most disorderly! And I won't have you blaming me for misplacing the duc's letter, which you must have put in your basket without thinking about it! It's probably been burnt by this time."

"And why burnt, you hussy?"

"Because," hissed Frédérique, slapping her hardy right breast with the flat of her hand, "you've told me a hundred times to burn the contents of your basket every morning! A hundred times, by my faith!" she protested, slapping herself again. "And may the Blessed Virgin and her Divine Son strike me dead if I'm lying!"

"It's *you*, you idiot," snarled the duchesse from behind her curtains, "who threw the letter in the basket! I never would have discarded a letter written by my beloved brother! And, sadly, now this letter has been burnt thanks to you, whore's bastard that you are!"

"I'm no bastard!" gasped Frédérique, badly stung by this phrase, and, pulling herself up to her full height, she countered, "I know both my mother and my father, who were well-to-do labourers in the countryside around Metz. And you know very well, Madame, that at court there are any number of high ladies who couldn't make the same claim!"

At this, the hulk of a lackey, who must have grown impatient with this endless bickering, presumed to cough.

"Who's there?" came the voice of the duchesse, as sour as vinegar and as stinging as mustard.

"It's Franz, Madame," replied the lackey. "I've brought you the Chevalier de Siorac."

"And you dared cough in my presence?!" yelled the Duchesse de Montpensier, her piercing voice reaching new heights. "Tell the major-domo to give you ten lashes with the whip right now!"

"Madame," said Franz, indignant, "all I did was cough! I didn't say a word! Nor did I say that you live in a pigsty!"

"You didn't say it, you knave, but you heard it! And to punish your indiscreet ears, tell the major-domo to give you another ten lashes!"

"Yes, Madame," muttered Franz, now red as a crayfish in boiling water. And, having made his customary bow despite his mute rage, he backed out of the room.

"Frédérique," came the voice from behind the curtain, "what do you think of the Chevalier de Siorac, since you're looking at him?"

"He's not very tall but well built," replied Frédérique, who approached me and looked me over closely, as if I were a bull she wanted to buy at the fair. "What's more, he's got hazel eyes, blond hair with a bit of grey around his temples and a ruddy complexion, and is, I believe," she continued, feeling my biceps, "fairly muscular. In short, Madame, he's very gallant and seems to enjoy looking at women's bosoms."

"What you mean is, you hussy," replied the voice bitterly, "that you're showing him enough to keep him looking!"

"Well, Madame, no more than is in keeping with today's styles!"

"Enough talk, you minx! Lead the chevalier over here by the hand. And make sure he doesn't step on any of my jewellery! He'd crush it into dust!"

My curiosity carrying the day against all the trepidation I'd felt since entering the lair of this she-wolf, I was now quite eager, after hearing her voice, to see this famous wild duchesse, who was the primary and principal enemy of my king in Paris, and who had used her vast wealth to turn the entire clergy of Paris into a counterweight bearing down on the populace, and to assemble around her a kind of counter-court, consisting of a bunch of debt-ridden noblemen (often quite high ranking ones), who were either disgraced, malcontents or ambitious, along with ladies of the same ilk, whom she made dance like puppets on a string for the greater glory of her brother and the greater detriment of my king. The most astonishing thing about this muddle-headed witch was that she found the time, occupied as she was with all the little intrigues of her household, to hatch an infinite number of political plots tirelessly and with infinite irascibility.

When the curtains were finally drawn, I found the duchesse seated, rather than lying, on her bed, propped up by a mass of pillows, and, though it was almost noon already and lots of natural light flooded the room, she had a candelabrum placed on her night table that provided even more light. What struck me immediately was how immodestly she was dressed, or rather undressed, since her night dress fell wide open on her bosom, which struck me as remarkably unspoilt by age, though she was already past thirty, after which age, in our country, a woman is no longer considered young. But her body certainly didn't look the least bit ravaged by time: her breasts were firm—though perhaps not as firm as Frédérique's—her eyes sky blue, her abundant blonde hair falling in tresses onto her well-rounded shoulders, her mouth large and her lips firm, with teeth that had not stood the test of time very well. As for her expression, there was nothing of the haughtiness of La Vasselière, but a sort of tranquil self-assurance, as though, being the sister of the future king of France, she had power over the life and death of every Frenchman alive, as legitimately as if they were the back of her poor lackey.

I had ample time to examine her, or rather to counter-examine her (though I did so with a pretence of respect), since, after my gaining entry into her little space, she considered me for quite some time (her pen held in suspense in her right hand over the escritoire she had placed in her lap, her bed strewn with various papers), with such an impersonal gaze that I felt as though I were a saddle horse, or a hunting dog she'd just acquired, or even a draught horse that she was examining to see whether it would be robust enough to pull its barge. Of all the varieties of haughtiness, this was probably the worst, since in its silence and disinterest there was no deprecation—the very idea of attaching any worth whatsoever to me would never have occurred to her. Or at least any *moral* worth, for she'd bought the allegiance to her brother's cause of so many priests and noblemen that she knew, to the nearest écu, the price of every man in the kingdom.

As she prolonged her examination, so did I mine—with no risk of offending her, any more than the gaze of a dog would offend a bishop. All the while I noticed that, in addition to the various papers that were spread over her bed, there was a disorderly collection of objects: pots of make-up, a mirror, jewels and other trinkets, a large plate of dragées, almond paste and dried fruits, which she was selecting with her left hand while her right hand was occupied by her pen. From time to time she'd grasp a handful of these confections and stuff them into her mouth (which was, luckily, quite large, given what she tried to force into it). She chewed on these various sweets while she talked, and, as soon as she'd swallowed a mouthful, she'd cram another handful into the maelstrom.

"Monsieur chevalier," she said at length, "please be seated."

"Madame," I replied, "forgive me, but I see no stool to sit on."

"Sit down on my bed. Am I so repulsive?"

"Madame," I replied with a deep bow, "my eyes have already told you with sufficient clarity that you are assuredly the most beautiful princess in Christendom."

"And yet they say that my cousin the queen, whom I haven't seen in a very long time, isn't so rotten that Henri couldn't give her a child if he were capable of it."

"Madame," I assured her with another deep bow, "the queen is certainly very beautiful, but she could never hope to compete with you, for all the innumerable graces that you possess!"

"Monsieur, please be seated," she said, evidently concluding that I knew well enough how to lay compliments on with a trowel that sufficiently conformed to the tone and flavour of her little court.

"Madame," I confessed, "I am entirely your slave."

I sat down on her bed. At this, she took me at my word, and asked me to remove the escritoire from in front of her and place it on the night table. This done, I had to collect and fold all the little notes that were spread over her coverlet, which I did, not without having glanced quickly at each one on the sly. As I collected them, she explained that these were the instructions that she was giving to her army of priests for their Sunday sermons. Far from hiding this sacrilegious and rebellious act, she behaved in such a way as to let the entire world know what was going on. Indeed, by manipulating these preachers, she was inflicting more damage on the king and doing more for the eventual triumph of her brother than all the armies that Guise had assembled in the east.

"Frédérique," she said, "tell Guillot to carry my sermons to each of the priests in person and to give each one ten écus."

"Ten?!" gasped Frédérique. "Ten, Madame? These sermons are going to ruin you! You gave them only five last week!"

"That's because," laughed la Montpensier, "this week the message I've asked them to spread is a little harder to swallow, so they will need to have a good drink before they regurgitate them and feed them to their flocks. My coins will lubricate their throats. Their zeal will do the rest. And Frédérique, when you've given the order to Guillot, don't come back here. I want to be alone with the chevalier."

"Madame," I observed, "the king himself has said that you have a remarkable talent for inventing stories."

"'Tis true," she gloated with an ironic smile. "And I'm delighted to be so praised by the king, who is so lacking in this talent."

"And which inspired you to claim that there were 10,000 Huguenots hidden in the Faubourg Saint-Germain, who were awaiting the signal from Navarre to execute their own St Bartholomew's day massacre on the Catholics."

"Well!" she laughed. "That was a good one! I didn't have them sermonize on it, but only repeat it during confession."

"Along with the story that Pierre de Siorac is said to have given 200,000 écus to Navarre from the king so he could wage war on his Catholic subjects."

"A story I had a lot of trouble denying after I'd spread it, since people tend to believe me when I speak through my clerics."

"So why did you say it?"

"So that someone would decide to kill you without my having to order it."

Madame de Montpensier said this straight out as if it had been the most natural thing in the world.

"Madame," I declared with a little bow, "I'm delighted that you retracted it."

"Well, I'm not sure that was the right thing to do," she replied, throwing me a sudden trenchant look with those blue eyes of hers; then she added, "Didn't you go to Boulogne to warn Monsieur de Bernay of Aumale's plans?"

"Not at all!" I said, following the inspiration of the moment. "That was not me!"

"And yet you were seen in Boulogne one week before the event."

"No again! That's not possible. I was never there!"

"But," she broke in, "you weren't in Paris either."

"No, Madame," I agreed, but suddenly felt on very shaky ground, which could fall away at any moment.

"So, where were you, Monsieur?"

"Madame," I temporized, feeling my alibi take shape little by little with each word I spoke under this intense inquisition. "Can I hide nothing from you? Am I at confession? Must I tell you where I was? And why not, while you're about it, ask me who I was with?"

"Who were you with?" queried the duchesse implacably.

"With a woman," I answered, trying to appear as confused and trapped as possible.

"Aha!" she laughed—I would almost say she "gave a belly laugh" given how much of her anatomy was exposed. "I've got you now, Monsieur hypocrite, you who are reputed to be so faithful to your wife! You went to play the beast with two backs in the provinces, didn't you, knowing that in Paris you couldn't get away with it?!"

"Madame," I said very awkwardly, "you've trapped me into confessing this with your knife on my throat, but I swear to you by the Blessed Virgin that I will not tell you where I was or who I was with."

"You don't need to, Monsieur," said the duchesse. "I believe you and was only pressing you to be certain. I already knew that it wasn't you who warned Monsieur de Bernay."

"And how did you know?"

"Because, when you returned, the king did not shower you with money, as he assuredly would have if you'd been involved in this affair. Which would have made me pity you, Monsieur," she added with a knowing look. "Anyone who crosses my brother doesn't live long enough to regret it."

"Well," I thought to myself, "what a relief he gave me the comfit box! Miraculous comfit box! How many thanks I owe you for saving my life!"

"Madame," I said, "I am very happy to have had the chance to speak openly with you, since our conversation has allowed me to leave your presence on my own two feet rather than in a sack tossed in the Seine!"

At this she laughed again, with the kind of cruel cackle of those for whom death is always other people's problem and not their own.

"Monsieur," she said, changing registers, "let us be serious. Do you want to work for me?"

"In what way, Your Highness?" I asked, open-mouthed.

"I'll pay you."

"Madame," I confessed after some reflection, "I cannot receive a salary from the king and, at the same time, one from his mortal enemy. I am not so crooked. And I don't need the money."

"You mean to say, Monsieur," she replied, with a sudden, not very benign light in her steely eyes, "that you're refusing me?"

"I mean, Madame," I countered with a slight bow, "that if I worked for you I would turn down any offers from your worst enemy. Does being a faithful servant mean nothing? Does the duc have so many of these?"

"Assuredly not," she replied bitterly. "He's only served by those who believe he can overthrow the king. And of this, none of his greatest allies can be sure. Not even Felipe. We've heard that Felipe wants us to take matters in hand—not for our house, but for his. When we've got rid of Henri, he wants to crown the daughter he had by Isabel de Valois as queen of France."

"The Rex Catholicissimus," I replied, "seems to care very little for Salic law!"

"Have patience!" she mused, her blue eyes drifting off into space and her expression suddenly very dreamy, as if she could already see her brother on the throne of France and herself at his side. "Do I understand," she continued, a bit dreamily, as if trying to shake herself out of her reverie, "that you don't want to serve me? It's really a shame, in my opinion, that a man as gallant as yourself should persist in serving this poor devil of a king—unless you're a poor devil as well!"

"Madame," I smiled, "if you were to spread such a rumour in your little notes to the priests, there's not a person at court who would believe you."

"Oh, I wouldn't dream of it!" she said with a shrug. "Other than to have you killed, what would I do with you? You're too small a grain to be ground in our royal mills."

"Madame," I replied, somewhat stung by this remark, "I'm not such small fry as you pretend. The Duc d'Épernon owes me his life."

"Unfortunately!"

"And if I'd been old enough at the time, who knows whether I wouldn't have been able to save your father when he was shot, since he was only wounded in the shoulder!"

"Monsieur," she countered, "it seems to me you're overstating your talents. If, God willing, you could only cure my indigestion, which," she continued, throwing off her covers and completely baring her stomach, "twists and distends my belly most uncomfortably."

And this said, she grabbed my hand and placed it on her belly. After palpating her abdomen here and there, I proclaimed:

"Madame, if you didn't spend the day sucking on sweetmeats, you wouldn't suffer from these little discomforts. A day of dieting and a few infusions will put an end to your obstructions."

"Ah, Monsieur," she cooed, "your hands are so soft and warm! And what an immense improvement these skilled and miraculous palpations are making! Keep going, I beg you! Already I feel all those knots melting away and I'm opening up where I was so closed!"

"Madame, I'm happy to have eased your discomfort somewhat."

"Somewhat, Monsieur! Your touch is so dexterous that I feel like a flower opening up to the sun! Let me guide your hand! The remedy will be even better!"

"Madame," I objected, "if my hand continues in the direction you're leading it, this will no longer be a cure, but a caress, and will be nothing but the prologue to a play that has nothing medicinal about it."

"But Monsieur, why delay? Let's act out the play if you're as hungry as I am to do so!"

"Assuredly I am, but why would you let a minnow such as me massage you? Am I not small fry?"

"Monsieur, let me be the judge of how low I can go beneath my rank. And are you still going to pretend that you're so faithful to your wife, when you've just told me that you've sown your seed elsewhere?"

At this I realized I was caught, and so, to my great shame, I let her continue to guide my hand in ways that allowed her to attain the proper "grist" she desired. Beyond the fact that it hardly seemed very gallant to discourage a lady of such noble birth, who seemed so ardently to desire to be satisfied, could I push this Fury away without mortally offending her, and especially without reawakening her suspicions regarding the role I'd played in the escapade in Boulogne? So I let my body do what it wanted—this vile creature (my body, that is) who, in defiance of every law of human decency, never asks for anything (in terms of payment) as its reward for walking into cannon fire and doing whatever I required it to do.

"My good friend," commanded Madame de Montpensier, sighing with pleasure as soon as I was in place, "that's just right, but don't move a muscle! I will do all the moving. Just remain stiff, that's all I require of you."

This was an order I didn't like, but understanding that she was one of those imperious women who only derive their pleasure from themselves, and take all the time in the world achieving it, I resolved to "present arms" as long as it took, only breaking her rules when I needed to do so to keep myself from weakening—which happened from time to time but was not even noticed in the furious activity she was engaged in, which was so stormy and tormented that I could never represent it fairly, my ears buzzing with the sighs and moans that accompanied her passion.

She took no account, of course, of my own enjoyment, which was greatly impeded by my being clothed uncomfortably in my starch collar, squeezed into my doublet and, as the tempest of her pleasure raged about me, too conscious of the Italian dagger that I had strapped on my back and that was sticking into my shoulder blade. And indeed, how I would have loved to penetrate the body of this enemy of the state with that other blade! And so I let my attention wander to the prodigious disorder that covered her bed and chanced to see, emerging from under her pillow, a small written note (which must have sought refuge there, no doubt, to escape the general devastation around it), which I now surreptitiously pulled from its hiding place; giving it a quick glance, I realized that it was in Guise's hand, and that it was precisely the note that the duchesse believed to have been burnt. The idea of taking it, and of the unspeakable peril that would be involved, struck me simultaneously, so much so that I nearly left off my ministrations, but caught myself just in time, yet began sweating profusely at the thought of what I was doing.

As far as I can calculate, it took the duchesse a good half an hour to reach her desired goal, which she did with high-pitched screams you could have heard on the other side of the Seine, accompanied by such convulsions that I thought they'd never end. Ultimately, however, they did, and she opened her steel-blue eyes and shoved me so vigorously away from her that I fell from the bed, whereupon she arose abruptly and left the room.

"Madame," I cried, pretending to be indignant, "where are you going?"

"Only to piss," came her reply.

Which, however uncouth it was, at least gave me time to hide the stolen letter in a pocket of my doublet. Hardly had I done so, however, when she reappeared (with Frédérique on her heels) and seemed positively astonished to see me there.

"What?" she said sullenly. "You're still here?"

"Madame," I replied, "I waited only for you to dismiss me."

"And so I do," she said, extending her hand rigidly to shake mine. "Did you know that the king had the effrontery to say out loud at the court that he would burn me at the stake if I continued to incite the priests against him? Well, Monsieur, since you are his faithful servant, ignoring the interests of the kingdom and your own, tell this poor devil of a king that it's sodomites like him who are burnt at the stake, not me!"

This said, she turned her back on me and sat down at a small desk and began writing furiously, as if she hoped to regain her strength by scribbling.

Frédérique, without saying a word, led me back to the small salon, where I found La Vasselière waiting for me, who said frostily:

"Monsieur my cousin, don't flatter yourself that you have gained the protection or favour of the duchesse by the little service that you rendered her here, since she never asks it of the same person twice, be he noble or low-born. You're alive. That's the main thing. And don't go bragging about these exploits at the court if you hope to remain so."

"Madame," I replied with a deep bow, "I shall remember your wise counsel."

At this she remanded me to the care of Franz, who, to judge by the way he was walking as he preceded me down the stairs, had already submitted to the punishment prescribed by his mistress for having coughed in her presence. Come to think of it, I'd been scarcely better treated than he, and despite his low birth and my noble one, we had ended up being companions in misfortune. Feeling suddenly that I wanted him to understand this, I caught up with him, slipped an écu into his hand and said softly:

"Franz, this is to console you for having been beaten on my account."

"Ah, Monsieur!" said my giant guide, staring at me in utter astonishment. "I thank you! I get more whippings than thanks in here and haven't been paid my wages for six months! Not that money's lacking in this house, but it all goes to the priests, to the soldiers and to the purchase of arms. I thank you, Monsieur!" he continued, looking at me with his benign and naive eyes. "I would have been very sorry if I'd been ordered to kill you!"

"What?" I whispered. "Does that really happen?"

"Oh, Monsieur! A lot more often than my conscience is comfortable with! Though our good chaplain absolves me on each occasion! Even so, I feel remorse from time to time."

I felt infinitely relieved to be able to step outside and to escape from the company of these two pitiless gorgons, and to find Miroul waiting for me, almost devoured by anxiety, given the long hours that I'd submitted to the various forms of inquisition these two women had practised on me. Their religious zeal and partisanship had succeeded in transforming their noble house into a veritable workshop of falsehoods and assassinations. 'Tis true, alas, that, given the examples that stretch from Blanche de Castille to Catherine de' Medici, including the Duchesse de Montpensier, the female of our species is to be feared every bit as much as the male when she applies herself to the affairs of the state, abandoning for these pursuits the sweet arts of love. Certainly, what passed between the duchesse and me in that bed would never merit the beautiful name I've just mentioned, and would drive me more to tears than sighs if I were given to crying. But such is not my temperament, and I'd much rather laugh at this insatiable gluttony that cannot get enough either of men or of sweetmeats.

I practically sprinted back to my lodgings, deaf to all of Miroul's questions, and only deigned to answer them when we were locked in my study. Of course, I omitted my ministrations to the duchesse and the theft of the letter, since I couldn't explain the latter without describing the former and I didn't want to put my Miroul in any danger by sharing with him these secrets. And then, realizing that from the windows of the needle shop opposite I could be shot, not only in front of my door, but in my very study if the shutters were open, I sent Miroul off to enquire whether anyone had rented the shop or the lodgings above it and, if not, to rent them at whatever price the owner proposed.

"Ah, Monsieur!" cried Miroul, his brown eye aglow. "Surely you're not serious! At whatever price the owner proposes! Have you become a papist to be throwing your money away like that? I'll bargain for the place, you can be assured of that! And you'll have it at the best price, as any good, self-respecting Huguenot would insist, even if I have to spend the whole day bargaining with the fellow."

"What a great pretext for spending the day wandering about Paris," I thought to myself, "once the deal is closed."

"So, Monsieur, who would you place in the room upstairs once you've acquired it? You'll need some thread to stitch this rent in your armour, and turn the place into a kind of gatehouse or watchtower for the house."

"I don't know," I replied, impatient for him to leave so I could peruse the letter which I could feel burning inside my doublet.

"But I," Miroul said with an air of great consequence, "have some little ideas which I'll share with you—unless I just keep quiet about them, as you seem to be keeping quiet about the events of this morning at the Hôtel de Montpensier, which have nonetheless left a sparkle in your eyes."

"Why, nothing happened, Miroul," I said, lowering my gaze, "nothing! I didn't hide anything from you! Get on with you now and stop this inquisition!"

And, taking him by the shoulders, I practically pushed him out of the little study, closed and bolted the door, and then shut the window, before daring to pull from my doublet the note from Henri de Guise to Felipe II of Spain, and examine it. It read as follows:

The difficulties and fatigue that Your Majesty has ever faced in the service of the Lord our God, in every land over which you hold sway, are ample witness of the piety and zeal that have produced such extraordinary progress in your royal enterprises. The help that we have received from Your Majesty's liberal hands is yet another proof of your piety and zeal. I cannot resist most respectfully thanking Your Majesty for being so obliging on our behalf. These obligations have created yet another connection between us, and I find myself today more closely engaged than ever before in carrying out Your Majesty's orders with my usual devotion.

I have already informed Your Majesty through your ambassadors and ministers of the happy progress we have made in our affairs. We are firmly resolved to push forward in this arena with all of the ardour that such an enterprise demands: I can say truthfully that nothing will be neglected on our part in pushing the king into an irreconcilable war against the heretics...

The note ended here, but what was stated was certainly enough to compromise the honour of a prince of Lorraine who claimed to be French, but had no shame whatsoever in receiving monies from a foreign sovereign, and submitting to that monarch's orders.

I was wise enough, no matter how hot my blood was boiling, to wait until the morrow and the hour of my usual visit to the king, before whispering to him, as I took his pulse, that I had matters of the gravest consequence to impart to him, and asked him for a private audience. To which he consented almost immediately, needing first to say his prayers in his chapel, and asking me to wait with Du Halde and Chicot in his chambers. Chicot, nose running as usual, said:

"Bloodletter"—which he called me because he knew that I had no use for this procedure—"you're going to find Henri in one of his happiest moods, since he's just engaged with the Huguenots in a game

372

of 'he who loses wins', waging war with them so fecklessly that he couldn't possibly defeat them—a discomfiture that would bring great comfort to Guise—and in the south has signed a truce for one year with Navarre, who, for his part, is not putting a knife to the king's throat."

When I'd taken Henri's pulse, I'd scarcely looked at him in the shadows of his bed curtains, but seeing him now in the light of his chambers, as he exited the chapel, he seemed to be in a good mood, his eyes bright, his face neither grey nor unduly wrinkled and the hand he extended to me quite cool, proof that in this long war of attrition with Guise he seemed to feel that he'd regained some of the ground previously lost in the Treaty of Nemours.

"Siorac, my child," he said almost joyfully, pointing to the stool next to his chair, "sit here, please, and tell me your news. I never feel I'm wasting time listening to you!"

And so I told him of the morning with the Duchesse de Montpensier, omitting nothing except the salacious and nasty words of this Fury, but reserved for later in our discussion the discovery of Guise's note to Felipe, which I was sure the king would be delighted to have in his possession since it was in Guise's own hand and thus irrefutable proof of the duc's felony.

My story delighted His Majesty, except the part in which it became clear that the duchesse had a mole working in his treasury, since she knew he hadn't made a disbursement to me upon my return to Paris.

"Sire," counselled the austere Du Halde, "you should tell your treasurer to sack all of the clerks and hire new ones."

"No, no!" countered the king. "I could never strike so many innocents to punish one guilty party! I'll deal with it some other way. Go on, Siorac."

So I continued my saga, and when I got to the chapter on my abdominal palpations and their grotesque aftermath, the king put his hand to his mouth and laughed like a schoolgirl, while Du Halde and Chicot guffawed good-naturedly, both at my predicament and to see the king so joyful.

"Ah, Siorac," cried the king, tears in his eyes from laughing so hard, "how diverting you are!"

"Diverting perhaps, but divergent from us, since he's just been baptized Guisard in the font of Madame Limp!"

"An accusation without foundation!"

"Ha!" said the king, laughing even harder. "Leave aside the foundation—this bell is supported by two unequal columns!"

"Nay, nay!" cried Chicot between two spasms of laughter. "Poor Siorac is in grave danger of hydrophobia, since he was bitten in his vital parts by the rabid jaws of the Enraged One!"

We all laughed so hard at this last witticism that we were bent double with hilarity, with tears in our eyes and nearly unable to breathe. But when we had quieted down somewhat, I ventured to say:

"Sire, there's an epilogue to this tumultuous farce that seems to me to have some consequence."

At this the king ceased his laughter and stood looking at me attentively with his jet-black eyes. And so I told him in detail about stealing the note from Guise to Felipe II. After which, I took the letter from my doublet and offered it to him, one knee on the ground.

His Majesty seized it and, rising quickly to his feet, began to pace back and forth in his chambers.

"Siorac," he said at length, with a smile, "though it's clearly a sin to steal anything from anyone, I absolve you of your crime with all my heart, in consideration of the service you have done the state in committing this felony. I'd had reports about the river of gold with which Felipe was flooding Guise to refresh him, but now, thanks to you, I have the proof! For this is definitely Guise's handwriting. My cousin the duc is so unsure of his French that he's forced to write out a draft before dictating a letter of any consequence to his secretaries.

And in this draft, observe, Siorac, the weaknesses of his style. The duc thanks Felipe for being so 'obliging' on his behalf—and, a little further on, he writes: 'These obligations have created yet another connection between us.' Guise doesn't know the difference between 'obliging' and 'obligations'. He thinks they're the same thing. Likewise, he writes: 'I cannot resist most respectfully thanking Your Majesty...' This 'I cannot resist' is very gauche. One would say that some exterior force is pushing Guise against his will to thank Felipe for his money!"

"So what should he have written?" asked Du Halde, astonished that the king should give us, on this occasion, a lesson in the French language.

"'I hasten'," corrected the king. "'I eagerly hasten to thank Your Majesty most respectfully.' Eagerness is the only sentiment a subject can feel towards his king, since his sovereign, in this case, seems to be Felipe and not myself. Here's another example of the weakness of his prose: 'piety and zeal' used twice in four lines. Nasty style, Siorac, nasty man. And the content of the note confirms this. What is at stake in this matter? Interests. And what is referred to in the letter? 'God'. 'Piety'. 'Zeal'. One hypocrite writing to another hypocrite, his pen dipped in the font. Guise and Felipe pour over the Lord all the sauces of their base cuisine, and these sauces—God knows that they've turned. That they're rotten. When Felipe conquered Portugal, he had 2,000 monks massacred, whose only sin was to love their country and to try to defend it against his invasion. This is the kind of 'service' to which His Majesty devotes so much 'piety' and so much 'zeal' in his 'royal enterprises'."

"Henri," laughed Chicot, "I'm astonished! To speak of your brother-in-law in such terms! That's a sin!"

"Well," said the king, "I'm Felipe's brother-in-law! I'm the brother-in-law of Mary Stuart! God save me from all these alliances that my mother was so enamoured of! What a lot of problems they've created!

They've all turned against me! Felipe wants to put my niece on the throne when I'm out of the way! And Mary Stuart, from the depths of her prison, is asking me to help her unseat Queen Elizabeth!"

"Sire!" Du Halde pointed out. "Navarre is also your brother-in-law!"

"Ah, but I like *him*! And I'm furious with the Pope for having excommunicated him as a heretic. The Pope has declared him ineligible to wear the French crown. What arrogance this Sixtus V exhibits! He shows none of the modesty and good sense of his predecessors."

"Henri," Chicot added, "did you know that when he was young, Sixtus was a keeper of swine?"

"Well then," replied Henri bitterly, "let him watch over his pigs and I'll watch over mine! What right does he have in my stables? And by what right does he pretend to decide the succession of established kingdoms like France? Let him explain how 'piety' and 'holiness' allow him to give away what isn't his! To take from others what belongs to them! To urge mutiny among vassals and subjects against their sovereign prince! To overthrow the very foundations of the political order!"

It was well said: with force, eloquence and reason. And the most marvellous thing about Henri's tirade was that he spoke in defence of a man against whom he was forced to make war, despite liking him and valuing him above all the other princes in Christendom.

"Siorac, my child," said the king as he sat down and held up his hand to me, "go home and take care of yourself. Once again you've served me well. I will know how to use this letter from Guise for my own ends, if God wills that I should successfully achieve the goals I've set for myself. Tomorrow, my Quarreller will bring you a modest expression of my gratitude."

This last was quite surprising: Henri had never before used Quéribus to send me a message, since I saw the king every day.

My Miroul didn't reappear at our lodgings on the rue du Champ-Fleuri until nightfall; when he did he was quite exhausted, or at least pretending to be, I don't know which, something that suggested that he'd spent most of the day wandering the streets of Paris.

"Ah, Monsieur!" he breathed, asking permission to be seated in my little office. "I had a lot of trouble and toil to find our man! I couldn't sit around, but had to use up a lot of shoe leather to locate him. He's lodging way out on the outskirts of Paris, and to get him to rent out the needle shop I had to work really hard. Without the tongue God gave me, which is as frisky and talkative as any they come, I would never have got him to agree! Ah, Monsieur, the obstinate hypocrite! The stubborn miser! He was a tough nut to crack, and he's more gluttonous than the devil!"

"And so?"

"Well, Monsieur," said Miroul, surprised by my interruption of his narrative, "I was able to get the needle shop for five écus a month."

"That's a lot!"

"That's a lot?!" cried Miroul indignantly. "Is that all the thanks I get for having run around like a madman all day, worn out the soles of my shoes and blistered my feet! Monsieur, am I your secretary or your messenger? A lot, Monsieur? Did you say a lot?! The fellow began by demanding fifteen, and I had to spend an hour knocking him down to five! And you're saying that's a lot, whereas yesterday you said you'd accept whatever he asked, as if you were a papist! Then, not content just to conclude the bargain with this fellow, and get the best price for renting the shop, I went and found you a tenant for the place! Ah, Monsieur, I'm furious! Is this the reward for my pains? You greet me coldly, put on a sour face, get all suspicious as though all I'd done was stroll around, instead of spending the entire day in your service! And then you interrupt my story and, worst of all, you say 'That's a lot!' as dry and hard as a stale crust of bread!"

"I'm sorry, Miroul," I answered, in as conciliatory a manner as I could (though I was still convinced that he'd spent the whole day happily strolling the pavements of Paris and taking in the street life, as he loved to do). "I've been very distracted, swamped by an ocean of worries."

"Which you haven't seen fit to share with me," replied Miroul bitterly, "as though you don't trust me."

"You must be kidding, Miroul," I cried, "I have total confidence in you! But I've discovered some secrets which, if you knew them, would put you in the gravest danger."

"All the more reason," objected Miroul, "that I should share these dangers with you, as I've done for these last twenty years, offering you advice and help—which you used to appreciate!"

"But, Miroul, these secrets do not belong to me!"

"Monsieur," moaned Miroul, standing up with an air of great sadness, "it is you who must be kidding! These secrets are yours because you know about them! You're just spouting false reasons because you no longer trust me as you did before you became so high and mighty and the king's confidant. Well, Monsieur, this is too much and I won't tolerate it! I'm leaving your service! First, you suspect me of wasting my time and make a face at me that would freeze the Devil! Second, you hide things from me. It would be understandable if you'd hide things from Angelina to avoid putting her in danger! But from me, Monsieur, me! Who have been practically your shadow for these past twenty years!"

At this I stepped over to him, took him by the shoulders and, pulling him up from his stool, gave him a powerful hug.

"Ah, Miroul, you're not a shadow, you're a beacon who's lit my way with your wise counsel."

"Which you disregard!"

"Which is always wise, even if I don't always follow it. Ah, Miroul, don't leave me! What would I do without you and all the scrapes and difficulties I get myself into?" I continued in this vein even though I pretended a degree of alarm I didn't exactly feel, knowing full well that he wasn't going to leave our household, given how much affection he felt for me and I for him. "My Miroul," I continued, "other than Madame my wife, who in this house holds a higher position, or is closer to me than you? Aside from being my secretary and majordomo, aren't you my friend and practically my brother?"

"What a shameful *captatio benevolentiae*," countered Miroul, though with a softer tone and as though calmed. "What is a brother from whom one hides so many things?"

"Well, tonight I'm going to think about how much I can tell you tomorrow, though I can't now promise to tell you everything. Does that satisfy you?"

"It satisfies me in proportion to your confidence. But, Monsieur, don't you want to know who I found to rent the needle shop?"

"Of course!"

"Mérigot."

"What, my assassin?"

"*Ipse.** Monsieur, he loves you so much for having saved his neck from the noose that in his devotion to you he'd walk right into the jaws of death."

"But will he leave his post as ferryman on the Seine?"

"Well, his post has left him! He fell from the mast of his boat and broke his left leg, and since it didn't heal properly he now hobbles about with a limp. So he's out of work."

"How much does he want?"

"All the gold in Peru: five écus per month for him and his wench to live on, and two arquebuses, so his wench can be loading one while he's firing the other."

"Five écus," I laughed, "is a lot! Ah, Miroul did you have to put me to such trouble for such a miserable little sum?"

---

* "The very one."

There was a knock on the door, and, at my invitation, Angelina appeared, looking very graceful in her nightgown, her blonde hair cascading over her round shoulders and her sweet doe's eyes looking at me with their usual candour.

"Monsieur my husband," she said, "what are you doing up so late? If your business is concluded, please don't delay any longer. Your bed is yearning for you!"

9

As the king had announced, Quéribus came to see me the following morning, not on horseback, but instead in his carriage, in which, to my surprise, he requested entry into my courtyard. Once inside, he had me close the gates to the street, and, having greeted me—and even before we embraced—he said, with a certain amount of pomp, that he had a small chest to give me on behalf of his king, and asked where he should have it brought.

"But Monsieur my brother," I said in surprise, "just bring it into my little study and place it on my desk!"

I meant the small secret cabinet where I'd placed the king's previous gift of the beautiful comfit box. At this, a robust lackey, dressed in Quéribus's brilliant livery, brought the coffer quickly into the study. It was about as long as my forearm and as wide as half its length, but beautifully worked in polished wild cherrywood, with hinges and fastenings in gilded bronze, representing women whose faces and breasts were visible but whose bodies faded into the bronze work. The handle on top represented a naked couple, who held each other in a close embrace, the man on top and the woman beneath him, so that when you grasped the handle, your palm touched the man's back and your fingers his obliging companion.

"Here's the key to the chest," announced Quéribus, with great ceremony. "But before I give it to you, and you put it to use—which you must not do in my presence—His Majesty wished me to inform you that he would have elevated your rank to baron had he not feared bringing the wrath of Guise down upon your head, and so, having by necessity to delay this honour until less troubled times, he begged you to receive from his hands this present, which he would have made less modest if the war had not so depleted his treasure. Monsieur chevalier," Quéribus continued, giving me the feeling that he was here more as herald and messenger of the king than as my brother-in-law, "I am your humble servant, and beg to take my leave of you."

"Well, my brother," I objected, as I placed the key in the pocket of my doublet, "don't rush off! Stay and dine with us, I beg you!"

"Monsieur chevalier," said the baron with all the stiffness that protocol required, "I thank you a thousand times and shall return here at eleven."

And then, without a hug or kisses, he made a deep bow, and, as he did so, I could see that he was wearing the collar of the Order of the Holy Spirit, which the king had conferred on him on 1st January 1584, but I'd never seen him wear until now.

Having accompanied him to his carriage to say goodbye, I passed Miroul, who announced that his missions had been successful and that he'd received the key to the needle shop from its owner and given it to Mérigot with orders to move in this very day.

"Miroul," I whispered in his ear, since the chambermaids who were cleaning our lodgings were buzzing around us like a swarm of bees, "follow me. You'll no longer accuse me of hiding things from you. And at the same time I'll show you what the king has given me."

"Ah, Monsieur," gasped Miroul, once we'd entered my study and closed the door behind us, "what a beautiful chest... one that," he added with a knowing smile, his finger running across the sculpted handle, "matches much more closely the disposition of him who receives it than that of him who gives it!"

I took from my pocket the beautifully worked and finely chiselled key, which was also made of gilded bronze, and unlocked the chest and threw open the cover. Well, I can only say that the king of the fairies, who, it is said, possesses a treasure of 25 million, could not have been happier than I was at the sight of all of these écus heaped in shining profusion against the black silk lining of this golden chest. With tremulous hands and scarcely able to breathe, I immediately began counting this treasure, assisted by Miroul, who, though normally so articulate and voluble, was silent as the grave. Neither of us had ever set eyes on such an enormous quantity of money since the day we had counted the plunder gleaned from the child murderer on St Bartholomew's eve. But here it seemed like we'd never finish the job, and the top of the desk was entirely covered with piles of coins, as we doubled then tripled the size of each stack, and still couldn't seem to exhaust the chest's contents. And although one never tires of counting one's own money, I was ultimately exhausted by this delicious labour, and my eyes dazzled by its brilliance.

But my astonishment hadn't yet reached its zenith. At the bottom of the chest I found a small sack of black leather, tied with golden thongs, and upon opening it I discovered three diamonds of the most beautiful purity, one of them surpassing in size the one that the Duc d'Épernon had offered me as payment for having cured the cankers in his throat, and two others that seemed to me nearly as large the first. The jeweller on the Pont au Change later offered me 1,500 écus for the first, and 1,000 for each of the other two. And although the total value of the coins surpassed 10,000 écus, a sum that surpassed the value of all my wealth, and made my temples throb for joy, the present of gems, though less of less consequence, I found incredibly moving, since the king, whom I'd told about the ring that Épernon had offered me and that had so delighted Angelina, had remembered this story and, in his customary generosity and benevolence, clearly wished to embellish the beautiful hands of my beloved with these new shining jewels.

That evening, after I presented this gift to my Angelina, I took Miroul aside in my little study, and provided him with the complete story of the adventures that I'd had, with but two exceptions: my travels from Paris to Boulogne with Alizon, which I'd happily enjoyed but suffered for in my conscience, and the morning's sport with the Duchesse de Montpensier, which I'd not enjoyed in the least but had in no way troubled my conscience.

Miroul listened to all of my adventures, his varicoloured eyes focused intently on mine with the worried and anxious expression of a mother (though we were the same age); and, when I'd finished, he immediately thanked me for having the confidence in him I'd displayed, and then said:

"Well, Monsieur, how many dangers you've been exposed to, and still are as we speak, for we know that Guise is trying to instil terror into every one of the king's allies in order to force them to quit his service, and surely they cannot doubt that you're among his most faithful servants, and are certainly planning your demise. So you're living on borrowed time, and we must be on guard day and night. During the day, you risk being shot in the street or being drawn into a fight, or getting knifed in a crowd. At night there's the danger of an assault on your lodgings, as there always is in Paris, without the watch or the royal guards ever seeming to arrive on time. So, as we did in Mespech, we must fortify your lodgings so as to be able to repulse such a nocturnal attack."

"But Mérigot is guarding me and is posted at the windows of the needle shop."

"Mérigot might sound the alarm and delay the assault for a while. But one man with an arquebus cannot do more than that. Monsieur, you need to raise the wall of your courtyard above ladder reach, since any miscreant could scale it. Put some corbels in the wall, and some slits so that you can fire on anyone trying to put an explosive device in front of your gate. Reinforce the shutters in all the windows that look out on the street. Double the thickness of the doors and plan some secret escape routes for Angelina and your children and all the servants."

"Secret escape routes!" I said, amazed.

"Well, Monsieur, we saw this only too well during our flight through the city on St Bartholomew's eve. The strongest house is only a mouse-trap when you can't escape from it through a secret passage!"

"Miroul," I laughed, "your imagination's run away with you! How on earth are we going to construct a secret door out of here when all our doors give onto the rue du Champ-Fleuri?"

"Monsieur," replied Miroul with great pride, "I've always thought that what you consider my biggest fault—that is, my delight in strolling around—is in fact my greatest asset."

"What do you mean?"

"Having observed that our neighbours on the right of the rue du Champ-Fleuri do not have a carriage gate giving onto our street, I realized that they must have one at the back of the house, exiting onto the rue du Chantre, which is parallel to this one. So, one day when you sent me to deliver a message—a task well beneath my station, as you know, but one that I was weak enough to agree to—I took it upon myself to explore the rue du Chantre and verified that our neighbours' courtyard and stables give onto that street."

"But this neighbour is a Guisard and would never allow us to flee, if necessary, through his house and courtyard!"

"This neighbour, however," Miroul pointed out, "is old and infirm, and planning to retire to the country, and hopes to sell his house in Paris…"

"Ah, Miroul! You're my eyes and ears, the first as precious as the second! But how on earth did you discover all of this?"

"But you know very well, Monsieur—by strolling around!"

Having landed this blow, Miroul fell silent, his lids half closed, a half-smile on his lips and having a modest air about him of one whose merits have finally been recognized.

"Go on, Miroul," I said gravely, but feeling dumbfounded by his astuteness, though he'd exhibited it at my expense.

"This would a very judicious use of your 10,000 écus," observed Miroul. "Buy this house anonymously, install Giacomi there and then engage a mason from Mespech to cut a secret passage between the two houses."

"Miroul, that's incredibly ingenious! You're more a mentor than a secretary! And I shall be forever grateful for the way you keep your eyes as open as your tongue is eloquent. From now on I swear that you can stroll to your heart's content! I won't stand in your way. And the only row you'll hear will be from Florine."

"Which is quite enough row for anyone to put up with," he laughed.

That evening, Quéribus and Catherine joined us for supper, and knowing that my sister would put on her finest gown, even for visiting her family, I suggested to Angelina that she purchase a new gown with the proceeds from our recent compensation to go with her new jewels.

"The king," said Quéribus, after we'd supped our fill, "is more liberal than any king in history. He seems to feel an almost irresistible impulse to give what he has, an impulse that some find strange, but that, for my part, I find marvellous and rare. I remember when I was with him in Poland—"

"Far from me!" broke in Catherine.

"Alas! Far from you, my dear!" echoed Quéribus. "And very sad to be so, not yet knowing whether the Baron de Mespech would give me your beautiful hand!"

"Monsieur," cooed Catherine, "you always say things I love to hear. And, as for me, believing that acts should always follow one's words, I very much hope that I should always be the only one in your heart and in your bed."

"Madame my wife," said Quéribus, though he blushed, it seemed to me, at this implicit faith, "you cannot possibly doubt it. 'Twould be to question my faith! But let me continue. When Henri was crowned king of Poland according to the custom of the church of St Stanislaus in Cracow, during the interminable rites and ceremonies that were unfolding, the king—clothed in his heavy robes and seated on his throne waiting to be anointed and to receive the sceptre and the globe—watched as his turbulent and magnificent subjects placed before him some rich, golden vases, full to overflowing with coins bearing his effigy: a gift from the Polish people to their king who had come from France. And seeing these vases, but not understanding a word of what was being said around him in a language entirely foreign to him, Henri, as he told us later, was seized, and almost tortured, by a frenetic desire to stand up and grab handfuls of these coins and throw them to the immense crowd of nobles and dignitaries who were attending his coronation. But he decided to resist this temptation for fear that it might mortally offend his new subjects, and cause them to consider him a scandalous madman; however, he had to exert such great pain and labour to remain seated and immobile that, despite the terrible cold in the church of St Stanislaus, in this month of February, he began perspiring profusely from head to foot, and huge pearls of sweat could be seen dripping down his forehead and flowing down his cheeks. Of course, those of us gentlemen who had accompanied him and who, though warmly dressed, were shivering with cold, believed that he was having a seizure when we saw how pale and sweaty he was, and were immensely relieved when, in the sacristy, where Henri withdrew after the ceremony, he explained to them the cause and motive of his indisposition, as if it were a commonplace."

"Well now," said Catherine, "that's very beautiful! Liberality becomes a king and whoever displays such generosity," she added, looking at Quéribus, "becomes, to a certain extent, a king in his own little kingdom and will be beloved by his subjects."

I frowned a bit at this statement, which I found a little too pointed, and unjustly so, since Quéribus was never stingy in dressing and bejewelling his wife. But, alas, my little sister Catherine was too haughty not to take advantage of such occasions to bite and scratch.

My dear friend L'Étoile, who was aware of everything that was happening in the capital at the time, from the deaths of octogenarians to the details of all the Parisian executions, likes to tell me I'm rather hazy with my dates, but I think it was in November 1586 that I was approached on the Pont Saint-Michel by a lady, who led me to a carriage nearby. After I climbed in, the valet closed the curtains so that I could hardly see a thing through the gloom within the carriage, but immediately recognized the melodious English accent of Lady Stafford, who said:

"Monsieur chevalier, you have so faithfully served your king and my queen in the affair of Navarre's letter that, if I could, I would like to serve your private and personal affairs. Have you heard of Babington?"

"Not very much, but what I've heard is not good."

"Well, this Babington is a young madman, who conspired with six other zealots to assassinate Queen Elizabeth and free Mary Stuart from her prison in the Tower. This plot was planned to coincide with the invasion of England by Guise and Felipe II. Fortunately, Babington, his six friends and the three Jesuits who were behind this plot, were all arrested, tried and executed on the twentieth of September. One of the Jesuits was named Samarcas."

"Good lord!" I shouted joyfully. "But what about Larissa?"

"She was shut up in a convent and has been named by Walsingham as a co-conspirator in Samarcas's plot."

"Well," I cried, "I don't believe a word of it! She's half-crazy and Samarcas was too astute to dare involve her in anything serious."

"Except as an unwitting tool," replied Lady Stafford, "and, unwitting or no, it's all the same thing to Walsingham, who's got the instincts of a bulldog. Once he's sunk his teeth into the flesh of a conspirator only Her Majesty can make him let go."

"But My Lady, couldn't you write to Queen Elizabeth and explain things?"

"Certainly I could," she replied, placing her hand on my forearm in sympathy, "but Walsingham receives all of my dispatches, and he is so fanatically devoted to his mistress that he likely wouldn't show her any letter of mine in which I was pleading the cause of Mademoiselle de Montcalm, who is a confirmed Catholic, and therefore would likely as not have supported the assassination plot."

I had no response to this, and my temples began to throb and the sweat drip down my back, due to both the anxiety I felt and my frustration at my inability to act.

"And what if I were to hurry to London and request an audience with the queen?"

"You'd still have to get by Walsingham, who's already learnt that you're the son-in-law of Montcalm, so you wouldn't get anywhere."

I could think of no answer to this and, feeling very downcast at the nearly insurmountable obstacles that seemed to bar my path, I began to imagine the wall that separated me from Larissa, and could almost hear her plaintive voice as she surrendered to years of captivity—or, worse, the scaffold and the tortures that were inflicted on traitors, which, from what I'd heard, were even worse in England than here.

However, as my eyes adjusted to the darkness inside the coach, I noticed a look that her lady-in-waiting threw at Lady Stafford, which seemed so pregnant with meaning and so conniving that it led me to surmise that they'd only cast me into my present despair in order to lead me insensibly to do what they wanted. "Well," I thought to myself, "these English ladies with their clear eyes and their musical voices are craftier than one would suspect at first glance! Indeed, I'll wager that, however noble and beautiful she may be, Lady Stafford is as politically savvy and acquainted with the affairs of state as her husband the ambassador, and that this lady-in-waiting beside her is not just a glorified chambermaid! I'd swear that there's some bargain being hinted at here that could well serve my own ends as much as it serves the English crown. Let's see what we can find out!" I thought. "If what they want does not thwart the interests of my king, but helps him as well in some way, why not see where it takes me?"

"Madame," I said, turning to look the lady directly in the eye, "counsel me in this predicament. I will obey you, knowing full well that you would never ask me to betray my king."

"I would never dream of such a thing!" she gasped, this time in French, her accent adding to her natural charm. "I could never stomach such a thing! But my suggestion does have a connection with your king's business, as your French finesse has already discerned. We know, Monsieur chevalier, that your master will soon send a special ambassador to my queen, in the person of Monsieur Pomponne de Bellièvre, to plead for Mary Stuart's life and try to prevent her execution. May I ask what the king thinks of this Pomponne?"

"My Lady," I replied coldly, "you're asking me to reveal information about the government of this kingdom that I cannot honourably impart, however much I may dislike this Pomponne fellow."

"Monsieur," she soothed, placing her hand on my forearm and leaning gracefully on my shoulder, her long neck bending towards me to look up at me more closely, "your point of honour is too delicate. You've reacted too quickly. Allow me to take up my cards and replay them in a way that will take account of your sensitivity."

I could not help smiling at this figure of speech, which struck me as much more English than French, and replied:

"As you wish, My Lady."

"Monsieur," she continued in her fluty, sing-song French, "I'm going to put my cards on the table and turn them over. I have reason to believe that your king does not like Monsieur Pomponne de Bellièvre, that he makes fun of his doltish eloquence and calls him 'Pompous Pomponne', that he believes he's Catherine de' Medici's creature and doesn't trust him, believing him to be secretly an agent of the League. Are my cards good, Monsieur?"

"As far as I can tell, yes."

"I also believe," said Lady Stafford, "that the king has no choice but to send Monsieur de Bellièvre to London. First, because Mary Stuart was his sister-in-law. Second, because the League would scream bloody murder if he didn't! But…" Here she broke off and squeezed my arm hard, looking at me searchingly with her blue eyes; then she continued, "But if Mary Stuart were to be condemned and executed, the king of France would make no effort of any kind to save her…"

"Well now!" I thought, lowering my eyes and falling silent for a long time. "That's the essence and substance of this business completely exposed in a single sentence. All Queen Elizabeth wants is to be assured of Henri's neutrality if Mary Stuart were condemned." Now I had a thousand reasons for believing that the king nursed very little tenderness for this princess, who was from the house of Lorraine on her mother's side, a cousin of the Guises, a fanatic papist, an idol of the League and a friend of Henri's worst enemies. What's more, Henri was far too occupied here in France with Guise and Navarre to be able to attempt any action across the Channel. But I realized I had a strong interest in not showing my cards right away, for I undoubtedly had the information these ladies desired but did not know what they were prepared to offer in return.

"My Lady," I proposed, after some hesitation and in the most circumspect tone, "this is a question that I must ask the king directly to be certain of his answer."

"Well then, Monsieur chevalier," replied Lady Stafford with a kind of ebullient gaiety in her voice and look that suggested that she was very happy with our interview, "let us make a few suppositions together, if you will. Let's suppose the king answers in the way we hope: that he wants to communicate his position privately to our queen; that he dispatches you for this purpose in the retinue of Monsieur de Bellièvre; that the queen, after the official communications given by my official ambassador, sees you in secret and hears from your mouth the assurances that I've just suggested. Don't you think that you'd then be in a remarkably strong position to serve the interests of your king, of my queen and of whatever private concerns you may have in this matter?"

"My Lady, there are a lot of 'ifs' in your proposal!"

"But all of them depend only on the first principle! So if, Monsieur, the king sends you to London, then all the rest of the 'ifs' will become deeds rather than guesses and cannot help but be realized! Monsieur, before leaving for London, you must come see me at the Maréchale de Joyeuse's salon, where, starting today, I'll be going every afternoon to bore myself to death!"

This said, she extended her gloveless hand, which I seized without kissing, instead looking at My Lady Stafford with delight for having unburdened my mind of this grave circumstance, and left me free to admire her beautiful Venetian-red hair, her imperious, yet oddly sweet look, her chiselled features, the dazzling pink glow of her skin and the pout which seemed naturally to round her lips. Finally, I said:

"My Lady, may I respectively and humbly suggest to Your Ladyship that this is not the way she last parted from her humble servant when he had the honour to be at her side in this coach."

To which Lady Stafford looked at me wide-eyed, unsure whether to laugh or to scold, and replied in English:

"Oh, you Frenchmen! Jane! Did you hear that?! This man is asking for a kiss! How impertinent! How mad! How French!"

"My Lady," smiled Jane, "after all, the man is well born and the son of a baron. And I've heard it said that his mother came from a very ancient family. And you know Her Majesty herself is very sweet to her servants, and teases her ministers, and goes so far as to kiss old Walsingham, who to my mind is remarkably ugly."

All of this was spoken in front of me as if English were completely incomprehensible to me, and they continued their disputation for a full ten minutes as the two weighed the pros and cons of the morality of such a "gift", and finally decided that the "pros" had carried the day, after which the kiss was ultimately granted—with, I'm happy to say, a good deal of ardour, since Her Ladyship never did things half-heartedly once she'd made up her mind.

The king nearly threw his arms around me when I reported this conversation to him the next morning.

"Ah, my good Siorac!" he cried. "It's Providence who always seems to put you right where you need to be! I've been worried about what this Pompous Pomponne would say to my cousin Queen Elizabeth, given that he takes his orders more from my mother than from me, and leans towards the League like a weeping willow over a muddy pond! He's a poor, snivelling braggart, who gossips like 100,000 chatterboxes. Ah, my good Siorac, I can already hear his pious, erudite ejaculations in London on behalf of Mary Stuart, whom I could tolerate well enough when she was the wife of my poor brother François, but whom I now abhor since she married the assassin of her second husband after having been complicit in his murder! She's a madwoman, and dared to write to Mendoza that she was bequeathing her kingdom of Scotland and her right to the English throne to Felipe II! Good heavens! Can you imagine more abject treachery? Her religious zeal has so entirely blinded her that she has delivered the valiant English people to the Spanish inquisitor!"

Here Chicot opened his mouth to voice one of his silly witticisms, but Henri raised his hand to shut him up and continued his monologue:

"When all is said and done, Mary Stuart is a Guise, a rebel and a traitor to her queen, just as Guise is to his king. Siorac, if you will consent, I propose to send you to London in the retinue of Pompous Pomponne. You will be his interpreter in the English language."

"But sire," cautioned Du Halde, "you've already ordered Hébrard to fill this function and he's packing his bags!"

"Then he'll unpack them!" laughed the king. "He's suddenly going to fall ill! I can sense it! I wish it! Within the hour, he's going to start feeling poorly and complain bitterly of his malady! Did you hear me, Du Halde? And please distribute 200 écus to the poor fellow to help with his cure. Let him keep to his chambers! He should not so much as take a step outside! Chicot, go wipe your runny nose! Siorac, off you go to London, and don't for one second trust my ambassador. Do you know his name?"

"Sire, isn't it Monsieur L'Aubépine de Châteauneuf?"

"The same. He's a bungling mischief-maker. He's in cahoots with the League. He's trying like the Devil to free Mary. Elizabeth communicated her displeasure with him through Lord Stafford, whom I greatly esteem, and to whom I'll *not* report your carryings-on with his wife in her carriage, Siorac, you devil!" And then, abruptly changing his tone, he added, "Is it not amazing that I can't even exile the prickly Aubépine to his estate without the League getting up in arms about it, and Guise sending me threats! Heavens! The knave has me by the throat and is practically strangling me!"

And, in a trice, Henri had switched from wild happiness to his most choleric disposition, turning pale, frowning, his dark eyes shooting sparks. Clenching his fists, he began walking back and forth across the room, casting mistrustful and suspicious looks every which way.

"Du Halde," he barked, "take these écus to Hébrard; and you, Chicot, go wipe your nose in my antechamber."

Stung to be thus dismissed from this saint of saints, but even more upset to see a return of the king's dark mood, they withdrew.

"My son," said Henri, taking my arm and inviting me to walk with him as he had done with the Cardinal de Bourbon, but this time with great seriousness, "what I have to confide in you is destined for your ears only, and for those of my cousin, Queen Elizabeth." And thereafter he gave me very precise directions in a voice lowered to a whisper (as if he feared that the tapestries in his chamber had ears, though these hangings were examined inch by inch every single day). And if some of the things he told me did not surprise me in the least, since his earlier monologue had prepared me for them, his final recommendation (which I will not relate here, since I want Queen Elizabeth to be the first to hear it in my account) left me almost dumbstruck, so unexpected and redoubtable was the secret imparted to me, and so much did I feel its burden on my fragile shoulders (whose adjacent head would be so easy to lop off), given the very humble rank Fortune had assigned me and how very close I was being brought to the great and powerful of this world.

Of course, I knew that kings often place more trust in their barbers than in their noble ambassadors, and that Henri, to return to him, had often used the venerable Dr Marc Miron to carry messages that he never would have trusted to the queen mother or Pompous Pomponne, or to any of his ministers. But I nevertheless stood there, stupefied and trembling to think that I was the one he'd chosen among all of his subjects (none of whom, it's true, had such easy access to him as I did) to be the means of his most secret project, which even Guise, had he learnt of it, would have termed monstrous, since it so thoroughly contradicted the politics this arrogant vassal had thought to impose on his master, but to which the king paid only lip service, while secretly despising and refusing to obey this ugly pretender from Lorraine.

Meanwhile, as I took my leave of Henri and left the Louvre, I began to regain my courage, telling myself that Guise's politics aimed at nothing less than the total extermination of the Huguenots—and already some of the most zealous of the League's supporters were writing tracts that argued that they hadn't finished the job begun on St Bartholomew's eve—and that in this work I was about to do, I was serving both my prince and my people, helping to thwart these bloody projects, especially since I'd always had, and would always maintain, a frightful horror of all kinds of persecution, and had always professed, like Henri himself, who has more intelligence and humanity than the entire Guise family put together, this inviolable axiom: *fides suadenda, non imperanda.**

Immediately after my midday meal, I hurried over to Madame de Joyeuse's salon, where, after listening stoically to her whining jeremiads on the excesses of power, riches and glory that the king lavished on her sons, I finally saw the Venetian-red hair of Lady Stafford appear across the room, and managed to move towards her gradually and as if accidentally, with an eye out for any Guisards who might be present. Luckily there were so many people amassed here that I could "bump into" Lady Stafford without seeming to have sought her out, and manage a quick conversation on a window seat. Speaking in English and so softly that I could scarcely hear her, she said:

"So, Monsieur, you're on your way. Is your message of a satisfactory nature?"

---

* "Faith must be obtained by persuasion and not by coercion."

"Indeed so! Beyond anything you dared hope!"

At this I saw her complexion redden and her body shudder so visibly that you would have thought she'd just seen a man enter the salon whom she was greatly attracted to—so much did the great affairs of state that she was managing displace and replace in her the feelings normally devoted to love.

"Monsieur," she said, "you have an eye for jewels. Do you see this ring I'm wearing? Can you describe it for me?"

"Yes, of course! It's an oval onyx stone with a heart-shaped ruby at its centre flanked by two pearls."

"When you arrive in London, you are to obey the orders of the person, be it a man or a woman, who is wearing this jewel."

"I will not fail to do so. My Lady," I continued, "may I, as well, hope to be as well satisfied in my own affairs as you are?"

"I hope it may be so," she replied, closing her eyes. "But I can promise nothing, since Walsingham is so harsh and obstinate."

And at this, she extended her hand for me to kiss. Though utterly crestfallen inside, I managed to smile, just as I would with the five or six other noblewomen to whom I would subsequently play the gallant—not out of any desire on my part, but rather to pull the wool over their eyes. I also wanted that smile to convince Lady Stafford that only her charms had led me to her.

When I thought over her last sentence, which had fallen like a heavy stone on my heart, I was persuaded that I needed to clip the wings of my hope of delivering Larissa from her jail, and though I had thought perhaps to inform Giacomi of the situation and bring him with me to London, I now decided against such a plan, not wishing to expose him to the cruellest of disappointments if I failed. So it was that I was accompanied only by Miroul, who was extremely vexed not to be in on the secret that necessitated this trip, but nevertheless greatly excited to be crossing the Channel and to be able to visit the great city of London, where, I had no doubt, he would be very excited to stroll about.

Not that our passage was easy. Quite the contrary. I'd never seen any sea other than glimpses of the Mediterranean from the hills of Montpellier, and that was in summer when she presented her most serene and happy visage. The body of water that separated us from England, however, seemed to me excessively tempestuous, grey and windy on the November day we set sail at daybreak from Calais, battered by a glacial rainstorm, in a great confusion of waves so violent as to make you cough up your guts right off, and a wind so bitter that it ripped one of our sails right in two. Things were so bad that after only an hour at sea we had to return to port and venture out only the next day, when the violent winds had died down a bit, but were now blowing directly against our course. As a result, we had to "tack" most of the way across, and so it took us no less than five hours to reach Dover. By land, this voyage would have been much faster and a thousand times more gentle on our intestines, which suffered so horribly on this occasion that Bellièvre, seeing the pitiable state of his retinue—and of their horses—upon our arrival, and being himself surprised at the quince yellow of his complexion as he looked in the little mirror he always carried with him (being so enamoured of his majestic appearance), decided we should rest for two days before heading out onto the highway from Dover to London.

The prickly Aubépine, as Henri called him, seemed a good deal less prickly than simply weak-willed and hapless in his judgements when he received Bellièvre and his retinue in the great salon of his embassy, being one of those simple-minded Frenchmen who, when abroad, are constantly boasting about France and Paris, openly denigrating the country they're living in and speaking its language poorly and with an atrocious accent, as I could tell immediately from the two or three English words that escaped him.

To hear him tell it, we could expect only trouble and disappointments in London. It was a very small city, occupying only the north bank of the Thames, and only half as grand as Paris, lacking the rich shops, the delicious meals, the healthy climate, the beauty of the women and the accommodating manners of the French capital. Of tennis courts there were but few, the players mediocre, the balls (except those imported from France, of course) lacking proper bounce. The English pastimes of bowls, archery, cockfighting and bear-baiting were all sad affairs. Aubépine warned, with special insistence, against setting foot in any English theatres such as Burbage's in Shoreditch or his son's in Blackfriars. Besides the fact that the plays were in English and insufferably silly, these theatres were known to be houses of ill repute where you could catch the plague or syphilis from a prostitute or by sodomy (the roles of women being played by boys).

"Avoid Southwark like the plague," he added, "which is a neighbourhood on the other side of the river from London, where brothels flourish, along with women whom I wouldn't touch with the end of my cane! And for the love of God, don't go sticking your nose into any of the city taverns, because someone is sure to pick a fight with you, since you're French, and we're greatly detested by the common people because we are of the Holy Roman religion and are all suspected of taking part in plots against the queen. When you let rooms and lodgings, as you must, since I cannot receive you all—only Monsieur de Bellièvre here—at the embassy, keep a sharp eye on your purse and don't go cavorting with the chambermaids: they'll fleece you like lambs. And finally, try to go out in groups, so you'll be able to defend each other if attacked."

I had no interest in this last piece of advice, wanting to get to know the English in London and not stay with the French, whom I already knew all too well from our contacts at court. Also, believing that it would be much easier for my secret contact from the queen to reach me directly if I were lodged alone and not surrounded by my compatriots, I gave myself permission to take "French leave"—or, as we would say, "to sneak off like an Englishman", each people being accustomed to attribute to his neighbours the worst of his own habits, as for example the terms for syphilis, which the northern Italians call "the Naples sickness", the French "the Italian sickness" and the English "the French sickness".

And so I took "French leave", claiming that I had a most unfortunate twisting of my bowels that necessitated my departure, and, mounting my horse, followed by Miroul and our packhorse, left the French embassy behind and headed for Whitehall, the most magnificent of the queen's dwellings. Estimating that I wouldn't be able to find lodgings in this wealthy quarter, where rich houses (which had nothing to envy in the most beautiful mansions in the grand'rue Saint-Honoré in Paris) bordered the Thames, I asked my way of an urchin who seemed like some sort of apprentice and who, rather than answering me, asked me where I was from; hearing that I was French, he gave me a terrified look and ran off as fast as his legs could carry him. I had no better luck with a milkmaid, who, when I hailed her, blushed like a poppy and, without a word, turned a cold shoulder.

"By the belly of St Anthony, Miroul," I mused, "could Bellièvre be right? The wenches are icicles in this country!"

"Well, Monsieur," laughed Miroul, "just wait a bit! There's no icicle that won't melt in a hand or a mouth. But ask that young man over there. He looks nice enough!"

"Sir," I said to this fellow, as I slowed my horse to a walk, "I've just arrived from the Low Countries and I'm looking for lodgings in the city."

The fellow stopped, and his face took on a very serious expression, as though I'd just asked him for a state secret. He looked me over in silence from head to toe, then looked at my horse, then at Miroul, then at his mount, then at the packhorse. This done, he remained silent, and I was just about to give up and set spurs to my horse when he said:

"Sir, I understand that you're Flemish. Then you don't have any love for Felipe II."

"None whatsoever."

"Nor the Pope?"

"Nor for him, either."

"Then sir, I suggest you take a room at the Pope's Head Tavern in Cornhill."

"Where, sir, is Cornhill?"

"Follow the Strand, then Fleet Street. Continue east behind St Paul's Cathedral. Cross Cheapside and Cornhill is there."

"Sir," I said, doffing my cap, "I thank you and salute you!"

"Sir," he replied, "may God protect you and give you succour!"

"Monsieur," said Miroul as he pulled his horse alongside mine, "I liked that fellow. He reminded me of your uncle Sauveterre."

"You're right! And Sauveterre would have certainly wanted to lodge at the Pope's Head Tavern."

"What does that mean?"

"It means a tavern with the head of the Pope for its sign."

"What, just the head? Do they think they've managed to behead him here, at least in thought?"

"I believe so."

And I had good reason to think so, knowing that the Anglican Church and the English queen had no more ferocious enemy than Sixtus V, who, with even more bitterness than his predecessor, had relaunched against them the Jesuits, Guise and Felipe II... and even, from what I'd heard, given his explicit blessing to the immense fleet that the Rex Catholicissimus was building in order to invade England, calling this great armada "my daughter".

At Cornhill, where we arrived after a good half an hour's walk, the first thing I saw was the tavern's sign, on which was painted the Pope's head, grimacing, pimply and quite devilish; under his tiara could be seen two diabolical horns and his hair was in the form of serpents. But as the inn seemed to be very presentable and clean, and was constructed of wood, stone and brick, I dismounted and, throwing my reins to Miroul, entered the common room, which also seemed quite clean and was, at this time of day, deserted. The innkeeper, who could have passed for a Frenchman from Provence, so dark was his skin and hair, asked me in rather abrupt tones what I wanted, since he didn't serve bread or wine until eleven o'clock.

"My friend," I replied, "we would like lodgings here for myself, my secretary and our three horses."

"Sir," he said, "who are you?"

"I am a French gentleman," I said, deciding that I must tell him the truth, since he would have to give a truthful report to the provost of London.

"Papist?"

"My friend," I smiled, "would I ask for lodgings here if I were?"

"Papist?" he repeated without a trace of a smile.

"No," I answered, imitating his brevity.

"Do you have the plague?"

"No."

"We'll see about that!" he replied. "Sir, come in here," he continued, preceding me by several paces, and without touching me at all, into a small room where, thank God, a bright fire was burning, since the morning was misty and chilly.

Once inside, he himself left, closing the door on me. My backside was quite sore from the long horse ride, so, instead of sitting down, I went to warm myself before the fire, my hunger increasing at the thought that we'd have neither food nor drink before eleven o'clock.

At length the door reopened and a young, buxom chambermaid entered, as blonde as the innkeeper was brown, but in her manner just as abrupt and cold as he had been.

"Sir," she said, waiting by the door, "please undress."

"What?" I protested. "In front of you?"

"Please undress," she repeated without batting an eye.

This did not please me in the least. But, since I did hope to eat and get some sleep, I consented, half amused, half ashamed to be treated like a pestiferous threat, and ended up putting on Adam's "clothes" in front of a woman who, for her part, without blushing in the least, examined me with great curiosity and very thoroughly in all my parts, telling me to bend over, spread my legs, raise my arms and I don't know what else. After which, still as taciturn as ever, she told me to get dressed, and left the room, no doubt to advise her master that she'd discovered no buboes or other signs of the plague, for the innkeeper now appeared with a register, in which he invited me, with scarcely more civility than before, to write my name, my condition and my religion, as well as my address in Paris and the reason for my visit to England. I had no problem with these precautions, and, indeed, would not change a single one. If only we had such rigorous precautions in Paris and a Walsingham to enforce them. There'd be much less for the king to worry about!

Once Miroul had been examined by the same buxom lass and found to be healthy and hardy, he was free to go and tend to our horses in the stable. Afterwards, he came to join me in my room, which was next to his, to see to my luggage; I gave him a hand with it, but we were so tired and hungry we said scarcely a word to each other, except to ask the chambermaid for some bread and wine—a request that was rudely rebuffed with the phrase "After eleven o'clock!" pronounced as drily as the crust which we so hungered for.

At the strike of eleven, I called the blonde chambermaid and again requested that she bring us some victuals, but was rebuffed a second time, as she threw over her shoulder the words: "In the common room."

We were very surprised, when we went down, to find the room full of fellows seated at the tables, sipping wine and smoking their tobacco pipes, whose smoke, though some physicians in France praise its medicinal properties, seemed to me to provoke coughing and inflamed eyes. We had to cross the entire smoky room before finding a table, a crossing that was not very comfortable since every eye was fastened on us with a suspicious air.

The chambermaid was a long time in coming to serve us, and even though I'd twice asked her that morning for bread and wine, she asked what I wanted. After having repeated myself, she indicated that we had to pay in advance (though it was clear she had not asked this of the others there), and, as I handed her an écu, she looked at it quickly and gave it back as if it were burning her fingers, saying in quite a loud voice that it was French and that she couldn't accept it.

At the word "French" I saw the eyes of the entire company fasten on me like arrows aimed at a target. Of course, I felt very ill at ease to be the object of such malevolence, and, at the same time, almost in danger of perishing from hunger despite the 300 écus in my purse. But after a moment, I reflected that a great merchant city like London must have money-changers, and then, remembering that I'd seen some near St Paul's Cathedral on the way here, I sent Miroul off with five écus that I pulled from my purse. The minute he'd left, however, I regretted having deprived myself of his company and help, given how increasingly menacing my neighbours' looks were becoming.

There were in this assembly of men, who looked better dressed than is the fashion in France, but two wenches, clearly whores, who were heavily made up with rouge and ceruse, and whose breasts were more outside than inside their bodices; they were the only ones not looking daggers at me. One of them, whether because she'd seen the coins I'd taken from my purse, or because the look I'd given her in my predicament was not unfriendly, arose and headed towards me.

But she didn't succeed in this attempt, for, as she was trying to pass between the tables to reach me, legs were stuck out on all sides, causing her to trip and nearly fall, whereupon, realizing the purpose of these obstacles, she frowned and returned to her seat.

My Miroul having returned with "healthy" English money, neither plague-ridden nor papist, the chambermaid came back to our table and rasped:

"It's a penny for a pint of wine."

"Here's tuppence. And the bread?"

"It comes with the wine."

"Now there's a pleasant custom," I thought, "that our Parisians would do well to imitate. Not stingy at all." Then I set about eating and drinking, leaving neither drop nor crumb, momentarily forgetting the general antagonism that was directed at us. But it wasn't long before we were reminded of it, for the thick cloud of smoke that hung over the room made me cough, whereupon my nearest neighbour turned to me and said with a provocative politeness:

"Sir do you object to my pipe?"

At this, I turned round, looked him in the face and, without batting an eyelid, replied calmly and quietly:

"Indeed, sir, I do not."

And though this exchange was followed by silence, I didn't doubt that the tavern was about to become a sort of arena in which the French bears were to be assailed and bitten by a pack of English hounds.

"Sir," said another fellow, rising to his feet and raising his glass, "I beg you to toast with me! I drink to the health of our gracious queen."

"Sir," I replied, leaping to my feet, as did Miroul, and doffing my hat, "I heartily drink to the good health of your gracious queen!"

Somewhat taken aback by this, the fellow sat back down, though I noticed he did *not* raise his glass to his lips. But the looks that came at us from all sides took up where the words left off, and those looks were full of hate and so furious I thought we should soon come to blows, were these English not so conventional in the fashioning of their quarrels, all of their effort going into putting me at fault without putting a foot wrong themselves.

"Is it possible," said another fellow after some moments, "that you're really sincere in toasting Her Majesty's health?"

"I am, sir."

"Perhaps not, sir."

"I am, sir."

"Sir, are you calling me a liar?"

"No, sir."

"Sir," he insisted, "I affirm and declare that you are not sincere in toasting Her Majesty's health, may God protect her."

"May God protect her," came a chorus of all the rest in the common room, who were now as grave and thoughtful as they would be in church.

"Sir," I said, "it's not enough to affirm. You must prove what you say."

At this, a silence fell over the room and the two assailants seemed to lack sufficient munitions in this battle of words, though they were fully armed with hate and determination.

"Chambermaid," I said, taking advantage of this respite, which I knew would be all too brief, "would you call the innkeeper, please?"

"I cannot," she replied, looking daggers at me, "he's gone out."

"Wench," I said, "in his absence you will be my witness of what is said and done here."

"No, sir," came her stiff retort. "I'm here to serve wine and bread, and not to hear or see what's happening between our guests."

At this, several vicious and conspiratorial laughs resounded in the room, which, joined with the absence of the innkeeper, led me to believe that our host was washing his hands of this bear-baiting, his absence keeping him as pure as the driven snow. And I'll wager that Miroul understood things this way too, since, though he'd been sitting across from me up until this moment, he stood up, took his stool and came and sat down by my side behind our table, which was situated nicely in the corner of the room and thus could serve as a kind of rampart between us and the hounds.

These latter had begun to make scolding and threatening noises, though, it seemed to me, they felt restrained by the desire not to break the law. In this regard, they are very unlike the Parisians, who are of such a rebellious and anarchic complexion that there's no law, human or divine, that can restrain them from their disorderly moods. However, I observed, not without some anxiety, that the chambermaid was leaning over a bloke with a very foxy face, and had been whispering something in his ear for quite some time, casting inflamed glances at us now and then. When, after this conversation, the fellows rose, I felt we must expect the worst.

"Sir," he announced in very polished English, "I understand you're in the retinue of the French ambassador who has come to speak to our queen regarding the fate of Mary Stuart."

At this execrated name, cries of rage arose from different parts of the room, and these were followed by a torrent of words so filthy and angry that I cannot repeat them here.

"Sir," I replied, rising to my feet, "it is the ambassador's mission to ask for a pardon for her, but not mine. I am merely his doctor and interpreter."

"And yet, sir," replied this fox-like fellow, "you cannot help, as a member of his party, but desire her pardon!"

"Sir," I objected, "not every Frenchman has the same opinion on this matter. Some think, as I do, that Mary Stuart was involved in the assassination of Darnley and in the attempts on the life of Her Gracious Majesty."

"Sir," he snapped, "how can a papist possibly hold this opinion?"

"Sir," I countered, "I am not a papist—I am a Huguenot."

The foxy fellow smiled at these words and, casting his eyes about those assembled in the room, he seemed to lick his lips at what he was about to say.

"That is, indeed, what you wrote on the registry of the inn. So you're a Huguenot, sir, as I understand you."

"That I am!"

"Sir," he proclaimed after a dramatic silence, "you're lying!"

"Sir," I cried, prey to an uncontrollable anger, which I was attempting to calm as quickly as I could when Miroul placed his hand on my arm, "what allows you to make this accusation?"

"Sir," he hissed, "I affirm that you are a papist wolf in sheep's clothing, and I can prove it! Wench!" he shouted. "Tell us what you saw around this man's neck when he disrobed for your inspection!"

"A medal of the Virgin Mary!" cried she, her charming face twisted in a grimace of hate, and her two hands held heavenwards as if she were reliving the horror of the sight that this idol had inspired.

This said, she seized a pitcher of water on the table next to her and, brandishing it, threw the water in my face.

I ducked.

"Monsieur, our stools!" cried Miroul, seizing his own from under him and holding it out as a shield.

I did the same, while pitchers, thrown from all sides, flew by and hit the table, the stools and the wall behind us.

"Monsieur," said Miroul, "in a moment we're going to have to fight it out."

The din was deafening given the tin pitchers banging about, and the angry shouts of "Traitors!" "Spies!" and even "Regicides!" hurled from every corner of the room. I saw Miroul lean over and check that the knives in his leggings were at the ready, and I checked that my Italian dagger was at hand—and even breathed the Lord's Prayer to myself, in the certainty that the pack of hounds would soon break free of whatever held them back and hurl themselves at us. Strange to say, however, even though I didn't doubt I was going to die, I felt no apprehension whatever, but simply a kind of mute astonishment that my medal, which had so often saved my life on St Bartholomew's day, would now be the certain cause of my death.

Suddenly, the terrible din ceased and, as I peeked out from behind my stool, I saw, standing in the middle of the room and appearing single-handedly to have ordered this silence, a very tall fellow with flaming red hair, which stood out despite the dense fog of smoke in the room. The man was dressed in a black velvet doublet and yellow leggings, cut quite short, as is the custom in England. He wore a yellow cape, unbuttoned and sleeveless, that fell to his boot tops. I judged him to be a gentleman—not so much because of his dress but because of a certain air of nobility and authority he projected, despite the derisive smile that curled his lips. He wore neither dagger nor sword in his belt and held only a silver-tipped cane, with which he tapped the tabletops around him in such a way as to petrify the entire crowd with fear as he passed among them, looking each man in the eye and calling each of them by name with a menacing smile. And, striding through the room, giving little taps to each table as he went, sowing consternation at each one, he arrived in our corner and greeted us most civilly, begging us to be seated, and assuring us that we would suffer no further molestation.

After this, he turned to the crowd with the same smile, something that appeared to freeze his audience with fear, and began to tap his left hand with the tip of his cane; then he said, in a perilously calm and polite tone:

"My masters, how come you to presume to create such a disturbance here? Why, you're rioting, if I'm not mistaken! Do you think you can pluck the feathers of this French cock while I'm not looking?

Is this your version of bear-baiting our French visitors? Throwing pitchers at their heads? Unsheathing your knives? John Hopkins," he said, addressing the fox-faced leader of the pack, "pick up the knife you dropped under your stool when I came in. Do you presume to take into your knowledgeable hands the queen's justice? May God save her!" ("God save the queen!" murmured the assembly in pious response.) "My masters, do you pretend to know *better than I*" (raising his voice on these last three words) "who is a friend of the queen, and who her enemy? Who is a papist and who is not? Who is plotting against her and who is not? Are you policemen? Are you judges? Are you executioners? *Who* is the law of the land?" (He pronounced this word with a quasi-religious emphasis.) "John Hopkins, what have you to say in your defence before I send you off to jail?"

"Sir," stammered John Hopkins as he rose to his feet, "the whole problem is that the innkeeper wasn't here—"

"I couldn't be here," explained the innkeeper, who was now standing near the door, but stepped forward after this accusation by John Hopkins. "As the law requires, I was making my report to Mr Mundane."

At this name, both Miroul and I started, and shot each other looks of utter surprise.

"But," Hopkins insisted, "the problem is also Jane, who got me all upset when she told me that this man who claims to be a Huguenot was wearing a medal of Mary around his neck."

"Wench!" growled the gentleman with the cane, "you gossip too much! Innkeeper," he said, turning to our host, "your chambermaid has too loose a tongue for the public good!"

"She's no longer my chambermaid," replied the innkeeper with some unhappiness, as far as I could judge. "Since her tongue creates public disturbances, she'll no longer work here tomorrow."

"Sir! Sir!" I broke in. "I beg you that there be no such consequence to this business, neither for Jane nor for Hopkins! Neither one could have known that I'm wearing a medal of Mary because my mother, who was a papist, made me swear on her deathbed that I would do so. Sir, once again, I beg you that no one be punished. Jane, pick up your pitchers, which, though dented as they are, can still hold a pint of good French wine, which you're going to serve everyone here at my expense, in order to drink to the health of Her Gracious Majesty."

"Well said and well done, sir!" beamed the gentleman with the cane, who, having made me a deep bow, left so quickly that I wasn't able to ask the question that was swelling my cheeks.

Such is the authority of the law in this country (and in those who represent that law, Mr Mundane being manifestly among the latter) that these people who were about to cut me to pieces began praising me to the skies, as soon as they were assured that I was not an enemy of their queen or of their faith.

It is assuredly a great strength of a country to be able to call on such prompt submission to legitimate authority, a strength that led me to believe that if the armies of Felipe II ever invaded this island, they would have a hard time overcoming the resistance of these English, who are so deeply and fervently committed to their queen. And this is all the more true since they don't sit around in idleness, as I would have occasion to observe, but are busily and industriously working on their defensive systems in London. They had already replaced the longbow ranges on Tassel Close at Bishopsgate with an artillery range, with earthen ramparts set up as targets. There I was able to observe the cannoneers from the Tower of London performing daily exercises to prepare for an invasion. It's a strange spectacle to watch these cannon fired in the middle of the city with a degree of precision that, I'll wager, our French soldiers are far from matching, and those of Spain even further. The noise and disturbance they made every day were proof that England knew that she was now in great peril of being besieged on her island by the enemies of her freedom and her religion.

Our pints of wine duly downed, scarcely had I regained my room before Jane, having knocked on my door, came in, with an austere and contrite air, to present, as she put it, her "humble apology" for having so grievously maligned me by calling me a papist, and, worse, for having lied. She also wanted to offer me "10,000 million thanks" (a phrase I later learnt was frequently voiced by the queen and therefore repeated by her subjects) for having allowed her to keep her place at the Pope's Head Tavern, without which she would have been reduced to famine since she had no family to fall back on. I presumed to beg a kiss from her as the sign of our reconciliation, which she gave me gravely and, I would almost say, religiously, since everything she did, she did with great seriousness, even this caress.

When she'd gone, I threw myself on my bed without bothering to bolt the door, and, exhausted by all the dangers and emotions of the events in the common room, fell quickly to sleep and was prey to a series of calamitous dreams. When I awoke, I was delighted to discover that I was alive, hale and hearty, and only gradually noticed that there was a candle burning on the bedside table that I was quite sure I'd not lit. And then I realized something else, which awakened me completely: sitting comfortably by my bed was an unknown woman, beautifully attired, who, seeing me open my eyes, removed her mask, smiled and, without saying a word, presented her hand, which, when I pressed my lips to it, she pushed hard against my mouth, bruising my lips with her ring—which I recognized.

"Monsieur," she said, "I must leave, and have but a few words to say: today is the twenty-second of November. On the afternoon of the twenty-eighth, my mistress will receive Monsieur de Bellièvre. And at nightfall on the twenty-eighth, I will come here to fetch you so you can meet him."

10

M R MUNDANE, who came to see me the next morning, thanked
me profusely for saving and healing his brother after Samarcas
had wounded him in a sword fight in Paris and begged me to tell him
of the circumstances of his death, an account he listened to patiently,
his blond lashes batting from time to time over his pale eyes, his lower
lip trembling, but with no other sign of emotion.

"I'm amazed," he confided when I'd finished, "that, after his duel
with John, Samarcas had the mad audacity to stick his nose into affairs
in London, where I put spies on his tail—whom, however clever he
thought he was, he couldn't shake. Ultimately, he led us to the Jesuit
Ballard, and Ballard led us to Babington. Monsieur, I'm very sorry
for your sister-in-law, who was, alas, the tool of this devil, without
ever being aware of any of his activities. Her fate is entirely in the
hands of Walsingham, whom you'll meet at the side of the queen on
the twenty-eighth. I am not able to say more: my orders seal my lips
on this matter."

It was then my turn to thank him most warmly for wrenching me
from the teeth of the hounds the day before in the common room.

"Well," he smiled, "it was nothing. As soon as your innkeeper brought
me his ledger and I saw your name, I rushed to your side, fearing the
worst. You see, Walsingham had given orders that I spread a rumour
about the city that Monsieur de Bellièvre had brought with him to
London not only the plague, but a bunch of hired assassins ready to

kill the queen. With this we hoped to paralyse, by means of popular hostility, the two or three spies of Guise who managed to insinuate themselves into Bellièvre's retinue. You were very wise, Monsieur, to part company with them as soon as you'd left the embassy."

"Very wise, perhaps," I agreed, "but very imprudent as well. Of course, my aim was to make myself available, so the queen's envoy could contact me without raising the suspicions of the Guisard spies you mentioned. But the very fact of having escaped their vigilance will have alerted them to the danger I represent, and I'm afraid that when I return to Paris, I'll be more suspect than ever to the Guisards."

"Yes, I thought of that," replied Mundane. "What would you think, Monsieur, if I asked you to leave the Pope's Head and take up lodgings with a beautiful widow, whom people will take for your lover? Our League spies could not fail to see you in her company. Wouldn't such a beautiful companion be reason enough for you to lodge elsewhere than at their inn?"

Dear reader, I realize you are smiling, indulgently I hope, though perhaps in disapproval, at seeing me so frequently sleeping in feather beds in the missions and travels of my adventurous life, but I'm happy to report that there were no sequels to this "affair"—not because I can lay claim to any virtue, which is indeed fragile enough, especially when I'm away from home and city, and even more so when I'm abroad, where it seems less of a sin than when at home, as if the divine and human laws that condemn infidelity suddenly lose their power once the border has been crossed. But Lady T., though very beautiful in her maturity, had reached the age when a woman gives off the last sparks of her feminine enchantments, which are all the more alluring in that they seem like the ultimate victory over death. But she paired this particular seductiveness with a nobility of soul that aspires more to an enduring friendship than to a brief and brutal dalliance. And her resolution not to sacrifice friendship to a passing affair was the first thing she told me upon meeting, and she assured me that whatever little attentions her role obliged her to display in public—smiles, looks, hands held too long and other signs of affection—must cease at the threshold of the lodgings where she received me. I assured her she had nothing to worry about in this respect. So we lived these few days together in good and amicable understanding, very chastely within her walls and very amorously without. I must add that I did not have to constrain myself much to surround her with my attentions and caresses, and was quite sure she enjoyed receiving them, since she played her role with such apparent conviction that I couldn't help feeling she was enjoying the whole thing.

And so I paraded my dalliance with the beautiful Lady T. in every part of London where we could be seen together by Monsieur de Bellièvre and his gentlemen, in such a way as to make sure that our affair was thought real, and gossiped about in infinitely detailed accounts, whose echoes reached Paris, as I shall recount.

I could not have wished for a better guide to London than Lady T., for she knew the city's history and loved it so well that she convinced me to praise it enthusiastically, although I must admit that Aubépine had not been wrong to say that Paris was larger and more populous than its English counterpart. The population of London is about 120,000, whereas our capital counts more than 300,000 inhabitants. Nor did I find London so rich in monuments or, especially, churches, for a large number of them had been destroyed when the monasteries were dissolved and sold by the crown to various rich people, who levelled these gracious chapels to build tennis courts or taverns or simply private houses. It was assuredly a great pity that this iconoclasm reduced churches to rubble and destroyed along with them a great number of works of art.

Which is not to say that St Paul's Cathedral and Westminster Abbey are not magnificent monuments, or that the Tower of London is not impressively spectacular, not to mention the various royal palaces of the queen (who is richer than the French king in this regard, having no less than a good half a dozen lodgings in London alone, as far as I can remember), but they adorn only the western part of the city: the rest, to the east (with the exception of the Tower), is a desert, composed of wooden houses with thatched roofs and sordid slums that have nothing to envy in the wretched abodes of the Faubourg Saint-Germain.

As for the streets, they're everywhere as dirty and putrid-smelling as those in Paris, channelling down their middles the shit and piss from the houses on either side; and as for the water of the Thames, I doubt it's any healthier than that of the Seine, given its odour, or less full of rats and dead animals. At the very least, one can credit the Londoners with more cleverness at drawing water from their river, since I saw, attached to one of the arches of London Bridge, a very ingenious wheel, which was turned by the rising tide and filled a reservoir from which the city could draw its water. As for its contents—I'd fear for my safety if I had to taste it, especially since the tide must make it somewhat briny.

The biggest marvel of the city of London in my opinion is the Thames, which is so wide and deep that great galleons can sail right into the city. This means that the English capital, without having the vulnerability of being a coastal city, nevertheless has every advantage, since it's both an inland city and a port where ships can drop anchor in total security.

Parisians cannot imagine how immense the Thames is, next to which the Seine is but a stream, nor the amount of engineering genius that was required to span it with the famous London Bridge, which boasts no less than twenty-two arches, if I remember correctly. And I do not wonder that it required so many, since the current of the river is so furious that ferrymen and sailors must use great skill when passing under the bridge to avoid their boats being dashed against the piles. Lady T. told me that when the queen travels to Greenwich from her palace at Whitehall, she walks down the steps to the Thames, embarks on her great royal barge, but then disembarks at the steps at the Old Swan before walking along Thames Street to Billingsgate, where she rejoins the boat—all of which allows her to avoid passing under the bridge, since the current is so dangerous there and has caused more than one fatality. Like Her Majesty, most of the English lords use the Thames as the Venetians use their canals, at least when travelling from west to east, as to go by river is much easier and faster than trying to make one's way through the crowded streets.

As soon as I'd set foot in Lady T.'s house, she ordered her tailor to dress me in the style that was all the rage in London, since my doublet and leggings would have immediately identified me as a Frenchman and exposed me to the peril of being beaten by passers-by, so great is their anger at the plots that Guise and the Jesuits have been hatching against their queen. So, twenty-four hours later, I became English, at least in my attire, and was delighted at Lady T.'s efforts to teach me the gait and the deportment of her compatriots. These lessons recalled the way my "little fly from hell" showed me how to move like a woman, since women enjoy playing mother even to their lovers and fashioning them to their own tastes.

Lady T. also convinced me to speak quietly and little, since my accent might give me away: a wise precaution, and one that I immediately forgot when, as we were walking along London Bridge, I saw the disembodied heads exposed along the parapets and walls of the Tower.

"Ah, how horrible!" I exclaimed. "Do they normally display the heads of those they execute?"

"No certainly not!" replied my Lady T. "Only those who have betrayed the queen. The ones you see there are, no doubt, Babington and his henchmen."

I know not what magnet drew me towards them, and as I got nearer I had to place my handkerchief over my mouth and nose so I could examine each of the heads. There were nine in all, and the ninth, clearly recognizable despite the wind and rain that had darkened it, and the work of the crows, was definitely that of Samarcas.

"Ah, My Lady!" I said with vehemence. "That's the Jesuit I told you about, who, while he was alive, hatched more plots and designed more intrigues than any son of the shadows in this world. His body was perpetually on edge, his brain hazy; he was zealous, always in a hurry, bustling about, in turn gentle, imperious, insinuating; a compulsive liar, false as Janus, without a trace of humanity or morals; he had a cross around his neck and a sword in his hand, dispatching his neighbours with a clean conscience and always in the name of God."

"Hush!" cautioned Lady T., taking me firmly by the arm and dragging me away. "You're talking too much and too loudly. Someone may have heard you!"

And, indeed, five or six rowdy young workmen who were hanging about, pushing and shoving each other, now came towards us. One of them, a large, fat and brazen fellow, at least six feet tall, blocked our way and asked my Lady T. with utter insolence:

"Madam, is the man a foreigner? A Frenchman?"

"He is neither," replied my companion, without blinking an eye. "He is Welsh and, alas, poor thing, a lunatic. He was talking to that traitor's head and expected it to answer him!"

And taking my cue from her, I began rolling my eyes and made so many grimaces with my mouth and contortions with my body that the young workmen burst out laughing and accompanied us to our coach, making jokes about my "poor condition". Lady T. later explained that some Englishmen find it diverting to visit the asylum at Bedlam of a Sunday and make fun of the inmates there...

Surrounded by her council, Elizabeth I received Monsieur de Bellièvre with great pomp and circumstance on 28th November, not at Whitehall, but at Richmond, another of her palaces, and very beautiful. As for me, I had eyes only for this great queen of the reformed Church of England, our ultimate recourse and last defence, without whom our Huguenot faith would be promptly and everywhere stamped out by Felipe II. As far as I could tell, given that she was seated on her throne, she wasn't very tall, but she held herself very straight. She was superbly bedecked with jewels, wore a purple and gold dress, of which I've never seen the equal, unless it was the dress Queen Margot wore for her wedding to Henri de Navarre. She wore a ruff that was open in front to permit the view of a necklace on which the largest ruby I'd ever seen was surrounded by a set of pearls. Her earrings were studded with another set of enormous pearls. Yet another set decorated the headband that adorned her immense, luminous forehead, which was framed by two ringlets of Venetian-red hair. She had, I must say in all truth, a somewhat masculine jaw, a nose that was slightly too long and thin, prudent lips. Her eyes, on the other hand, were very beautiful and lively—eloquent, even—and full of mirth, looking constantly about her, yet never losing sight of the essential, which, on this occasion, was the behaviour and bearing of Monsieur de Bellièvre.

The Pompous Pomponne, who had been polishing and repolishing his little speech ever since we'd left Paris, certainly lived up to his sobriquet and spoke for a full hour, much happier with himself than the queen was with him, and infinitely more boring than a rainy day in London. Everything got thrown into the pot: Alexander the Great, Homer, Virgil, David and Saul, Caesar and Augustus—this last cited as the most beautiful and rare example of clemency in history. As the translator of the ambassador, I had to interpret as he pronounced, and was constantly trying to attenuate his language, especially when he evoked some veiled threats that the king of France was said to have made as to the consequences were his sister-in-law Mary Stuart to be condemned. I could tell that Elizabeth appreciated my softening of his speech, for her eyes shone with a particular luminosity when I did this, and I decided that Lady T. had been right when she claimed that Her Majesty spoke very good French, Italian and Latin in addition to her native tongue. I suspected that if she didn't interrupt me to say that she understood Monsieur de Bellièvre quite well without my help, it was to allow her counsellors, some of whom must not have been as good linguists as she, to follow the thread of this voluminous verbiage.

When Pomponne de Bellièvre had finished, she replied in French with a thoroughness and a vehemence that left the ambassador speechless, since she spoke both as a queen and as a woman, and reduced him to silence both by her reasons and by her volubility.

"Monsieur de Bellièvre," she said in a voice both sweet and strong, "I have a very clear sense of your speech, having heard it twice—once by you and a second time by your interpreter. I have understood it so well than I haven't missed a single word. And I'm quite angry, Monsieur de Bellièvre, that a person of your character should have crossed the Channel to speak to me of an affair in which there is neither honour nor profit for anyone in attempting to change my will in this matter, because the thing is so clear and the cause so evident. Although Mary Stuart is of an inferior rank to me—since she is in my kingdom, not I in hers, from which she was exiled by her subjects after her murder of Darnley—I offered her my infinite friendship. But this did not deter her from her ill will towards me, so that I no longer feel secure in my lodgings, or in my own kingdom, but assailed and spied on from all sides. She has incited so many enemies against me that I no longer know which way to turn. I am no longer free, but a captive. I am her prisoner rather than she mine! If she were to triumph, it would be, as you know all too well, the end of me and of my people, whom I've sworn before the Lord God to protect. I would perjure myself, Monsieur de Bellièvre, if I granted you the pardon you're asking of me—a pardon I would never ask of the king of France, my good brother and your master, in circumstances that would threaten his person or the safety of his state, as is the case for me and my kingdom in this affair. Indeed, on the contrary, I desire, pray for and wholeheartedly wish that my good brother the king of France be protected and preserved from all his enemies, as I am from mine, who am but a poor woman and have such trouble resisting the assaults and snares that threaten to overwhelm me."

While the queen was speaking, my eyes wandered from Monsieur de Bellièvre and the gentlemen in his retinue whom I judged to be Guisards to the faces of the counsellors of Elizabeth, gleaning very different impressions from the French and the English. As for the first, despite the courtesy of the court, which had polished their faces somewhat, I found them troubled, bitter and uneasy, especially when Elizabeth spoke of the enemies of her good brother Henri—which could only mean Guise and the League. As for the second, they seemed both happy with the adamant firmness of their sovereign and very moved by a virile sense of protectiveness when she spoke of being "but a poor woman" assailed by snares on all sides—or, at least, all of them who spoke French, who were quietly translating her words for the others. As for me, I found the queen extremely dexterous at capturing the hearts of her subjects, deploying at the same time, in her effort to seduce them, the force of her resolution and the weakness of her sex.

Monsieur de Bellièvre, who, despite the pomp with which he strutted, knew very well the ways of the court, and was not so stupid that he didn't understand the sense of what the queen had said. He clearly felt that that nothing was to be gained by insisting further and ended up delivering a long speech of thanks for her benignity in receiving him. The queen responded with a few amiable compliments (although she'd laid into him brutally during her speech) and gave him leave to depart. His counsellors, who weren't so obliged to counterfeit their feelings, remained as stony-faced as the cliffs of Dover.

As we left Richmond, I asked my leave of Monsieur de Bellièvre, who granted it straightaway, while some members of his retinue betrayed knowing smiles as they watched me climb into the elegant coach of Lady T., who was waiting for me in front of the palace.

"Well, My Lady!" I cried, taking her hand, as soon as the curtains had been drawn around us, and covering it with kisses. "What an admirable queen! What a marvellous mind—a remarkable mixture of masculine and feminine! How perfectly she understands statecraft and how to govern her subjects! How I would love her and wholeheartedly devote my life to her service if I were English!"

"Monsieur," she countered with a delicious smile, "I beg you not to lick my hand so much: you go at it with such French fury that one would think you were going to swallow it whole!" (At this the chambermaid sitting opposite us burst out laughing so hard she nearly choked.) "Besides, this swallowing isn't necessary since we're not in public."

And with her free hand she reached over and gave me a tap on my hand as a sign that this reproach was really a form of tenderness, one that expressed her affection mingled with her English sense of humour. As for me, sitting nestled by her side in this cosy coach, leaning against her beautifully rounded shoulder, I looked at her delightedly through the lens of our complicitous friendship and thought how much she might have loved me had we not each been constrained by our obligations to others. It occurred to me that, rather than resent a woman who refuses us, we should be grateful for her virtue (if that's the reason she rejects our love), which makes her even dearer, since this is such a rare quality in these times and elevates our esteem for her sex.

"The queen," observed Lady T. as we sat enjoying a light supper in her lodgings, "is as royal in her throne room as she is affable in private, and loves to give her ministers nicknames, calling Leicester her 'Eyes', Hatton her 'Eyelids' and Walsingham 'the Moor'. The late brother of your king, the Duc d'Alençon, for whom she had special

422

affection—though she never resolved to marry him because he was Catholic—she called 'the Frog', and his private ambassador, the charming Monsieur de Simier, 'my Monkey'."

"And why does she call Walsingham 'the Moor'?"

"Because he has such dark skin and hair, you'd think he was born in Algiers. You're going to find him quite terrifying when you make his acquaintance."

Just then we heard noises in the antechamber, and the chambermaid showed in the "lady of the ring" who had woken me up from a deep sleep on the morning of the 22nd at the Pope's Head Tavern.

"Monsieur," she said, "it's time." (My heart started pounding so fiercely against my ribs, I thought she would hear it!) "Please put on this mask."

When the mask was removed a few minutes later, I found myself in a throne room—not at Richmond, but in another palace whose name I never learnt. This particular room is called the "Presence Chamber", a term that seemed particularly fitting since it draws attention not so much to the throne but to the presence of the sovereign, who, even when she's absent, is still venerated there. This was demonstrated by the way the servants—who were setting the table for the queen, bringing in succession tablecloth, salt, plates, knife and wine—knelt three times before the throne as if Elizabeth were seated there as they entered or left the room. These ceremonies certainly lengthened the time of my interview, but what lengthened it even more was the function of the "lady taster", who, when the plates arrived, was not there to taste each dish to prevent the poisoning of the queen, as one might have expected, but rather to distribute morsels of food for that same purpose to each of the servants there. The servants seemed to derive a sense of great honour from this custom, as perilous as it might be for them.

This precaution having been taken for each of the dishes, and no one having expired as a result, I expected that the queen would appear, but in her place there appeared a giant usher, carrying a gold-embossed baton, who preceded a swarm of pretty young chambermaids clad in colourful dresses, whose job was to remove everything from the table, including the tablecloth and the place settings; they swirled around in their ample hoop skirts and then disappeared through the door from which they'd just entered. I guessed that the queen had decided to take her supper in her private apartments, and so I prepared myself for an hour's wait for her to finish her meal. But not ten minutes later, the gentle giant reappeared, announcing that Her Majesty had finished her meal and wished to see me. I supposed (a supposition that was confirmed later by Lady T.) that, unlike her father, Henry VIII, who was excessively fond of wine, meat and women, Elizabeth ate little and drank even less. As for men, although she had herself called the "Virgin Queen", and was celebrated as such by her poets, it didn't seem, from what I'd heard, that she practised as much abstinence in this regard as she would have wished her subjects and the wider world to believe.

Although ever since I'd arrived in London I'd daily rehearsed what I was going to say to the queen, my legs were shaking beneath me and my heart was beating like a drum as the usher brought me into her presence. She didn't see me at first because she was occupied in reading a letter, observed very closely in this activity by a gentleman seated on her right, whom I recognized as Walsingham by the dark colour of his skin—rather than by his hair, of which only a few strands of white emerged from under his skullcap. This little cap clerically crowned his long, thin and austere face, which ended in a sad little pointed beard. His body seemed sickly, old, infirm and broken, though he was but fifty-six, but I found it very hard to tolerate the brilliance of his black eyes, which were sunk deep in their sockets. Behind him stood Mr Mundane, whom I assumed must be his assistant, and who was the only one to smile at me as I entered. As for Lady Markby (the "lady of the ring"), she was standing behind the queen, reading over her shoulder—but with the queen's consent—and waiting for her to finish before turning the page.

"Well then," said the queen at last, "that's all very good, my Moor—you must dispatch this letter tomorrow."

"May it please Your Majesty to sign it," replied Walsingham, dipping a pen in ink and handing it to the queen.

"Alas, my Moor," answered the queen petulantly, "I have a sore thumb and can't hold the pen. I'll sign it tomorrow."

"If Your Majesty's thumb is suffering from gout, then we must have it looked at," counselled Walsingham.

"What?" cried Elizabeth, angrily leaping to her feet and beginning to pace back and forth in the room, casting indignant looks at Walsingham, Mundane and Lady Markby. "Who dares accuse our royal thumb of having gout! For the love of God! I've never suffered greater impertinence! This thumb," she continued, brandishing it before her as if to accuse it of lese-majesty, "has committed the grave fault of being hard, swollen and painful. But by all the wounds of the Lord, I affirm that this thumb does not have gout! By God! It wouldn't dare have gout!"

This said, she smiled suddenly, as if amused at her own declaration, and continued, half seriously, half in jest:

"Moreover, who said I was in pain? It doesn't hurt in the least! And if I don't sign this letter tonight, it's because I don't want to. Did you hear me, Moor?"

"Yes," sighed Walsingham, while Mundane and Lady Markby, taking advantage of the fact that they were standing behind the throne, smiled at each other. As for me, I thought to myself that if the English were reputed on the continent to be of a lunatic disposition, it most assuredly comes from on high.

"It is possible," continued the queen, "that some people at court are not in such good health, but I would ask everyone to remember, and to publish it abroad, that the prince of this kingdom is in adamantine health!"

"I shall not fail to do so, Your Majesty," conceded Walsingham.

"And while you're at it," she added, with an affectionate look his way, "have it reported that her secretary of state is also at the peak of health."

"As you wish, Your Majesty," replied Walsingham with a sigh, followed by a dry cough, while a shadow passed over his eyes, as he was already suffering from an illness that he couldn't cure: his passionate service to his queen, an immensely fatiguing undertaking, without respite or rest, which would literally cost him his life four short years later.

"But," said the queen, suddenly catching sight of me, "who is this?"

At this, Lady Markby leant over and whispered a few words in her ear.

"Approach, Chevalier de Siorac," said the queen.

Which I did, though my legs were trembling so badly when I knelt before her that I wasn't sure I'd be able to regain my feet. After considering me quite curiously for a moment, the queen gave me her hand, which I kissed; after this, on a sudden impulse, she gave me her hand a second time—I placed my lips on it again—while with her other hand she patted my cheek several times and said:

"Monsieur, I like your eyes. They are warm and good."

I can only say that I felt absolutely astonished and incredibly moved to see her so graciously condescend to me in this way, and I'm not exaggerating when I say that, had I not been a Frenchman and in my own king's service, I believe I would have dedicated the rest of my life to her. Later, reliving this scene (which was similar to many others that Lady T. described to me in which Elizabeth, in a couple of well-chosen words, forever captured the goodwill and devotion of one or another of her subjects), I could appreciate the role of artifice and politics in these little cajoleries of Her Majesty. And yet, at the same instant, I discerned that, far from being false, the sentiment she had just expressed came directly from her heart, which only served her purpose better, since her very sincerity made her caresses even more irresistible.

Meanwhile, the queen had not failed to notice the effect she'd produced on me, being too much of a woman not to feel the heat of my affection; on the other hand, she was doubtless aware, from the dispatches Lord Stafford had sent, that I was bringing her a message from my king that was very different from that which Monsieur de Bellièvre had presented. But she also had to pretend, no doubt, not to be impatient to hear what I had to tell her, since her impatience would have betrayed some fears unworthy of her royal dignity, and so she allowed herself to indulge, for the present, in a kind of joyous, jocular playfulness.

"Markby," she said, smiling at her friend, "what shall we do with this nice little Frenchman? Marry him off to one of our English beauties so we can keep him here at court?"

"If it please Your Majesty, marry him off to me!" laughed Lady Markby. "I like those hungry eyes, which seem to eat you right up!"

"But Markby," laughed Elizabeth, "have you forgotten that you've got a husband at home in Shropshire?"

"Would that I *could* forget him!" said Lady Markby pouting.

"Then let's marry him right off to our Lady T.," continued the queen, "since she's a widow."

"Your Majesty," I laughed, joining in, "nothing would please me more, given the affection and respect I feel for Lady T., but I'm already married in Paris."

"Oh, what a pity!" cried the queen, who was certainly already aware of my situation. "Well then, Markby, if we can't marry him at least let's give him a nickname! That way we'll make him ours, capturing his essence in the word we choose for him!"

Her Majesty seemed very pleased with this idea, since she shared Henri's delight in the verbal games that were all the rage in both her court and ours—and also in Italy, where this craze for linguistic games, metaphors and alliterations had originated.

"Markby! Mundane! Walsingham!" cried the queen petulantly, clapping her hands. "Lend me your ideas! Let's find a nickname for the Chevalier de Siorac! My Moor," she said, smiling at Walsingham, who seemed quite out of sorts at all this attention being paid to a Frenchman, "a nickname for Monsieur de Siorac!"

"'The Fox'," said Walsingham disagreeably.

"No, no!" laughed Lady Markby. "If he got in our henhouse, he'd caress all the chickens instead of eating them!"

"How about 'the Frog'?" offered Mundane.

"Well, Mundane," returned the queen, laughing, "You lack imagination. We already used that on the Duc d'Alençon, who was so small, twisted and charming. But we're not going to call all the Frenchmen 'frogs'. Let's reserve the name for poor Alençon, whom I would have married if my ministers hadn't objected so strenuously."

"Well, I'm not so sure of that," objected Walsingham. "Your Majesty never followed any advice but her own will!"

"Indeed," confessed the queen. "Markby, a nickname, quickly, for Monsieur de Siorac!"

"'The Ferret'!" proposed Markby.

"That's better," agreed Elizabeth. Ferrets are fairly pretty, supple, alert and valiant. But they're too bloodthirsty. And I can't imagine Monsieur de Siorac taking the life of another, except in self-defence. No, Monsieur de Siorac is not a cruel animal. He flies! He flies!"

"Then let's call him 'the Lark'!" proposed Lady Markby.

"'The Lark'!" cried the queen, clapping her hands. "You win the prize, Markby! The Lark is a great find, I find! Monsieur, I name and consecrate you henceforth my little French Lark to the end of time.

Aargh!" she winced. "I hurt my thumb again clapping! By God! This thumb is a traitor thumb, and I'll have it tried and cut off tomorrow!"

At this Walsingham smiled in such a knowing and formidably sinister way that I was amazed.

"Tom," cried the queen, "bring a stool for Monsieur de Siorac!"

The gigantic usher hurried forward, carrying a stool as if it were as light as a feather, and so I stood (having been on my knees all this time in front of Her Majesty) and then sat down, my temples throbbing, and feeling almost intoxicated by the incredible kindness that the queen was displaying for me—which, even though I knew very well it was ultimately directed to my master, Henri, I found quite overwhelming; I almost felt that I was sprouting wings, as my nickname would have me do!

"My Lark," cooed the queen in French, sitting very straight on her throne, her two hands on the armrests, and suddenly adopting a grave and imposing tone, "sing me your song of France and let it be as pleasant to my ears as the singer is to my eyes!"

This was too much for me! For my heart was beating like a cathedral bell; my legs went weak and my throat went dry and tightened up, and I stood there dumb as a lamp post—the beautiful speech that I'd prepared and polished, just as Pomponne had, suddenly went straight out of my head like water out of the cask of the Danaids.

"Well now!" said the queen, who, like my master Henri, loved using terms of endearment. "Has my little lark lost his voice?"

At this Lady Markby and Mundane had a good laugh, and even Walsingham smiled, though in a different way this time—his ferocious and swarthy face suddenly took on a much more tender indulgence than I'd seen so far, which led me to believe that he secretly idolized this queen whom he served so zealously, confusing this love with the great and exigent love that he bore the state. Would that God had only provided us with ministers in France who were as honest and

429

resolute as this man, more devoted to maintaining the grandeur of the kingdom than to his own life!

"Mundane," laughed the queen, "give my own little French Lark a beakful of wine in order that the nectar might free his voice!"

Oh, how avidly I emptied that cup, which restored my courage and my voice—both of which had been overwhelmed by the patience, goodness and astonishing display of friendship that this queen had proffered me!

"Your Majesty," I said, "everything I'm about to tell you was told me in secret by my master Henri III without any witnesses, charging me to repeat what he said word for word without adding or omitting anything, to his beloved sister the queen of England."

"Did he really say 'beloved'?" asked Elizabeth, arching her perfectly trimmed eyebrows in surprise.

"That's exactly what he said, Your Majesty."

"Oh, how charming these French are!" laughed the queen, her eyes shining with pleasure. "They sprinkle love everywhere! But let's hear the rest."

"My master," I continued, "believes that Your Majesty is the sole judge of her security and of the measures she must take to preserve her person and her kingdom from the attacks of her enemies, whoever they may be."

"Did my beloved brother," asked the queen, "really say 'whoever they may be'?"

"Yes, that's what he said."

"This is," remarked Elizabeth, "a most Machiavellian diplomacy! After Pomponne, the anti-Pomponne. Which one should I believe?"

"The second, Your Majesty," I replied emphatically.

"My Moor," said Elizabeth, "what do you think?"

"That the king of France is so hard-pressed on all sides that he cannot help but be Machiavellian."

"My Lark," the queen continued, "am I to believe that the king approves of the trial?" (And I had to admire the way that, once again, although Mary Stuart was continuously present in this conversation, she was never named.)

"Not at all!" I replied.

"Not at all?" cried the queen. "Where is your Gallic logic? My Lark, your conclusion refutes your premises!"

"No again, Your Majesty! My master believes that, touching crimes of lese-majesty, the execution should *precede* the sentence and not the inverse."

"That the execution should precede the sentence," repeated the queen. "My Moor, what is does this jargon mean?"

"That we must dispatch the traitor without giving her a trial."

"But that's an assassination!" exclaimed the queen with indignation. "And very repugnant to the customs of my people, who believe that the guilty party must be tried according to form, even if the sentence be not in the least in doubt."

I smiled somewhat at this, but said not a word, for I could not see any difference between the pike that killed Coligny and the executioner's axe, when it was responding with such docility to the will of the sovereign.

"The French," observed Walsingham, who had noticed my smile, "have very different customs from ours, and have less respect than we do for the letter of the law. When the sovereign and his advisors have decided that a vassal is a traitor, they condemn him to death without trial or judges, and leave the execution to the king's killer."

"The king's killer!" cried Elizabeth. "Is there such an office in France?"

Since I did not wish to answer, Walsingham answered yes with a nod of his head.

"Continue, my Lark," urged the queen, who, however much she'd questioned the French system, did not wish to pursue the point for fear of appearing to criticize her "beloved brother".

"Meanwhile," I said, "my master also believes that you are better positioned than anyone else in the world to decide how best to maintain your own security and preserve the peace in your state."

"One could never claim, after listening to you," said the queen with a smile, "that subtlety was the French king's weak point. Continue, my Lark."

"What I will now say," I continued, not without some emotion, "has no relation to the person we've been discussing, but is, instead, a secret of such immense consequence that my master recommended that I share it only with Your Majesty."

"Sing, my Lark, sing!" urged the queen. "All of the ears in this room, though they may belong to different heads, are mine—and I have every bit as much confidence in them as I do in myself for forgetting or remembering what we shall hear."

"Your Majesty," I continued, though with some difficulty in recovering my breath given the enormous strangeness of what I was about to say, "my master has learnt that his brother-in-law and friend, the king of Navarre, against whom he has waged war most half-heartedly and only when absolutely forced to, has asked Your Majesty for some subsidies, monies and subventions that would enable him to recruit in Germany an army to support him in this fratricidal conflict. Your Majesty, what I am about to tell you is so surprising that I scarcely dare say it for fear of being disbelieved."

"I believe I have a good idea of what you're going to tell me," said the queen, her nostrils quivering. "Go on, my Lark."

"My master," I continued, trying to strengthen my voice, "believes that if the refusal Your Majesty has made to these requests up until now is based on her fear of alienating the king of France, this monarch would not be take umbrage if this fear were to be overcome by Your Majesty's government."

"My Moor," gasped the queen, "did you hear that?"

"Yes, Your Majesty," whispered Walsingham as if he were holding his breath.

"Go on, go on!" urged the queen.

"My master believes, in fact, that such an army would effectively counterbalance the forces of the Duc de Guise, and that if…"

"And that if…" urged the queen…

"…that if this army, having crossed the border, were to occupy Lorraine and ravage that area without moving farther into France, it would infallibly provoke a counter-attack by the armies of the Duc de Guise, which, God willing, would be weakened or defeated, leaving the king of France free to make a pact with the king of Navarre, with whom he has always enjoyed a good relationship, and whom he has already recognized publicly as his successor to the throne of France."

A pregnant silence followed my explanation, during which the queen and Walsingham exchanged very animated looks, as did Mundane and Lady Markby behind them.

"Despite the total madness of such a scheme," observed Elizabeth, "there is, indeed, method in it, since the same worm that is gnawing at your throne is also munching on mine."

Making a sign for Lady Markby to lean over to her, she whispered something in the lady's ear, but it seemed to be an agreeable message, for she smiled upon hearing it and went forthwith to repeat it to Walsingham, who, though he did not smile, gave a nod of his head and made a sign to Mundane, who, bowing to Her Majesty, left the room.

"Sweet Siorac," said Elizabeth, seeming suddenly to have forgotten my nickname and preferring this alliteration, "please give your master, my beloved brother, 10,000 million thanks for the reassuring friendship that he has shown me in my present predicament. Tell him that I hope wholeheartedly and will pray to the Lord God every day for the preservation of his life and his continuance on the throne, as I try to continue on mine. And lastly—touching his last message, which is of the greatest consequence—tell him that I am going to discuss it with my council and that he will soon see from our response what was decided."

This said, she held out her fingers; I knelt before her and placed a devout kiss on them, and then presumed to articulate the words that were burning my mouth:

"May it please Your Majesty, regarding the fate of Mademoiselle de Montcalm—"

"Monsieur!" broke in Lady Markby. "Etiquette forbids that you address the queen after she has presented her hand."

I rose, silent, ashamed, my lips sealed shut by this sharp remonstration, and backed from the room, making three humiliating bows to Elizabeth on my way out. Lady Markby, imitating my bows, followed me into the antechamber, and, once we were outside, took my arm and whispered:

"Sweet Siorac, be patient. Give the queen and Walsingham time to think about this and the matter will resolve itself."

"But why?" I asked, as she handed me the mask I had worn on my way to my appointment. "What need is there for it in here?"

"Because we never know," she replied, "whether some agent of Felipe's has slipped in here."

"In the queen's palace?!"

"Why not? Money can accomplish anything. Would we be tasting every dish set before the queen if we didn't live with this fear?"

Before arriving at the lodgings of my affectionate hostess, Lady Markby again put her hand on my arm and said:

"There is a gift waiting for you at your lodgings that the queen had brought there. Which is why you saw Mr Mundane leave the room before we did."

"Ah, Lady Markby," I replied, "I am infinitely grateful to Her Majesty for her gracious liberalities, but, being in the employ of my master in France, I could not accept anything from the hands of a foreign sovereign, however much love and reverence I bear her."

At this, Lady Markby laughed, being of a naturally gay and sprightly nature, and whispered teasingly in my ear:

"Just wait a moment before refusing the gift that's awaiting you in Lady T.'s drawing room."

When I attempted to kiss her hands as I descended from her coach, she directed my lips to a more delectable target. These caresses, though very brief, led me to believe that, in order to spare my conscience undue trouble, the queen had asked for me to be placed with Lady T. and not a lady who might have conveniently forgotten that she had a husband in Shropshire…

Wondering what the queen's gift could possibly be, I headed to Lady T.'s drawing room, where, looking around as I entered, I saw nothing that I hadn't seen the previous evening. I felt a strange pang of disappointment, though I was quite resolved not to accept any gifts from Her Gracious Majesty. A bright fire burned in the fireplace and I spied in the mirror above it my hostess standing to my left, holding a fan open in front of her face, as if cooling herself before the heat of the fire. I thought, naturally, that it was Lady T., given her blonde hair and the pale-blue brocaded dress that she'd been wearing the day before. Wondering whether I shouldn't simply withdraw from the room in order not to disturb her reverie, I was about to retrace my steps towards the door when the lady lowered the fan, caught sight of me in the mirror, leapt with a cry of joy from the couch where she'd been sitting and threw her arms around my neck.

"Ah!" I cried, my voice strangled with emotion. "Larissa!"

I was unable to say another word, for she held me to her and covered my face with kisses, and I could only hug her to me in silence, overwhelmed by the immense joy of finding her healthy and free. I was struck anew by her extraordinary resemblance to her twin, not just in her features, hair and build, but also in her skin, which was, like Angelina's, fine, smooth and perfumed. My heart swelled with gratitude for the *delicatezza** of Queen Elizabeth, which wasn't simply in her granting Larissa her freedom, but also in the way she'd turned it into a surprise, at the very moment I'd given up hope.

Nothing multiplies as marvellously as joys do, for scarcely had I felt the immense relief of recovering this sister after so many months of worry before I was suddenly filled with concomitant pleasure at the idea of returning to Angelina the sister she'd so worried about, and to Giacomi the woman he'd so long adored and desired.

From what I was told, Monsieur de Bellièvre intended to remain in London until the condemnation of Mary Stuart, in order to attempt to influence the queen's decision; but, knowing what I knew after my secret meeting with Elizabeth, he had no more chance of succeeding than if he were attempting to throw a rope around the horns of the moon, and so I asked the ambassador's permission to return to France without waiting for the outcome of the trial (which threatened to take a long time, given the English people's attachment to the forms and formalities of the law). I told him that it had been evident ever since our first meeting with her that Queen Elizabeth spoke such excellent French that my services were no longer needed. For his part, Pompous Pomponne was not sorry to see me go, since he'd no doubt got wind, from a certain member of the League, whose English was quite good, that my simultaneous interpretation of his speech had included many unfortunate softenings and attenuations. He was quick to grant my request, believing, no doubt, that this other gentleman would render him more faithful service than I.

---

* "Thoughtfulness."

We parted company nevertheless with a few forced expressions of friendship, which, for his part, sounded more like venom than honey, but which he enveloped in the usual court "varnish" and his inevitable verbosity. And Lady T. was nice enough to bring me to Dover in her coach with a large escort (English roads being as unsafe as ours, and frequently interrupted by toll booths operated by local landowners, who stopped us to exact remuneration for maintaining their section of the route). My Lady insisted on seeing me embark at Dover with Larissa before she left, and our parting brought tears to her eyes and a knot to my throat.

My Angelina was absent from our lodgings when we arrived in Paris, and I left Larissa there in order to hurry to the Louvre to inform the king of my success. Henri was of course delighted that Queen Elizabeth seemed willing to ally herself with him against Guise, a plan that struck me personally as tortuous and problematic, given that Henri was willing to connive in the invasion of his own kingdom by a foreign army in the hope that Guise's forces would be crushed. But his happiness was short-lived, since the king was rapidly overwhelmed by a series of plots that were constantly being hatched in Paris by the League (which seemed to grow them like the Hydra did heads), with the intention of invading the capital, assassinating his council, seizing his person and shutting him away in a monastery.

On 18th February 1587, Mary Stuart was beheaded in the great hall of the castle at Fotheringhay, on a scaffold draped in black. That she was guilty no one could doubt, other than a few zealous League members, who quickly presumed to elevate to "sainthood" this adulterous accomplice in the murder of her husband, a traitor queen who, not content to bequeath her kingdom and that of England to a foreign sovereign, had plotted the death of Elizabeth and encouraged a foreign invasion. Still, the news of her execution didn't fail to move me, since the killing of a woman is so abhorrent and unimaginable to me that, even had she been a thousand times more guilty, I would not have wished her to be punished, or beheaded.

In consequence, there fell on Paris a rain of the most furious sermons, pamphlets, libels and satiric verses, both in Latin and French, which, on the one hand, praised to the blood-soaked heavens the "splendid soul" and "royal virtues" of the "martyred saint" Mary, while, on the other, condemning Elizabeth to the worst tortures, public obloquy and outer darkness. She was labelled "wicked", "whore queen", "dirty bitch", "impious brothel-keeper", "a prostitute who wants to cure her leprosy with innocent blood" and, finally, this, which raised their invective to the height of the ridiculous: "the execrable egg of a sacrilegious crow" (Henry VIII being the crow, since he'd rejected the Pope and established the Anglican Church, which made him a crow forever, and his "egg" despicable the moment she'd seen the light of day).

If my memory is correct, it was towards the middle of June that the king learnt that a foreign army was massing on our eastern border, a force that Elizabeth had funded by channelling money through the king of Navarre (as my secret embassy to the queen had suggested she do); indeed, I saw that, on learning the news, Henri was not in the least aggrieved, since this army served his Machiavellian aims and, above all, provided him an argument with which to convince Guise to renounce the inexpiable war he'd been waging against the Huguenots, given the threat of this invasion by the reiters, especially since they were invading his own duchy of Lorraine, from which he drew most of his revenues.

It was not easy getting Guise to sit down with the king—because, of course, the former suspected that, no matter what display of goodwill Henri attempted to project and the amiable letter his monarch had sent him, the king secretly hated him, and might well be planning an ambush or some other surprise to undo him. Ultimately, the queen mother, Catherine de' Medici, who openly supported the League over the king (despite the fact that he was her son!), agreed to mediate, and went to see the duc in Châlons (where he'd set up his headquarters), where she persuaded him to come to Meaux to speak, face to face, with the king. In the end he did, though he temporized for several days, during which we learnt the sad exploit perpetrated at La Motte Saint-Eloi by the Duc de Joyeuse (for whom I'd once fashioned an entire army of carved wooden soldiers!). Some four or five hundred Huguenots who were besieged there agreed to surrender under on condition that their lives be spared, but were, against the duc's word of honour and all the laws of warfare, pitilessly slaughtered—all but one, who escaped, and of whom I'll have more to say later.

This act was considered excessively cruel by the king and everyone at court—more worthy of one of the League's brigands than of one of His Majesty's lieutenants—and seemed entirely at odds with the frivolous, whimsical and ebullient character of the Duc de Joyeuse. The poet Agrippa d'Aubigné met him shortly thereafter and asked him why he'd done this.

"Well," explained Joyeuse, "can't everyone see that the kingdom is coming apart and falling to pieces? And I, who want to have a role in the aftermath of this tragedy, understand that I must conform to what's being preached in Paris. So this massacre, which I ordered with a heavy heart, is entirely in keeping with what our priests are saying in Paris—more so than if I had won and then shown mercy to my prisoners!"

"Certainly, he is frivolous," sighed the king to Chicot, after having heard the account of this massacre, "but he's also frivolous in his ugly excesses. To dispatch, against all honour, 500 prisoners in order to be praised by the priests in their pulpits—that's a pretty terrible judgement on both the priests and Joyeuse."

The other duc, the one who wanted to empty my master's throne so he could sit on it, screwed up his courage enough to venture to Meaux, where the king and court were waiting for him, and arrived with a large retinue on 2nd July. I hadn't seen him for a long time, and found him little changed, being, with the possible exception of Épernon, the tallest, most handsome and most vigorous, agile and dexterous of all the princes in France. There were few who could rival him in beauty of his face: he had gentle, almond-shaped eyes, fine features and a thick moustache that curled up from his ravishingly well-sculpted lips. And yet, as handsome and imposing as he was in the flesh, I couldn't help detecting in him a false and hypocritical air.

Not that the king couldn't play his part as needed. The two men exchanged a tender embrace and amicable looks, along with suave protestations of friendship, though we know all too well what looks are worth—they cover the thoughts that cannot be expressed. But the real feelings disguised by these niceties were not at all the same. The king desired peace and worked ardently to achieve it, whereas Guise burned to walk through the blood of the French and the misery of the people (these idiots who so loved him) to clear a passage to the throne, his soul able to accept anything except the possibility of not reaching this goal.

The venerable Dr Marc Miron having given him an enema that very morning, the king, despite his discomfort, received the Duc de Guise in his chambers. But not wishing to encourage the duc with the hope that he was suffering and that the throne would soon be vacant, he made the effort to get dressed before his dangerous visitor arrived, and had a table set with bread, wine and two capons. He then ordered Miron, Du Halde, Chicot and me to eat some of the capons before he himself sat down at table with a drumstick in his hand, pretending to tear at the flesh with his sharp teeth, when the guest from Lorraine entered, smiling broadly. Seeing at first glance the half-eaten feast laid out on the table, his face fell, but he then tried to regain his earlier sunny countenance.

"My cousin," the king said blithely, "I had an enema this morning, and was feeling quite empty, and so, as I was as hungry as a dog, thought I should gorge myself. Will you join me, cousin?"

"Nay, sire," Guise demurred. "'Twould be too great an honour, and I've already breakfasted!" He was then forced to kiss the king's hand, now greasy from the capon, and barely brushed it with his moustache, albeit with as much respect as he could manage.

"In any case," announced the king as he rose from the table, wiping hands and mouth with the napkin Du Halde presented to him, "I've stuffed myself to the limit! A man shouldn't be such a glutton that he can't moderate his excesses! *Corpus onustum hesternis vitiis animum quoque praegravat una,*"* he continued gravely, but with an amusedly conspiratorial air, as if he'd forgotten that Guise knew no Latin. "But, my cousin, we must maintain clear heads to discuss our affairs, since they are of such great consequence for the future of our unhappy kingdom, which is so torn by questions of religion."

"Alas, sire," replied the duc, joining his two hands together sanctimoniously. "Would that it pleased God to make all of Your Majesty's counsellors as zealous in the defence of the Holy Catholic Church as I am."

"Or as I am," agreed the king with a somewhat haughty tone, "for you cannot doubt that I am strongly resolved to allow no other religion in my kingdom than the Catholic one. But we must be prudent, my cousin! You cannot be unaware that a great foreign army is being amassed on our eastern frontier, which, were we to take up arms against Navarre once more, would not hesitate to invade us, devastating our provinces,

---

* "When the body is too heavy with the excesses of yesterday, it weakens the mind" (Horace).

causing incalculable suffering and trampling the poor people to death as it goes. Such is the sad state of our affairs, and necessity has put a knife to our throats, so shouldn't we agree to purchase a good peace rather than risk such a hazardous war?"

"Well, sire!" cried the duc. "That's not how I see it! I cannot accept a peace that doesn't guarantee that the faith of our fathers would be saved! Indeed, sire, I beg you to cast your eyes on our dying religion and embrace its conservation with all your heart, believing that no sacrifice is too great or too perilous to achieve this noble end. Sire," he continued, "your people can imagine nothing worse than the fall of heaven. And the Bible assures us that with our Lord's cross as our standard, we can destroy all our enemies on earth."

Such hypocritical language—designed to hide the traitor duc's crude ambition under the cover of religion—sickened the king, I think, for he turned his head away with a tremble in his upper lip that he couldn't control, and began pacing back and forth, his hands behind his back.

"My cousin," he said at last, pausing before the duc, "aren't you aware that peace offers no advantage to the Huguenots, since we profit from their realization that the only way to advance their affairs is by converting to Catholicism, which is necessary either to obtain a place in the government or to marry, since there are many more Catholic women in this country than the reformed kind. Clearly, we need time to achieve this reconquest, but it can be achieved by gentle means and persuasion, whereas by the knife we merely create martyrs, whose blood nourishes and multiplies their Church. The persecution against them began under my grandfather, and was continued by my brother Charles IX. I myself tried the sword at Moncontour, at Jarnac and at La Rochelle. And what have we gained from nearly half a century of combat, sieges, massacres and executions if not that the king of Navarre is stronger than ever, and that a great army of German reiters is menacing our frontiers? Is it nothing to you that, in order to invade our kingdom, they must pass through Lorraine and devastate the duchy from which you've issued?"

"I will face this danger for the greater glory of the Catholic Church," replied the duc, as proudly as if he were St George called personally by God to defeat the dragon of heresy, "and you, sire, swore to combat it in the Treaty of Nemours."

"Ever since it was signed, there have been nothing but infractions and contraventions of it—"

"On your part, sire!" cried Guise, interrupting His Majesty, and shouting in a tone so loud, so abrupt and so insolent that Épernon put his hand on his dagger, but the king gave him such severe look that the arch-favourite dropped his hand to his side.

And yet his gesture did not pass unnoticed by Guise, who spun around as though he feared to be stabbed in the back, a movement he executed deftly but also with the stiffness of one who is wearing a coat of mail underneath his doublet. Seeing only Du Halde and me behind him, who were calmly and peaceably leaning against the tapestry (though our thoughts would have immediately dispatched the man if they'd had the power to do so), he seemed reassured, and continued his violent speech, though in a different register.

"I must protest, sire, against the terrible treatment that has been directed at those cities that demanded the extirpation of the pretended 'reformed' Church. *Someone* ruined the citadel in Mâcon! *Someone* took Valence! *Someone* disgraced Brissac, Croisilles, Gessan and Entragues because they belonged to the League! *Someone* redirected the monies that we'd amassed for the war! And therefore," he continued bitterly (this series of "someones" clearly designating the king), "it would certainly seem as though *someone* wishes heresy to continue in our kingdom!"

"And yet," the king fired back, "there's not a prince in this world who has worked harder than I at extinguishing it! But I think that the members of the League are going about it very badly. Which makes me think"—his black eyes suddenly sending sparks at the duc—"*that they're aspiring to much more than that.*"

These words, accompanied by that look, were so clear that the duc actually paled, opened his mouth to speak and abruptly closed it, looking around him with a suspicious air. But seeing Épernon seated on a stool, his arms crossed, his eyes lowered, and all the others as immobile as logs, he seemed to regain his confidence, but with the much less assured air of a hypocrite who has seen his mantle of sanctimoniousness suddenly stripped, and feels naked and ashamed.

"But, sire," he continued, more softly and finding it difficult to regain his self-assurance, "is there any evidence—"

"There's a good deal more of it than I'd like!" broke in the king. "Who in this country is ignorant that *they* have asked me to construct strongholds to protect against Huguenots in places where there's no reason to fear them? That *they* have stolen a march on me and taken Dourlens and Pondormy? That *they* would have surprised me in Boulogne, if the valiant Captain Le Pierre hadn't put down their coup? That *they* had Captain Le Pierre killed in a fight to punish him for having faithfully served his king? That *they* built a citadel at Vitry-le-François against me? That *they* refused to accept the governor that I'd named at Rocroy? And as for the money that you're so bitterly complaining about"—moving from "they" to "you" with a sudden light in his eyes—"didn't you waste the 100,000 écus that you were given to build a citadel at Verdun? And that's not all! There are lots of things I'm not mentioning out of respect for your honour…"

"My honour, sire!" cried the duc, who had suddenly lost all the colour in his face, and who now leant against the wall after this brusque, frontal assault by his king, seemingly needing to regain his waning strength to make his escape, his honour (which in reality had now been demolished) not allowing him to remain here a minute longer.

Seeing this, and not wishing a complete break with Guise, which didn't suit his plans—since he calculated that if there was to be war, as seemed increasingly inevitable given the uncompromising position of the League, the huge foreign army would likely overwhelm the duc's forces—the king suddenly changed his expression, his tone, his gestures and his look with surprising litheness, and, taking Guise by the arm in an almost friendly manner, he said playfully:

"My good cousin, let's speak no more of this! You allege that I've failed to uphold the Treaty of Nemours; I allege you've done the same. The two allegations counterbalance each other. What we need is to restore order to our kingdom, if possible. Now, however, we need to figure out how to combat the Huguenots and how to defeat the army of reiters amassed on our borders when they attack. But before we join forces, as I hope we shall, I would ask you to reconcile your differences with the Duc d'Épernon, who so aspires to be your friend."

The king said this last without a trace of a smile, though he knew, as everyone in the kingdom did, the strident hatred that separated these two men, who each aspired not to friendship with the other but to his death, Guise believing the "arch-favourite" to be the staunchest supporter of the throne that he wished to occupy, and Épernon considering Guise to be the arch-enemy of his king.

However, the king had no sooner expressed the desire to see them reconciled than Épernon rose from his stool and came over to the duc and stood before him, his face all smiles and full of goodwill. Guise stood and returned his smile. There couldn't have been a more surprising spectacle than to see these two felines pull in their claws and show only velvet paws with such a gentle and benevolent air.

"Monseigneur," said the Duc d'Épernon with a bow, "I request the honour of becoming your most humble, closest and most devoted servant."

"Monsieur," replied Guise (who, however honeyed and full of nectar he managed to be, could not condescend to call the king's arch-favourite

"Monseigneur", since Guise believed he was a parvenu of the lowest extraction; indeed, the Duchesse de Montpensier had told all her priests to spread the word that he was the son of a notary and not descended from Nogaret as he claimed), "I ask you for the same honour and have no greater wish than to serve you as well."

"Monseigneur," continued Épernon, "since I know no one greater or more noble than you in this kingdom, I beg you to dispose of my person and all my worldly goods as if they were yours."

"Monsieur, I shall not fail to do so. And as you have required this of me, I ask only the same of you. I will treat you as a brother; we will be as inseparable as two fingers on my hand."

"Monseigneur, in truth, I place you so far above all the lords of this kingdom that whatever you shall order me to do in the service of the king, I shall unfailingly execute your command."

"Monsieur," replied Guise, who no doubt sensed the subtle derision in Épernon's words, replied, "I too shall execute yours."

"Monseigneur, I am overwhelmed. Would you permit me to embrace you?"

"Monsieur, the honour and pleasure will be mine!"

At this our two great tigers placed their paws around each other's necks (which they happily would have opened with their teeth) and gave each other an embrace that lasted so long, was so strong and affection-ate, with so many pats on the back and kisses planted on each other's cheeks, that you would have thought they were the two best friends in the world. Ultimately, the king (who seemed very happy with this spectacle) had to separate them, reminding them that his council was expecting all three of them in half an hour.

There is a game that the urchins in Paris play in the street in which one of them dresses up in a crown of paper and a large tattered garment in place of an ermine gown, carrying a wooden sceptre and an orb made of rags, and sets up his thrown on a stone marker, pretending to be the king. Gradually his "subjects"—the other urchins, all dirty and snotty—walk up to him, genuflect and call him "sire" or "Your Majesty", and decorate him with other titles. Each one, however, as he backs away from the "king", robs him of one of his ornaments: one will take his crown, another his sceptre, the next his orb and yet another his great gown. In the end, the poor king, as honoured as he is, finds himself entirely naked.

This trick, which I've often observed at various crossroads on my way from my lodgings in the rue du Champ-Fleuri to the Louvre, and which these ragamuffins seem to adore, is called "the farce of the fleeced king".

Now on Tuesday, 7th July, as the king was preparing to mount his horse to return to Paris, Guise came up to him to take his leave of him, kissed his hands almost on both knees, with much bowing and scraping and great repeated protestations of his zeal to serve him and promises and guarantees of the subjection of the members of the League to his throne—compliments that all of those present, including myself, considered so exaggerated as to be injurious, but that the king suffered in courteous silence and with a benign air.

When the duc had left, at the head of a suite of almost royal proportions in terms of number, array and splendour, Épernon frowned and said to the king, with his hand on his dagger:

"What's the duc playing at?"

"Don't you know?" replied Henri with clenched teeth. "He's playing the farce of the fleeced king."

And with an unusual glint in his black eyes, he added these three words, which I, and all of us, have reason to remember:

"But have patience!"

After this, with a grimace, as if he regretted having said too much, he turned to his retinue and shouted in a strong, clear voice:

"Gentlemen, saddle up!"

*

447

We got back to Paris around nightfall, and, taking leave of His Majesty, I hurried to my lodgings with Miroul, the darkness rendering the Paris streets less safe; and, once arrived at my door, I was happy to see Mérigot, faithfully watching from his post at the needle shop across the street.

Everyone had already gone to bed when I reached my rooms, but seeing no candlelight I assumed that my Angelina had gone to sleep; so, not wishing to trouble her, I undressed in the little cabinet adjoining our room, where I lit a small oil lamp. When I entered our room, I slipped between the sheets, where I found the warm and smooth body of my beloved, but was careful not to touch her to avoid troubling her sleep. Sighing in relief after all the riding and fatigue of my trip, and happy to be in this bed, where I had never known anything but sweet delight, I was about to blow out the lamp, when I heard a very sad sigh.

"But, my Angelina," I said, taking her sweetly in my arms and trying to see her face through her dishevelled hair, "you're crying! What's the matter? Why are you so sad?"

"You know all too well," she said in a mournful and muffled voice, her body heaving with convulsive sobbing.

"I know all too well?!" I repeated, astounded. "Angelina what are you saying? Have I done something that has wounded you? If I have, you must tell me immediately so I can make it better!"

"This wound," she managed to gasp between her convulsive sobs, "you won't be able to sew up like you do your wounded patients!"

"What?" I protested, greatly alarmed, but trying to laugh at her confusion. "What can be so terrible? Have I committed some capital and grave fault towards you that you should treat me so bitterly?"

"Indeed you have!" she moaned.

But nothing else would she say, for, her sobs at an end, and despite my insistent questions, protests and the tenderness inspired by my immutable love for her, she refused to say another word; instead, pushing me away, she turned her face from me so that I could only see it in profile, and remained as silent as if she'd turned into a statue of salt, her eyes staring into emptiness, her body stiff. I spent the next hour attempting to coax her out of this mournful immobility, but I began to suspect that her grief had to do with a jealousy that she had too much self-respect to admit. It suddenly occurred to me that she might have got wind of my travels with Alizon to Boulogne, since I had this adventure very much on my conscience, and thus I began to damn myself for engaging in a scenario that might well have cost me the love of my life.

Not knowing what else to do or to say after all my useless supplications and prayers to confide in me, and tired of turning over and over in my bed as if already I could feel the flames of hell licking at me (which are always inside us and come not from God, who is too merciful to have created a hell), I decided to get up and, going to get my clothes, dressed without a word, my throat so dry I could hardly breathe, and headed downstairs to seek the comfort of my little study, where I'd at least have the relief of my books.

Angelina was so surprised at my behaviour that she recovered her voice all of a sudden and said very bitterly:

"What are you doing? Where are you going? Are you returning to London?"

Sometimes it happens in life that you have something to hide from your lover and, when accused in the heat of an argument, you discover with infinite relief that she believes you to be innocent where you are not, and guilty where you are innocent (and can prove it). One can imagine how Angelina's words immediately undid the knot of anguish that was caught in my throat.

"What?" I said, laughing almost uncontrollably. "England! So you've heard stories about the beautiful Lady T. and me!"

"Beautiful!" cried Angelina in the tumult of her anger. "Do you dare use the word beautiful to my face?"

"But she is," I said, still laughing, "and what's more, she's very virtuous, and so faithful to her queen that she consented under orders from Elizabeth to lodge me and pretend to be having an amorous relationship with me that had neither marrow nor substance."

"Are you mocking me?" said Angelina, raising herself on her elbow, the better to look at me. "What on earth would be the interest or need for such a pretended connection?"

"It was of capital importance for my safety, since I was supposed to meet with the queen in secret and provide her an account of the king's plans without Bellièvre and his gentlemen getting wind of it. Which is why I couldn't stay at the inn with them."

Innocence is infinitely comforting in that it provides a great strength that keeps you from protesting too much—quite the opposite of lying, which has a tendency to feed on itself and multiply itself in unwelcome sprouts. My laughter was a relief, and my affirmation of Lady T.'s beauty (something that a guilty husband would have denied out of cowardice), the reticence I had to maintain about the object of my mission (a silence my wife was quite used to) and, above all, the ease with which I cleared myself, all convinced Angelina that the gossipmongers of the court had abused her, and she all but apologized for having doubted my faith and loyalty, an apology that I nipped in the bud by kissing the lips that might have uttered it.

We talked for another full hour of the charms and worries of our domestic life, of our children, who, thank God, were beautiful and healthy, of our plan to knock through the wall of the house next door, which I'd bought to house Giacomi—both as part of the strategy of retreat that Miroul and I had conceived in the event of some popular uprising, and to please my spouse, who loved the idea that, now that she was married, after the past ten years of cruel deprivation, she would have her twin sister nearby. Ultimately, quieted and reassured, she fell asleep in my arms; and I, by the light of the little paraffin lamp, looked, with a combination of tenderness and a little remorse, at those beautiful cheeks, on which the tears had now dried. But, alas, as everyone knows, the bad thing about our bodies is that though they give us much they also take much away: sadly, you can't fall asleep in your lover's arms without your entwined members in time growing tired and stiff, and so, eventually, it was necessary to let go and move away from her.

My thoughts of her also wandered away; I found myself thinking about the interview at Meaux and was excessively chagrined that the hypocritical party of war (ah, Guise's beautiful eyes, so clear, so blue, so lying) had carried the day once more against my master's basic humanity and worries about his poor subjects in this doleful kingdom. Well, I just have to say it again: everything seemed so ugly and base in the Magnificent! What a cockroach's soul inhabits that lordly envelope! What honeyed mendacity in his eyes, his voice, his thought and his word, he who had dared beg the king to "cast his eyes on the dying religion". Papism is dying? Can one possibly articulate such a palpable fallacy without batting an eye? God grant that papism might exist in this world with a little less health, corpulence and bloodthirstiness! It would think less about bleeding our poor Huguenots, whom the sword, jail and execution have so assailed in this country these last forty years!

If you press this handsome duc, the only thing that comes out are falsehoods like pus out of a boil! It's almost as if he were claiming that it was the Catholic Church that was being persecuted in our country! Moreover, such a thing has already been claimed!

If your steps happened to take you to the Saint-Séverin cemetery during that torrid July, you would have seen, among the thronging crowds, a great painting that Madame de Montpensier had ordered to be displayed there to whip up popular sentiment for war from a credulous people. You could see represented there in hideous colours the cruel torments and strange inhumanities that were supposed to have been committed by Queen Elizabeth against her Catholic subjects. You could see pincers, the brodequin, the strappado, impalement, dismemberment, castration, hanging—all the means of torture were there, not to mention images of women being raped and children roasted alive. To look at these horrors, which I never saw a trace of in London, our poor wenches in Paris wept and our good boys gnashed their teeth, and when they got home, they sharpened their knives to use on the Huguenots. There was even a fellow there with a pointer, who gave a commentary on this sublime painting, and repeatedly told his audience—and did so as if it were gospel—that there were 10,000 Huguenots hiding in the slums of the Faubourg Saint-Germain, waiting only for a signal from Navarre (who had been conniving, he claimed, with the king) to throw themselves on the Parisians!

11

I N AUGUST 1587, although I can't remember the exact day, the king sent me to Sedan to carry a message to the prince of that town, the young Duc de Bouillon. This was a very secret mission, which, because of its nature, put the messenger in great danger, and so the king ordered Fogacer to circulate the rumour that I had retired to Saint-Cloud at the home of the Baron de Quéribus in order to attempt to cure a sickness that carried a high risk of infection—this to keep the spies of the League from sticking their noses into the business. And so I left, ostensibly for Saint-Cloud, quasi-prostrate in my coach and swabbed with ceruse to appear as pale as possible (Miroul telling our neighbours that I was *in extremis*), but accompanied by a large escort provided by Quéribus, made up of the men who'd already accompanied me to Boulogne, and whose loyalty I'd ensured by the means I've previously recounted.

The king having spared no expense for this mission, I remained in Saint-Cloud long enough to purchase three good horses, knowing that the countryside around Sedan was infested with Guise's troops, who, though not explicitly laying siege to the town, kept a close watch on it despite the fact that the king had several times ordered him to withdraw his forces from that area since their continued presence was creating problems for him. You see, the king was ostensibly supporting the Duc de Bouillon, though the duc was a Huguenot, as he didn't want his small duchy to fall into the hands of Guise. This last had already seized Toul and Verdun (but had failed to capture Metz), with the design of closing the border by which the German princes might come to the aid of either the Huguenots or the king of France.

The reason I wanted very healthy, lively and spirited mounts was that if we met any of Guise's men as we approached Sedan, I thought our only hope would be to outrun them. This calculation proved to be correct not once but twice, in encounters in which we barely had time to discharge our pistols before turning tail and, thanks to our horses' strong legs, quickly leaving our enemies for dust.

The young Duc de Bouillon, Prince de Sedan, was barely twenty years old, and he would have exuded charm and vigour had not his health been so compromised, leaving him feverish and congested, as I'd already heard and was confirmed by my first glance. Which led me—since there were in his entourage a number of very suspicious-looking faces that I immediately distrusted—to announce myself as Dubosc, one of the king's physicians, whom His Majesty had commanded to come to see if I could cure the duc's malady. In this way I was able to examine him in private, sheltered from the prying ears of his retinue, and to transmit the secret message from the king, to wit: that he should take control of the great army of reiters, of which he shared the command with the Prussian Fabien de Dhona; that this army should stop in Lorraine and pillage that duchy; and that they should not continue their invasion beyond that point, but instead try to attract and defeat the army of the Duc de Guise, knowing that if, unhappily, they did not succeed, they could easily escape back to their German bases, since they were so near the border.

"Well!" said the young duc, who assuredly was not lacking in intelligence. "That's all very clear and well presented! And I would certainly wish to oblige my king, who protected me from being ripped apart by the violent oppression of the Duc de Guise. But I doubt I could succeed in what you're asking, since Fabien de Dhona would never accept the command of anyone other than a member of the royal family, and neither Navarre nor Condé would venture this far east. Dhona would never accept my command nor listen to my advice, since he's almost twice as old as I am and thinks I'm wet behind the ears, which is true, and brainless, which is not true. Brains have nothing to do with age!"

"But, Monseigneur," I urged, "you could tell him that it is the express desire of the king of France, who, should the reiters be defeated, will guarantee their safe return to their country. It is of the greatest consequence that you understand, Monseigneur, that my master has distributed his forces in such a way as to allow him to remain in control of the situation. On the one hand, he had to provide Guise with a fairly large army, strengthened even further by the forces of the League. This is the army that you and Dhona will have in front of you in Lorraine, if your wisdom prevails and you accept this command. On the other hand, since Joyeuse has gone over to the League, he has fallen from the king's favour and Henri has provided him with a force too weak to defeat Navarre, but strong enough to contain him. The king has set up camp along the Loire with the greater part of his army to prevent Navarre from joining the reiters, if Joyeuse can't stop him, and will thus be able to dictate the terms of peace to all involved if, as he hopes, Guise is beaten in Lorraine and Navarre is stopped in Gironde."

"What a Machiavellian plan!" smiled the Duc de Bouillon. "And one that does honour to my beloved cousin the king of France, who manages to treat his adversaries as friends, and his friends as adversaries!"

"Which assuredly they are, Monseigneur. Who could doubt it? And who is ignorant of the fact that the king of France conducts this extremely distasteful war with reluctance, since he fears almost as much winning as losing? If Guise won in Lorraine or Joyeuse in Gironde it would shake his throne."

Two days later, I left the Duc de Bouillon, so handsome, so amiable and so mortally sick.

In taking my leave, I doubted he'd live more than a few months, or even manage to stay on horseback during the campaign, or even that he'd be able to convince Fabien de Dhona to remain in Lorraine, since the latter's appetite for plunder would doubtless attract him and his troops to Paris, a veritable magnet for the armour of the reiters.

As the king and I had agreed, I didn't return directly to my lodgings in the rue du Champ-Fleuri, but went back to Quéribus's house in Saint-Cloud, arriving after dark so that no one would see me on horseback. As I was dismounting, I asked Quéribus how my Angelina and children were, and he replied that the king had ordered them to be taken to my estate of the Rugged Oak, since, during my absence, my house in Paris had been attacked one night by a good dozen ruffians, who'd tried to break in, taking axes and sledgehammers to the doors and attempting to set fire to the place with petards, which thankfully Miroul had extinguished by throwing water from the roof. From his window in the needle shop, Mérigot had fired on them with two arquebuses (his wench recharging one while he fired the other). Giacomi had joined in from his lodgings with two pistols, and ultimately the rascals had fled, carrying off their wounded and leaving their dead behind. However, one of those left for dead survived, and confessed to Nicolas Poulain that their company had been paid by the major-domo of a great house. This convinced Mosca (or Leo) that Guise had had a hand in this attempted massacre.

Upon hearing this story, which Quéribus told him the next morning, the king began trembling for my safety, especially since he'd just heard the day before that the brave Grillon, who had replaced Monsieur de Bernay as governor of Boulogne, had miraculously escaped an assassination attempt that the Duc d'Aumale had financed. Henri thus concluded, on the one hand, that the League had not swallowed the fable of my illness and believed—perhaps without knowing exactly where—that I was on a mission for His Majesty, and, on the other, that the princes of Lorraine had taken up again their plan of assassinating one by one his most faithful servants and officers to strike terror into the survivors and thereby create a void around him.

"The king," Quéribus concluded, "wants you to take refuge at the Rugged Oak and stay away from the dangers that surround you in Paris, until the war has ended."

"Well," I confessed, "how it saddens me to hear that! What is he saying? That I wouldn't even be safe in his encampment at Gien-sur-Loire surrounded by his troops?"

"He thinks not."

"What about my mission?"

"He begs you to share the fruits of your discussion with me and I will speak for you."

"Not such fruitful fruits! Bouillon wants what the king wants, but he cannot manage it. The strength of the German army is in its size. Its weakness resides in the fact that it's composed of reiters, Huguenots and Swiss, who do not get along with each other, and are commanded by two generals who don't trust each other: Bouillon, whom Dhona considers a child with no experience, and Dhona, whom Bouillon considers an idiot. Moreover, the poor Bouillon is devoured by consumption, which will soon kill him."

"Those are pretty meagre fruits all right," observed Quéribus, "given how much money this three-headed army has cost three kings."

"Three?" I said. "How do you calculate that there are three of them?"

"Navarre, Elizabeth…"

"And the third?"

"Henri."

"What?" I gasped. "Henri?"

"Secretly, through Bouillon. At least, that's what they're saying at court."

"You mean among the League?"

"No, no! Among the most faithful officers of the king. Oh, my brother! If this is true, it's way too deep for me! To pay someone to invade your country!"

"Not at all, my Quarreller!" I smiled. "To invade Lorraine, devastate it and vanquish Guise!"

"Well!" said Quéribus taking his head in his hands. "Machiavelli! Machiavelli! Machiavelli! Did you know that Navarre has also asked Bouillon to go to Lorraine? He only wants the reiters to create a diversion, not to try to join forces with him, since he doesn't want to owe his eventual victory to a foreign army or to confront Henri in his encampment at Gien-sur-Loire. Apparently, Henri keeps saying, 'I'm using my enemies to take revenge on my enemies!' The king says this in Latin."

"In Latin it goes like this," I said, parading my knowledge of that language: "'*de inimicis meis vindicabo inimicos meos*.'"

"Ah, Pierre, how knowledgeable you are! How I regret, when I hear you speak Latin, that I never studied anything but military arts when I was younger!"

"And you're the finest blade in the kingdom, and at more than thirty years of age you still you cut a figure that turns a lot of heads…"

"This is true," conceded Quéribus, prancing a bit to display his wasp-like figure. But it sounds like you yourself made some conquests in London…"

"Silliness and nonsense! I was wasting my time! I merely flattered a flower who had no interest in being picked, or even admired."

My Quarreller was not unhappy to hear this: having conceded my abilities in science, eloquence and politics, he didn't want to vie with me to be the most seductive member of the family.

"Ah, if only I could have come with you to London, I could have been your second!"

"No, you would have been the leader of the expedition! For I have no doubt that as soon as you arrived you would have said, like Caesar, '*Veni, vidi, vici!*'"

"And that means?" he said, raising an eyebrow that was, like the king's, plucked and painted.

"I came, I saw, I conquered."

"Excellent!" cried Quéribus, delighted and amused. "Most excellent! Oh heavens! What a proud motto! Pierre, you must write it down for me in Latin so that I can memorize it and use it on occasion! Better yet, I'll have it embroidered in gold on my hose so that I can always have it in mind when I'm undressing!"

It was not without some sadness that I watched him ride off the next day on a pretty bay mare with his escort, heading for the king's encampment at Gien-sur-Loire, envying the wild insouciance of this worldly-wise favourite of the court, as if that were not a contradiction in terms. At least, whatever his coquettish frivolities, Quéribus was faithful to his king. Not that he understood where His Majesty wanted to lead him, but he followed nonetheless as a point of gentleman's honour, however perilous this fidelity might be, since the League had sworn to bring about the deaths of all the supporters of Henri and the ruin of their houses once victory had been declared.

All that autumn, I champed at the bit in my little estate—not that there wasn't a lot to keep me occupied there, finishing the fortifications on the model of what we'd done at Mespech, and managing my estate according to good Huguenot economy. I'd been able to enlarge my domain over the years, thanks to the largesse of my master. And it must be said that I would never be one to feel the time drag even in the middle of a desert, being a man who enjoys the charms of his household and marriage. Angelina, my beautiful children, my books, my rides through the forest of Montfort-l'Amaury and the evenings spent in front of the fire with neighbours, men of lesser nobility, richer in rustic virtues than in money. And yet I languished so far from my master's service, for this work had become the very stuff of my life, since, in serving the king, I was persuaded that I was also serving the conservation of the state, the maintenance of peace and the victory of tolerance.

Heavens! How many times in my forced rustic inactivity did I dream about and relive, though without ever satisfying this thirst, my many memories of comic or dangerous events on my missions in Guyenne, in Boulogne, in London and in Sedan! It seemed to me that I was fully alive at those moments, and the more so the more dangerous and useful I was, serving as a weaver's shuttle in the hands of His Majesty, going and coming, returning again, according to the orders Henri gave me, but always at the centre of the warp and weft of the enormous tapestry he wove to defend his throne against those who sought to overthrow him and trample the people under the scourge of war, massacres and the Inquisition.

I often invited the priest Ameline to Montfort, who was a good enough fellow, prudent, not more invested in the League than was necessary for his well-being, never preaching against the king—and only rarely against the arch-favourites—and moderate in his habits, his behaviour and his body. He was neither tall nor short, neither thin nor fat, neither hairy nor bald, neither young nor old, neither puny nor hale, neither wanton nor entirely chaste, neither too fond of the bottle nor rejecting of it, neither stingy nor liberal, neither gluttonous nor abstinent, neither a dolt nor a wit, neither eloquent nor stuttering, neither wise nor foolish, neither cowardly nor brave, neither a zealous worker nor a lazy one—and whatever he said, or suggested, or condemned, it was never entirely fish or fowl.

Of his face, one couldn't quite say whether it was round, oval or square (or a bit of each); whether his look was frank or false; which his nose was, thin or obscene; whether his teeth were good or bad, since he never showed them when he smiled; or whether his voice was strong or weak, since he opened his mouth so little to let it out.

"Well, Monsieur chevalier," he said, sitting down at my table on the chilly 16th November that remains today so vivid in my memory, after greeting me neither coldly nor warmly in response to my welcome, "I had Monsieur the abbot of Barthes visit me yesterday, who comes by fairly often, since he has some land at Mesnuls. He is, as I believe I've mentioned to you, the confessor of Chancellor de Villequier, and since he was coming from Paris, he brought me news of the war that we're waging."

"And what is the news?"

"Neither good nor bad," answered the priest.

I knew he would say that, I swear! And seeing him sitting there silently chewing on his ham, I waited until he'd finished to say:

"Please tell me about it!"

"For the moment, here's how it stands," said Ameline. "The army of Monseigneur the Duc de Joyeuse was entirely broken and defeated at Coutras by the king of Navarre on the twentieth of October, and a large number of Catholic noblemen were killed. Monsieur de Joyeuse himself was thrown from his horse, upon which he brandished his gauntlet and cried, 'Ten thousand écus to spare my life!' but had his head shattered by a pistol shot fired by the fellow who was the sole survivor of the massacre that the duc had ordered at La Motte Saint-Eloi."

"The trouble with massacres," I noted, "other than their inhumanity, is that they always leave behind a witness or an avenger, but that's a lesson you never get to profit from since that lone survivor will end up killing you."

That was all I could think of to say, since I didn't want to rejoice at Navarre's victory or pretend to be disappointed by it.

"The strangest part of the business," continued Ameline, "is that once Navarre had won the battle, he disbanded his army and disappeared. It was even rumoured that he'd died. But I don't believe it. If he'd been killed, they would have paraded his body around *urbi et orbi*. So he's still alive."

"So what's the good news?" I asked, fearing the worst.

"The great foreign army, which people said would remain in Lorraine, has spread out over the kingdom, one leader pulling to the left and the other pulling to the right in total confusion, and ultimately it was surprised at Vimory and defeated by the Duc de Guise, who killed 2,000 of them."

"So where did the other 20,000 go?"

"I don't know," replied Ameline, who seemed momentarily surprised that I didn't rejoice at this victory as he had expected.

But seeing this, I quickly added with some gravity:

"In my opinion, the good and the bad are sometimes counterbalanced. We must wait to see how things play out with Navarre on the one hand, and the remaining presence of the reiters on the other, to see whether there's any reason for celebration."

"Well," Amine corrected, "there's already a reason! The Duc de Guise's victory is being greeted everywhere with great joy! In Paris there are fireworks; stories of the victory are being printed and proclaimed at every street corner, and the standards seized from the reiters are on display. In every church a *Te Deum* is being sung, and outside public prayers and Ave Marias."

"Ah," I thought to myself, "the League is very busy, indeed! I'll bet the Duchesse de Montpensier is busily buying streamers to attach to all the standards taken from the enemy—and she's got an infinite litany of praise for Guise issuing from every pulpit of the city!"

I had some difficulty hiding my teeth-gnashing from Ameline, and instead feigned moderation, which he could easily identify with, since he never bragged and, by nature, avoided all extremes. And in the end, fearing that he should remember my indifference later, I slipped him a few écus, knowing that he was engaging in redoing the roof of his vicarage, having now finished the one for the sacristy.

I'd known Anne de Joyeuse back in Montpellier, when he was scarcely five years old and was certainly the cutest little fellow in creation, his pink cheeks, blue eyes and golden hair looking angelic, and his manners so sweet, so open and so affectionate that you couldn't look at him without delight. His father, the Vicomte de Joyeuse, was governor of Montpellier; I'd first seen him at breakfast, eating with one of those little forks—an unheard-of refinement at the time—that looked like a tiny pitchfork, whose use was later introduced by Henri III at court, causing a great scandal among his pious courtiers, and which was later dubbed a *fourchette*.

Anne, whose image remains so indelibly fixed in such vivid colours in my memory, was just tall enough to see what was on the table where his father was seated. He wore a pale-blue cap and a large flattened collar. He seemed to me to be lively, mischievous and funny, but a well-behaved lad, who kept looking lovingly from his father to his father's plate, on which he was cutting his meat, and each time Anne saw a morsel he liked, he'd point with his little finger and say in bird-like, sing-song tones:

"May I, Monsieur my father?"

And Monsieur de Joyeuse, smiling, would answer with great civility:

"You may, Anne."

Later, I saw Anne quite often, since I'd had my friend Espoumel carve a set of little wooden soldiers, some with French, some with English uniforms, and place them in the miniature fortifications that we'd made for Anne's birthday, and re-enacted for him the siege of Calais—which I knew well, since my father had fought heroically in that battle alongside the father of the current Duc de Guise. And, passing him the stick by which he could move the soldiers about in the construction, advancing into or retreating from the breaks in the walls that our cannon had made, I sadly watched him repeat over and over the same mistakes, using up his reserves too quickly, failing to protect his rear and pushing too far ahead with his avant-garde.

I had the occasion to encounter him again at court, when, at eighteen years old, he conquered the affections of the king. He was, at that age, so amazingly good-looking that one of our poets could have compared him to a flower without anyone smiling at it. But sadly, the person most amazed by this beauty was Anne himself, being so enamoured of himself, so drunk with his own charm, that he lost all reason and abandoned himself to every caprice, including constantly changing his moods.

All of these defects—which so exasperated the king that occasionally he went as far as to beat his arch-favourite—made up the essence of his charm, which, like that of some children, was composed of his inaccessibility, his lack of conscience and his thoughtlessness.

He gave proofs of this instability that astonished even the most phlegmatic of his friends. Showered by Henri with favours, titles, lands, chateaux and an immense fortune, and married off to a princess well above his own rank, he consorted with the Duc de Guise and became a member of the League, in hopes of maintaining and increasing these exorbitant privileges once Henri had died. After which, he felt exceedingly unhappy when the king lost interest in him and his younger brother, the Comte du Bouchage, and locked himself away in a monastery so as not to have to choose between the king and him.

Poor little Joyeuse was so empty-headed that he thought he could betray Henri without losing his love, massacre unarmed prisoners at the battle of La Motte Saint-Eloi and continue to be admired as a humane leader, and have this massacre celebrated in the sermons in the capital while retaining the esteem of the king, who hated both massacres and the sermons!

He was called the "arch-favourite" but he should have been called the "arch-spoilt child", for his insane lack of discipline caused him to lose the first important battle he ever fought; and when, on the battlefield, he shouted, "Ten thousand écus to spare my life!" his cry had no other result than to attract a pistol bullet that was not so light as his brain, and represented a judgement that exacting vengeance for the massacre of La Motte Saint-Eloi was worth more than an heavy pile of écus.

In memory of the child he was, I felt some regret at the death of this young man, but shed not a tear, since tears were inappropriate, given his treason and his cruelties, whatever the lack of responsibility and thoughtlessness that led him to commit them. *Fructu non foliis arborem aestima.**

Around 1st December, I was strolling through the woods of Montfort-l'Amaury with Miroul and three of my domestics, all of us well armed, when, approaching the pond that lies along the right-hand side of the road called "Great Master's Road", I heard some cries. Believing that it must be some travellers under attack by highwaymen, I galloped furiously towards the lake, followed by my company, and there saw some woodcutters in a small boat trying to pull a wench from the water, who, far from making their task easy, was vigorously resisting their efforts and screaming at the top of her lungs that she wanted to die and that neither God nor the Blessed Virgin could prevent her from doing so. Luckily, she was screaming in Provençal, a language

---

* "One must judge a tree by its fruits, not by its leaves."

not comprehensible in the Île-de-France, so that the woodsmen didn't understand, or they might have been horrified by her blasphemies and just let her drown. Unhitching another boat, Miroul and I jumped in and rowed over to this desperate stranger, who seemed to be unable either to pursue or to abandon her enterprise, since her saviours were keeping her afloat with their oars, yet couldn't persuade her to grab on to their boat. But since we came up from behind her without her seeing us, while she continued her impious and strident invective, I was able to seize her by her chin and, with Miroul's help, pull her aboard despite her nearly capsizing us with her desperate defence. Finally, having laid her out on the bottom of our craft and with my full weight preventing her from escaping (though this was far from pleasant since she was soaked with icy water), I seized both her hands in one of mine to prevent her from scratching my face, and, as she began to quieten down a bit, with my other hand brushing her long, wet hair away from her features, I succeeded finally in uncovering her face and recognized… Zara.

"Ah, Zara!" I exclaimed.

I said no more until we had her up behind me on my horse, and Miroul tied us together with a rope, after having given a few coins to these woodsmen, who doffed their hats to us and offered us "10,000 million thanks", just as Queen Elizabeth would say, as they left. Not only had they doubtless earned more in these few minutes on the water than in an entire week splitting logs, they had also walked away with a thrilling story that would be retold every night until Christmas!

I could just as well have not tied up Zara, since she had now calmed down and was shivering from head to toe, gripping me with all her strength and whispering to me not to gallop since she was terrified of falling—that she was falling! that she was dying of fear! I looked back at her and assured her that it was better to die from fear than from drowning, especially in December. Now, with her charming lisp, she told me she could see that I had turned against her, conniving with everyone else to reject her, to point fingers at her, and I could only surmise from all this that she was regaining the will to live, since she was protesting so vigorously. Then, having said all that, she suddenly gave me a wet kiss on the back of my neck and hugged me tight, adding, without any fear of contradiction, that I was the only one—the only one!—for ten leagues around to show her any tenderness or consideration.

Since Angelina wasn't at home, I had a great fire lit in her room and, having undressed my poor Zara so close to the hearth that we were almost touching the flames, since she was now blue from the cold and shivering uncontrollably, I gave her an energetic rubdown, a task that, other than warming me greatly, had its own recompense, since her body was as beautiful as her face, and it would have been a great pity if she'd removed herself in her distress from the human race.

The chambermaids having refilled the bath with hot water, I jumped in beside Zara and continued my ministrations until she turned as pink as a crayfish, her face regaining its colour and her eyes recovering their sparkle. Then, hearing a noise at the front door, I let Florine take over and ran to the door, which Miroul opened, admitting Angelina, surprised to see me soaked through and dripping water, followed by Fogacer and Silvio, whose arrival evoked an equal degree of surprise from me since they'd just arrived on horseback from Paris, having sent ahead a letter that we had never received. Not wishing to inundate them with my embraces, I told Angelina that Zara was in her room, and, when she'd finished her bath, to avoid asking her any questions until I'd returned, having now to bathe and change my clothes to prevent catching my death of cold.

When I returned to Angelina's room, a full hour later (having remembered that I owed Pierre de L'Étoile a letter and that I had to write it before the courier from Montfort left), I saw that my wife, as generous and caring as ever, had accomplished miracles, having washed

Zara's hair and dried it before the fire, then dressed her in her own most beautiful gown and adorned her with her most beautiful jewels—a triangular necklace of diamonds. Florine had brushed and arranged Zara's hair, found slippers for her and applied make-up, eyeshadow and lipstick so that she was now as beautiful as I'd ever seen her.

Night was falling as I entered the room; the shutters were closed and the curtains drawn; the fire, to which Miroul had generously added new logs, was flaming brightly, and the room was pulverized with sweet perfume. It was all the cosier since one could hear the bitter winds of December howling outside, and brilliantly illuminated with all the candles that Florine had lit to pamper Zara. I was transported by the joy of seeing my beloved and Florine, so beautiful themselves, serving with such affection our Zara, in an effort to pull her from her despair (whose cause they did not yet know; all they knew was that she'd tried to drown herself)—sweet physicians that they fancied themselves, healing the soul by means of the body, and returning to Zara some appetite for life through this act of beautifying her.

They were just finishing their ministrations when I entered; then, each taking Zara by the hand, they illuminated her with a chandelier, and led her, not without some pomp and mystery, over to a large Venetian mirror that I'd given Angelina for her last saint's day, and there Angelina told her to open her golden eyes, whereupon Zara cried out loud to see herself looking so beautiful, and then just as suddenly fell silent, lost in contemplation. I must say, speaking as a doctor, that this sudden and unexpected joy so infused her blood with vitality that her animal spirits were reinvigorated and her humours were realigned. And, immediately relieved to see her reborn and ascend from the depths of suffering into which she had fallen—so deep that she'd rejected God and the life that He had given her—we all surrounded her with love and caresses, and I told her repeatedly (with a knowing look at Angelina so that she would forgive my hyperbole) that there was no one on earth more delicious to behold and that our world would be desolate and deserted if we were to lose her.

And I must say that it is quite true that, apart from my Angelina, there was no more charming object than Zara on our earthly globe, which would be a mournful hell if her sex had been exiled from it. While receiving our embraces, squeezes, pats and kisses, though these last had to be very light in order not to ruin her make-up, my Zara was throwing me smiles and glances in the mirror, all the while twisting her long, lithe, buxom body into poses that showed to great advantage her sculpted profile, long and flexible neck, and beautiful green sparkling eyes with their tiny gold specks.

And when she was quite satisfied with all this attention, we had practically to force her to eat a bowl of hot soup, half a goblet of Bordeaux wine and an almond tart. When she had enjoyed of all of this without leaving a drop or a crumb, she announced she was renouncing food, drink and sleep for the rest of her life, so mortified was she at the terrible wrong she'd suffered.

"But what wrong is this, my Zara?" asked Angelina, fixing her beautiful, tender black eyes on her.

"Well, Mademoiselle Angelina," cried Zara, her green eyes darkening with spiteful anger, "do you not know? Dame Gertrude has dared hire a personal chambermaid, a slattern of a scullery maid, a horrible imp who thinks she can take my place simply because she's young."

"But, Zara," soothed Angelina very innocently, "Gertrude has not sent you away! Far from it! She simply wants to ease your burden by having Éloïse help you. The girl's neither dirty nor ugly, from what I've seen."

"Madame!" cried Zara, pacing back and forth in front of us, her eyes inflamed and wringing her hands. "You must not have looked carefully! The imp is not attractive, I can tell you. Her tits are bubbling out of her blouse, like milk boiling over on a fire, and her stomach is so big it touches her knees—and as for her arse, which I've seen naked, I swear, I can tell you it has hair on it!"

"What?" gasped my credulous Angelina. "On her buttocks? You really mean on her buttocks? Zara, that's very strange. Couldn't it be removed?"

"But to what barber at the baths would the slut dare show these horrors?" continued Zara, practically grinding her teeth. "Not to mention that she also has a very menacing and idiotic look, a snotty nose and smelly feet! Ah, what a beautiful chambermaid my mistress has hired… whom she presumes, Madame—hear me carefully, I beg you!—whom she presumes to have sleep with her, preferring her to me!" she lamented, beating her breast. "Ah, Madame! Madame! What an affront Dame Gertrude has made to me! What an abject affront! To prefer her to me! To me—the one who's loved and served her!" she continued, glancing indignantly at her image in the Venetian mirror. "She's taken this pile of filth and stuffed her in her bed! Monsieur chevalier, how can one who has flown so high end up landing in the manure pile?"

And at this thought, tears began to well up in her eyes. Seeing this, Florine cried:

"Madame, if you cry you're going to ruin all my work!"

I know not by what miracle Zara managed to restrain her tears, but her eyes did remain dry, though they weren't any the less full of sparks, projecting the heat of her Italian anger, and she managed to lift her head in pride, arching her back like a mare rearing and beating the air with its front hooves.

"But Zara," soothed Angelina, her candid eyes opening wide, "I understand that many mistresses like the company of their chambermaids in bed, and the custom is quite widespread. After all, Zara, sleeping in one place or another is not so important. What difference does it make?"

"Not so important, Madame? My place in bed not so important? I've served Dame Gertrude with the most ardent devotion all these years and the first imp that comes along takes my place in her bed! No, Madame, I won't tolerate it! And I'll never set foot in Dame Gertrude's house again until she's sent this dirty scullery maid back to the manure pile from which she was spawned!"

"Now Zara," said Angelina, "don't talk this way! The poor girl has a human mother and father just like you!"

"No, Madame," came Zara's retort, as if she were quoting from one of the Gospels. "I affirm that she grew in the manure pile like a mushroom!"

"Zara," I pointed out, thinking the moment had come to introduce a little realism into her inflamed hysteria, "it doesn't look as though your mistress is going to obey you and send away this wench, if she's grown accustomed to her. What are you going to do in this predicament?"

"Go back to the pond you fished me out of!" cried Zara, crossing her arms over her chest. "What else can I do?"

"Ah, Zara," cried Angelina, rushing over to her, "you're not going to repeat this infamy! You'd be rejecting God and will lose your eternal salvation! No, no, my Zara," she said, taking her in her arms and covering her with kisses, "if you don't want to go back to Gertrude, we'll keep you here in our lodgings with us."

At this, showering us with infinite thanks, our Zara began to perk up a bit, preferring to be overwhelmed by our insistence than to return to her encounter with death (since, as she confessed later, she had developed a horror of water, to the extent that she frequently awoke at night feeling the pond closing around her and vines wrapping around her legs, pulling her under like so many hands).

And so it was that Zara came to take her place in the constellation of our household, a place that was honourable but not well defined since she seemed to have no role among our domestics other than an ornamental one, given that she never consented to dirty her hands with any sort of task, even of the lightest kind. So, for lack of any other function, she became a companion to Angelina, an office that was for my poor wife much more of a cross to bear than a pleasure, since her companion spent her time interminably and repetitively chewing over her recriminations against Gertrude in pathetic tones, her eyes shining, her mouth drawn in bitterness and her shoulders shaking in a flood of words so continuous and precipitous that they made you think of a rushing river and the inexorable mill wheel that it turns round and round. My poor Angelina emerged from these frenetic monologues with her head buzzing and her heart stricken, and in the end she begged me to serve as an intermediary with Gertrude to attempt to resolve this quarrel, which had come to seem of greater consequence than the war that was ravaging the kingdom and dividing our people.

I did my best, but failed completely to persuade the proud Norman lady to send Éloïse away and take Zara back, even though it seemed to me that she was beginning to tire of the former and regret losing the latter. But as we all know, a sense of pride and some small point of honour in not giving in often play a large role in such matters.

On the evening of their arrival at my little estate, I retired with Fogacer and Silvio to my library (whose books had increased greatly in number since the king had begun to shower me with wealth), and I assailed Fogacer with questions about the news from Paris. Standing on one leg like a heron, he stretched out his tall, thin silhouette in front of the fire, clothed in black as usual, standing at ease with his left hand on his hip; Silvio straddled a stool, and looked much bigger and stronger, with a beard sprouting on his chin.

"Well, *mi fili*," said Fogacer, "the problem with being Machiavellian is that when double-dealing doesn't work, you lose doubly: both the stakes and the consideration of the other players, since cheating is universally scorned. And so it is with our poor Henri. The large foreign army of Swiss and reiters, shaken by Guise at Vimory, was hit again at Auneau. These were small engagements that the League trumpeted as sublime victories, accustomed as they are to making every little Guisard cat into a tiger. And the reality is that they're only giving these laurels to Guise to diminish any successes of the king, who heads a huge army that could exterminate the remains of the foreign army if he wished. But the king will have none of it. Why? *Mi fili*," continued Fogacer, looking me in the eye, his eyebrows arched in confusion, "you did ask me to come here, but why?"

"I don't know if I requested you to come," I laughed, "but it turns out that I do need you here."

"Well, I heard you! *Primo*, the king, who is human, abhors blood and massacres. *Secundo*, he doesn't want to antagonize the reiters and the Swiss, since he thinks he may need their help soon against Guise. He's in discussions with them and is paying them to leave his kingdom."

"He's paying them!"

"He's paying them in linens, silks and in écus for their departure. *Exeunt* reiters and Swiss."

"That's good news!" I observed.

"It's very bad news!" corrected Fogacer, stretching his long spidery arms so that they seemed to fill the library. "Because they're now beginning to say in Paris *that the reiters were called for, paid and sent home by the king, given how well he's treated them*! Now Paris is full of shouting! Clamour! Sermons! Raised fists! Henri is now almost universally hated and despised by the populace. And the Sorbonne—you've heard no doubt—the Sorbonne (that is to say, forty crusty pedants) got together to have a drink and concluded that it's legal for them to remove the government from the hands of the king if things aren't to their liking!"

"That's rebellion!" I said.

"Open and frenzied! Ah, *mi fili*, Paris is boiling! The throne is beginning to wobble!"

This said, Fogacer threw himself down on the armchair I'd offered him when he came in, and, pointing at a cushion nearby, he said:

"My Silvio, come and sit here."

I was very surprised to see Silvio—whom I'd seen so many times sitting at the feet of his master—openly pout and reply:

"Venerable doctor, with your permission, I'd rather stay where I am."

This reply so startled Fogacer that he visibly paled and fell silent, his eyes closing and his upper lip beginning to tremble. This display left me surprised and, in a way, disappointed, since I'd always imagined that my former teacher at the school of medicine in Montpellier was able to rise above human emotions, both through his science and by the cold scalpel of his mind. Alas, these days I know all too well, now that I'm older, that one whom we may venerate as a demigod or hero in our childhood sometimes descends from his pedestal in tears, stung by the ingratitude or betrayal of a friend, who causes him all the more pain the closer he is to his heart.

Aware of this silence as it continued, and of Fogacer's brown eyes fixed with astonishment on Silvio's, still blinking as though the tyro had slapped him, and that he was unable to think of what to say or do in the pain he was feeling—not so much in his sense of honour as in his raw affections—I decided to break the cruel ice that had closed over his soul, and, attempting to distract him from the throes of this cruelty, I said:

"So what's this about Navarre disappearing after Coutras, when he so unexpectedly disbanded his army?"

"Well," explained Fogacer, his voice gradually regaining its timbre, "that was not a surprise to Henri. It's proof that Navarre and the king never stopped working in concert. As you know, Navarre has always had the wisdom to pretend to be a madman. He disbanded his own army in order not to have to attack the army of the king, who is his declared enemy and secret ally. And so, to cover his inactivity, he hurried to lay a laurel wreath at the feet of his mistress, the beautiful Corisande. He's still there, as profligate as a rat in straw."

"Does Guise know this?"

"He didn't learn it immediately," said Fogacer as he stood up, his eyes still looking very sad under those arched eyebrows, his hand grazing, as if by accident, Silvio's face with a constrained, almost furtive air. "He didn't know it," he repeated, turning away, his voice suddenly recovering its mocking and sarcastic tone, "and seeing the king warming himself by the fire, just as I am doing now, and believing—or wishing to believe—that Navarre was dead, as rumours had it in Paris, Guise asked His Majesty for news of him. At this the king gave him that sidelong glance that makes his Italian eyes so bright, and said with a smile, and in a tone that I can't imitate, 'I know about the rumour that's circulating, and why you're asking me about it. Well, he's as dead as you are.' Did you hear that, *mi fili*? 'He's as dead as you are'! All the pedants in the Sorbonne, putting their heads together, could spend the rest of time glossing that little phrase and find millions of meanings in it, the most obvious not being the right one. For example: 'He's as dead as you are alive,' which is flat. Or again: 'He's dead like you, who are, alas, alive.' This is even better: 'He's dead like you, whose death I hope for.' Which is excellent."

This said, arching his satanic eyebrow, he smiled his slow, sardonic, sinuous smile, which quickly turned into a bitter grimace, all his features contracting, hollowing out and shrinking into an expression of such bleak torment that, seeing it, I fell silent, unable to say a word. Then, suddenly, Fogacer took leave of me in a strangled voice, rose and turned away, casting the same constrained and furtive look at Silvio over his shoulder, and left the library.

The silence that followed his departure was deafening, and I expected that Silvio would also take his leave, but the young man just sat there on his stool, like a log, his eyes on the fire and his expression resolute, though looking both sad and terrified, so I finally decided to wish him a good evening and withdrew.

Six weeks after this terrible evening, which was doubly sad for me (since I'd both learnt of the failure of my master's projects and witnessed Fogacer's heart-rending troubles with Silvio), after having taken breakfast before heading out for my usual morning ride with Fogacer through the forest of Montfort, I was astonished to enter the stables and discover that he and his horse were not there. I called Miroul, who appeared looking very troubled and holding a letter from Fogacer, who'd left at daybreak for Paris, begging Miroul not to wake me. Miroul reported that Fogacer had told him that the circumstances of his sudden departure would be explained in the letter. Alarmed that he'd decided to run the risk of travelling alone on these dangerous roads all the way to Paris, I tore open the missive and read:

Mi fili,

I have never known in my troubled existence a wound that grieved me more than this one. Even the executioner, to whom I'm doubly destined—by both my nature and my unbelief—would be a briefer torment and provide me with a merciful death. *Mi fili*, forgive me for running off like an Englishman and for leaving Silvio there, who knows perfectly well why I've done so. Alas, the further I continue in this miserable life, the more I discover that to love is ultimately to suffer and suffer again. Grief is such a very long process.

I pray and beg you, *mi fili*, turning to you as my only and immutable friend, to take good care of this little unfortunate. I couldn't stand to see him cast into the street, hungry and homeless, still loving him as I do, despite his betrayal. As soon as you return to Paris, I will pay you whatever expenses you have incurred to keep him with you. *Vale, mi fili.* My eyes are full of tears as I write this. Please do not say anything to your adorable wife about this, who is to me like a mother, a daughter, a sister and so much more. *Mi fili*, one more embrace! Since I cannot pray, I can only ask that you think of me from time to time.

Your affectionate,

Fogacer

Well, I offered him a thousand times more in friendship than he asked, but I found several things in his letter that were confusing, and so I resolved to ask Silvio to enlighten me, and went to find him in his room. Hearing no response when I knocked, I presumed to open the door, and, to my great surprise, found Zara and Silvio there, both fully dressed—the former was sitting like a queen on an armchair, looking very proud and stiff; at her knees, with his hands joined, his face wet from tears, was the latter. The sight of me seemed to strike such terror into him that he would have run away had I not seized his arm and forced him to sit down on a stool.

"Silvio," I exclaimed, "what's going on? What's Zara doing in here? What were you doing on your knees? What's the meaning of these tears?"

But Silvio only lowered his head at these words, paralysed by shame, and continued crying copious tears. I turned to Zara with an inquisitive look, at which the beauty, with a very haughty and disdainful air and a look of triumph, said calmly:

"I asked Silvio, with no promise of faith or fidelity, to make me pregnant, and now that it's done, this silly child refuses to accept his dismissal, which I'd carefully warned him would be forthcoming, and wants to stick to my skin like a louse in a monk's hair!"

"What?" I gasped, hardly daring to believe my ears. "Zara, you're pregnant? With Silvio's child? You who've always said you hated men?"

"Oh, but I do hate them," snorted Zara contemptuously, "but since I wanted to get pregnant to take my revenge on Gertrude, I chose this lad, who's scarcely a man, being so young and soft."

"Soft!" cried Silvio, tears gushing from his eyes with this new affront. "Soft!" he repeated, shaking his brown curls indignantly. "You have every reason to believe the contrary!"

"You know what I mean," sniffed Zara with crushing haughtiness. "And do you flatter yourself, you good-for-nothing, that I'd promise to marry you? You or anyone else?"

"But, Zara," I asked, stupefied, "if you don't want a husband, how are you going to manage raising the child your carrying?"

"Well, Monsieur," she said proudly, "trust me! I'll manage! If I have to, I'll work with my hands!" she added, looking at her beautiful long hands, as if the idea of asking them to do any work would have astonished even her.

"Ah, Zara, Zara!" I cried, not knowing whether to laugh or be angry with her bizarre unreasonableness. "Is this what you had to do to express your anger with Gertrude? Is it not madness to get a bloated stomach just to spite her? Do you really think she'll give in to your wishes when you have brought a child into the world?"

"I don't know," she conceded, her eyes suddenly filling with tears. "I cannot believe that she doesn't love me any more after so many years that I've loved her, and that she'll completely forget me and won't want to help me or have me near her! My life has no meaning or substance without her!"

The real Zara, so close to tears, speaking her heart without any pretence or hauteur, convinced me that this baby was a kind of appeal and that she wanted, hoping against hope, to share it with Gertrude and for them to raise it together. I was so moved by this thought that

I took her in my arms and gave her two kisses; then I sent her back to her room, asking her not to share any of this with my Angelina, who would be most discomfited, and promised that I'd speak to Gertrude. Hearing this, Zara leapt to her feet and said, in a cutting tone, that she forbade me to do so. But I know that, secretly, she hoped I would not obey this order.

Silvio, who hadn't said a word this entire time, made a movement to get up from his stool when Zara headed for the door, but, sensing his movement, she whirled around and gave him such a withering look that the poor fellow sat straight back down, wounded by such manifest scorn.

I felt enormous compassion for him at that moment, since it appeared that he was the great loser in this business, having renounced one love without winning the other. And since I had to tell him about Fogacer's departure, I took care to soften this terrible news by informing him of his master's generosity on his behalf, which, if it didn't replace his tutorial presence, at least assured him of bread and shelter in this dangerous world. He paled at first, and then began shedding hot tears, and was unable to say a word, so acute was his pain. So I just stood there, quietly contemplating him, waiting for him to regain his composure. He was a likeable fellow, who would never lack for women in his life, since it was now clear that he was inclined in that direction; he had something of the Moor in his colouring, being fairly brown-skinned and black-eyed, with curly, crow-black hair and handsome features, with a virile look in the design of his cheek and neck that would not fail to interest the opposite sex. He had, in addition, a lively mind and a ready tongue, and spoke eloquently and, from what I'd observed, candidly.

"Ah, Monsieur!" he moaned, rising from his stool, his tears subsiding. "What a strange loss I've had! And how empty my life seems! Such a good master! The wisest of men! And the most benign and humane! He didn't just pull me from the mire—he educated me. He was both mother and father to me and I'm immensely grateful, and there's no mother's son in the kingdom for whom I'll ever have more respect and immutable friendship."

"And yet you hurt him pretty badly in my library, and it seemed to me that, during these last few weeks, you'd become estranged from him."

He didn't quite know how to reply to this, and blushed, lowering his eyes, overcome with shame. I waited quietly, however, and at last he said, his voice very constricted by the knot in his throat:

"Monsieur, you're touching there on a point that might have given offence to anyone but yourself, for I know from my master Fogacer, who has so often praised you, that you are nourished by the true milk of the Gospel, and accept his person and his nature just as they are, without blame or condemnation of any sort. But for me, you must know that I am not made of the same stuff that you accept in him. I am not naturally inclined to homosexuality—since it must be called by its name—and only consented out of gratitude towards him. So, in the end, I had to become a man in all respects, and discontinue our relationship. Which is why, Zara having made the overtures that she did, I hastened to agree, and went at it quite passionately, very curious about the body of a woman, something that was unknown to me, and became quite enamoured of it as soon as I was able to possess it. Alas, Monsieur, I found Zara only to lose her as well…"

"And yet, Silvio," I soothed, "give the woman her due: she never promised you anything. She didn't fool you or cheat you."

"'Tis true enough. But how rough and rude she was when she'd got what she wanted from me! Ah, Monsieur, what a pity that this marvellous body does not enclose a heart as tender and benign as my master's!"

"Silvio," I smiled, "the members of this gentle sex are not all without hearts, as you'll discover someday, being as young as you are and having the vast world at your feet, populated with such an infinite variety of people. Meanwhile, Silvio, we're going to keep you with us, and Miroul will find work for you that will distract you from these terrible losses that you've endured."

He stammered his thanks in his confusion, and I left him, fearing that the arid dismissal by Zara, who was still living with us, coupled with the absence of Fogacer, would make life thorny for him for a while. But what could I do? And who is at fault in this strange world, when we don't love those who love us, and love where we are not loved?

Luckily—or unluckily—this situation lasted only one day, for that very evening my Quéribus arrived, followed by his usual lordly escort, that included not only a dozen robust valets, but also a masseur, a barber, a fortune-teller and a fool.

As soon as he had paid courteous homage to Angelina, he asked to speak to me in my library, and, once closeted there, said to me with immense seriousness:

"Monsieur my brother, I've come here on behalf of the king, who requires your presence in his Louvre."

"Ah, my brother! My brother!" I cried, overwhelmed with joy, since I'd been champing at the bit these many months I'd been confined to my house and fields. "At last I'm going to serve him! And do you know the reason?"

"Yes, indeed. He explained it, though I confess it's Greek to me! It seems that the king would like you to re-establish contact with a certain 'Mosca', unless it's 'Leo'. I'm repeating this as I believe I heard it, since I know no one bearing these strange names at court. Which, by the way, my brother, you will find quite abandoned by all those lords who've gone off to join Guise."

"Are things going so badly?" I said, my throat tightening.

"Ah, Monsieur my brother!" replied Quéribus with a bitterness that was quite unusual for him. "They're going worse than badly!

When you walk through the streets of Paris, all you hear are rogues saying, 'Let's take this blackguard from his Louvre and lock him in a monastery!' And no one dares argue or challenge the knaves for fear of being torn to pieces by the populace, so great is the execration directed at Henri for not having crushed the Huguenots and reiters. Is it not incredible that the king should be treated as a traitor to the Church for having been human?"

"So that's how things are?"

"That bad and worse!" replied Quéribus. "My confessor has come down with a fever and has withdrawn his support. So I went to make confession to one of the wretched priests in Paris. And do you know what the first thing this fellow said to me was? 'My son, are you for the League?' 'No, my father.' 'In that case, my son, I cannot hear your confession, since in good conscience, I could not absolve you.'"

"But that's crazy!"

"Indeed," replied Quéribus with a degree of bitterness I'd never heard in him. "Words are too feeble to condemn this confusion of the political sphere with the spiritual. Oh, Pierre! Religion has become nothing but hatred! We think we're hearing our priests crying 'Give us this day our daily blood!' Outside the extermination of the heretics there is no faith! No hope! No salvation! That's what it has come to, my brother!…"

12

R ECOLLECTING THE INJURIES and attacks against my lodgings launched by the Guisards while I was in Sedan visiting the poor young Duc de Bouillon, I decided to leave for Paris without taking Angelina, whom I left with the children on my little estate of the Rugged Oak, sobbing and discomfited; I myself was very melancholic with the thought that I'd be so long deprived of her presence, which was milk and bread to me. On the other hand, I brought with me, besides Miroul and his Florine, sad Silvio, whom I didn't want languishing under the same roof as Zara, so that his heart wouldn't be torn by seeing her every day without being able to so much as touch her with the tip of his finger.

Meanwhile, before my departure, I hurried over to embrace my Samson, as ever so happily absorbed by his glass jars that he knew very little about the crisis in the kingdom, and, taking Gertrude aside, tried, without presuming to give her advice, to sound her out about her feelings. Learning that, after the initial novelty, her feelings for Éloïse had considerably cooled, and that Gertrude was now whinnying for her former oats, I dared tell her that Zara had begun to weigh on Angelina with her inconsolable sorrows, especially given my wife's sadness about my coming departure. I told her that she would considerably brighten the spirit of my household if she would consent to pay a visit, throw a bridle on her fugitive horse and bring her back to her stable.

At first she trembled, as though infused with a new hope, but then frowned and said a very stern "No!" But then she excused herself and softened her resistance, and confessed, with tears in her eyes, that certainly she had loved Zara, and Zara's constancy, for all those years, but that Zara suffocated her with the weight of her love. She confessed, however, that she was astonished that she could neither live continuously with her nor permanently without her, and that it would require some reflection—so she promised to think it over.

I left her to her ruminations, quite surprised that she considered Zara's adventure with Silvio so inconsequential, and left quite sure that the scales would tip in favour of Zara's return to the apothecary by Christmas, lightening the burden on Angelina inflicted by Zara's moods. Believing that, henceforth, order and serenity would be restored in my household, I found myself free enough of these worries to turn my attention to the affairs of my king. But no sooner had I set foot in Paris than I discovered that matters were even more desperate than Quéribus had reported.

I arrived there at night, and sent Miroul out the next morning to wander about near the Grand Châtelet to try to reconnoitre with Mosca on the sly, and ask him to pay me a visit at night. I myself set out that morning to feel the pulse of this angry and rebellious city, with a visit to Pierre de L'Étoile, who seemed better able to hear what was going on in parliament, at the university and at the court than any mother's son in France.

Although he was as affectionate with me as always, I found him buried in the darkest depression and trembling more than a hare in its burrow, dreading in the coming year of 1588 the end of his house, of his kingdom and of the entire world.

"My dear chevalier," he said, embracing me warmly, "everything is being torn to pieces: this globe, this kingdom and myself!"

"You, my good friend!" I laughed. "Well, for a dying man you seem hale and hearty! Your colour is good, your beard is thick and your lips are as red as roses!"

"My health is good enough," he agreed, sighing. "But not my soul, for it is so troubled by my sins that I'm afraid to die and afraid to continue living." (This was a phrase I'd heard him repeat at least once a year for the last sixteen years.)

"Your sins?" I laughed. "You mustn't go exaggerating either the weight or the number, since you are universally considered a great man, except of course by those rascals in the League—which is a compliment to you!"

"Well, my friend," he said, sitting down in an armchair and indicating another for me, both of which faced a fireplace so enormous that you could have roasted a calf, and where huge logs were burning, their heat providing wonderful comfort from the raw and bitter winds in the street. I loved this room, which was bright and well lit by a series of large windows with beautiful transparent glass—not those little squares of colour that have for so long darkened our lodgings. "My friend," he continued, "I do not deserve the renown that has been given me, at least when it comes to the virtue that is expected of an old man who is married, like me, who has passed the age of forty, and yet who disports himself shamelessly with a young woman who makes fun of him, bleeds his purse dry and then runs off with the first rascal who comes along."

"My dear L'Étoile," I advised, "don't rein yourself in so much and you won't feel the bit! And take the spurs off your conscience! Then it won't prick you so painfully!"

"I wish to God I could! But you, my dear Siorac, don't you fear the hereafter?"

"Not to the point of spoiling the here and now!"

"Or the end of the world?"

"Is it so near?" I asked, laughing.

"Near!" cried Pierre de L'Étoile, rising to his feet and turning away from the fire to warm his back. "Near! We can practically touch it with our fingers, because it's coming in this disastrous year of 1588. We're there, chevalier!"

"But who is telling us that this abomination of despair should be our lot? Most assuredly a dreamer!"

"No, not at all! A wise man! A very wise man whom you must know: Regiomontanus. The one who established the map of the stars that permitted Christopher Columbus to find his way to the unknown lands of the Americas."

"From the fact that the stars guide our way at night, we cannot deduce that they influence the destiny of the earth."

"That's not what Regiomontanus claims. He has calculated that an eclipse of the sun will take place in February 1588 and that, at that moment, the stars will be in the most fearful conjunction: Saturn, Jupiter and Mars will be within the house of the moon."

"I don't doubt the conjunction, since he calculated it. But what have I to fear from it?"

"I don't know."

"Could it not be that Regiomontanus is both a mathematician and a poet? It would appear that the conjunction that he foresees is a calculation, and the dark prophecy is a dream. And it's a dream that just happens to fit well with the sinister state of things in this kingdom and with your very sombre mood."

"I don't know," repeated L'Étoile, who seemed shaken, but not entirely persuaded by my reasoning, since it's always easier to think something than to stop thinking it, once you believe it.

"Would you like me to tell you the prediction that Regiomontanus made, elegantly couched in verse?"

"What," I smiled, "a mathematician who writes verses? Wasn't I right? Isn't he a poet?"

"Listen carefully," countered L'Étoile with a hint of impatience, crossing his arms over his chest, "and when you hear this you won't be able to keep from trembling, given how precise the prediction is!

> *"A thousand years after the Virgin gave birth*
> *Five hundred others flowed rapidly by;*
> *In the eighty-eighth year, prodigious things swirled,*
> *But in their terrible wake there'll be no mirth:*
> *We'll see at year's end if it's the end of the world—"*

"Well, that's reassuring!" I laughed.

"But let me go on," L'Étoile answered, somewhat annoyed at being interrupted in the middle of his prophecy, which was supposed to leave me trembling like a leaf.

> *"We'll see at year's end, if it's the end of the world!*
> *All will be o'erthrown; vast empires will fall*
> *And everywhere mourning will hold us in thrall."*

"Well then!" I cried, leaping to my feet and throwing my arm over L'Étoile's shoulder. "France is safe!"

"Safe?" he frowned. "How do you conclude that?"

"Because ours is not a 'vast empire', since we have no possessions beyond the seas, except in Italy, where there's the Marquisate of Saluzzo. No, no, my dear L'Étoile, the 'vast empire' can only mean Spain. And if the prediction miraculously comes to pass, believe me, it'll be the opposite of what Regiomontanus says: mourning will not 'hold us in thrall'! Neither England, nor Holland, nor any among the Lutheran princes in Germany, nor Huguenot Switzerland, nor Navarre, nor even the court of the king of France!"

"Well, you're just reading into things!" he countered, not wishing to be reassured at any price, since he found a kind of comfort in his malaise.

"Indeed, I *am* reading into things, but what else is Regiomontanus doing if not reading into an eclipse and a conjunction of the stars?"

"Dear chevalier," replied L'Étoile, now throwing *his* arm over *my* shoulders, "even though I hold you in particular affection and your joyful and lively humour delights me each time I see you, your reasoning will not comfort me, so many and so terrible are the manifest signs of the coming desolation. For example, on the Sunday preceding your arrival in Paris, there arose in this city and in the surrounding areas a great and thick fog such as has never been seen in living memory: for it was so black and dense that two people walking together through the streets could not see each other and were obliged to light torches to see their way, even though it was only three o'clock in the afternoon. And the next day, they found hundreds of wild geese, jackdaws and crows that had bumped into walls and chimneys because of the sudden darkness."

"My dear L'Étoile," I replied, "a fog is a fog and that's all. And what does a momentary fog have to do with the machinations of Guise?"

"Ah, those terrible plots defy the imagination!" agreed L'Étoile bitterly. "Have you heard about the 'happy day of Saint-Séverin'? The expression designates, in the League's language, the day when the king calamitously attempted to arrest the three most insolent priests in Paris and failed, since the people sounded the alarm and, taking up arms, fortified themselves with the priests in a house in the Saint-Séverin quarter and repelled not only the sergeants and commissioners, but even the king's guards."

"What!" I exclaimed. "Fighting in the streets? Here? In Paris? Because of two or three tonsured priests? And the king couldn't calm the public outcry?"

"Ah, my friend! My friend!" cried L'Étoile, raising his hands heavenwards. "There's worse! Have you ever made the acquaintance of Madame de Montpensier?"

"Yes, I know her quite well," I said without batting an eye.

"Well, chevalier, she's a demon! A female demon! A succubus! A she-devil! A Fury from hell! On fire everywhere, even her arse!"

"As everyone knows," I observed. "And who is unaware that her missives to the Paris priests inspire their invective against the king?"

"Well, chevalier, our king, lord and sovereign calls her into his presence and scolds her, telling her that he knows what she's doing and more, that she invents and creates myths about him and then sends them to the priests, whom she pays to spread them to their congregations. She thinks she's the queen of Paris, he tells her, and that she is raising the city against him, who has been so patient with her; but his patience is at an end and it's he who is in command. Then he tells her to get out. She answers not a word to any of it, not a shadow of an excuse, makes a short curtsey and leaves, proud and limping; then she goes to throw herself on the neck of her Lorraine cousin the queen, and on the queen mother, who now swears only by her Lorraine grandson, on Chancellor de Villequier and the ministers, who have been 'Lorrainized' right down to their kidneys, whereupon all of these—the queen, the queen mother, the chancellor and the ministers—go and invade the king's chambers, like ticks on a dog, and remonstrate with him that he can't exile Madame Limp without provoking a popular uprising and mortally offending the Guise family."

"And what did the king do?"

"He gave in and she's staying. Oh, my friend, the king has become so soft and timid!"

"Soft! Timid?" I said indignantly. "Soft, the victor at Jarnac and Moncontour?"

"I grant you," said L'Étoile with a sigh, "that he was once a coura-geous prince, but at present he looks like a warhorse whose warrior is lying on a stretcher."

"I don't believe a word of it," I replied. "The king is just feigning this lack of spine and his madness. He'll strike when he's ready."

"I don't think so," answered L'Étoile, frowning and scowling. "The king has been too enervated by his pleasures. Did you know that at the request of the ladies, he prolonged the fair at Saint-Germain by a week? And that he goes there every day and allows his favourites to hurl nasty insults at the wenches—some women, others mere girls—whom they see there? And as if these villainies were not sufficient, he brings women from all over Paris to certain houses where he takes his leisure—the most beautiful and the least well bred, with whom he puts on ballets, masquerades, dinners and, even worse, diversions that he calls his 'little pleasures', into which he throws himself with abandon, as though the kingdom were enjoying a period of lasting peace and as though there weren't priests, the League, the Guisards or Guise at his heels."

"My dear L'Étoile," I laughed, "you love morality more than you love yourself! And I frankly don't see whether you're reproaching the king for his taste in men or for his taste in women!"

"Both!" came L'Étoile's sombre retort.

Thereupon, after a powerful embrace, I left him, amused to see him so unforgiving in his statements about the king—him who was carrying on a secret liaison with a strumpet—but also quite alarmed at the same time to hear that the situation of the king had so worsened that one could not help fearing the outcome of this sedition here in Paris, in his capital, in the symbolic seat of his royal power.

Scarcely had I opened the door of my lodgings before Miroul handed me a sealed but unsigned note that he said had been handed to him by a masked lady as he was strolling near the Grand Châtelet. He added that he believed she was the lady-in-waiting of Lady Stafford, because she handed him note with her ungloved hand, allowing him to see the ring that we both knew so well. Hearing this, I broke the seal and read:

> Friends of the Moor, who have eyes to see and ears to hear, have advised ER's little French Lark to vacate his nest, which is dangerously threatened day and night, under a different plumage and to find a friendly nest.

"Read this, Miroul," I urged, seeing his varicoloured eyes looking at me tremulously.

"Well," confessed Miroul, "this is about as clear as Guise's conscience, and I can make neither head nor tail of it. Who is this 'Moor'? And who are his friends?"

"'The Moor'," I explained, "is Walsingham. And his friends, I surmise, must be his agents in Paris."

"And who is this 'ER'?"

"Elizabeth Regina."

"What? The queen of England! And who is this 'little Lark'?"

"The nickname she gave me."

"The Lark!" cried Miroul, breaking into a laugh. "Well, Monsieur, that's very sweet, and fits you to a tee!"

"Miroul, this is no laughing matter. Knowing what you know about its source, what do you think of this warning?"

"That we must pay close attention to it! Especially since Mosca, whom I just saw, refuses to visit you, even at night, arguing that there are too many spies who've got their eyes on the door of your house."

"Miroul," I said, making my decision in the blink of an eye, since our lives depended on it, "I'm going to disguise myself as a bonnet-maker and go to stay with Alizon. As for Silvio, Florine and you, I can't keep you with me any more since your two-colour eyes would give you away anywhere, so you'll lodge with Giacomi."

"No, Monsieur!" declared Miroul firmly. "I'll dye my hair black and put an eyepatch on. As for Florine, she's handy enough to do some sewing in Alizon's shop. You'll need a messenger even when you're staying with Alizon and I need Florine in order to live, move about and be who I am."

"All right then!" I laughed. "Since the valet is now giving the orders and not the master! A pretty faithful image of the kingdom we're living in!"

"Monsieur," corrected Miroul, holding his head high, "I'm your secretary, not your valet!"

"Well then, Monsieur my secretary," I said, embracing him, "may I ask you to please tell Mosca, or Leo, to visit me at night at Alizon's shop."

"But are you sure, Monsieur," he replied, his hand on the doorknob and his brown eye sparkling while his blue eye remained cold, "that Alizon would want to have you stay with her?"

"Ah, Miroul! Miroul!" I laughed. "Why didn't I apply the rod and beat you more often when you were younger so I wouldn't have to put up with your impertinence!"

"A good question, Monsieur, though if you had I wouldn't love you," observed Miroul. "Things come bundled together, Monsieur: impertinence and affection!"

"Miroul," I laughed, stepping towards him with my hand raised, "do I have to beat you?"

"Fie, then!" he said, feigning terror. "A lark is about to peck at me."

"Miroul," I added as he was about to leave, "when you come back, take these ten écus to Mérigot in the needle shop, and use the back door. And please tell him that since I've returned, he needs to redouble his vigilance."

Even though Florine was bustling about, trying to arrange our affairs all by herself since our chambermaids had remained at the Rugged Oak, I felt quite lonely with Miroul gone, and when I went to knock on the secret door that joined our lodgings to Giacomi's I learnt that the *maestro* and Larissa had gone out and wouldn't be back until that evening. So, exhausted from my long trip, I went to lie down and tried to fall asleep, but even though I was physically tired, my mind remained very active and my soul (which I believe is different from the mind, being, as it were, our breath, our impetus and our instinct) was so exalted at the thought of the adventures I was to have that I felt my chest dilating and my nostrils swelling with a sort of intoxication, as if I were pawing the ground and shaking my mane, impatient to throw myself towards new horizons, whatever obstacles or troubles might await me in this headlong gallop!

Recalling the beautiful image that Pierre de L'Étoile had used, comparing the king to a warhorse whose bold warrior lies wounded on a stretcher, I considered that the long rest at the Rugged Oak had in no wise softened me (quite the contrary) and that the danger in which I now found myself—the measures, ruses and stratagems by which I would escape the claws of the enemies of the state, my disguise as a bonnet-maker, my stay with my "little fly from hell", the (delicious) perils that I'd faced there, my comings and goings, my steps and actions, watchfulness and waiting, the traps I'd have to set to escape from other traps—that all this would allow me, in the near future, to extricate myself from the rut and furrow of an existence altogether too orderly and too safe. All these thoughts threw me into a state of excitement so great that I felt a rush of *joie de vivre*—even in the teeth of death—that was completely unknown in my daily life.

I was then thirty-seven years old and had arrived at the age when it is customary in our country to treat a man like an old greybeard and expect him to retire, as Michel de Montaigne had done before the age of forty. But I didn't feel the slightest need to cut back on any of my activities or projects, or loves, feeling that, quite the contrary, their cessation would be a cowardly capitulation to old age and death, which, in my view, a man should never give in to except after a long fight, his back to the wall, his strength ebbing, his sword falling from his hand.

Night had fallen, and since Miroul had not yet returned to the fold, I was lying uneasily on my bed when I heard a knock at the front door and Florine came to tell me that a man named Franz was asking to see me with some urgency. I racked my memory, and suddenly recalled that this was the name of Madame Limp's gigantic valet, to whom I'd given an écu to comfort him for having been whipped by the major-domo of his mistress. And even though I didn't imagine that the fellow meant me any harm, since gratitude comes more easily to these simple people than to our strutting cocks of the court, I strapped a dagger behind my back and a pistol in my belt before peering through the peephole, where I recognized the man, and opening the door, upon which he immediately handed me a note, which I read immediately since I could see he was waiting for an answer.

Monsieur my cousin,

My cousin would like to see you this evening in her hotel at the stroke of ten, and, as you know, she is not someone who accepts disappointment. I am therefore counting on your prompt acceptance of this invitation, which you may impart to the bearer of this note.

I am, Monsieur my cousin, in expectation of your presence here, your humble and devoted servant,

Jeanne de La Vasselière

Having read this, I felt very perplexed that Madame de Montpensier should have so quickly learnt of my return here, and, this circumstance causing me some mistrust, I felt very little appetite for throwing myself into the mouths of these ogresses, but felt equally worried that by not going I would incur their wrath. Seeing that Franz was watching me with his big blue eyes as I inwardly debated with myself, it occurred to me to say:

"Franz, you can see my confusion and you can guess the cause. Give me some friendly advice. Should I go or not?"

"Monsieur," replied Franz with great gravity and, surprisingly, great eloquence, despite his thick accent, "I'm the one who's embarrassed. I am faithful to my mistress, who is, however, less stingy with the whip than with her money."

"In that case, why are you so faithful?"

"She's from Lorraine, as I am, and of higher birth than I, being a princess. Which is why I must ask you, Monsieur, not to ask for my advice—advice not being part of my job."

"And if I were to ask, what would you do?" I asked, amused, despite the seriousness of the moment and his very stiff formality.

"Having some obligation of friendship towards you, I would be forced to tell you not to go there. Which I would deplore, since I want to be a good servant, whether my master is a good master or not."

"In that case, I'm not going."

"Monsieur, I didn't hear your answer, since, if I heard it, I would be obliged by my position to stab you to death before your door."

"What? Right here in front of my house? While I've got a pistol in my hand?"

"Even then."

"Well, Franz," I observed, "I like you way too much to trade my death for yours. And so I now understand that the correct response is to say that I have every intention of going to see your mistress."

"Assuredly so, Monsieur. What you do after this doesn't concern me. Especially since, by this answer, you will have gained a few hours."

"A few hours to do what?"

"To pack your bags and flee the city."

"Very good, then. Tell your good mistress that I will happily accept her invitation. And Franz, please accept from me, in recognition of our friendship, this écu, which is certainly worth much more than a ball from a pistol."

"Monsieur," Franz explained, his good, square face reddening like a slice of ham, before becoming rigid again, "it isn't part of my job to accept money from a gentleman I was supposed to stab to death, either here or at ten o'clock on the way to our lodgings. I would be too afraid that, in accepting it, I would be in the delicate situation of having betrayed my mistress."

"Franz," I smiled, "night is falling, the street is quite deserted. You have a lantern in your hand. Suppose that, quite by accident, I dropped this écu through the peephole of my door. Would you fail to find it as you left my doorstep?"

"I can manage not to fail to find it," said Franz with the utmost gravitas. "Providence sometimes smiles on unfortunate people. Monsieur, I salute you most humbly," he continued, as he watched me toss the coin through the peephole, his ears pricked in the direction it had fallen so that they could hear it land on the pavement.

"Well," I said to myself as I closed the door, "the Moor's friends were right! I have to flee this place!"

Hardly had I turned away from the door when there came another knock and, risking a sidelong glance through the peephole, I saw Miroul.

"Miroul," I said in Provençal, fearing some ambush, "are you alone? Is there anyone pressing a knife to your back?"

"*Degun me vol aucire o menaçar*,"* he answered in the same language.

I opened the door. He was alone, but very pale, and blinking, his lip trembling and his breath very laboured.

---

* "No one wants to kill me or is threatening me."

"Monsieur," he said panting, "they've just killed Mérigot and his wench! I saw three rascals running from his shop by the front door when I came in the back. They surprised them and cut their throats. Ah, Monsieur, I would have pursued these miscreants like a hunting dog if they hadn't taken the arquebuses with them."

"My Miroul," I gasped, my throat suddenly parched, "sit down and drink a glass of this wine. I've never seen you so overwhelmed!"

"Well, Monsieur," he replied, the colour gradually returning to his cheeks as he drank, "the poor couple were still panting when I came in, and what a horrible scene: their throats were slit from ear to ear! I could hardly keep from throwing up at the sight of so much blood! You would have thought you were in a slaughterhouse! I've never seen anything this cruel except during the St Bartholomew's day massacre! I can't understand what led poor Mérigot to unlock his door to these murderers. He usually fortifies his house at dusk!"

"Perhaps he knew these fellows from his work on the river, fellows who were, as he was, on the lam, or maybe they were old drinking companions—who knows? All those poor workers are so ignorant and hungry they can be bought for a few coins. These mercenaries fight the wars, Miroul, while Madame de Montpensier is stuffing herself with dragées and prunes on her silk cushions."

I told him about the letter from La Vasselière and my conversation with Franz.

"Ah, Monsieur," he said resolutely, "it's all very clear. They sent for you to visit them at Madame Limp's hotel in order to ambush you on the way, and, once you were dead, they could attack the house and massacre your family, which is why they killed Mérigot, to have their way clear here. Monsieur, we've gone back fifteen years! Another St Bartholomew's day massacre is being prepared and these murderers are the first buds. And what else can we do except what we did in '72—flee? Monsieur, we're the wandering Jews in this kingdom!"

"You're right, Miroul! Go wake Silvio, who's sleeping like a log, and pack our bags, if you've already unpacked them. I'm going to warn Giacomi of our predicament."

Very luckily, I found him at home, along with Larissa, and informed him of the situation. If he hadn't had to worry about Larissa, he might have accompanied me, but I urged him to stay and allow these thugs to eviscerate and pillage my house in order to remain hidden himself, and so that he would be able, should we need it, to offer us a refuge or hiding place, since his house was so close to the Louvre. He ended up consenting to this plan, at which point Miroul observed that we'd need our horses (who had already proved themselves in Sedan), and so we decided to lead them from our stables, passing through the secret door, and take them down one floor to stable them in Giacomi's courtyard. This was *not* an easy task, since, as one can imagine, horses have a particular antipathy to stairs, especially when they have to go down, and are terrified by the void they see deepening beneath them.

The next difficulty was to gain admission to Alizon's workshop, given the late hour and the very dark night, but as soon as the door was opened and our horses stabled, my "little fly from hell" led Miroul and Florine with their baggage into a tiny room and left them, saying:

"Truly, the bed's not very wide, but given the way you look at each other, I think you'll manage to accommodate yourselves to it!"

And, laughing, she gave Florine a kiss, and presented her hand to Miroul as if she were a royal princess; then, taking me by the arm, she dragged me, almost running, to her room, where, having closed the door behind us, she threw her arms around my neck and kissed me passionately (and I confess I gave as good as I got).

"My Pierre," she explained, "you're going to be very upset given your Huguenot morals, since the only room I might have given you is the one I've just given Miroul and Florine. Of course, I could have taken Florine with me, like certain high-born ladies do who like to sleep with their chambermaids, but how could I in good conscience"—and she laughed as she pronounced this word—"separate Florine from her husband? It would be too cruel! The only other room is Baragran's, who loves sleeping there since the chimney passes through one of the walls and gives out enough heat to comfort his poor twisted bones. My Pierre, do you think I should kick Baragran out of his room and throw him into the damp eaves so you can have it? Is that what you want?"

"Well, my friend," I replied, seeing where all this merciful generosity was leading, and finding myself too tired (and too softened by her kisses) to resist, as I should have, "you have put yourself out so much in order to hide us that I could not possibly displace poor Baragran from the warmth of his room after his day of labour. No, no, I'll sleep in the loft and won't notice the cold and damp there once I'm asleep."

"Blessed Virgin!" cried Alizon, redoubling her kisses since the idea of my sleeping in the loft provoked in her even greater compassion. "Do you think I could ever agree to lodge you in such a dark, damp and malodorous place as that loft, where I wouldn't even put a scullery maid? You, a noble gentleman and great venerable doctor! Really! I can't imagine it! I would die of shame! My Pierre, if you can't bear sharing my little bed," she said with a sigh that would have rekindled a forge, "I shall suffer in the loft and leave you this room—"

"You're not serious, my little chick!" I said, giving her delicate soft neck a grateful kiss.

"Not content to invade your house with Miroul and Florine, would I rob you of your room and your bed? Fie then! Do you think me so shameless as to put my good hostess in such discomfort? And to set up camp as though I were in a conquered country, stretching out comfortably in your bed while banishing you to shiver in the loft? Zounds! It's out of the question! I'll sleep on the floor at the foot of your bed, if perchance you have a blanket to give me."

"Alas, I have none!" Alizon replied, without missing a beat. "And I cannot bear the thought of having you bruise your bones on the parquet. But, my Pierre, enough squabbling. Let's eat a morsel and drink a pitcher or two of my Bordeaux and leave the decision to the inspiration of the moment."

Which we did. But before I went to bed, Mosca, whom Miroul had been able to contact a second time at the Grand Châtelet earlier in the evening, came knocking on Alizon's door, accompanied by a large escort, and spent more than an hour talking with me. Some very disturbing things concerned with peace in our kingdom were discussed during that hour's talk, which I'll recount later, since I had to repeat the substance of it to the king the next day. For this meeting, I sent Florine to tell Quéribus that he should admit into the palace, by a discreet door, not the Chevalier de Siorac (who'd apparently left Paris), but a master bonnet-maker named Baragran. This was accomplished by means of a token bearing the royal seal, which I was able to present at the Porte Neuve, which gives on to the Tuileries Garden, and from there gain admission to the Louvre by a secret door—both gate and door being heavily guarded so that the king's envoys could enter and leave the palace without having to pass through the streets of Paris, which, even had they not been in a state of rebellion, were seething with the League's spies and so full of carts and carriages during the day that one could scarcely make one's way through them. Thus, thanks to the Porte Neuve, the speed and security of these secret messengers of the king were assured, and the king himself could, if and when he judged it useful, reach the farmland around the city without having to pass through its streets. This wise and prudent disposition will be shown to have had the greatest consequence as this story unfolds.

As for me, there were obvious advantages to this itinerary, which I followed more than once to go to provide the king with information. Leaving Paris with Miroul (who had dyed his hair and put a patch over one eye, just as I had adopted the dress of a master bonnet-maker) through the Porte Saint-Honoré, we directed our horses through the faubourg of the same name and out into the countryside, where on either side we could enjoy the sight of charming windmills; next we crossed the Seine to the left of a pretty village called Roule and then, riding along the river, crossed back at the foot of the Chaillot hill (from the name of the village that sits atop it)—a place that we sadly remembered as the part of the Seine where, fifteen years before, we'd seen the bodies of the Huguenots, victims of the St Bartholomew's day massacre, lying everywhere among the tall grasses and reeds along its banks.

Heading back up to Paris, we re-entered the capital through the Tuileries Garden by the Porte Neuve (carefully watched by the king's guards and avoiding the Milice gate, which was infested with partisans of the League). There, having shown our royal passports, we dismounted, leaving our horses in the king's stables, and were led to a secret door by a sergeant. Miroul followed behind with a basketful of clothes and accessories that we were supposedly selling, and these were carefully searched by a detachment of the Forty-five Guardsmen, the personal guards of the king, who watched this entrance day and night, and had never left the Louvre since things had become so tense between His Majesty and his Parisian subjects.

One of the more pleasant reasons for taking this journey, which had us leave Paris through the Porte Saint-Honoré and return to the Louvre through the Porte Neuve, a long and leisurely ride that allowed us to enjoy the roads, villages and windmills of the countryside before returning to the city, was that it allowed us to ascertain whether we were being followed. We took the particular precaution, when we rode through the village of Roule, of going round the church (which was some distance from the road) so that we could see whether there was anyone behind us who followed us off the road to spy on us.

*

I hadn't seen the king since the month of August 1587, and when Du Halde showed me into his chambers early one morning (followed by Miroul with his basket, who was thrilled to be invited into the king's intimate rooms) I was surprised by the enormous changes in his appearance in a few short months: his cheeks looked hollow, his hair whitened at his temples. As for his body, his back was bent, his chest sunken and his shoulders sagging, and he seemed thinner on top but swollen lower down—despite the fact that His Majesty had been eating so little, which greatly worried Du Halde. His skin and colouring were ample witness to his excessive pleasures (which L'Étoile had denounced, forgetting his own), the lack of fresh air and exercise, and the terrible worries of fourteen years of exercising power in conditions that could not have been more vexatious and unstable, bearing the weight on his shoulders of a kingdom that was torn by factionalism, plots and fratricidal wars.

I couldn't believe my eyes when I saw how much my beloved sovereign had aged—though he was the same age as me, he looked at least twenty years older. And yet I didn't allow myself to get overly alarmed, knowing as I did that his corporeal form responded to his moods and that a bit of good news or a new hope could suddenly transform him, so that twenty minutes later his eyes might be shining, his head held high and his posture straight as a board; he could recover, if not the rosebuds of his youth, at least the green leaves of his maturity.

"Well, my son!" he said, holding out his hand. "Seeing you here is like Fortune smiling again on this court, whose ranks have so thinned as so many ingrates have fled, their hearts following their heads, which turn whichever way the wind is blowing. But," he said, observing my disguise, "how oddly you are dressed, my Siorac!"

"Sire," I explained as I knelt before him, "may it please Your Majesty to remember that Siorac is gone, having fled the many attempts on his life by the League, and that you have before you the master bonnet-maker Baragran. As for the one-eyed assistant you see there with his basket of goods, that's my secretary, Miroul, who is the most faithful servant of the kingdom."

"Like master, like servant," observed the king; and, in his great benignity and condescension, he made a welcoming sign with his hand towards Miroul, who blushed with pleasure. "Baragran," he said, turning back to me, "what account has Mosca given you? Blue or black?"

"Black, with the blackest ink, sire. The great Pig was secretly in Paris the day before yesterday, and was accompanied by a swarm of the biggest shit-eating flies in the League."

"Ah, Bloodletter!" laughed Chicot, his nose running as usual. "I've always thought so, but now I'm sure: you're a poet."

"Silence, Chicot!" snarled the king. "So, Siorac, the Duc de Guise's brother, Mayenne, was in Paris the day before yesterday."

"Yes, sire. And this Mayenne was proclaiming his great exploits and the sublime victories he'd won in Guyenne against the heretics."

"In truth," broke in Chicot, "the Pig killed a tiny little rabbit that happened to be running under his backside, and that, in his retelling of it, has become an entire pack of wolves."

"To please our good Paris sermonizers, that's the way you have to tell it—a massacre. No one is appreciated or accepted by the League unless he uses this language. But go on, Siorac. And not a word out of you, Chicot!"

"Henri," objected Chicot, "what's the use of listening to the Bloodletter and his one-eyed assistant when I know the A to Z of what the Pig and his Leaguers are plotting?"

"And that is?" asked the king.

"To take your city!"

"But I need details of this plan!" cried the king.

"There's no lack of them, sire," I said. "Here's what I learnt from Mosca, who was present at the meeting between Mayenne and the

League. First off, in order to take the Bastille, about a hundred or so of our good Leaguers will knock on the door at night, and if no one opens up to them, a guard in their pay will slit the throat of the nightwatchman and open the doors. If the nightwatchman opens it himself he'll be dispatched along with all the men who are with him who are known to be 'political'. While they're doing this, other detachments will go to the houses of the first president, the chancellor, the attorney general and other major officers of the crown, and kill each of them, their reward being the pillaging of their houses. As for the Arsenal, the League has men working inside who will kill the provost; for the Grand and the Petit Châtelet, the League intends to gain entry by disguising some of its men as sergeants bringing prisoners in during the night; and for the Palais-Royal, the Temple and the Hôtel de Ville, the League foresees no trouble in taking them, probably in the morning after they open their doors. And, as for the Louvre—"

"Yes, what about my Louvre?" said the king with a glint in his eye.

"The League intends to occupy it, seize Your Majesty and kill your council and all the officers who have remained faithful to you, and replace them with its own men, sparing your person on condition that you do nothing to oppose it."

"I find them most evangelical!" laughed the king.

"But by what means will they occupy it?" asked Du Halde, who, up until that moment, hadn't said a word.

"Once the League has seized the Bastille, the Arsenal, the Châtelet, the Temple, the Palais-Royal and the Hôtel de Ville, its emissaries will spread out through the city shouting 'Long live the Mass! The city is taken!', and call all good Catholics to arms and send them to the Louvre, where all the doors will be blocked. This done, they'll simply starve out the king's guards until they surrender."

"But anyone can see," said Henri, "that the minute they hear this appeal to the people, thousands of thieves and lowlifes will run into the streets and begin murdering and pillaging in every quarter of Paris!"

"Sire," I replied, "the League has understood the ruin and confusion that would reign for all the inhabitants of the city, and they've thought of a way to combat that eventuality."

"And what is this way?" asked the king.

"Barricades."

"Barricades?" frowned the king quizzically. "What are you talking about? What novelty is this? What do they mean by this word 'barricade'? Du Halde, have you heard of such a thing?"

"No, sire," replied Du Halde. "But we talk about 'barring the way' when one wants to keep people from entering a passage. From which, I suppose, you get the word 'barricade', meaning a way of keeping people from entering."

"That's true and false, my dear Du Halde," I replied. "Certainly, the idea is to block the way, but it's not, as you suggested, from the verb 'to bar', but from the word 'barrel'—when filled with dirt, barrels are placed across the street to obstruct passage, and the space between them is filled with paving stones that have been dug up. Thus, no one can pass these 'barricades' without presenting a badge that has been distributed by the League. In this way, they can prevent, on the one hand, the beggars from leaving the slum districts of the Cour des Miracles and spreading throughout the city, and, on the other, gentlemen and 'politicals' from travelling from their various houses in Paris to help the king in the Louvre. Of course, these faithful servants will immediately be accused of heresy and their throats will be cut wherever they appear."

"'Sblood!" cried Chicot. "People are breathing blood and snorting massacre in this Paris that surrounds us!"

"So," said the king, chin in hand, and looking vacantly across the room with a thoughtful and dreamy air, "that's what they call a 'barricade'! *È ben trovato!** It goes without saying that a dozen or so rascals fortified behind these barricades with arquebuses could hold off two or three companies or squadrons of seasoned guards, especially if the adjoining houses were held by their partisans, which would obviously be the case."

The king's words struck me powerfully, and the events that were to follow proved his clairvoyance. In them I recognized the acute military genius of the warrior prince of Jarnac and Moncontour; he had certainly not fallen so deeply asleep "lying on a stretcher", as L'Étoile had put it, that he wasn't still able to evaluate the pitfalls and advantages of a given situation. Indeed, his observation comforted me a great deal, however pessimistic it was, since it reconfirmed the trust I had in his subtlety, in his lucidity and in his supple talent for escaping from the most dangerous setbacks.

"*È ben trovato*," he repeated, shaking his head and resorting to Italian, not so much because of his Florentine heritage on his mother's side, but simply because he loved the language, and I'd heard him say more than once that he found it more elegant and flexible than French.

And, shaking his head again, he repeated:

"*Bene, bene, bene*: 'barrels', a 'barricade'—what could be simpler? What a discovery, my Siorac. And so inexpensive: some casks, some dirt, a few paving stones! And the king's regiments are completely blocked! Our good Leaguers are not so stupid as I thought. Du Halde, hatred seems to make them smarter!"

"But sire," observed Du Halde, his long, austere face expressing the alarm he felt at hearing this, "in such a case, a prince could never restore order and reason in a seditious city!"

"Oh, yes he could," countered the king, "but only by means much slower and more considered than street fights, which are always so

* "That's well thought out!"

costly in human life for both sides, and spill rivers of blood for an uncertain outcome. The proof is in what our good Leaguers call the 'happy day of Saint-Séverin', when two or three stinking priests and three dozen rascals held my guards in check. To win that struggle, we would have had to use cannon, and massacre an entire quarter."

"But sire," said Du Halde stiffly, "if that's the way to ensure ultimate victory—"

"No, no, my good Du Halde!" interrupted the king animatedly. "A king must never put himself in the position of slaughtering his subjects! It is an unnatural act, and as useless as it is inhuman! That's the lesson I learnt from the St Bartholomew's day massacre."

Hearing these beautiful and noble words, and recognizing the courage the king had had to display in downplaying his own successes at Jarnac and Moncontour, I was so overcome with feeling that I threw myself at his feet and presumed to seize his hand and kiss it.

"Well now!" he said with an affectionately derisive smile (and giving me an affectionate pat on the cheek as he pulled his hand from mine). "Now now, Siorac, look at how happy you are that I denounced the St Bartholomew's day massacre! Aren't you a good Catholic?"

"Sire," I replied, "if being a good Catholic means plotting against the crown, and being hateful and seditious, then no, I'm not. But if being a good Catholic means hearing Mass and serving his king, then, sire, count me as a member of that Church."

"Well said, Siorac," smiled the king, giving two taps with his hands to the arms of his chair. "My own Church is one of good and honest people who do not want to use the sword to exterminate heretics, but rather reason to persuade them. My own Church is also one that believes in pardon, which I shall use, Du Halde, with all of my subjects who are acting so blindly, since I desire neither their blood nor their lives, but rather their preservation, as fervently as a father would that of his children."

"Sire," asked Du Halde, "would you use such mercy towards the one who is blinding them?"

"I don't know yet," answered the king with a thin, sinuous smile, looking at Du Halde out of the corner of his beautiful black eyes. "But why not, if he were to become truly repentant?"

"I wouldn't believe it," laughed Chicot.

"What wouldn't you believe, my fool?"

"Neither his repentance nor his forbearance. You're a sly dog, Henri. Guise has his moment now, but you'll have yours tomorrow."

"Amen!" breathed Du Halde.

"Siorac," said the king, not wishing to pursue this conversation, and seizing the watch that hung around Du Halde's neck and giving it a quick glance, "it is almost time for my council. Is that all you learnt from this fly who believes he's a lion?"

"No, sire. He heard from a very reliable source that there is also a plot against you being hatched by Madame Limp, who would love to be queen. Having determined that when you return from Vincennes you pass by a house in Roquette that belongs to her, she has planned to hide some forty *spadaccini* there, who will seize your carriage as you pass by and kill the five or six gentlemen in your retinue and take you prisoner."

"Ah, sire!" cried Du Halde. "I told you that your escort was too weak!"

"Who would have thought," said the king, paling in anger, "that this wicked woman, who sent the queen and the queen mother to beg me on their knees not to exile her, far from desisting from her execrable designs, would dare, so soon after her pardon, to attack my royal person? And yet, if I press her too hard on this occasion, she'll proclaim her innocence and accuse me of calumny and send off a note to her priests to the effect that I'm attacking a weak woman, because I don't like her sex. Du Halde, I will satisfy you! From now on I won't leave the Louvre without the protection of my Forty-five Guardsmen, fully armed. And as for the desperate enterprises of those of my subjects who have taken up arms against my authority, I shall fortify all the strongholds in my capital in such a way as to rid those seditious rebels who would attack them of any further taste for doing so! Siorac," he said, rising and presenting his hand to me, "continue, I beg you, to serve me well, and be as affectionate in the future as you always have been, bringing me from time to time the buzzings of this good fly who swoops over the dungheap of the League to discover its deliberations."

I have reported this conversation exactly as it happened, without polishing or pruning the king's words, because I wanted to give a detailed portrait of the king just as he was: sometimes familiar and witty, at others serious and majestic, but always using language in the same refined way that he dressed, having a great appetite for art and a great love of words—for he'd studied rhetoric with Pibrac, and founded an academy with him. He was, moreover, a great admirer of Rabelais, Ronsard, Villon and, ever since they'd first appeared, the *Essais* of Michel de Montaigne, whom he revered for his luminous lucidity, his supple style and his reasonable approach to life. And I can well remember in this respect how, at Chartres, Henri was upset and angry with the League for having thrown Montaigne in the Bastille (if only for a few days, and until the queen mother had him released), since they so hated a mind whose gentle humanism was at such odds with their fanaticism.

During the four months that followed this conversation, I saw the king several times, while disguised as Baragran, to keep him informed of the seditious plans of the League in Paris, and notably of their intention to assassinate Épernon at the fair at Saint-Germain in February or March 1588 (my memory is not very precise about the date). Épernon was very brave and high-handed, as I've already indicated; and, the king's council (most of whose members were creatures of the queen mother, and were more or less supportive of the League) having hypocritically questioned the information provided by Mosca as being possibly of Huguenot inspiration, the duc wanted to be certain of the value of the information. So he secretly put on a coat of mail under his doublet and had himself followed at some distance by a large escort as he walked around the fair. There a group of students from the university suddenly surrounded him and tried to start an argument, pulling out their knives, and would have surely cut him to ribbons had not the escort rushed up and put them to flight.

I was very glad that this experience reaffirmed the king's trust in his "fly" and, of course, in me, who brought him these "buzzings". And may I just say here, without too much fanfare, that I advised the king to have all the students at the Sorbonne disarmed, since the shitty pedants who taught there had turned them into turbulent and dangerous fanatics, and they had frequently been found to be the source of various disturbances at public events. The king found this idea good and expedient, and sent his prosecutor to the part of the city known as l'Université to search for and remove all weapons, both swords and firearms. But the booty turned out to be very slight, which led the king to believe that l'Université had been forewarned by the members of his council who'd been won over by the League, and that the arms had been hidden in convents in that quarter, which were already overflowing, according to Mosca, with arquebuses, pistols and pikes that the League had amassed in these inviolable places in preparation for the insurrection it was planning almost openly against the king—which, it was rumoured, would break out any day now.

Except for going to see the king very early every morning, I rarely left Alizon's lodgings, fearing to be recognized by the League's spies, though this was improbable given the disguise I had, and, in addition, the beard that I allowed to devour my face. At this time Quéribus was operating as go-between for the king and me, just as I served this function for the king and Mosca, and my brother-in-law would visit me at Alizon's under the pretext of accompanying Catherine there, who was having my "little fly from hell" make many additions to her wardrobe. I well remember their last visit to the shop, which took place towards the end of March, in which he informed me of the manoeuvres of the Duc d'Aumale in Picardy, which the duc held almost entirely in his hands, save for the cities of Calais and Boulogne, despite his repeated attacks on the latter.

"Well, Pierre!" exclaimed Quéribus. "Please excuse me, but I don't think I could embrace you, dressed the way you are! I simply cannot get used to your costume! Fie then! A merchant! And that beard! These clothes! Your untended hair! Ah, Pierre! I'd rather die from a thousand sword thrusts than descend to this level of baseness!"

"But I'm doing this for my king!" I explained, somewhat put off by his attitude. "And I'm defending him in a way no naked sword would do."

"Oh yes, of course, of course," grumbled Quéribus, "but in disguising yourself in this way you show a degree of self-denial that I could never achieve. As I look at you dressed like that I don't know whether to laugh or cry."

"I would be sincerely wounded," I replied stiffly, "if my clothes caused you to despise me, since I believe I have other claims to your affection."

"Ah, Pierre," blushed Quéribus, "this is too silly of me! You are worth infinitely more than I, who am, when all is said and done, but a courtier whose only merit is that he is faithful to his sovereign. Please forgive me, I beg you. Your hand on it, Pierre."

I gave him my hand immediately, and noticed from his expression that he was very disappointed not to see the rings I usually wore on it, but didn't dare say so since he was so ashamed of having wounded me.

"Pierre," he confided, "the king wants you to contact again this fellow whom he calls Mosca—what a strange name!—since he's so worried by the developments in Picardy. The Prince de Condé, who was the titular governor, has just died, poisoned by his wife, and in his place the king has named the Duc de Nevers."

"Nevers? I've heard tell that he was courting the League."

"That love affair didn't work out," replied Quéribus with a smile, "and Nevers has come back to the king, who, as I said, named him governor of Picardy. But Aumale, who has occupied Picardy for his cousin Guise, refuses to step down."

"What?" I cried. "He's refused? He refuses to accept a governor named by the king! That's open rebellion!"

"It gets worse. Aumale, at the head of 1,200 arquebusiers, has taken Abbeville in Guise's name, and, to the king's envoy who asked for an explanation of these actions, he dared reply with the utmost insolence that the Picard gentlemen will not suffer in their province either royal garrison or a Gascon governor. Which response, as you can imagine, my Pierre, was not well received by the king, who sees Picardy as a key piece in this game."

"And why so?"

"Ah, my Pierre," protested Quéribus, "don't ask me! As you know I don't have a head for politics and never get involved in its twists and turns."

"But what can Mosca tell me about Picardy, since he lives, as I do, in Paris?"

"I know not."

"Is that all?"

"Yes, indeed! Except," he continued, stroking his moustache, "that the king did me the favour of finding another nickname for me! He no longer calls me 'my Quarreller Quéribus', but instead 'my cocky cockerel'! Isn't that sweet?" he continued, standing up to contemplate himself in the mirror, his hands on his hips and turning this way and that to exhibit his figure. "So, my Pierre, what do you think? 'My cocky cockerel'! Isn't that just a superb nickname? Could His Majesty have discovered a more gallant alliteration?"

"Or one that suits you better," I said seriously, "for I have to admit that there are few gentlemen more dashing than you at court."

"Ah, Monsieur my brother!" gushed Quéribus. "You're blinded by your affection for me! Some people claim that Laugnac de Montpezat would be able to turn many a pretty head if his inclination were in that direction."

"Laugnac! The head of the Forty-five Guardsmen! Ah, my brother! Leave that swarthy fellow to his cut-throats! He's so ordinary-looking it makes you sick!"

"My brother," laughed Quéribus, his eyes shining, "your hand! I must take my leave. 'Sblood! You can't see your face behind that merchant's beard! I must leave whether Madame my wife has finished or not with Alizon. You know how frivolous these women are! There's no limit to their gabbing when it comes to finery! But the king ordered me to go to the Maréchale de Joyeuse's salon this afternoon to speak with Lady Stafford."

"Really! On what subject, if I may ask?" I asked, frowning, somewhat stung that the king sent him to hunt in my woods.

"But *you're* precisely the subject! 'Sblood! I completely forgot! What a feather-brained fellow I am! The king wants to know if you feel that it would be useful for me to tell Lady Stafford where you're staying presently and under what name, so that your contact with the English could be re-established. The king fears inviting Lady Stafford to the Louvre, since there are so many spies about. He can't even trust his own walls! So, what do you say? Is it a good idea? Should I tell Lady Stafford?"

"Certainly! But with extreme discretion—and whisper it in her ear and *only* to her. You can identify me simply as 'the Lark'."

"The Lark!" echoed Quéribus, breaking out laughing, with his hand covering his mouth (in imitation of the king and many others at court). "My brother, I shall not forget that! And, speaking of birds, what do you think of the peacock that I had embroidered on the left sleeve of my doublet? Quite stylish, no? Its eye is a ruby and its wings are rimmed with real pearls."

"And what are those three embroidered *vs* coming out of its mouth?"

"*Veni, vidi, vici.*"

"Ah, my Quéribus!" I laughed. "If I weren't afraid of annoying you with my beard and clothing, I'd embrace you!"

"The intention is as good as the act!" Quéribus threw over his shoulder as he pivoted towards the door. "I must go! Do you know, Pierre," he added, with his hand on the doorknob, "why the Demoiselle de La Trémoille had the Prince de Condé poisoned by her page?"

"No."

"She was having an affair. The prince found out about it and wanted to shut her away in a convent. So she had him killed. And now it won't be a convent she's locked in but a jail cell! This is the way of the world, Pierre..."

"And whom was the affair with?"

"Why, her page, of course! Isn't that what you imagined?"

"What did they do to the page?"

"They would have had him castrated before drawing and quartering him for cuckolding a prince. But they couldn't catch him. He scandalously scampered off! My Pierre," he continued with a laugh, his hand over his mouth, "what do you think of my alliteration?"

"By my conscience," I replied, imitating the high intonation of our courtiers, "I find it wonderfully cute!"

"Truly?"

"Truly!"

"In that case, I'll repeat it to the king."

And at that he departed with the usual spring in his step, leaving in his wake the smell of his musk perfume and the brilliance of his multicoloured plumage. Oh, my handsome Quéribus! So frivolous and so silly! Yet so faithful to the king amid the great haemorrhage of French nobles, who were continually flowing out of the Louvre towards Guise at Soissons, like impatient rats leaving the ship of state, which appeared to be sinking, to climb aboard a vessel that was sailing towards the throne.

Poor, great England—her freedom, her religion and her queen so sorely threatened by the immense armada (blessed by the Pope, who actually referred to it as "my daughter") that Spain was readying to invade her shores. Their queen must have been excessively on the alert to judge by the alacrity of my Lady Stafford in reopening the lines of communication with my king, for, by eleven o'clock the next morning, Alizon came to tell me that a lady of quality, masked in black and speaking strange gibberish, begged to see me.

"My Pierre, I told her she was mistaken, that there was no one named Baragran here."

"And what was her response?"

"That she couldn't be mistaken. That she would wait for you and, what's more, that you knew her well."

"What does she look like?"

"I couldn't say. She refused to take off her mask, even though I asked her to."

"Ask her to come up."

"What! Here! To our room?"

"My friend, if she is who I believe she is, her visit must remain a secret," I replied, sitting down on the bed after having pulled the curtains.

"What?" cried my little fly from hell. "On the bed! You're going to cuddle in here! What's the meaning of this?"

"Nothing, Alizon," I laughed. "I have to see her from behind the curtains and ask her to take her mask off before I reveal my identity to her."

Which was done, except that when the mystery woman took off her mask, I was amazed to recognize, not as I had expected the lady-in-waiting of Lady Stafford, but the black, almond-shaped eyes of Lady Markby, the very one who had awakened me at the Pope's Head Tavern in London by pressing the ambassadress's ring to my lips.

"Well, My Lady!" I said in English (since I suspected Alizon had her ear at the keyhole). "What are you doing here? Can the Moor and your mistress do without you in London? And don't you have a house and husband in Shropshire?"

"Must you remind me?" she laughed. "When I'm trying so hard to forget it, especially when I see you dressed as you are, and covered with all that make-up. But, thank God, your eyes are still the same, which so agreeably devour my feminine charms. My Lark, I can't hold out any longer. Your lips, I beg you!"

"Ah, My Lady, nothing would please me more, but it's not possible. We're being watched."

"And by whom, other than this little brown Fury on the other side of the door who let me in?" asked Lady Markby bursting out laughing. "My Lark, I might have known that there would be some roses hidden among the thorns of your life in hiding!"

"No, My Lady, against all appearances, you're mistaken. But please sit down, I'm dying to know what's brought you to Paris!"

"*Sono qui una persona nuova*,"* she explained (having the tendency, common to Windsor and the Louvre, to break into Italian for no good reason). "Lord Stafford's house is now surrounded by so many spies, both from the League and from Spain, that no one can go in or out

---

* "I'm a new person here."

without being followed by at least two of them. I'm not staying at Lord Stafford's and no one in Paris has ever seen me—so at least for a while I can move about freely."

"So, My Lady, I'm listening."

"Picardy," she said, arranging the folds of her hoop skirt, which were emerging on every side from her chair, "is the reason I'm here."

"Aha!" I said, pricking up my ears. And in the sudden interest I took in her words, I momentarily forgot her bewitching beauty, adding, "I heard yesterday that my master is very worried about the events there."

"And no less so my queen, but for very different reasons. My Lark," she continued, "I'm going to shed new light on this situation as long as you'll sing my song to your king."

"My Lady, may your heart be ever assured of this: I will never stop singing *ad maximam gloriam Henrici et Elizabethae reginae.*"*

"Here's my new light: Aumale and Guise are taking one after another the king's cities in Picardy and putting the royal garrisons to flight, disobeying his orders and refusing to accept his governor."

"We knew that already, beautiful dawn."

"But did you know why? *Primo*: in Picardy, lots of money can flow from nearby Flanders to help Guise and his rebellion. *Secundo*: in a sign of reciprocity, Guise will try to take Calais, Boulogne or Dieppe, to provide Felipe II with a harbour and base for his 'Invincible Armada'."

"Calais is too big a morsel for Guise's throat. And Aumale already failed to take Boulogne."

"Which leaves Dieppe," answered Lady Markby with shining eyes. "And if Guise takes Dieppe, and gives it to Spain, my mistress will be very displeased."

"Dieppe? I'd never really thought about Dieppe."

---

* "To the greater glory of Henri and Elizabeth Regina."

"Guise has. Otherwise would Aumale have taken Abbeville? It's only a skip and a jump from Abbeville to Dieppe."

"Well, I thank you, my dawn! You're bringing welcome light to the situation. Now I understand why the king is so worried!"

"But stay!" said My Lady, separating each of her words like so many arrows that she was letting fly towards a target. "It would be enough if the king of France were to throw some troops into Rouen to lock up Normandy and prevent Guise's garrison at Abbeville from taking Dieppe."

"The king," I conceded after ruminating on her suggestion, "will hesitate to take troops out of Paris to reinforce Rouen, since his capital is already practically under siege."

"On the other hand," Lady Markby pointed out, "Guise will hardly want to dispatch troops that are in Picardy to march on Paris, if there's a royal presence in Rouen that could cut him down from behind."

"Ah, that's very well thought out! But this must be weighed by much finer and wiser royal scales than the ones I have here."

"But will you suggest it to your master?"

"That I will, and wholeheartedly."

"We have reason to believe," Lady Markby continued gravely, "*that Felipe II will launch Guise against Paris on the day he launches his Invincible Armada against us.* That day is coming very soon. God save the king of France if Elizabeth falls under the assault of this immense fleet."

"Amen!" I said, tears suddenly streaming from my eyes, so abhorrent to my imagination was the frightful thought of the Spanish mercenaries sowing brutal desolation across our two countries, on whose heels would come the greatest scourge of all—the Inquisition! I could easily see and conceive how this predicament would go far beyond France. The fate of the entire world would be at stake the minute the sails of the Invincible Armada filled with wind: if they were not repulsed by the bastion of England, all of Christianity would be subjected to the fanatical zeal of the monks, who would everywhere extirpate, with slow, meticulous and methodical cruelty, the nerves and tender roots of freedom of conscience.

"And is this day," I managed to say when I'd overcome my emotion, but still trembling, "so near?"

"We believe so," replied Lady Markby, seizing my two hands and squeezing them hard. "My Lark, these are the oats that have nourished us on this occasion. I'm giving them to you, so that your master can make good use of them in his turn."

"I hear you."

"We know that in the first days of April, Felipe II sent to Guise, in Soissons, Moreo from Aragon, who urged Guise to march on Paris in the first days of May, promising him 300,000 écus, 6,000 German foot soldiers and 1,200 lancers."

"Guise knows the Spaniard, and knows what his promises are worth."

"They will be kept if, at the same time, Felipe II launches his fleet against us. My Lark, time is passing, and I must away. Your little Fury behind the door must have her ears ringing with our English. I'll be back to visit you if necessary."

"My Lady," I said, kissing her hands, "I am so happy for myself and for my king that we have had this talk, and doubly happy that Elizabeth sends on her missions a woman of such amiable beauty as yourself."

"Is she not a woman herself?" said Lady Markby proudly. "Are we necessarily stupider than you just because we don't have a fencing foil behind our flies?"

"Fie then!" I laughed. "I neither said that nor thought it. Quite the contrary, I think there's more diplomacy in your little finger than in the large member that you mentioned."

"A beautiful lie from an able tongue!"

"Which is all yours…"

"I shall remember that promise," smiled My Lady, "if we ever get out of this storm, you and I. My Lark, I've got you in my net and I'm going to pluck you!"

"Ah, My Lady, nothing would please me more than to be slow-roasted on your fire."

"Well, Monsieur," she replied in French, "don't make me laugh! I can scarcely don my mask. Are you so light-hearted? Can you laugh and still laugh when the apocalypse is upon us? Did you know that each of the ships of the Armada will be carrying in its hold monks, torturers and instruments of torment to return the people of England to the Pope's religion?"

"Madame," I replied, "laughter is also a weapon against fanaticism. May I give you a kiss?"

"You're too late! I've already put on my mask."

"But there's a little place for my lips just behind your little ear."

"Ah, Monsieur, you're going to take that from me?!"

"Madame, every kiss that I steal is stolen from the priests who are our common enemies."

But as comforting as I found this banter, I who'd been living for months far from the diversions and luminaries of the court in a dark little house and wearing sad clothes, as soon as this lady had departed (a devil in angel's clothes?) I felt very lonely and very worried; and my worries increased that night, when I received word that, in Paris, the League had dispatched a fellow named Brigart to Guise in Soissons practically to *order* Guise to come to Paris with the greatest urgency, since the members of the League there were losing heart as they saw the king well fortified in the Louvre, and the Bastille and the Arsenal reinforced and impregnable. They were so discouraged that they imagined themselves arrested and hanged, and they threatened to abandon the League if the duc didn't come as he'd promised to do so many times. Let him come! Let his presence re-establish their dominance! Let him be the yeast that will raise the crust!

"Épernon, did you hear?" said the king to his arch-favourite when I repeated to him the next day all I'd learnt from Lady Markby. "The terrible storm is coming that will carry off both the throne of Elizabeth and mine. What do you think?"

"Sire," replied Épernon with a derisive laugh, "this man Guise in Soissons is only asking for a few little favours: the title of lieutenant general of the kingdom, the establishment of the Inquisition in France, the extermination of all of your Huguenot subjects and the designation of the Cardinal de Bourbon as the heir apparent."

"Henrikins," said Chicot, "Épernon is right. The Magnificent one only wants the throne. So let's give it to him. Her Majesty the queen mother would be delighted, and she could nickname him her 'walking stick'!"

"A stick with which she could beat her son," smiled the king sourly. "Épernon," he continued, turning serious and his black eyes shining, "the more we cede to Guise, the more he demands. This is not a moment to trim our sails—it's time to go full sheets to the wind! Elizabeth is right, and I thought of it even before she did: we must throw reinforcements into Rouen, in order to seal off Dieppe and cut off Guise from the rear if he presumes to march on Paris. Monsieur colonel general of the French infantry, I hereby name you governor of Normandy, and you will command our forces in Rouen."

"Sire," replied Épernon, kneeling before his king, and looking up at him with his beautiful, strong face, "I will obey you."

"At the same time I will dispatch Monsieur Pomponne de Bellièvre to Soissons to ask Guise not to come to Paris unless I expressly require it; and to tell him that if he does come, things being what they are here, his arrival might cause an uprising, for which I would hold him forever guilty."

"There's little evidence," Chicot noted, "that the Pompous Pomponne would speak that way to the duc, since he shits in his pants at the very sound of the man's name."

"Pomponne," observed Du Halde, "belongs to the queen mother. He'll say to Guise, 'No, no! Yes, yes!' That will be 'No, no' from the king and 'Yes, yes' from the queen mother."

"Who wants her 'walking stick' right here," added Chicot. "Henri, the only sure way to handle this is to send the Bloodletter."

"Most assuredly not!" replied the king. "Siorac wouldn't last an hour in Soissons, if he got there at all! I'll write a letter to Guise that Pomponne will deliver to him. And Monsieur colonel general," he said to Épernon, "order Lagny to move my Swiss Guards towards Paris, and billet them in the faubourgs of Saint-Denis and Montmartre. That will give our Parisian rebels and rabble-rousers something to think about!"

Épernon in Rouen, Bellièvre in Soissons and his Swiss Guards at the gates of Paris: excellent measures, all well conceived, promptly taken and well executed, and that would demonstrate, contrary to what L'Étoile and De Thou were saying, that the king was neither soft nor indolent, and that he knew how to act, and act decisively when he judged the moment opportune.

Sparing no expense, he gave Épernon the lion's share of his army: four companies of heavy cavalry and twenty-two squadrons of foot soldiers, keeping for himself only the 4,000 Swiss Guards billeted in the faubourgs of Paris. Moreover, to give Épernon's departure more importance, he himself accompanied the army out to Saint-Germain-en-Laye, where he took his leave of his general, and went to enter the monastery of the Hieronymites at Vincennes, saying that he wished to do seven days of penitence and that, during that time, he would not speak to anyone.

This was a strange decision to be sure, given the troubled times and the precarious predicament that, normally, he would have wished to follow hour by hour. But then, every man has his weaknesses, and this was the king's particular foible. He went on pilgrimages; he processed; he flagellated himself; he mortified himself in cold cells without heat, endlessly praying with his rosary of death's heads, asking a thousand thousand pardons from his Creator for the pleasures he could not resist and that overwhelmed his conscience with an insufferable weight. At this price, for one whole week, his poor soul seemed to find some peace. And subsequently, the memory of this quietude being so powerful, he ended up almost falling in love with monasteries, calm cloisters and his hair shirt, so much so that the sight of a monk, perceived by chance at court, excited him. And, as everyone knows, he died because of it.

I saw Mosca twice during the week that the king spent in penitence, which I spent as a recluse (though not sanctimoniously) with my little fly from hell, and each time he told me that the reinforcements of the king in and around Paris had so struck terror into the hearts of the League that they had disbanded, and debauched themselves to the point that if Guise didn't appear in the capital, or if the king decided to deal severely with them, the League would collapse.

"But Mosca," I said, "do you think he'll come?"

"Ah, Monsieur," Mosca replied, "who will ever understand Guise? He has so many different faces that he doesn't even know himself which is the real one. Moreover, having decided to march towards the throne by imperceptible degrees, and not straight on, but sideways like a crab, he must feel very uncomfortable to have to cross the Rubicon in one fell swoop and appear within our walls. What's worse is that he faces a difficult choice. He has too few forces to maintain an army in Picardy while attempting to occupy Paris. And it would be awkward to pretend he's here in friendship after having stripped the king of so many cities in Picardy. However, if the Spaniard and the League push him hard enough I think he'll end up coming, though in very bad grace, and timidly. But even then, God save the king! For the Paris mob will rise up against him."

13

O N 9TH MAY, finding myself in the king's apartments a little later
than usual, and the king having some affairs to attend to but
having asked me to await his pleasure, I sat down on a trunk that was
in a dark corner, my hat pulled down over my eyes, since there were
quite a few people there besides Chicot and Du Halde. These included
François d'O, Pomponne de Bellièvre, the venerable Dr Marc Miron,
Fogacer (who pretended not to know me), Monsieur de Merle (the
king's butler), Alphonse d'Ornano, whom they called "the Corsican"
since he commanded His Majesty's troop from that island, and the
little abbot d'Elbène, who was very welcome in His Majesty's presence
since he was a royalist and anti-League. As such, Henri had sent him
in Épernon's retinue to Angoulême, a city in which the abbot had been
besieged in his house by an uprising fomented by the League, in which
he almost lost his life.

He was a lively little fellow, with sparkling eyes, not without some
resemblance to a squirrel, and a man who had no faults other than his
stinginess and appetite for hoarding money. Otherwise, he was a very tidy
abbot of the court, soft-spoken, making frequent reference to Scripture,
and very fond of Alphonse the Corsican, who was at least two heads taller
than he—he was a giant of a man: square-shouldered, rough-skinned
and loud-voiced, as well as haughty and arrogant in his behaviour.

About eleven o'clock, the Cardinal de Bourbon asked to be presented
to the king, who received him thinking that he had some news to impart

about the arrival or the non-arrival of Guise in Paris; however, it was immediately apparent that the Great Halfwit knew nothing about it, and that he had come in his capacity of prelate to gain acceptance for his point of view that the death of Condé was a good thing since he'd been excommunicated by the Pope at the same time as Navarre, both being considered heretics.

"There now, sire," he said, shaking his head and spreading his arms unctuously as if he were speaking from the pulpit, "that's what it is to be excommunicated!"

"But my cousin," observed the king, feigning naivety, "I heard tell that Condé was poisoned by his page."

"Assuredly so, sire," said the Great Halfwit, "but who put the page up to it?"

"They say," said the king, "that it was Condé's wife."

"Assuredly so, sire, but what inspired the Demoiselle de La Trémoille to commit this murder?"

"Her adultery, from what I've heard," said the king ingenuously.

"Possibly," admitted the cardinal. "But, sire, we have to look higher than all these contingent causes and search out the necessary cause."

"Which is?"

"The will of God."

"But wait, my cousin! Are you claiming that God ordered Mademoiselle de La Trémoille to commit adultery, and ordered the page to assassinate Condé?"

"Well, sire," said the Halfwit, "we have to look at causes as originating in a much higher place. As for me, I don't attribute the death of Condé to anything but the lightning bolt of excommunication by which he was struck down."

"'Tis doubtless true, my cousin," said the king, taking the cardinal by the arm and leading him by degrees towards the door. "It is true that that a lightning bolt is to be feared, and yet all those who have incurred God's wrath must not necessarily die! There would be an awful lot of people dying!"

"Nevertheless," said the cardinal (whom the king was, step by step, pushing out of the door with every appearance of courtesy), "Condé is dead as a result of it."

"Helped along by a good and devout poison," observed the king with a smile, as he presented his hand to the cardinal.

Seeing this, the cardinal had no choice but to kiss the hand and take his leave, which was indicated so graciously and with such regard that the king actually accompanied him all the way to the door and patted him affectionately on the shoulder as he left.

The king seemed cheered by this conversation, which had distracted him from his sombre concerns, and returned smiling to the group of noblemen whom I mentioned (all of whom were visibly amused by this little comedy that His Majesty had enacted with his "heir apparent"). When he caught sight of me, however, he remembered that he'd begged me to visit him, and so he came over to me and I rose, doffed my merchant's cap and knelt before him, thinking he would present me with his hand. And, indeed, he was preparing to do so when Chicot, who'd been standing by the window giving onto the courtyard, observed in his usual humorous way:

"Who is this I see coming on foot, escorted by the queen mother in her chair? He looks as big as ever but a good deal less natural. Who else but the Duc de Guise?"

At this the king dropped the hand he'd extended towards me, paled and cried in fury:

"Chicot, if you're lying, I'll beat you with my bear hands!"

"Henrikins," said Chicot without budging an inch, "I'd much prefer to be beaten and kicked by you than to see what I see! But it is, alas, the Magnificent! There's no doubting it."

At this, everyone ran to the windows to see whether the fool was telling the truth.

"Sire, it's him!" said Alphonse d'Ornano in his loud voice, placing his right hand on his sword. "And he's only escorted by five or six gentlemen."

The king staggered over to a little table, put his hand on it to steady himself, then sat down on the trunk that I'd just abandoned and covered his face with both hands—a gesture that he always made in moments of great anguish. Du Halde claims that he heard him say quietly, "He'll die for this," but I don't know whether he merely imagined this afterwards, since I was quite close to His Majesty and heard nothing of the sort, and can only report that his visage was distorted by a furious expression when he pulled his trembling hands away from his pale face.

"Sire," said Alphonse d'Ornano in his brusque loud voice, "has someone injured you?"

"That's an understatement," replied the king, who was, little by little, regaining his colour. "But the problem is this, my Corsican. I forbade Guise to return to Paris, and now, disobeying my orders, he has dared to come, knowing full well that his presence in Paris will set off an explosion."

"Sire," replied Alphonse d'Ornano, squaring his powerful shoulders, his voice as resonant as an organ, "if it please Your Majesty to give me the orders, I will today throw Guise's head at your feet before any man can move or prevent it."

At this, the king, his head and eyelids lowered, reflected for a moment, no doubt sorely tempted to acquiesce, but held back from saying yes by the thought of the unpredictable consequences such an execution would have in a city (and a kingdom) that idolized the duc—not to mention in Spain, where it could well furnish Felipe II with the pretext he needed to invade France and, at the same time, conquer England. For it must be said that there were few men in this month of May 1588 who in their wildest dreams imagined that Queen Elizabeth could ever resist the Invincible Armada, whose arrogant galleons and superb sails could be seen weighing anchor behind the tall silhouette of Guise as he crossed the courtyard of the Louvre, apparently without any other escort than five or six gentlemen, but supported by the zeal of the innumerable clergy and the adoration of an uneducated people, in addition to the inexhaustible riches of the most powerful monarch in Christendom.

What's more, my master, far from being able to improvise such a momentous decision on the spur of moment, was really a man of his study, a political mind, a Machiavellian, whose thought was more suited to waiting and temporizing, to knotting and untying the many threads of an action well in advance. And finally, as I've said many times already, he had a deep repugnance for shedding blood, and would only do so if every other possibility seemed closed and out of reach.

"Sire," said Alphonse d'Ornano, his enormous frame trembling from head to foot from the affront to the king—he was like a mastiff pulling on its chain with its teeth bared as it watches its master being assailed by his enemies without being able to come to his aid. "Sire, shall I do this thing?"

And, except for Pompous Pomponne, who belonged to the queen mother and was more or less a partisan of the League, everyone present, indignant that Guise had presumed to insult the king in this way, stood silently watching the king, holding his breath and desperately praying that he would consent to d'Ornano's proposal.

"Sire," said the little abbot d'Elbène, his suave and fluty voice cutting through the silence, "permit me, touching our present predicament, to cite the Holy Scriptures."

"Go ahead, abbot," said the king without looking up.

"'Smite the shepherd, and the sheep shall be scattered.'"

"Sire, shall I do it?" d'Ornano suddenly repeated, as though encouraged in his violent scheme by the authority of the sacred word.

Whether it was because of the clarion voice of d'Ornano (which, even when he murmured, gave the impression he wanted to be heard by the entire regiment), or, instead, because of the weight of all of our expectant looks bearing on him, Henri raised his head, presented his calm and composed face to us and, casting his beautiful dark eyes on d'Ornano, said, with the affectionate derision that he liked to take with his closest servants:

"No, my courageous Corsican. I do not wish it. There is no need for that yet."

Unlike L'Étoile, De Thou and so many others, I couldn't decide whether my beloved sovereign was right or wrong by opting for the longer road of patience. It is the tantalizing nature of history, whose outcome produces such unbearable regrets, that we project our own desires with childish impatience onto the great actors of the drama and yearn to give them a nudge so that they can make the decisions that our knowledge of hindsight shows us to be the most desirable ones. Having such convenient knowledge of the future of the prince, the historian falls prey to the temptation to think he's wiser than he, forgetting that the prince was confronted with an opaque present.

Whoever didn't see the tall, handsome Duc de Guise enter the king's apartments—looking truly magnificent in his white, pearl-studded doublet, accompanied not by his gentlemen but by the queen mother, his cousin the queen and the latter's usual companion the Duchesse d'Uzès, the three of whom seeming to flank and protect him like frigates alongside the admiral's galleon—can't imagine the impression of power and invincibility that he projected, as if the wind that was carrying him towards the throne were the same one that at that exact moment—9th May 1588—was swelling the sails of the Armada off Lisbon, as it set out for England.

As soon as he saw the king, the duc made him a deep bow, to which Henri responded with a slight nod of his head, but without presenting him his hand, his expression and eyes cold as ice, and his teeth clenched:

"What is this? Did I not forbid you to come here?"

"Well, sire!" said Guise, with blatant hypocrisy. "If you'd expressly forbidden it, I would have died rather than disobey you."

"So, Bellièvre!" said the king, turning to the Pompous Pomponne. "Did you not repeat my words to Monsieur de Guise? Didn't you give him my letter?"

At this, Bellièvre made a bow to the king that seemed to be intended as much for Guise as for Henri, but said not a word, since he didn't dare, tortured by the risk of offending the king, or the queen mother, who'd given him a message for Guise exactly contrary to the king's, or the duc, whom he believed to be his future sovereign—if the duc were able to leave these apartments alive, which he began to doubt, in which case his betrayal would have been in vain.

"Well, Bellièvre?" said the king, whose glacial look seemed to penetrate, one by one, each of the embarrassing calculations of his ambassador. "Did you or did you not deliver my message to Monsieur de Guise?"

"Assuredly, sire," stammered Bellièvre, whose uncertain look was fixed respectfully on the king, as if he wished to take back his ambiguous words, which appeared to answer two contradictory questions but in reality answered neither one.

"Sire," said Guise, who was doubtless too concerned about his own safety to worry about helping Pomponne out of his predicament, "I did indeed receive Monsieur de Bellièvre in Soissons. But if I had understood that you were ordering me expressly—"

"Did he not give you a letter from me?" continued the king, interrupting him in the most abrupt fashion. "And have you not read this letter? Did I not have you confirm its contents by Monsieur de La

Guiche? How many ambassadors must I send you to persuade you to obey me?"

"Sire," answered Guise, looking around him uncomfortably, for he'd just seen Crillon, the chief officer of the Louvre, enter, who, far from politely doffing his hat to the duc, had furiously pushed it farther down on his brow, and gone over to stand next to d'Ornano, who was posted by the door, after which the two began speaking to each other in hushed tones and throwing Guise angry looks, while fidgeting with the handles of their daggers.

"Sire," said Guise, "Monsieur de La Guiche does not have the same authority as Monsieur de Bellièvre and it's the latter whom I believed."

"Your Bellièvre here is as quiet as a carp," cried the king, his black eyes flashing in anger.

"Sire," said Bellièvre, who was now trembling from his capacious stomach to his double chin, "there must be some misunderstanding. The Duc de Guise did not understand my words as he should have."

"That's enough, Bellièvre!" the king cried furiously, and, turning his back on Guise, he went over to the window, glaring murderously over his shoulder at both Bellièvre and Guise.

And, whether his legs were suddenly too weak to support his large body, or whether he meant to anticipate a sword thrust in his back, Guise went over to sit down on the chest on which the king had just been sitting, and, as he did, threw a desperate look at the queen, his cousin, who, understanding this mute message, went over to him, took his hand affectionately and sat down on the chest on his right. Whereupon the Duchesse d'Uzès, seeing a look from the queen mother, went over and sat down on his left. In this way the two women made it impossible for the king to proceed to his arrest or his execution.

"'Sblood!" murmured d'Ornano (though his murmurs could easily be heard by all). "Nice work to have two petticoats serve as your protection!"

At this remark, a complete silence fell over the room, while the queen whispered something to Guise, and the king, for his part, stood with his back turned, tapping on the windowpane with his finger, and shaking with anger from head to foot.

The queen mother stood silently looking at her son, her large eyes protruding, her lips twisted in pain from her gout (having got out of her sickbed to take Guise to the Louvre, fearing that without her august presence they might have killed him right then and there). She now felt helpless, since the king had let his mask slip and allowed his anger to explode against the duc, against Bellièvre and, clearly, against her too, given that he had neither looked at nor greeted her when she'd entered his apartments.

She seemed to me to hesitate over whether to join him at the window, and perhaps felt that she didn't have the strength to go over to him alone, since she walked with such difficulty, as I'd observed when she entered, her left hand grasping the arm of the Duchesse d'Uzès, and her right the arm of Guise, her "old woman's walking stick", as she dared say. She also seemed to me, moreover, very sickly: her cheeks, which had always been so round, now seemed swollen and wan, and her lower lip hung so loosely that she seemed to have difficulty joining it to the upper one when she tried, from time to time, to do so. She looked like nothing so much as a toad, especially with her protruding eyes and her drooping eyelids.

"Bellièvre," she said to this creature of hers, extending her arm to ask for his. But when the gentleman ran over to her, his back bent to her command, she doubtless decided that she could not, without some danger, approach the king in his company, and so she said:

"No, not Bellièvre—Du Halde!"

To which Du Halde obeyed, but with a good deal less enthusiasm than Bellièvre had displayed, since he had no love for Catherine, seeing as she had tried so many times, out of jealousy and hatred of him, to have him removed by the king, although she had failed each time.

"My son," she said, suddenly in tears (a commodity she'd always been able to produce on demand), "won't you listen to me?"

"Madame," replied the king without turning his head, "my ears are tired."

"Ah, my son," said the queen mother, redoubling her tears, "what will they say of me when they see that I, whom God chose for your mother, find myself rejected by you?"

"Madame," replied the king without turning to look at her, "I am not rejecting you. It even seems that I'm listening to you, whether I like it or not."

"Well then, my son," said the queen mother, "if I must tell the truth, it is not to affront you that Guise has come, but at my request, to answer the calumnies that your Huguenots have spread about his activities."

"At your request, Madame?" said the king. "It's because you invited him that he's here? This is another of your wicked tricks!"

"But," parried the queen mother, "he's only here to ask for forgiveness for his mistakes and to find some way to make his peace with you and give you back your cities in Picardy."

"Madame," said the king quietly but his voice full of fury, "you're nothing but a very confused old lady! You're muddled and you meddle too much. Give me back my cities in Picardy? That's not what this is about! Did you dream this?"

"I'm going to keep trying day and night even if I sacrifice the little life that remains to me!"

At these words the king turned round, looked at her and, surprised at the change he discovered in her, found that he felt some compassion for her; so he said, more gently:

"Madame, you are not well. Go back to your bed. You shouldn't have left it."

"My son," she murmured, throwing all her battalions into the breach, "I will not return to my bed unless you promise me that you will not persecute the duc."

"Madame," replied the king with obvious weariness, "I'll do as you wish, but I beg you, go back to bed!"

Under the watchful eye of her son, the queen mother pursued her absurd speech about reconciliation, which Du Halde, who was listening, later described as making as much sense as claiming that the fox had entered the chicken coop in order to have a reasoned discussion with the hens. Watching the king, Du Halde could tell that Henri had truly loved his mother when he was a youth, but that he had become embittered when he'd watched her ally herself first with his brother Alençon and subsequently, and more disastrously, with this most mortal enemy of the throne and the state—but Henri could not resign himself to hate her, since this was a sentiment that simply could not take root in his benign character, which was too noble and forgiving to harbour such a trait, one that would have easily dominated a less generous soul.

That Guise had come, as she dared pretend, without bitterness, to explain and justify his actions, to make peace with the king, to return to him the cities he'd seized in Picardy, and to promise to behave himself from now on, Henri didn't believe for one single moment. And if, ultimately, he seemed to accept her version of events, it was because, having decided not to kill the duc, since he could see the forest of the Invincible Armada's masts emerging behind his back, he wanted to give this apparent gift to the queen mother in order to maintain her services as "interpreter" between the duc and himself, so that he could, at any given moment, get an idea of his dangerous but vacillating enemy's intentions through her. It was a subtle, Machiavellian game: Catherine undermined her son's power in pretending to serve him, while he feigned belief in her in order to ascertain the duc's underhand treachery.

"Madame," he said finally, "if you will do everything you can to return the cities in Picardy and persuade the duc to leave Paris immediately, since his very presence here is an affront to me, I will be infinitely grateful to you. I'm already in your debt for the innumerable gifts you have bestowed on me. If you would oblige me even more by making peace between the duc and me, your good offices will serve to cut the roots of the calamities that now risk falling upon us. But, Madame, you are pale, suffering and not well at all. I beg you, return to your bed and do not leave it until you are in better health! As for me, I'm going to be much more gracious with the duc."

Bowing to her with apparent good grace, he left the window recess and walked over to Guise, still surrounded by the ramparts of the queen's and the Duchesse d'Uzès's dresses; and, looking the duc in the eye, but with a less severe but still somewhat cold expression, he said, in a much calmer voice:

"My cousin, I must take my breakfast. You must do likewise. Return here when you've done, and we will continue our conversation."

So saying, he presented his hand to the duc, who, dropping to one knee, bestowed a fairly devout kiss upon it. This done, he stood, made a deep bow to the king, not wishing to be sparing in his genuflections; then, without taking any more notice of the queen mother than if she'd been a dead goat—she who had apparently just saved him—he headed to the door, while Crillon and d'Ornano shot him murderous looks. And, in my estimation, if ever a man felt astonished to be leaving the Louvre alive, after the welcome he'd at first received, it was on this 9th May, and that man was Guise. And that he should have later forgotten, in his overweening conceit, the peril he'd ventured into that day is wholly astonishing.

Scarcely had Guise departed before the king dismissed the rest of his visitors, with a singular dearth of tenderness for Bellièvre, and for the royal skirts that had protected the duc, retaining only Du Halde, Chicot and me (whom he'd pretended to forget in my corner), and told me that it was no longer enough to speak with Mosca, but that I should immediately head out into the streets and public squares of the capital to try to take the pulse of the people. He had no scruples in asking me to do this since he didn't think it so dangerous, for he'd noticed that not one of the people who'd just been there, despite the fact that they all knew me, had recognized me with my beard, unattractive hair and merchant's clothing. He requested that, once my mission was accomplished, I return through the Porte Neuve, the Tuileries Garden and the secret entrance, no matter what the hour, and share my observations with him.

I was delighted that the king would make such use of me in the almost desperate predicament he was in, and Miroul and I spared no effort in running around the city, talking with its labourers and inhabitants, pretending that I was a bonnet-maker from Boulogne who was visiting a friend in Paris. I was careful to wear my medallion of the Virgin proudly displayed on the front of my doublet, and a mother-of-pearl rosary wrapped around my right wrist, and to proffer many League-ish observations, much like the ones I was hearing everywhere in the shops, in the markets and on the steps of the churches throughout the capital. Once inside the churches, I pretended to be very assiduous, my nose in my missal, giving generously to the collection, and listening with devout nods of the head to the seditious, disloyal and criminal sermons that were being preached and that, at another time, would have had me drawing my sword from its scabbard in anger.

On this occasion, I was careful not to wear a sword, but to carry a dagger concealed on my back and two pistols in my wretched leggings. Miroul's were no less ridiculously puffy and bourgeois than mine, and also concealed two pistols, plus several knives that he could throw should necessity require it.

I learnt from Quéribus, who visited me that evening at Alizon's lodgings, that during these two days I spent wearing out my soles on the paving stones of the capital, Guise had not left the king's side, having returned with a large escort, visiting him at Mass or at dinner, where in his role of grand master of France he offered him his napkin, or else at the Convent of the Repentant Daughters, where the queen mother was lodged. It seemed, from what transpired at these discussions, that the king was trying to persuade Guise to leave Paris, and Guise was assuring him of his obedience, on condition that the king promise that, once Guise left the capital, the lives of his supporters in the League would not be endangered. On his part, the king reproached Guise for his capture of the cities in Picardy, whereupon Guise swore that he held them in the king's name and that he'd return them once Henri, instead of giving ear to his enemies (meaning Épernon), recognized Guise's good service and made peace with him. And when the king defended Épernon tooth and nail, Guise made a deep bow and replied, with a smile full of malice, that "out of love for the master, he'd love even his dog". So, as Du Halde (whom I saw for a few minutes on the 11th) reported it, it was clear that Guise was toying with the king and playing for time.

It was quite clear to me why Guise wanted to gain time, and I shared this with the king: everywhere I went, I found the capital more stirred up than ever. The Leaguers—who, until his arrival in Paris, had been losing heart and had more or less fallen into debauchery— had regained their courage as soon as he had arrived, and, like flies to honey, were organizing nearly open sedition and inflaming the delirium and adoration of the people for the duc. Guise, however, had not shown himself in public very much, except on his arrival on 9th May, when, as soon as he was recognized, he couldn't take a step in this city that idolized him without crowds gathering and pressing him on every side, the good people acclaiming him and kissing his hands, his boots and his horse's shoes—some even rubbing their rosaries on his coat to sanctify them.

During these two days, I saw everywhere men organizing, openly carrying both swords and firearms, polishing their weapons in the back rooms of their shops and having heated discussions, their hats frequently decorated with white crosses, reminiscent of the murderers of St Bartholomew's eve, who were now going about bragging of their former exploits, which they hoped soon to renew. Many preachers were giving sermons in the street and I don't know how many barrels were being rolled into the streets and piled in places that had been indicated in advance so that, when the time came, they could be filled with uprooted paving stones and placed strategically as "barricades".

Of the three areas of the city—la Ville, the Île de la Cité and l'Université—this last seemed to me by far the most fearsome in its resolution, the professors, monks and priests having insufflated a frenetic papist zeal into the population of ecclesiastics and students, who, because of their youth and quarrelsome nature, were only too inclined to pillage and revolt. As for the right-bank area of Paris, called la Ville, the people seemed more political than zealous, and more interested in removing the king's favourites, who were wasting huge amounts of public money, than in deposing the king himself. But within l'Université the sedition was animated by the taste for blood, combat and regicide. Everywhere there was talk of assembling Guise's troops, who were being hidden by the monks in the innumerable cloisters, colleges and monasteries of this quarter, of rushing down the rue Saint-Jacques, across the Pont Saint-Michel, through the Île de la Cité and across the Pont Notre-Dame, and then "going to seize the blackguard in his Louvre". And as for what they would do with him when they had taken him—I would fear to dirty my pen by repeating what I heard in the mouths of the clerics.

I couldn't help noticing during the two days that I spent crossing and recrossing Paris with my alert Miroul (who knew the capital better than anyone), that if the Duc de Guise affected to appear a stranger to what was happening here, seeing the king twice a day and trying to lull him with language that was both conciliatory and ambiguous, his lieutenants, particularly Captain de Saint-Paul and the Comte de Brissac, went about very actively—the latter especially in l'Université— organizing a public uprising.

The Comte de Brissac, a large, well-built man with red hair and green eyes, would have been very good-looking had he not had a squint in his left eye and if his mouth did not have a tendency to pull to the left, which, together, gave him on second glance a shady and false expression. Having chosen a career in arms, he'd done little to distinguish himself in terrestrial combat or in the unfortunate naval engagement in the Azores, which had led the king (who could never resist a bon mot) to observe that "Brissac was good neither on land nor at sea". When he'd heard these words repeated, Brissac had conceived a homicidal hatred for his king and become a Guisard, vowing to rid his country of this monarch if he could, sparing neither pain nor effort during these two days to prepare an insurrection in the streets, and repeating—with his mouth ever more twisted—that, if he weren't good on either land or sea, he'd show His Majesty that he was good on paving stones, where he'd finally found his element.

On each of these days I saw Mosca, who was very well placed amid the knot of League vipers, and he confirmed the imminence of the tumult that was being prepared. He cited the "quasi-miraculous" appearance of the duc (as the sermonizers had labelled it), and his "quasi-divine presence within our walls" (so many rosaries had been sanctified by contact with his coat), and said that he had reawakened the deflated resolutions of the people and inflamed their passions to the heavens.

I saw the king on the evenings of the 10th and the 11th, and repeated Mosca's observations, as well as my own. He listened very attentively and related that all of the accounts he'd heard came to the same sinister conclusions about the great popular uprising provoked by the Leaguers and the Guisards, and that what worried him the most were the reports of a large number of soldiers being hidden in the quarter of l'Université, who would bolster the rioters with their pikes.

During the second of these two visits, I overheard a few words that His Majesty exchanged with Du Halde, to the effect that Henri had finally convinced Guise to leave Paris and that he could see all too well that the Lorraine duc had secretly had a hand in planning the revolt, all the while pretending hypocritically to be involved in vain negotiations; however, the king had decided to put an end to this commotion by bringing his Swiss Guards into Paris from their garrison in the Faubourg Saint-Honoré, so that the Leaguers could be reminded of their duty and in the hopes that even Guise himself, seeing so many troops, would withdraw to Soissons.

On the evening of the 11th, Lady Markby came to see me and, once we were alone in my room, began furiously kissing me, which at first distracted me from my troubles, but then discomfited me excessively when Alizon went at me tooth and nail after discovering these goings-on.

Lady Markby, who already knew about the king's decision to bring the Swiss Guards into Paris—given how excellent the spies of the Moor were—told me that Lord Stafford predicted that the people, far from being intimidated by these new troops, would be spurred to anger like a taunted bull.

"My Lark," said Lady Markby with a delicate smile, "Lord Stafford has asked me to tell you that if you're feeling threatened or in danger of being recognized in your peregrinations though Paris, you're welcome to take refuge in his embassy on the quai des Bernardins, which you should enter not by the main gates but through the bakery next door, which has a secret passage leading to it. It will be enough to show this sign," she explained, handing me a coin displaying the image of Queen Elizabeth and that had been pierced in its centre, "and you'll be admitted immediately. As for me," she added, her black eyes shining and her carnivorous teeth showing brightly, "if I have to seek refuge there as well, I will immediately make good on the promise I gave to pluck a certain lark of its feathers…"

I slept little and badly on the night of the 11th to the 12th May and, finally nodding off at daybreak, I had a nightmare in which I found myself in my shirt on the gibbet, the rope already round my neck; and, though my hands were tied behind my back, I was struggling like the Devil in a baptismal font, and shouting with indignation at the hangman, who looked just like the Comte de Brissac, with his sinister eyes and mouth, telling him that I was a gentleman of the court and that as such I should not be hanged but beheaded. At this the executioner responded derisively that he'd never seen a gentleman dressed like me, and, moreover, even if what I said was true, he couldn't satisfy me—however eager he was to satisfy his customers—since, no more than the king of France, he was not in possession of a sword or axe that would be sharp enough to decapitate all his felons. Saying this, he tightened the rope about my neck and I woke up with a cry, and found my little fly from hell, fully dressed, shaking me by the shoulders with her two little hands, assuredly much softer than the rope, whose bite I had felt on my skin only an instant before.

"Pierre!" she cried. "My Pierre! The guards! The Swiss Guards are in Paris!"

And, very happy to discover I was alive and still possessed of all my parts in this soft bed, with Alizon on top of me, though only a moment before I had seen myself passing into the beyond, badly washed of all my sins, I added to those sins by pulling her to me and kissing her with great joy, as the very symbol of all those pleasures the rope had very nearly deprived me of.

"Ah, my Pierre!" cried Alizon, struggling like the supple eel that she'd always been. "Have you gone mad? This is not the time to start fooling around! Can't you hear the drums? And the Swiss Guards' boots on the pavement? Ah, we're doomed! They'll kill us all! Pillage everything! Truly, soldiers in Paris! Is that not shameful! 'Tis a vile and abominable violation of the Paris privilege!"

"What privilege?" I frowned.

"Well, my Pierre," explained my little fly from hell, frowning back in anger, and escaping from my embrace, "haven't you yet wiped the Périgordian dust off your feet? Truly! The pretty Parisian you pretend to be! Don't you know that Paris has the privilege to defend itself by calling on its bourgeois militias, and that no garrison of troops has ever been allowed within the city walls? This is just another dirty trick by your devil of a king!"

"He's also yours!"

"And by his arch-favourite!"

"Who couldn't be involved since he's in Normandy!"

"Ah, my Pierre," she cried, throwing herself in my arms, "let's not quarrel any more! I'm terrified at the thought of losing everything I've worked so hard for over the last twenty years! Truly! If they don't murder us, these nasty Swiss are going to pillage our homes and rape all our women! I could endure that since the pain doesn't last forever, but my property! They're going to take it and plunder it! Oh, Pierre!" she continued, seeing me getting dressed. "Help me! Take your good sword, I beg you, your pistols and your daggers, and, with Miroul and Baragran, escort me to the nuncio!"

"To the nuncio?" I asked, astonished. "To the Pope's nuncio? And to what end?"

"To put my gold in trust. Some of the artisans in our street did this yesterday and the day before yesterday to protect it from the popular uprising, and so I'd be very well advised to do the same, if you'll only give me a hand."

"Well, I'm not sure!" I said derisively. "In my view that would be going from bad to worse. The nuncio is no different from anyone else! He'd never renounce any gold he could get his hands on! Will he give it back when the tumult has passed? Since I am still, as you put it, my fly, an unwashed peasant from Périgord, I'm going to share a *langue d'oc* proverb with you."

"In *langue d'oc*?" she cried in disappointment and anger. "I don't want to hear it! Enough of that jargon! I don't understand a word of it!"

"I'll translate it for you: 'Monks and lice never satisfy their lust: they'll eat anything, even the crust.'"

"Ah, Huguenot!" she shouted, tears of rage spurting from her eyes. "You're attacking our good priests, you heretic! Instead of helping me, you torture me!"

"You crazy she-wolf," I said, seizing her by the arm as she was pacing frantically back and forth in the room like an unhinged lunatic. And holding her tightly in my arms I continued, "What does this mean, 'Huguenot'? 'Heretic'? 'Torturer'? Is this your Pierre you want to sink your teeth into? Can't we have different opinions? Am I a heretic simply because I don't say 'amen' to every decision you make? If you absolutely want to give your gold to the nuncio, go ahead, my sweet madwoman! I'll help and cooperate, however much I disagree with the decision."

Hearing these words, she softened and melted into my arms; and, transformed from wolf into cat, she began purring a thousand thanks in my ear, giving me loving looks, kissing me and caressing my head and neck in ways she knew full well would please me. And having me thus wound tight in her web, she would have wanted to leave right away if, opening the window, I hadn't advised her to wait until the Swiss Guards had passed, their advance marked by the sinister rhythm of their drums, the menacing undulation of their flutes and the hammering of their boots, as they marched four by four down the rue de la Ferronnerie, heading, I judged, towards the walls of the Saints-Innocents cemetery, their swords at their sides and on their shoulders their arquebuses—which, from what I could see with some misgivings, had their wicks already lit, which meant they were loaded and ready to fire. This detail didn't escape the notice of Alizon, who, clenching her fists, cried between her clenched teeth:

"Ah the accursed soldiers! They want to fire their lead into our chests and make a St Bartholomew's day massacre of the Catholics! If I had a stone here, I'd throw it at them!"

This sentence, now that the street was quiet, all the fifes and drums having passed, and the pale labourers and inhabitants frozen and silent at their windows, was heard by one of their officers, who, looking up at our window, cried mockingly at the spectators:

"Bourgeois, put some fresh sheets on your beds! We'll be back tonight to sleep with your wives!"

This nasty phrase made the rounds in Paris, and was everywhere received with angry rumblings that we heard from virtually every side when the troops had passed and barricaded themselves within the Saints-Innocents cemetery. After they'd passed, Miroul, Baragran and I set out, pushing a cart with a locked chest on it, armed to the teeth, which didn't surprise anyone, since at this point there wasn't a mother's son who wasn't out on the streets, some with pistols, others with arquebuses, pikes or skewers, or even butcher's knives—but all with fire in their eyes, seditious slogans on their tongues and fists raised in defiance.

The nuncio lodged in the Saint-Antoine quarter, and in each street we passed we could see increasing numbers of people emerging from shops and houses with the same angry expressions and furious shouts that the king had violated the Parisians' privilege, all of them very resolved to protect their families from his mercenaries.

Once we'd arrived the nuncio's palace, we had to stand in line for a good two hours given the numbers of merchants and bourgeois who'd had the same idea. But, to tell the truth, however much of a papist this cardinal was, he impressed me with his honest and good face, and his frank and open expression. He even joked that it was a pity that these were all merely deposits and not offerings—for, he said, with all this gold he could defeat the Turks and establish Christianity in the Holy Land!

Returning to Alizon's lodgings around noon, we were surprised to see that our way was blocked by barricades, which were springing up here and there like mushrooms. They were made of barrels filled with paving stones, just as Mosca had reported. Each barricade had an opening just large enough for a pedestrian or a man on horseback to pass through, but the space could be filled by a cart like ours, which could be wheeled into place and used as a kind of door in the barricade.

We managed to cross two of these barricades without firing a shot. However, as we reached the third, which, like the first two, was bristling with arquebuses, halberds and pikes, a large, fat fellow who was parading and bragging a lot, and told us haughtily that his name was Fessard, informed us that we had to have a man named La Chapelle-Marteau provide us with stamped documents, without which we'd be forbidden to continue and considered to be "politicals"; we'd also have our cart confiscated by the League, who would use it as a door for their barricade.

We retraced our steps and began to ask various people what they knew about this man, La Chapelle-Marteau, whom I'd discovered, through reports from Mosca, to be one of the most bloodthirsty and influential of the Leaguers, and who was a counsellor to the Court of

Accounts. One fellow told us that he held court in a tavern that he'd had reopened under his authority, all shops and boutiques having been closed by their owners as soon as the Swiss Guards arrived, out of fear of both the soldiers and a popular uprising, so we went looking for this place. Meanwhile, I was trying to calm my Alizon, who was spitting like an angry cat at not being able to get back to her shop. She was worried that she hadn't been able to fortify it properly, and that it was now protected only by the weak arms of Florine, a bonnet-maker, an embroiderer and a little messenger.

I was able to get her an audience with La Chapelle-Marteau, a large lump of a man as yellow as a quince, with a twisted nose and a jaundiced look, who was so full of self-importance that he could already imagine himself as a minister under the future king, and who, after having looked rudely at us, and noticed the medal of the Virgin on my doublet and the rosary wound around my wrist, finally softened his stance somewhat and was willing, he said through tightly closed lips, to give us a pass if we would donate two écus for the war chest of the League. Seeing my Alizon ready to take out her claws again, I secretly squeezed her wrist, and said devoutly to La Chapelle-Marteau that I was only too happy to make such a donation, since it would serve the greater glory of the Catholic Church, which had been so buffeted by those Huguenots and the political friends of the king. La Chapelle-Marteau was very pleased with this language, since it was in such words that he revelled every day, but, being of a jaundiced and sickly complexion—both outwardly and inwardly—he observed, as I reached for my purse, that if those two gentlemen (meaning Miroul and Baragran) were in our party, it would cost another écu. At this Alizon's eyes blazed hellfire, but I quickly and unobtrusively stepped on her foot and silenced her. Presently, La Chapelle-Marteau furnished us with our passes, on which my name was listed as "Baragran, Étienne, master bonnet-maker from Boulogne".

I was not sorry to be done with this miser, who vividly recalled Captain Bouillargues, who did quite a brisk business in passports during the Michelade in Nîmes, for the poor Catholics who had money enough to escape those executions.

My little fly was too furious even to buzz about this (she was as angry about the loss of my écus as she would have been had they been her own); Baragran was silent—since, as usual, he had nothing to say—and even I was too concerned about what I was seeing to speak: the windows of each of the houses along the street were full of people with guns, or, on the windowsills in front of them, piles of stones, and I could see that the Swiss Guards, forced to stop by the barricades in front of them, would be stoned and fired upon from the houses on either side of them. Miroul was the only one of us who opened his mouth between one barricade and the next, to observe jokingly that it was no wonder that La Chapelle-Marteau was the counsellor in charge of the Court of Accounts, since he was so good at settling his.

Hardly had we returned to our lodgings when I decided to head back out again to gather more information, but Alizon didn't see things that way: she wanted me to have some nourishment and to join me in that repast, for, despite being as thin as an eel, she was as hearty an eater at table as she was frisky in bed, her night-time activity quickly burning up the fuel of the other kind of nourishment so that she never seemed to get heavy.

Our meal finished, the bonnet-maker, the embroiderer and the little messenger were sent home, and both doors and shutters of the house were locked and bolted closed. Once this was done, Alizon asked Baragran and Miroul to collect any stones they found in front of the house and in the courtyard behind, and to make piles in the windows to throw at any Swiss Guards who tried to force their way into the house. This done, and since her house and workshop—which had been transformed into a fortress, like each of the others in the street—were now unoccupied, her workers having been sent home, she would have liked to be comforted more completely in her anguish, being accustomed to having recourse to a remedy that never failed her. I, however, refused to consent, knowing full well that, once she had me captive in her arms, I wouldn't be able to get away until after dark, and would be too tired to do anything but fall asleep. So I tore myself away from her tender wiles, very sorry to see her sobbing at the perils I would be exposed to, but in a great hurry to extricate myself, since her rages always seemed to follow her tears.

Miroul and I headed first towards the Saints-Innocents cemetery, passing the barricades without firing a shot, thanks to the passes that La Chapelle-Marteau had provided us with, the barricaders assuming that I was an envoy of the League, which seemed more likely to them since I was well armed. Once at the cemetery, I realized that it was surrounded by fortified streets of the sort I had walked through, so that the Swiss Guards wouldn't be able to get out without being caught up in a kind of battle they were not at all used to, exposed as they would be on all sides, and trapped between the barricades on one hand and the windows and roofs of the houses on the other. Moreover, from what I'd heard they were very unhappy with the orders they'd been given not to fire on the people, who, emboldened after their initial terror by the apparent passivity of the guards—who'd made no more move to attack on them than if they'd been stone statues—began to insult them, and had dared to intercept the convoy of supplies sent by the Louvre, eating the bread and drinking the wine right in front of the hungry soldiers. The Swiss were now prey to great discomfort from hunger, thirst and the sweltering heat—and especially from the view of this city in arms, whose thousands of voices were calling for their immediate extermination.

And indeed, this is what I was beginning to fear, for I could see people who were not necessarily sympathetic to the League, but who were determined to defend this notion of the "privilege" of the Parisians and to boot out of their city these troops that the king had dared put there. It now seemed as though, faced with this affront, what had been merely a revolt of Leaguers had now become a universal uprising. I could see that on this day, Thursday, 12th May, an entire people had rushed to bear arms—the artisan dropping his tools, the merchant his wares, the schoolboy his books, the hauler his sacks, the lawyer his liripipe and the grave counsellors their very robes—to dress in doublets and take up pikes, so enormous was their indignation at the insufferable offence that had been made to their city.

From the Saints-Innocents, I headed to the place de Grève, where I heard that other Swiss and French Guards had been stationed and then beset on all sides by barricades, and were perhaps in a worse predicament than their colleagues whom I've just described. Here the inhabitants and workers of the Saint-Antoine quarter that surrounded them had seized a convoy bringing gunpowder to the troops, and had distributed its contents to those on the barricades who had firearms. Now, it seemed the people would be better armed than the soldiers themselves if it came to a battle.

But of all of the spectacles I encountered, the most upsetting for me, as a faithful servant of my king—though, of course, it would be thrilling for a member of the League—was the scene that awaited me on the Île de la Cité, when I crossed the Pont Notre-Dame: here the Swiss Guards, according to what I heard, had been pressed so hard by the mass of the people that they'd taken refuge at the back of the Marché-Neuf, and the companies that had advanced across the Pont Saint-Michel had fallen back under a hail of stones thrown by the clerics and students of l'Université under the leadership of the Comte de Brissac. Colonel Crillon, the same man who'd pushed his hat farther down on his head rather than bow to Guise, now having had to retreat, was nearly consumed by his rage at the order not to fire.

The strangest part was that those on the barricades and those in Swiss uniforms could see each other clearly. And since they hadn't begun firing, the League leaders and the royal officers began trading comic insults very much in the Parisian manner. It's a pity and ironic to consider that those men preparing to kill each other over the issue of the reformed religion all belonged to the same papist faith. Indeed, it has been confirmed that, on that 12th May, everywhere in France Catholics were split between the royalist and Guisard causes—in Paris, at the court, in the great body of the Estates-General, in the provinces, in the entire nation; every city, every neighbourhood, every street, every family and even the brains of individual men were divided.

Thus it was that I recognized, among the royalists, François d'O, and, among the Leaguers, his brother the Marquis d'O; or again, among the officers was Colonel Cossein, and within the barricades one of his best friends, a counsellor of parliament, who, raising his voice and calling him by his name, asked him jocularly if he was happy where he was. Cossein, who was never slow to respond to a joke, answered:

"It's not so comfortable here, but it's the fault of the provost of the merchants!"

"And how so?"

"He promised the king 30,000 labourers and inhabitants of Paris. And I see that he didn't keep his promise, for I see thirty of the king's men here and 1,000 for Monsieur de Guise."

Whether candour or cleverness inspired this banter, it was very flattering to the men on the barricades, and, having made them laugh, made them feel a bit better about the soldiers, who still hadn't killed anyone, however badly wounded some of them had been by the stones.

"Why don't you withdraw?" shouted one the heads of the Leaguers, who, perhaps a bit less zealous than the others, found it enormously absurd, as I did, that Catholics of various stripes should be exterminating each other over the question of whether the Huguenots should be exterminated—who, by the greatest irony of all, were not even included in this fight at all, since the few who were still in Paris had disappeared when these troubles had begun.

"I'd like to, but I can't!" cried a captain, a man named Marivaux.

"Marivaux," shouted a Leaguer friend of his who had recognized him, "where are you supposed to go?"

"To the Louvre! With my Swiss Guards!"

"But that's what we want too! We just don't want you in Paris!"

This reply was so well received within and without the barricades, and ultimately welcomed by both sides, that in the end each side sent negotiators, who, according to what I heard, decided after a lengthy discussion that the Swiss Guards should withdraw along the rue Neuve and the Pont Notre-Dame. Once they'd crossed the river they were to follow the quai de Seine to the Louvre.

And, when reason had finally prevailed, the Swiss Guards began their retreat, with Monsieur de Marivaux leading them, accompanied by a League negotiator, who had the barricades opened so that they could pass. And, curious to see how this strange retreat would be managed in this insurgent city, I followed them, along with many of the barricaders, with whom I mingled and who, deliriously happy with their victory over the king's troops, forgot that they owed this peace to the king himself, who had given the order that under no circumstances should his men fire on the people.

However, scarcely had the first column entered the rue Neuve when the people in that street—who were leaning out of their windows, armed with pistols and arquebuses or piles of stones—began shouting at them to extinguish their fuses, fearing that an inadvertent shot might wound someone on the barricades or at a window. This cry was taken up by all the onlookers, who thoroughly understood its urgency, and suddenly the air was filled with a hubbub of vociferation that left the poor Swiss all the more stupefied since they took them for cries of hatred, and simply couldn't distinguish the words "Extinguish your fuses!" Tragically, since the soldiers couldn't comply with these shouted demands without an order from their officers, and since all the officers were at the head of the column, and couldn't make out this request among the general pandemonium, nothing was done. To add to this concatenation of confusion, on that 12th May Paris was afflicted with a nearly insufferable heatwave; none of the Swiss Guards had had anything to eat or drink since daybreak; and, though they were fearsome soldiers in the open field against declared enemies, they were unhappy to be opposing these civilians whom the king had brought them here "to control". And to top it all they were under strict orders not to fire, but no one had told them to extinguish their fuses.

As one might have predicted, from the midst of this hungry, thirsty, overheated troop a shot was unfortunately fired that killed a bourgeois in a window. Shouts of vengeance followed immediately, and all the arquebuses in the other windows spat out their deadly charges at the poor Swiss, while, worse still, a hail of rocks, stones and window glass descended on them, cutting them down on all sides. Those who attempted to find refuge under the corbels of the houses were taken out by the marksmen on the other side of the street. The more reasonable among them simply fell to their knees and, pulling out and brandishing their rosaries, cried lamentably (since they thought the Parisians believed them to be Swiss Huguenots): "Good Swiss! Good Catholics!"

These naive appeals, cries of pain and brandished rosaries, along with the moans of the dying, ultimately produced a general feeling of compassion among their assailants, and as the Swiss fell back towards the Marché-Neuf, the people allowed them to retreat without further harm and regroup in a butcher's shop. From what I've heard, while this was going on along the river, the two other garrisons of the Swiss at the Saints-Innocents cemetery and at the place de Grève were hardly better off, surrounded by barricades and lacking food or ammunition.

There now seemed to be a wave of hesitation among the insurgents and the Leaguers, and, since they had no natural hatred of the Swiss, who had never fired a shot at them, other than the accidental one, and now seemed to be the innocent instruments of the king—neither royalists, "politicals" nor Huguenots—no one really knew what to do with them, having no further taste for attacking them and fearing in case they were forced to fire their weapons in self-defence.

It was onto this ambiguous and embarrassing situation that the Duc de Guise descended from the heavens like a *deus ex machina*.

He was magnificently clad in a doublet as white as his soul and as pure as his intentions; on his head was a great white-plumed hat, and in his hands was no other weapon than a walking stick with a silver handle. He was preceded by two pretty blond pages looking like cherubs, one carrying his sword, the other his sceptre (so that it would be eminently clear *urbi et orbi* that there was also some of St George in this archangel of peace). Addressing the people in the streets, he praised their valour for having turned aside the threat to their city and protected their immemorial privileges. He explained hypocritically that he'd been closeted in his lodgings all day, unaware of what was going on outside until he'd received a request from the king urging him to go out, calm the tumult and lead the troops back to the Louvre safe and sound. He asked their permission to do so in the name of divine mercy and prayed to God and to the Holy Church to keep him safe for evermore.

At this, from every street and every quarter came a burst of acclamation, delirium and hallelujahs, with people kneeling in front of him, kissing his boots and rubbing their rosaries on his white tunic, which was a good deal less white by the day's end—so much did the naivety of these Parisians, who are so much more gullible than in any other city in the kingdom, cause them to be besotted with Guise. They were so charmed by his voice that he began inventing all kinds of lies, including that he'd had nothing to do with this riot, whereas his lieutenants were known to have been plotting it since the 9th. The noise of acclamation was deafening, as the people shouted "Long live Guise!" and "No more delays! Let's lead Guise to Reims right now!"—which of course meant that they intended to crown him king of France immediately, since the vox populi desired it. At this, Guise hypocritically pushed his large hat down over his eyes (so they wouldn't see him laughing?), and, extending his two hands in front of him, said modestly:

"My friends, that's enough! Messieurs, it's too much! Don't shout 'Long live Guise'—shout 'Long live the king'!"

At this, of course, the shouts of "Long live Guise" increased dramatically, and could not be drowned out even by the church bells, all of which began ringing joyfully to notify the Most High in heaven of the stunning victory of the Holy League over the king.

"My friends," repeated Guise, who, as he advanced through the streets in his immaculate doublet, simply couldn't get enough this incredible pleasure of not being obeyed, "don't shout 'Long live Guise'—shout 'Long live the king'!"

"Ah, the poor king!" I thought. "What a dark day! An immense loss! And of peace first of all! How can they not see it? Whoever controls the capital controls more than half of the kingdom! If Guise is king of Paris, he will bring the Spanish within our borders, reduce the legitimate king to nothing and impose on him a war of extermination against the Huguenots, which will be followed by the Inquisition!"

I was thus plunged in my dark thoughts amid the general joy of the crowds around me, when I felt a tug at my sleeve, and Miroul whispered in *langue d'oc*:

"Monsieur, I beg you, put on a happy face. There's a lady in Guise's retinue who's been looking at you all this time from behind her mask, and who looks as though she might be Marianne."

Having said this, Miroul began waving his arms wildly and shouted more loudly than any of our neighbours "Long live Guise!" This turned out to be a grave mistake, for amid all the shoving in the crowd, his eyepatch slipped from his blue eye—he put it back as quickly as he could, but the damage was done. The watchful lady had had time, I believe, to recognize his varicoloured eyes, and quickly beckoned over a pretentious-looking fellow, whom I immediately recognized as the major-domo of Madame de Montpensier.

"Let's get out of here, Miroul," I hissed. "They're going to cut us to pieces!"

Unfortunately, to make our escape we had to head in the opposite direction from our lodgings and refuge, retreating back across the Pont Notre-Dame and ending up in the Île de la Cité, where I knew of no friendly haven. This we did at a walk, since the crowds were so thick we thought we might be able to escape by simply melting into the mass. But when we got to a more open space, we saw ten *spadaccini* sprinting after us, and we had to make a dash for it.

"Miroul," I cried, "these rascals are gaining on us. This next street is deserted, the mob busy shouting 'Long live Guise!', so let's unsheathe our swords and wait for them!"

"Monsieur, you can't be serious!" whispered Miroul. "There are ten of them—ten to two is too many!"

"All right then, let's play Horace in the fable. At the next corner, we'll take out our pistols and shoot the first two in the bunch. Then run for it again, and do the same again later. Six to two is much better odds."

"Monsieur," replied Miroul, "I don't know who this Horace fellow was, but he must have been pretty smart!"

So we did what I'd suggested, which had the effect not only of diminishing their number (may the Lord pardon us for killing our assailants to save our skins) but also of slowing them down, since, after seeing what had happened to the first four, none of them wanted to be the leader of the pack, and consequently we left them for dust. However, when we left the tiny twisting streets of the Île de la Cité and came out onto the Pont Notre-Dame, which was unfortunately as straight as a carpenter's ruler, our pursuers fanned out across the width of the bridge (which was lined with houses on each side) and had at us like winged devils. Miroul had just time to drop one in his tracks with a throw of his knife. The rest were on us in a flash; there was nothing we could do but draw our swords, and, as soon as we crossed blades, I immediately understood the immense danger we were in. This wouldn't be a spot of light fencing—these men were professional swordsmen.

"Use Jarnac's thrust, Monsieur!" cried Miroul in *langue d'oc*. After having learnt this secret from Giacomi years previously, I'd promised him I'd never use it except in the last extremity, but I prepared to use it now on the most fearsome-looking of the three assailants who still faced me after I'd slashed the fourth on the arm. Just then, out of nowhere surged a young masked man, who called in a sweet and sing-song voice:

"Five against two, that's too many! I won't tolerate it!"

So saying, he unsheathed his weapon and ran to my side. This freed me from one of my adversaries and, with the wounded man quitting the fight, I began to regain some hope, despite the expertise of the *spadaccino* who now faced me. I tested his skills so slyly with a quick thrust that he leapt backwards two steps as if he'd been stung. This retreat gave me time to glance at the young gentleman at my side; I noticed in the blink of an eye his beardless cheek, his bright eyes behind the mask (which stopped at his nose) and the delicacy of his ringed hand.

"Monsieur, I thank you!" I said, but he said not a word in response, so, seeing my *spadaccino* retreating again, I advanced towards him and said, "Well now, you cad, you don't seem to have much desire to continue!"

"Monsieur," he said, saluting me from afar with his sword, "excuse me, but it seems to me that the way you first engaged me, you have some secret trick."

"Rascal," I replied, "would it be a secret if I bragged about it? Come on then! You can see for yourself!"

"Monsieur," he said, suddenly bowing and calmly resheathing his sword, "my job is to kill and not to be killed. I won't engage you further, I swear by the Blessed Virgin."

Hearing this, the only *spadaccino* still in the lists—Miroul having wounded one of his two assailants and the beardless gentleman having dropped his opponent on the pavement—didn't wait around to be dispatched to another world by our three swords, and showed us his heels.

"Messieurs," said the gentleman with the sing-song voice, "I have a refuge a stone's throw from here. Let's head over there. It's not a very sure thing to be for the king given the state things are in here."

So, off we went in a trice. I kept my eye on him as he ran beside me and noticed that he was far from being as adroit at running as he was at swordplay, and, for his part, he kept smiling at me with a genteel but somewhat humorous look from under his wide hat.

"Miroul," I asked as we ran along, "where are we?"

"Quai des Bernardins, Monsieur."

"Monsieur," I said to the stranger, "are you for the king?"

"No, Monsieur," he said with a shrill and fluty voice, "for Elizabeth Regina. Here's the place, Monsieur. It's a bakery that by some miracle is still open. I think you know why, and at the word 'bakery' you must realize where you are."

And even though I did indeed know where I was, the gentleman gave himself the pleasure of explaining things as soon as he'd shown his token, and I mine, and we had been ushered through a hidden door into a small room that was boarded up and lit by candles, even though it was still light outside.

"Sir," I said, "how can I ever repay you for the help you brought us! I owe you my—and our—lives!"

"Repay me?" replied the gentleman with a little laugh and that sing-song voice that seemed to me so charming. "Well, certainly, you can!"

"And how?"

"With a kiss."

"With a kiss?" I said, astonished.

"On the mouth."

This of course made me look at his mouth, which seemed sud-denly familiar, as did his voice, even though it was disguised. And so I proceeded carefully, and then, as soon as I recognized my saviour, with great excitement.

"So, then!" said the gentleman scornfully. "Do you like men or not?"

"Lady Markby," I laughed, "is it sodomy to love your pretty lips?"

"Ha!" she cried, removing her mask. "You must truly be a Frenchman to have recognized me that way! But, Monsieur, even though you're certainly gallant, your eyes look tired and sad to me. Wait here a moment. I'm going to ask Lord Stafford to have a chamber prepared for you."

As soon as she'd left the room, I threw myself on an armchair and gave full vent to my despair, my throat tied in a knot. Seeing me thus, Miroul came and sat down on my right on a stool.

"Monsieur," he comforted, "all is not lost! The king still has his Swiss Guards and he's still in his Louvre."

"Ah, Miroul! A city is like a woman. You can't keep her if she doesn't want to be kept! From now on, Paris belongs to Guise. She gave herself wholeheartedly to him. Now he's her prince."

"But, Monsieur, there's still the kingdom!"

"What good is a decapitated kingdom? Is Henri still the king of France when Guise is the king of Paris?"

14

THAT NIGHT I COULDN'T sleep for agonizing thoughts about my poor master, who was going to find himself besieged in his Louvre (as soon as Guise slyly threw the reins to the people), and only fell asleep at dawn as daylight was filtering through the shutters of my room. Doubtless I could have slept till evening if Lady Markby hadn't entered my room, followed by a barber and a chambermaid carrying a brilliant new suit of clothes.

"Zounds!" she exclaimed, using Elizabeth's favourite swear word. "What kind of lark is this that lies in its nest sleeping instead of greeting the new day with its radiant song? My Pierre, it's time for you to hop out of your nest and fly to your meeting with Lord Stafford, who will see you in an hour and share some news with you."

"Good or bad?" I cried, my heart pounding in my chest.

"Bad and good. In a word, Henri is safely out of Paris."

"Thank God!"

"Wait a moment before you thank Him. If the Invincible Armada is launched, Elizabeth and Henri will drown together. But enough about that. Every day brings its particular distress. My Pierre, you cannot see Lord Stafford dressed like that. He's very particular about etiquette and won't even look in the mirror if he isn't properly dressed in his collar and doublet. So I asked for a barber to shave off your merchant's beard and curl up your poor untended hair. What's more, I've borrowed a suit of clothes from one of our young gentlemen that will be more appropriate to your rank and this serious situation. Beautify yourself, my pretty fellow! 'Truly', as your Alizon would say, to whom I sent a messenger this morning to let her know that you're safe. Am I not a good angel?"

"Beautiful and beneficent!"

"Ah, I recognize your golden tongue there! 'Truly', as your silly impertinent girlfriend would say, who shot me dead with her look each time she saw me, yesterday I had little interest in kissing those lips of yours hidden away in that nest of a beard. So, my Pierre, I'll be back for you in an hour."

With a somewhat bloodthirsty laugh she was away, her hoop skirts sweeping out of my room, more lively and rapid than a panther in peril. But danger seemed to provide her with a kind of nourishment without which she would have starved and withered away, so that it was little wonder that her house and husband in Shropshire saw so little of her. She simply wasn't made for domestic bliss.

Lord Edward, Baron Stafford—to whom I was introduced in my new (though borrowed) plumage, and whom I'd only seen once before in my life, at the door to the king's apartments—responded with but a brief nod to my bow to him. He had a natural hauteur that matched his physical height and his majestic frame—straight as a board—with square shoulders and not a trace of stomach (though he was past forty years of age); his long face encompassed a closely trimmed beard, a short moustache, cold grey eyes and a long nose. He was superbly clad, though in the English manner, the collar of his doublet extending far up his neck, and above it a thin ruff that framed his jaw. He wore no jewels other than the Order of the Garter, on which a crimson cross was surrounded by a sun, each of whose golden flames ended in a pearl.

His doublet was of the English style, worn quite tight around the body (quite the opposite of ours at that time), and very tightly buttoned as well, which nicely set off his trim waist and athletic frame. In his carriage he was stiff and disdainful, as rugged as the Dover cliffs, but not without a twinkle in his eye that shone from time to time either in amusement or in benevolence—at least towards me, whose great love of his country and his sovereign he appreciated, but it didn't take long to discover that he could be biting and disdainful with another, whom I will shortly name. In short, he had the appearance and the demeanour of a great lord who never forgot that he was in Paris, so hateful to his religion and his queen, who was the visible incarnation of a great kingdom of Christendom, a country justifiably proud of itself, all the more brave and intrepid now that it was threatened from without.

"Monsieur chevalier," he said, after I'd presented him with both my respects and my thanks for his benevolent help, "I'm pressed for time and so I must be brief in informing you of news regarding your master. The Parisians, drunk with their victory over him, which they owe only to the excessive benignity of his heart, last night put up barricades around the Louvre in an effort to capture the palace and seize the person of the king. Henri has no expectation that Guise will calm the people, since he knows that secretly he's egging them on, and, not wishing to engage in a bloody combat (a wise decision), he decided to quit the palace with his 4,000 Swiss and French Guards and to withdraw to Chartres. He managed to do this quite dexterously yesterday afternoon, without saying anything to the two queens, since he knew he couldn't trust either of them. Sneaking out of the Louvre through the secret door, he pretended to be taking a walk in the Tuileries, managed to reach his stables, mounted a horse and left through the Porte Neuve, the only gate that was still in the hands of his troops. Once outside the walls, they took off and left this ungrateful city behind them—a city that Henri has deeply loved, as you know. Is it not strange," Lord Stafford continued, "that he has been a king in two countries and has had to flee his capital in both? The first time from Warsaw and the second from Paris."

"But," I asked with a terrible knot in my throat, "doesn't his departure signal that he's lost his country?"

"Not at all!" replied Lord Stafford. "I'll say it again: your master was very wise. No power in the world could win a street fight in such a large city against an armed populace in revolt, supported by a powerful segment of the nobility—unless possibly they were willing to resort to cannon fire and massacre."

"So having lost his capital, what advantage will the king have in Chartres, apart from his Swiss Guards?"

"His legitimacy," answered Lord Stafford gravely, "which is an immense power. And one that the Duc de Guise cannot lay claim to at this time, something he understands only too well, since he has dispatched the Comte de Brissac to speak with me—and to what end I can easily imagine. Monsieur chevalier, the comte is waiting in my antechamber and I would like to ask you to be a witness to this conversation, so that you can repeat it verbatim to your master. If you will oblige me by going into this little room here, I'll leave the door partly open so that you may hear our words without being seen by the comte. Would you agree to cooperate?"

"Monseigneur," I replied, "wholeheartedly, especially given your part in acting frankly and nobly with my poor master in the dangerous predicament he finds himself in—and in which you yourself are caught, since your embassy is situated in the midst of a people who are rioting and who are hostile to your queen."

"But she is protecting me even here since I am her representative," said Lord Stafford with an expression so proud and fearless that I foresaw that Brissac was going to have more trouble than even the poor Swiss Guards, who, even under a hail of stones, were forbidden from firing on the people. "Forgive me," Lord Stafford continued, "for enclosing you here in this dark, windowless cabinet, and for leaving the door open only a crack, but I must take my precautions, for Brissac is very fox-like and I don't want him to get wind of you. Moreover, the darkness will allow you to put your eye to the crack and watch us without being seen."

Scarcely, however, had I entered the little room when a strong, finely manicured hand seized my right wrist in the darkness and a voice I recognized immediately whispered in my ear:

"It's me, Pierre."

"What?" I hissed. "Are you spying on Lord Stafford in his own house, Lady Markby?"

"Not at all! He has the entire confidence of the queen and the Moor. I'm just here to hide you if Brissac happens to open this door for whatever reason."

"Hide me? Is there a hidden door or cupboard in here?"

"No, but I'm tall and my hoop skirts are remarkably ample."

"What? Are you suggesting I'd hide behind a woman's skirts?"

"Not behind," she corrected. "That wouldn't be safe enough if the comte decided to walk around me."

"Then I don't see where the hiding place would be."

"Think on it," she murmured in my ear, nibbling on it. "You are a Frenchman. I leave it to your imagination."

This said, she placed her hand on my mouth—and it was a good thing she did for, despite the gravity of the situation, I nearly burst out laughing, having finally understood this rascally kitten.

Anyone who'd seen the Comte de Brissac in profile, as he entered Lord Stafford's house, would have thought him a very handsome fellow, since his squint-eyed and lopsided expression would have been hidden. His true face, if I may phrase it thus, could only be appreciated head-on. Which reminded me that his master, Guise, also had two very different profiles, since the scar that he had near his left eye made it water from time to time. The result was that, when he laughed, one could see him laughing on his right side and crying on his left, having, like Janus, two faces—but both of them false.

It became quickly evident, listening to him from within the cabinet, that in hypocrisy and dishonesty, Brissac was every bit Guise's equal, since he began by heaping protestations and promises on Lord Stafford of his great friendship, which were meant to be golden but which his ridiculous exaggeration turned to lead. Meanwhile, at the end of this string of compliments you could see the fox's ears emerging, when he proposed to Lord Stafford, on behalf of the Magnificent, to place a guard in his house to "protect" its occupants from attacks and pillaging by the angry mob outside—who were, he claimed, "running around like mad bulls" that nothing in the world could restrain but the duc's hand.

"Comte," replied Lord Stafford, who understood perfectly well that they were offering him this protection solely in order to establish a diplomatic link between Guise and him (which, of course, would imply that he had officially recognized the duc's authority in Paris), "if I were just any individual living here, I would gratefully accept the safeguard that the Duc de Guise has the generosity to offer me, and would go immediately to see him and thank him in person. But living in Paris in my capacity as minister and ambassador of Queen Elizabeth to the king of France, I could not, and would not want to, accept any guard or offer of safety and protection from any authority but the king's."

This was stated courteously and in French, but had a resolute and decisive ring to it, though Brissac had spoken to him in English, a language he spoke quite passably. However, in his next response to Lord Stafford, which he delivered with some heat, the comte fell back on his native tongue.

"Monseigneur," he said, "we are all resolutely faithful subjects of the king." ("Ah, by God," I thought, "if only the air, which must suffer everything, would turn red each time a man tells a lie, this comte would have turned crimson!") "The Duc de Guise," Brissac continued with more unctuousness than a monk, "did not come to Paris to make trouble and difficulties for the king, but to extend a protective wing over the good people of this city, whom he loves, but whose well-being was threatened by a plot that had filled the Hôtel de Ville with gibbets and executioners—an indubitable fact that I beg you, Monseigneur, to report to Her Majesty the queen of England."

"I've heard rumours of these gibbets," replied Lord Stafford stiffly. "An odious fact, were it true—but it requires proof, and proof that would have been easy to furnish by producing these very gibbets, which the League, once the Hôtel de Ville was in its hands, didn't judge it expedient to do. Moreover," he added, not without some derision in his tone, "those who form such great plans are not required to confide their secret designs to anyone, only to reveal them at the desired moment, painted with the colours that they are pleased to give them."

This statement, which, however diplomatically it was expressed, was dosed with equal amounts of oil and vinegar, made Brissac wince and twist his mouth even more.

"And yet, what I reported to you," he said much less resolutely, "was but the pure truth."

"The truth is rarely pure," said Lord Stafford gravely. "And true or false, whatever the pretext invoked for justifying the insurrection in Paris against the sovereign, foreign princes will receive the news very badly, since it creates a dangerous and indeed disastrous example of the valet raising himself over the master and chasing him out of his house."

"Nevertheless," replied Brissac, quite mortified by what he'd just heard, "I would be very grateful if you would report to Her Majesty the queen of England the facts that I've just reported."

"I shall do so, my dear Brissac," replied Lord Stafford, smoothing his words with a bit of oil, "out of friendship for you, and out of consideration for your master, but, at the same time, I would like the Duc de Guise to know that, as ambassador to the king of France, I cannot be, nor do I wish to be, his interpreter or his go-between with my sovereign. However, as I just said, I will inform the queen of what you've said, without judging your words in any wise, leaving this work to Her Gracious Majesty, who will know what she ought to think, being much more intelligent than I."

"Then I am completely satisfied," replied Brissac, who manifestly was not satisfied in the least, having a bone so firmly stuck in his throat that he could neither chew it nor throw it up. "But, My Lord," he continued, not without a threatening tone in his voice, "touching this safeguard that the Duc de Guise proposes to give you here, I would very strongly advise you to accept it, since you have everything to fear under the present tumultuous circumstances, the Parisians being excessively embittered against your nation, given the cruelty that the queen exercised against Mary Stuart."

"Cruelty, Monsieur!" cried Lord Stafford, interrupting him vociferously. "I will not accept the word 'cruelty'. The person you just mentioned was the object of a long judicial procedure conducted according to all the forms and rules of the law. And as for the Parisians, I don't see what reason they'd have to hate me so much, since I've never offended any of them."

"Well," said Brissac, whose bitterness was beginning to seep through his honey, "rumours are flying in Paris, among its inhabitants and labourers, that you have arms hidden in this house."

At this Lord Stafford immediately burst out laughing.

"Comte," he said with a mocking sneer, "are you repeating this hypothesis in private, as the personal friend that you are, and as your uncle, Arthur de Cossé, was?"

"Certainly," replied the comte, who looked quite embarrassed by the turn the conversation was taking, steered by the ambassador.

"In that case, I would answer that if I had come here as a private person, it's possible I would have taken the precaution that you suggest. But being clothed in the dignity and responsibilities of my office and the inviolable title that is mine, I have to tell you that the rights of men and public faith are my only and my sufficient defenders."

"Again speaking to you as a friend," snarled Brissac in an openly hostile way, "my duty requires me to inform you that you may be invaded from one moment to the next by a people in revolt, who will search every corner of your house—and so I advise you, Lord Stafford, to close and lock your doors."

"No, no!" cried Lord Stafford proudly. "The lodgings of an ambassador must be open to all—I shall not close my door until I see such a mob arrive. And if they want to break in by force I shall defend this house to my last drop of blood and my last breath! My death will mark this kingdom with infamy, and it will be reported to the end of time and throughout the world that the rights of men were odiously violated in the person of an English ambassador!"

"May it please God to see that that never happens!" said Brissac, who added to the end of this pious ejaculation I don't know how many protestations and compliments, all uttered with evident hypocrisy, while his squinting eye seemed increasingly drawn to the door of the cabinet in which we were hiding. Lady Markby clearly divined from this behaviour that he fully intended to head towards the wrong door as he was leaving and open this one. And seeing him already moving this way, she quickly whispered to me to hide in the place we'd agreed. Which I did, pulling my legs as close to me as I could just in time, since the hoop skirt fell over me at the very moment the door was flung open with a great crash, and I heard Lady Markby say in the most derisive tones:

"Well, Lord Brissac! This is very strange indeed! Will you search this house? Or me, for that matter? Are you French lords so indiscreet?"

"Madame," said Brissac, whose steps I could hear circling her on the parquet, "I make you my humblest and most regretful apologies! I seem to have used the wrong door!"

"I hope that's so," said Lord Stafford in dry and icy tones. "Otherwise, how could I ever have forgiven you this invasion of my private apartments?"

At this, Brissac continued to babble his excuses in profusion, never being short of words or of impudence.

"We'll speak no more of this, Brissac," said Lord Stafford, who didn't wish to drive the stake in too far. "I would prefer we parted as friends, since tomorrow I must leave for Chartres."

"For Chartres!" said Brissac, clearly taken aback by this news. "You're leaving Paris for Chartres?"

"Of course, since I am not assigned as ambassador in Paris," he replied calmly, "but ambassador to the king of France, and therefore must follow him to Chartres, where he is setting up his court."

At these words, which sounded the death knell for Guise's hopes of keeping the English ambassador in Paris and, in this wise, gaining his official recognition, Brissac took his leave, and Lord Stafford showed him out, as I divined from hearing their voices and steps grow fainter; but even though Lady Markby was pushing me with both hands under her petticoat, I didn't want to emerge—until I heard Lord Stafford return to the room and say:

"Chevalier, the weasel has left and my door has closed behind him. Come out of your amiable hiding place so you don't suffocate!"

Which I did, red from the heat and my hair ruffled, and when Lord Stafford saw me he fell into an armchair and began to laugh hysterically, a spectacle that quite amazed me, given how stiff and cold he'd been with Brissac.

"Ah, Madame," he said in French to Lady Markby, "if I ever see our gracious sovereign again, I'll amuse her no end by telling her to what extremities you've pushed your zeal of serving her."

"*Honi soit qui mal y pense!*"* cried Lady Markby, quoting the motto of the Order of the Garter and feigning outrage—though, only a moment later, she herself burst out laughing and added, "In any case, My Lord, I'll tell Lord Markby that it was your idea!"

"Yours, Madame, yours!" cried Lord Stafford. "Let it never be said in this house in front of a French gentleman that the head of an English ambassador could ever consider such an idea, one so beneath the dignity of his charge."

"What?" replied my Lady Markby, throwing him a look so subtle and conniving that it gave me much food for thought. "You expect me to take responsibility for this? Wasn't it your suggestion? Am I going to sacrifice my reputation once again to maintain your good name?"

At this, a shadow of embarrassment came over Lord Stafford's face and Lady Markby's regained its composure as she said:

"My Lord, you said a moment ago 'if I ever see our gracious sovereign again'. Are you apprehensive about what's going to happen to us in Paris?"

"In Paris? Not at all," he replied. "The Magnificent wants to appear, above all, magnanimous, as he proved when he liberated all those poor Swiss Guards. We'll be able to leave here unharmed, and will pass outside the walls of the city without incident and without being searched. My fears are more long-term and concern this single question: does the benediction of the Pope have any power with the Master and Sovereign of Heaven?"

"The Pope's benediction!" I cried. "My Lord Stafford, what do you mean?"

"Well, didn't Sixtus V solemnly bless the Armada, calling it 'my daughter'? If this benediction is effective, then the Armada will really be as 'invincible' as its name suggests. With England invaded, our

---

* "May he be shamed who thinks badly of it!"

beloved queen will disappear, your king as well, chevalier, and as for us, ambassador or not, the gibbet will be waiting for us."

"Well, I for one won't be afraid to climb onto it," cried Lady Markby, choosing to laugh rather than cry. "Anyone who's got a reputation as infernal as mine ought to perish on a pyre!"

Lord Stafford took me with him in his travelling coach, with all the curtains lowered, and, as he had predicted, there was no trouble at the Porte Saint-Honoré, neither from the Leaguers nor the bourgeois militias there, since the Comte de Brissac, to whom the ambassador had communicated the hour of our departure, was waiting to ensure our safe passage so that we would not be held up by any bloodthirsty zealots. Meanwhile, although I was very eager to see my beloved master and to offer him my immediate services in whatever way I could be of help, when I saw the coach take the road through Montfort-l'Amaury, moved by the compulsion of the moment, I asked to be let out there, feeling a very strong desire to embrace Angelina and my beautiful children, whom I hadn't seen in so long. And only later did I realize how lucky a decision this was, when I learnt that a large party of Leaguers, acting on their own and without orders, had stopped the coach at Rambouillet, and, in the teeth of the ambassador's most vehement protest, searched it—luckily not finding me. Otherwise, I would never have had the opportunity of writing these lines—or for that matter any of the ones that precede them, my great love of my family saving my life on this occasion. Meanwhile, having taken leave of my host, I begged him to tell my king when they arrived in Chartres that I would rush to his side the moment he sent for me, a call that didn't come until August, as I shall recount.

Since my history here concerns a moment of such great import for the future of the kingdom, I will not dwell on the felicities I found in my sweet, bucolic and conjugal retreats, after the all the intensity of

Paris, and, alas, in all the sinning as well, my conscience stinging me as usual—not that this would prevent such sins in the future, or heal them, such guilt in the aftermath always being in vain. Indeed, I wonder whether there isn't some ambiguous hypocrisy in remorse thanks to which we can satisfy our consciences while gratifying our flesh. And many of the king's subjects also had their reasons for remorse, when it came to public affairs, for having chased the king out of Paris, even if they were partisans of the League. This was a subject that I wanted to discuss with various of my friends in Montfort-l'Amaury—in particular Ameline, the priest of the town, who was neither a committed Guisard nor a complete royalist (like many other French people in these uncertain times). Ameline wondered, indeed, whether he ought to congratulate the League on their victory or deplore the fact that the king had been reduced to such an extremity and the necessity of fleeing his capital.

Ameline, who got his news through the abbot of Barthes, confessor of the minister Villequier, informed me that not one, but several delegations of Leaguers had gone to find the king in Chartres to ask him to return to the Louvre, but that the king, while receiving them with his usual benevolence, and assuring them of his pardon, had not consented to their request. Ameline also told me that Henri had employed the venerable Dr Marc Miron as his go-between with the princes of Lorraine in order to try to make peace with them, and that an agreement had been reached in which the king had acceded to all the demands of the Duc de Guise, who forced him to agree that Navarre would be blocked, as a heretic, from any claim to the throne, that Épernon would be disgraced and that Guise himself would be named lieutenant general of the armies. In addition, the Estates-General would be convened in the autumn to address the abuses of the kingdom—a project that should have begun, in my opinion, with the suppression of Guise himself!

Quéribus, followed by his elegant escort, came to see me towards the end of August, and, in his usual humorous fashion, recounted the affairs of the "little court in Chartres", reporting that there weren't many people there—the setting sun attracting less attention than the new day that one could see dawning in Paris.

The strangest thing in these last days of August was that the weather was not seasonal but remarkably unsettled at the Rugged Oak, with lots of rain and wind, and constant storms coming down, according to Gertrude (who had just returned from her native Normandy), from the Channel, where an incredibly violent tempest had been raging for a month without pause. The damp cold so penetrated our bones that I kept a huge fire going in my library, which at least brightened up that part of the house.

"My brother," I said as we stood warming ourselves in front of that fire, "can it be possible that the king has ceded all of his power to Guise?"

"The truth is that my poor Henri," replied Quéribus (who never missed a chance to flaunt his familiarity with the king of France—a familiarity that was in truth merely superficial, since the king maintained some distance from his favourites despite his courteous manners), "when he acceded to Guise's demands, had one eye on Paris and the other on the Invincible Armada that was making its way towards the English coast, and whose victory he considered ineluctable, all the while praying on his knees that it might not be so. So having his eyes fixed on two different scenes, he was squinting like Brissac... (What do you think of that comparison, my brother? Isn't it gallant?) In which state he considered Guise's demands baseless and bumbling, and so he answered yes to the whole proposal in principle, but reserved the right to reject any parts of it that he objected to and has been systematically undoing everything he agreed to. Moreover, in Chartres, there's a remarkable dearth of funds, not even enough money to pay the Swiss Guards, who, as good Swiss, have nevertheless remained faithful to him. Which is part of the reason the king agreed to meet with the Estates-General, hoping to wrest some money from them under the pretext of pursuing the war against the Huguenots—which monies, once obtained, he'll use for his own ends, as he's always done."

"But what about the disgrace of the Duc d'Épernon?"

"Merely for the sake of appearances, as was your exile. Épernon has traded control of Normandy for the control of Angoumois, where he can establish a secret liaison with Navarre, who controls the armies in that region."

"So you think that the king is just 'trimming his sails', as he likes to say?"

"I'm quite sure of it. Listen to the rest, which will entirely confirm this: after the agreement between the king and Guise, which was called the Edict of Union (so named, of course, since it's preparing the *dis*union of the country and a civil war), Guise freed the queen and the queen mother, whom he'd been holding under house arrest since the king's flight to Chartres."

"What? He had the temerity to hold them prisoner?"

"With all sorts of kissing of their hands, flattery and genuflections—you know how that sort of hypocrisy works! But still, they weren't allowed to leave Paris until the Edict of Union was signed. And so they're both coming to Chartres, the queen mother more of a Guisard than ever, since she believes that Guise's ship is in full sail and that the Armada will be victorious. So she has attached herself to the king like a horsefly to the arse of a mare!"

"Did he kick her off?"

"I'll tell you. The scene took place in the king's apartments in the bishop's palace in Chartres, and I was among the very few who attended. If some people in the court want you to believe that they were there, don't trust them, for the only people present were Du Halde, Chicot, François d'O, Alphonse the Corsican, Crillon, Laugnac and me."

"I shall remember, my brother," I said gravely.

"Anyway, the queen mother arrived on Bellièvre's arm."

"What, he was also there?"

"Yes, and a few others whose names I've forgotten. Catherine came in looking very ill, but heavily made up with lots of ceruse and whitening, clothed in her perpetual black dress, dragging her foot like a wounded crow, and, the minute she crossed the threshold, croaking like one. At this the king, who'd at first appeared happy enough to see her, suddenly closed up like an oyster.

"'My son,' she said, 'what are you doing here in Chartres, where you're nothing but a kinglet without a palace or a court and confined to the bishop's palace, instead of coming back to your Louvre in Paris and living as befits your rank?'

"'Madame,' he replied with visible bitterness in his black eyes, 'I am infinitely grateful for your wise counsel, but the same reasons that made me leave my Louvre continue to keep me away from it, and these reasons haven't changed since last Friday, the thirteenth—in fact, quite the contrary.'

"'Ah, my son,' she replied, 'how can you say that since you've signed the Edict of Union with the Duc de Guise?'

"'In which I've ceded everything to him.'

"'Well,' she cried, 'that's nothing! If we'd had to give him half the kingdom to preserve the other half, wouldn't we have done it?'

"'Madame,' objected the king, with a very unhappy glance around the room, as if he were ashamed that such words, so unworthy of a queen, should have been spoken in front of so many people who might repeat them. 'Madame, a kingdom is a whole. He who has only half has nothing.'

"'Well, thank God it hasn't come to that,' rejoined Catherine, 'since the duc has sworn to obey you.'

"'As he has and will always do,' snarled the king through clenched teeth." (And Quéribus, pivoting on his heels to emphasize his wasp-like figure, added, as if to show off what excellent hearing he had, "And I heard him quite well, even though he scarcely murmured this last sentence.")

"'And as for you, my son,' continued the queen mother, 'you display too little confidence in Guise by refusing to return to Paris. Your presence here makes it seem as though you harbour some resentment for what happened on the twelfth and thirteenth of May!'

"'Madame,' replied the king, his eyes shining with particular brilliance, 'I've never held a grudge against anyone: you know my natural goodness.'

"'Ah, Monsieur, I know it well!' replied the queen mother, who had completely missed Henri's derisive tone. 'Of course, I know it for having often profited from it myself, and have always known you to be benevolent and extremely forgiving.'

"'Extremely well said, Madame. Sometimes I have trouble forgiving myself for being so accommodating. Perhaps I would have had fewer failures if I'd been more demanding.'

"'Well, my son!' she said, her head bobbing with age and infirmity, her heavy eyelids half closed over her large protruding eyes. 'You shouldn't be ashamed of your good qualities!'

"'I thank you, Madame. And I thank you for asking me, in the name of my natural benevolence, to return to Paris and to my Louvre. But I must ask you: what would I be doing if I agreed to return, other than putting myself back in the hands of the very people who, on the twelfth and thirteenth, chased me out of Paris?'

"'But you've made peace with these people since then!'

"'True,' agreed the king, but turned away to hide his face from the queen mother and from the rest of us looking on, and went to stand in the window bay (as he'd done in their previous meeting), where, making a sign to Bellièvre to give her his arm, the queen mother followed him, puffing at the effort, her fat lips gaping like those of a fish out of water.

"'My son,' she insisted, 'I cannot but beg you, with the greatest urgency, to return to Paris, since I gave my word that you would do so and I would lose my credit and my authority if you refused.'

"'I understand you well,' said the king, his back obstinately turned and throwing her a frigid look over his shoulder, 'and also understand that the duc is speaking through your mouth. Assuredly, he could not find a better interpreter than you. But, Madame, hear me well. Anything you could ask of me, I would grant you instantly... except this that you are asking of me now, and I beg you humbly, Madame, not to trouble me further. You would make me very angry.'

"'Ah, Monsieur!' cried the queen mother, bursting into tears (but you know very well, Pierre, that to a hard heart tears come easily). 'How cruel your words are! What will people think of me if you reject me? What respect will I ever have then? How will people care about me if you throw me out? Denied and rejected by you—me, whom God chose to be your mother!'

"'Madame, the entire world knows how much I love and have obeyed you, but in this present business, it will not be so. I will not—I repeat *not*—go to Paris.'

"'Oh, Monsieur my son!' cried the queen mother, tears flowing down her fat cheeks. 'I see what the problem is! It's all about the barricades, which have blinded you and caused you to lose your reason!'

"'Reason for you is pure folly for me!' snapped the king without turning to face her.

"'Ah, my son! Have you suddenly lost your natural benevolence? I've always known you to be such an accommodating, sweet person, with an easy and forgiving disposition.'

"'What you say is true, Madame,' agreed the king, now turning to face her and smiling wryly, 'but what can I do? Others have changed me! That is also true.'

"Then, with a sudden burst of laughter right in her face, he cried:

"'It's that wicked Épernon, as everyone knows, who ruined my natural goodness! Which is why he has earned my disgrace!'

"And this said, he laughed in her face with the greatest derision, made a deep bow and, abandoning her there, strode rapidly from the room."

Having heard this report, I complimented Quéribus on the pretty tale he'd recounted for me. And, of course, having heard these compliments and lapped them up, he attempted to go one better, as was his wont:

"Did you observe," he cooed, "how I used a clever alliteration: 'baseless and bumbling'? Wasn't that rather cute? I am able to do these without study and scarcely trying. How did you like it?"

"Very sweet."

"The king adored it! As preoccupied as he was by affairs of state, he deigned to smile at it. And it's no mean compliment when Henri, who speaks so exquisitely, admires your words! I made an account of this while we were at dinner with his gentlemen, and, seeing the king looking sombre, I wanted to cheer him up, and so I said, 'Sire, do you think we could now refer to things inconsequential as "baseless and bumbling?"' And at that moment, my brother—"

"He smiled."

"Yes! He smiled!"

"It's abundantly clear," I said, "that you are very solidly in the king's favour and I'm very pleased that your credit at court is equal to mine."

"Well, my brother," he replied pretending to speak with some modesty, "I do indeed believe that the king loves me well enough. And as for me, you know very well that I would give my life for him."

This statement, unlike many of those self-satisfied phrases that preceded it, did not make me want to laugh, because it was true, as true as the Gospels. Quéribus's foibles may have floated too often to the surface, but his heart was loyal, unlike those of some noblemen I could name, whose beautiful bark of obedience hid a very corrupt sap.

"This break between Catherine and the king," Quéribus continued, "took place on Saturday, the thirtieth of July. Guise arrived in Chartres on the second of August, and, my brother, you can imagine, knowing him as you do, the doffing of the hat and the genuflections of the Magnificent before the king, who raised him to his feet, embraced him warmly—oh! that he had suffocated him!—kissed him on both cheeks and invited him to his table. When the cup-bearer had poured each of them a goblet of wine, the king turned to Guise and said, quite playfully:

"'My cousin, whom should we toast?'

"'Well, sire,' the duc replied, 'whomever you please! It's for you to propose the toast. I'd be very happy to obey.'

"'Well, then!' said the king with a sly smile. 'Let's drink to our friends the Huguenots!'

"'Very well, then!' agreed the duc, understanding the mischievousness of the king's proposal.

"'But let's also toast,' said the king, 'our good barricaders in Paris. Let's drink to them as well, and let's not forget them!'

"Guise managed to laugh at this, but it was a laugh that didn't come easily, for he was quite confused by the king's mixing together Huguenots and barricaders, who were thrown into a common sack as rebels to his throne, whereas Guise considered the first his enemies and the second his friends."

Having spoken so long, and having now spoken of wine, Quéribus had got thirsty, and told me so, whereupon I signalled to Miroul, and he left the library to ask that we be served a bottle of wine, but returned immediately, since he didn't want to miss any of Quéribus's story, especially since the fate of the world was hanging in the balance at this moment when Guise and the Armada were threatening to destroy two kingdoms. Fixing his varicoloured eyes on Quéribus, who'd fallen silent as he waited to be served, Miroul seemed to be counting his heartbeats, as was I, to measure the minutes that separated us from an uncertain and dangerous future.

During this pause in the narration, I realized how astonished I was that the queen mother had asked her son to return to Paris. And as I thought about it I couldn't decide—and have never really resolved to this day—whether the queen mother, had this request been consented to, would have put her son's life and liberty in the utmost danger. Was it a monstrous act or a completely naive one? In the latter case, I can at least imagine that perhaps she thought that if she served Guise's interests, she would acquire so much credit with him that she could protect the king if the worst came to worst.

I confess that this question still troubles me today and makes me doubt the intelligence that is often attributed to Catherine de' Medici, this great Machiavellian. Adding to my doubts about her, Pierre de L'Étoile told me that he'd seen a copy of a letter she'd sent years previously to Queen Elizabeth, in which she proposed to marry one of her sons to Mary Stuart, who was at that time already a prisoner of her queen! I repeat: she suggested that the Catholic Mary Stuart, ex-queen of Scotland and pretender, even in her jail, to the English throne, in whom Elizabeth placed as much trust as she would have in the tooth of the most viperous viper (which is why she kept her in jail), should marry the son of the French queen mother, who would then have been able, if the situation presented itself, to uphold her pretensions to Elizabeth's throne! Can one possibly imagine a proposal less likely to seduce the sovereign, to whom Catherine, with a candour that approached the most block-headed stupidity, had the gall to suggest this? On this occasion, and on the one I just mentioned, involving the return of the king to Paris (a disastrous request that the king, despite his benevolent nature, could never forgive), I can't decide whether one should attribute Catherine's behaviour to the perfidy of a hateful mother or to a degree of credulousness that, in this aged weaver of innumerable intrigues, might seem hard to believe. I confess that, ever since the St Bartholomew's day massacre, I've held Catherine in such profound abhorrence that I don't trust my judgement and wouldn't want, even in her case, to be unfair.

"My brother," said Quéribus as he put down his goblet to launch back into his report on Guise's reaction to the king's toast, "the Magnificent looked confused and saddened when he heard the king put Huguenots and barricaders under the same banner, but that was nothing compared to the ugly face he made when he heard the news three weeks later."

"What news?"

"The defeat of the Invincible Armada…"

"Did I hear you correctly?" I shouted, jumping to my feet (along with Miroul). "The Armada defeated? The Invincible Armada vanquished! Are you sure?"

"Entirely!"

"'Sblood! Is it true? Has it really happened? Are you in your right mind, my brother?"

"Completely!" laughed Quéribus. "Do you think I'm a madman? A babe in arms? A raving lunatic?"

"Heavens!" I yelled at the top of my lungs, my arms and head shaking as if I'd lost my mind. "I'm the lunatic! The Armada defeated! Miroul, did you hear? The Armada defeated! My brother, why didn't you tell us straightaway?"

"Pierre," laughed Quéribus, "a good storyteller has to arrange the parts of his story carefully, like a cook a good meal, and keep the best for last!"

"But the Armada—good God! The Armada defeated! Ah, you English, what a great country! Valiant people! A sublime kingdom! And forever blessed by the Lord!"

I jumped up, grabbed Quéribus and pulled him into a victory dance, giving him a hug and another to Miroul and then another to Quéribus, who, to my considerable surprise, embraced Miroul, commoner that he was.

"Heavens!" I cried, throwing myself into an armchair, worn out by my excitement and the excessive joy I felt. "What an immense weight has been lifted from our hearts by the bad fortune of the Armada! May the Lord be praised throughout the centuries!"

"Amen!" agreed Miroul. And looking at each other, each of us with tears in his eyes, we suddenly fell on our knees and said a fervent prayer to the Almighty.

"Ah, you Huguenots," observed Quéribus when we'd done. "It's a strange thing to go praying just anywhere, outside a church, chapel or oratory!"

"God is everywhere," observed Miroul.

"Certainly! Certainly!" agreed Quéribus, using this adverb in jest since it was reputed to be in great usage among those of the reformed faith. And at this, we all had a good laugh.

"My brother," I said when we had all calmed down after such unexpected joy, "tell us about this stunning victory, which cuts the heads off the hydra that is the Inquisition for the time being!"

"Well, not all of them, alas!" replied Quéribus. "We still have some in France! But in truth, I don't know very much about the defeat of the Armada except that Admiral Drake, with a navy of much smaller, lighter and more mobile ships than the heavy Spanish galleons, and better armed with cannon, threw his ships, one against ten, towards this enormous fleet, and made terrible ravages on the first day, and on the second caused even more terrible damage, and then used the tides to send eight burning ships into the harbour where the Spanish had taken refuge. Forced to flee the harbour, the Armada was exposed to a violent storm that finished the work Drake had begun. But, my brother, the best news of all is that Mendoza has gone to see the king."

"What? Mendoza in Chartres? I thought that he was the only foreign ambassador who'd remained in Paris with Guise."

"That's true enough. But having heard a false rumour that the Armada was victorious, he galloped all the way to Chartres to make this triumphant announcement to the king. Mendoza—the zealous, twisted, arrogant Mendoza, who, before being Felipe's ambassador to France, held the post in England, where he hatched so many vile plots against Elizabeth that England finally threw him out of the country like a doctor puncturing a boil to rid it of pus."

"What an image, Quéribus!" I laughed. "Will you tell it to the king?"

"I thought of it myself! But I must continue. Mendoza arrived in Chartres, jumped right out of his carriage and ran to the cathedral to thank the Blessed Virgin for this wonderful victory—who, if she'd not been made of stone, would have shivered to see such a wicked man addressing her."

"That's a phrase worthy of a Huguenot!" observed Miroul sotto voce.

"From the cathedral he rushed to the bishop's palace, where the king is lodging, brandishing a letter he had received in Dieppe, and with true Spanish bombast yelled at the top of his lungs, '*Victoria! Victoria!*' The king received him with a quiet, suave and benevolent air, and said, in the most exquisitely polite tone:

"'Alas, Monsieur, alas! I fear that my beloved cousin the king of Spain is going to be excessively disappointed to learn, as I've just done, through a courier from Dieppe, that Drake sank twelve of his vessels and killed 5,000 men.'

"'Sire, that's not possible!' cried Mendoza, turning ashen.

"'Alas, Monsieur,' soothed the king in honeyed tones, 'I regret that it's not only possible, but has actually happened. I have in my court 300 Turkish galley slaves from a vessel that went aground off of Calais. Would you like to see them?'

"'Those Turks,' snarled Mendoza, 'belong to the king my master. I demand that they be returned to us!'

"'Monsieur, my council will certainly consider your request,' replied the king with utter calm; and he presented Mendoza his hand, which the Spaniard would have bitten if he'd dared. But not daring to do so, he hurried back to see Guise, who assured him of his support and went to plead his case with the council.

"'France,' replied the king gently, 'does not recognize the condition of slavery. Whoever steps onto French soil is a free man. I say, therefore, that we return to the sultan, who is our ally, those poor Turks.'"

This opinion, despite being eminently just, only carried the day in the council after a most bitter debate, at which one could judge which of the members of the council were Guisards by the way they openly opposed the king's recommendation.

"The king," continued Quéribus, "from what I heard from François d'O, made some reflections at the council about those of his disenfranchised ministers who were favouring Spain, and about the remedy that it would ultimately be necessary to bring to bear against their partiality."

My Angelina did not welcome Quéribus with much warmth, suspecting as she did that he had come, on the king's orders, to whisk me away from her, and as soon as she learnt that she had not been mistaken in her conjectures, she threw herself into my arms and burst into tears. This offered me an exquisite excuse to comfort her, moved as I was not only by her beauty, but also by her emotion and by our mutual tenderness, which the years had not dulled. On the contrary, it seemed to me that our feelings had become more acute over the years and penetrated more easily into our hearts—after all the trials they had endured—than in our first years together, when we were less assured of each other and a misunderstanding was more likely to cause some distance.

Although Angelina had borne me six children, she had lost none of the freshness of her youth. Of course, she was older, but she was still beautiful, although possessing another kind of beauty, without any thickening of her girth, her bosom high and vigorous, and her face, though showing some wrinkles, more serene and soft than in the first bloom of her youth. She had wonderful, wide eyes that communicated her gift of always anticipating and enjoying my needs. In a word, she was infinitely more touching than when I'd first met her and my senses had galloped out ahead of my heart, but now the latter had taken the lead, nourishing the lifeblood of the former. For, as soon as she was in my arms, her nightdress flowing in the evening breeze, undone by her tears and by her appearance, I experienced a tenderness that made me tremble from my neck to my heels, and I felt myself melting into a kind of pity and limitless love that fortified my thirst for her and, once satisfied, only multiplied.

She asked me, feeling her legs weak with desire, to carry her to her bed, where, stretching out beside me, she looked at me with her soft black eyes, the most beautiful in the universe, and told me that she'd been devastated to learn from Giacomi, who'd written to her, that our lodgings in Paris had been invaded and pillaged by the Leaguers to the point that there remained no furniture or tapestries that those holy people had not carried off in their zeal. Seeing me once again preparing to depart, she confessed that she was afraid she'd never see me again… And I, wishing to divert her from such morbid thoughts—and, I confess, wishing to divert myself as well—followed my natural inclination, which was to caress her insatiably as soon as I held her in my arms, and, in our present troubles, with so much more ardour and melancholic joy, because of this sudden realization that I could indeed die in the service of my country.

Our tumults at an end, she nestled her blonde head in the hollow of my shoulder and said with a sigh:

"Monsieur my husband, do you really have to join the king in Blois? What will you do in this Estates-General to which you've not been elected? Haven't you done enough? And haven't we paid dearly enough with the pillaging of our house in Paris? Do you have to risk the well-being of your wife and children, your estate and your own life in such perilous service? Can't they do without you?"

"Can any timepiece work without even its tiniest cog? Did I have any effect on the events in Guyenne? In Boulogne? In London? Or at Sedan? Would the League harbour such great hatred for me if I weren't so useful to the king? Did you know that Guise demanded His Majesty disgrace the venerable Dr Marc Miron simply because he served as a go-between for them in the drafting of the Edict of Union and Guise found him too zealously invested in the cause of his master? Did you know Guise is pressing the king to get rid of Chicot?"

"What! His fool?"

"Yes! Quéribus told me about it. And if even a fool is so useful to the king in Guise's view, wouldn't I be even more so? Could I be so cowardly as to quit his service when so many of his faithful subjects are disappearing?"

"Ah," sobbed Angelina, "you love your king more than me, more than our children!"

"My friend," I said somewhat stiffly, "I'm surprised at you! Can you imagine what would happen to you, to them and to me if Guise were to triumph? You must understand that the reality of the situation is not that I serve my king, but that in serving him I serve my nation and my family—"

"And your Church!" she said, not without some bitterness, which was softened by her voice.

"No, no and no!" I cried, now feeling really indignant. "I serve no Church to the detriment of another! I work to ensure that they coexist and that everyone be free to choose the religion he wants!"

Seeing that my mind was made up, and that she wouldn't be able to change it, and perhaps shaken by my justifications for my decision—though she pretended never to give in to my decisions, since being convinced felt too much like a defeat—she fell silent, wiped away her tears and spoke no more of matters of any consequence, but instead of things "baseless and bumbling", as Quéribus might put it. And during the next month, which was September, Quéribus leaving on the 2nd and returning on the 30th to present the king's request that I accompany him to Blois, Angelina displayed a Roman—or should I say a Montcalm-like—degree of calm, nobility and strength of spirit, overcoming her tears, complaints, sighs and frowns and displaying a united front with me, entirely persuaded, as she would say later, that she would never see me again, and, for this reason, wishing me to be happy for the last month of my life.

As we passed through the gates of my little estate and on into the forest of Montfort-l'Amaury, Quéribus seemed so jubilant and excited about the future that I pulled my horse alongside his and asked what was making him look so happy.

"Hardly had the king arrived in Blois," he answered, "when he dismissed several of his ministers!"

"Which ones?"

"Can't you guess? The Leaguers and Guisards. In short, the ones his mother had placed in his entourage and thanks to whom he couldn't flip an egg without her knowing."

"That would be Cheverny, Villeroi, Pinard, Brulard…"

"And Bellièvre."

"Yes, I saw him at work in London. In addition to being the biggest hypocrite in creation, he exuded Spain out of every pore in his body. So *exit* the Pompous Pomponne and *exeunt* all the other idiots who take their orders from a Lorraine duc, a king in Spain or a Pope in Italy—in short, from anyone in the world except the king of France. And whom did he replace them with?"

"With a group of good, honest and obscure men who have the advantage of knowing nothing of the court, who are amazed to be so honoured, who will be mute as tombs and who will be obedient in all things to His Majesty."

"Finally! And thank God! Do I know any of them?"

"You know Montholon. He's the uncle of your friend L'Étoile. And Revol, who was Épernon's bursar."

"Well, that shows," I laughed, "how thoroughly Épernon has been disgraced!"

"Well, my brother," asked Quéribus after a moment and squinting at me sideways, "what do you think of this shake-up?"

"That it's a sea change to have brought in all these new players to replace those self-satisfied creatures of the queen mother, who are now cast into darkness."

"So what do you think will come of it?"

"The same as you," I replied with a smile.

"Which is?"

"I think that the king is about to make some great decisions that he wishes to keep secret."

"May the Lord God hear you!" answered Quéribus with a gravity that was unusual for him and that quite surprised me. "Did you know," he continued, "that the king has exiled Chicot for three months?"

"What!" I cried. "He gave in to Guise's demands?"

"That's what some people think."

"But you don't believe it."

"Assuredly not," he replied. "I've often heard the king complain of living constantly with him and that his fool knew too many things."

"Where's the danger? He's loyal."

"He is loyal," Quéribus confirmed, "but perhaps a bit too garrulous. Sometimes he'll sacrifice a secret to make a good joke. I heard that one day in the king's chambers he scratched the stone floor with his knife and said, '*J'ai... guise.*'"*

"That's correct, I was there."

"The joke seems to have displeased the king," explained Quéribus, "attributing to him as it did a thought that he had never put into words."

At this he looked at me, and I returned his look, but judging that we'd said enough about this, we fell silent.

It took us five days to reach Blois, and, in truth, we would have arrived sooner if Quéribus had been less interested in pursuing his pleasures at each inn.

So as to avoid being identified by any Leaguer spies, we entered the city at nightfall and by a gate that was strictly watched by the French Guards, where Quéribus showed his royal pass. Despite the late hour, the streets were thronging with horses, carriages and sedan chairs; a host of torches and lanterns were held aloft to light their way. In addition to the 500 deputies assembled there for the Estates-General, hundreds of noblemen and -women, cardinals and bishops, each with a retinue, had also descended upon the city, such that there was barely room to lodge a pin anywhere in the town. I began to worry that, with this many people arriving en masse, I would struggle to find a spot in any of the inns in Blois, but Quéribus informed me that the king had

---

* "I'm sharpening it" [*aiguiser* = to sharpen] / "I have Guise!"

reserved rooms for Miroul and me at the Two Pigeons Inn, where a whole wing of the place had been reserved to house a dozen of his Forty-five Guardsmen, since there wasn't room for them in the chateau.

I was to share a room with two of them, who were to ensure my safety that night and take me to a barber the next morning to have my hair cut and my beard and moustache shaved and blackened; then they were to furnish me with uniforms similar to theirs in order to allow me to pass as one of them the next day when they returned to their duties at the king's side. Evidently my blond hair would have been far too visible among the guardsmen, who were all from Gascony and thus very dark-skinned and dark-haired—as I saw when I joined their troop.

Other than Laugnac, who had rudely stopped and searched me when I returned to the king's chambers after my return from Guyenne, I knew no one among the Forty-five, who'd been ordered by the king not to frequent anyone in the city or at court but to keep to themselves in order to prevent anyone from attacking them, poisoning them or, at the very least, picking a fight with them. For the same reason, and to prevent them from getting caught up in any intrigue against the king, the Duc d'Épernon—or, if not him, his intendant, Revol (when he wasn't acting as one of the secretaries of state), or some assistant— furnished these men with whores, whom I saw, while I was at the Two Pigeons Inn, arrive every Monday at our wing of the inn in a large platoon. One of their number proffered her good offices to me, but I refused, having no appetite for such corrupt and rustic affairs—these wenches were girls from the surrounding villages who'd fallen into prostitution after a swelling of their bellies had seen them chased away by their parish priest.

The two Gascons who welcomed me into their room were named Messieurs de La Bastide and de Montseris, both very noble and very destitute, being young noblemen in a very poor province, and would not have been so hospitable to me had I not spoken Provençal, a language very similar to theirs. This immediately broke the ice and they happily accepted Miroul and me since they hated the people from the north of the Loire valley in exact proportion to the disdain their neighbours to the north heaped on them. The League and Guise hated them since they believed that the Gascons had built an inconvenient rampart between the king and their aspirations. Madame Limp and her preachers in Paris invented all kinds of lies about them, claiming, among many other horrible rumours spread about them, that at night they roamed the streets of Paris like tigers thirsting for blood, cutting the throats of passers-by and throwing them in the Seine. They covered the guards with insults, calling them "the king's slicers", his "ham-stringers" or else his "Gascon devils".

Whether La Bastide and Montseris were demons I know not, but I found them good devils and very thankful to the king for treating them so well, as they received 1,200 écus a year and were fed for free. And, of course, here they were getting wenches for free as well, and as many as they wanted. They were quite happy with this life after their miserable existences in dilapidated Gascon chateaux.

Moreover, these two, La Bastide and Montseris, were good men, but simple, unwashed of the dirt from their native soil, smelling strongly of garlic and sweat, scarcely knowing how to read, understanding French, but speaking it very badly, and very focused on athletic exercises, on pistol shooting and fencing, which they practised in our room, almost from dawn to dusk, yelling at the top of their voices as if they were really going to cut each other's throats, though they loved each other like brothers. This noise was extremely bothersome and was often worse at night, when their twin snores deafened us from dusk to dawn, one starting up just when the other miraculously ceased his racket. Not to mention Mondays, when the wenches arrived and, for reasons of security, we had to remain in the room, where we could not help witnessing their diabolical sarabands, which lasted the entire day, their activity and especially their noise passing imagination, since the guards polished off these poor wenches as if they were assaulting them, with cries of "*Cap de Diou!*" and "*Mordi!*" and other terrifying oaths; once done, however, they were not the least bit brutal or wicked, but held them sweetly in their arms and sang them some very delicate Provençal romances, which the poor girls couldn't understand since they were from the Loire valley. Physically, La Bastide and Montseris weren't very tall, but they were very vigorous and well built, with not an ounce of fat—despite the fact that they ate like ogres (perhaps to make up for the famine back at home). They were both agile and dexterous and were so alike in aspect that I could hardly tell them apart, especially since their thick black beards seemed almost to connect with their eyebrows and devour their faces, with the exception of their noses, which were large, and their eyes, which, set in the midst of this sombre underbrush, shot out dark but lively sparks. Their teeth were very white, and their smile, when it broke out, was naive and simple, like a child's.

The barber, who arrived at dawn, did wonders for my hair, turning it jet black, but could do nothing for the colour of my eyes, which remained steadfastly blue, which was why La Bastide (unless it was Montseris?) advised me to keep my hat pulled down over my eyes and to walk in the middle of the troop—which I did, keeping my eyelids practically closed until we got to the chateau, where Laugnac, captain of the Forty-five, seeing that I was there, took me to see my master. He led me up a little staircase to the second floor, and then to a room that he informed me was called the "old cabinet", which opened by one door onto the king's chambers and, by another, onto the council's meeting room. This door—and I emphasize this detail because it will end up being of the greatest consequence later—had been walled up, by order of the king, as soon as he'd arrived at the chateau, so that one couldn't pass from the council's meeting room to the "old cabinet" without passing through His Majesty's chamber.

Laugnac, who was a very tall and handsome gentleman with the skin and beard of a Saracen, was very welcoming, all honey and smiles, and yet looked me over very carefully; he was, I imagine, reassured to discover that I was not too young, being as he was one of the little favourites of the king, convinced that there were rivals everywhere and extremely jealous of Bellegarde—and even of the Duc d'Épernon, who'd had him appointed. But there was something desperately hungry in his look that I didn't like, and even made me question the confidence the king had placed in him.

"Monsieur," he laughed when he saw me, "they should have dyed your skin walnut colour since it looks so pale in the middle of this black hair!"

"Laugnac," I joked in return, "aren't there any blue-eyed blonds among your Gascons?"

"Indeed there are," he conceded, "five or six of them, I believe, but they stand out and are all well known to the League's spies, which is why we had to disguise you with the dominant colour. Usher! This is the Chevalier de Siorac. Please announce him to the king!"

I found His Majesty, after the several months we hadn't seen each other, looking pale and thinner, but appearing very resolved, despite the almost ridiculous situation he found himself in—or perhaps because of that situation—as if all the resources of his soul had banded together for one last combat, having as he did his back to the wall and with very few in the kingdom betting on him. With him, as I entered, were Du Halde, Alphonse d'Ornano, known as the Corsican, and Revol, his new secretary of state.

"Siorac, my child," said the king, looking very tense and yet his manner still majestic and suave as usual, "I'm very happy to see you, especially now that I need all my friends around me, protecting me with their swords, for this is the ultimate endgame—which, if we lose it, will signal not only the end of my throne and of my life, but of the kingdom as we know it."

"Well, sire, I am all yours, you know very well, whatever you command and no matter how dangerous the mission I must undertake."

"*È meglio un buon amico che cento parenti*," laughed Henri, who added between clenched teeth, "*o che una madre*"* (proof that his conversation with his mother in Chartres was still very much on his mind). "Sweet Siorac," he continued, "as my beloved sister Queen Elizabeth calls you, who has, thank God, conquered the Invincible Armada, leaving me to contend here with another group of galleons we have here in Blois, swelled with Spanish gold, stuffed with paternosters and followed, alas, by a besotted people, the present Estates-General being so partial to the League that they make my hair stand on end. Siorac, I haven't been able to see Lord Stafford either in Chartres or in Blois. The League would have decried my connivance with the heretic, but he sent me a note, telling me that you were witness to a conversation he had with a certain lord who, *if he's not good on land or sea, is at least good on paving stones*. So, my child, what can you tell me?"

And I, astonished that the king, in the very jaws of death, should take so much pleasure in his exquisite language, recounted, with as much humour as possible, the exchange that took place between Stafford and Brissac, and the king burst out laughing several times at Brissac's hypocrisy, but also seemed very touched by the ambassador's behaviour.

"The Englishman," he observed when I'd done, "has an excellent sense of the necessity of dignity in his position. It's a trait I admire in this valiant nation—perhaps even more so than its bravery. I will take from this a very good opinion of Elizabeth, and hope to convey it to

---

* "Better one friend than a hundred relatives" (Seneca); "or than a mother."

her myself if I live long enough. But, Siorac, I didn't tear you away from your estate simply to see your good and honest face, although I am truly comforted by your presence, as I must look at so many bigoted and sanctimonious faces every day. Siorac, in a word, here's the target for your arrow. There is in the Magnificent's retinue, not yet invited to his table, but certainly among his hangers-on, a Venetian actor by the name of Venetianelli, who from what I've heard is *un gran birbone**—amusing, lively, but as unscrupulous as they come. Siorac, I'd like you to sound this rascal out to see whether, if you drop a pailful of gold into his well, it comes back full or empty. Do you get my drift?"

"Completely. But, sire, may I leave the Two Pigeons Inn?"

"Only at night, but the first contact will be made by Giacomi, who has the advantage of being Italian."

"Ha!" I gushed happily. "So the *maestro* is here!"

"He'll come see you after your noon meal. Siorac, one word more. I've asked Revol to write to the great judge in Montfort-l'Amaury, to have the Rugged Oak inscribed in the registry there as 'Siorac'. You will therefore be Siorac twice, whereas your father is only Mespech once."

"Sire, I'm infinitely obliged to you!"

"Alas!" replied the king. "This is not very much. But I don't even have enough money to pay Larchant's guards here, so that the only thing I can give you, Siorac, is your name."

"Sire, I can only say that the man who bears this name serves you with all his heart."

"I know!"

This said, his two hands resting on the arms of his chair, presenting a very regal, proud appearance and looking me directly in the eye, Henri said gravely, but without any pomp or raising his voice:

"I'll see you soon, Siorac."

---

* "A great rascal."

"Ah, sire!" I cried, understanding now, and throwing myself at his feet, but I couldn't say another word. His Majesty presented me his hand, and, unable to speak after having kissed it, I attempted to express my utmost gratitude with my eyes, and withdrew from his presence on unsteady legs, Du Halde accompanying me at a sign from the king.

"Du Halde," I asked, once we'd stepped into the old cabinet and closed the door, "what's happening with the Estates-General? Are things as bad as the king says?"

"Ah, Baron!" replied Du Halde. "Worse! The worm is in each of the three orders—and deeply. The clergy is entirely for the League, as are more than three-quarters of the Third Estate and more than half of the nobility, for God's sake! Do you know who each of the three orders has elected as president? The Third Estate elected La Chapelle-Marteau, the nobility Brissac, and the clergy the Cardinal de Guise! Guise is, as you know, a furious zealot. Blessed Virgin! My master will get nothing but thorns, spitting and flagellations from them."

At this tears began to flow down his long, austere face, and, embracing him sadly, I rejoined my guardsmen colleagues in the Gallery of the Stags, my throat so constricted I could hardly speak, having no thought for the title of baron that had just been bestowed on me (something that would have overjoyed me at any other time), but on the misery and death that would ensue when the throne collapsed.

Since I couldn't leave the chateau without them, I had to wait around for two long hours with the Forty-five, who whiled away their time smoking, playing cards and throwing dice with their usual ruckus, completely unconcerned with the future of the state as far as I could tell, and finding life very good indeed—with a roof over their heads, good wages, good food and wenches every Monday. If their simplicity wasn't exactly saintly, it wasn't any the less happy for all that, in these times when just thinking about the future of the kingdom threw you into the darkest of moods.

Giacomi came to see me at the Two Pigeons Inn after the noon meal. La Bastide and Montseris, however generally rough-mannered, had the decency to quit our room as soon as they saw him, to leave us alone to talk. I was so grateful for their discretion that I sent the chambermaid to bring them a pitcher of Cahors wine in the common room of the inn. With his spidery arms, which reminded me of Fogacer, my Giacomi embraced me fondly, with many kisses, and laughed to see me so dark-haired. He told me that he'd scarcely left the king's side ever since the barricades, sharing His Majesty's nomadic life, riding from Paris to Chartres, from Chartres to Rouen, from Rouen to Mantes, and from Mantes back to Chartres—then from there to Blois. Larissa had remained in Paris and had not been molested, nor had her lodgings, since Giacomi was protected by the Duc de Mayenne, who had been one of his fencing students. In the meantime, Paris had become a kind of bourgeois republic, under the rule of the "Sixteen", so called because each of the sixteen quarters of Paris had elected a representative to participate in the governance of the city. These Sixteen were more fanatical than the League and more papist than the Pope, subjugating the parliament, lambasting the "politicals" and scarcely obeying Mayenne or Guise. All of this was of enormous concern to Giacomi, who feared for his Larissa in the midst of all of this fanaticism, so he wrote asking to take refuge at my estate in Montfort-l'Amaury with their children—which he was very relieved to hear that Larissa had done, having received that very morning a letter confirming her arrival there.

"The king," he continued, "didn't explain this Venetianelli business, except to say that you wanted to meet him and that we had to approach it with kid gloves since the man belongs to Guise. I've never laid eyes on him, only heard about him since I know his *dona de cuori*,[*] whom they call La Cavalletta."

"Which means?"

"The grasshopper."

"Because she has long legs, or because she devours wheat fields?"

"Both. La Cavalletta arrived here on the heels of the Estates-General and immediately opened a welcoming little house for all three orders where one can eat, drink, gamble and carouse."

"Aha, *maestro*!" I laughed. "Even though I think it's better to wallow in a whorehouse than to rob an innocent damsel of her honour, I'm surprised that you haunt such places!"

"I only go there to gamble," confessed Giacomi a little shamefacedly, since he was possessed of this vice, albeit in moderation.

"And you're hoping to use this this noble lady as a go-between with Venetianelli?"

"Not without some misgivings, since La Cavalletta is a noblewoman, or at least passes for one: she dresses like a princess, is very decorous, puts on high airs and disguises her whores as honest chambermaids. I'm scarcely of sufficient rank to be admitted to her table, desiring as she does to play host to great lords, unctuous prelates or rich bourgeois."

"So," I said, smiling at the portrait, "Venetianelli is the favourite of this pretentious madam?"

"That's the rumour. But I've never laid eyes on him in this good house, which is exquisitely appointed with all manner of paintings, rugs, furniture, crystal, silver, chandeliers, numerous servants, costly wines and delicacies. La Cavalletta is growing very rich from this. And, it is said that she has secretly married Venetianelli."

"Well," I confessed, "I'm very disappointed. How can I succeed if he's so well off thanks to his wife?"

---

[*] "Queen of hearts."

And suddenly, without really thinking it through, I decided to take a serious risk, and said:

"Giacomi, perhaps you could tell La Cavalletta, without mentioning my name, that I'm an officer of the king, and that Venetianelli might want to take some precautions and protections on this side *as well…*"

Giacomi immediately threw me a concerned look and said pensively:

"We'd have to exercise extreme caution. Ah, my friend, swordplay is but child's play in comparison with complicated manoeuvres like this!"

The day after this conversation with Giacomi, which took place on 9th October, was the opening of the Estates-General, which I attended, lost in the middle of the Forty-five (and apparently nobody noticed that there were now forty-six of us!), who were stationed in front of the platform on which Henri and the two queens were seated, forming a crescent around them, with the gentlemen of the house standing some way behind the guards. This platform was not very high and had been constructed in front of the immense fireplace that occupied the middle of the long room, and in which great pine logs were burning (it being an unusually cold October). The royal dais was therefore situated right in front of these flames, which illuminated the violet velvet hangings with gold fleurs-de-lis that surrounded the king, and heated and illuminated him from behind so that his sombre silhouette, clothed as he was in black velvet, seemed to have a halo of light around it. This was already impressive, but when the king stood to deliver his speech, the fire crackled, sending sparks flying from behind him as if he'd commanded the flames that illuminated his royal person. This fiery performance left the three orders of the Estates-General stupefied, since it was the complete opposite of the submissive presence his bellicose subjects were expecting from their sovereign.

This hall, which was immense, happened in fact to be the work of Henri himself, for it had only included, at the time of the comtes de Blois, a single, splendid vaulted ceiling, like an inverted ship. But, twelve years previously, in his sure instinct for the beauty of things, Henri had doubled this with a second, identical and parallel to the first. It was linked and supported by a line of columns that ran in arcades up the centre of the hall. Thus, the two ships seemed to have been anchored side by side with their keels resting on the heavens above. In this way, the king had doubled the volume and surface of the hall without in the least destroying its harmony. The only inconvenience that resulted from this addition was that the windows situated on the smallest sides of the rectangle, though they were fairly large, weren't sufficient to light the entire room, and so had to be augmented by the light from candles, set in chandeliers hanging from the middle of the arcades. But as many candles as there were, they provided only a fraction of the light that was now generated by the enormous fireplace, whose vigorous flames illuminated the king.

The Duc de Guise, in his office of lieutenant general of the kingdom, was seated on a stool at the foot of the platform, half turned to face the three orders to his right, but half-turned to face the king on his left in apparent respect. This ambiguous position couldn't have been more symbolic, since he drew some of his power from the people he represented, but simultaneously drew the weakness of his position from the king, whom he might well be plotting to overthrow, but whose legitimacy he could not undo! He was wearing—and assuredly this was not by chance (since he wanted to resemble the archangel sent by God)—the same white doublet that he'd worn on the day of the barricades, which, being too light for the season, caused our beautiful archangel to sit there shivering with the cold, something that afflicted everyone in the hall save the king. His seat, supported on four sculpted legs, was garnished with a velvet cushion, but had no back, which seemed to hinder the duc in his attempt to strike various affected noble poses.

The poor queen mother, a martyr to her gout, had been dragged from her bed to her throne on the right of the king, usurping the place that should have been reserved for the queen, Louise, but which Catherine would never have consented to vacate, so ardently did the desire to hold on to the vestiges power burn in her dried-out heart. (In fact, that power was as useless and desiccated as her heart itself: the king had refused to accept the ministers she'd chosen for the council and now locked himself in his old cabinet to read his dispatches.) When the king rose to give his speech, her pale, swollen face betrayed her anger at the fact that he'd written the address himself and refused to provide her with a copy—and indeed, within the magnificent homage he paid her at the beginning of his speech was hidden a nearly insufferable derision, when he called her "mother of the state and the kingdom", entities that seemed quite resolved to do without her.

The queen mother was wrapped, as was her custom, in the dark, funereal robe that she had worn since the death of Henri II, and, since the king was also dressed in black, one could only be grateful that Queen Louise had chosen a pink satin gown; she looked wonderfully composed, her face fresh and her blue eyes shining with innocence, being lucky enough to have no understanding of politics and to have never been asked to play a role in the affairs of state. Her sole occupation, it would seem, since Henri had never given her a son, was to be his doll—he loved to fuss over her, to do her make-up and run a silver brush through her long, golden hair. Here, in this austere assembly, she was a balm for the eyes, as were most of the court ladies in the gallery, who were much more interested in being seen than in listening to political disputes. I couldn't help casting my own eyes on them from time to time, enjoying not only their beauty but also the wafts of perfume that reached me. I would much rather have been seated in the midst of these beautiful, gold-embroidered dresses than standing among these rough and malodorous Gascons.

Although the king was dressed in black velvet, he had not forgone under the circumstances any of his jewellery—rings, rows of pearls and earrings—which he loved to display, or his favourite hat, believing that he shouldn't omit any of his baubles simply because some of his subjects ridiculed him for wearing them. In the same independent spirit, he broke with the tradition whereby the king sits on his throne while speaking to the Estates-General; instead he spoke standing, thereby giving more force to his words. No one in the room had any idea of what he was going to say, since he'd written this oration alone in the privacy of his old cabinet, refusing to share it with the queen mother or with any of his ministers—and especially not with his lieutenant general, Guise; instead he had had it printed so that it could be distributed immediately to the deputies of the three orders, and sent to the governors and seneschals of each province, as well as to the members of the parliaments in Paris and in other major cities.

Standing tall and majestically, holding the printed pages of his speech in his gloved hands, looking radiant in the halo of light coming from the fireplace behind him, he began his speech quietly and somewhat haltingly, but, suddenly finding a voice that matched the tenor of his words, his voice became strong and imposing.

I would like to invite my reader, at this historic moment, to bring his or her compassion to bear on the suffering of this oh-so-human man, my beloved master, whose overwhelming desire was, above all, even at the peril of his life, to preserve his people from a bloody civil war, and a significant number of his subjects from extermination. He stood before a large congregation of fanatical clergymen, powerful and ambitious princes, much of the French nobility and ignorant commoners. And in this immense hall of the Château de Blois—where the dark, inverted twin ships above seemed already to symbolize the shipwreck of the state, their keels reaching towards a pitiless heaven— fewer than 100 of the 500 deputies present shared the wise and peaceful ambitions of the king. The Third Estate, the clergy and the nobility, all in the name of a "God of love and forgiveness", were panting for blood, already tasting murder, dreaming of massacre, despising the king and his long patience, and yearning only to submit to the double yoke of Guise and the Spanish king. But this lonely king—betrayed by so many of his followers (and by his mother before any of them), almost three-quarters defeated, clearly at bay, financially ruined, supported by unpaid soldiers, controlling but a handful of faithful cities in his kingdom—had suddenly turned to face this pack of rabid dogs and was defying them. He was standing up to their assault! He was parrying their every blow! Henri deserves, I believe, our tenderness and our unlimited admiration for the incredible bravery and fortitude he displayed, faced with this bloodthirsty mob.

And what did this king without a capital say? Nothing but what he would have said at the summit of his power, without compromising any of the principles or prerogatives of the throne. Let's listen to him as he defies the victory of the so-called Holy League:

"All leagues that are not under my authority will not be tolerated. Neither my duty to God nor my duty to the state will allow me to legitimize them; rather, they force me to oppose them. For all leagues, associations, practices, movements, plots, drafting of troops and raising of monies by or from anyone within or outside the kingdom" (clearly a reference to Spanish gold) "must be made by the king and, in any well-ordered monarchy, will be considered crimes of lese-majesty if undertaken without the express permission of the king."

And his speech included this statement, clearly directed at Guise and the Lorraine princes:

"I am your king by God's decree and am the only one who can truly and legitimately make this claim!"

And he added this, under the guise of a pardon granted to the errant rebel, but in fact condemning any future such attempts:

"Some of the great lords of my kingdom have made leagues and associations, but, in witness to my accustomed beneficence, I am willing to put the past behind us. But as I am obliged—as we all are—to preserve the dignity of the throne, I declare that, now and henceforth, any of my subjects who engage in such activities without my express consent will be tried for the crime of lese-majesty."

There was at these words a terrible commotion in the hall, which rippled through the 500 deputies of the three orders and agitated them like a wind of hurricane force through a field of grain. To say that Guise and his followers would be accused of the crime of lese-majesty if they did not desist was nothing less than to hint at their death sentences, since there was no likelihood that they would consent to abandon their plots, having the king at their mercy as they did. And that the king in such dire circumstances would have the incredible audacity, in the name of his legitimacy, to threaten Guise with the executioner's block, in front of the assembled Estates-General, left the duc aghast. I saw him waver in his chair, his face drained of colour and self-assurance, hesitate between fear and anger, and then glance at his brother the cardinal, who was seated in the first row of the clergy. This last, despite his robe (which he willingly exchanged for a coat of mail or a breastplate), did not pride himself on manners or mercy as his older brother did, whom he resembled not a whit, being dark-skinned, with furious, sharp, black eyes that gave off sparks of hatred. He was quite handsome, although not very evangelical by nature: in his private life he was a great whorer and, in public, seemed interested only in murder and massacre. Nor did he hesitate very long about what to do, but rose, pale with rage and gnashing his teeth, and left the hall without bowing to the king, to be followed by the duc, the Comte de Brissac and La Chapelle-Marteau, as the king continued to read his speech in a strong and firm voice, his face inscrutable, as if it were of no consequence to him that his grand master and the three presidents of the orders had left the hall.

As for me, I felt extraordinarily happy and comforted by the brilliance with which the king had shaken the pack of wolves that were biting at his heels, and very curious too as to the political consequences of it all. I was unhappy, however, that I had to continue to blend in with the Forty-five (a good hiding place, since they were so despised by the Leaguers that the latter refused even to look at them), and was prevented from running outside to learn what was happening.

Thirsty for news, barely had I returned to the Two Pigeons Inn before I sent off the chambermaid to Quéribus's lodgings to ask him to visit me. But she returned without having delivered my message, the bird having flown from his cage—fluttering about, no doubt, from beauty to beauty, with his "*veni, vidi, vici*". And it was quite fortuitous that, the next afternoon, while I was practising swordplay with La Bastide in my room, he paused to catch his breath and said:

"*Cap de Diou*, Baron! Here we are wasting our time with our good blades, making buttonholes in each other's tunics, when it's through the heart of that monster Guise that we should be driving our points!"

"*Passinsa amic*," I replied. "*Que mienja lo gal del rey, cent ans après raca las plumas.*"*

Bastide laughed and replied:

"We have the same proverb in Gascony, but it's worded a bit differently—which reminds me that before our exercise this afternoon I saw an older gentleman in the common room of the inn, with about as much hair as I've got on my hand" (an inapt expression since his hand was so hairy!) "who was asking his valet to bring him some wine and whose accent was so close to yours I thought he must be Périgordian."

---

* "Patience, my friend. He who eats the king's chickens will throw up the feathers a hundred years later!"

"What did he look like?"

"He was a nobleman, more of the robe I'll warrant than of the sword, although he was wearing one. He seemed a good man, not so haughty, but I thought he must be high enough in the kingdom, since he was wearing the Order of Saint-Michel."

"By the belly of St Anthony, there are not many men in Périgord who belong to that order and I think I know who it must be!"

So saying, I rushed from the room, silently descended the staircase that led to the common room (which I never entered), crouched down, peered through the railing and—true as gospel!—whom did I spy, happily ensconced at a table and greedily devouring his food, his tall forehead topped by a bald pate, with high cheekbones, long, aquiline nose and wise eyes focused on his meal, but Monsieur de Montaigne!

"Hey, La Bastide," I cried, rushing back upstairs, "ask Margot, I beg you, to carry a note to this gentleman, whom I know and love, requesting him to meet me in our room and not in the common room, for obvious reasons."

"Is he a friend of the king's?" asked La Bastide as he twisted his moustache.

"Indeed he is!"

"In that case, no need to ask Margot! I'll take your note to him."

Monsieur de Montaigne, who seemed to carry his fifty years with great vigour, had some trouble recognizing me, not only because I had dark skin and black hair, but because so many hard years had passed since we'd last met in 1572, sixteen years previously. Back then I was but a lad and had scarcely finished my studies. To tell the truth, he knew my father much better than he knew me, having entertained him frequently at Navarre's court, and rumour had it that Montaigne had served—and perhaps still did—as a messenger between the king and the Béarnais. In any case, he was a faithful friend to both men, and one of those "politicals" whom the League hated because they seasoned their faith with some grains of tolerance.

"Well, Monsieur!" I said. "Is it true that the Leaguers arrested you and threw you in the Bastille on the day of the barricades?"

"Indeed it is!" he laughed. "Why didn't I have the sense to stay peaceably at home on my sweet estate?" (By which he meant the Château de Montaigne, near Bordeaux.) "What a terrible time I had of it on that trip! I was attacked on the road by highwaymen, who robbed me of everything I had, but at least didn't take my life. But scarcely had I arrived in Paris, where I was arranging for the publication of my *Essais*, when I was thrown in jail by the Leaguers, who, less merciful than the beggars who robbed me, would have killed me if the queen mother, who luckily still cared for me, hadn't interceded in my favour!"

"At last, something to be grateful to her for! Without her, this kingdom would have lost a wise man, not to mention those essays of yours, which we have been eagerly awaiting since you whet our appetites with your first volume."

"Ah," said Montaigne, with half-sincere, half-feigned modesty, "I'm not sure I believe that!"

"Well then, ask the king, who adores them and constantly reads and rereads the ones that have been published!"

"As beset as he is by his affairs, he didn't fail to tell me so this morning," Montaigne replied. "And he had great things to say about you! He insisted I stay at this inn so that I would see you, and might perhaps take news of you back to your father, if Fortune allows me to see him on my return to Bordeaux."

As he said this, Montaigne smiled a slow and conspiratorial smile, which led me to believe that he continued to serve, on these occasions, as a messenger between the king and Navarre, since he couldn't be seen with my father at Navarre's court. In this capacity, he was like

Monsieur de Rosny, whom I'd caught sight of in the streets of Blois the day before, the brim of his hat pulled down and his face buried in his collar.*

I mentioned to Monsieur de Montaigne that I'd sighted Monsieur de Rosny, whose presence in Blois he confirmed, saying that, as far as he knew, Navarre had offered the king, in his present predicament, both military and financial support, which the king had not refused, but that it required further negotiations. Navarre wanted a city or town along the Loire in order to ensure his safety while he and the king were meeting. There was still some degree of mistrust that hadn't entirely disappeared between the two, who had spent so many years fighting each other, though always with a certain amount of mutual restraint and consideration.

I heard all this with the joy one can imagine, since I'd always thought that the king could never defeat Guise and the League without Navarre's help.

"Monsieur de Montaigne," I asked, after calming down, "how did you find the king after his angry speech yesterday at the Estates-General, and the bitter anger of the gentlemen of the Holy League?"

"I observed the same resolve when I met the king in his chambers this morning. He was seated in a very simple chair in an alcove covered with fleurs-de-lis when I entered, and scarcely had he said, 'Monsieur de Montaigne, I'm delighted to see you and thank you for your devotion to my service...' when there was a loud noise at the door, and the king sent Du Halde to see what was happening. Du Halde half-opened the door and returned, to announce:

"'Sire, it is the Cardinal de Guise, who demands to be received immediately by Your Majesty.'

"'Immediately?' said the king in surprise. 'He said "immediately"?'

---

* Rosny was later known as Sully, one of the advisors of Navarre.

"'Sire,' said Du Halde, 'he said it twice, adding that if he weren't received within the hour, he would leave Blois.'

"'Monsieur de Montaigne,' said the king without batting an eye, 'you can see how things are. The Church cannot wait. May I ask you to withdraw into this alcove with François d'O? I'll see you after I've received the cardinal.'

"Whereupon, Du Halde having opened the door, the cardinal burst in furiously, as if mounting an assault, his long, purple robe flowing behind him, his figure tall and thin, his handsome face twisted in anger and his nostrils aflame as if he were breathing gunpowder. The king, sitting erect in his chair, his two hands on the armrests, immobile and majestic, did not present his hand, and his visitor scarcely bowed before him. Of the Duc de Guise and the cardinal," Montaigne continued, with a derisive smile, "the least hypocritical, the least genuflecting and the most sparing in manners, smiles and unctuous phrases is, as you know, the cardinal, who, brandishing in his hand a printed copy of the king's speech, scolded the king and took him to task as if he were some schoolboy for having dared to write and publish that 'some great men of his kingdom' had made 'leagues and associations against his authority'. The imputation was clear, he said, and injurious, and he would not suffer it, any more than would his brother the duc—or the clergy, since everything that had been done had been for the sole defence and preservation of their dying religion. He demanded that His Majesty reprint the speech, removing the sacrilegious phrase, before distributing copies, and warned that if His Majesty did not satisfy these demands, the clergy, having duly deliberated, would leave the Estates-General immediately, and depart from Blois, followed by the Third Estate and perhaps the nobility as well. He concluded by saying that the duc, his brother, had decided to retire to his house and no longer serve in any capacity, given this dissolution of the Estates-General."

"Well," I cried indignantly, "the damnable impudence of this doctor of lies, who, denying that black is black, dares affirm both that his party has not hatched plots against the king and that these plots were religious! What did the king do?"

"What else could he do but capitulate?" replied Montaigne. "The cardinal had a knife to his throat. If the Estates dissolved there would be no money! And if Monsieur de Guise were to leave Blois, there would be war! And you can't fight a war without money!"

"So what was the king's expression as he gave in?" I asked after a moment's reflection.

"Inscrutable! The cardinal made him read and sign a retraction of the 'sacrilegious phrase'. But, while the king was reading, the weather—which ever since dawn had been rainy and dark—suddenly got much darker. And, indeed, so dark did it get that they had to light a candle so that the king could continue reading the note and then sign it at the bottom. This all led François d'O, who was standing in the alcove with me, to whisper that it was the king's last will and testament that they'd written there, and that they were lighting the candle to watch him draw his final breath."

"Ah!" I cried. "No! No! The last breath drawn in this affair will not be his, of this I'm sure! The king has declared to the Estates, with all his might, the principles of his politics. He has rightfully condemned Guise, and now, faced with superior forces, has cleverly given way, is tacking and 'trimming his sails', but will never lose sight of the shore where he wants to land."

"Fortune will decide!" mused Montaigne, who surprised me by using the word "Fortune" rather than "God"—as he does throughout his *Essais*, as I noticed later, something that led Rome to censor his writings. Which reminds me that Montaigne also said during this conversation that, having known Guise and Navarre well, he thought that the first was hardly Catholic and the second not very Protestant…

And as for me, having reflected on these words of Montaigne, the use of the word "Fortune" in place of the word "God" led me to believe that he himself was scarcely the one and not very much the other. I say this here without in any way wishing to detract from the merits of this great man.

"The worst part of this," he told me the next morning as he was taking leave of me, carrying in his bags a letter I'd written to my father, "is that the king, after this retraction, is going to appear soft, timid and a coward, and that there won't be any affront that the Estates, the League and Guise will not direct at him."

In this, he was not mistaken, except that the word "affront" was far too weak to describe the rebuffs that the king had to endure over the next two months. The hatred and disdain that the League-supporting Estates felt for him knew no bounds, as I was to witness every day, placed as I was among the Forty-five during these interminable sessions.

To the king—who didn't want Navarre to be stripped of his rights to the crown without having listened to him, and who said, "It would surely be just at least to have a discussion with him and determine whether he wants to convert!"—the Estates replied, with great clamour, "A king *who was once a heretic* shall never govern us!" Even if he were to convert, they wanted none of Navarre! The zeal of these fanatics took them even further than the Pope would have gone.

The Estates held the strings of the purse, and, far from loosening them, tightened them considerably, so that it was clear that they were trying to strangle the king. They wanted him to declare all-out war on his Huguenot subjects but refused him the means to do so: neither subsidies, nor contributions, nor extraordinary subventions would they offer, and all taxes that had been established since 1576 were suppressed. The king pleaded reason to these fanatics. "Messieurs," he said, "how can I be expected to make do with the taxes agreed all those years ago when the cost of living has increased so much? How do you propose I live? To refuse money is to defeat me and to defeat yourselves and the state with us." One of the deputies shouted in reply: "*Then don't be king any more!*"

At the beginning of December, one of the deputies of the Third Estate proposed, "as a demand from the Estates to the king, that he reform his household by dispensing with the Forty-five", and this was heartily applauded, since most people thought that this had been suggested to him by Guise. When we returned to the Two Pigeons Inn and heard a report of this motion, La Bastide and Montseris began pacing up and down in our room, rolling their eyes, and La Bastide exclaimed through clenched teeth:

"*Cap de Diou!* These Guise brothers are devils incarnate! They want to take the bread from our mouths!"

"Am I going to have to go looking for work at my age?" moaned Montseris, who was almost thirty.

"Or return to our Gascon misery?" said La Bastide. "'Sblood! I won't stand for it! It's clear that this shithead Guise wants to take the wasp's sting away before crushing him."

"You're right!" added Montseris. "What are we doing here but being the dogs protecting this lamb! Whoever chases the dogs away wants to devour the lamb! There's not a man who doesn't understand this! *Cap de Diou!*" he continued, his hand on his dagger. "Let the king give me this Guise and I'll make lace of his liver!"

I repeated these words to the king, who, having gathered his Forty-five around him in the chateau at dawn—a time when Monsieur de Guise, who slept at the chateau, was still asleep, exhausted by his revels with Madame de Noirmoutiers—told them that in no case would he consent to be separated from them, holding them each in such affection that he considered them his sons; that he loved them in proportion to the hatred others directed at them, not without reason, since they were his sword and shield; and that even if they reduced him to one capon for his dinner, he'd share it with them.

"*Captatio benevolentiae*," observed my secretary, Miroul, when I repeated these words to him. "I think the king will prevail. He knows men so well. And he's so clever…"

As for me, I was champing at the bit, for the simple reason that, after two months, and I don't know how many attempts by Giacomi, I hadn't been able to meet La Cavalletta, much less Venetianelli, since his lady, more distrustful than a weasel and sensing that my overtures originated with the king, couldn't help but rebut them, since her favourite was linked to Guise's fortunes.

Towards mid-December, however, having heard from Giacomi that La Cavalletta was now engaging in the magical arts, selling very expensive bewitched dolls and potions (which may have been poisons), I had the *maestro* show me her window (since it seemed that she had a weakness for him); then, having persuaded the king to lend me five of his Forty-five (including La Bastide and Montseris) for this expedition, we managed to enter her room at midnight by means of a ladder and a broken pane, and found a blazing fire waiting for her to finish her damnable activities.

As we had quite a while to wait, I began to examine the place, and was lucky enough to discover, in a sewing basket, a doll that resembled the king, and whose heart was pierced through by a needle. To tell the truth, the resemblance was limited to the fact that the effigy was male and wore a crown, as well as earrings on both ears and pearls on each side of its face. The strange thing was that the pearls were sewn directly into the cheeks, the ears having been omitted to simplify the labour.

Hearing steps on the staircase, I barely had time to stuff my discovery in my breeches and put my mask back on, since I didn't want La Cavalletta to be able to describe me to anyone if I ended up being unable to persuade her. But Fortune smiled on me on this occasion, for, as the door opened, I saw that she wasn't alone: her favourite was following her, and I immediately recognized Venetianelli from Giacomi's description. Seeing them both caught in our net and that the door was locked from within by the favourite, my Gascons and I emerged from our hiding places, whereupon, all six of us having surrounded them with daggers in hand, I said, with the greatest calm:

"I would like you to remain silent. Any cry would be fatal for your throats."

At this, La Cavalletta, who certainly seemed to have earned this nickname of "grasshopper" given the length of her legs and arms, her long face and very bright eyes, said, without batting an eye:

"What do you want? Money? There isn't any."

"Fie, Madame," I answered, "do I look like a bad boy, I who have to hunt them down? You don't understand who you're dealing with!"

"Monsieur," replied La Cavalletta very proudly, and no more discomfited than if our daggers had been made of paper, "I know that in any case I have no business with you!"

"I wouldn't bet on it!" I answered, surprised at her insolence. "The rope has plenty of business with the hanged and the executioner with witches! And I doubt that you're incombustible, no matter how well placed your friends are, who would prefer to see you sacrificed if the practices in which you engage are seen to be criminal enough to compromise them! You cannot be unaware of the great care these lords take in their good reputations."

"Monsieur, I don't understand you," replied La Cavalletta.

"Madame," I replied with a special emphasis on the word, "it's *magical* that you don't understand me, since my assertions are so clear and since I have the proof in my breeches…"

At this she threw an anguished glance at the basket of rags and paled, though she managed not lose her composure—unlike Venetianelli, who looked visibly undone by our daggers and my words. I could see that his legs were getting very shaky.

"Well, Monsieur," she conceded, though maintaining her haughty air, "I'm listening. What do you want?"

Instead of responding, I just stood there silently looking at her, noticing that she was put together in an unusual way: her head (though quite oval, with a pointed chin) was very small, her shoulders puny and her torso oddly short; her legs, however, were very long, to the point that, since I couldn't actually see them under her hoop skirt, I might have thought she was walking on stilts! As for her arms, which were momentarily folded, her hands over her stomach, I had the impression that if she extended them they'd reach all the way to the wall behind me. And yet, despite this disproportion, La Cavalletta was not ugly. She had bright, black eyes, a straight nose and nicely formed lips. As for her bosom, given how narrow and short her torso was, it was surprisingly luscious, firm and milky. Looking again at her face I realized that I couldn't have seen her turn pale as I thought, because she was so heavily made up—rather, I had been given this impression by her nostrils, which had pinched up at the mention of the words "witches" and "magic".

"Madame," I said at length, "I want nothing more than a private interview with Signore Venetianelli, in this little cabinet here. Will you consent to this?"

"Seigneur Venetianelli is not a suckling babe! He can talk with whomever he wishes."

"Signore," I said, "will you agree to the conversation?"

"Yes, Monsieur," he murmured, after having cast a desperate at La Cavalletta, who had closed her eyes and was nibbling furiously on a lace handkerchief.

"Madame," I said, "I will ask you to be seated on the stool and not to move a muscle or say a single word during our conversation. Montseris," I said in Provençal to my Gascon roommate, who was standing next to me, "be sure not to accept *anything* from this *drola*,[*] neither a bite to eat nor any wine—and that goes for the lot of you."

This said, I sheathed my dagger, took a candle from the bedside table and lit it from the chandelier; then, seizing Venetianelli by the arm, I pushed him into the little room and closed the door behind us.

"Signore, are you going to kill me?" stammered Venetianelli, who I could see by the candlelight was trembling from head to foot.

I laughed in response and looked him over more curiously than I'd done previously, when I'd been focused on La Cavalletta, never having seen anyone like her. And, in truth, Venetianelli had nothing strange about him, being a pretty little *signore*, whose very diminutive size was the most amazing thing about him: he was a head shorter than La Cavalletta, with a soft and fearful demeanour—in contrast to hers, which was so arch and commanding.

"Signore," I began, "my job is not to go killing people, but to protect the king and his loyal subjects from assassination, which would include murders committed from afar using bewitched dolls and other damnable practices. If I were to arrest you right now, along with La Cavalletta, not even the Cardinal de Guise could protect you from being burnt at the stake."

"But I'm not involved in her work!" he pleaded, his lips atremble and sweat pouring down his cheeks.

"Who will believe you?" I said staring him in the eye. "And who could possibly believe you're not since you're her husband and thus must surely have taken part in her witchcraft?"

At this, Venetianelli fell silent, and so did I, but I was careful to drop my threatening looks. His eyes gradually lost their fear and began to gleam with a certain Italian finesse, though he was still uncertain and tremulous.

---

[*]   "Girl."

"Monsieur," he whispered, his mouth so dry that I could see by the candlelight that filaments of saliva were drying on his lips, "is there any way that I could correct this unfortunate impression?"

"Well, there *is* one, Signore. I hear from time to time reports from a fellow who, being a valet of the Lorraine household, serves at their table and listens to their conversations. You wouldn't know or even suspect him. However, another story, coming from you and whispered in my ear, unconnected to the first but corroborating it, would be very precious to me."

"Precious? How precious, Signore?" breathed Venetianelli, regaining his breath and looking infinitely relieved.

"Precious enough for me to let sleeping dogs lie."

"Ah, Monsieur! That wouldn't be enough to satisfy La Cavalletta," he countered. "She'll require you to return what belongs to her so that she can destroy it."

"Signore," I smiled, "I'm not a man to make your *signora* unhappy, who can *giocare con sua bambola** as soon as my master has left Blois and your stories have, as I believe they will, satisfied me. Signore, do we have an agreement?"

"*Chi tace acconsente*,"† said Venetianelli. "Tell me where to meet you and my mouth will be there, unbeknownst to my conscience, not wanting to bite the hand that feeds me."

"Signore," I laughed, "the scruples of conscience are much less sharp than a needle in the heart of a doll. I can be found at the Two Pigeons Inn every night. You'll find my ears wide open if you'll just ask Monsieur de La Bastide. Signore, I wish you goodnight and advise you not to leave Blois—your departure might be interpreted as a flight by the suspicious."

*

---

* "Play with her puppet."
† "Silence means consent."

This all took place on the night of 15th December, and I didn't have long to wait, for, on the evening of the 18th, La Bastide, who was rolling dice with Montseris in the common room, brought Signore Venetianelli up to see me. Whereupon La Bastide left and I hid Miroul with an escritoire behind the bed curtains so that he could take careful notes of this conversation. I myself put on a mask, having little confidence in the man, who, when he entered the room, looked with such suspicion at the drawn curtains that I laughed:

"Signore, I didn't hide any *spadaccini* there to kill you! Sit down here on this stool, next to me, and tell me your story, which I'm most curious to hear and to compare to the one I've already heard." (Of course, I hadn't heard any other story, but had made up the bit about the other spy so that he wouldn't embroider his own version too much.)

"Monsieur," Venetianelli began, "you therefore already know that there was a dinner given by Monsieur de Guise, last night, to which he invited the Cardinal de Guise, the archbishop of Lyons, the aged president of Neuilly, La Chapelle-Marteau, Maineville and Madame de Montpensier."

"Yes, I know who was there," I confirmed, though feeling quite uneasy since the only guests at this dinner were Guise's council of rabid zealots, all of whom hated the king—not least the archbishop of Lyons, whom Henri had accused of simony and incest with his sister, and who, in retaliation, had written a libellous accusation against Henri and Épernon. Neuilly, who couldn't say two words without whining, had such a tender heart that, sixteen years previously, he had taken advantage of the St Bartholomew's day massacre to have the president of La Place assassinated so he could take his place. La Chapelle-Marteau, the lanky, bent-nosed thief who'd taken three écus from Alizon and me on the day of the barricades, was a counsellor at the Court of Accounts who "knew how to feather his own nest". The Seigneur de Maineville turned up frequently in Mosca's reports as having served as a go-between for Guise and the League at its beginnings, and I knew him, without having met him, as a cold, cunning fellow, who cared no more for the life of a man than for that of a chicken. As for la Montpensier, she has lit up so many pages of this account with her sulphurous flames that I can leave it to my reader to judge her.

"Monsieur de Guise," Venetianelli recounted, "seemed somewhat disquieted, and when his brother, the cardinal, asked him the reason, he said that he'd heard so many accounts from so many different people that the king wanted to dispatch him, that he wondered if it wouldn't be better for his personal safety to leave Blois.

"'No, no!' cried the archbishop. 'Monseigneur, you must not think of it! He who leaves the game loses it! Will we ever have a better chance than this given that the Estates are ours? The king is not a madman, he wouldn't want to destroy himself trying to destroy you. Moreover, he's more woman than man and will never have enough resolve to arrange an assassination, even if he's thought about it!'

"Monsieur," Venetianelli continued, "you doubtless know that the archbishop is expecting to be named a cardinal, and that he fears his chance will founder if Guise flounders."

"Yes, I know," I answered gravely, "but go on, Signore: your 'founders' and 'flounders' are very gallant. One can see, thanks to your native Italy, that your talent for these *concetti** has enhanced the elegance of your French."

"Monsieur, I thank you," gushed Venetianelli, who seemed delighted with my compliment, since he was, in general, so full of himself. I noticed that, as he spoke, he kept admiring his hands, or else his image in the mirror opposite. "The president of Neuilly," he continued, "spoke next after the duc, with tears in his eyes, as usual, pleading both sides of the argument without being aware of the contradiction.

---

* "Elegant plays on words."

"'Well, Monseigneur,' he said, 'you must certainly look out for your safety, since your loss would mean our collective loss. And yet, I believe that you must ignore the warnings you've received, and remain here, unless you'd like to leave in order to better preserve your life, which is so precious to us, since ours so depend on yours.'"

"Well, that's as clear as mud!" I laughed.

"The next speaker was worse!" smiled Venetianelli. "It was La Chapelle-Marteau, and he drove home the point.

"'We shouldn't be afraid,' he said in his raucous voice, 'since we're the stronger party. And yet I don't trust the king. We must not flee but strike first.'"

"Did he say 'strike'?" I said, frowning.

"In truth, I'm not sure whether he said 'strike' or 'act'. You know, the fellow hardly opens his mouth when he speaks, he's so miserly and doesn't want to share his breath."

I encouraged my Italian spy with another smile at this little joke, sensing that the more Venetianelli let himself go with his natural verve, the more he'd reveal about the dinner.

"As for Maineville (whom the king calls 'Maine-League', as you know), he spoke furiously, horns lowered, with that bull's face of his.

"'The archbishop of Lyons,' he noted, 'is completely wrong to say that the king isn't a madman. And as for saying that, being more female than male, he doesn't have what it takes to strike—that is a huge mistake, Monsieur! The king *is* mad: he'll strike without regard for the consequences. And as for having 'enough resolve', did Catherine de' Medici have 'enough resolve' to kill Coligny? So if the mother didn't lack what it takes, then the son may not lack it either, since he's of the Florentine race and therefore capable of poisoning and assassination! Be very afraid of the Medici family! My advice is that we shouldn't dawdle here. If we don't flee, then we must act and do so before the king does.'"

"Signore," I said, "I'm not surprised you're an actor! You are an entire theatre all by yourself! Your scene is well presented and your actors so lively! I can't wait to hear what the duc will say!"

"Well, Monsieur, you're going to be very disappointed!" replied Venetianelli, who stole a look in the mirror and appeared to be quite satisfied with his corporeal form. "The duc didn't play his role very well. I expected him to be more trenchant, but he seemed vague, evasive, yet very full of swagger:

"'If I were to see death coming through the window, I wouldn't rush out the door!' he cried. But as for a decision, there was nothing in the slightest, which made his brother so impatient that he shouted furiously, his black eyes shooting sparks:

"'Monsieur my brother! You always do things by halves! If you'd listened to me, we wouldn't be in such difficulty with the king as we are today!'

"'That's the way to talk!' applauded la Montpensier, who, rising from her chair, limped over to her brother-in-law the cardinal and kissed him on the mouth. ''Sblood!' she continued. 'Let's bury this king–queen in a convent and be done with it! Monsieur my brother, you can hold his head between your knees and, with my scissors, I'll tonsure him and make his third crown in the centre of his head… Messieurs, I think this Valois gentleman will make an excellent monk, since he's already so practised at self-mortification and fasting that the Lord will not wait long before calling him to His side…'

"This so amused and tickled the cardinal that, rising, he raised his cup majestically and shouted:

"'I drink to the future king of France!'"

"Signore," I reflected after a moment's thought, "this is beautifully told! I don't doubt that the advice of the zealots will carry the day, but the strange thing is the way the duc continues to beat about the bush!"

"But that's because he feels so great, so strong, so supported and loved by the people and so sustained by the three orders that he believes he's invincible—like the Armada," said Venetianelli with a smile, "or like Goliath."

"Signore," I laughed, "you don't seem very unhappy to be forced by me to bite the hand that feeds you!"

"That's because," Venetianelli snarled, his dander up, "he doesn't feed me at his table, but standing, in the kitchen, with the skivvies and the scullions—which I consider a great injury to my talent. The Doge of Venice never treated me that way!"

"Signore," I reassured him, placing my hands on his shoulders with apparent respect, "I am neither the Doge of Venice nor the Duc de Guise, but I would be very honoured to have you at my table, seeing as I'm dealing with a man of quality and who serves so honourably the Muse of comedy. Signore, please continue, I beg you, on the other hand, to serve the king, and you will thereby discover many other advantages than the destruction of an unlucky *bambola*."

At that I embraced him warmly, and, having walked him to the stairs, left him as happy with me as he was with himself (which was no mean amount) and returned to my room to remove both my mask and my pretence of civility—for, by the end, I couldn't stomach this rascal, who, I believed, was something of a blackguard and, worse, was the favourite of a well-known procuress.

Miroul emerged from behind the bed curtains, exclaiming:

"Well, Monsieur, that was very entertaining, listening to him miming the voices of these great lords on whom our happiness or unhappiness depends. And isn't it extraordinary that this little worm, Venetianelli, is inserting in the wheels of these great intrigues an infinitely little grain of sand that risks having such a huge impact on history! His story is a powder keg! And who do you believe will be blown up?"

"Ah, you're asking me? I'm not sure it's right to pray to the Lord to kill a man, but, 'sblood! I'm praying for it!"

I then spent two long hours with Miroul, going over his notes and my own recollection of what was said, so that we'd have the entire conversation verbatim, and could preserve the essence and substance, as well as the eloquence, of his remarkable story.

This done, I would have run immediately to the chateau, despite the dark and rainy night—but, alas, I couldn't without the Forty-five, in whose ranks I was, by order of the king, to conceal myself at all times. Therefore, I had to wait until morning, and, as is easily imagined, I was able to get very little sleep during that interminable night, tossing and turning on my bed while the Gascons serenaded me with their snores—and swearing, for they swore even while sleeping, La Bastide in particular, who dreamt every night that the Forty-five were being chased by Guise and the Estates, and that he had to seek shelter.

Laugnac announced me to the usher, Nambu, early the next morning, and Nambu announced me to Du Halde, who came out to find me in the old cabinet and told me, since I'd asked after the king's well-being:

"Winter is not his best season. Although he's easy enough to serve at every other time of year, at times of bad weather he becomes almost insufferable. As soon as it clouds over, he grows gloomy. He complains when the wind begins to blow. When it's raining he's practically in tears. And when it's freezing? He gets stiff. Don't even think of talking to him about pleasurable distractions at such times. He lives like a hermit in his cell, stays up late, sleeps little, gets up early, works from dawn till dusk, nearly kills his four secretaries with all the work he gives them, wears out the chancellor, is unforgiving of mistakes, denounces excessive expenses (imagine!), and becomes, in short, incredibly meddlesome, fussy, worried, suspicious, quick to anger and bitter—he believes the entire world is plotting against him and that even the rain has betrayed him!"

"Well!" I thought, as Du Halde led me into the king's chambers. "What His Majesty is going to hear from me and read from my pen is not going to cure him of his choler and dark mood!"

The king was standing on the other side of the room, warming himself in front of a meagre fire, and I could see from his wrinkled brow and the downward turn at the corners of his mouth that Du Halde was right.

"Ah, my son!" he said as he withdrew his hand almost before I'd kissed it. "I never see you any more! You've abandoned me! And enough, I beg you, of these grimaces and genuflections! I know from experience that the one who genuflects the most is the greatest traitor! And what a traitor and how excessively stupid was the architect employed by my grandfather who designed this room with the throne at one end and the fireplace at the other in this ridiculous alcove, as if a king, just because he's king, wouldn't feel the cold! I have been suffering from it ever since this pitiless sky hid the sun from me two months ago, since when I haven't caught even a glimpse of it! Ah, my son! This world does not love us, which forces us to live interminably in the shadows, cold and rain. Du Halde, it's midnight in here at high noon! Have more candles brought in and throw some more logs on the fire! Have we really been reduced to such misery that the king of France doesn't have enough logs for his fire? The Estates want us to catch our deaths of cold even before we starve!"

Meanwhile, Du Halde had the valets bring in more logs and candles to light up the room, and the king, bending over the fire, whispered to me:

"My son, you must have found your man, since you're here. And what did he say? Speak sotto voce since this floor might have ears."

And so I quietly recounted the story Venetianelli had told me, while the king listened without batting an eyelid or pursing his lips, but with his eyes closed, his head to one side and his body immobile in a very meditative air. Afterwards, he said not a word, other than to thank me for having minutely copied out the words of Venetianelli, whose name, I noticed, he refused to pronounce, calling him "the man" or "the fellow". Barely, however, had he taken the manuscript from my hands when there was a knock at the door that led from the king's chambers down, via a spiral staircase, to the queen mother's room, which was located directly beneath his. Which is why, I believe, he'd said that the floor might have ears.

"Sire," said the usher, passing his head through the very narrow opening he'd made, "it is Madame de Sauves, who is bringing Her Majesty the queen mother to be received by you."

"Monsieur," answered the king, looking at him coldly, "what's the point of placing you at my door, and three of Larchant's guards in the stairway, if you let yourself be besieged by my mother's creatures? Repulse the woman, Monsieur!"

"But sire," said the usher, looking most unhappy, "Madame de Sauves can hear you! She's right behind me!"

"Well then," screamed the king in fury, "since she can hear me, I want her to know that I do not like her sticking to my door like a louse in the hair of a tramp!"

"Sire," the usher cried, "she's running away, her hands over her ears!"

"Well," shouted the king at the top of his lungs as he walked over to the door and stuck his head out, "her *ears*! They're just the part of her I hate! Monsieur," he screamed at the usher, and no doubt at Larchant's guards, "make damnably sure, henceforth, that no ear-bearing being, male or female, is able to put the tip of his or her toe on the first step of that staircase. Do you hear me?"

624

"Sire," observed Du Halde, with a discreetly reproachful air that he alone dared take with the king, "the queen mother will have heard you."

"I hope so!" replied the king, calming down suddenly. "Otherwise, would I have shouted so loudly? Du Halde, am I not the king at least in these few square feet of my rooms? Must I be constantly spied on? My son," he continued sotto voce, turning to me (but, I noticed without naming me), "take Laugnac and a dozen of the Forty-five out to the little pavilion at the end of the gardens. Have a great fire lit and wait for me to join you there with a few trusted friends once the council is done. Also," he added with a sad smile as he offered me his hand, "you, my son, who are so bright, find a way to make this interminable rain stop! By the holy fog, it will be the end of me!"

It was well after noon and the council long since finished when I saw, one by one, the "trusted friends" of the king arrive at the little pavilion at the end of the park: François d'O, Rambouillet, the great *écuyer* Bellegarde, Alphonse d'Ornano, called "the Corsican", the Maréchal d'Aumont, secretary of state Revol, minister of justice Montholon and, finally, the king himself, accompanied by Du Halde, who was trying to keep the diluvian rain from his monarch by means of an Italian *ombrello* so little that it encumbered his arm more than it protected the head of the king. So ineffective was it that the plume on His Majesty's hat was so soaked with rain that the feathers all remained stuck together. Bellegarde pointed this out to the king as he entered the pavilion, and so the king gave his hat to Du Halde and asked him to place it near the fire to return its lustre, but not so near that it burned. All of those present could observe, as I did, the excessive anger of the king at this incident, despite the fact that he had many other subjects, and graver ones, to be vexed about. However, as the flames in the fireplace rose high and bright, and the little room was comfortable and well lit with candles (the pitch-black skies making them necessary), the king's mood lightened by degrees and he joked that it was much better to have a little pavilion where he could be comfortable than a huge, cold chateau where the walls had ears.

As for me, unsure as to whether or not I was invited to be present at this council, I began to leave the room, but the king caught sight of me and asked me to stay, saying that he would need me as a witness. As he sat down with his back to the fire, the king asked Revol to fetch a small leather wallet, from which he drew three or four papers that he held on his lap and quoted from or read to support his words. These papers constituted the proof, he said, of the Duc de Guise's rebellion, of his felony, of his connivance with foreign governments, and of his ongoing plot to assassinate his royal person.

Touching this assassination plot, he read a letter from the Duc de Guise, signed by his hand, in which the duc said to his correspondent that he had the Louvre "so closely surrounded" that he could "answer for what was inside".

"What was inside, Messieurs," said the king with a wry smile, "was me."

He handed this letter to Du Halde for him to carry to his assistants, and then continued, in a measured tone, his indictment, in which he claimed to have proof that the duc was soliciting monies from a foreign prince in order to provide resources for his enterprises against the crown; as proof, he produced the letter that Guise had written to Felipe II and that I'd been lucky enough to steal from la Montpensier. The Maréchal d'Aumont wanted to know how I'd been able to appropriate this document; the king bade me explain, which, as you would expect, made me feel somewhat ashamed, but His Majesty insisted, and so I consented in the end to tell the embarrassing story, which did not fail to produce some smiles, particularly from the Maréchal d'Aumont, who was a Frenchman of the old school, very devoted to his country and to his king, and who said to me, half-joking and half-serious, that there were no lengths one would not in good conscience go to serve one's sovereign.

The king denounced the League's plot, and the Estates for reducing him virtually to impoverishment by refusing to grant him any funds, and for conniving with Guise's plot to seize his person. In support of this claim, he read Venetianelli's report exactly as I'd written it down, and this produced a very powerful effect—although it was less powerful than the one I produced by removing from my leggings the bewitched doll that I'd taken from La Cavalletta's basket. I did this in answer to François d'O's question as to how I'd been able to get such a hold on the actor, and the king was the most surprised of all, since I hadn't had time that morning to show him the magic *bambola* by which they had planned to kill him from a distance.

The king then discussed his resentment of the Duc de Savoie, who, in October, had seized the Marquisate of Saluzzo, the last of France's possessions in Italy, and there was no doubt, given the connections between the Duc de Savoie and the Duc de Guise, that the former would never have risked such a venture without the latter's assent. And no doubt Guise had offered this assent in return for promises of troops and money to wage war on his own king.

"Messieurs," said Henri, "the thing is clear and I've now acquainted you with all of the proofs which show and make certain and assured that Monsieur de Guise has plotted to seize the kingdom, after having destroyed its foundations. Well, Messieurs, given that you are the firmest of those foundations, whose destruction would closely precede or follow mine, I must ask you, what do you advise me to do in this predicament?"

Having said this, he turned towards the minister of justice, Montholon, who was, with Revol, one of the ministers appointed after the firing of the queen mother's puppets, and assuredly a very honest man and very faithful to the king, but whose large eyes in the middle of his round face betrayed not a whit of intelligence or talent.

"Sire," said Montholon, "it is my opinion that, in this troubled and dangerous state of affairs in which the hand of Monsieur de Guise has played such a destructive and major part, it would be best to arrest him and bring him to trial."

"Rambouillet?" said the king, his face inscrutable.

"By my faith, sire, I agree with Montholon."

"Revol?"

The secretary of state, Revol was as much a man of the law as Montholon, and one would have expected him to acquiesce to the proposition of the minister of justice, especially since his weak and timorous demeanour seemed to predispose him to it, being very feeble, with a long, white face that made him look as though he were turning into chalk. But he created considerable surprise when he said in his gentle and timid voice:

"Sire, if you arrest Monsieur de Guise, where will you find the place, the judges and the witnesses to conduct this trial? Cato, the wisest of the Romans, said that it was much better to strike a traitor to one's country down than to have him arrested and then consult as to whether to condemn him to death. When the state is in peril, the execution must precede the judgement."

"D'Aumont?"

"Sire," the maréchal replied in his raucous voice, "we would be dishonoured and our swords as well, if we were to tolerate for one more day the insults of this traitor! The more we bend, the more he puts his foot on our chests! To hell with the trial! When the crime is lese-majesty, a prompt death is the only punishment."

"François d'O?"

"Sire," said François d'O, "I am also of this opinion."

"Bellegarde?"

"Sire, d'Aumont has said what we must do."

"My Corsican?"

"Sire, as Revol has said, the punishment must precede the judgement."

"I believe so as well," said the king, after a moment of silence, "since I've debated with myself for quite some time and decided that a trial would be completely impossible in the straits in which I find myself. And yet, I have difficulty reaching the decision that you're recommending since I abhor bloodshed. But in the end, I believe that since my arch-enemy is ever pushing his advantage further, allowing him to continue living will mean my death, the deaths of all of my friends and the ruination of my kingdom. Guise is too powerful for us to be able to arrest and try him. To throw him in prison would be to throw a net over a wild boar that can easily tear through the string."

"Sire," said Rambouillet, who, despite not being a flatterer in the least, nourished unlimited admiration for the king, along with a naive and sincere affection for the man, "if your position does not agree with mine, then mine must be wrong. I will take your side in this."

The king smiled and turned to Montholon, who, however, remained silent, having as he did the obstinacy of an ass or a mule, which made him persevere on the wrong path simply because it was the path he'd chosen. I believe that this silence was the reason Henri dismissed him a short time afterwards, on suspicion that Montholon was in league with Guise—something that, in my opinion, was false.

In any case, Montholon said not a word, his eyes closed in defiance, and the king elected to say no more, but turned to Du Halde and asked him what time it was according to the watch that hung around his neck. Then, saying that he should not remain too long outside his principal lodgings, he gave us leave to depart, either because he wished to meditate some more on his decision, or else because, his decision made, he wished to keep the date and the circumstances of its execution secret.

On 20th December, a Tuesday, I received a visit at nightfall at the Two Pigeons Inn from Venetianelli, who seemed quite jubilant at the idea of satisfying his anger at his protector by dropping in my lap some news that was swelling his cheeks. However, sensing the weight and value of this new information, he first wanted to bargain with me on an acceptable price, and asked me to return the *bambola* before he even opened his mouth. Unwilling to consent to this, yet being very anxious to conserve the good graces of this vain and touchy fellow, I flattered him up and down, and, as Margot brought me my dinner, urged him to share his news with me, claiming that since I felt such friendship and trust in him, I didn't want to hide my face from him any longer. So saying, I removed my mask (which I was forced to do in any case by my repast) and assured him that, the next time, I would reveal my name and parentage to him, hinting that they were among the highest in the kingdom. As for the *bambola*, which I placed between us on the table, I begged him to agree to let me decide when I would return it to him. To which Venetianelli ultimately agreed, so impressed was he by my civility and condescension.

"Monsieur," he said, as soon as Margot had brought our meat and pitchers of wine, and closed the door behind her, "what I have to tell is but one word, but this word is worth an entire book, such heavy and huge consequences does it have for the great men whom it concerns: the 'great man of Blois', as Nostradamus would say, by which the king is clearly designated, and his 'friend', which can designate only Guise."

"Well," I said, only advancing my paw in this matter to withdraw it, "you know Nostradamus's prediction!"

"I know it," said Venetianelli, with an air of immense and incommunicable wisdom, "and I believe that it is entirely certain, since it affirms that the 'great man of Blois' cannot help but kill his 'friend' since it is written in the stars."

"Ah, yes, the stars!" I smiled. "Which, according to Regiomontanus, have already predicted the end of the world in 1588! We are but ten days away from 1589 and the world is still here, as solid as ever, and seems little disposed to disintegrate under our feet."

"Monsieur," replied Venetianelli, "if you don't believe in the stars, believe at least in personalities. If I were to tell Guise that he would be killed tomorrow, he'd laugh in my face. What's the use of handing a mirror to a man if his power blinds him? Guise is from Lorraine, and even if the court of France has cleaned him up a bit, he still suffers from a certain Germanic dullness that cannot help being trumped by the Florentine finesse of the son of Catherine de' Medici. Moreover, the king is a sodomite—and who says 'sodomite' says 'actor'."

"Signore," I smiled, "I admire your Venetian lucidity, but, I beg you, don't keep me in suspense! Tell me the 'word' that you mentioned and I shall decide whether it's worth, as you claim, an entire book."

"Or at least a doll," he replied. "Monsieur, here it is. Try telling me it's not charged with powder to the maximum: tomorrow, Monsieur, at the very latest, after Mass or vespers, the Duc de Guise will tell the king that, being tired and bruised by all the suspicions that have been directed at him by His Majesty concerning his most innocent actions, he has decided to resign his title of lieutenant general and leave Blois."

"Well," I said, open-mouthed, "this seems to me to be excessively threatening. But, Signore," I added, heaping on the compliments not with a spoon but a trowel, as if I were addressing a lady, "you, whose penetrating vision pierces the most arcane hidden intentions, can you tell me what the duc's motivations are in this half-break from his king?"

"He hopes that the king, terrified by his departure, will try to retain him by promoting him to the position of constable of France or, which amounts to the same thing, that the Estates will beg the king to confer this title on him, threatening to dissolve and leave him penniless if he refuses."

"Well, Signore!" I replied. "I would never have imagined such an exorbitant and arrogant request! If I remember correctly, we haven't had a constable of France for twenty years, given how much our kings have feared to invest anyone with such immense powers as to make him the rival of the sovereign. Guise, constable! He who is already king of Paris! And the king of the Estates-General! 'Sblood! He'd be an enormous cat, with the king a very little mouse."

"But then," said Venetianelli with a conspiratorial smile, "he would only have more reason to get rid of the cat, before it can fatten itself on him!"

That was exactly the thought that occurred to me at that very moment, but I had no interest in divulging it to this actor, especially since he wouldn't have many more occasions to share his precious provender with me, so I contented myself with saying:

"Signore, you didn't disappoint me: the one word spoke volumes. Here is the *bambola*. It's yours. But permit me, before you return it to La Cavalletta, to remove this needle from its heart—such an insult to and contradiction of the stars and Nostradamus. If, however, by the end of this week, you hear any news of great consequence, may I count on your friendship to inform me of it?"

Venetianelli assured me of it, as he said a fond goodbye with such an effusion of friendship that I felt somewhat ashamed of the underhand means I had employed. But can't a rascal who's proud of his knavery also have some natural naivety that makes him amiable and tolerable?

15

I T WAS AT SEVEN O'CLOCK the next morning, Wednesday, 21st December, that I was able to see the king and report what I'd heard as he was removing his earrings. He was astonished at my account; then, having glanced at Du Halde, he looked at me with total incredulity.

"Well, my son! This is unexpected! But it's so imprudent that I can't believe it! Even from Guise! In any case, I'll see him at Mass at eight o'clock in the Saint-Calais chapel, and afterwards, and if he speaks to me, I'll have a clear heart, or, if your man is correct, a very confused one. Du Halde," he continued, "since my lazy secretary hasn't arrived yet, may I ask you to write a note to Madame de Sauves?"

"Happily, sire!" replied Du Halde, before going to fetch an escritoire and settling it on his knees.

"Here it is," said the king.

Madame, I would be most unhappy if you were not to consent to the prayer that I make you in these sad lines, that you be willing to forgive me for having dared to speak ill of your ears, which, I remember, are the prettiest in the kingdom—and would be even more so if you were to oblige me by accepting these jewels from me. Your humble and devoted and affectionate servant, Henri.

"Sire," objected Du Halde, his austere face becoming even longer, "you're being too delicate with a creature, who, on orders from the queen mother, consorts with the Magnificent. These people are already too quick to find you soft, timid and infinitely forgiving."

"Let them believe that! I wouldn't be a bit sorry if they did right now," said the king, throwing me a conspiratorial look. "My son, please wait in the old oratory; I'll see you after Mass."

This old oratory was situated to the left of his chamber as you looked out of the windows, and to reach it you had to pass through a very low door, like most of those in this wing of the chateau, which is all the more strange in that this part of the chateau was built by François I, who was unusually tall, and must have had to bend over a lot. This door was adorned with a tapestry, no doubt to keep out the cold.

The oratory itself was a small rectangular room, empty of any furniture since it was no longer used for Mass, and lit by a large and beautiful window that opened onto an Italian loggia. Opposite this window was another low door, which gave onto the "old cabinet", a square room with a large table and five or six stools in it. A fireplace was set into the walls in the old cabinet, which were covered with wooden carvings, some of which opened by a secret mechanism that was hidden in the skirting board to reveal hiding places, where I imagined that the king kept his most precious documents. Du Halde told me later that the cabinet of the queen mother on the second floor was likewise adorned with fine wooden panels that hid cupboards, but that hers were on the exterior side of the room, whereas his were on the courtyard side. I'll take his word for it since I was never able to put the tip of my toe in Jezebel's den.

I spent more than an hour waiting for the king in the old oratory, biting my nails and shivering, since the room wasn't heated, finally seeking refuge in the old cabinet, where I found, thank God, a blazing fire and six of the Forty-five, whom I knew pretty well and asked in Provençal if I could join them, to which they agreed very politely. But seeing them happily occupied in a game of cards, I went over to the window that looked out on the courtyard and the Louis XII wing, which I loved, since both walls and adjoining tower were constructed with a pleasing mixture of brick and stone. Although the use of brick is unknown in my native Périgord, since we have such beautiful ochre stone to work with, the noble rusticity of this wing somehow reminded me of my crenellated nest at Mespech. This association turned quickly from pleasurable to melancholic, since I found myself pining for the countryside of my youth, all the more so given the perpetual rain falling outside, so typical of the Sarlat region in winter, and whose dank odour is still in my nostrils now, mingled with the smell of chestnuts, which were always roasting in the fireplace.

I was in the midst of these thoughts about my youth when I saw a group of men emerge from the Saint-Calais chapel across the courtyard, two of whom broke away and strolled off together: the Duc de Guise, in his grey satin doublet, and the king, dressed in black velvet with the Order of the Holy Spirit attached to his collar and his head coiffed under his plumed hat. The two began to walk along under the covered gallery of the Louis XII wing, the columns obscuring their faces every now and then, which I would have wanted to study, knowing as I did the subject of their conversation. They talked for more than an hour, but I was unable (as were, no doubt, the group of men watching them) to discern whether their discussion was angry or animated. The only thing I noticed was that, at several different moments, Guise removed his great plumed hat, whereupon the king begged him to put it back on with a gesture from which I could conclude nothing, the duc being so prone to doffing his cap at all times, and the king so courteous.

Ultimately, the two men parted ways, and the king crossed the courtyard under driving rain dressed only in his doublet. But, strangely, when Du Halde ran up to him brandishing his Italian *ombrello*, the king spun around impatiently and scolded him furiously, whereupon poor Du Halde had to conclude that his services weren't needed. The king had begun to climb the staircase, and, since the door between the oratory and the king's chamber was open, I raised the tapestry and waited in the doorway, ready to respond to the king's call, sensing from his treatment of Du Halde that he was in one of his angry moods. But this one surpassed any I'd previously witnessed, for as soon as he'd entered his chamber, and the door having scarcely closed behind him, he ripped off his plumed hat and threw it furiously on the floor. This gesture reminded me of his brother, Charles IX, who, sixteen years before, as he was playing tennis with Guise, Téligny and me, was suddenly beside himself with rage when he heard Yolet tell him that there'd just been an attempt on the life of Coligny, and threw his racquet on the ground.

"Sire!" Du Halde said reproachfully as he picked up the hat. "Look! You've broken the crest irreparably!"

"'Tis a symbol, Du Halde!" screamed the king at the top of his lungs. "A symbol! And you know very well of what!"

"Sire," said Du Halde reproachfully, "you're going to awaken Madame the queen mother, who is in a very bad way and took some medicine this morning."

"Bah!" snarled the king, grinding his teeth. "Women have seven lives like cats! Madame my mother will bury me and follow my funeral cortège, her arm resting on her 'old woman's walking stick', as she likes to call him. Du Halde," he continued, holding his hand up to his ear and looking very bewildered, "where are my earrings?"

"But sire, you made Madame de Sauves a present of them this morning!"

"Heavens!" roared the king. "Should I despoil myself while I'm still alive? Make the Magnificent constable! And give my earrings to his whore! Ah, my son," he choked, seeing me standing there in the doorway, "your man wasn't lying!"

"Sire," cautioned Du Halde, "the walls have ears!"

"No, they don't, my Du Halde," said the king, his voice falling by several decibels. "This entire chateau is one immense ear, so fine that even my heartbeats can be heard. And one minute, Du Halde, one minute after my great anger, the Magnificent will know all about it. Du Halde," he continued, speaking more softly and more rapidly, his teeth clenched, "I want to see d'Aumont, Revol, Rambouillet, Bellegarde, François d'O and my Corsican immediately in my old cabinet. Right away, do you hear?"

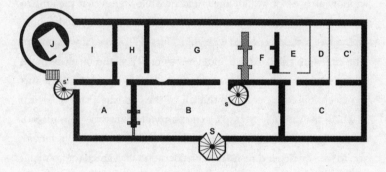

Reader, I have drawn a plan of the second floor of the Château de Blois that will be essential in understanding what follows. *S* designates the marvellous staircase that leads from the courtyard to the various floors, but it is doubled by two others: *s*, which connects the chamber of the queen mother on the first floor with the king's chamber on the second—this is the spiral staircase that we've already seen, since it was on this staircase that Monsieur de Nambu and three of Larchant's guards repulsed Madame de Sauves and her ears; and *s'*, which links the old cabinet (*A*) to the outdoors and allowed the Forty-five to have access to the king's apartments without using the central staircase. *H* is the old oratory, next to the king's chamber, where Henri told me to wait while he went to Mass that Wednesday; as for *I* and *J* (of which

J was in a tower called, God knows why, the "Mill Tower"), they were rooms that served as guards' rooms for the Forty-five, when the king wanted them to assemble nearby. The door in the old cabinet that opened onto *B* (the council room) had been walled up by the king on his arrival in Blois, no doubt to isolate his "cut-throats" (as the Leaguers injuriously labelled them) from the rest of his apartments. When you came from the council room (*B*) into the king's chamber (*G*) you had on your right the great fireplace (which Henri complained was too far away from his throne); opposite the door were two trunks in the window alcoves, on which one could sit while waiting for the king to call one and present his hand. To the left was the king's bed, whose blue velvet curtains, covered with gold fleurs-de-lis, were always drawn. The king didn't like this bed and never slept in it, claiming it was puny, preferring his queen's bed and the warmth of her body since he was so susceptible to the cold. To the left of the bed was a sort of alcove in which the throne—a simple armchair with armrests—was placed. To the right of this chair was a stool, on which the king would invite you to sit—or, depending on the consideration he wanted to show you, *not* invite you to sit—during an audience with him. On the other side of the room, to the left of the great fireplace, was a door that opened into *F*, the "new cabinet". In fact, the king also received visitors on the other side of his apartments in the old cabinet, but he preferred to work in the new cabinet since it was a small room, and especially because it was well heated by the great fireplace.

Two doors opened into the new cabinet: one from *E*, the king's wardrobe, and another from *D*, the new oratory.

I never set foot in *C* or *C'*, and so can't describe their layout; these large rooms were the queen's apartments and so it's possible she had them subdivided…

In the king's new oratory was a small, very pretty altar, which was surmounted by a large crucifix; opposite the altar was a wooden prayer stool covered in gold leaf and cushioned with blue velvet, on which the king knelt for morning prayer and later for a Mass said by his chaplain, unless he decided to go out, cross the courtyard and attend Mass at the Saint-Calais chapel—as he had done this Wednesday morning, 21st December—where he encountered Guise and "was to have his heart cleared or excessively confused".

And that the said heart was pushed beyond all tolerable limits was clearly what this sudden outburst on his return from his conversation with Guise had demonstrated; and, even though the king had finally calmed down, I saw clearly when he came out of his wardrobe, from the worry in his eyes and the twist of his lips, that he had taken the duc's threat to quit the Estates and leave Blois very hard. He was wearing, in the place of his damaged plumes, a pale-blue doublet; on his head was a hat of the same colour but devoid of any feathers, and even though his attire was much more gay and lively than the black velvet he'd been wearing, I could see that he was struggling with very dark thoughts from the anguish in his face.

"My son," he said when he caught sight of me, "run and see if my friends are waiting for me in the old cabinet."

I returned to him with news that all were there save Revol, but that Du Halde had gone to fetch him, according to the others; so the king hurried in, only to find that there were also five or six of his Forty-five there, smoking and playing cards, who, when the king suddenly appeared, were very embarrassed to be so engaged. But the king, speaking to them with his usual benevolence and calling them "my children", sent them off into his chamber to prevent anyone from coming in. Once there they set about their cards again in front of the great fireplace, but were careful to abstain from smoking since the king abhorred tobacco.

Revol arrived, running, preceded by Du Halde, who, on a sign from the king, opened wide one of the windows to clear the awful odour that had filled the room (and which wasn't just from the tobacco!). The king invited us to be seated on the stools and, after having spoken quite a while very softly in Bellegarde's ear, withdrew from our circle and went to stand in front of the fire until the air was clear and the windows could be closed.

Bellegarde was a very handsome gentleman who was fond of petticoats—or, rather, they seemed uncommonly fond of him—but he was of a serious and quiet disposition, entirely faithful to the king, and would have been perfect in every aspect if he not had, like Chicot, a runny nose that continually threatened his ruff and doublet, an infirmity that was the reason the king (who was excessively annoyed by this trait) chided him ceaselessly, despite loving and esteeming him very much.

"Messieurs," said Bellegarde in the raspy voice of one who does not speak much (and without ever naming Guise except by the designation of the *tertium quid*, a strange expression he'd borrowed from mathematics and that means the "third element"), "here is a sketch of the plan that concerns us, and for which, since he'd like it to be fleshed out in greater detail, His Majesty wants your enlightened opinions."

I am not going to reproduce this sketch here, since it was greatly modified in the debate that followed. Nor do I believe that I should identify those who made amendments to the plan, since there would obviously be some danger for them, even today, in being named as the authors of suggestions that contributed to the success of the venture. Hot coals still smoulder beneath the cinders of this civil discord, and proud as one might be to have been among the king's faithful servants in those times, one might also feel alarmed to have one's name exposed to the ongoing vindictiveness of our adversaries, if one were to be credited with the conception of a ruse that our foes might libellously term atrocious or Machiavellian. And, certainly, our plan might well deserve to be so described by a mother, a brother or a wife of one of our enemies, and I would agree to such a designation if there had been any way at all, other than death, of stopping Guise's march towards the throne, the subsequent extermination of "politicals" and Huguenots, and ultimately the subjection of the entire kingdom to the Inquisition.

It was quickly apparent in our debate, conducted in lowered voices and whispers, with Guise referred to only as the *tertium quid*, that the principal difficulty was to isolate him from his followers, since a confrontation between his gentlemen and ours, with all the hazards of combat, might well lead to many casualties, except perhaps the very person whose death would be useful to the state. This was not least because this *tertium quid* (who sensed that he had reason to be constantly on the alert) usually had himself accompanied by all his men right up to the king's door, except on the days the council met, when the hangers-on of all the great men in attendance were so numerous that they waited in the courtyard outside. It was therefore decided that the attempt on his life must made be on a day the council would be meeting (in the room marked *B* on the drawing), and that, in addition, this meeting should be called early in the morning in the hope of reducing his entourage to a very few gentlemen, most of whom would still be in their beds.

Meanwhile, as we were trying vainly to find some justification for holding a meeting at seven o'clock in the morning—an hour at which in December the sun wouldn't yet have risen—the king, who was standing facing the fire, proposed, without even turning round and speaking in nearly a whisper, that the reason could be that he needed to leave for his house in la Noue for a retreat, and hoped the council could meet before he left. Hearing this, one of our number added that the king could use this pretext the night before to demand the keys to the chateau from the *tertium quid*, which he held as grand master of France, in order to close the doors of the chateau after the council had arrived. This would have the effect of closing the trap once the fish was inside.

This precaution was adopted, but wasn't judged to be sufficient to ensure that the *tertium quid* would be separated from his followers, which we resolved to make sure of by having our men block the three staircases that led to the king's apartments (indicated by *S*, *s* and *s'* on the floor plan).

But then we encountered another difficulty that took us a long time to resolve, for though there was no problem in having the Forty-five take over the staircases *s* and *s'*, since they'd be hidden from view there, if they were to occupy the grand staircase of honour (*S*) as the *tertium quid* arrived, they would no doubt alert him to the danger of the situation, since he well knew how much the Forty-five hated him and that they had very good reason.

The king overcame this objection immediately by proposing that Larchant could occupy the grand staircase with a few of his men on the pretext of demanding from the council the back pay that they were owed. Moreover, Larchant could warn the *tertium quid* the night before that he intended to take this action, so that the latter wouldn't be alarmed at seeing them there. There followed a debate about where the *tertium quid* would be dispatched, but the king interrupted it, saying that he'd already decided this privately and that there was no point in raising it and discussing it on this occasion, especially since he hadn't yet decided on the date for the council's meeting. He thanked us for our views and repeated his most strenuous insistence that our discussion remain absolutely secret—"*even from God in our prayers*", a qualification that astonished me coming from the mouth of a prince who was so devout.

I remember that, when I came back to the Two Pigeons Inn that evening, I had an attack of dizziness and vertigo that lasted only a moment but felt as if the world were spinning out of control. But as it was over so quickly and never recurred, I concluded that this dizzy spell was moral rather than physical and had its source in the feeling that had been needling me ever since the meeting I've just described: that events were now spinning out of control with no possibility of being stopped, and that destiny was advancing so quickly because blood was about to be spilt.

At dusk, to my considerable surprise, since I thought I'd seen the last of him, Venetianelli came to visit me. As usual, I made him many hyperbolic compliments and invited him to sit down at my table, facing the mirror behind me that he made such use of, and share my dinner. I asked him no questions, but simply waited for the fruit to ripen and fall off the tree into my mouth. And indeed, as soon as my guest had relaxed into the welcome I'd lavished on him, he told me that Guise had learnt of the fury of the king that Henri had displayed on returning to his apartments after Mass that morning, and that His Majesty had held a long meeting with his closest advisors in the old cabinet. As nothing appeared to have come from that meeting, Guise had become very worried and had made a decision to leave Blois at noon on Friday the 23rd.

After Venetianelli had left my room, La Bastide and Montseris having excused themselves for the obvious reasons, I felt a terrible knot in my throat and sweat began to pour down my cheeks; my legs felt so weak I could hardly remain upright, and my hands were shaking uncontrollably. It took me some moments before I understood that my reaction was due to the certainty that I was a tiny but crucial cog in the implacable chain of events that was unfolding: certainly, I could decide not to share Venetianelli's words with the king. But if I repeated them to him, as was not only my duty but also my inclination, it was clear that I would be helping the duc set the date and the hour of his own death, for the vehement desire of the king was to prevent his departure, which would have been fatal to his cause.

The next day was 22nd December, and as soon as I arrived at the chateau with the Forty-five, I asked the king's usher to alert

Du Halde that I had something of great importance to say to His Majesty. Du Halde came up and embraced me warmly. In a hushed voice I asked him how the king was. Du Halde answered, in the same tones: "On the surface, very calm, but inside he's boiling and feverish." He led me across the king's chamber (where I saw only one valet, who was putting logs on the fire) to the new cabinet, where the king was seated before a table on a simple stool, his back to the flames, reading dispatches that secretary of state Revol, was handing to him one by one. Seeing me, His Majesty interrupted his reading and presented me with his hand; he told me to take a seat, and told Du Halde to stay, then continued his reading. I watched him closely as he read and noticed that although his face was inscrutable, his interior agitation was betrayed by his eyelids, which from time to time fluttered uncontrollably, and by his lower lip, which was disturbed by the twitching of a muscle spasm—a reaction Henri must have been aware of, because at each spasm he raised his hand to calm it. However, his hands, which were holding the dispatches, did not tremble in the least.

As I was standing on his right and the candelabrum that was lighting his reading was set to his left, his face was etched by this luminous halo, and, though he looked thin and wan, I found him very handsome, his profile so refined, prolonged by his short black beard, which was now streaked with white, as was his hair. The more I looked at him (which I could do without offending him since he was reading), the more I admired the sensitivity in this fine and noble visage. Many of the ladies of the court sang the praises of Guise, nicknamed Magnificent by Chicot, but I did not like the falseness of his slanted eyes, the heaviness of his jaw or the gross fatuousness of his arrogance. He was a carnival king, made of cardboard, tall and well painted, but lacking the Italian finesse that one appreciated in Henri's eyes.

Having finished his reading, the king put down the dispatches, glanced over at me and asked: "*Quid novi, mi fili?*"*

Before I could answer, Bellegarde entered and told the king that Madame de Sauves begged His Majesty to receive her so that she could thank him for his marvellous present, and because she had a message to deliver from the queen mother. The king consented to her visit immediately and, at a sign he gave me, I stood up and moved away from the light of the candelabrum over to the darkest corner of the room, having little fear that Madame de Sauves might recognize me since I now had a full black beard and wore the velvet cap of the Forty-five.

Madame de Sauves, who continued to be called by the name of her late husband, despite her subsequent marriage to the Marquis de Noirmoutiers, entered the king's cabinet preceded by Monsieur de Nambu, and the king rose to greet her with his usual courtesy (showing as he did the ladies of the court, except when he was furious, the greatest regard). He presented his hand and Madame de Sauves bowed graciously before him, revealing her fine figure and generous bosom, which was decorated with a little pink lace collar, sprinkled with a very expensive plethora of pearls.

But it would be unjust not to mention that the lady displayed a grace that her years did not seem to diminish, not only in her body but in her face, which was so angelic that the most perspicacious saint would have been fooled by it: beautiful blue eyes, gorgeous pink skin, a dreamy mouth, a long neck and something so disarming in her physiognomy that even a tiger would not have remained insensitive to her charms. But she was a devil in her heart, and in her innate haughtiness already imagined herself the next queen of France, since she'd been consorting with the Magnificent. Meanwhile, in a meek

---

* "What's new, my son?"

but hypocritical display of deference, she remained kneeling at the king's feet—at all of our feet, I should say, since Du Halde, Bellegarde, Nambu and I also gazed down at her, as she knelt and endeavoured, in her apparent submission, to better dominate us with the yoke of her all-powerful beauty.

"Madame, you may rise," said the king, giving her his hand and leading her to a chair.

"Ah, sire!" she replied sweetly, in her deep, musical voice. "Your condescension overwhelms me completely, and I'll never be able to thank you enough for the marvellous present of the pearl earrings you bestowed on me, which are all the dearer to me for your having worn them! And I swear to you that I shall wear them every day that God grants me before the end of my terrestrial life."

Madame de Sauves continued in this vein for ten long minutes, which must have dragged unbearably for the king, but which he made no attempt to shorten, responding to his guest with that language of the court that manages to stretch the least phrase into ten lines and to use ten words where one would have sufficed.

"Sire," she continued, "knowing how much the affairs of state press and occupy you, I wouldn't have dared ask Your Majesty to receive me if the queen mother hadn't requested that I intervene on her behalf. Since she must keep to her room, she has asked the Duc de Guise to come to her chambers at two this afternoon, and, since she has got wind of a cooling in your relations after Mass yesterday, she would be very desirous of providing a prompt remedy so that you can make peace with each other for the greater good of the state."

"Well, Madame," replied the king with a sweetness of tone and look that left me astonished, "what infinite gratitude I owe you for this sweet embassy; with what joy I shall visit my mother this after-noon and with what redoubled happiness do I welcome the chance to see my cousin Monsieur de Guise, with whom I would never want to have a quarrel without wanting immediately to smooth it over! I would be infinitely unhappy if Monsieur de Guise were to think that I had so black a soul as to wish evil on the firmest pillar of my throne. Quite the contrary, I swear and declare here that there is no one in my kingdom whom I love more than him, or anyone to whom I am bound by so many obligations—as I hope to prove before too long, for the greatest good."

These words were proffered in such a sincere, spontaneous and naive tone that for a split second I doubted the king's true intentions. But when I saw him rise and present his hand to Madame de Sauves, seize hers and kiss it in turn, I understood the enormous and secret derision that lay behind the farce this great comedian was playing for the woman whom, that very morning, he'd called "Guise's whore". After having told her, as he kissed her hand, that "he was only king by right of succession, whereas she was queen by her incomparable beauty", he walked her to the door of his chamber as if she were a royal princess, a favour and an honour that appeared to enchant the lady, given how true it is that we mortals lose all perspective and clarity of vision when our vanity is caressed.

Meanwhile, after the lady had left by the spiral staircase that led to the queen mother's chambers and that was heavily guarded by Nambu and three of Larchant's men, the king returned to his new cabinet, walking quickly and with a very sullen expression, as if the comedy he'd just had to play to calm the suspicions of the queen mother and Guise had given him indigestion.

"My son," he said very tersely as he sat down, indicating that I should sit in front of him, "*quid novi?*"

Seeing him thus harried by so many disquieting worries, I didn't want to weave a story, but told him in a few words what I'd learnt about the *tertium quid*'s intention to leave Blois at noon on Friday.

"Well!" said the king; but then he fell silent for a long minute and sat there as immobile as a rock, his eyes staring straight ahead, but without the flutter I'd noticed when I came in, or the little spasm of the muscle under his lower lip. His whole body seemed petrified, with the exception of his hands, which he'd joined as if in prayer, and which were so tightly pressed one against the other than I could see his fingers turning white.

"It seems," he finally said in a deep, firm voice, "that our council will be meeting on Friday morning at seven."

Bellegarde, Du Halde and I looked at each other for a moment in silence, without any of us desiring to add anything, words being now superfluous since the day and the hour had now been decided. But Bellegarde, who, being so young, still had something of the child in him, said:

"Sire, if I understand you correctly, you won't be going to visit the queen mother this afternoon?"

"Ah, Bellegarde! Bellegarde!" said the king with a wan smile. "You're not thinking politically! Of course I'll go! Now more than ever! For fourteen years," he continued in a very meditative vein, his finger pointed at the floor, "that lady and author of my days has been meddling in my affairs and trying to get me to meddle in the Devil's work, whether Alençon or Guise be the Devil; and she has worked single-mindedly to make me give up everything I had, whether it be half the kingdom or the position of constable of France! Well then, by God, let's let him have everything! Tomorrow we'll see the effects! A dead man cannot hurt us any more."

The king asked that only Bellegarde accompany him to the queen mother's chambers, for the simple reason that Bellegarde was so quiet and so little engaged in politics that he'd never offended anyone and no one could accuse him of influencing the king. Many years later, when I'd gained his confidence, he told me that during that afternoon the king proved himself to be the most dazzling performer of the *commedia dell'arte* that he'd ever seen. Apparently, Guise was very defiant, distant and cold at the outset, but the king overwhelmed him with grandiloquent demonstrations of friendship and hinted at promises of his future greatness, wrapping it all in so many little pleasantries, small compliments and gracious gestures, including offering him dragées from his comfit box, that Guise ultimately melted like snow in the sun—and, of course, the queen mother, watching this from her bed, was so ecstatic to have effected such a reconciliation between the two that you would have thought you were at a wedding!

As he was leaving, the king took Guise aside and said in a confidential and affectionate voice:

"My cousin, we have much business on our hands that must be expedited before the end of the year. In this wise, come tomorrow morning at seven and we'll take care of some of it, though I have to leave for several days for a retreat at my house in la Noue. You can send me what you've resolved."

I asked Bellegarde to repeat twice the king's words, and later the ambassador from Tuscany, Filippo Cavriana, who'd come to visit the queen mother and was present at the end of this conversation, confirmed them verbatim. Cavriana admired the king's Machiavellian finesse, since by leaving Guise to preside over the meeting in his absence, he was already assigning him the functions of a constable of France—a piece of bait that must have been impossible to resist and overcame any caution Guise might otherwise have exercised in this situation.

The king had told me before his visit to the queen mother to remain in his new cabinet and to sleep the night of the 22nd to the 23rd in his wardrobe with Du Halde, who slept there every night on a bed that he rolled up at dawn and locked in a closet. But since His Majesty hadn't explained exactly what service he expected of me, I found myself quite at a loose end, my only work being to write a letter to the Cardinal de Guise that the king dictated, for lack of his secretary. The cardinal hadn't attended a meeting of the council for nearly two months, and the king requested that he attend the meeting scheduled for the next morning, since it was the last one of the year and so the matters discussed there would be of great consequence. This letter was so amiable in expression and so favourable in substance, and the addressee had been so insufferably arrogant with the king, having demanded a retraction of his speech the morning after the opening of the Estates, that I understood that the plan was to allot him the same fate as his brother. Wishing to understand this situation better, I asked Du Halde what he thought of the cardinal. And Du Halde, after a moment of reflection, replied:

"He's worse than the duc. He's a furious zealot. He breathes only blood."

At nine that evening, the king had Larchant brought to him and made sure that the officer had told Guise that he wanted to present him with a request the next morning, at the foot of the grand staircase, regarding the pay of his guards, so that the duc wouldn't be surprised by their presence there. The guards, the king added, were to be assembled there at seven o'clock with no other instructions than that they should secure the grand staircase after the duc and the archbishop of Lyons had entered, and to forbid anyone else to pass in either direction. After Larchant, the king saw Laugnac, and asked him to assemble his Forty-five at five the next morning in the Gallery of the Stags, at the bottom of the stairs that I've labelled *s'* on the floor plan. I observed that the king didn't say a word to Laugnac about the true purpose of the Gascons' presence, perhaps because he felt some mistrust of Laugnac or, possibly, because he feared that a secret that was shared among so many men couldn't be kept.

Once Laugnac had left, the king gave Du Halde and me leave to go to bed in his wardrobe, which we did, though the bed was somewhat narrow for two men who were anything but narrow themselves, especially since the cold obliged us to sleep with our coats on. Being separated from the new cabinet only by a door, I could hear the king speaking quietly with Bellegarde for quite a while. After which, I heard the king's steps in front of our other door, from which I concluded that he'd gone to sleep with the queen. At this moment, Bellegarde, a candle in his hand, opened the door a crack and said:

"Du Halde, the king demands that, on your life, you should not fail to wake him at four in the morning."

"Well, Monsieur," answered Du Halde, his voice full of anxiety, "may I ask you to hold your candle up to my clock so that I can set the alarm?"

Bellegarde came into the wardrobe and obligingly knelt next to Du Halde and held his candle up to the alarm clock that the latter had removed in order to set it. Leaning on my elbow, I watched him try to set the alarm, but his hands were trembling violently out of the fear that he might not set it at the right time, since the numbers were so small and the light so weak and flickering. Not a word was spoken during this scene; the only sounds were the noise of our breathing and, from time to time, the noise of gusts of rain whipping the windowpanes.

"Baron," said Du Halde, his voice trembling with anxiety, "did I set it correctly?"

"I believe so," I replied, but as I reached over to take the clock to verify it, he put his hand on my wrist to stop me, saying that the watch must not be shaken since the least motion would put it out of order.

Once Bellegarde had left, I tried in vain to get a little sleep, but I was filled with terror at the idea that the tiniest detail going wrong at the last minute could completely undo the king's designs. However, after finally dropping off, I was awakened by such a loud noise that I doubted that it could be Du Halde's snores. Sitting up, I saw Du Halde trying to stoke up the fire with a large pair of bellows, which explained the noise I'd heard. I asked him if he were cold, and he answered that he wasn't, but that he needed the light of the fire to see his alarm clock. I could see he was covered in sweat for fear of missing the fateful hour.

"Don't you trust it? Has it ever failed you?"

"Never."

"So trust it now!"

"Ah," replied Du Halde, "the risk is too great!"

"What time is it?"

"Three o'clock," replied Du Halde after reviving the fire enough to see the face of his watch.

"Has it ever stopped?" I asked, looking at it.

"Never. It's fairly new. I bought it on the day of the opening of the Estates-General in Blois, knowing how much Blois is famous throughout the world for the excellence of its watches and alarm clocks."

"Has its alarm ever failed to sound at the prescribed hour?"

"Never," affirmed Du Halde, throwing a stick on the fire that was about to burn his fingers.

"Well then, go back to sleep."

"I can't," confessed Du Halde, "I'm too terrified of letting the hour pass and everything failing on my account."

"Well then, stay awake!"

"If I stay awake," complained Du Halde, "I'll end up being so tired that I'll fall asleep without realizing it!"

"Well then, Du Halde," I laughed, "stop tormenting yourself! Let's roll up this bed and stow it in the closet; then we'll wait up together, on those two stools, and the first one to fall asleep will fall off the stool and wake up! That'll pass the time pretty quickly!"

Du Halde consented, and we did as I suggested, but the hour did not fly by—quite the contrary, it crept along like a slug on a lettuce leaf, so occupied were we at keeping the fire burning brightly so that the king would be warm when he got dressed. When at last we managed to breathe life into the fire, the sudden light illuminated the long, austere visage of Du Halde and his two bony hands extended towards the flames—this man who had served the king ever since he'd been the Duc d'Anjou, following him to Poland and fleeing that country with him; he had shared in Henri's shadow many good and bad days, leaving Paris and the Louvre with him after the barricades, and, had it been necessary, would have followed Henri to hell without a second thought. My great, immutable friendship with Du Halde really dates from that night, when, sitting in front of the fire on our stools, we listened quietly to the ticking of the watch, the crackling of the fire and the gusts of rain against the windowpanes. Du Halde was Seigneur and Baron d'Avrilly, and governor of Étaples, and could have aspired to higher office than this if he'd consented to abandon his humble and daily functions for the king. His only title was "ordinary manservant" and he hadn't been paid a single sol since the day of the barricades.

At four o'clock, the faithful timepiece tintinnabulated, and Du Halde stood up as if a crossbow had shot him off his stool. A look at the floor plan will confirm that the door of the wardrobe leading into the passage that led to the new oratory was opposite the door that opened into the queen's chambers. Which is why Du Halde, who had no candle, left the door of the wardrobe open to allow the firelight to guide his way. I got up when he did, but was careful not to block his light as he knocked on the queen's door.

I heard a woman's voice asking:

"What is it? Who is it? Aren't you ashamed to disturb the king's sleep?"

"It is I, Du Halde. Tell the king that it is four o'clock!"

"I will *not*!" said the voice bitterly. "I won't do it! The king is asleep! And the queen as well!"

"By God," cried Du Halde in anger, "wake up the king this minute! Or I'll start yelling so loud and for so long that they'll both wake up!"

And I saw him raise his fist as if he were going to knock again furiously, but he was dissuaded by the voice of the king from within.

"What is it, Piolant?"

"Sire," replied Piolant (who was, I imagine, the queen's chambermaid, and who, like Du Halde, slept on a bed that she unrolled on the ground), "it's Du Halde, who says it's four o'clock!"

"Piolant!" came the king's voice. "My boots, my robe, my candle!"

Hearing this, Du Halde returned to the wardrobe, still trembling with anger, and said, between clenched teeth: "That ninny Piolant!" and then tossed an entire log onto the fire, sending sparks showering onto the floor just as the king entered. He seemed very pleased to see such a display and exclaimed:

"Thank you, Du Halde, for such a beautiful fire!"

But I noticed that he didn't present his hand either to Du Halde or to me (whom he didn't even seem to notice), and I attributed this oversight to the thoughts that must be agitating him. In this I turned out to be wrong, for—after Du Halde had removed the king's robe (which was thickly lined with ermine), administered a rough rub-down over his entire body with spirits of wine, dressed him from head to toe in black velvet, combed his hair, placed his cap on his head and hung around his neck the Order of the Holy Spirit—the king, turning round to look at himself in the mirror, said:

"Du Halde, am I presentable?"

"Indeed, sire!" confirmed Du Halde after inspecting his monarch meticulously.

And it was only then that the king presented his hand to us, first to Du Halde and then to me, since, as we were both barons, Du Halde had precedence over me: he was the king's manservant and I only his physician. In this capacity, I wanted to take the king's pulse, but he said that he felt fine, and that he'd feel even better if the affair didn't fail.

Just then we heard a noise that seemed to be coming from the courtyard of the chateau, and since the windows in the king's apartment looked out over the countryside, the king sent me to the old cabinet, which overlooked the courtyard, and I could see by the light of their torches that the noise came from the king's carriage and the service horses, which the coachmen had tied up to the right of the grand stairway: a deception that His Majesty had staged in order to make it look as though his departure to la Noue were imminent. Retracing my steps, I bumped into Bellegarde in the old oratory, who was returning from the Gallery of the Stags, where he said the king had sent him to ascertain that the Forty-five were assembled there.

Returning together to the room, we found it full of the advisors and officers whom His Majesty had convoked for five o'clock, namely, the Maréchal d'Aumont, Rambouillet, François d'O, secretary of state Revol and d'Entragues. With the exception of these last two, whom the king kept at his side, he sent the others into the council room, a valet lighting their way with a candelabrum.

Laugnac finally appeared at the door of the old oratory, and the king, now showing signs of impatience, asked him rather abruptly if all of the Forty-five were now assembled in the Gallery of the Stags.

"Yes, sire," confirmed Laugnac, "all but two or three."

"Good enough," approved the king. "Have them tiptoe upstairs to the room next to my old oratory. I shall meet them there. And tell them on their life to keep quiet. The least noise might alert the queen mother, and that would spoil everything. Du Halde," he continued, "I'm hungry. Is there nothing to eat here?"

"Sire, all we have are some plums from Brignoles. Shall I bring you some?"

"Thank you, yes," confirmed the king, who only nibbled two or three of them, proof that he wasn't so much hungry as worried at being potentially weakened by his fast, having risen so early.

Laugnac having returned to report that the Forty-five were now at their posts, the king asked me to take him to them and to point out to him La Bastide and Montseris, no doubt remembering that I'd told him that my two companions were highly inflamed against Guise, since he wanted to steal their livelihood by sending them home to look for work in Gascony. Having traversed the old oratory, he stopped on the threshold of the room in which the Gascons were crowded, standing silently at attention. I whispered to the king the descriptions of my two companions and he nodded that he'd understood me.

"Messieurs," he said softly, "some very evil people have made plots and threats against my person and my life. I am going to need to depend on your strong arms and your courage. I am going to ask you to raise those same arms *without saying a word*, if you agree to do as I command this day no matter what I order you to do."

All the arms in the room were raised as one, and in the most absolute silence. The king nodded in particular to Bastide and Montseris and then withdrew, leaving me alone with Bellegarde, who stepped next door into the old cabinet and returned a moment later, his arms full of daggers, which he'd doubtless removed from the secret drawer in that room.

"There are eight of these," explained Bellegarde. "Don't say a word. Raise your hand if you want one."

Many, but not all, of them reached for the weapons, among them La Bastide and Montseris in the front row.

Bellegarde brought the eight Gascons that he'd just armed into the king's chamber, and told them to hide their weapons behind their backs in the Italian manner so that they would be concealed under their capes. One among them asked quietly why they'd need knives when they were wearing swords at their sides. Bellegarde explained in the same quiet voice that it was a matter of an execution of a traitor to the king condemned by His Majesty and not a duel, and that the king did want any Gascon blood to be shed on this occasion.

At this moment, the king, who'd been in his new cabinet with Revol and d'Entragues, entered the room; he stepped up to the eight, stood quietly in front of them and looked each of them in turn in the eye as if he wanted to remember them. Then he said, sotto voce:

"My friends, I thank you for your zealous devotion to my service. The traitor is the Duc de Guise, and he must die."

One of them, whose name, I learnt later, was Sarriac, then said in Provençal:

"*Cap de Diou, sire, iou lou bou rendraï mort!*"*

It was now about half-past six, and Du Halde came to tell the king that his chaplain and his almoner were asking Monsieur de Nambu if they could pass through his room into the new oratory, where His Majesty had asked them to say Mass. The king then had his eight Gascons return to the old oratory, no doubt so that the priests wouldn't see them, and received the latter with his customary civility, telling them to prepare to say Mass, which he regretted he wouldn't be able to hear, in which case they should sing it without him.

The priests had scarcely left the new oratory when Larchant arrived to announce that his men were now assembled at the bottom of the great staircase.

"Ah, Larchant!" said the king. "Place five of your men and an officer on the first floor in front of the queen mother's door, and if Guise attempts to see her, have him told that she has just taken her medicine and refuses to see anyone. Moreover, your guards must

---

* "By God, sire, I'll kill him for you!"

prevent *anyone* from entering the queen mother's room—and anyone from leaving it, including any chambermaids. And assign three guards to Nambu to be placed on the spiral staircase between my rooms and my mother's."

Once Larchant had departed, the king sent Bellegarde to choose twelve from among the Forty-five to place in the old cabinet, so that if Guise succeeded in escaping from the eight Gascons posted in the king's chamber he'd find them there with their swords drawn.

Having thus finished his orders, and having now to await the outcome of his enterprise, the king became suddenly very animated, and, though he usually liked to wait, whether sitting or standing, as immobile as a statue, he suddenly began pacing up and down in his room, his eyes fixed on the floor and his hands behind his back. In truth, I'd already seen him agitated before, but never this feverishly—now consulting the watch that Du Halde wore around his neck, now looking out of the windows and complaining about the torrential rain, now complaining that the sun wasn't coming up and that it was "the darkest, most shadowy day he'd ever seen".

As for me, I was surprised that he'd required my presence—I couldn't imagine to what use His Majesty would employ me or why he'd insisted that I sleep in his wardrobe with Du Halde and not leave him. And even when he called me over and asked me to deliver a message, its contents were not so sensitive that it required a messenger of my status. Quite the opposite. And so I felt that it was ironic that I, who was not a Catholic other than by lip service, had to cross the new cabinet into the new oratory on behalf of the king, to carry a message to his chaplain and his almoner.

The chaplain was named Étienne Dorguyn and the almoner Claude de Bulles, but for the life of me I can't remember which was which, since they both had rounded shoulders and round paunches and round red, faces with scatterings of white hair on their pates.

"Messieurs," I announced, after greeting them with all due respect, "His Majesty requests that you not wait any longer for him but begin your devotions immediately and pray to God that the king succeed in the enterprise that he has undertaken in order to bring peace to his kingdom."

At this speech, the two priests looked somewhat astonished, and asked what the enterprise was that required their prayers, as it were, blindly. But since the king's message did not specify this, one of them, the almoner I believe, who'd already put on the alb and stole to celebrate Mass, said:

"Monsieur, please assure His Majesty that we obey his order and that we will both pray for the success of his enterprise."

After having bowed to them, I left them, but not without some uneasiness, Huguenot that I am, at the strange things that men— priests and the faithful alike—ask of the God that they adore, and whom they pretend to obey. For I fear that the Mass that day in the new oratory was neither requested nor said in good conscience, but was, both for the king and for his chaplain and almoner, reduced to the level of pure superstition.

When I returned to the king's chamber, I heard Henri order his butler, Monsieur de Merle, to hurry to the Cardinal de Guise's chambers to remind him that the king was expecting him to attend the meeting of the council, as he'd indicated the previous evening in his letter. And catching sight of me at that moment, the king asked me to post myself at the window of the old cabinet, which overlooked the courtyard of the chateau, and to tell him when the duc appeared, who would be crossing the courtyard to enter the Louis XII wing and mount the great staircase of honour.

I found the twelve Forty-five waiting in the old cabinet, mute as carps, but not at all peaceful since they were constantly adjusting the handles of their swords as if they were itching in their scabbards, and even though the king (despite the fact that he'd done so to the eight in his room) had not yet told them the name of the traitor whom, if necessary, they would have to prevent from escaping, I could see from their determined expressions that they had no doubt as to his identity and little love for him, since he sought to break up their band and send them back to their poverty in Guyenne.

As I glued my forehead to the window, I watched the day dawn pallidly, the oblique sheets of the driving rain and morning mist so obscuring my view that I couldn't have distinguished a grey cat from a white one. There had been some movement in the courtyard as various dignitaries arrived for the council meeting, but I had to wait for what seemed a very long time before I caught sight of the duc, who was accompanied only by his secretary, Péricard, a valet carrying his *ombrello* and another who preceded him with a lantern. I immediately recognized the duc by his height (which exceeded that of any other lord at the court) and also by his doublet and light-grey coat—Guise, aspiring to the status of archangel, preferred light colours.

I could see him very well, since the valet carrying the lantern was walking backwards despite the risk of falling on the wet pavement, in order to light his master's way. As the great staircase projected several feet into the courtyard, I could also see Larchant's guards waiting to present their respectful demand for back pay, but whose orders were to occupy the staircase as soon as the duc had passed, closing the trap behind him, all the other staircases also being guarded by the Forty-five. The duc, who had but a few yards to traverse to arrive at his death, seemed to me already to be walking with great fatigue, assuredly tired by having spent the night in the bed of Madame de Sauves. As for me, at that moment, as great a traitor as he was, paid by Spain and working for the ruin of the state, I was seized as I saw him approach the first step of the great staircase with a feeling of compassion, sensing that he was ready to fall from the arms of a woman into the hands of God, sallying from a night of voluptuous pleasure into eternal night.

He entered. I ran to announce his arrival to the king, whose eyes suddenly lit up and who said, turning to Bellegarde:

"Bellegarde, order the porters to close the gates of the chateau as soon as the Cardinal de Guise and the archbishop of Lyons have entered, and tell Nambu that no one other than the Duc de Guise is to cross the threshold of my chambers."

And then, turning to the eight, he said:

"Sit down on the trunks here and remain calm. But stand up as soon as the duc enters and follow him respectfully to the door of the old cabinet. Be very careful to avoid being hurt by this man. He's tall and powerful and I'd be very sad if any of you were wounded."

As the duc passed through the door that was so well defended by Monsieur de Nambu and entered the council room, a shudder seemed to run through all those present, as I learnt from François d'O and d'Aumont, who recounted the scene to me later.

At the instant the duc entered, his head held high, greeted by a deep bow from everyone in the room, magnificent in his light-grey satin, his long coat thrown over his left arm, and his great plumed hat in his right hand, there was no evidence of any council in progress. The counsellors were standing scattered about the hall, or walking in small groups from one fireplace to the other, which were heating the room only feebly since the valet of the wardrobe had neglected to stoke them after the entrance of the Maréchal d'Aumont.

Finally, the archbishop and the Cardinal de Guise arrived, and if Heaven had granted them a miraculous increase in their hearing, they might have heard the gates, doors and drawbridge of the chateau closing behind them. But the council did not yet begin, since they were waiting for the arrival of secretary of state Martin Ruzé to bring the day's agenda.

The old Maréchal d'Aumont, who'd been my friend ever since he'd heard from my mouth how I'd managed to steal, from Madame Limp, the damning letter from Guise to Felipe II, told me later that the counsellors in the large hall had grouped themselves by affinity: on one side the Leaguers—the Duc de Guise, the Cardinal de Guise and the archbishop of Lyons; on another the less zealous royalists—the Cardinal de Gondi, who was the archbishop of Paris, the Maréchal de Retz, the secretaries of state Marcel and Pétromol, and the idiot Montholon; and lastly the ardent royalists, the very ones the king had enlisted in the secret plot—himself, Rambouillet and François d'O. Each group, François d'O told me later, was looking furtively at and spying on the others, trying to hear what they were saying. But since they all feared being overheard, they limited their conversations to the most banal subjects, as demonstrated by following from the Cardinal de Guise to the duc:

"Where's the king going in such bad weather?"

"I hear," replied the duc, "he's going to attend a retreat at la Noue for a few days, as usual."

"My dear d'O," I said looking at his lively and intelligent face as he recounted this scene much later, "what do you think Guise was thinking at that moment?"

"Why, nothing!" said d'O, raising his eyebrows in surprise. "Nothing! Big body, little brain. In short, a Goliath!"

"A Goliath!" I said. "But he was a hypocrite, a sneak, a liar…"

"Yes, of course," agreed d'O, "but his lies were grotesque, his plans obvious and his hypocrisy transparent. Because the king didn't have d'Ornano kill him on his return to Paris, Guise imagined he'd never dare do it. God knows he received plenty of warning in Blois! He didn't believe any of it! He understood nothing about the character of his king. Because Henri is good, Guise thought he was a coward. Because he had a feminine side, his cousin thought him weak. But weakness and womanhood are not synonymous. Guise should have known this given how easily Madame de Sauves wrapped him around her little finger."

"But wouldn't you have thought that the duc's face would betray some degree of apprehension on that morning given that he was alone without his retinue in a chateau that was unfriendly to him?"

"Not at all! The duc displayed everywhere he went that natural bravery of men who don't think. That morning, he was cold and he was hungry. He was cold because, being foppish, he was wearing only his light-grey satin doublet, which was much too thin for the season. He was hungry because he slept too late in la Sauves's pretty arms and forgot to take any breakfast. What's more, his valet forgot to furnish him with his comfit box full of the Damascus grapes that he usually ate each morning for breakfast."

"Péricard," said the duc to his secretary, "I'm so hungry I'm like to faint! Be good enough to find my valet and ask him for my comfit box."

Péricard had scarcely left when Larchant entered the room with several guards and played his role to perfection (which was all the more believable since he had the frank, regular and tanned face of a good soldier who would never be involved in anything dishonest). He bowed to the duc and said:

"Monseigneur, these poor men begged me to pray the council to be allowed to remain here until His Majesty arrives so that he may hear their complaint that if they aren't paid they'll be forced to sell their horses and return home on foot."

"Monsieur de Larchant," replied Guise, "I will help them and I will help you as well. It's entirely reasonable that this be straightened out."

"But," broke in secretary of state Marcel, quite innocently since he wasn't in on the plot, "I see a notation here in my book that indicates that 200 écus has been set aside for them."

Hearing this, Larchant withdrew with his guards from the council room, but not, of course, from the stairway.

Meanwhile, since Péricard still hadn't returned with the duc's comfit box, the duc turned to Monsieur de Saint-Prix, the king's first manservant, and said:

"Monsieur de Saint Prix, I seem to be without my comfit box. I wonder if I might ask you for a few crumbs from the king's?"

"Monseigneur," replied Monsieur de Saint-Prix, "would a few Brignoles plums be acceptable?"

"Certainly, Monsieur," said the duc.

At this, the council's usher, Jean Guéroult, brought the king's comfit box and explained that the guards had blocked Péricard's re-entry when he tried to return. The duc thanked him, ate the plums and some Damascus grapes, and then placed the beautifully wrought box on a table nearby. Then, suddenly penetrated by the dankness in the air, given his summery attire, he rose, approached the fire and, shivering profusely, proclaimed:

"I'm cold! My chest hurts! Have them light the fire!"

Once a valet had thrown another log on, the duc sat down on a stool next to the fire, but whether he had gone too quickly from cold to hot, had eaten the plums and grapes too quickly, or else was too exhausted from his night with Madame de Sauves, his symptoms worsened and his nose suddenly started to bleed. He looked for his handkerchief in his breeches, but couldn't find it, and said:

"My valet was in such haste this morning that he didn't provide me with what I need. Monsieur Guéroult, may I ask you to try to have Péricard admitted so he may bring my things?"

But Guéroult seemed to have disappeared, so Monsieur de Saint-Prix brought the duc a handkerchief belonging to the king, and, Martin Ruzé having just arrived with the agenda for the meeting, the members of the council took their seats around the table, where they were joined by the duc, his comfit box in one hand and his handkerchief in the other, which he rolled into a ball since his nosebleed had stopped.

Here I interrupt François d'O's account, and turn to my own observations of what happened. I was at that moment in the king's apartments, that is, in the new cabinet, with the king, d'Entragues, Bellegarde, Du Halde and secretary of state Revol, to whom the king now said, his face calm and his voice resolute but quiet:

"Revol, it's time. Go and tell Guise that I'm waiting for him in my old cabinet."

Revol opened the door of the new cabinet that led to the king's chamber and raised the tapestry, but suddenly reappeared.

"My God, Revol!" said the king. "What's the matter? What's happened? You look pale! You're not going to spoil everything! Rub your cheeks! Rub your cheeks, Revol!"

"I haven't turned pale, sire. This is my natural complexion."

"But why have you come back? What's the matter?"

"Nothing's the matter, sire. It's Monsieur de Nambu, who won't open the door to me without your order."

The king raised the tapestry, since the door was still open, and said to Nambu, who was guarding the door to the council room:

"Nambu, let Monsieur Revol leave and then let the duc back in here—but *only* the duc!"

Nambu obeyed, and the king dropped the tapestry, continued standing behind it and called me to his side (though I had no idea why); I was glad of it, since between the length of tapestry and the door frame there was a small crack that allowed me a view of the room.

The council, François d'O told me later, was debating a proposal that had been submitted by the committee on finance when Revol entered, seemingly on unsteady feet, his face so white and his body so frail of substance that he seemed to have been awakened from the dead, and it was indeed death that he was bringing as messenger to the Lorraine duc. As he approached the man, he made a deep bow and said in a voice so timid and weak that it seemed to be his last breath:

"Monseigneur, the king requests your company in his old cabinet."

After which, he stepped away, or rather, was obliterated—almost reduced to nothing—when Guise rose, in all the majestic symmetry of his enormous frame, so powerful, well built and muscular that he appeared indestructible, and at this moment luminous, because of the pale-grey satin in which he was clothed, the strings of pearls that adorned his doublet, his blond hair and his azure eyes, which were never fixed on a lady of the court without her nearly swooning, her virtue already compromised. When he'd stood to his full height, he leant over and took from his comfit box a few of the Brignoles plums that Monsieur de Saint-Prix had brought him, and threw the rest negligently on the tablecloth, saying playfully:

"Messieurs, who would like some?"

This said, he smiled, his long, carnivorous jaw opening to reveal a set of brilliant teeth so straight it seemed that a jeweller had set them in place. He seemed entirely recovered from his sudden attack of illness, except that his scarred left eye was watering—but we were so accustomed to this double face, half sad, half smiling, that we thought nothing of it. He was, no doubt, convinced, after all the recent affability and compliments the king had showered on him, that His Majesty was inviting him into his cabinet to discuss his appointment as constable of France. Throwing his cloak over his shoulders, he playfully draped the tail over his right arm, then his left, with a conniving smile to us all, as though asking us to witness that the hang of this garment was more important to him than any interview with the king. Having tried out several poses, the implied derision of which escaped no one, he threw the tail of the cloak over his left arm, in two loops, "in the wildest manner", took his comfit box and his handkerchief in his left hand and his plumed hat in his right, and, bowing in a royal gesture, said in a very loud voice, "Adieu, Messieurs!"; in two steps he was at the king's door, where he knocked once. Monsieur de Nambu immediately opening it, the duc entered, upon which Nambu quickly closed and bolted the door, though perhaps a little more forcefully than usual, a gesture that startled the Cardinal de Guise, who suddenly looked disquieted.

As for me, with my eye still glued to the crack between curtain and door frame, I didn't see Guise enter the king's chamber, but I heard his step and I saw the eight Gascons rise from their seats and raise their hands to their black velvet hats as if to greet him. The duc walked around the king's bed to reach the door of the old oratory, his step majestic and nonchalant, and was followed by the eight, as if they were a respectful escort, their left arms hanging down, but their right arms already reaching behind their backs under their short capes for their daggers. This double progress towards the door seemed impossibly slow, and the Gascons, all of whom were a full head shorter than their prey, looked like nothing so much as a group of panthers, dangerous in their supple and padded steps, pursuing a great tiger.

Since the both of the duc's hands were encumbered, the left by his comfit box and the right by his hat, he raised the tapestry over the door with his elbow, and leant down to duck under the low door. But, as he did so, he glanced back over his shoulder at the Gascons, who were circled very close behind him, their faces so tense and drawn that he exclaimed, half in surprise, half in anger:

"Eh, Messieurs!"

He never said another word. La Bastide seized his arm and Montseris struck a blow at his throat, believing that the duc must be wearing a coat of mail, and that he could only be wounded there. At this, all of the others fell on him with cries of "Kill him! Death to the duc! Kill him!"—some seizing his arms, others his legs and one his sword, to prevent him from drawing it, striking him repeatedly all over his body now that they realized he had was wearing only a shirt beneath his doublet. The duc continued to struggle with prodigious force, shaking these cats from his body and striking them with his comfit box and his fists, but he was ultimately submerged by their number and weakened by the wounds to his vital parts, from which blood was flowing and staining his satin doublet. All that could be seen now was a confused melee of furious little men swarming over this giant, like a pack of hounds over the flanks of a wild boar. Once he stopped resisting, they stepped away from him, thinking he'd fall to the floor.

But the duc, still standing, though staggering, his mouth open and emitting a whistling sound as he struggled to breathe, held out his hands in front of him, his eyes already unseeing and half-closed, and stumbled forward towards the royal bed, as though he were trying to get to the door that Monsieur de Nambu was guarding. Seeing this, Laugnac—who up until this moment had remained immobile, his arms crossed, sitting on a trunk, his sword, unhooked but not unsheathed, on his knees—stood up, and, at arm's length, struck him in the stomach with his scabbard, at which the duc collapsed at the foot of the bed, his head on the step and his great body staining forever a small Bohemian rug that was placed there.

Meanwhile, according to what I heard later from François d'O, hearing the cries and tumult from the king's chambers, there ensued a great commotion in the council room. Everyone leapt to their feet and the Cardinal de Guise shouted, "All is lost!" and rushed to the door of the king's chambers, banging furiously on it. Then, realizing they wouldn't open it, he ran to the door of the queen's chambers to attempt to flee. But the Maréchal d'Aumont, stepping in front of him, drew his sword and cried:

"In the name of God, don't move, Monsieur! The king wants to see you!"

Immediately the hall was full of Larchant's guards, who didn't hesitate to seize the Cardinal de Guise and the archbishop of Lyons and lead them to a little garret on the third floor, which had been prepared for his Capuchin monks by the king. There was no doubt in anyone's mind as to what would happen to them—or at least to the cardinal—as soon as the king had found a man who would dare stain his holy purple with blood.

As for me, I remember very well that, after the duc fell, it seemed an eternity before the king moved, his face petrified, as though he couldn't believe that this arch-enemy of his throne, of his life and of his state had ceased to be able to harm him. And when he was finally convinced of the immobility of his nemesis, he stood on the threshold of the room, turned to me and said:

"My son, you are a doctor. Please confirm that he's dead."

And suddenly I understood why he'd kept me with him ever since the previous evening.

In truth, one look would have been enough for me to make my declaration, but understanding the king's need for absolute certainty, I knelt beside the body, which seemed to me even bigger than when it was standing. This thought was later ascribed to the king, but he never said it, any more than he kicked the cadaver or pierced it with his sword; nor did the queen mother truly exclaim, when she learnt of the duc's murder, "My son, that's nicely cut, and now you have to sew it up."

I closely examined the duc's wounds and found one on his neck, another below his left breast, another above his right eye and four more in his stomach. I suppose that there were other wounds in his back and kidneys, but I didn't see the necessity of turning him over since his body was so heavy and bloody and his death so obvious. However, to satisfy the king, who evidently couldn't believe his eyes, I took from my leggings a small mirror, which I held up to the duc's lips, but it didn't cloud up at all. I held it there for quite a while, having trouble, myself, accepting that this great zealot of intolerance, author of the civil war and the massacre of the Huguenots had finally given up his soul to whoever wanted to receive it from his lips.

"Beaulieu," said the king to one of his secretaries of state, "look and see what he has on him."

Which Beaulieu did, rather unhappily, kneeling down and attempting to avoid being stained by the ocean of blood.

He found, tied around Guise's arm, a small key attached to a golden chain. In his breeches there was a small purse containing twelve écus and a piece of paper, on which the duc had written: "To keep the war going in France, we'll need 700,000 livres every month." This message was thought to have been intended for Mendoza, and was additional proof, if any were needed, of Guise's treason.

The king seized the note that Beaulieu handed to him and asked him to remove from the duc's finger a ring bearing a diamond shaped like a heart; and, taking this ring in his fingers, the king looked calmly around at the men assembled there and said, without raising his voice:

"The king of Paris is dead. I am now the king of France and again master, and not a slave and captive, as I have been since the day of the barricades."

After which, giving me a sign to follow him into his new cabinet, and having closed the door behind us, he said:

"My son, please take this ring to the king of Navarre. He will recognize it. His shameless wife gave it to Guise when she was consorting with him. And when he sees it, Navarre will know that we shall henceforth be in league against the League!"

PUSHKIN PRESS

Pushkin Press was founded in 1997, and publishes novels, essays, memoirs, children's books—everything from timeless classics to the urgent and contemporary.

Our books represent exciting, high-quality writing from around the world: we publish some of the twentieth century's most widely acclaimed, brilliant authors such as Stefan Zweig, Marcel Aymé, Teffi, Antal Szerb, Gaito Gazdanov and Yasushi Inoue, as well as compelling and award-winning contemporary writers, including Andrés Neuman, Edith Pearlman, Eka Kurniawan, Ayelet Gundar-Goshen and Chigozie Obioma.

Pushkin Press publishes the world's best stories, to be read and read again. To discover more, visit www.pushkinpress.com.